D1246226

THE SINGERS OF NEVYA

LOUISE MARLEY

FAIRWOOD PRESS
Auburn • Seattle

THE SINGERS OF NEVYA
A Fairwood Press Book
November 2009
Copyright © 2009 by Louise Marley

Fairwood Press
21528 104th Street Ct E
Bonney Lake WA 98391
www.fairwoodpress.com

Cover and book design by Patrick Swenson

ISBN: 978-0-9820730-4-9
First Fairwood Press Edition: November 2009
Printed in the United States of America

For my guys

Ice Cliffs
Manrus
The Marik Mountains
Perl
The
Filus
Conservatory
The Frozen Sea
Clare
The Southern Timberlands
Tarus

CONTENTS

BOOK ONE:

SING THE LIGHT

Prologue

The Old Singer closed her papery eyelids and concentrated. A web of wrinkles etched her pale face like cracks in the Great Glacier. On her *filhata* she played a melody in the second mode, *Aiodu,* as she reached far, far away with the thread of her thought, lengthening, narrowing, stretching it beyond all known limits. Past the thick stone walls of Conservatory, across the great ironwood forests of the Marik Mountains she reached. She followed events by listening to the mind of Sira, her protégée, who was in the gravest possible danger.

The old Singer's psi, so often used to speed the motion of the tiniest parts of air around her, to stir it into giving off heat and light, now carried her many days' ride away, to a lonely campsite where Sira, the youngest of Nevyan Singers, lay wounded, bleeding into the snow that covered her. The old Singer had followed the shadowed patterns leading to this, had sensed the evil that pursued Sira from the safety of the great Houses out into the deadly climate of the Continent. She felt in her mind how the cold that all Nevyans feared began to seep into Sira's body as night fell and the warmth of the *quiru* above the campsite waned. Around Sira was death and more death, and the old Singer sensed her shock and grief, and her fear.

Then, as she listened with all her mind, the echo that was Sira's thought faded from her hearing. The Singer struggled to find it again. She cast about in the darkness, her *filhata* flung aside on her narrow cot. But try as she might, she could hear no more from Sira. In desperation, the old Singer prayed into the night for the Spirit of Stars to help her beloved student. As always, the unknowable Spirit sent no answer.

Chapter One

Sira listened in shy silence as the riders chatted and talked around the little softwood fire. So much talking aloud made her uncomfortable, but she supposed she would get used to it, in time. Her *quiru* shimmered warm and secure around them all. Stars glittered icily beyond it, and enormous ironwood trees loomed around the campsite like ghosts in the night.

"Cantrix, would you like more *keftet*?" Rollie hunkered next to Sira, holding out the pot and spoon. "Or maybe you'd like to go out of the *quiru* for a moment?"

Sira hesitated. She was not sure she understood the other woman's question. "Go out?" she asked softly. "Rollie, do you mean–do I wish to relieve myself?"

The rider's laugh creased her weathered face and made Sira blush. Rollie put out a hand as if to touch her, then, remembering who she was, pulled it back.

"I'm sorry, young Cantrix," she said. "Those are just not the words I would have used."

"I am not much used to conversation," Sira said.

Rollie made a wry face. "I don't know if riders' talk can truly be called conversation." She indicated the darkness beyond the *quiru*. "I'll take you out now."

The two women left the circle of riders in the glow of the *quiru* and stepped a few feet away to the privacy of the irontrees. "Remember, now, Cantrix," Rollie said, "we never leave a *quiru* by ourselves when we're traveling. Always in twos, at least. If I have to go out with one of the men, then I do it. Never alone."

"Why is that, Rollie?"

"More than one reason, Cantrix," Rollie replied. Her face was dim in the vast darkness. "The cold can get you quick. Or you could fall, and no one would know until it was too late."

Sira nodded in the dark, then realized Rollie couldn't see her. Sira was not used to darkness, either, having lived virtually all her life in the light of Houses. "I will remember, Rollie," she said gravely. "Thank you."

"And don't forget the *tkir*, either, Cantrix," Rollie added. Her voice was deeper, harder, when she gave this warning. "They won't attack in a *quiru*, but they will in the dark. A person alone hardly has a chance."

Rollie kept behind Sira as they made their way back to the *quiru*. It shone in the starry, snowy night, an envelope of light, the little cooking fire a spark within it. Sira breathed deeply in appreciation of its beauty, and in satisfaction at having created it.

Rollie heard her sigh. "Something wrong, Cantrix?"

Sira shook her head. Her bound hair caught on her fur hood, and she wished she could wear it cropped short as Rollie did. "Nothing, Rollie," she answered. "There is so much beauty, out here in the mountains."

The *quiru* light reflected on Rollie's leathery cheeks. "I love being outside," she said. "We need our Houses, but the best life is out here, in the trees, in the snow."

Sira turned her eyes up to the brilliance of the night sky. "I have not seen the stars since I can remember."

"Best get into the *quiru* now, young Cantrix," Rollie said. "The deep cold season isn't over yet."

Sira obeyed, stepping back into the warmth of the *quiru* she had herself created a few short hours ago. It was like stepping into the warm water of the *ubanyix*. She shook herself with pleasure, and wondered how anyone who had never experienced the cold of outside could really appreciate a *quiru's* warmth.

The riders were rolling themselves into their bedfurs, and Sira saw two of them returning from outside the *quiru*, together, as Rollie had said. She slipped into her own bedfurs, nestling down into their warmth, offering a little prayer of thanks to the *caeru* who had provided them. As she stretched her long legs under her furs, she felt the beginnings of the saddle soreness that would develop tomorrow, and she liked it. Today had been her first day as an adult, her first day riding *hruss*, her first day as a full Cantrix. The soreness was confirmation that it was all real, that what she had spent her short life preparing for was about to happen.

She was Cantrix Sira v'Conservatory, soon to be v'Bariken. These riders, this camp in the Marik Mountains, this very day, were all for her. She felt a rush of happiness as she closed her eyes to sleep. Her whole life lay before her in a rosy glow of hope.

Maestra Lu lay alone on her bed in her tiny room at Conservatory, but sleep would not come. She felt the absence of Sira in the House as a sharp wound, a feeling that some essential part of herself was missing.

Lu had said goodbye to many a young Singer in her years of teaching. With Sira it was different. No student had ever affected her in the way Sira had, and as she had watched the ceremony this morning, standing in the wintry sunshine on the broad Conservatory steps, Lu was overwhelmed with premonition.

As always, it had been a mostly quiet ceremony. The riders, mounted and ready, provided a dark and restless backdrop as they waited to be on their way. Sira, tall and thin and so terribly young, sat high on the big, heavy-boned *hruss* Bariken had sent for her. She wore new furs, and had newly-made bedfurs tied to her saddle. Her *filhata* was carefully wrapped and slung on her back.

Everyone waited as the students of Conservatory wished Sira goodbye in their silent way.

Goodbye, Sira . . . Cantrix! This was sent by Isbel, Sira's best friend, who was better at a mental giggle than any student Lu had known.

Good luck, Cantrix Sira!
The Spirit protect you!
Congratulations, Cantrix!

One or two students sent nothing, but Lu knew Sira was used to their resentment, and would be unaffected. At least there were no taunts on this day.

Magister Mkel stood smiling at the top of the stairs, listening. His mate, Cathrin, waited patiently for the part of the ceremony she could hear. She was fond of saying she was not burdened by the Gift, and preferred normal conversation. Maestra Lu, as the senior teacher, stood with Mkel and Cathrin, her face stiff and her eyes dry. Her own farewell she saved for last.

At length the mental chatter among the students ended, and Mkel cleared his throat and spoke aloud.

"Cantrix Sira," he said. Sira's grave eyes brightened at the sound of her newly-earned title. "Every Singer's true home is Conservatory. We will always await your return. Good luck. Serve well." He bowed, deeply and formally.

Sira's eyes shone darkly within the yellow-white *caeru* fur that circled her face. She bowed from her high-cantled saddle. "Thank you, Magister."

Lu treasured the sound of that deep young voice, knowing its power and the immense talent behind it. She felt her already-stiff features harden to ice as she controlled her emotion.

Sira turned her face to her teacher. *Thank you,* she sent. Her thought was warm with affection. *Maestra Lu, thank you. I will miss you.*

Lu bowed, delicately and deliberately. *Farewell, Cantrix Sira. May the Spirit of Stars be with you always.*

And even as she sent her goodbye to her protégée, the premonition struck her like a blow. She was quite sure, in that moment, that she would never see Sira again in this life.

As the traveling party made its way through the passes toward Bariken, Sira rode in silent awe of the majesty of her surroundings. How different from the sheltered life most of her people lived, protected behind the walls of their great Houses! Only those whose work it was to ride between the Houses saw the magnificence of the Continent. The scattered ironwood forests, the huge boulders that marked the landscape, the deep snowpack that never disappeared—all these were no less wondrous to Sira than the magic of her *quiru* was to the riders.

To the south was Clare, where she had been born, where the thick paper all the Houses used was manufactured. To the north, Perl, where the people wove cloth and rugs. Northeast, four more days' ride, her new home of Bariken, known for its limeglass. For a moment, she envied the itinerant Singers who plied the mountains all their lives. They saw the glories of the Continent every day, every week, in all seasons.

But for her, each day brought her closer to Bariken. Soon, the life she had always sought would be hers.

"Cantrix?"

Sira started, realizing Rollie was speaking to her. So lost in thought was she, and so unused to her title, she had not noticed. "I am sorry, Rollie. What is it?"

"We'd like to camp here, if it suits you."

If it suits me? Sira thought. She looked around at the riders, all considerably older than herself, and nodded. She knew nothing of campsites. She knew only her music.

Blane, the guide for the party, gave a respectful nod. "Rollie, thank the young Cantrix." Like Rollie's, his face was weathered to a rich brown. "Ask her if she would be so good as to raise the *quiru*, and we'll make camp."

Rollie jumped nimbly off her *hruss* and came to hold Sira's stirrup, careful not to touch her inadvertently.

Sira had less than four summers to Rollie's six, but she was stiff and sore. As she slid from the saddle, a small groan escaped her, though she meant to suppress it. She gave Rollie a small, rueful smile. "I am sorry. The Spirit did not pad me much."

Rollie chuckled. "Wouldn't matter, Cantrix. You're just saddle-sore." She untied Sira's bedfurs and spread them on the snow.

Sira said, "I believe I will stand." Rollie grinned.

Sira laid her *filhata* on her bedfurs. She carried her *filla*, the little flute that was perfect for a traveler's *quiru*, inside her tunic. She brought it out now and put it to her lips.

She played a traditional melody in the first mode. Her psi, focused and amplified through the music from her *filla*, reached into the air around her, speeding and warming its elements to protect the people and *hruss* from the deep cold of the Nevyan night.

The small *quiru* needed for a campsite took only half her concentration. She was aware, as she played, of the riders listening. She embellished the melody here and there, making it as much a musical as a functional performance. Heat and light billowed from where she stood, reaching up into the dusk of the evening and out to the shaggy *hruss* at their feed. Sira had been warned beforehand that if the *hruss* were not included in the *quiru*, they would crowd into the light, putting the riders at risk of being stepped on by their broad hooves. She made sure the animals were well inside her *quiru* before she stopped playing.

When she put down her *filla* there was a brief silence. At Conservatory there would have been silent comments, criticism or praise. Sira became suddenly aware of her loneliness. There was nothing to hear but her own thoughts. There was no Gift here but hers.

After dinner, the riders talked of the seasons.

"Softwood's almost impossible to find now," Blane said, to murmured agreement from the other riders.

"My mate said they ate cold food from Bariken to Lamdon last trip," said one burly man.

Sira listened with curiosity, then turned to Rollie. "Why would they eat cold food?"

"The softwood trees are almost gone," Rollie said. "If summer doesn't come soon, there'll be nothing to burn."

Sira looked around their campsite, and saw that it was true. There were none of the thin, fragile softwood trees that sprouted only in summer. Ironwood would not burn.

Blane spoke from where he sat on his bedfurs on the other side of the fire. "I have a son born in the last summer, and he's almost five years old. The Visitor better show up soon! Kel's driving us crazy wanting to know when he'll have one summer."

Everyone laughed. The common practice of counting summers instead of years was cumbersome, but popular. Sira thought of her own brothers and sisters, and wondered how many summers they had counted up now.

She had not seen them since she was seven, with only one summer. It seemed a lifetime ago. She could not remember what her mother looked like, or the sound of her father's voice. She barely knew her siblings' names.

She murmured to Rollie, "I can hardly remember what the Visitor looks like."

"I feel the same," said the rider. "But it shows up in the sky every five years anyway, thank the Spirit. Otherwise we'd all be under a hundred feet of ice by now."

"Is summer almost here, then?"

"So it is, Cantrix. This makes the fifth deep cold since last summer. The days are getting longer. It's time, sure enough."

A little silence fell around the fire as the riders contemplated their constant and unrelenting enemy, the cold. One or two of them looked up at the *quiru* above them, appreciating its protection, perhaps thinking of their homes. Sira felt a wave of nostalgia for Conservatory, and she thought of the ironwood plaque that hung over its great double doors:

> SING THE LIGHT,
> SING THE WARMTH,
> RECEIVE AND BECOME THE GIFT, O SINGERS,
> THE LIGHT AND THE WARMTH ARE IN YOU.

She remembered stumbling past that carved creed on her first day at Conservatory, in the company of all the other Gifted ones newly arrived. She had not wept, though many of the others had. It was a day of parting from everything and everyone they knew. No Singer ever forgot it.

Lost in memory, Sira reached inside her tunic for her *filla*. She looked above her *quiru*, where the mysterious stars wheeled in their mighty dance, and a melody came to her mind. She put the *filla* to her lips. She played in the fourth mode, *Lidya*, raising the third degree. After a few bars she shifted into the fifth mode, *Mu-Lidya*, dropping the third degree down in a subtle cadence. The stars seemed to shine brighter as she played, as if her Gift could reach into the very heavens, and the darkness beyond the *quiru* receded a bit more.

Sira lost herself in the music, assuaging her loneliness, recalling her true home. When she finished, and lowered her *filla*, she realized with a rush of self-consciousness that the riders had ceased speaking and were watching her.

Her cheeks flamed. "I am sorry if I disturbed you—I—I forgot where I was." She looked down at her *filla*, cradled in her long, thin fingers.

"It was beautiful, Cantrix," Rollie said, just loud enough for everyone to hear. "Does it have a name?"

"I was improvising," Sira said shyly. "I am glad if you liked it."

"It should have a name so we can hear it again."

"I will name it, then," Sira said. A new melody was an important thing, something tangible, with its own meaning. "It is 'Rollie's Tune.'"

Rollie grinned around the circle. "Now, isn't that a nice thing to happen to an old mountain rider?" Her chuckle was comfortable, and one or two of the others ventured to nod to Sira. It was a moment like those Sira had dreamed of during the long years of her training. She tucked her *filla* back into her tunic, enjoying the sudden sense of belonging. If this was being a Cantrix, she thought, she would like it. She would like it very much.

Chapter Two

Isbel had been Sira's closest, indeed her only, friend in their class at Conservatory. They were as different as they could be, Isbel plump and pretty, with auburn hair and flashing dimples, and Sira tall, thin, and solemn.

Isbel sought out Maestra Lu after Sira had been gone from Conservatory for three days. She found her in the great room, in a rare moment of idleness, seeking the warmth of the sun as it filtered through the thick green windows.

"Excuse me, Maestra?" Isbel asked aloud. A student never sent thoughts to a teacher without invitation.

Maestra Lu did not turn, but she smiled up into the weak sunshine. *Good morning, Isbel.*

Isbel bowed. *Good morning.* Lu indicated a place on the bench next to her, only turning when Isbel sat down.

The Maestra looked more frail than ever, her pale, papery skin nearly translucent over the sharp bones of her face. Isbel thought her own ruddy, freckled skin seemed extravagantly healthy next to Lu's. But she kept these thoughts low in her mind, not wishing to offend her teacher.

Maestra, I was wondering if you are following Sira.

Lu looked at her sharply. *And how could I be following Sira?*

Isbel dimpled, and the Maestra's lips twitched gently. *Maestra, we all know you have the longest reach of anyone. Maybe the longest ever.*

Maestra Lu sighed a little. *And how do you all know that?*

We have heard the stories!

Maestra Lu turned to gaze out the window. For a moment Isbel thought she had forgotten her presence. The look of memory was on the old Singer's face. Surely Maestra Lu, who had twelve summers, must have many memories. Isbel waited until she turned back to her.

Sira is fine, Lu sent. *That is all I can sense, but it is enough, is it not?*

Isbel nodded, content. *She will be a wonderful Cantrix.*

Indeed, I hope so.

Do you remember her first quirunha?

Very well.

Isbel leaned against the cool glass of the great window. *The others were jealous.*

Lu raised her eyebrows, though this was hardly a revelation.

Yes, Isbel went on. *It was two years earlier than any of the rest of us could perform the* quirunha. *They teased her that day at breakfast.*

Tell me about it, Isbel.

Isbel loved stories, her own or anyone else's. No one knew more of them, or invented more, than Isbel. Sira had loved to listen to her tales, especially when the two girls lounged together in the *ubanyix*, floating lazily in the scented warm water. Now Isbel straightened, ready to make a story of Sira's first *quirunha*.

She was only fourteen.

Maestra Lu nodded. Individual birthdays were put aside when the Gifted children entered Conservatory. Each summer, a class came from the Houses across the Continent, Gifted children of six and seven, sometimes eight, delivered by their families. From then on, they shared the same birthday, the anniversary of their first day.

In the great room, the students tormented her. One in particular— Isbel looked sideways at her teacher, not wishing to cause trouble for one of her classmates. Lu seemed not to notice.

One was asking her if she was nervous, going on and on about how the whole House would be there, and listing all the things could go wrong. Sira was trying to eat—you always tell us to eat before we work— Lu's lips twitched again. Isbel saw, and her dimples flashed.

Finally, I am afraid I lost my temper. I told them all to stop it. All around us the House members were calmly having breakfast, not noticing our argument. Sira could not eat her keftet, *and she stood up.*

She sent to me, so that everyone could hear, that I was not to worry. That she was not nervous. Then she turned to—to the one who was teasing her, and she told her she had better not miss the quirunha. *She might learn something!*

Lu began to smile.

Sira went striding out of the room. You know how she walks, with her back so straight. Lu nodded, sharing the memory of Sira's tall, narrow form pacing the halls. *And of course you remember the* quirunha, *because you were her senior that day. It was beautiful. It was perfect.*

Lu took Isbel's hand. Only a Gifted one could touch another one of the Gifted, and the contact soothed and connected them, one to the other. *So it was, Isbel. And you need not have worried about your friend.*

I was still angry.

I know. But Sira would not have worried about what her classmates thought. She is always most critical of herself. Had she been disappointed in herserlf, that would have been something to worry about.

Isbel grew thoughtful. *I am sure she will be a great success at Bariken.*

A shadow passed between their two minds, and the Maestra withdrew her hand. Isbel looked searchingly at her, sensing something amiss.

She will be a fine Cantrix, Lu sent. *And so will you, my dear. Perhaps you should be practicing now?*

Isbel giggled. *Yes, Maestra.* She jumped up from the bench beneath the window and bowed. *Thank you.*

Lu watched her leave the great room. She was such a pleasant student, neither complicated nor difficult, reasonably hard-working, and with a pretty, warm voice. Sira had been her most challenging student, intense, talented, driven. Her only weakness was in healing, but both Mkel and Lu had thought her new senior Cantrix could continue training her. In the end, Lu felt certain, Sira would be a better Cantrix than she herself had been. She had not been a great healer either, but had been renowned for her singing. And, of course, as Isbel and the other students knew, for the strength and reach of her psi.

She hoped Sira's great Gift was not wasted on Bariken. She had protested the assignment, but the shortage of Conservatory-trained Singers had reached a critical point. Lu rose from the window seat, grimacing with the effort. There was something not right at Bariken, something hard for Conservatory and Lamdon to identify. And now Sira, young and inexperienced, was their Cantrix. It was out of Lu's hands.

The journey from Conservatory to Bariken took five full days. Traveling had a rhythm of its own, Sira discovered: riding, resting, meals. There was little talk during the day. Sira often did not speak at all, and the odd silence of being with unGifted people added to the strangeness. As her saddle-soreness began to ease, Sira studied the riders to see how they sat their *hruss,* how they handled their reins, how they used their feet. In the evening, around the fire, the riders told stories and jokes, but never spoke directly to Sira. She was the reason for their journey, and she was their protection. But it was not for them to hold unnecessary conversations with a Gifted one. Only Rollie, assigned to Sira for the trip, spoke to her. Sira was grateful for Rollie's warmth and humor, Gifted or not.

On their last day in the mountains they made their camp rather late, in purple twilight. Blane found a spot ringed by huge ironwood suckers. Sometimes the long thick shoots that connected the great trees lay hidden under the snow to trip *hruss,* but tonight they were welcome, as the riders leaned against them for support.

Sira made the *quiru* rise swiftly, and Rollie sat next to her, grinning in appreciation. "I'll be sorry not to hear you do that anymore."

Sira frowned. "I do not understand."

"We'll be at the House tomorrow, just after midday," Rollie said. "If the Spirit allows."

"I see." Sira tucked her *filla* into her tunic and smoothed her bedfurs. But you can attend the *quirunha,* can you not?"

Rollie's tanned face changed subtly. "It's not my custom."

"But at Conservatory, even the Housemen and women hear the *quirunha.*"

"Things will no doubt be different at Bariken from what you're used to, Cantrix," Rollie said gently.

"But I would like you to attend," Sira said. "I know no one else there."

Rollie looked out beyond the *quiru* into the deepening dusk. "I'll be around," she said. "If you want me, just tell that Housekeeper. He'll send for me. But he won't like it."

Sira wanted to know more, but with Conservatory courtesy, she did not press. Rollie went to the fire for Sira's tea and *keftet.* As the riders began the meal, the silence was broken only by the gentle crackling of the little fire.

In the quiet, Sira's sensitive ears picked up a sound. "Rollie!" she called softly. "There is someone approaching."

"Not likely, Cantrix." Rollie stared out past the *quiru,* listening, then shook her head. "Why do you think so?"

"I hear it!" Sira turned toward the direction of the sound. "Out there, up the hill. *Hruss.*"

"Blane!" Rollie called. "I don't hear it, but the Cantrix says there are *hruss* up on the hill." She pointed.

Blane stood up. *Hruss* could survive in the deep cold, but if there was a person there, leaving him or her in the lethal darkness was unthinkable. "We'll go see," he said. "I'll take Chan." The other man was already beside him. They pulled on their heavy furs, and plunged out of the *quiru* into the blackness beyond.

Sira stood with her head bowed, listening to their progress up the hill. To send people out of the safety of the *quiru* was a serious thing. Following them with her ears, she opened her mind as well. She sensed fear, and sadness, a man lost out there in the freezing dark.

Those in the *quiru* did not have to wait long. The sounds from the hillside grew until everyone could hear them. As they watched, Blane and Chan led two *hruss* into the warmth and light of the campsite. A man clung to the stirrup of one saddle, stumbling as he came into the *quiru*, falling clumsily to his knees as his strength suddenly failed him.

Blane crouched beside him and dropped an extra fur over his shoulders. "Take your time," he said quietly. Everyone in the *quiru* was silent, stunned by awareness that the stranger had been within heartbeats of freezing to death.

The man's *hruss* were still outside the circle of *quiru* light. Ice hung from the long hair under their chins, and clogged their forelocks. Sira pulled her *filla* out of her tunic and played briefly until the *quiru* swelled, its warmth and light expanding to include the half-frozen animals.

The stranger turned, stiffly, to see who was playing.

Blane said, "This is a party from Bariken. I'm the guide."

There was a long silence, and Sira could see the man's lips and face were too cold to move. At length he mumbled, "Devid," through still-rigid lips. He managed his House name, "Perl", then fell silent again. They all waited for his circulation to return. Every Nevyan knew it was a slow and painful process.

At length he gave a ragged sigh. "My Singer . . ." he struggled to say. His pain was unmistakable through the shield of Sira's mind. "My mate. She died last night."

Chan brought the man's bedfurs from his saddle, and helped him to sit down. Devid pulled his hood back, uncovering a lined, weatherbeaten face and graying hair. "She was ill." Another pause. "We were going to Conservatory for help."

Rollie had built up the fire, and now she pressed a cup of hot tea into Devid's icy hands.

"We're bringing our new Cantrix to Bariken," Blane told him, with a nod in Sira's direction. Devid stared at her, too exhausted for courtesy. "You can come with us."

"No metal," the traveler said miserably. "My mate hasn't worked in some time."

Blane put up a hand. "Not necessary," he murmured. "Nevyans help each other." The other riders nodded.

"Thank you." Devid turned to bow stiffly to Sira. "Cantrix."

Sira nodded in return. It felt odd to be treated with deference for doing only what every Conservatory student over three summers could do. "I am sorry about your . . . Singer." She stumbled over the word. She had known, in a rather distant way, that itinerant Singers took mates. No Cantrix or Cantor would dare to do such a thing, unless—like Magister Mkel—they intended to leave the Cantoris.

"Thought we could make it," Devid said to the riders, his eyes reddening. "Thought Conservatory could help. But she wasn't strong enough."

The riders sat staring into the flames, honoring Devid's loss with their silence. Tragedy struck often on the Continent, and there were few whose lives had not been touched by it.

The deadly cold ruled the lives of Nevyans. The snow and ice, which receded only once every five years, was as much a part of their surroundings as the sky or the rocks. Survival required almost all their energies.

At length Sira ventured to ask, "What troubled your mate?"

Devid lifted his face, and it seemed the lines in it grew deeper by the minute. "Pain in her side." He indicated the right side of his body. "We were in Deception Pass, on our way home. We turned for Conservatory, but the pain got so bad she couldn't ride."

"There's no road there," Blane said.

"Right. We tried to make a shorter trip of it, but the irontrees are so thick, and the drifts twice as tall as *hruss* . . . . Thank the Spirit, at the end she couldn't feel the pain anymore."

"She's with the Spirit of Stars now," Chan offered.

Devid nodded. "Yes. But our children will miss her. And I—" His voice broke, and he hung his head. Almost whispering, he finished, "I had to leave her there. In the snow."

Sira took a breath. Of course, if a Singer mated, there could be children. But the idea embarrassed her. She looked away, out into the darkness beyond the yellow *quiru* light.

"You can go back in the summer," Chan suggested.

"Better get into your bedfurs now," Blane said. "Warm up quicker."

Devid obeyed. There was really nothing else anyone could do. The other riders began to roll into their furs. Rollie and Sira went out of the *quiru* briefly, and returned to find the others already sleeping. Rollie said good night, and Sira slipped into her own bed.

Devid lay wakeful. Sira heard small sounds as he turned and shifted under his furs. When she sat up, she saw his hair tangling as he twisted.

"Traveler?" she whispered.

Devid lifted his head to see who was speaking. The skin around his eyes was gray and worn, and his lips trembled.

"May I help you sleep?" she asked quietly.

He looked confused, and didn't answer. She hesitated a moment, then began to sing, softly, a simple *cantrip* the older Conservatory students sometimes sang for the young ones who lay awake crying for their mothers. It was as familiar to her as the memories of the dormitory, where the narrow cots of the first- and second-level students lined the walls in neat rows. She used the gentlest touches of her psi to soothe the sorrowing man into sleep.

It did not take long. Soon his fretfulness stopped, and sleep stole over him. No one else seemed to have been disturbed by her singing.

Sira was satisfied, thinking how simple her job was, really. Looking up, she saw her *quiru* warm and bright above the travlelers. Reassured, she too lay down and closed her eyes.

She was surprised to hear Rollie say, "Sleep well, Sira."

In her drowsiness, Rollie had forgotten her title. The omission, in a strange way, made Sira feel at home.

Chapter Three

The riders, with Sira in their midst, clattered over the clean-swept paving stones of Bariken's courtyard just after midday. Sira looked up at the big doors of the House, and took in the sweep of its wings stretching east and west from its center hall. It was smaller than Conservatory, but she could imagine the fullness of the life inside, the great room where the House members met for meals, the huge kitchens, the apartments where families lived, their children tumbling over each other on the stone floors. At the very center would be the Cantoris, where she would do her work. The glassworks would be between the wings in the back, as would the nursery gardens.

One of the riders had galloped ahead to announce their arrival, and several people were assembled on the steps of the House.

Rollie murmured, "Perfectly natural to be nervous, Cantrix."

"Do you know my thoughts, Rollie?"

The rider chuckled softly. "You're the mind-listener, Cantrix, not me!"

"Rollie, I have not done so," Sira protested, and did not realize until a moment later that Rollie had been teasing her.

They reached the front of the courtyard, and Rollie slipped off her *hruss*. She came to assist Sira, but Sira dismounted on her own before she could reach her, her young body adapted already to the rigors of days in the saddle. Rollie untied her charge's saddlepack as a little, wrinkled Housewoman left the group on the steps to come and take it.

Rollie bowed quickly to Sira and stepped back. "Good luck, Cantrix." It sounded like goodbye.

"But I will see you, Rollie?" Sira's words hung in the clear air like those of a forlorn child. She wished she could take them back. She would have liked to touch Rollie's arm, but that would be a breach of custom. Rollie bowed again without speaking.

"Cantrix, Rhia is waiting for you," said the wrinkled Housewoman. She fidgeted impatiently, shifting the saddlepack in her arms, and looked up at the steps of the House.

There were two men and two women waiting before the big doors. The Housewoman said again, "She's waiting. Best hurry."

Sira had no idea who Rhia was, nor did she know the identity of this little Housewoman who spoke to her so brusquely. Taking a deep breath, she pulled her wrapped *filhata* from its place on her back, and slipped it into its more customary position, under her arm, a badge of office to give her confidence. Then she strode to the steps, her back arrow-straight. Blane walked close behind her.

"Rhia," Blane said. One of the women stood a little apart from the others. Her face was as smooth and still as the ice cliffs of Manrus, her bound hair glossy and pale. She seemed to be measuring Sira with her eyes. Unconsciously Sira put a hand to the binding of her hair.

Blane went on. "This is Cantrix Sira v'Conservatory."

Sira still unsure of who the woman was, bowed politely.

"I am Rhia v'Bariken," the pale woman said. "And this is Cantrix Magret, and Cantor Grigr." There was no mention of Magister Shen, although Sira had expected him to be in her welcoming party.

The blonde woman bowed the shallowest of bows, but Cantrix Magret, middle-aged and plump, smiled warmly at her new junior, her eyes crinkling cheerfully. Sira noticed, however, that she sent nothing.

"Welcome to Bariken, Cantrix," Rhia said, in a voice as dry and crisp as a softwood leaf.

"Thank you."

"I hope you had a good journey," Magret said aloud. Her voice was resonant, a Singer's voice. "I can hardly wait to hear all about Conservatory."

"Welcome, Cantrix Sira," the older man, Cantor Grigr said. His hair was nearly white, and his face was marked with illness. "We are so glad to have you here."

Sira bowed deeply to him, in respect. "Thank you, Cantor."

"Rather young, aren't you?" Rhia observed.

"Yes." Sira regarded the woman curiously. Surely youth was nothing to apologize for, but there was implied criticism in Rhia's manner. There was something extraordinary about every aspect of her appearance and bearing, the binding of her hair, the cut of her tunic. She spoke with authority, yet she bore no title. Sira hardly knew how to respond to her.

The dark man standing next to Rhia spoke now. "Magister Mkel of Conservatory spoke very highly of Cantrix Sira."

Rhia nodded. "Yes. Of course." Rhia lifted a graceful hand. "This is my Housekeeper, Wil. He will show you to your room." As an afterthought, it seemed, she added, "We all look forward to hearing you sing."

Sira doubted the sincerity of this very much, but she pressed the thought low so as not to offend her new senior. Rhia turned and went into the House, the elderly Housewoman trotting after her like a *caeru* pup after its dam.

Sira turned back to say farewell to the riders, but they were already leading the *hruss* out of the courtyard toward the back of the House, where the stables would be. The traveler Devid went with them. Only Blane still stood next to Sira.

"Thank you for escorting me," she said formally. She bowed to him, too, feeling tall and awkward and out of place.

His bow was deeper, and when he spoke, she sensed his sympathy. "Good luck, young Cantrix," he murmured. "We're sure you'll be a great success."

Sira straightened her shoulders and looked up at the great House awaiting her, expecting her to warm and light it, to serve its inhabitants. "By the will of the Spirit," she responded, and started up the steps.

*

Sira had expected, once she joined her new senior, the silent and easy communication she was accustomed to. It was a surprise to her that Magret persisted in speaking aloud as they sat together over their evening meal. The great room of Bariken was very like that of Conservatory, though smaller. The biggest difference, Sira thought, looking about her, was one of adornment. At Bariken, every surface was carved and molded into rich detail. The brightly colored clothes of the Housemen and women looked familiar, but the dark tunics worn by those of the upper class were heavily embroidered and embossed. Every wall bore hangings, and all the floors were laid with rugs. Conservatory was austere, its hard surfaces left bare to enhance their resonance. The first thing Sira planned to do tomorrow morning was remove the extraneous decorations that cluttered her own room.

"We are so glad you are here at last," Magret was saying. "Poor Cantor Grigr was not sure he could cope much longer."

Sira looked down the table to where Grigr sat, leaning on his elbows. His hand, as he lifted the wooden spoon to his mouth, trembled. She felt a rush of compassion that the old cantor must have sensed, for he turned to her. She thrust the feeling down, sorry to have disturbed him, and bowed respectfully from where she sat. His answering nod was tired, and full of understanding.

Since her senior spoke aloud, Sira did, too. "Can you not discover what is wrong?"

Magret shook her had. "Perhaps Nikei can help him. But you know, my dear, Cantor Grigr has eleven summers. He would have retired before this had there not been such a shortage of Singers."

Sira nodded. This was why she had been graduated so quickly. As a general rule, Cantors and Cantrixes did not step into a Cantoris before the age of twenty. Sira was only seventeen, not yet having four summers.

"Cantrix Magret, where is the Magister?"

Magret's smile faded. "I do not know where he is tonight, Sira. He may be hunting. He likes it very well."

Sira raised an eyebrow. Her mind was open, waiting for closer communication from her senior, but Magret, looking up at the central table, sent nothing. Sira followed her gaze.

Rhia, who Sira now knew was the Magister's mate, was deep in conversation with the Housekeeper. At Conservatory there would have been people coming to the table, asking questions and advice, being given directions. No one approached Rhia's table. Wil lifted his dark, narrow head occasionally to scan the room, but he and Rhia were left in privacy.

Sira turned back to hear Magret say, "Would you like to bathe now? After all that traveling . . ."

Sira accepted gratefully. It had been a busy afternoon, and a long, warm bath would be a great pleasure.

She and her senior both fetched clean clothes, and Magret led the way to the *ubanyix*. Here, as elsewhere at Bariken, there was an abundance of decoration. The great ironwood tub was scrolled and sculpted all around its edge, and Sira marveled at the number of *obis* knives that must have been worn to slivers in its making. Scented flower petals floated on the water, and piles of woven towels from Perl, familiar to Sira, were set out on the benches.

The two women stepped out of their tunics and trousers and hung them on pegs above their furred boots. As they slipped down into the tub, Sira stretched joyously, relieved to be free of the clothes she had worn for so long. Her body under the water was as lean and taut as a child's, while Magret's was curving and plump, with generous breasts and hips softened by the passing of years and comfortable living.

There were bars of soap from the abattoir in carved niches around the tub, and the soap, too, was scented. The Housekeeper must be very good at his job, Sira thought.

"Cantrix Magret, shall I warm the water a bit?"

Magret nodded. "That would be nice.

Sira got out of the tub to fetch her *filla*, then stood naked, unselfconscious, as she played a little melody in *Doryu*, the third mode. The temperature of the water rose sharply, until Magret held up her hand.

Very good, Sira, she sent.

Sira smiled, relieved. Now they could really talk to one another. She stepped back into the tub and began to unbind her hair for washing. *Maestra Lu sends her greetings to you.*

Is she well? Magret asked.

I think she is tired. And worried about me, Sira sent.

Magret lifted her head, her forehead creasing with a sudden frown. Softly, but aloud, she said, "We have a need to keep our thoughts private here."

Sira looked up through the wet, dark strands of her hair. Confusion made her abrupt. "But why?"

Her senior's frown softened and she reached out to push a lock of Sira's hair away from her eyes. "Everything is different here," she said. "It is difficult to explain. But there are Gifted people in the House who can hear us."

Sira leaned back in the water to rinse the soap from her hair. She could only follow her senior's lead, of course. If Magret wished to explain to her, she would. If not, Sira's duty was to accommodate her.

I know it is strange, Magret sent. *Try to be patient.*

Sira nodded, unsure what was expected of her. As they stepped from the tub to dry themselves and dress, she told herself she must simply wait and watch. Surely her questions would have answers soon enough. Surely Magister Shen would attend her first *quirunha* tomorrow, and perhaps she would understand more then. In any case, she had only to fulfill her duties. She was confident of her ability to do that. The politics of the House could not possibly matter, she thought.

She was mistaken.

Chapter Four

Alone in a practice room, Isbel labored over inversions in the fourth mode, trying to fill the emptiness created by Sira's absence. The fingering was complex, and she did it again and again until her fingers grew tired. She stopped to rest, laying down her *filhata* and stretching her arms. Strands of hair fell over her shoulders, and she combed them back with her fingers. As she started to redo the binding, the sensation of her fingers in her long hair brought up a memory, one she had avoided thinking of for a very long time. She pulled her hair loose and let it fall about her shoulders as she dwelt for a moment in the past. Her loneliness had begun in her babyhood.

Isbel had been born between summers, and she was two and a half years old when she first stepped outside into the light from Nevya's two suns. She remembered seeing the Visitor for the first time. She also remembered the look on her mother's face at day's end.

Isbel's mother, Mreen v'Isenhope, had smiled at her little girl running back and forth over the smooth cobblestones. Isbel squirmed when Mreen caught her up, laughing, tugging at the mass of curls that already fell halfway down Isbel's back. For a moment Mreen hugged her little daughter, then released her to run again.

Isbel was Mreen's only family. She had lost a child, a little boy who never saw a summer, to a fever the Cantor could not control. Her mate had died of the same fever. On this first summer day, Mreen sat with other parents, all of them smiling as they listened to the squeals and laughter that filled the courtyard.

When a woman began calling, "Karl!" with fear in her voice, the laughter stopped. More urgently she called again, "Karl! I can't find Karl!" Isbel remembered the bright afternoon seeming to dim all around them.

The adults in the courtyard were on their feet, looking behind the benches, hurrying off to look in the stables. Some went to the edge of the forest and called between the huge irontrees.

Isbel, unhappy at the interruption, ran to her mother. "Mama, Mama, play!"

Mreen picked her up. "Not now, darling. Ana can't find Karl. I must help her. You stay right here and wait for me."

The children were unaccustomed to the freedom of outdoors. It was rare for one to have the courage to walk away from the House. Isbel recalled sensing fear in the air, as sharp as smoke. She had held tight to her mother's neck.

"But, Mama," she said. "I know where Karl is."

"You do? Show Mama, then." Mreen put her daughter down and Isbel immediately trotted to the edge of the courtyard and into the woods.

"Isbel, where are you going?" Mreen called, hurrying after her.

"Show Karl, Mama." The beginnings of softwood shoots greened the earth under the ironwood trees and filled the air with their spicy scent. Isbel led Mreen into the chill shade of a broad tree that obscured the view of the House. Karl was curled up in the crook of an ironwood sucker, sound asleep.

Mreen swept him up in her arms and hurried back to the House. Karl was just waking as she handed him to his frantic mother. The adults gathered round, laughing in relief and asking Mreen where she had found him. She said, "Isbel found him," then looked down at her little daughter, realization dawning in her eyes. There was only one way Isbel could have known where the missing boy was.

Still, Mreen searched for another explanation. "Did you see Karl leave the courtyard?"

Isbel shook her curls. "No, Mama. I heard him."

"What do you mean, you heard him?" Mreen asked, her voice harsh with a new fear.

"I heard him sleeping," Isbel said, pulling her hand away from Mreen's. "I heard his dream. Didn't you?" She looked up into her mother's face, and watched the light go out of her face as surely as the suns would set a few hours later.

Mreen began, inexorably and deliberately, to withdraw from her daughter from that day forward. Isbel could not understand until much later that her mother simply could not bear the loss of another loved one. Mreen knew the pain that was coming. She also knew her duty. Her little Isbel was Gifted, and that meant she belonged, not to Mreen, but to Nevya.

Isbel was two and a half that summer. There were five years until Conservatory claimed her, and Mreen did what she had to do. But Isbel never saw her mother smile again.

Eighteen-year-old Isbel, now a third-level Conservatory student, dashed tears from her eyes and smoothed her hair back into its binding. She picked up her *filhata* again. Maestro Takei would want to hear the inversions tomorrow. That was what mattered now. Her mother had long ago gone with the Spirit beyond the stars.

The evening meal in the great room cheered Isbel. She took comfort in the familiar routine, seeing Mkel and Cathrin at their table in the center of the room, with Maestra Lu and the other teachers next to them. The students, Isbel's class and the two lower levels, all sat together at one side. Their tunics were drab, but their faces and eyes were bright. The air was thick with their silent chatter, for those who could hear it. At the other side of the room, the colorfully dressed Housemen and women conversed aloud, in the rich blend of Gifted and unGifted that was Conservatory.

Who is next, do you think? Kevn, one of the third-level students sent to the group.

No one for a while, I hope. This was Jana, the youngest of their level. *It is too soon.*

Not too soon for Sira—I mean, Cantrix Sira, Kevn responded.

Maybe it was, though, Jana sent back. *She is still not a strong healer. And not close to four summers.*

Closer than you! Kevn teased, and Jana smiled.

Isbel smiled, too, but the sadness of the afternoon flooded over her again. She looked down the table at her classmates, her friends. *There are so few of us,* she mused.

Kevn looked at her, his smile fading. *Only one for each House. A heavy responsibility.*

They were all silent for a moment; only the first-level class was oblivious to the turn their conversation had taken. No one needed to mention that the newest class was even smaller, not even one young Singer for each of the thirteen Houses. Isbel felt, somehow, that her memory of her mother and the students' concern over small classes were in some way connected, but she couldn't think how. She shook her head, frustrated, and saw that Kevn was watching her.

What is it? he asked.

I do not know, she sent. *Something I was thinking of earlier, but it is gone now.*

Kevn turned away to tease Jana. Isbel tried to join in the general conversation, but as one of the oldest students, she felt she hardly fit in anymore. When she pushed away her *keftet* and rose from the table, she was surprised to see Magister Mkel's eyes on her. He smiled gently, and she bowed. She knew he understood that she missed Sira, and that she shared his concern over her friend's assignment. As she left the great room, she felt heavy with the burden of the Gift, a weight that could never be put down.

She looked back as she reached the door. The students and the teachers in their plain tunics, together with the House members in vivid red and green and blue, made a lively scene in the bright light of Conservatory's *quiru*. They had gathered almost all of them, for the *quirunha* earlier. After the evening meal some would go to their family apartments, others to the *ubanyor* or *ubanyix*. Some would stay here to talk and tell stories, one of Isbel's favorite pastimes. She hoped Sira found the atmosphere at Bariken as congenial, but however pleasant Bariken was, Sira would feel as they all did, that Conservatory was home. It was now lost to her for years to come. Before long it would be lost to all of them.

Sira, her hair carefully bound and her *filhata* impeccably tuned and shining with fresh oil, waited for Cantrix Magret outside the Cantoris. Memories of Conservatory *quirunhas* rose in her mind, and she pictured the Cantoris there, an austere room, with rows of plain ironwood benches filled with students, teachers, and visitors. They would be silent, concentrating, preparing to support the Cantors in their work.

Usually two Singers worked together in the Cantoris, although there could be more. At Lamdon, the capital House, there might be as many as four at the daily *quirunha*. Lamdon was famed for the intensity of its House *quiru* and the abundance of Singer energy it could expend.

Cantrix Magret appeared now, smiling at her junior, and led the way into the Cantoris. Sira looked around curiously.

There was only a scattering of people, all in dark clothing, seated on ornately carved benches. They were chattering and laughing as if this were a social occasion. There were none of the vivid tunics of the working Housemen and women.

Since Magret appeared unsurprised, Sira had to assume this was typical. She kept her mind open, but her senior sent nothing. Sira, with her *filhata* under her arm, followed her up onto the dais. She must clear her mind now. She could think of these things later, when the ceremony was accomplished.

Those attending the *quirunha* rose and bowed to the Cantrixes. The chatter subsided, and the atmosphere grew solemn at last. This was the function for which Singers trained. Without the *quirunha*, the House would grow cold and dark. The plants would droop and die. The people would shiver in the cold, and as it crept through the stone walls, they, too, would die. The *quirunha* was the reason families dedicated their Gifted children at a young age, relinquishing them to Conservatory. It was a great sacrifice, and it was necessary.

Magret bowed briefly to her junior, sat, and began the ceremony with a quick strum of her *filhata's* strings. Her high, delicate voice had a slight vibrato, a fragile sound like the chiming of icicles striking together. Sira's own dark, even tone contrasted dramatically with Magret's. Their *filhatas*, schooled in the same tradition, made a disciplined counterpoint.

Sira followed her senior's lead easily, thinking perhaps Magret, using only the first mode, was keeping things simple for their first *quirunha* together. Lacy drifts of melody rose to fill the high-ceilinged Cantoris as they concentrated their psi together. The room brightened, and began to grow warm. Sira reached out with her mind to the glassworks, the apartments, the stables, and the nursery gardens, all places she had not yet seen with her eyes. She imagined each seedling and plant in the gardens stretching out its green leaves to receive the blessing of warmth.

When the *quiru* was strong and warm once again, Magret laid down her instrument. Sira looked out into the faces in the Cantoris. Wil, the Housekeeper, sat at the end of one of the long benches, his long legs stretching into the aisle. Cantor Grigr sat close to the dais, tremulously nodding appreciation. Rhia was absent, nor was there any man present who loooked as if he might be Magister Shen. Sira's pride was hurt. How could both the Magister and his mate ignore her first *quirunha* in their House?

Magret rose then, and Sira did, too, bowing formally to her senior as the assemblage rose. Together they chanted the traditional prayer:

SMILE ON US, O SPIRIT OF STARS,
SEND US THE SUMMER TO WARM THE WORLD
UNTIL THE SUNS WILL SHINE ALWAYS TOGETHER.

The ceremony was complete. Magret sent, *Thank you, Sira. You are as talented as Maestra Lu said.*

Sira was relieved to be able to send to her senior for amoment. *You are very kind, Cantrix Magret. It wa a lovely* quirunha.

Magret made a deprecating face. *Future* quirunhas *will be more interesting, perhaps.*

Sira caught a flash of wordless feelings, and understood that Magret, in keeping their music simple, was protecting Cantor Grigr's feelings. Sympathy welled in her. She could think of no heavier loss than losing the Gift. She thought of Maestra Lu, aged and yet still musically and mentally so strong. Perhaps Maestro Nikei really could restore some of Grigr's health. She sent a brief prayer to the Spirit that it might be so.

The Housekeeper came to the dais and stood by as first Magret and then Sira stepped down. He was very tall, half a head taller even than Sira. He looked down at her with narrow, dark eyes. "A charming *quirunha*, Cantrixes," he murmured as he bowed. There was an undercurrent of something in his voice, laughter or boredom, Sira couldn't tell which. When she glanced up at him, his thin mouth curved, and she looked away. She felt tall and awkward and childish, not at all the way she wanted to feel. She tucked her *filhata* under her arm, hugging its weight to her body.

"Thank you," Magret said to Wil. She put her hand firmly under her junior's elbow. "Come along, Sira, and I will show you the garden before the evening meal. Grigr and I had Cantoris hours this morning, and for now I am free."

Sira, glad to escape Wil's intense gaze, bowed goodbye to him, and went with Magret out of the Cantoris. She felt the Housekeeper's eyes on her back as she walked away.

Just outside the Cantoris the wrinkled little Housewoman who had been on the steps with Rhia when Sira first arrived stepped up to Magret with a sketchy bow. "Cantrix Magret, Rhia wants you to come and warm the *ubanyix* for her."

Sira drew breath to offer herself for the task, but Magret nodded to the Housewoman and turned down the hall toward the *ubanyix*. Sira opened her mind, but Magret sent nothing. Uncertainly, Sira followed her, expecting some instruction. The little Housewoman trotted busily in front of Magret. Sira sensed only resignation from her senior.

Still, this wasn't proper. Sira called, "Cantrix Magret, please. Allow me this small task. You are senior now."

Magret looked back in surprise. "That is very kind, Sira," she said. "But it is better if I do it today. We will have our walk in the gardens later." Her voice had gone rather flat, but her face gave no indication of her feelings. She hurried away, following the old Housewoman.

There was nothing Sira could do but turn and walk on alone, wondering. Magret had accepted a peremptory, even discourteous command, and she had complied without demur. Sira did not understand why a senior Cantrix, with her heavy responsibilities, should be treated in this way. Naturally, customs would differ here, but such disrespect surely should not be tolerated.

Sira wandered down the long, broad corridor. The intricate carvings that lined the walls reflected the yellow *quiru* light from curved and faceted surfaces. It was distracting. There was so much to look at, everywhere. It must have taken many summers to decorate every inch of Bariken in this way. Several people passed Sira. They bowed, but they did not speak. There were no voices in her mind. There were no friendly smiles.

A wide staircase opened up before her, with a carved banister that rippled and flowed like a slender river of wood. It was beautiful, and extravagant. She knew very little about *obis* carvers, but the ones who had made this banister had invested it with real artistry. It invited her hand to caress it as she climbed.

She wandered up the stairs, stopping to admire the wavy limeglass window above the first landing. The glassworkers also had much to be proud of.

On the floor above, the hallway was similarly wide, with apartment doors spaced far apart. Sira thought she must have come upon the Magister's wing, where he and his staff would have the largest rooms. She heard the murmur of conversation and ongoing family life behind the doors she passed, a homely and familiar sound. Her fur boots whispered across the stone floor as she walked.

She was sure she must soon come to another stairwell that would return her to the first floor. As she paced the corridor, she heard a door open behind her.

"Cantrix Sira!" The voice resonated in the hall. It sounded, in fact, like the voice of a Singer, the soft palate lifted, the vowels open. Sira turned to see a plump, middle-aged woman in the dark tunic of the upper class, standing in the doorway of one of the largest apartments. A child called something behind her.

"Yes," Sira said, wondering how this woman had known she was passing.

"I believe you have lost your way," said the woman. She closed her door and came forward, a woman as ample in her proportions as Sira was spare. She bowed rather casually. "I'm Trude. May I show you back to your room?"

"It is not necessary. I will find it."

"Very well. At the end of the corridor, turn right down the stairs and then right again." Trude smiled, her expression reminding Sira of Wil's odd one. "I enjoyed your *quirunha* today. Certainly a relief after listening to old Grigr's wobble."

Sira frowned. "I am sure he gave long and devoted service," she said stiffly.

"Too long, Cantrix. You're a refreshing change." Trude looked Sira up and down. "You certainly look like a Singer. No danger of you going astray, is there?"

Sira's eyebrows lifted. "I beg your pardon?"

Trude laughed, and Sira heard again the overtones of Conservatory in her voice. "Never mind, young Cantrix. I'll leave you alone. If you really don't want a guide, then—" She bowed again, still smiling.

"Thank you." Sira spoke coldly, and made a deliberately shallow bow. She turned her back, and was some way down the hall before she heard Trude's door close behind her.

Sira shrugged off her irritation as she went looking for the stairs. Someone, she thought, should teach the House members of Bariken how Singers should be addressed.

She took her *filhata* from under her arm and stroked its glowing surface, remembering the Houseman at Conservatory who had so painstakingly carved and polished and tuned it. She recalled the ceremony with which he had presented it to her. He would have disapproved of the manners of these people. Maestra Lu would have been furious.

Sira was always an early riser, preferring to put in an hour of work before the morning meal. On her third day at Bariken she rose even earlier than usual, and gently sought Magret with her mind, careful not to intrude.

When she determined that her senior was still in her room, Sira hurried out. She carried her *filla* in her hand, and moved quickly among the few people who were in the halls at that hour. When she opened the door to the *ubanyix*, she saw with satisfaction that the big carved tub was empty. The air was redolent with the fragrance of herbs left to soak overnight.

Her little melody in the third mode, with its plaintive raised fourth degree, floated out across the water. She played until curls of steam rose from the surface into the yellowish light.

Magret came in just as she was about to leave. A Housewoman was behind her, carrying a stack of woven towels.

"Sira? Are you bathing so early?"

Sira bowed. "No. But a senior Cantrix should not have to perform this small task."

"Ah. I see." Magret's cheeks curved with her smile, making her look younger than her seven summers. "Thank you." She hesitated for a moment, her eyes half-closed, listening to something. The Housewoman was on the other side of the room, busy with towels and cakes of soap. Magret opened her mind briefly.

There are problems here, she sent. *You are very thoughtful. But please be cautious.*

Sira raised one eyebrow, and waited for an explanation, but Magret shook her head. "Let us go to the great room together."

Sira inclined her head. She would follow her senior's lead, of course.

On the point of leaving the *ubanyix*, Magret turned back. *Keep your thoughts shielded*, she sent briefly. *Always.*

Sira's eyes widened, but she nodded once again. It was strange advice. She followed Magret out into the corridor, wondering. She and all Singers learned in their early years to observe the courtesy of mental privacy. Shielding should not be necessary. She drummed her fingers against her *filla* in frustration. Were these trivial things the lessons that could not be taught? They seemed a waste of a Singer's time.

She ate in silence, with a healthy appetite for the nursery fruit and spicy *caeru* stew. She and Magret sat alone at a table, basking in the bright light from one of the tall windows. Mealtime at Conservatory had been a time of community. The great room here at Bariken, Although filled with people, seemed cold and foreign.

She wondered what Rollie would be doing on such a clear morning. Perhaps she was outside, riding after the *caeru* in the sunlit hills.

Chapter Five

Cantoris hours began right after breakfast. Sira and Magret, *fillas* ready, seated themselves on carved armchairs at one end of the long room, and House members seeking healing lined up before them. Sira's role would be mostly one of observation at first, but she was nervous just the same. This was the weakest part of her Gift. Only the small bumps and ailments of the dormitory had been within her scope. Maestro Nikei had been frustrated with her. Maestra Lu thought the skill would come, with practice. But Sira had practiced, and practiced hard, and the knack of sensing others' discomforts still eluded her.

The first few patients were easy, a bruised elbow, two mild colds. One infant, held by a sweet-faced, tired young mother, had a toothache. Magret asked Sira to treat it while she watched, and supported her with her own psi. Sira closed her eyes, and sensed a new tooth making its slow way into the little one's mouth. It was easy to slip past a baby's unformed mind. She played a soothing melody, and the child stopped crying, distracted by the music. Encouraged, Sira extended the tune, and used the gentlest nudge of her psi to ease the gum tissue away from the little tooth. Magret showed her how to quiet the tiny nerves, and Sira followed closely. The baby sighed with relief. Sira did, too.

"Oh, thank you, young Cantrix," the mother whispered. She was no more than four summers old, Sira was sure, but her eyes were smudged and swollen.

"You are welcome," Sira said. "You need rest, Housewoman."

The young mother shook her head. "You've never raised a baby," she said tiredly.

Sira raised one eyebrow. Magret said sharply, "All right, Mari. You may go now."

Mari blushed and put her hand over her mouth. "I'm sorry," she said, with a wary glance at Cantrix Magret's stern face.

As Mari hurried off, Sira sent, *I do not think she meant to offend, Cantrix.*

We must discourage familiarity, Magret responded. *It hampers our work.*

Sira wondered why disrespect was tolerated from some and not from others, but others were waiting, and there was no time to ask. It would bear consideration, when she had time.

As Mari carried her baby from the Cantoris, Sira could see that it was sound asleep, and she felt a rush of satisfaction. She felt like an adult at that moment. She felt like a professional. She had much to learn about Bariken and its ways, but this first small success delighted her.

She sat back in her chair, her *filla* cradled in her long fingers, and found Wil watching her. Outrageously, he winked one narrow eye. Sira flushed, and looked away to the next patient. Surely the Housekeeper's behavior could be called disrespectful. Something about him disturbed Sira, even offended her. She pressed her lips together. It was all very confusing.

A man with his arm in a sling was next in line, but a Housewoman stepped in front of him. Sira expected Magret to tell the woman to wait her turn, but the senior Cantrix only gave a long and audible sigh.

"Cantrix, Trude wants you to see her boy upstairs," the woman said to Magret.

Sira turned to her senior in protest. Working Housemen and women were waiting, and in her experience, no House member received consideration above another. Magret, however, did not return her glance. She rose without comment to follow the Housewoman. Sira opened her mind, but Magret's thoughts were firmly shielded.

A flood of exasperation at these mysteries brought Sira to her feet. Without stopping to consider, she said, "A senior Cantrix is not summoned like a cook or a stableman." Her deep voice rang in the Cantoris with authority beyond her years, beyond even her own intent. The people in line looked up in surprise, and she sensed Wil's sudden movement. But she could not stop now. "I am junior, and if the boy is too ill to come to the Cantoris, I will go to him."

The Housewoman looked bewildered. "Trude said—Cantrix Magret," she blurted.

Magret opened her mouth, but Sira forestalled her by stepping forward. "Let us go," she said, "so that I can return to assist Cantrix Magret here. People are waiting."

The Housewoman hesitated, looking about for guidance. There was a sibilant hissing of people whispering to each other. Sira strode from the Cantoris swiftly, before Magret could demur. As she passed him, Wil grinned, openly amused.

Sira knew where Trude's apartment was. She turned in that direction, her long legs moving too fast for the fat Housewoman, who puffed as she hurried after her. Wil caught up with them at the foot of the stairwell.

"Cantrix," he said, matching his own long steps to hers. "Are you sure about this?"

Sira did not look at him. She feared losing the sense of purpose that had carried her out of the Cantoris, and she was trying to hide her lack of confidence in her ability to heal the child. She used the energy of her irritation to quell dismay at her own rashness. "Of course I am sure. Cantrix Magret has great responsibilities."

"But customs at Bariken—"

"Are different. So I have been told." The fat Housewoman was far behind them now. "Some things never change. A senior Cantrix must be respected."

"Perhaps I can smooth this over," Wil said. Sira glanced at him. Clearly, he was enjoying himself. She wondered how bad it might be.

She slowed her walk a little. She had acted impulsively, but she knew she was in the right. Her doubts assailed her then, and she turned her *filla* over in her hands, looking down at it. "If I cannot heal the boy," she said diffidently, "naturally I would call on Cantrix Magret."

"Naturally."

They reached the upper hall, and Wil stepped ahead of Sira to knock on Trude's door. His smile vanished, though his eyes still gleamed. Trude opened the door, looking perfectly composed. Her eyes met Wil's directly, as if they knew each other well.

"Is Denis ill?" asked Wil. "Your Housewoman said you needed one of the Cantrixes."

Trude frowned as she caught sight of Sira. "I asked for Magret."

Sira frowned, too, at the omission of Magret's title. The Housewoman came panting up behind her.

"Cantoris hours were busy this morning," Wil said easily. "Cantrix Sira offered to help."

"A child to heal a child?" Trude turned back into her apartment, and Sira sensed a wave of anger from her. She wondered at the strength of it. Usually unGifted people did not broadcast their emotions so strongly.

She followed Wil into the apartment, where a boy of about two summers, perhaps nine or ten years, played on a *caeru* rug on the floor.

"Is this Denis?" Sira asked. She knelt beside the child, and he looked up at her suspiciously. Sira sensed Trude behind her, still angry. When she looked around for permission to proceed, she saw a glance pass between Trude and the Housekeeper. Wil gave a slight shake of his head.

Sira turned her attention back to the boy. "What is bothering you?"

"My ear hurts." His face and voice were sullen now, though he had seemed happy enough when Sira came in. Her doubt receded. Earache had been a common complaint among the little ones in the dormitory.

"Please sit very still," she told him. He looked up at his mother, then put down his wooden toy. Sira raised her *filla* to her lips and began to play.

The music carried her quickly out of herself. She could see Denis's inner ear with her mind, the slight redness deep in the curving recesses, the swelling that was the cause of the pain. It was a matter of only moments, a melody in the healing third mode, a gentle probing of psi to release the congestion and diminish the swelling. From the pocket of her tunic she drew a scrap of soft cloth and fashioned a tiny cushion which she put in the boy's ear.

"What's that for?" he asked, curious in spite of himself. Sira smiled at him, and got a small, knowing smile in return.

"It is to keep the cold from your ear," she told him. "Take it out when you think your ear is healed."

She stood, her *filla* by her side, and spoke to Trude. "This was not serious. Denis could have come to the Cantoris."

Trude's temper grew, palpably filling the room with its energy. Sira felt it as surely as if Trude were one of her Gifted classmates. Wil's face was still, but Sira saw laughter in his eyes once again.

"When we need healing, young Cantrix, the Singer comes to us," Trude retorted, biting off the words. Her soft face looked older, harder, in her anger. "Denis is the Magister's son, after all."

Sira's eyebrow arched in surprise, but she said nothing. When neither thanks nor explanation were forthcoming, she bowed the briefest of courtesy bows, and turned on her heel. The door shut with satisfying sharpness behind her, and she paced down the corridor as swiftly as she could.

Wil caught up with her at the top of the stairwell. She flashed him a look without stopping.

"Trude can be temperamental," he said, grinning broadly now. Sira did not speak, but started down the stairs.

"She was Cantrix, you know," Wil went on conversationally. "Before Denis's birth."

The revelation stopped Sira in midstride, one foot on the landing. "Her voice—"

"Yes," Wil said. "She was Trude v'Conservatory. She came here as a girl of four summers."

Sira couldn't speak. A Cantrix . . . who had a child. She knew what that meant.

Wil nodded. "It was almost a disaster," he said. "Cantor Grigr saw what was happening, of course, and Conservatory sent Cantrix Magret before it was too late." He gestured with his long arm, and they resumed walking, more slowly now. "Perhaps you can understand that Trude is somewhat—sensitive."

Sira shook her head with profound disapproval. "She, especially, should know better."

Wil chuckled. "Ah. So young, and so sure. We'll see, young Cantrix." They reached the door of the Cantoris, and Wil bowed elegantly. "Well done, Cantrix Sira." He straightened, and looked directly into her face. It was a look of challenge.

Sira felt the rising flush on her cheeks, and she stiffened. She was no Trude, to be dallied with and seduced. She was a full Cantrix, and she took her duty to heart. She turned her back on the Housekeeper, and tried to ignore his chuckle as she went through the door.

As she came in, Magret looked up with a worried expression. Sira felt a fresh surge of resentment that a senior Cantrix in the midst of Cantoris duties should be bothered by trivial things.

But she calmed herself. There were still people who needed help. It was the work that mattered most, after all. Let Trude and Wil play their games. It meant nothing to her.

She sat once again beside her senior, and took up her *filla*.

Cantoris hours sped by, and Sira was surprised to find it was time for the midday meal. The *quirunha*, after the meal, filled the early afternoon. When it was completed, with no more House members attending than the day before, Sira addressed the problem of her room.

It was situated in the same wing as the Magister's apartments, but on the lower level, close to the Cantoris. It would suit her well once the hangings and rugs had been removed.

The Houseman who came to take away the offending decorations was carefully formal. "What can I do for the young Cantrix?" He was far shorter than she, having to turn his brown, wrinkled face up to look at her.

Sira wondered briefly if the word "young" were to be forever attached to her title, but she thrust the thought aside as unimportant. "These hangings. They dampen the resonance."

The Houseman nodded, though he looked blank. Still, he obediently pulled down the hangings and rolled up the rugs, piling them in the corridor. "Will there be anything else, Cantrix?"

Sira shook her head. He bowed from the doorway, and she realized that, besides herself, this Houseman was the only person who had been in her room since she arrived.

"Excuse me," she said, before he could pull the door shut. "Do you know where Rollie might be today?"

The Houseman said, "If you need something else, Cantrix, I've been assigned to help you."

"No. Never mind." She could hardly tell him she only wished for company. It would be beneath her dignity. And worse, it might make Rollie uncomfortable if she asked to see her. "Thank you," she said. "There is nothing else."

When he had gone, she picked up her *filhata* and began to work.

She was deeply immersed in a melody combining the fourth and fifth modes, searching for the perfect modulation from one to the other, when there was a sharp knock on her door.

Automatically, she cast her mind out to discover who was there, but she did not recognize her caller. She went to the door, the *filhata* under arm, and found the petite, white-haired Housewoman who attended Rhia. Sira nodded to her. They had never been introduced.

"The Magister wants to see the young Cantrix," the woman said. Her bow was much shallower than that of the Houseman, and executed as if it were an afterthought.

"Oh, certainly," Sira said.

The Housewoman's faded blue eyes sparkled with malice. "Trude's been to see him," she said with obvious satisfaction. "Something about you."

Sira let this pass. She was about to meet her Magister at last. She put down her *filhata* and followed the Housewoman out, closing the door behind her.

The Housewoman cast her an upward glance. "Your hair?"

Sira put her hand to her head, and found that thick strands of hair had burst free of their binding. She tucked the errant locks back, and straightened her tunic. She shortened her steps to match those of the Housewoman.

"Do you know about Trude?" the woman asked.

"We have met."

The woman cackled. "You want to be careful with her. Denis is the Magister's only child."

Sira, offended by the Housewoman's intimate tone, disdained to ask if the Magister were angry about what she had done. It was not the first impression she had hoped to make, but there was nothing to be done about it now.

"Rhia has no children," the woman prattled, as if Sira had expressed interest. "Not one."

She grinned, making deeper wrinkles in her sunken cheeks. "Nice for Trude."

Except for Rollie and Blane, Bariken had not impressed Sira. She was unaccustomed to secrets and rudeness, but she hardly knew how to reprimand the woman. She walked faster. The Housewoman had to trot to keep up, and breathlessness put an end to her gossip.

They went up the staircase with the intricately carved banister and the beautiful limeglass window. The glow of Bariken's *quiru* shone beyond the glass, fading the sunshine. In the upper corridor, Sira let the Housewoman go ahead to show the way. They passed Trude's apartment. At the next door, the Housewoman stopped, and opened it without knocking. She stood back to gesture Sira into a room with furs and tapestries everywhere–on the chairs, on the walls, on the floor. Sira had never seen a room so full of furniture and rugs and hangings. She had not known there were so many colors of thread for weaving, red and purple and blue and lavender all worked together.

"Magister?" the Housewoman called. Sira noticed that her tone was polite now.

"Here, Dulsy." A stocky man of middle height with thick, graying hair and beard emerged from a back room. When he saw Sira, he grunted, and dropped into a big carved chair. She knew intuitively that her height bothered him; he sat so he wouldn't have to stand looking up at her. Politely, she bowed. When Dulsy only stood to one side, watching her in silence, she introduced herself.

"Magister Shen. I am Cantrix Sira v'Conservatory."

Shen nodded a curt greeting, muttering, "Welcome," or something like it. His face was ruddy and creased, and Sira remembered that he loved to hunt. He looked more like her father than he did Magister Mkel. He stared at her for a moment. "How old are you?"

Sira was weary of the question. "Almost eighteen, and fully qualified as Cantrix."

"How many summers is that?"

"It will soon be four." She met his eyes steadily, and after a moment he turned his gaze away.

"Well, young Cantrix," he said. "I need peace in my House. I don't want these women coming to me with their problems. Listen to Rhia. Don't cross Trude. That's all."

"Is that all?" Sira said quietly. Her temper rose like a softwood blaze, and the air around her began to glow. He had not met her, had not bothered to hear her sing, and yet he called her here . . . ordered her here, just to scold her! Was she supposed to respect a man like this?

She put her hands behind her back to hide their clenching. "Do you suggest, Magister, that your mate should supervise your Cantrixes?"

Shen's face darkened. "Now, listen," he began.

Rhia forestalled his answer, walking gracefully into the room. "Magister," she said, giving the title an odd, exaggerated inflection that made Sira's psi tingle. "I didn't know you had met our young Cantrix."

"Trude complained about her," was his curt answer.

Sira saw a flash of triumph brighten Rhia's face, then die away as her fine features resumed their usual icy composure. "Trude interrupted Cantoris hours," she said smoothly. "I think Cantrix Sira handled the situation very well."

"Wouldn't hurt Magret to go see Denis," Shen said.

"Cantrix Magret is senior now," said Rhia. "Cantrix Sira was perfectly able to take care of Denis."

"Denis was not seriously ill," Sira offered. She had meant it to be a reassuring remark, but she saw with alarm that the Magister's face flushed a dark red. Dulsy stood watching with her arms folded, eyes bright with enjoyment. Rhia noticed her, too, and waved a dismissive hand. Dulsy obeyed without ceremony, banging the door shut behind her.

At the sound, Shen's temper snapped. He smacked his fist against the arm of his chair, and shouted, "By the Six Stars, Rhia! Can't you keep this women's business out of my hair?"

"House business," Rhia said, her voice low and even. She touched her glossy hair, briefly hiding her eyes with her hand.

"I'll take care of House business," the Magister roared. "Trude, and her boy . . . you take care of them! And these silly Cantrixes!'

Sira sucked in her breath as if she had been slapped. Her own temper made the air around her glitter with power. She struggled to control it, lest some ornament shatter under its force.

Shen, oblivious, sprang from his chair, his muscular vitality out of place in the ornate surroundings. He stamped out of the room, and another door banged shut.

Rhia stood frozen in her graceful posture. Her face was still, but when she lifted her eyes to Sira, they gleamed. "The Magister—" she began, then stopped. Sira watched her take control of her emotion, rein it in as if it were a rebellious *hruss*.

Rhia began a second time. "Magister Shen has no patience."

Sira's own temper subsided as she watched the other woman.

"He has no idea that he insulted you," Rhia said. "Other things occupy his mind."

The atmosphere in the apartment was charged with emotion. Sira felt it like waves of heat and freezing cold. Rhia's words sounded as if they were meant to protect her mate, and yet beneath them there was something else, some perverse pleasure in the scene Shen had created. Sira's disappointment at the Magister's reaction to her was overridden by her wonderment at the strange relationships these people had.

"You may go now," Rhia said.

Sira eyed her, wondering if Rhia realized her curtness was nearly as rude as the Magister's careless insult. She asked, "And Trude?"

"I can handle Trude." Rhia turned away. "You'll find I am the one who handles it all."

Sira folded her hands together, and bowed.

"I'll call someone to show you back to your room," Rhia said.

"It is not necessary. I know the way."

Rhia nodded, and remembering herself at last, bowed. A muscle quivered in her jaw, marring its smooth line. Sira walked to the door, and opened it just in time to admit a Housewoman with a stack of ledgers in her arms. As Sira closed the door, she saw Rhia and the Hosuewoman sit down at a large desk with the thick books between them. If Rhia managed the inventories and the Cantoris, settled disputes and acted as intermediary for Shen, then what did the Magister do? It seemed that it was Rhia, indeed, who handled everything. Who did the Magister's job.

Sira wished she could find it in herself to like her.

Chapter Six

Isbel, like all Conservatory students, loved to see travelers. No matter who they were, travelers brought with them the essence of the mountains and glaciers and irontree forests of the Continent. For the students, as for most of the people of Nevya, life was bounded by stone walls year in and year out. Only in the brief summers did their world expand to include the sky, the earth, the smell of fresh breezes. Riders coming in from the great outside seemed adventurous and free. For Isbel, the storyteller, they were also mines of information.

When word passed among the students that travelers were riding into the great cobbled courtyard, Maestro Nikei released Isbel from her third-mode exercises so she could join her classmates in the window seat to watch the party dismount.

They were a bedraggled-looking group from Perl, the poorest of the northern Houses. There were three rather small, thin men, and one who was big-shouldered and strong. This one wore his shock of curling blonde hair short, shorn in the manner of those who travel for their livelihood.

That is Theo, one of the students sent. Isbel recognized Jana's voice, and she remembered that Jana was from Perl. *He is a Singer, an itinerant. I have met him.*

What is that fur he wears? asked Kevn.

Urbear, Jana sent with a shiver. It was silvery-gray on its surface, with a layer of dark gray showing beneath. *Be glad they do not leave the coast.*

Who are the others? Isbel asked.

I only know one, the one with gray hair. He is Housekeeper at Perl.

What do you suppose they want?

No one had an answer. The party were now off their *hruss* and were coming into the hall, shrugging off furs and stamping their cold feet. The young Singers untangled themselves from the window seat and reluctantly went back to their lessons. In the hall, Isbel watched Cathrin greet the travelers and invite them to bathe and eat.

The broad-shouldered itinerant, Theo, looked up and met Isbel's eyes. He recognized her, no doubt because of her dark tunic, as one of the students. He bowed, and when he straightened he caught her eye and smiled at her. Isbel dimpled and ducked back out of sight, hurrying up the stairs toward the students' wing.

By the time the House gathered in the great room for the evening meal, all the students knew why the travelers had come. Perl, as Bariken had been a few weeks before, was in need of a Cantor. Cantor Evn, who had only eight summers and should have been able to work for some years yet, had something wrong with his fingers. His junior had been unable to relieve his disability, and unable to play either the *filla* or the *filhata*, he was nearly useless.

At the Magister's table, the students saw Perl's Housekeeper and Magister Mkel looking at their table. Shivers of excitement went through their ranks.

Cantor Evn must be worried, a second-level student sent. *What if he can never play again?*

That would be disaster, Kevn sent. *No one can sing that way.*

So it will be one of us. That was Arn.

I am ready, boasted Kevn

We are all ready, Arn responded, but several of his classmates shook their heads in doubt.

Perhaps they will send Jana, someone put in. *It is her home.*

Jana's sending was forlorn. *Conservatory is my home, just as it is yours.*

There was a long moment of silence. The first- and second-level students looked with wide, respectful eyes at their seniors, who were so close to adulthood and professional life. All the older students knew that the day of their departure was close, whether this year or the next. Now it appeared that someone, besides Sira, would be leaving early.

Isbel looked around at them—tiny Jana with the dark eyes, Kevn tall and thin and craggy, Arn plump and slow-moving, but with quick fingers on the strings of the *filhata*. There had been thirteen. Now there were twelve. Soon they would be only eleven. They were her family, as were all those at Conservatory. Cathrin had given Isbel more affection than she had received from her own mother.

She lifted her head to gaze around the great room. Theo, the itinerant Singer, was seated at a table with several stablemen, but he was watching the students with a strange expression. Daringly, Isbel opened her mind to see if he would send to them. She heard nothing. Still, his eyes seemed full of longing as he looked from one to the other of the students. Isbel wondered about him. What must it be like, a life spent forever traipsing back and forth between the Houses? Everything about him spoke of the outdoors, of sun and wind and the deep cold. She glanced at Maestro Nikei, at the Magister's table. He was about the same age, she guessed, but as white and slender and fragile-looking as Maestra Lu.

Isbel forced her attention back to her friends. Perhaps she would have a chance to speak to this Theo before he rode out with the party back to Perl. He must have many stories to tell.

When the evening meal was over, the youngest of the students begged a story. Isbel sat in one of the broad window seats, and the first-level students clustered around her. They were very new, having been at Conservatory only a few months. They still cried for their mothers at night. Isbel and the other third-level students indulged them at every opportunity, prompted by poignant memories of their own misery when they had first arrived.

With one child on her lap and others leaning against her, their little hands on her arms, in her hair, tugging on her tunic, Isbel told them the story of how the Spirit created the thirteen Houses. Because the story was one of the legends, she chanted it aloud on three scale degrees of *Mu-Lidya*. She sang the old, old words without embellishment.

THE SPIRIT OF STARS, THE GREAT SOWER OF SEEDS,
LOOKED DOWN AT THE EMPTY WORLD AND LAMENTED ITS BARRENNESS.
SO THE SPIRIT REACHED OUT ITS GREAT HAND
TO GATHER THIRTEEN STARS FROM THE ABUNDANT SKY.
THEY SPARKLED IN ITS PALM.
THE SPIRIT BREATHED ON THE BURNING STARS TO COOL THEIR FIRE,
THEN IT THREW THEM ACROSS THE CONTINENT.
AT MANRUS THEY FELL, AND AT ARREN,
AT PERL AND ISENHOPE, AMRIC AND CONSERVATORY.
AT LAMDON, BARIKEN, SOREN, AND CLARE,
    AND TARUS AND TREVI AND FILUS.

The children sighed, each having waited to hear the name of his or her own House as Isbel chanted it. One put her cheek in Isbel's hand, and Isbel cupped it as she sang. Feeling other eyes on her, she looked up to find the itinerant Singer watching from a distance.

THE STARS TOOK ROOT, AND THE HOUSES GREW,
AND THE SPIRIT BREATHED ON THEM A SECOND TIME,
TO FILL THEM WITH NEW LIFE.
THE PEOPLE CAME, AND *CAERU* AND *HRUSS.*
FERREL AND *URBEAR, WEZEL* AND *TKIR.*
THE SPIRIT LOOKED DOWN AND SAW THE EMPTINESS FILLED,
AND WAS CONTENT WITH ITS CREATION.
BUT THE PEOPLE CRIED OUT TO THE SPIRIT
THAT THE WORLD WAS COLD, AND THEIR SEEDS WOULD NOT GROW.
THE SPIRIT OF STARS GREW SAD THAT ITS PEOPLE WERE DYING.
A THIRD TIME THE SPIRIT BREATHED,
AND FROM ITS OWN FIRE CREATED THE GIFT,
THE SPARK THAT WOULD WARM THE WORLD.

That is us, sent one sleepy child.
Isbel ceased her chant for a moment. *You are quite right, Corin. That is us.*
Go on, please, sent several others. One girl was already asleep on Isbel's shoulder.

THE SPIRIT OF STARS, THE SOWER OF SEEDS,
LOOKED DOWN ON THE WORLD WITH ITS HOUSES AND SINGERS
AND SMILED TO SEE IT.
WHEN THE SPIRIT SMILED, THE SUMMER CAME,
THE LAST AND GREATEST OF THE GIFTS.

Several children joined in the last lines, the prayer that ended every *quirunha.*

SMILE ON US, O SPIRIT OF STARS,
SEND US THE SUMMER TO WARM THE WORLD
UNTIL THE SUNS WILL SHINE ALWAYS TOGETHER.

There was a silence when the song was ended. The Housemen and women who cared for the young ones came forward to gather up the sleepy children.

The Singer Theo waited until they had all left the great room, and he and Isbel were alone. "That was beautiful."

"Thank you."

He looked about to say something else, but several House members came in to set the long tables with bowls and spoons for the morning meal. Isbel bowed, her mind open for the Singer to continue his thoughts, but he only bowed in return. She knew no other way to invite his friendship. She went off to her bed, leaving him in the great room watching the preparations.

Magister Mkel and Maestra Lu had to decide quickly, and the students knew it. They waited only two days before they learned that Arn would become Cantor at Perl. Although by the common reckoning, all the third-levels were the same age, measured in years Arn was the oldest of them, just short of twenty. His ceremony and departure were scheduled three weeks hence. His classmates congratulated him, touching his hands, encouraging him, understanding his anxiety despite his avowed confidence. Cantor Evn would remain at Perl to smooth the transition, since except for his stiffening, painful fingers, he was healthy.

In the *ubanyix* that night, the third-level girls stayed so long they had to warm the water twice. They gathered at one end of the ironwood tub, treasuring their moments of leisure.

Even Arn will grow thin at Perl, sent Olna, who was plump and fair. Everyone laughed.

No. He will make them improve the kitchens, Ana sent.

I am afraid they are beyond help, Jana sent, somewhat disloyally. They chuckled, and then a silence grew among them.

Soon we will all be saying goodbye, Isbel sent, unnecessarily.

There were nods, and their young shoulders seemed to bow with the great responsibility each of them bore. One by one, they climbed out of the bath and dried themselves, and helped each other to rebind their hair.

Isbel was the last to leave. As she pulled the door of the *ubanyix* closed behind her she saw Theo, the itinerant Singer, coming down the corridor from the *ubanyor*. His blonde hair was damp, and a bit of metal on a thong around his neck shone in the *quiru* light.

"Good evening," he said.

"Good evening, Singer," she responded. She kept her mind open, but he sent nothing, though they walked side by side down the long hallway to the stairs. She glanced sideways at him, appreciating the bright blue of his eyes and the vigorous curl of his short hair.

He caught her glance and smiled. "I'm Theo."

She smiled back. "I am Isbel." They walked a few more steps. "Why do you speak aloud so much?" she asked, bluntly, as a curious child might.

Theo laughed, the resonating laugh of a Singer. It made Isbel laugh, too.

"My talents are different from those of Conservatory-trained Singers," Theo said. He was still smiling, but Isbel was sensitive, and she heard pain in his voice.

She wondered why that was, but she said only, "Oh. I did not know."

He shrugged. "It's a big Continent. There's much to know."

Isbel said impulsively, "Would you like to see our gardens?"

He bowed. "A pleasure, Isbel. If it's not too late for you?"

She shook her head, and led the way down the lower corridor to the back of the House, where the seedlings and plants of the nursery filled a huge, steamy space with a thick glass roof. The smell of rich earth and melted snow-water met them even before she opened the door.

"We are especially proud of our gardens," she told Theo. They strolled down a path between flats of plants just starting to grow. A gardener stepped out between them and bowed deeply to Isbel. She bowed in return.

"We have more fruit trees even than Lamdon." She pointed to the southeast corner where small trees in raised boxes stood against the outer wall. The kitchens were on the other side of the same wall, so that no breath of the deep cold should penetrate into the gardens and harm the fragile trees or their fruit.

There were benches here and there, and Isbel chose one. They sat, the itinerant keeping a careful distance. "It's wonderful here," he said. "I rarely see this part of the Houses I visit."

"What House are you from?"

"No House." Sensitive Isbel heard pain in his voice again.

She said gently, "How is that possible, Singer? Who on Nevya has no House?"

He chuckled. "The son of two itinerant Singers has no House."

"But other itinerant Singers have Houses," she protested. "I know a story about one, Tarik v'Manrus. Every Nevyan should have a House."

"Perhaps you're right, Isbel. But not everyone does."

"I never knew that."

"So there are some things they don't teach you at Conservatory!" Theo laughed. He lifted the thong that held the bit of metal around his neck and showed it to her. It was strangely marked, and she could not read it.

"This belonged to my mother, and her father before that," he told her. "We come from a line of Singers past remembering. Healers, cutters, itinerants. Perhaps this makes up, in some way, for having no House."

"I have only seen metal once before," Isbel said. "Do you earn great amounts of it?"

Theo laughed again. "There is no great amount of it on the whole Continent! I earn enough to keep me supplied. A few bits for each traveler, a few more for healing. It's enough."

Isbel felt suddenly weary. She was unused to so much speaking aloud, and the quiet of the nursery gardens made her aware of how late it must be.

Theo seemed to sense her feeling. "It's very late," he said quietly. "You should surely be in your bed by now."

She nodded to him. Evidently his Gift was intact, though apparently he could not send. "You are right, Singer. I must go up." They rose and walked back through the gardens, down the deserted corridor to the stairwell for the students' wing.

"Will you wait here at Conservatory for Arn?" Isbel asked before turning to the stairs.

"No. Magister Mkel has arranged a party for me to Arren."

Isbel's eyes widened. "So far," she breathed. "All the way to the Southern Timberlands."

He grinned at her. His eyes were ice-blue, like a cloudless sky above a snowfield. "It's my specialty," he said. "I know the southern Houses better than anyone."

"Sometime you must tell me about them." Isbel stifled a yawn with her hand.

He bowed. "With pleasure. Sometime when you're awake!"

She dimpled, and bowed too. Experimentally, as she started up the steps, she sent, *Good night, Singer*. But although he waited politely as she climbed the stairs, he made no response.

Chapter Seven

The long-awaited summer was beginning at last. The distant speck of the Visitor, the wandering sun, glimmered above the southern horizon. Children who had never been out of doors in their lives scrambled over each other to peer through the rippled window glass, hoping for a glimpse. The firn began to diminish on the lower slopes of the Mariks, and the snow that seemed eternal now dropped from the trees in large, mushy chunks.

Sira, who had seen only three summers herself, was no less excited than the little ones at the coming season. She came into the great room before Cantoris hours and watched them at the window for a few moments before sitting down to her meal. Several House members bowed to her from a distance.

Sira would have liked to crowd into the window seat with the children to watch the changes outside, but she knew if she did, they would pull back, keep their distance, be careful not to touch her. If they didn't, their parents would speak to them sharply, even fearfully. As Cantrix of Bariken, Sira had only her senior for real company.

She looked around the great room as she drank her tea. By now she could distinguish between the House members and their guests. Some were here to trade for limeglass, bringing worked leather goods from Amric or *obis*-carved ironwood implements from Tarus. In the far corner of the great room, two itinerants sat negotiating with the Housekeeper for work. Summertimes could be difficult for itinerants. For a few short weeks, Nevyans could move between Houses without hiring Singers to protect them. Itinerants had to find some other work to do while both the suns shone.

Sira leaned her head on her hand, remembering the visit her family had made to Conservatory last summer, five years before. Her mother had been silent and worn-looking. Her father was awkward and formal. Though Sira had not yet reached the status of full Cantrix, they did not touch her. They held themselves apart, as if she had become something alien, something awesome. She had been relieved when they departed, leaving her to her music and her friends. Since then, as before, she had received one message a year, carried by some traveler for the price of a small bit of metal, on the anniversary of her entrance to Conservatory.

Sira was not sure how many children her mother had. When she left, there were already three older than herself, and two younger. Of all her family only her father seemed vivid in her memory, full of energy after a hunt, striding into the family's apartment with a joy in life her mother had never shown. Sira had not liked the rough-and-tumble of her siblings, and once her mother had accused her of thinking herself better than her brothers and sisters because of the Gift. That memory stung, partly because there was a substantial amount of truth in the criticism.

Good morning, Sira, Magret sent, sitting down opposite her.

Good morning, Cantrix. Sira welcomed the interruption of her dark thoughts.

Summer at last. Magret and Sira had fallen into the habit of sending everyday pleasantries. Less trivial thoughts they spoke aloud.

Sira looked again at the children crowding against the big windows. She now knew a few of them by name. Denis was among them.

Magret followed her gaze. *In a few days, they will be playing outside.* Magret sipped her tea, and spoke aloud. "Last summer," she said softly, "Denis ran off into the woods, and Trude had the whole House looking for him." She shook her head. "The Magister treated it as a joke, but Rhia was furious. None of the children were allowed out again the rest of the summer."

"That was hardly fair."

"Certainly not. And it still did not change Denis's behavior."

Sira finished her meal, but waited politely for her senior. It was burdensome to speak aloud with another Gifted one, but Trude sat at the Magister's table, reminding her of the need.

The *quirunha* went on as usual, since the thick stone of the House walls shed the warmth of summer as effectively as it did the more cold of the winter. The daily ceremony was Sira's chief pleasure, the more so as she and Magret grew to know each other's musical inclinations.

Cantrix Magret seemed to be almost without ego. She allowed Sira to dominate the *quirunha*, enjoying the freshness of her ideas and the effortlessness of her technique. Sira enjoyed each opportunity to perform, though the sparse attendance was still a disappointement.

Magret, one day, saw her searching the listeners when the music was over. "You know, Cantrix Sira, it is only important to sing; it is not so important for whom you sing."

"I am sorry, Cantrix," Sira said, abashed. "Of course you are right." It was not wasted on her that Magret had spoken her rebuke aloud, so that Trude should not hear.

Magret put a soft hand on Sira's arm. Sira started, and realized it had been many weeks since she had felt someone's touch. "I am not angry with you, Sira," Magret said. "It has not been so long since I was a junior Cantrix, you remember."

"So I do, Cantrix," Sira said. "And you are generous with me."

Magret shook her head, as if that were not important. Sira marveled at the older Singer's ease with her Gift. She appeared tranquil, content, while in Sira's own breast the fire of ambition burned hotly. Sira wanted applause; she wanted to be presented in concert, as Maestra Lu so often had been, simply for the sake of her beautiful music. She cared what her listeners thought of her work. Cantrix Magret evidently cared only for the work itself.

From the first hint of the Visitor's arrival, the summer came on quickly. In a very few days, Magret's prediction came true, and the children were playing outside in the courtyard, with a few Housemen and women watching over them, and enjoying the suns on their own faces.

Sira was lingering over the morning meal, watching the courtyard, when she saw a man she recognized ride up, two long-legged boys on *hruss* beside him. It was Devid, the man her traveling party had encountered on the last day of her journey to Bariken. The boys were so like him, hair and eyes and build, that she had no doubt they were his sons. She pressed against the casement to watch them, putting her forehead to the cool glass. They all dismounted, and Devid sent the taller boy around back to the stables with the *hruss* while he and the other boy turned into the entrance.

After the *quirunha* that day, Sira saw the younger son once again. He sat in the back of Cantoris, on the bench furthest from the dais. His eyes were intent on the two Cantrixes as they stepped down. Sira tucked her *filhata* under her arm and strolled toward him.

He rose as she approached, brown eyes shining up at her in awe.

"You are Devid's son?" Sira asked.

He nodded, and a flood of feeling swept out of him and over Sira as he stammered his compliments. "It was a beautiful *quirunha*, Cantrix. Wonderful! Your voice—and your melodies— Do you change them? I don't know that many modes, but—"

Sira, almost laughing, put up her hand to hush him. His thin cheeks flushed red and he stopped talking, but the tides of emotion did not recede. There was elation, and pleasure, and a spate of longing that was unmistakable.

"What is your name?"

"Zakri, Cantrix." He ran nervous fingers through his brush of brown hair, and made her a clumsy bow.

"Your father did not mention to me that one of his sons is Gifted."

He gaped at her. "Can you tell? How did you know?"

"Zakri, your thoughts flow out of you like spilled water, going in all directions at once."

He blushed again. "I'm sorry, Cantrix! My mother was trying to help me with that—but she died. She was a Singer." The last he said with youthful pride and sorrow.

"Yes. I am very sorry about your mother." Sira looked about her. The Cantoris had emptied. "Zakri, how old are you?"

"This summer makes three."

"But in years, how old?"

He frowned, concentrating. "I—I think I am twelve."

"You should have been at Conservatory long ago!" Sira spoke without thinking, and she knew she had blundered when tears welled in the boy's eyes. He dropped his head, not answering, and Sira wished her words unspoken.

Devid's bulky form appeared behiind him. "Zakri, your brother needs your help in the stables." The boy looked up at his father, and his eyes flashed. Devid stepped back suddenly, holding up a warning hand.

Zakri took a ragged breath, then bowed stiffly to Sira and rushed out of the Cantoris. It made Sira's heart ache to watch his thin back as he hurried away. Undisciplined emotions poured from him, even after he was out of her sight.

She turned to Devid. He bowed, and was on the point of leaving.

"Your son needs training." She spoke as a full Cantrix, with the authority of her position.

"His mother was teaching him," Devid said. "Now I must find someone else."

"Why did you not send him to Conservatory?"

"There was no need for that." Devid's gaze was hard, and his mouth looked stubborn. "His mother was a Singer. And we didn't want to part with him. We needed him at home."

"But he longs to be a true Singer."

An old anger sparked in Devid's eyes. "He will be! I will apprentice him to an itinerant Singer and he'll learn all he needs to know, just like his mother did."

Sira frowned. "It is very late for him, but you could still send him to Conservatory. I can send a message to Magister Mkel."

Sira was so intent on her purpose that she was caught by surprise when Devid punched one big fist into his other palm. She jumped. She had not realized he was losing his temper.

"Why do you Cantors always think yours is the only way?" he thundered.

Sira had no answer. He was right. For a Conservatory-trained Singer, there was only one way. She stood tall, keeping her gaze steady. For a frozen moment they stared at one another, until Devid suddenly remembered himself.

He looked down at his furred boots. "Forgive me, Cantrix," he mumbled. "You saved my life, and now I've offended you."

Sira looked away, up at the dais where she had so recently sat and played. She tried to soften her own voice. "Nevya needs every Gifted person to be fully trained and capable. My class at Conservatory had barely one Singer for each House. We cannot afford to waste any."

"We love our children," Devid said, and there was fresh misery in his voice. "To send one away so young—we couldn't do it."

"But a Gifted child suffers without training," Sira said, turning back to him. "If he hears other thoughts, sense other feelings, and cannot direct his own, he will go mad. He will be dangerous to those around him."

"It's been hard on him since his mother died. But I'll find someone. He'll be all right."

Sira had no further argument to offer. She bowed to Devid in grim silence, and left the Cantoris. Poor, unhappy Zakri. If his father could feel his emotions as she did, he would know the child wanted nothing more than to go to Conservatory to train, late or not.

Sad and thoughtful, she went to her room and spent her emotions in long, painstaking practice with her *filhata*. Later she heard from Magret that young Zakri had stood in the hall outside her room for an hour, listening.

The brief weeks of summer fled by. The children grew brown and strong with running in the woods around Bariken. They laughed and chattered at dinner, and ate prodigiously, making the adults smile. The hunters ranged far, bringing back many *caeru* to be skinned and dressed, preserved for leaner times. One trip netted them a *tkir* pelt, and the entire House gathered to exclaim over its tawny, speckled richness, and to praise the hunters who had brought it down. They saved its great serrated teeth to be made into cutting tools valued in the abattoir. The children clamored to touch them, and when they were allowed to do so, cautiously, they put one finger to the yellowish points and then ran away, shrieking with mock fear.

In the forest around the House, the softwood shoots sprang up, growing visibly every day. Even the children were careful with them, never stepping on them or pulling them. Every Nevyan knew how much they were needed.

Sira had time to spare after the *quirunha* each day. She took to spending it in the courtyard, enjoying the suns, and playing little tunes on her *filla* for the children. Zakri sat near her one afternoon, and she smiled at him. She offered him her *filla* to play, but he shook his head, embarrassed. A leather ball lying near his feet suddenly rolled away over the cobblestones to smack against the side of a bench. Sira watched, trying not to show her surprise.

Zakri possessed a powerful Gift. It would cause serious problems if not harnessed soon. She tried to open her mind to him, but he didn't know how to respond.

Sira remembered her first days at Conservatory, when the dormitory grew quieter and quieter as the young Gifted ones, surrounded by their own kind, began to speak with their minds and not their voices. She wondered if Zakri's mother would have taught him how.

The next day Zakri and his father and brother were gone, in search of the mother's body to take home for burial. The softer ground of summer always meant burials, but it meant more sadness for Zakri. Sira sent up a prayer to the Spirit for him. It was all she could think of to do.

Another day, when the summer had passed its zenith, Sira sat in the courtyard in the long afternoon playing a lively melody for a little girl who danced, laughing, on the cobblestones. Denis and several other children were watching and applauding, in accord for once. Sira was startled when a shadow fell over her. Still playing, she glanced up above her *filla*.

Rhia was standing over her, frowning. "Must you play here?"

Sira abruptly broke off her music and stood, deeply offended. The little girl who had been dancing dashed away. Denis and the others stepped back, watching.

Rhia's jaw was set and she was pinching the material of her tunic, over and over. As Sira searched for some response, Rhia turned and called to one of the Housemen who had been nearby a moment before. "Bors! Bors! Come here!" Her voice was harsh in the bright air.

Sira was both fascinated and repelled. Rhia was angry about something, and clearly the other House members were afraid of her.

"Bors!" The Houseman appeared from around the corner, and bowed quickly to Rhia. "Where is the Magister?" she snapped.

"I believe he is away from the House," the man offered. He looked as nervous as a *caeru* being pursued through the forest. "There was a report of a *caeru* den—"

"Hunting. Just when he is needed, naturally!" Rhia said bitterly. Waves of her deep and helpless anger swept over Sira.

Deciding this situation had nothing to do with her, Sira started to walk away.

"Cantrix." Sira stopped. Rhia's eyes glittered, and Sira knew that her anger was out of control. "Don't play out here again," she said.

Sira stood tall, looking down at the older woman for a moment as she secured her own composure. "I see no reason not to entertain the House members with my music."

Sira? Do not argue with her. Come in, please.

It was Magret, sending clearly and strongly to her junior.

Sira, of course, obeyed immediately, but her cheeks burned with shame at being called away like a child. With her back arrow-straight, she spun about, and stalked into the House.

Cantrix Magret was waiting just inside the door. She gestured to Sira, drawing her toward their apartments. *Sira, I am sorry, but . . .* Magret looked up quickly, and Sira saw Trude leaning against the door of the great room

"Did Rhia find the Magister?" she asked lazily. "The Committee member is waiting."

"I do not know," Magret answered quickly. Sira was lost in the currents of anger, fear, and envy swirling through the atmosphere.

"Don't mind Rhia, young Cantrix," Trude went on, straightening, turning toward the stairs. "It's hard for her. She can't win either way." Trude did not bother to shield her enjoyment of the conflict.

As Trude's generous figure disappeared up the stairs, Sira turned to her senior. *What is happening here?*

"It is better we speak aloud," Magret said softly. "The mind's ear extends far beyond the physical one. Come to my room, and I will explain as best I can."

Sira followed Magret, but fresh anger made the air glisten around her. By the time she sat down in Magret's apartment, her jaw ached from clenching it.

"A member of the Magistral Committee is making the rounds of the Houses to arrange a congress," Magret told her. "She expected to talk to Magister Shen, and Rhia is embarrassed that she cannot find him."

"What does that have to do with my playing in the courtyard?"

"Nothing, Sira. Nothing. But Rhia is not kindly disposed toward Singers in general. Trude and Denis constantly try her patience. It is one reason the House members avoid the *quirunha*. She was angry, and you were there— that is all. But she can be dangerous. When she loses her temper, she abuses her power." Magret whispered her last remark.

"In what way?" Sira asked.

Magret kept her voice very low and her eyes averted. "She banished one or two Housemen who crossed her, and they and their families had to go begging for another House. And through the Housekeeper, she controls privileges certain families receive. Some of them are essential, and families suffer."

"But what could she do to me?"

"I do not know. But she is a clever and determined woman. And not a forgiving one."

Sira looked down at the fists she had made in her lap, and released them, stretching her long fingers. "This is a strange House."

"All Houses have their strangenesses. You will become accustomed to it."

Sira brought her gaze up to her senior's. "We have trained and worked all our lives to serve our Houses. I do not think I will become accustomed to disrespect."

"We have no choice, my dear. Where Conservatory sends us, we go. And serve." Magret sighed. "Choice is a luxury beyond a Cantrix's reach."

Sira said nothing more, but she could not accept Magret's statement. There would be more to her life than compliance and obedience. There had to be, or she would be as frustrated as young Zakri.

Chapter Eight

The softwood shoots sprang up in abundance during the weeks of summer, their tender green needles flourishing under the light of the twin suns. The ironwood trees, thick and dark, looked heavy and ancient among them.

Now the summer was fading. The faraway disc of the Visitor dropped lower and lower toward the southern horizon, and the air cooled sharply. The steady trickle of summer guests dwindled, and itinerant Singers began to offer their services to those who had stayed late, to ensure their safe journeys home.

It was on one of these last summer days that the Housekeeper Wil bowed to Sira after the *quirunha* and asked her to come to the Magister's apartments. "Rhia wishes to see you, Cantrix," he said, adding with a deprecating smile, "at your convenience, of course."

Sira nodded, though she doubted her convenience had little to do with the summons. She followed the Housekeeper out of the Cantoris. They were both tall and slender, and they drew many glances as they walked through the corridors. Sira tried to look oblivious, but for once she felt graceful, not awkward, in her great height.

Rhia was waiting for them with tea and a tray of refreshments. Trude was also present, sitting near the window and selecting tidbits from the tray with her plump hand in the manner of one long familiar with her surroundings. It was odd to see the two women together. What a strange relationship they had: Trude, the former Cantrix, mother of the Magister's son; and Rhia, childless mate of the Magister.

Rhia bowed nicely, and Sira's answering bow was polite but deliberately shallow. The flash in Rhia's eyes showed she understood. Still, her attitude remained courteous.

"I won't keep you long, Cantrix," Rhia said. "I want to discuss something with you." She gestured to the refreshments, but Sira shook her head. The Housekeeper stood behind Rhia's chair, and Sira, watching the older woman sink elegantly into her seat, felt suddenly and distressingly gauche. Rhia's dark tunic and trousers were simple, but impeccably draped. Sira tried to unobtrusively smooth her own plain tunic. She stopped when she saw Wil's slight smile. She dropped her hands and composed her face, deciding not to look at him again.

"The Magister will be making a trip to the capital, to Lamdon," Rhia was saying. "There is to be a meeting of the Magistral Committee. I—that is, we would like you to accompany him. It will be a three-day ride, and he needs a Singer."

With Trude so close, Sira kept her thoughts low. She could indulge in excitement later. But Lamdon! Lamdon, with its eight Cantors, and people coming to the Cantoris from all over the Continent! She was so delighted she almost forgot an important question. When it occurred to her, her spirits sank as quickly as they had risen.

She blurted, "Why me?"

Rhia smiled, and reached for her teacup. "We would prefer Cantrix Magret to stay here, to sustain the House *quiru*. Now that Cantor Grigr has retired, we are again shorthanded. Naturally, Cantrix Magret has managed it alone many times. We feel there is less risk that way."

She did not mention the possibility of hiring an itinerant Singer, and Sira did not want to bring it up. Perhaps they felt an itinerant was not adequate protection for the Magister. Knowing Trude was watching from the window, Sira hid her elation. She felt like a child hiding a sweet.

"In that case," she said rather stiffly, "I will be happy to travel with the Magister."

Rhia nodded. "Good." Her smile was gracious. Sira could hardly reconcile this charming woman with the furious one who had insulted her in the courtyard not many days before. "Thank you, Cantrix. You leave in a week, then, and you'll be gone eight days. The Magister only expects to stay at Lamdon two nights."

Sira nodded. Rhia rose, signaling the end of the discussion. Wil and Trude stayed behind as Sira paced back to her own small room, her step and her heart light with anticipation.

Magret found her later in the *ubanyix*, lazing in the warm, scented water.

"Well, Sira, this is unusal for you, is it not?" Magret smiled at her junior as she hung up her tunic. "Is the water hot enough?"

"It is fine, Cantrix," Sira said, returning Magret's smile. Magret eased herself into the warm water with a pleasurable sigh. There were only two other women in the ironwood tub, washing each other's hair at the far end.

Magret reached for the soap in its carved niche. "What did the Housekeeper want?"

"Rhia wanted to see me." Sira tried to speak casually. "They want me to go to Lamdon with Magister Shen."

Magret dropped her eyes. Sira feared she was upset, or perhaps resentful. She opened her mind, hoping for some sharing of Magret's inner thoughts. She weas relieved to feel neither anger nor envy, only a brief moment of concern before her senior shielded her mind.

Sira said in a rush, "It should have been you, should it not? So I said to Rhia."

The lines around Magret's mouth deepened. "Perhaps. In another case it might have been I. More likely, they would have hired an itinerant. Perhaps because of your youth . . ." She sighed. "Perhaps they hope the journey will give you experience."

Sira understood Magret did not believe this. There was something else. She waited for an explanation, but Magret only shook her head. "I do not know, Sira. I do not know what might be in Rhia's mind." She glanced at the other women in the *ubanyix*. "I beg you to be cautious."

Sira nodded. "I will, Cantrix. Although I do not know what to be cautious about."

Magret's chuckle sounded weary. "I do not usually hear any doubts from you. And I cannot tell you exactly what to be on guard against. Perhaps—just be aware of everything.

"You will meet Cantrix Sharn, senior at Lamdon. She is a wonderful Singer, and an old friend. You can give her my regards. And enjoy yourself!"

"I will." Sira stretched her long arms above her head in joy, pushing away any doubts that might cloud her pleasure. Lamdon! It was a dream come true.

When the day came, the sight of her old friend Rollie in the traveling party added to Sira's delight. The rider, her tanned face swathed in the yellow-white fur of her hood, came forward to secure Sira's furs and saddlepacks and to help her mount. Patting the *hruss*'s heavy neck, she winked at Sira. "So here we go again, young Cantrix!"

Sira grinned. "I am so glad to see you, Rollie."

A great adventure lay ahead, and here was Rollie to share it. Not even the Magister's gruff presence could darken Sira's mood. And unless he chose to freeze to death, he would have to hear her sing, something he had not done in all the months of her sojourn in his House.

The last halfhearted days of summer were a week past. The Visitor had dropped below the southern skyline, and the travelers were in full cold-weather gear. It was a small traveling party, with only two other riders besides Rollie. Big-shouldered men, looking even larger in their furs, rode at the head of the group.

"Alks is the one on your left, Cantrix," Rollie whispered. "Mike is the other one." She gave Sira a conspiratorial smile. "Not too sociable, you'll find."

Sira loved the feel of the saddle, though she knew that after all these months she would be saddle-sore once again. The cold air was exhilarating, and the prospect of Lamdon filled her with energy. Having Rollie to ride beside her made everything perfect. There would be news of Maestra Lu, also. Lamdon had everything. Sira hummed a little tune as she rode.

As the day wore on and the party climbed steadily upward into the

Mariks, snow began to fall. The Magister, boisterously cheerful and clearly in his element here in the mountains, told Alks to make camp as soon as they dropped into Ogre Pass. Sira caught a snowflake on her tongue, then blushed when she realized what she had done. Rollie chuckled, and Sira did, too. She supposed, just for the moment, she could forget the dignity of the Cantoris.

Ogre Pass was in itself exciting to Sira. She had never traveled through it before. In fact, she had never been further north than Bariken. A wide canyon with steep, wooded sides and a flat floor, Ogre Pass wound through the Mariks, south to north. Lamdon and Isenhope were at the northern end. Its southern mouth opened to the Houses on the Frozen Sea. There were no Houses to the east unless, as legend had it in one of Isbel's songs, the Watchers had a House there. Sira looked eastward to the fierce jagged peaks on the horizon, and doubted anyone could build a House in that terrain.

Alks chose a campsite in a hollow between stands of immense irontrees. Conscious of the Magister listening, Sira created her warmest and swiftest *quiru* that evening. As the melody in the second mode wafted from her *filla*, the envelope of warm, brilliant air sprang up around them, as tall and bright as she could make it. Shen gave no sign that he noticed.

Drifts of snowflakes tumbled past the *quiru* as Rollie and Mike built a cooking fire with softwood from their packs. Everyone's furs sparkled with tiny, transitory jewels as the snowflakes, dropping through the light, quickly melted. Alks and the Magister were already seated on their bedrolls. Alks pulled a big leather flask from his saddlepack.

Sira saw Rollie roll her eyes at Mike, and she wondered why. But when the hot food and tea were ready, she soon learned that the Magister was more interested in the flask than the food. His face began to flush the dark red she had seen once before.

"Never mind, Cantrix," Rollie muttered from her place next to Sira. "Alks knows how to handle him. They've traveled together many times."

Mike leaned back against his bedroll, eating in silence. Alks and Shen handed the flask back and forth between them. Rollie finished her meal, and rose. "Magister, more *keftet*?"

She bent to take his half-empty bowl, and Shen grinned up at her, seizing her legging with his free hand. "You've got something I'd like better, Rollie!" He and the other men roared with laughter. Rollie frowned at them, pulling her leg free and nodding pointedly in Sira's direction.

"Oh, I know," Shen laughed. "Our very young Cantrix! Too young for my jokes, you think, Alks?" He took another pull on the flask, then held it out to Sira. "Want some? I'll swear by the Six Stars you never had this at Conservatory!"

Sira had no idea how to respond. She hid her confusion behind a frozen countenance.

Shen bridled. "Too high and mighty? Well—you're my Singer, aren't you? Sing, then!"

Sira turned her head to look at Shen. She thought of refusing him. She thought of spilling his wine flask with a burst of careless psi, or tweaking an ember from the fire to land on his boot. Instead, she reached inside her tunic and drew out her *filla*. Her long fingers caressed its smooth surface even as she kept her gaze on Shen's face, and she put it to her lips. She turned her eyes away from him only when she began to play.

It was not the way Sira had pictured her first performance for her Magister. In the haven of her *quiru*, with the snow drifting down around them, she played the merriest tune she could think of, a jaunty fifth-mode melody with a dance rhythm. After the first statement of the tune, she toyed with it. She embellished and modified it into something that fit the mountain campsite with its fluttery curtains of falling snow.

Then, in the middle of the music, Shen abruptly rose and went outside the *quiru* to relieve himself. He didn't go far. Alks followed, and Sira, hearing the repulsive sounds they made, stopped playing.

Rollie swore under her breath. Mike kept his face averted, gazing down at the snow slowly melting under his bed of furs. Where Shen had been sitting, the flask lay flat and empty.

Shen reeled back into the *quiru* a few moments later, brushing roughly past the *hruss*, who huffed and stamped nervously. "Sing!" he cried loudly. Alks stood behind him, holding his arm as he collapsed, laughing, onto his furs. "You're my Singer . . . Sing!" He laughed harder, belching, thrusting his booted feet toward the fire.

Sira bowed from her cross-legged position. The more revolting his behavior, the stronger was her sense that she must maintain absolute control of herself. There was a feeling of sympathy around her, and she wondered why. Surely no one could think the behavior of a boor like Shen could hurt her. But then, they could not know.

Sira let her *filla* rest on her knee, and she began to sing. She did not trouble to disguise the lullaby, one she had learned as a child at Conservatory, and had sung to the little ones as she tucked them into bed. It was a lullaby to soothe the hearts of children weeping for their mothers.

Her voice, so dark and even, rolled over her audience. Rollie's weathered face relaxed, her frown smoothed away. Both Mike and Alks sat still and silent, watching, listening.

Sira wove a sleep *cantrip* into her song, delicately and accurately directing it at Shen.

> LITTLE ONE, LOST ONE,
> SLEEPY ONE, SMALL ONE,
> PILLOW YOUR HEAD,
> DREAM OF THE STARS,
> AND THE SHIP THAT CARRIES YOU HOME.

> LITTLE ONE, SWEET ONE,
> DROWSY ONE, LOST ONE,
> THE NIGHT IS LONG,
> THE SNOW IS COLD,
> BUT THE SHIP WILL CARRY YOU HOME.

Shen's eyes grew heavy and his face slack. He nodded quickly into snoring sleep, still sitting fully dressed on his bedfurs.

Sira concluded her song. Alks rolled himself into his furs and turned away from the fire. But Mike watched Sira, his face set as if to resist her,

Louise Marley

as if it were he she had tried to sing into sleep. It seemed an odd reaction.

Rollie smiled and shook her head, eyes wet with emotion. "Beautiful, Cantrix," she whispered. "We'll have peace now. And he'll never figure out what hit him. Tomorrow I'll ask you for 'Rollie's Tune'."

"Thank you, Rollie," Sira said. "I will be glad to play it for you."

In the quiet, Rollie murmured, "I knew you would do well at Bariken, Cantrix."

Sira laughed a little. "I am not so sure I have, Rollie. Rhia is not fond of me."

Rollie glanced at Mike, but he, like Alks, had rolled into his bedfurs and turned his face away. "Rhia's a disappointed woman," Rollie said softly. "I came with her when she was mated to the Magister. She grew up thinking she would be Magistrix at Tarus, but a younger brother was born when she already had three summers."

"Were you born at Tarus, then, Rollie?"

The rider nodded. "It's very different on the coast. Sometimes whole islands of ice appear overnight. Once one crashed against the cliffs when we were sleeping, and we thought the House was coming down around us." She shrugged. "Bariken's been a big change, but after three summers, I'm used to it."

Their talk dwindled, and Rollie began to yawn. She said good night, and went to bank the fire. Sira crept into her bedfurs. Rollie covered the Magister, then she, too, lay down. As Sira closed her eyes the irontrees creaked, groaning in the deepening cold.

Just before dawn, Sira woke from a vivid dream of being trapped under an icy cliff, with icicles sharp as knives crashing around her. It left her with an overwhelming sense of dread. A warning, she thought. I have had a warning, but of what?

She sat up quickly to assure herself the *quiru* was holding. It shimmered securely about all of them, undisturbed by any wind. It would stand for hours after they had moved on in the morning. The silent snow continued to fall.

Uneasily, Sira lay down again. She knew the dreams of a Singer were never to be ignored. There was danger somewhere, of some kind. She pondered it, but without success. Eventually the fatigue of her long ride in the fresh air stole over her, and she slept again as the night faded slowly into an icy dawn.

Maestra Lu, six days' ride to the southwest, could not capture sleep again at all that night. Awakened by the same alarm as Sira, she lay on her cot at Conservatory, trying to fathom what danger hung over her protégée.

Chapter Nine

Shen woke the next morning complaining of a headache. The party could not break camp until Sira had treated him.

"Do whatever it is Grigr used to do," the Magister growled. His breath was sour with wine, his beard and hair uncombed. Sira pressed her lips together, but she brought out her *filla* despite her revulsion. He was her magister, but she wondered what Maestro Nikei would think about this use of her Gift. Mike and Alks and Rollie squatted around the camp, while Shen lay on his furs and Sira knelt beside him with her *filla*.

It was a simple enough thing Sira played, a straightforward melody in the third mode. She directed her psi to relieve the constriction of the tiny channels that carried blood around the body and into the head. For once she added no refinements to her music. Her playing and her healing were unsubtle.

The Magister grunted as the pain eased and the blood flow grew easier. Sira heard him, and gooseflesh rose on her arms. As she put down her *filla*, she felt the disdainful curl of her lip, but Shen did not notice.

"You're a handy one, Cantrix," he said jovially, sitting up and running his fingers through his unkempt hair. "That's a useful skill!"

Sitting close to him, Sira saw the broken red lines in his cheeks and nose, and knew why his face grew so dark when he was excited. "You should not indulge so much in wine, Magister. Your health will suffer."

"Hear that, Mike? We should not indulge so much! Ha! We should be like those fancy Cantors, no mating, no wine, no hunting!" Mike joined in his laughter as Sira rose from her kneeling position.

"You should have known my father, Cantrix!" Shen called as she turned her back on him and went to tie on her saddlepack. "He drank twice as much as I do, and never suffered for it!"

Rollie came to help Sira, and whispered across the *hruss*'s back, "His father never saw twelve summers." Alks and Mike and Shen were laughing together as they mounted up.

They rode out of camp with the rumps of the *hruss* draped with bedding furs, wet from melted snow, to allow them to dry in the cold air. Mike and Alks rode ahead, large and stolid as *hruss* themselves. The Magister followed. Sira and Rollie brought up the rear, their hoods pulled well forward to hold in warmth. Snow fell intermittently all day, frosting their furs with white, freezing on the open bedfurs in lacy patterns. Ogre Pass was cruelly cold, even in daylight. The *hruss*'s big hooves made little sound as they plodded through the soft powder.

They stopped just before dark to make their second camp. The season was one of long days and short nights, and they had ridden far. They were so close to Lamdon they could see the glow of its *quiru* on the mountain slope ahead, a distance of about four hours' ride. The snow-bleached sky and the pale peaks melded into one indistinguishable landscape at this hour, and the circle of Lamdon's warm light seemed to float in the air, as if suspended above the ground. As their own *quiru* grew around them, the larger one sparkled vividly beyond and through it like the first star of evening.

Alks's wine flask had been emptied the night before, and the camp was quiet this night. Sira lay on her furs wondering what Lamdon would be like, and listening to the Magister reminisce with Alks and Mike about their boyhood years. Several stories included Shen's father, usually with Shen on the receiving end of some rough joke.

Sira thought of her own father, the familiar smell of him when she was tiny, the odors of softwood smoke and snow that clung to his furs. She fell asleep trying to remember his face, and woke in the morning grateful there had been no more night terrors.

It was the following midday when the travelers rode into the great courtyard of the capital House. The *hruss*'s hooves clattered on clean-swept paving stones, a startling sound after three days of snow-muffled hoofbeats. Sira sat straight in her saddle, trying to see everything at once. Lamdon was even larger than Conservatory, perhaps twice again as big. Its great doors looked as if four people would be required to open them. Its lavish *quiru* sparkled and gleamed, coruscating in the snowy setting.

Their approach had been noted, and a formal welcoming party was assembled on the broad front steps. *Hruss* and saddlepacks neatly disappeared into the hands of several Housemen, and a bewildering variety of people were introduced. Sira was grateful when a small man with a merry expression bowed, and seemed ready to take charge of her.

"Greetings, Cantrix," he said, his voice surprisingly deep for a person of small stature. "I am Cantor Rico. Welcome to Lamdon."

Sira bowed in return, a deeper bow to honor a senior Cantor. Rico gestured to the enormous doors. "Please come in and meet the other Singers who have gathered. They are all in our senior Cantrix's apartment at the moment, talking Conservatory, I should think."

"Thank you, Cantor Rico," Sira said. The riders were going off toward the back of the House. Magister Shen had been formally received by some Committee official. Sira followed Rico, stumbling once on the steps as she gazed up in wonder at this largest House on the Continent. Its *quiru* was so warm that people were wearing sleeveless tunics, and no fur at all indoors, not even on their feet. Sira had never seen a sleeveless tunic before. The unaccustomed heat made her feel breathless.

As Rico led her down a long hall, she caught a glimpse of the great room to her left, and the Cantoris to her right. It was much, much larger than any she had ever seen, and she had to tear her eyes away from it in order not to lose sight of Cantor Rico. He led her to the north wing, and down another long corridor to a large apartment.

There were eight Singers for Lamdon's Cantoris, Sira knew. The senior Cantrix was a person of significant influence, second only on the Continent to the Magister of Conservatory, or so Sira had been taught. The senior Cantrix at Lamdon served as advisor to the Magistral Committee and was also liaison between Conservatory and Lamdon. If a Cantor or Cantrix was recalled, it would be by her order. If one was reassigned, the decision was made jointly by her and Magister Mkel. Such issues were grave responsibilities, matters of life and death, and the shortage of the Gift was their most vital concern.

Cantrix Sharn's apartment was crowded with at least twenty Singers, of all ages and sizes, and it was absolutely silent.

Cantor Rico, please take Cantrix Sira's furs for her; she will be so uncomfortably warm.

Sira turned to see a slender white-haired woman of about twelve summers. Rico helped her with her furs, then introduced her. *Cantrix Sharn, this is Cantrix Sira v'Bariken.*

Sira bowed deeply. *Cantrix Sharn, I am to give you my senior's greetings.*

Sharn smiled warmly at Sira. *I have greetings for you as well. From your teacher.* For a moment, the image of Maestra Lu, created by their joined memories, filled Sira's mind with an intensity that made her close her eyes.

Sharn waited until the moment passed, then indicated two chairs close together. They sat down, and Sira looked around the room.

The apartment was almost as bare as Sira's own, though there was more furniture. It looked like a room one could practice in, Sira thought. When she looked back at the senior Cantrix, Sharn was smiling again.

Indeed it is, my dear, and I do it every day, even now.

Sharn gestured to a passing Housewoman, who carried a tray of refreshments. Sira took a piece of dried fruit containing a kind of nut she didn't recognize, and she sipped thirstily at a cup of tea. Sharn helped herself to a tidbit, and Sira noticed her long, slim fingers. Good hands for the *filhata*. She hoped she would have the chance to hear Cantrix Sharn play.

Again Sharn heard her idle thought. *Actually, Sira, I was hoping you would play for us.*

Sira nodded, though the thought caused her a thrill of nerves to run through her.

Rico returned, and stood by her elbow. *We are all very curious, Cantrix Sira, to hear how things are at Bariken.*

All is well there, I think, Sira responded carefully. She kept her mind as clear of doubts as she could.

And how do you find working for Magister Shen? Rico pressed.

Sira was disconcerted when she realized all the other Singers in the room were listening for her answer. She took a moment to collect herself before she nodded politely to Rico. *The Cantoris is a good one, with Cantrix Magret as senior. She is very helpful.*

Rico surprised her by chuckling aloud. He patted her shoulder lightly with a small pale hand. *A diplomatic answer, friends! Our young colleague should be a great success!* There was general friendly laughter, and several Singers sent warm wishes to Sira.

Shr turned to Sharn, uncertain what Rico had meant. Sharn was smiling, too. *Do not let Rico's teasing disturb you. He is searching for crumbs of gossip to offer round at dinner.* There was more laughter.

We all knew of your early assignment, offered a middle-aged Cantor. *We have been thinking of you.*

Sira was touched. She bowed to him, and sent, *That is very kind, Cantor.* She was relieved when the conversation turned to other topics.

The Singers were especially concerned with the reason for the Magistral Committee's meeting that had brought so many visitors to Lamdon. The Committee was to discuss the shortage of Cantors and Cantrixes, and in particular the failure of many families to dedicate their Gifted children to Conservatory. Penalties had been proposed.

Magister Shen, Sira thought privately, would have little interest in such a discussion. He was not concerned about Singers or Conservatory, or anything except his own pleasure. It was a disloyal thought, and she shielded it well.

A young Singer of about five summers nodded to Sira from across the room. She recognized him. He had been a third-level student when she was in her second level. She basked in the glow of their mutual history. When Sharn's attention returned to her, Sira sent, *I would like to send a message to Maestra Lu.*

Yes, you should do that.

I have no metal at all. Will it matter?

Sharn shook her head. *I will see to it for you. Now, I will tell you all the news I have from Conservatory, and you tell me all about Magret, and anything else interesting!*

In Sira's guest room there were several nursery flowers gathered into a little stone vase. At Conservatory, herbs were grown, but no flowers. Bariken grew flowers, but they were for scenting cakes of soap or sweetening bath water. Using them strictly for decoration seemed an extravagance worthy only of Lamdon.

After a brief bath in the enormous *ubanyix*, Sira rested, waiting for the evening, and thought about Cantix Sharn. The older woman's charm had drawn more from Sira than she had offered to anyone in a long time. Still, Sira had been careful. For all their strangeness, Magister Shen and Rhia were her employers, and she did not wish to be disloyal. She had told the senior Cantrix about Shen's drinking and her treatment of its aftermath, however.

Sharn had not seemed surprised. *We were not really trained for that, were we, my dear?* she sent, then gracefully turned their conversation to lighter subjects.

Sira drew her spare tunic over her face to shut out the brilliance of Lamdon's light, hoping to sleep for a little while. In a short time, she would observe the *quirunha*, and this evening there would be a concert given by Lamdon's own Singers. She was part of it all, one of them, the Singers of Nevya. How satisfying it all was! She wished Rhia and Wil and Trude could have seen her in private conversation with the senior Cantrix of Lamdon. They could hardly laugh at her then.

The *quirunha* at Lamdon was elegant and polished. Cantrix Sharn presided. A Cantrix named Becca led, with a fluting soprano and small, quick fingers on the *filhata*. Two Cantors assisted her, one of them particularly skilled in the use of harmonics, pressing his fingers lightly against the strings of the *filhata* to make sympathetic overtones ring out an octave and more above the melody. The walls and ceiling of the Cantoris resounded until the room itself became a musical instrument. The Cantoris had such a live acoustic, in truth, that without the audience's presence to soak up some of the vibrations, it might have been overwhelming.

Cantor Rico, escorting Sira to the Cantoris, noticed the flush on her cheeks, and assured her someone would lend her cooler clothes. *It is our little conceit*, he sent. *Abundant warmth.*

But now Sira floated on the tide of music and psi, sitting as straight as if she were on the dais herself. She forgot how warm she was. She thought of nothing but music for the space of the *quirunha*. Her fingers lifted and danced in her lap, following Becca's leads.

When the prayer had been said and the *quirunha* was complete, Sira sent to Cantrix Sharn, *Everything was beautiful.*

Sharn smiled. *Thank you. I have an idea that a compliment from you is an honor.*

Sira blushed, hoping she had not been effusive. She had been sincere. Indeed, she was always sincere, and that could be considered a fault. She could only hope these sophisticates would not find her naive.

Rico, true to his promise, sent a Housewoman to Sira's room with a cooler tunic. The Housewoman held it out to her, a lovely thing, deep brown, embroidered in green and yellow thread. It had no sleeves.

"I am not sure I can wear this," Sira said.

The Housewoman tilted her head to one side, regarding her. "Oh, yes, Cantrix, I think it will be fine. May I help you?" She waited for Sira's nod of permission before reaching out to help her remove her heavy tunic and replace it with the lighter one. She smoothed it down over Sira's trousers. "I'm sorry we have no cooler leggings for you. Your legs are so very long."

Sira looked down at herself. "I know."

"No matter." The Housewoman pulled a brush from her pocket, waiting again for Sira's consent before she began to brush and rebind her hair. Having someone else dress her hair felt as strange to Sira as wearing a sleeveless tunic. Her bare arms made her self-conscious, and she kept them pressed to her sides.

The Housewoman bowed deeply when she left. Sira stood uncertainly in the middle of the room, not sure what would happen next. It was a relief when Cantor Rico came to fetch her.

The meal in Lamdon's great room was a wonder of fresh vegetables and abundant grain in a *keftet* also dotted with spiced fruit. Afterward, everyone gathered in the Cantoris for the formal recital. All of the Magistral Committee were there, along with many of the House members. The Cantoris was full. Even for Lamdon, it seemed, this was an event of note.

She was enchanted. She sat on a bench between Rico and a Cantrix from Tarus. The audience preened itself. Sira noticed people looking at her and whispering to each other. She lifted her head, pretending not to see. It would seem everyone knew who she was, the youngest full Cantrix on the Continent, and she didn't mind that at all.

When the music began, Sira was ready to immerse herself in it, as she had done in the *quirunha*. But with an ear meticulously trained by Maestra Lu, she found there were faults. Surely that cadence was a little rushed, and one of Lamdon's Cantrixes had a tendency to sharp on rising melodic lines. The harmonies were not particularly inventive, either. After the concert, her compliments to the performers were modest. Fortunately, no one seemed to notice. Other members of the audience were generous in their praise.

During the refreshment period afterward, Sharn joined her. "How did you like the music?" Sira had noticed that Sharn usually spoke aloud when non-Singers were present.

"I enjoyed it very much," Sira said truthfully.

Sharn's smile told her that the senior Cantrix understood. "Yes," she said blandly. "There were some nice moments." And then, "I would be very pleased if you would play for us while you are here."

A fresh thrill of nerves tingled beneath Sira's borrowed, embroidered tunic. She bowed politely. "I will if you would like me to, of course, Cantrix."

"May I lend you my *filhata*?"

"Thank you. I am sure I will play better on your instrument than on my own."

Sharn nodded approval of this formal courtesy. "Perhaps after the evening meal tomorrow. Will that suit you?"

Sira murmured assent, glad of the day to practice. Sharn signaled to a Housewoman, and took from her a *filhata* beautifully wrapped in a piece of Perl's best fabric. Sira accepted it from her hands with another bow. "Would it be rude of me to excuse myself now?"

Sharn shook her head. "Of course not. I am sure you are tired. Let me call Rico."

Sira allowed her to do that, not sure she could have found her way back alone. She did not correct Sharn, but she felt sure Sharn knew it was not fatigue that sent her to her room. She wanted to play.

She cradled the borrowed *filhata* under her arm as she walked next to Rico, trying to listen to his social chatter. The instrument felt warm and heavy and full of history, and she could hardly wait to feel its strings under her fingers.

Sira had no appetite for the delicacies offered at the evening meal the next night. She had not felt so nervous since her very first *quirunha*. She let the feeling flow over her, experiencing the quiver in her stomach and the tremble of her fingers. It was better to allow the nerves to have their moment than to pretend they didn't exist. Cantor Rico smiled in understanding.

Cantrix Sharn had invited all the Singers in the House, except the itinerants, to her apartment after dinner. There were more than thirty of them. When they had all been served a cup of tea, Sharn beckoned to her.

Sira paced the length of the room, already concentrating on the music she had in mind, oblivious to the faces that smiled at her as she passed. She did her best to carry herself with poise. She tried to forget that she felt too tall and too young. She felt the critical eye of her former schoolmate, and was aware of a tingle of resentment coming from him, but she was accustomed to this. It was so familiar a feeling as to be almost comforting. She thrust it aside as she always had; she could not help others being envious. She must think only of the music.

Her anxiety disappeared as if it had never been the moment she took up the *filhata*. She sat quietly for a long moment, shaping the first phrase in her mind, breathing in its mood and the attitude of her listeners, and then she began.

It was a piece she knew very, very well. She had studied and polished it with Maestra Lu herself. It began slowly, with an instrumental line. When the voice entered, the meter changed, then changed again, without marring the fluid legato. She had chosen a nostalgic text, and its appropriateness for this audience was in itself a triumph:

> SING THE LIGHT,
> SING THE WARMTH,
> RECEIVE AND BECOME THE GIFT, O SINGERS.
> THE WARMTH AND THE LIGHT ARE IN YOU.

Her dark, even voice rose and fell, embellishing and modifying the melody. Three times she sang the verse, and the music was different, deeper, broader, with each repetition. She ended with a recapitulation of all of the motives of the music in a graceful coda. When she finished, there was a long silence, which she extended by keeping her gaze down, her hand flat on the strings. When she looked up at last, she saw several Singers with glistening eyes. One gray-haired Cantor covered his face with his hand.

Sharn rose and came to her, holding out both her hands. *Thank you, Cantrix Sira*, she sent, her eyes glowing. Each of her many summers seemed imprinted on her face at that moment. *I think I may speak for all of us. If you are representative of the students coming out of Conservatory in these difficult times, we are all honored. Bariken is most fortunate in their newest Cantrix.*

Sira kept her face as still as she could, tempering her elation, but she knew it had gone well. She bowed to Sharn, and handed back the *filhata* with careful thanks. There was a wave of approbation from the company, and she bowed to them all.

It was only later that Sira had time to wonder why, as the Cantors and Cantrixes clustered around her, Sharn's smile faded as she resumed her seat. Her mouth set in hard lines and her eyes were distant. She looked angry.

In celebration of their time together, the Cantors and Cantrixes retired to bathe before beginning their journeys home. In the *ubanyix*, Sira marveled at the Singer energies it must take to keep the water warm. Forty people could recline in this tub at one time, though now there were just eight Cantrixes. Sira folded her long form on the bench next to Sharn, tucking her legs under her. Dried flowers floated on the water that lapped gently about her shoulders.

Sharn opened her mind. *Sira, I must tell you of our concerns about your assignment.*

Sira watched her, wide-eyed.

We at Lamdon feel that something political may be happening at Bariken.

Sira shook her head slightly. *I have heard nothing, Cantrix.*

I know Rhia, Sharn went on. *I have sensed her desire to rule Bariken.*

She already does in many ways, Sira ventured.

Sharn nodded. *Yes. So I understand. But I believe she does not find it satisfying.* She leaned back against the side of the tub and closed her eyes. *She wants to be Magistrix.*

Sira gazed into the gently rolling clouds of steam that floated from the surface of the water to the ironwood ceiling high above. Sharn had broken their psi connection, but Sira understood what she had been told. Sharn had trespassed on Rhia's thoughts. Sira could guess that Rhia had accompanied Shen to Lamdon on some occasion, bringing her into Sharn's range. Perhaps Sharn had even done so under instruction from her own Magister.

Sharn was warning Sira, and Sira had already had a warning from her own instinctive mind. Should she tell Sharn of her dream? But what could it mean? And how, Sira wondered finally, could any of these circumstances be a threat to her, a Singer?

Sharn's eyes were still closed, her lashes as pale and delicate as the rest of her body. She sent, very faintly, *Your first responsibility is to protect yourself, whatever happens. Nevya needs its Singers. It is possible for some to forget that.*

Sira felt a sudden chill, and she rubbed her cold shoulders.

Come, Sira you are getting cold. Let us get something hot to drink. As if their enigmatic conversation had never taken place, Sharn led Sira to the stack of linens, and they dried and dressed themselves.

Later, as they said good night, Sharn appeared as serene as always. Sira moved away from her down the hall, tired after an exciting day, preoccupied. She didn't mean to listen to Sharn's private thoughts, but she caught the echo of them as she turned toward her room. Sharn was regretting the need for a Singer so young to bear the burdens of a troubled world.

Chapter Ten

It was a dull group of travelers that headed back into Ogre Pass on the return journey from Lamdon to Bariken. Snow fell heavily, and a nasty wind snapped at them as they rode. Even the middle hours of the day were shaded and gloomy. Sira huddled in her furs, rocking with the *hruss*'s movements, lost in her own thoughts.

Shen, debilitated by too much of Lamdon's wine two nights in a row, was also withdrawn. He had not mentioned either the Magistral Committee meeting or its purpose. Alks and Mike rode ahead, and Rollie, getting little response to her occasional tries at conversation, also lapsed into silence.

They left Lamdon very early, and rode until late that day, covering half again the usual distance for a day's travel. Darkness was closing in, and Sira's *quiru* in the evening took a few extra moments. The cold reached frigid fingers inside everyone's furs to chill any skin it touched. Sira's lips were stiff with it, and it was difficult to play.

When the *quiru* bloomed above them, Mike started the cooking fire. The party relaxed with the light glowing securely about them. Alks and Shen gossiped about Lamdon and its people while Rollie prepared the *keftet* and boiled water for tea. Only Mike remained impassive. When Sira looked at him, her psi prickled, and she thought something must be troubling him.

As the group settled down for the night, Sira spoke to Shen. "Magister, I think this *quiru* may need replenishing before morning. The wind may break it down."

In fact, the snow was falling slantwise, and the tops of the irontrees soughed and danced above their campsite.

All right," Shen said. "Rollie, you waken the Cantrix mid-night, then sleep."

Rollie nodded, and propped herself on her furs to take the watch. Mike and Alks had already gone outside the *quiru* with the Magister to relieve themselves. Now they stepped outside for the second time that evening, ducking their heads against the icy snow.

Sira was kneeling, unrolling her bedfurs and thinking only of warmth and sleep, when her psi suddenly screamed a warning. Her nerves flared, and she dropped her bedfurs and threw up her head. Instinctively, she cried, "Rollie!"

It was too late. Even as she heard her voice ring across the *quiru*, she whirled toward Rollie. It seemed to her shocked senses that a fur-tipped arrow simply appeared in Rollie's bare throat. The rider's face went slack as she fell backward, sprawling off her furs and into the snow.

Sira turned swiftly to Shen. A second atrocity unfolded so quickly she had no time to absorb it. An arrow pierced the Magister's furs, and a long-handled knife followed a heartbeat later. His shock of graying hair reddened as blood leaped across it. He gave a long groan, and fell to one side to lie unmoving on his bedfurs.

Sira bit off another outcry. She could see no escape for her. She could not see the assailants in the darkness, while she and Rollie and the Magister were perfectly illuminated by the warm glow of her *quiru*. She straightened her back where she knelt, and was still. Her own arrow, bitterly punctual, pierced her body just below her collarbone. She, too, was meant to die.

Sira knew instantly that her wound was not mortal. By instinct, just the same, she let its impetus drive her down, prostrate her like the others. The point of the arrow drove through her flesh, and dug into the freshly fallen snow. She lay still, as if her spirit had fled beyond the stars, and she waited.

Hushed, tense voices sounded from outside the *quiru*. The killers were coming to assure themselves that everyone within was dead. The cold would have driven them into the warmth in any case. Assuming it was Alks and Mike, how were they planning to save themselves once the *quiru* dissipated?

All this Sira thought in a flash, while she lay motionless. She felt little at the moment, though she knew that when her body's reaction to the danger wore off, she would feel the pain of her wound. Shen and Rollie were already dead, their minds past her hearing. She must convince the assassins that she was, too.

She allowed herself no surprise when not two, but four people came into the *quiru*. She knew them all. It was Mike who came to confirm that the three victims were dead. Sira sensed him leaning over Shen, with his double wounds, and poor Rollie, who had at least died instantly. As he came toward where she herself lay, she drew a veil over her mind, the darkest she could imagine. Mike bent low for a moment, as if listening for her breath. He could not bring himself, it seemed, to touch her. She sensed, even through the veil, his inability to overcome the tabu. She also sensed his repugnance for the task he believed he had accomplished.

Sira's breaths were as shallow as she could make them. She lay listening to the voices.

Alks and Mike crouched around the fire with the two new arrivals. Wil, Housekeeper of Bariken, was there, speaking to the the two riders. Another voice joined in, a voice that shocked Sira, a voice she could hardly believe. There was no precedent for a traitorous Singer, but she was there: it was the former Cantrix, plump, sly Trude.

Sira thickened the veil over her mind. She dared not react to the double betrayal. Trude, despite her years of undisciplined living, would pick up her thoughts if she did not bury them. Sira smoothed the waves of her mind until they were as flat and opaque as the lifeless rock beneath the snow.

Wil said, "We'll cover the bodies as soon as we've had a chance to get warm. This campsite is enough off the trail, I think."

"What about their things?" Trude asked.

"Their gear stays," Wil answered. "If the story is that they got separated in the storm, their *hruss* and possessions would be lost, too."

"It's just—" Trude's voice dropped. "Her *filla* . . ."

"Everything," Wil said flatly. "No exceptions."

There was a silence. So deeply had Sira forced herself below conscious thought that he heard their voices as if in a dream, a slow nightmare of cold and pain and shock. She hardly noticed as Alks and Mike piled snow over her body and the others. She suppressed even the faint hope that flickered at the knowledge that her *filla* would be left, still tucked beneath her tunic.

Through her blanket of snow, she heard the slaughtering of the *hruss* that had carried her. Like herself, it was buried in snow. It seemed an unecessary cruelty. *Hruss*, after all, could survive the cold on their own, though they preferred the company of people. But Sira could not risk reacting to this, either, nor allow herself to experience her own rising pain, or the deep cold of her tomb of snow. Her infrequent breaths kept a pocket open above her mouth. Otherwise, she perfectly mimicked the corpses whose grave she shared.

A few hours before dawn she heard Trude playing a *filla*, competently enough, apparently, to strengthen the *quiru*. Sira waited. Some deep level of her mind knew her body was getting dangerously cold, but she suppressed her instinctive need to move, to warm herself. She lay still through the long hours, listening, breathing, but not thinking.

At last she heard shuffling and brushing sounds as the men obliterated the traces of the campsite. Distantly, Wil asked Trude some question.

"It will be gone in two or three hours, in this wind," Trude said. Sira knew they meant the *quiru*, her last hope of survival. Still, she could not react, could not feel. Her hands and feet had gone numb, and she feared frostbite. She had been feigning death for hours.

The sounds of *hruss* and their riders faded away from her hearing. Sira thought she would wait another hour before attempting to break through her covering of snow, but when she began to feel warmer, she knew she did not dare. All Nevyans learned as children that the illusory sensation of warmth was the first sign of freezing to death. She feared her spirit might drift away after all if she did not move.

The snow was the dry, powdery snow of the mountain passes. Her searching arm reached the air quickly. It hurt to move, but she dug in reverse, making a hole upward through the drift until she could see the remains of the *quiru*. Mike's arrow, crusted with snow, ground against her bones as she struggled.

Her left arm, the side where the arrow was, caused her too much pain when she tried to use it. It took half an hour of flaking away the snow cover, a single handful at a time, until her torso, and at last her legs, were free. She was too cold to know if she was still bleeding.

Her *quiru* faltered around the site, inadequately strengthened by Trude. She thought she had perhaps an hour before the last shreds of it dissolved. The remnants of the fire had been covered with snow, along with all other signs of human or *hruss* presence.

Sira feared using her *filla* now. Her betrayers could not be more than an hour's ride away, and Trude's ears, though dulled by years of abuse in everyday House life, might still be sharp enough to hear its bright timbre at a distance. Falling snow obscured the sun, which she supposed must be well overhead. The cooling *quiru* would be warm enough to sustain her for a little while, and she could address the problem of her wound.

As her body began to warm again, the pain of the offending shaft sharpened and grated, and its position inhibited her movement. It had to be removed. She felt fairly strong, considering the horror of the night she had just passed, which led her to think she could not have lost too much blood.

Casting about for a way to extract the arrow, she dug in the snow until she found a long thong that had been used to tie her pack onto her saddle. Rollie had fallen closest to her, and Sira reached, shuddering, beneath her friend's furs to take the long-handled knife from her belt. She paused a moment with her hand on Rollie's frozen one, offering a silent prayer for her safe passage beyond the stars.

It took her some minutes of sawing on the shaft of the arrow to cut all the way through it. The movement made the wood chafe against bone and flesh, and Sira had to rest several times until the nauseating pain subsided. Perspiration trickled over her body, and she gasped for breath. When the knife finally broke through the wood, the furred flight fell at her feet, and she drew a deep breath of relief.

She tied the thong around the smallest of the nearby trees. The hardest part was to reach behind her with her right arm to try to secure the other end of the thong around the arrowhead. She tried to stretch her arm over her shoulder, then down behind her back, but pain forced her to stop short of her goal.

After some thought, she made a loop like a *hruss*'s noose in the thong. She turned her back to it, and wriggled, trying to catch the arrowhead in the loop. She twisted and writhed, trying to find it, gritting her teeth against the pain when the arrowhead scraped the trunk of the tree. It was like trying to thread a needle in the dark, and it seemed impossible to accomplish. When she finally succeeded, her eyes stung with tears of pain and triumph.

She pulled the little noose tight, not wanting to chance the arrowhead slipping free again. When it was as tight as she could make it, she stood for a moment, effectively lashed to the tree behind her. She calmed her breathing and her mind. The last step would take mental as well as physical strength.

When she was ready, Sira took one deep breath, tested the noose once again, then, pushing off with all her strength, sprang away from the tree.

The arrow jerked out of her body and hung by the thong, grisly and broken. Sira fell face first into the snow, sobbing with pain and the disgusting feeling of the wood yanking through her flesh. Fresh blood soaked her back, but she was too glad to be free of the arrow to care.

She rested for some time, until she noticed the air growing colder around her. Raising herself on her arms, she saw the last fragments of the *quiru* scattering before the wind and snow. She had to do something soon, or her efforts thus far would be wasted.

She was stranded halfway through Ogre Pass, without *hruss*, or food, or guide. The swirling snowstorm obscured the landmarks. A trickle of blood burned against her back.

For today, what she needed was a *quiru* and a chance to stanch her wound and rest. She recovered her saddlepack from beneath the snow, mentally bade farewell to Rollie and even to Shen, and began her difficult trudge through the deepening snow to find a spot where she could rest away from the fatal campsite. She did not trust this place.

The wind intensified, making it difficult to listen for *hruss* and riders. Her pack was not heavy, but as she slung it over her shoulder, she winced with the pain of her wound. She would walk, she decided, for one hour, then call up a *quiru*. When she was rested, she would think what to do, and how to get somewhere safe.

Maestra Lu was haggard from a night spent first in grief and anxiety, then a terrible confusion. When Sira had drawn the veil over her mind, her teacher had felt the loss of her thoughts as surely as if she had died. Then, when Sira began once again to think and feel, Lu's heart fluttered with hope.

She leaned now on the doorjamb of Magister Mkel's apartment and knocked weakly. Cathrin opened the door, and drew a sharp breath when she saw Lu. "Maestra! Why, whatever are you . . . you should have sent your Housewoman to us!"

"I am fine, Cathrin. And there was no time. Please get Mkel for me, will you?"

"Of course, of course I will." Cathrin led Lu to a soft chair near a window. She did not touch her, but her warmth was tangible as she hovered over her. "Let me get you some tea."

"After," Lu said tiredly. "I must see Mkel immediately."

Cathrin disappeared into another room. In a moment she came back with Mkel, still arranging his dark tunic, at her side. He carried his boots in his hand, and sat to pull them on.

"Something has happened to Sira," Lu said, without preamble.

"Maestra?" He waited, one boot still in his hand.

"Last night, something happened . . . I felt it. I thought she was dead."

Cathrin gasped, but Mkel held up his hand. "Where was she?"

"I cannot tell. Far away."

"There was a congress at Lamdon," Mkel said. "Possibly she was there. But that is too far for you to hear her, surely."

Lu shrugged that off. "Something happened to her, and through the night I could not feel her at all. Then, at first light this morning, I heard her clearly for just a moment. There has been a disaster of some kind. We must send riders to Bariken."

"But how could you hear anything so far away, Maestra?" whispered Cathrin.

Lu shook her head. "I do not question my Gift."

"Nor do we," Mkel said. He thrust his foot into his boot and stood. "I will dispatch riders to Bariken right away."

"They will need a Singer, someone strong," Lu said urgently. "And they must hurry."

Mkel nodded, and Cathrin wrung her hands. "Now will you drink some tea, Maestra? And you must rest. You look exhausted."

Lu leaned back in her chair, her strength ebbing suddenly. "Tea, yes. Thank you, Cathrin. I will rest when the party is on its way."

A Housewoman brought Lu some tea and *keftet* while she waited for news. Mkel went straight to the great room, where the House was assembling for its morning meal. He came back soon after with two riders and a blonde itinerant.

"Maestra, of course you know Jane and Gram," Mkel said. The two riders bowed to her. "And this—" Mkel indicated the itinerant. "This is the Singer Theo."

Theo bowed also, and Lu inclined her head to him.

"Something is wrong at Bariken," Mkel told the three. "The Maestra has heard something, and feels Cantrix Sira is in great danger."

Jane and Gram nodded. The Singer Theo frowned, but was silent, waiting.

"There is no time to lose," Maestra Lu said. Her voice scratched in her throat. "Jane, Gram, please do all you can to find her."

"We will ride immediately," Jane said. "To Bariken, then?"

"I do not know where she is. You will need to begin there." She turned to the itinerant. "Singer Theo, this is of the greatest importance. Will you help us?"

His bow was as elegant as that of any Cantor. "Of course I will help, Maestra," he replied. She found his voice resonant and reassuring. He turned to Mkel. "Magister?"

"Yes," Mkel said. He turned to lead the riders out of the apartment. "We'll make arrangements for provisions and mounts. And your pay, Singer."

Lu just heard the Singer's answer before they closed the door. "My pay can wait."

A moment later the room was empty except for Cathrin and Lu. Lu let her head drop back and her eyes close. She felt the softness of a *caeru* rug fall around her. She took a deep, sighing breath, and fell asleep where she was.

Chapter Eleven

Snow and wind harassed Sira as she struggled to put some distance between herself and the campsite. Her muscles strained, and blood trickled steadily down her back. Her skin was cold and clammy, and her head felt as it were floating free of her body. As if from another lifetime she recalled Maestro Nikei talking about the effects of bleeding. The remedies circled vaguely through her mind as she pressed on. None of them were available to her now.

When she judged she had waded through the powder for an hour, working her way off the road into the forest, she allowed herself to collapse against an ironwood tree. She reached into her tunic for her *filla*. She could go no farther until she was warm all the way through.

Sira's Gift almost failed her at that moment. When she took a breath to play, pain from her injury stunned her. Her lips were icy, and her mind fluttered with fatigue and weakness. Her psi felt as distant as the safety of Conservatory. For one terrifying moment she could not think of the mode she needed.

She stiffened her spine. "I have not come this far," she said aloud, to convince herself, "to let my body get the better of me." The iron will that had seen her through the hours beneath the snow cleared her thoughts. She bit at her lips to increase the circulation, and began to play. No emotion, no physical sensation, did she allow her mind to register until a slender, intense *quiru* was born about her, as warm as she could make it under the cirumstances.

Then, while her body warmed in the safety of its warmth and light, she gave in. She crumpled to the ground, pulled her furs around her, and sobbed against her knees for her pain and fear and betrayal. The softness of the *caeru* fur soaked up her tears and muffled her weeping.

Several hours passed while she rested. When she felt a little stronger, she remembered that she should drink. She used her *filla* again, the briefest *Doryu* melody, to melt snow in a hardwood cup from her pack. The icy water tasted of wood and rock. She had to do it again and again to get enough water, but she kept at it until her thirst was quenched. She had a little food, a gift package of dried fruit and nuts. Cantrix Sharn had given it to her only two days before. It seemed a time past remembering.

She chewed a piece of dried fruit and a few of the nuts, and began to feel stronger. She could think of no way to bandage her wound, but the bleeding seemed to have ceased for the moment. She took some of her extra linen from her pack, and pressed it between her back and the tree, thrusting it down the back of her tunic as best she could. The entrypoint of the wound, below her collarbone, was already closed and scabbing.

She decided to rest the night through before setting out again. Lamdon was the only safe place for her to go, and it was also the closest House, as far as she knew. If she worked her way back to the road, she should be able to find the way.

Now, as she settled in for the night, she tried to take in what had happened. Mike and Alks had evidently been part of an assassination plan. Magister Shen had been their target, of course, but it was shocking to think that neither of them, nor Wil or Trude, had cared who died with him. Sharn, and even Magret, had tried to warn her, but she had been too blind to see how bad the situation was in Shen's House. What had she missed? What evidence had she, in her eagerness to go to Lamdon, ignored?

A picture rose in her mind of Rhia, now a beautiful, pale widow, Magistrix at last. She would be flanked, Sira supposed, by Wil and Trude. Perhaps Wil had conceived the intrigue. Trude was surely not so clever. And Alks and Mike? They would straggle in to Bariken with a dramatic story of storm and separation, a not-unheard-of tragedy in the Mariks. So sad, everyone would say, the loss of the brilliant young Cantrix.

Sira huddled lower inside her furs. There was no way for her to know what was happening now at Bariken. She didn't know whom she had to fear most. But she was certain she must hide the fact of her survival until she reached safety. Cantrix Sharn would know what to do. Until she could reach her protection, she would have to protect herself.

Shen's party had come one long day's ride by *hruss* from Lamdon. Sira estimated it would take her three days to cover the same distance on foot. It was a daunting prospect, but there was nothing she could do but accept it. She lay down, hoping for a healing sleep. Outside her slender *quiru*, snowflakes danced a menacing pattern in the cold and wind.

I can do it, she thought. One step at a time, I can do it.

It would be a hard and lonely three days, but at the end of it would be the safety and warmth of Lamdon, the comfort of Cantrix Sharn to confide in. The important thing—the saving thing—was that no one knew she was alive. Mike and Alks would not be coming back for her.

Maestra Lu and Isbel sat close together in a window seat at Conservatory. Lu sent, *I have heard Sira's thoughts. I know only that she lives. For a time I thought we had lost her.*

But what has happened? Isbel begged. *What did you hear?*

It is hard to explain. Something frightened me in the night, and when I sought Sira's mind, it seemed it was gone. I could hear nothing, as if she had gone with the Spirit beyond the Stars. Then, hours later, I heard her again.

Your reach is so long, Maestra, Isbel sent sadly. *I wish I could doubt you, but I do not.*

Lu put out her fragile white hand, and Isbel took it in both of hers. They clung together that way, the old Singer and the young one, sharing their fear for one of their own.

I think someone died, Lu sent a few moments later. *Not a Gifted one, but someone with Sira. There was grief in her thoughts, and shock.*

But she lives, Isbel sent.

Lu squeezed Isbel's fingers. *She lives. We have sent Gram and Jane to Bariken to discover what is wrong. She is their Cantrix, and they will surely help us to find her.*

We must save her, Isbel sent, tears springing to her eyes.

We must. Nevya needs her. And I need her.
Soft-hearted Isbel, in an unusual display of emotion, put her arms around her teacher. Lu accepted her embrace, and they wept together.

Sira managed a few hours of sleep despite her circumstances. She woke once to replenish her faltering *quiru*, the wind having torn at it through the night, then slept again. A bright day woke her, fading the light of her *quiru* to a dim glow. Her wound was stiff, and she moved carefully, hoping not to start the bleeding again.

She made a brief meal of fruit and nuts again, carefully wrapping what little was left and stowing it in her pack. She hoisted the pack gingerly to her shoulders, trying to avoid chafing her injury, and set out to retrace her steps of the day before. Her only real danger, she thought, was getting lost. She could manage without food for a little while.

The road they had followed to Lamdon and partway back again was one established by tradition and landmarks rather than improvements. Occasionally blocking trees were cut down, or boulders rolled aside. But snowfall shrouded Ogre Pass most of the year. Footprints rarely lasted more than a few hours.

But Sira knew Lamdon lay northeast of Bariken. Holding that in her mind, she could find the way. She would allow herself no doubts, but envision her welcome by Cantrix Sharn, a beacon to guide her to safety.

She intended to start by returning to the campsite where Magister Shen and Rollie lay entombed by snow. She would take her bearings there, where she would recognize the landmarks. Though it meant retracing an hour's worth of steps, it seemed a prudent beginning.

The wind died down with the coming of day, and it gave her the added protection of her acute hearing. She could detect the approach of any riders. By this time, Wil and Trude and the others would already be at Bariken, and were perhaps even now sending messages about the accident that had taken the lives of Bariken's Magister, its junior Cantrix, and one faithful rider. She shrank from thinking how grieved Maestra Lu would be.

She did not make good time. She was hungry, and weak from bleeding. The powdery snow had grown even deeper, and she had to wade through thigh-high drifts at times. Her trail had vanished, but she trusted her instinct to keep her moving in the right direction. When the moment came, however, she almost went right past the campsite.

She was plodding past a snowfilled clearing, which looked as if a clutter of boulders had been covered by the snow, when a crooked irontree caught her attention. It looked familiar. She stopped, and turned to look back the way she had come. The configuration of irontrees and their great twisting suckers jolted her memory. She went to one of the snowy boulders to clear it with her hand, and she found, as she swept away the powdery layers, that it was Rollie's frozen body, freshly buried by the steady snowfall.

Sira set her teeth against a wave of sorrow for her friend, and began to scrabble through the snow to find Rollie's pack, then Shen's, hoping to find some food.

There was very little. Rollie had a little dried *caeru* meat, and Shen had a small flask of wine. A Cantrix, of course, never touched wine, but Sira's hand hovered over the flask for a long moment. It would be warming, and she supposed it had some nutrition. Still, if it were to interfere with her ability to make *quiru*, its other qualities would be of no use. Instead, she took Shen's long-handled knife, and thrust it through her belt next to Rollie's. She had never used one except to rid herself of Mike's arrow, but it might be useful. She intended to survive.

She took one last glance around the site. There was nothing else to be done here. She whispered, "Goodbye, Rollie," before she turned her back on the awful memories, and began plowing her way back up the road to Lamdon.

Chapter Twelve

Theo feared his tired muscles would fail him by the time he and the two Conservatory riders galloped wearily into the courtyard at Bariken. He didn't know how the *hruss* had survived the pace the riders had forced on them since leaving the stables at Conservatory. He himself was exhausted, and he fell as much as slid out of the high-cantled saddle. He had been an itinerant Singer more than half his life, and was a saddle-hardened man of six summers, but this journey had been exceptional. Gram and Jane, who had neither rested nor eaten since dawn, had to be almost past endurance as well. Still, they refused refreshment, demanding to be taken at once to the Magistrix of Bariken. Night was hard on their heels as they entered the House.

Bowing to the Magistrix in her spacious windowed apartment, Theo was uncomfortably aware of how dirty and disheveled they all must look. Never, in the all too many Houses he had worked for, had he encountered a woman more beautiful than this one. Wishing he looked more presentable, he tried to smooth his hair. It sprang back immediately into a curling tangle.

Gram and Jane spoke urgently of Maestra Lu's psi impressions. Rhia bent her glossy head and listened as Theo tried to ignore the trembling of his legs. He had heard this story in detail at Conservatory, but he listened again, still not comprehending how even a Conservatory-trained Cantrix could pick up thoughts at such a great distance, as Lu claimed to have done.

Theo's parents had been itinerant Singers, like their parents before them. They had refused to consider Conservatory. Like all Nevyans, they revered the Cantrixes and Cantors who warmed and protected the Houses, but they never aspired to the Cantoris, not for themselves, not for their son. They were proud of the accomplishments of their line, and they were satisfied. They had not offered Theo a different choice, and he had never thought to ask.

The Magistrix was speaking. "Is it really possible?" Her eyes were clear and sympathetic in her smooth face. "Could your Maestra have heard someone's thoughts at so great a distance?"

"Maestra Lu can," Gram insisted. Jane nodded. Both stood straight, despite their weariness, intent on their purpose. They were whip-thin, weather-worn. Gram looked angry, and Jane worried. "We need riders to go back up the Pass with us, at the earliest possible hour."

"Of course," Magistrix Rhia said. "And of course, we all hope Cantrix Sira is, indeed, alive." Her Housekeeper, a long-limbed, dark man, sat still as stone behind her, while she leaned forward in her carved chair, concern in every line of her graceful body.

"We feel the loss of our young Cantrix deeply," she went on. "You must have met our messengers on the road."

"So we did," Gram said. "They went on to Conservatory."

Rhia spoke over her shoulder to the Housekeeper. "Wil, please arrange for the search party without delay."

He stood, and bowed.

"At first light, please," Jane begged. "There may be no time to lose."

Theo watched the Conservatory riders with admiration for their dedication, even as envy, his old, unwelcome companion, welled in his heart. He tried to thrust it aside, even to deny it. Surely by now, as old as he was, it was a pointless emotion.

"Our men will be ready at dawn," Wil said. "Now let me arrange beds and baths."

"Yes," said the Magistrix. "You must rest. You will want to be fresh. Singer, will you ride with them tomorrow? We have no other Singer here but Cantrix Magret, and of course we can't spare her from the Cantoris."

Theo bowed as elegantly as he knew how, despite his chagrin over his grimy appearance. "Of course, Magistrix. I agreed to this at Conservatory."

The three travelers followed Wil out the door. Theo didn't know which he craved more, hot food, a bed, or a bath, but he meant to make the most of each. He was, however, to be kept from all of them for some time yet. An anxious and saddened Cantrix Magret, lonely and overworked, pressed him with questions, searching for a hopeful clue about her young colleague's survival.

As the first flickers of morning light edged the horizon, the search party gathered in the courtyard. The Conservatory riders met those from Bariken for the first time over a quick breakfast in the great room. The Bariken men, called Alks and Mike, were large and grim-faced. Theo's friendly overtures were met with little more than grunts, and he soon gave them up.

He was still tired from the day before, but eager to be moving. He shivered inside his *caeru* furs. These northern mountains felt the beginning of the deep cold sooner than the southern timberlands he had recently traveled through.

Jane was a shadowy blur in the twilit morning, her breath a shifting cloud before her hood. Gram raised his hand to the other riders, and the party was off, the *hruss* slogging through fresh powder from the night's snowfall. Alks and Mike led the way, and Theo trailed behind Jane and Gram. With a little chill of apprehension, Theo noticed that Jane had a long knife strapped to her waist. He was sure it hadn't been there before. As they rode, he wondered what intuition had caused her to arm herself so visibly.

As the light grew, Theo realized that all the riders but himself carried weapons. Tension flickered under his breastbone. Only once before had he been inadvertently involved in violence between humans. Usually the struggle between man and the environment was enough to occupy those who lived on the Continent. His senses sharpened, and the very air seemed alive with danger. As the saying goes, he thought, the drifts are deep in this one.

The powdery snow that hindered the search party's progress also obscured the hooofprints of the *hruss* that preceded it. Maestra Lu sensed this, wrestling with her fears at Conservatory. She could not have proved it, but she knew in her bones that two others had ridden out from Bariken, ahead of Jane and Gram and the Singer Theo. They were pushing their mounts up into the Pass as fast as they were able.

Lu paced her room like a *wezel* in a cage, long past being able to make wild rides into the Mariks. There was nothing she could do but fret and pray, in the age-old manner of mothers.

Sira awoke from her second night alone in Ogre Pass stronger, but desperately hungry. She had seen a *wezel* the night before as she called up her *quiru*, but the little meatless creature hardly seemed worth the trouble of killing. This morning, though, she felt she could have eaten even its scruffy hide.

She had a scrap of dried *caeru* meat left, and she chewed it as she broke camp. She saved the last of the dried fruit for midday. She supposed she could come across a living *caeru* today, but she doubted she would be swift enough to bring it down. There was so little wildlife in the mountains, and most of that terrifying. She had no desire to encounter a *ferrel* by herself, although she supposed if the feathers could be pulled off, there might be some meat on the long bones. She had seen one as a child, swooping down from a mountaintop to pick up a *caeru* pup in its beak as if the little thing weighed nothing. She could not bear even to think of the *tkir*. She promised herself an early *quiru*, so there would be no risk of being caught by darkness.

She had walked all day yesterday, not quickly but steadily. Two more days should get her there if her sense of direction was true. A lifetime spent within the walls of her parents' House, Conservatory, then Bariken had not prepared her for a trek through Ogre Pass.

She walked through the day, stopping only to finish off the dried fruit. She sucked on snow until it melted in her mouth, feeling almost constantly thirsty. The snow chilled her, and made her teeth ache. She had to balance her thirst with the dangers of the encroaching cold.

At least the snow had stopped. The sky was gray, but the clouds lifted above the peaks. By evening, Sira felt she had been walking through deep powder all her life, as if her memories of Houses and other people were only dreams. She felt entirely alone in a cold white world.

Her muscles ached with the unaccustomed exertion, and her wounded shoulder was stiff as she sat against a softwood tree at last and dug out her *filla*. What would she have done if Trude had taken her *filla*? She shuddered to think of it.

Darkness slipped down from the mountaintops as she played a little first-mode melody. The *quiru* grew around her, a fragile little home, all there was between her and the malignant night. She warned herself firmly to stay alert. It was hard, though, so very hard. The emptiness of her belly made her feel disconnected and drowsy.

She settled in under her furs. Her *quiru* hung suspended and still, undisturbed by any breeze. Only the creaking of the ironwood trees around her campsite disturbed the silence.

As her eyes grew heavy and her mind drifted in a fog of hunger, Sira thought she saw the rounded, furry back of a yearling *caeru* pup slipping into her *quiru*. She imagined she could see the yellow-white blotch on the snow, just inside the circle of light, and that she smelled its acrid odor. Only her eyes showed out of her own *caeru* furs, and she dreamed that she and the animal looked the same, curled on the snow, two mounds of yellow-white fur in the glow of the *quiru*.

There was a faint cry, distinct and insistent, in her mind. Sira could not resist its direction. She blinked, and came out of her dream.

A half-grown *caeru* lay near her. It was as beguiled as she, drowsing in the warmth, unaware that the other furry mound was not one of its own.

Moving instinctively, pushed by that distant voice in her thoughts, Sira reached for one of her knives. Slipping it from beneath the furs, she felt its shape and heft, and measured her target. She tested the action in her mind before she moved, once, twice, three times; then she leaped. Her knife struck true, just behind the foreleg and up, straight to the heart of the sleeping animal.

She jumped aside as the *caeru* twisted in its death throes, but not quickly enough. A long yellowed claw caught her forehead, and hot blood streamed over her cheek. She dared not get near enough to cut its throat, but had to wait as it pumped out its lifeblood over the snow.

Plucking a bit of fur from her bedfurs, she pressed it over the gash in her forehead. There was no time to worry about this new wound. Swiftly, she carved out the *caeru*'s heart and liver. She ate them warm and raw and dripping, kneeling there in her *quiru* under the lonely stars.

Maestra Lu released the long, fragile tendrils of her thought at last. She could no longer keep her mind extended so far, reaching out into the wilderness. Commanding the *caeru* had taken all her energy. She put down the *filhata* that had been her tool, and leaned her head into her hands.

She smiled to herself, weary but triumphant. Sira was no longer so hungry nor so weak. Lu had never reached so far before, or done something with such effect, and if the *caeru* hunters knew what she could do, they would give her no rest.

But the effort had taken all her energy. Like Sira, it had been two days since she had slept a full night or eaten properly. All at once, her reserves of strength evaporated like snowflakes in the sun, and Maestra Lu collapsed, unconscious. Her Housewoman found her lying on the cold stone floor the next morning.

*

By the light of morning, Sira stared unbelieving at the *caeru* carcass inside the fading boundary of her *quiru*. A thousand questions tumbled through her mind. Had she really done this, or had it been a hunger-induced nightmare? She had never killed anything in her life.

She looked down at her hands, and was shocked and rather queasy to find them crusted with blood, the nail rims dark. Then she nodded to herself, grimly. "At least," she muttered, "it is not my blood."

Her own blood had dried uncomfortably on her forehead, but, fearful that this new wound would bleed again if she cleaned it, she left it as it was, crudely bandaged with a scrap of fur.

Before departing the campsite, she clumsily carved out what meat she thought she could carry, wrapping the grisly bits in a section of hide to put in her pack. Soon she was walking again, finding the Pass growing steeper and steeper as she toiled through the snow. She left the remains of her kill to freeze solid where they were.

Chapter Thirteen

Sira pressed on, working her way steadily northeast. The floor of the Pass widened and flattened, and the wind blew the powder from the snow-pack, making it easier to walk.

She made her next camp at the first sign of darkness. Her *quiru* trembled in a sudden breeze that had not troubled her all day, and she felt the vastness and unpredictability of the Continent around her. Once she thought she heard a distant roar, but it might have been only the soughing of the wind in the treetops. She hunkered down with her arms around her knees, remembering Rollie's warnings about *tkir*. She strengthened her *quiru* until it flashed with energy in the gathering gloom, but still she felt small and vulnerable. Thinking of Rollie pierced her with grief. The hours of darkness seemed an eternity of solitude.

Though the night passed slowly, she felt infinitely stronger for having eaten. She slept fitfully, but she did sleep, and in the morning she set out with a will. Her pack bounced lightly against her back, and the wound from the arrow did not begin bleeding again as far as she could tell. She kept her *filla* close to her body, the most essential tool of her survival; the two long knives were stuck through her belt where she could reach them in a heartbeat.

At midday she rested and forced down more of the raw *caeru*, refusing to gag at the texture and taste of uncooked meat. She remembered with longing the platter of nursery fruits and nuts she had barely touched at Lamdon.

She grew hot with exertion, but she knew better than to remove her furs and feel the bite of the cold. She was grateful for the distant pale sun that illumined the tops of the trees and occasionally reached past their great branches to fall on the floor of the Pass. No more snow fell, and Sira whispered thanks to the Spirit of Stars for not having to ford a foot of new powder. Once she looked back the way she had come, and could see her own tracks clearly, far into the distance. She supposed that could be a good thing. If she lost her way, she would be able to retrace her steps.

Gram and Jane pled with the riders from Bariken for more haste. Alks said, "Doing our best." Mike said nothing at all.

Theo chafed at the strain in the traveling party. There was something wrong with his *hruss*, indeed all three *hruss* Bariken had provided. They were either old or underfed, and no matter how the riders urged them, they could not seem to pick up their pace. There was no conversation to fill the hours, only the constant tension, like an extra traveler in their midst.

As they worked their way into the Pass, the deep powder gave way to an easier snowpack. Gram pointed down, beneath his *hruss's* feet, and Theo saw Jane lean from her saddle to see something. Theo kicked his struggling *hruss* so the beast would catch up, and he, too, bent to look down at the tracks in the snow.

"More than one person passed here," he said. "And *hruss*."

Jane and Gram exchanged a look, and Gram said, "You're right, Singer. I don't like the look of this."

"You don't think it could simply be other travelers?"

Jane said, "Let's hope so."

Gram lifted his reins. "I think," he said darkly, "that Bariken has done everything they could to delay us." He thumped his poor *hruss* with his heels, and was rewarded with a stumbling trot. Jane made a disgusted noise, and did the same.

Theo touched his beast on its neck. "Sorry," he said. "But you're going to have to keep up." He gave it a sharp kick in the ribs, and hurried after Gram and Jane as best he could. When they caught up with Alks and Mike, they were forced to slow again to a flat-footed walk. Theo saw Jane pounding her fist against her thigh in fury and frustration.

Sira took a brief midday rest, turning her face up to catch the weak sunlight. She just might reach Lamdon before dark. The thought renewed her energy. She swung her pack into position, and started walking once more.

Topping a rise, she stepped around an outcropping of rock that thrust up through the old snowpack. The snow was deeper here, some drifts coming to her knees. She was about to drop down into a little gulley when she felt the sharp, warning prickle of her psi. It had been three days since she had any contact with living humans. Her senses were instantly alert, with an almost physical sensation, as if she had heard a noise tear through the silent forest.

Her nightmare experiences had turned Sira into a wary creature. She had been both predator and prey in the last few days, and as her nerves flared, this new Sira wasted no time in questioning her instincts. She cast about immediately for a place to hide.

The snow was so deep at the sides of the road, and so easily marked, that she could see no way to escape without making deep and unmistakable tracks. The irontree branches began far above her head, too high for her to reach.

She hurried on, her mind open to receive whatever clues might come her way. Someone's mind was insufficiently shielded, or she would have received no warning at all. Now, as she concentrated, she felt little tendrils of uneasy thought leaking from the careless one, like smoke curling from a cookfire. Someone, a Gifted one, was agitated. And that someone was not far away.

Sira's body began to drip with perspiration under her furs, and her thigh muscles to burn. She panted as she forced her way through the drifts. Struggling over the far side of the arroyo to look down at the long valley beyond, she wasted a moment in gasping for breath. No clouds obscured the pale sky, and the air was so light and empty that she could see, looking ahead to the steep slope at the end of the valley, the peaked roofs of Lamdon and the great curve of the nursery gardens behind them. So near did they seem, she felt she could reach out and touch them. In truth, they were surely at a distance of four hours' walk. The danger she sensed behind her was much, much closer.

On the near slope of the valley there was a little stand of softwood trees, young and slender. The branches of several stretched just an arm's reach above her head. Her shoulder was still stiff, and she wasn't sure she had the strength to pull herself up. But she had to try.

As she loosened her pack to free her arms, she thanked the spirit of the little *caeru* that had given her its life's energy.

She chose the thickest tree in the little grove. With another prayer, she jumped off the snow and grasped a low limb with both hands. Pain flamed in her shoulder, but she ignored it, scrabbling with her boots for purchase on the trunk of the tree. She pulled herself up, bit by painful bit, grunting with effort. Fresh blood leaked from the wound in her back, but she hardly noticed it, so hot was she from her struggles.

With intense effort, she reached the lowest limb with one foot, and wriggled upward until she straddled it. The branches above were thinner, but offered more camouflage. She climbed until she thought she had gone as high as she dared without breaking through.

She stood with her legs braced on different limbs, one a little higher than the other. Her back pressed against the spongy bark, and she looked down through the leaves to the road below. She felt like a *caeru* at bay, and she knew the hunters were closing in. In a last attempt to save herself, she concentrated all her psi energy into one powerful broadcast for help. The mind leaking warnings behind her would hear it, too. But she was trapped. She poured all her strength into one long, silent scream of terror.

Theo's breath caught in his throat at the scream that seared his mind. He had experienced only the vaguest of psi impressions since his childhood; his parents had carefully taught him to close his mind to them. But this one broke through with incredible strength, and a definite impression of distance. Crude though the cry was, Theo was certain of what he had heard.

"Jane! Gram!" he shouted, urging his *hruss* forward. "I've heard something—something I've never—it's the Cantrix, in my mind!" Unfamiliar though his impressions were to him, certainty drove out any doubts. "She's up ahead, and she's in danger. Now!"

Jane pierced him with a glance, then nodded to Gram. The two kicked and whipped their weary *hruss* into a gallop, forcing them past Alks and Mike and on up the road at a dead run. The Bariken riders looked back at Theo, then hurried their own much stronger *hruss* to catch up.

Theo's psi might have been blunted by his parents' training, but his years on the road had sharpened his instincts for danger. His gut told him what they had to fear in that moment, and he gave a hoarse cry as he kicked his *hruss* hard, brutalizing it into a faster pace.

"Gram!" he shouted. "Watch out! Watch out behind you! They—"

He saw Alks draw his long knife, and rein his *hruss* around to face him. Theo had not time even to slow his own beast as Alks pulled back his arm and threw the knife with wicked speed. He watched it come for what seemed an interminable time, sawing on his reins, bracing himself. When the knife reached him, the impact knocked him completely out of his saddle. He fell hard on his back into the snow.

Shock immobilized him and stole his breath. Theo couldn't tell how badly he was wounded, or even if he still lived. He heard the cries of the other four riders as from a distance. He knew a battle ensued, but he couldn't tell who was victorious, and before its sounds ceased, darkness closed over his head, as sure and complete as midnight in the Marik Mountains.

Sira waited, her nerves on fire with suspense. The mental spill from one of her pursuers tormented her, and it grew worse when she began to hear them with her ears, too. They had given up any effort at stealth, and were racing toward her as fast as their *hruss* could carry them. One of them had heard her silent cry. It had forced them to deal with her as swiftly as possible.

The leaves of the softwood tree rattled around her, vibrating with the strength of her psi. She drew a deep breath, and quieted her mind. The leaves ceased their trembling, but there was nothing she could do about the deep tracks she had made in the snow.

A moment later two strong *hruss* charged over the rise into her little valley. With curses, their riders reined them in, and called questions to each other as they cast about for her path.

Sira knew their voices. Wil and Trude had found their way to her once again. In moments, they stood below her slender softwood tree, peering up through its branches.

Wil's familiar voice was redolent of easier times. "Cantrix Sira, are you there? You must be so frightened! Come down, and let us escort you safe to Lamdon. This political struggle has nothing to do with you."

Sira gritted her teeth. The old Sira, the innocent one, might have believed his words. But that naive girl was gone, leaving in her place one who trusted no one. Her breath whistled slightly in her throat, and her legs trembled with fatigue from bracing on the uneven branches.

"Cantrix Sira?" This time it was the sweet, low-pitched tone of Conservatory. Trude's *hruss* pressed close to the softwood tree as Trude tried to project sympathy and concern. The effect was awkward, her mental discipline too long unexercised. She forced her psi in a way that would have shamed any second-level Conservatory student.

She tried again. "Sira, you poor thing! You've been alone up here so long. Let me help you down, won't you? I'm sure you need hot food and a bath, and—"

Hot temper, born of the fear and grief of the last days, flooded Sira's mind. In a fury, and without making a sound, she sent an angry blast of psi to Trude that made the older woman gasp in mid-sentence.

Traitorous bitch, Sira sent. *You are not fit to touch a true Cantrix!*

She heard Trude mutter something to Wil, and then there was an ominous silence.

Theo struggled up from the depths to wakefulness once again. Something was pressing tightly against his stomach. With difficulty, he forced his eyes open to see Gram bending over him, tying something around his middle, beneath his furs.

"Theo," said the rider in a tight voice. "Can you hear me?"

Theo meant to say yes, but all that emerged from his dry throat was a choked sort of croaking sound. He caught Gram's eyes, and managed a brief nod. The muscles of his face were stiff with shock and cold.

"We need to hurry, and that means we have to leave you here for a while." Theo's eyes tried to close again. His head lolled, and he had to exert all of his will to remain conscious. "You'll need a *quiru* in about five hours," Gram went on. "We'll be back for you, but maybe not till morning."

Theo, with a great effort, forced his rigid tongue to work. "Cover me," he rasped. "In case . . ."

"Yes." Gram's face gave away nothing, and Theo understood there was no time for emotion. "Jane's hurt, too, but she says she can ride, and I need her. I think you ought to try to stay awake. You're still bleeding, I'm afraid." While he talked, Gram spread Theo's bedfurs over and around him, tucking him tightly into them. Theo saw a long knife lying in the snow where Gram must have tossed it. Blood–his own blood–smeared the blade. He looked away.

"Got your *filla*?" Gram's voice was rough. Both men were aware that Theo would freeze to death if he was unable to call up a *quiru*. Gram didn't apologize, nor did Theo expect it. There was no choice to make between the life of an itinerant Singer and that of a full Cantrix.

Theo felt with his fingers until he had his *filla* in his hand. When he nodded, Gram touched his shoulder once, then disappeared from Theo's line of sight.

Theo fixed his eyes on a nearby ironwood tree as he listened to the sounds of the two *hruss* departing. He held onto consciousness with all his strength. He was warm, at least for the moment. He felt shockingly weak, but then, he told himself, he didn't have to go anywhere. He didn't have enough energy to laugh at his own unspoken joke, but it made him feel better.

Suddenly he realized that he didn't know what had become of the Bariken riders. Lifting his head hurt too much, but he could twist his neck enough to look about him. Two fur-covered figures lay not far away, legs and arms askew in attitudes of death. Gram and Jane had let them lie where they had fallen. Their *hruss* stood nearby, shifting their weight uneasily on their wide hooves. They were still saddled, reins hanging to trail in the snow. Two still had bedfurs strapped behind the cantles. Only Theo's had been removed.

Gram and Jane had killed Alks and Mike, just as one of them had tried to kill him.

Well, Theo thought. I don't feel like dying this afternoon.

His fingers found the bit of metal that had been his mother's, and he held it in his hand. He lay still, but he kept his eyes open, and concentrated on gathering his strength. One thing he knew well, and that was how to heal the injuries that befell those who plied the icy roads of the Continent. Weakly, he concentrated his psi on the wound in his belly. He had little energy, and he couldn't play his *filla*, not yet. But he could try to slow the bleeding. If he could stay awake.

Sira's softwood tree began to quake, and she knew someone was coming up. It was easier for Wil, because he had his big mountain *hruss* to stand on. His boot found the bottommost branch with ease, nothing like the painful effort it had cost her.

She looked above her for a way to escape, but the boughs over her head were so thin, and already shaking with the impact of Wil's approach, that she was sure they would never hold her. Her breathing slowed. She felt distant, separate from her fear. She became that trapped *caeru*, an animal at bay, with an animal's instincts.

She found, to her surprise, that she had drawn Shen's long knife out of her belt. The heft of it felt good in her hand. She turned the point downward, holding it behind her, away from her body, as the tree shivered and swayed under Wil's weight.

Wil seemed unconcerned about his own safety. She was not surprised at that. She was a Singer, after all, and they were known to be a gentle breed, soft, even effete. She supposed Wil could not conceive of her as dangerous. He did not hesitate, but climbed higher and higher until their eyes met through the quaking branches of the softwood tree.

Sira's eyes narrowed as she gazed at him, and her purpose crystallized to an icy focus.

Keeping the knife behind her, she worked her way around to the opposite side of the tree. Wil cursed as he struggled to follow. He weighed more than she did, and the branches began to bend and crack beneath him.

But at last he ascended to the same branches she had been been standing on. His lean hand reached around the trunk.

She breathed steadily, silently, as Wil stretched one long leg out to a limb on Sira's side of the swaying tree. He found his foothold, then pulled his body around with his hands.

Just as he came around the trunk, fully in her sight, Sira switched the knife in her hand so that it pointed outward. Wil pulled himself up beside her, his arm reaching for her, his fingers spread to seize her throat.

She gathered all her strength, and plunged the long blade into him, past the skin and muscle, as far into his body as she could thrust it.

Part of her mind knew that the memory of the act, of the resistance of flesh and tendon and muscle to the knife, would be too ghastly to bear. But at this moment, her mind was no part of the event. It was her body that acted, driven by the need for self-preservation. It was the culmination of three days of a struggle to survive.

Wil fell, crashing through the tree branches. The knife went with him. Sira stared down at her hand, shockingly empty now, the air suddenly cold against her palm.

As if from a great distance, Sira heard Trude scream, and scream again, not with her mind but with her throat as Wil, already dead, thudded to the packed snow under the softwood tree.

Sira heard, but felt no pity. *Shut up*, she sent, in a cold fury.

Trude ignored her, and the waves of shrill sound went on. Sira hissed aloud, "Shut up!" Still Trude screamed.

Sira had never used her psi for ill, not even taking part in the teasing dormitory games at Conservatory, which too often left younger students in tears. But she was more animal than Singer at this moment. She sent a tide of psi into Trude's mind, anything to stop her screaming.

Shut up or I will kill you too!

Trude's ululation broke off abruptly. There was a moment of silence before she screeched, "You great idiot! Do you know what you've done? I'll see to it you never step foot in a Cantoris again, you whore, you—"

Sira did not stop to think. She was, in fact, not thinking at all. She cut through Trude's mind with her psi as brutally as a carver cuts through a chunk of ironwood with his *obis* knife. It was a wordless, formless blow, with all the power of a great Gift behind it. Trude fell instantly, and permanently, silent.

Sira shuddered, coming to herself as if waking from a nightmare. She took a horrified breath, and reached out with her mind to see if Trude still lived.

The former Cantrix did still live and breathe. But there were no thoughts in her mind, no emotions to sense. Her mind was completely, and Sira feared irretrievably, broken.

But there was no time for sympathy. Sira pulled out her remaining knife, Rollie's knife, and held herself poised to strike again. Her heart felt like a piece of chiseled stone, and her lips pressed together until they stung.

She waited. She had no sense of passing time. Her mind and her emotions were frozen as solid as the blue ice of the Great Glacier.

She had no way of knowing how many hours it took for Gram and Jane to reach her. When she heard their voices beneath her tree, it took her some minutes for her to relax her muscles enough to move.

"Cantrix Sira?" called Gram urgently. "Are you there? Sira? It's Gram, and Jane . . . from Conservatory. Maestra Lu sent us when you–when she—"

Sira's voice cracked when she spoke. "I am here. I will come down."

"Are you hurt?" Jane's voice sounded glorious to Sira, familiar and strong.

"I was wounded three—no, four—days ago, but it is almost healed. I am well."

Sira gingerly descended a branch, and then another. Her muscles trembled with sudden weakness, and the aftermath of crisis. "I need a hand down. I have not eaten in some time."

Gram and Jane together reached up to her, and she slipped down into their waiting arms. Trude was a huddle of yellow-white furs against the snow, crouched beside Wil's inert body. Only when Gram had satisfied himself that his young charge was all right for the moment did he turn to look at her.

"Who is this?" he asked.

"It is Trude v'Bariken." Sira spoke without inflection. "She is harmless now. Her mind is gone."

"Are you sure?" Jane had let go of Sira the instant she was safely on the ground, but she stayed so close, Sira could feel the rider's breath against her own face.

"Yes," said Sira. She added indifferently, "She was a Singer once."

"And this?" Gram prodded Wil's body with his booted toe.

"That was the Housekeeper of Bariken." Sira looked away. "His name was Wil. I have killed him. Is Maestra Lu all right?"

"She's very worried about you," Jane said.

There was no more talk. Sira brought out her *filla*. Gram busied himself bringing the *hruss* close, spreading out bedfurs, bringing food and cups. He rolled the Housekeeper's body away from the makeshift campsite, but pushed Trude onto his own bedfurs. Her face was blank. From time to time she gave a wordless moan, but she seemed unaware of the activity around her.

Sira played, and the *quiru* blossomed. When it glowed warmly around them, they ate, especially Sira. Her young body craved nourishment. Gram and Jane fussed over her, coaxing her to eat and drink just a bit more.

"Sleep now, Cantrix Sira," said Jane.

"We'll be at Lamdon by midday tomorrow," Gram added.

Sira lay down at once on her furs. Jane found Trude's own bedfurs and rolled her into them without gentleness. She slipped into her own, while Gram stoked up the little fire of softwood from his pack, and prepared to stand night watch.

"I hope Theo's all right," Jane said.

"Yes," said Gram, gazing out into the darkness. "He's good, for an itinerant."

"We'll send him help from Lamdon. We owe him."

"We'll see he's repaid." There was a pause, and Gram added softly, "If he lives."

There was no answer from Jane's bedroll but a deep sigh as she eased into sleep. Trude seemed to be sleeping as well.

Sira lay with her eyes open, staring up at the stars twinkling faintly beyond the light of her *quiru*. Only when she realized Gram was watching her did she close them.

Chapter Fourteen

Theo admired the pale remnants of his *quiru* in the brilliant morning sun. Look at that, he thought. Still holding, and no one to admire it except three old *hruss*.

It had been a long night, full of nervous wakings and odd sounds exaggerated by solitude. The wound in his belly ached, and he felt weak as a newborn *caeru* pup. But he was alive, and he was warm.

He wondered about the young Cantrix, ten years younger than he, alone in the Mariks for at least three nights. Itinerants thought of Conservatory Singers as delicate, protected, their esoteric Gifts nurtured and pampered like nursery flowers. His own career had seasoned him early, but an eighteen-year-old Cantrix . . .

In truth, he didn't expect to meet Sira v'Conservatory alive.

He tried sitting up, but feeling a fresh wash of blood into his bandages, gave it up after the first attempt. It seemed he would have to lie here, helpless as a babe, until someone came for him. His *filla* was close at hand, and a flask of water. He couldn't have eaten even if he had food. There was nothing to do but lie still and wait.

From time to time through the day and then through the second night, Theo played his *filla* just enough to keep his *quiru* steady. Deep breaths sent blazing pain through his belly, so he kept his *quiru* just big enough for himself and the *hruss*, who crowded close to him. The legs of a corpse stretched inside the envelope of light, with the upper body abandoned to the darkness, made a surreal and chilling sight. As there was nothing Theo could do about it, he tried to remember not to look in that direction.

To pass the time, he tried listening with his mind, searching for the reflex that had responded to Cantrix Sira's mental call. Something he thought suppressed since childhood had come alive in that moment of need. But now, he heard nothing but the wind stirring the branches of the ironwood trees. He remembered how strict his mother had been about shielding his mind, how many times she had scolded him for hearing her thoughts before she spoke them. She had been convinced–and had convinced him–that hearing others' thoughts would only drive him mad. But now, dozing on and off, he wondered.

On the second morning, he drifted out of sleep to find *hruss* and riders emerging from the forest into his clearing. When he was sure he wasn't dreaming, he grinned crookedly at the welcome sight of Gram, who leaped from his mount and hurried to bend over him.

"Hello, again," Theo said. His voice was hoarse with disuse. "Back so soon?"

Gram gave a huge smile, gripping his shoulder. "Thank the Spirit! No more lives lost."

Another man, slight and pale, knelt by Theo, and gently folded back his bedfurs. "I'm Cantor Rico v'Lamdon," he said. "We were horrified to hear what happened." He peeled back Gram's hasty bandages, and scowled at the wound. "You've stopped bleeding," he said. "Though I don't know how you managed that. But you'll have to ride in a *pukuru*."

"Just so I don't have to stay here another day," Theo said. "I'm tired of the view."

Cantor Rico pulled a square of cloth from his pocket, and began to rebandage Theo's belly. "You did well, Singer," he said. Theo knew it was anger that made the Cantor's voice shake. "You will want to know that Cantrix Sira reached Lamdon safely. She and Jane will meet us on our way."

"Good news," said Theo. Then, wearied by the brief conversation, he let his eyes close. He was glad to know the young Cantrix was safe. And now perhaps he could rest for a time.

Rico finished with his bandage, wrapping strips of felt around Theo's waist to hold it in place. He sat back on his heels then, and played a healing *Doryu* melody on his *filla*. Theo's flesh responded to Rico's psi with a warm, prickly sensation that left the injured area tingling when it was over. Theo had often healed such wounds in others; it was a strange feeling to be the recipient rather than the giver. Rico finished by playing another melody in the first mode, and Theo promptly fell into a sound sleep.

He woke as they lifted him, bedfurs and all, and laid him in the *pukuru*, then slept again. When he woke a second time they already were on their way, the *pukuru* lashed behind one of the *hruss*. The bone runners glided over the snow with hardly a bump. Rico saw he was awake, and gave him a draught of some herb-flavored drink. He drank, then slept again.

When the party stopped for the night, they unhitched his *pukuru*, and he woke. The mountain peaks were already disappearing in the folds of night. He was reaching for his *filla* to call up a *quiru* when he heard someone else begin to play. He remembered he was not the only Singer in the party. It was a beautiful sound, sweet and clear in the gathering dusk. He listened to the precise intonation, the liquid phrasing, and in his weakened state, tears formed behind his eyelids. He blinked them away as the light swelled around him, a *quiru* not of his making.

It flared up into the twilight with startling swiftness. He tried to twist his head to see who was playing. Gram saw this, and turned the *pukuru*, sliding it sideways on the snow so Theo could look into the circle of people around the crackling campfire, and find the Singer.

It was a girl, a tall, lean young woman with a bandage over one eye. She needed no introduction. When she lowered her *filla*, he regretted the end of her melody.

She felt his gaze, and looked across the fire at him. "I owe you thanks, Singer." Her voice was deep, and it sounded tired, too old a sound to be coming from such a young person.

"No thanks are necessary, Cantrix Sira," Theo said. His own voice sounded weak and thready. "I am glad to see you . . . well." He had been going to say "alive," but felt it was perhaps not tactful.

"Yes, I am quite well," she said dryly. Theo understood she was aware of what he had almost said. He grinned at her, and though she did not smile, she nodded acknowledgment.

There was a flash of psi around the circle, drawing Theo's attention to Cantor Rico's grim face. Theo supposed he was sending something to Sira.

He gritted his teeth in frustration at being unable to follow.

Sira gave no indication that she heard anything. Her lips were set firmly together. The yellow light of the *quiru* gleamed dully on her bandage, and her face looked sallow, with deep lines etched in the youthful skin.

I am not the only one who needs to heal, Theo thought. But my wound is only of the body.

He was surprised to find his old friend envy supplanted by a wave of pity. He stirred restlessly, trying to ease the pull of his belly wound.

Rico pulled his bedfurs close to the *pukuru*. "May I help you sleep, Singer?"

Theo hesitated, hating his weakness, then acquiesced. He closed his eyes as Rico began, in an oddly deep voice for such a small man, a short *cantrip*. It was easy to let the focused psi of the *cantrip* into his mind, and drop down into sleep, but it made Theo, who had been a Singer on his own for three summers, feel more like a child than the man he had been for so long.

Hours later, with the *quiru* still strong in the blackness of the night, Theo woke again. He looked about the circle of sleeping forms. Only Sira was sitting up, her bedfurs pulled around her shoulders. She was very still, gazing into the graying embers of the fire.

Sensing Theo's wakefulness, she glanced across at him. He raised one eyebrow in silent question, not wanting to disturb the other sleepers. Sira gave the slightest shake of her head and turned her eyes back to the fire.

Something fine has been destroyed in this misadventure, Theo thought. Though he had never met this young woman before, and though he could not hear her thoughts, he could feel that something in her had shattered. He doubted she would ever be the same again.

What a pity, he mused, as he began drifting into sleep again. What a waste.

Chapter Fifteen

Theo had never traveled with so large a group, nor had he often traveled with another Singer. Conservatory and Lamdon had mounted a party of twelve between them, and Cantor Rico and Cantrix Sira handled all the *quiru*. Not, Theo admitted to himself, that he was up to participating. His belly was beginning to heal, but the herbal draught from Lamdon and Rico's frequent ministrations meant that he spent the long hours of travel mostly asleep. By the second night of their journey, Theo knew they were on their way to Conservatory.

When he could, he watched Sira. She spoke only when spoken to, and then in the briefest of sentences. Her face was closed and unreadable, and Theo saw Rico and Jane exchange frowns above her head. No one offered to tell Theo exactly what had happened in Ogre Pass, but he could guess it had been something shocking.

Sira insisted on being the one to bring Theo his tea and *keftet* in the evenings. On the third night of their journey, as the others were helping themselves from the cooking pot, she knelt beside his furs and held out his bowl and cup.

"Cantrix, you shouldn't wait on me," he protested.

"You must allow me to," she answered in her odd deep voice. She helped him to a sitting position, propping his saddlepack under his bedfurs so he could lean against it. She did it so naturally that he forgot to be surprised at the touch of a full Cantrix.

"Join me then," he said, smiling. She looked at him somberly. The fire-light glinted on the angles of her lean face. He thought she was going to refuse, but then she nodded, and he knew it was to indulge him. It was reason enough, he thought.

She went to the fire and bent over it. When she returned, her bowl held only a scant few mouthfuls of food. He looked into it and laughed without thinking, then gasped with pain when his belly wound reminded him it was still there.

It took him a moment to recover while Sira watched him, her bandaged eyebrow lifted. "That little bit of food was hardly worth a trip to the fire, Cantrix," he said when he could speak. She looked into her bowl and shook her head.

"Just not hungry?" he asked. She didn't answer. Theo said as gently as he could, "I know you've had a bad experience. But when you're traveling, you need to eat and drink when you can."

She turned her dark eyes to him. "Thank you, Singer," she said gravely. She took a spoonful of *keftet* and put it in her mouth.

"Cantrix." Theo cocked his head at her. "You should probably chew it, too."

Obediently, but still solemn, Sira began to chew her food. Theo sighed, and leaned back, adjusting his bandages. "If I were healthy, Cantrix," he said, "I'd sing you the song about a *ferrel* that picked up a *wezel* and then dropped it because it was too thin to bother with. Dropped it right into the courtyard of Filus and they turned it into a pet. It got so fat it needed a room all its own, and when the *ferrel* came back for it, it was too heavy to carry." He winked at her, and despite herself, she smiled a little at the silly image.

"Is that the kind of song you like, Singer?" she asked.

"So it is," he said. "Also the only kind of song I know."

This earned him another smile. Theo tried to conceal that so much talking had tired him, but Sira saw his fatigue. "You must rest now," she said, and reached for his bowl.

"Tomorrow," he said sleepily, "you must teach me a new song. One I don't know."

"Yes," she said. She helped him to lie down, moving his saddlepack to just within reach. "Now sleep," she told him.

"Good night," he murmured.

He felt relaxed and lazy, as if he were floating in a warm bath. When a faint tickle in his drifting mind said, *Thank you,* he was not really sure he had heard it. If he had, it would have marked only the second time in his adult life he had truly heard someone's voice in his mind, and both times had been the voice of this surprising young Cantrix.

*

Sira, from her saddle, was the first to see the roofs of Conservatory above the trees as the travelers made their slow way up the snowy ride. The pace of the journey had been leisurely, adjusted for the *pukuru*, and restricted by the shortening hours of daylight as the season of deep cold approached. They had been riding for six days.

She glanced down at the fur-bundled figure of the itinerant. He was sleeping again.

She knew Cantor Rico was watching her, but she pretended otherwise. She had ignored the looks passing between Gram and Jane. There was nothing she could do to ease their fears. Anything she said to reassure them would be deception. She wanted only to see Maestra Lu, rest in her presence, and unburden herself of the awful things she had done.

Over and over again she recalled the knife plunging into Wil's flesh, and the slice of her psi through the fabric of Trude's mind. She recalled the rush of triumph as the weaker mind broke under her attack. Only Maestra Lu could tell her how to live with those moments.

The shaggy *hruss* filled Conservatory's courtyard with their noise and bulk, and a somber group appeared to assemble on the steps. The day was brutally clear, sunlight glancing off snow and rippled glass windows. The Magister himself stepped forward to greet the travelers.

"Conservatory welcomes you," he said. Sira saw Theo awake, and twist his head to try to see who was speaking. "We are very grateful to you for bringing Cantrix Sira home to us."

Home, Sira thought. Perhaps I will never be at home again. She willed away the tightness in her throat, staring fixedly above Magister Mkel's gray and venerable head. Maestra Lu was not in the gathering on the steps, but Isbel was, and all her old classmates except Arn.

Sira slid off her *hruss* to bow to Mkel. Hooves clacked and slid on the paving stones as the rest of the party dismounted, stretching, smiling with relief at reaching their destination.

Mkel's eyes were on Sira, the patterns of wrinkles in his face deepened by the harsh light. "Are you well, Cantrix?"

Sira nodded, holding herself rigidly upright. The bandage on her forehead felt enormous.

Jane came to stand beside her. "The Cantrix is tired, Magister," she said. "We have been riding for hours today."

"Of course," said Mkel. "All of you must come in and bathe and eat." He gestured to several Housemen, who came forward to take the reins of the *hruss*. The doors of the House opened wide, and the students led the party inside. Two Housemen came out to unhitch the *pukuru*. They each took an end to carry Theo up the steps, but he waved them off.

"I can walk," he said. "Just lend me an arm." With help from one of the Housemen, he struggled up from the *pukuru*. Sira turned back, thinking she would help him, but he shook his head at her, and she understood that he wanted to walk into Conservatory under his own power.

Sira's classmates stood apart, watching as she entered the House. They bowed when she passed them, formally as strangers. She knew they were curious, and trying not to show it. They were waiting for her lead, as they would for any other full Cantrix. Only a few short months ago they would have plunged into a lively, silent conversation, full of questions and jibes and jests. But she was one of them no longer. She was Cantrix Sira, and she could not go back.

Mkel made his way to her through the cluster of people. "Cantrix Sira, we will talk after you have refreshed yourself."

"Thank you, Magister. I will not be long."

"Take the time as you need. I will speak with Gram and Jane first. And Cantor Rico."

Rico bowed to the Magister, and they turned toward the stairs. Sira looked up, and found Isbel standing before her.

Isbel, her rosy face solemn, bowed. She sent, presuming on old friendship, *Cantrix Sira, a bath first? Or are you hungry?*

"A bath, please," Sira said aloud. Isbel took a sharp breath. Sira looked straight ahead, trying not to see Isbel's hurt. "And something to drink."

Kevn appeared from somewhere, and bowed. "I will get tea," he said aloud. Sira wished they would tease and taunt her as they used to. She wished Isbel would take her hand, or put an arm around her waist. But she could not bring herself to initiate the contact.

She started down the corridor toward the *ubanyix*, and Isbel followed. When they had left the others behind, Sira said, "Where is Maestra Lu?"

Isbel looked up at her old friend, meeting her eyes. "I will bathe with you, Cantrix," she said quietly. "And I will tell you about Maestra Lu."

Sira saw the small widening of Isbel's eyes that meant she was opening her mind. Sira shook her head, a small gesture of helplessness. "I cannot do it right now," Sira whispered through suddenly trembling lips. "Please tell me."

They had arrived at the door of the *ubanyix*. Isbel opened the door. "Spirit of Stars," she said lightly. "It is empty."

She led Sira in, and closed the door behind them, then turned. Her eyes brimmed with sorrow. "I am so very sorry to tell you, Cantrix Sira, that our old teacher died ten days ago."

Sira closed her eyes, and struggled to breathe as she counted back over the last days. When she dared open her eyes, she slipped her furs off her shoulders with shaking hands, and stepped out of her soiled trousers. She unbound her hair, and pulled her tunic over her head. Isbel took everything to drop on top of the mound of discarded furs.

Sira, feeling as if every inch of her hurt beyond bearing, stepped down into the warm water. Mechanically, she began to wash crusted blood from her wounds. She had grown shockingly thin. All her bones seemed exposed. Her stomach was concave, and her breasts, always small, had shrunk almost to nothing. Only her hair, dark and heavy, hung past her shoulders to trail in the water.

Can we talk now, Cantrix? Isbel sent gently. *Sira?*

Sira felt dizzy with grief. "I cannot," she said tightly. "Not yet."

The warm water lapped around her shoulders. She remembered being in this same bath with Lu, and the ache in her breast threatened to choke her.

"Mkel told us Maestra Lu knew you were safe before she died," Isbel said. She leaned forward in the scented water. "Sira. You were her favorite."

For a long moment Sira could not speak. When she did, her lips felt stiff, her words clipped. "I caused her death," she blurted.

Isbel sucked in her breath. "No, Sira, no. Of course you did not! How can you think that? Whatever Maestra Lu did, she did because she had to. You cannot take responsibility."

Sira closed her eyes and leaned her head against the carved ironwood tub. She heard the little splash of water as Isbel moved closer. "Sira, this—this thing that happened—you bear no blame for it. You were just their Cantrix . . ."

"Just their Cantrix. That is it, is it not?" Sira said, her eyes still closed. "All the years of study, of struggle for perfection . . . and they own us, like well-trained *hruss*." She drew a shaky breath. Her heart felt as if it could burst. "It is the way we speak of itinerants. Oh, he's just an itinerant, we say." She splashed her face with water to disguise her threatening tears.

Isbel stared at her for a long, painful moment. Finally she said, "Shall I warm the water?"

Sira nodded, to allow her friend to do something for her. She could not help wondering why she had struggled so to survive. What had it been for?

She longed for the sound of Maestra Lu's voice to guide her, to soothe her. Maestra Lu's reach had been long, but no one, however Gifted, could reach from beyond the stars.

Isbel's *filla* trilled. The water temperature rose and the scent from the floating herbs intensified. The familiar walls of the *ubanyix*, the robes hung on hooks on one side, even the tidy stacks of towels, pained Sira. Everything looked as it always had, but everything had changed.

Isbel slipped back into the tub, her countenance solemn in a way Sira had never seen. "Open your mind to me," she whispered.

Sira said flatly, "I love you too much to do that. You do not want these memories."

Tears sprang to Isbel's eyes. "I want to help you. What a terrible ending for your first assignment! We were all so proud of you, so glad for you—you are the best of us."

"The worst is," Sira said slowly, "that I worked deliberately to be the best. I thought that was what mattered . . . yet in the end, it did not count for anything."

"Your next assignment will be better."

Sira did not answer.

In silence, the two girls washed and dried themselves, dressed in clean clothes, and bound their hair. The tea had been left outside the door. Other bathers came in while Sira drank it. Isbel bowed and left her when she turned toward Magister Mkel's apartment. Her memories dragged at her, slowing her steps as she walked down the corridor.

"Cantrix Sira, come in." Cathrin greeted her warmly. For as long as Sira could remember, Cathrin, motherly and bustling, had been part of Conservatory, busy with her own brood or fussing over one of the Gifted ones. Cathrin was unGifted, generous, and comfortable.

She led Sira to a chair and set a tray of nursery fruits and nuts near her, with tea and a cup of water. Sira drank some water to please her, but she had lost her appetite somewhere along the long road she had traveled.

"Cantrix Sira," said Mkel, coming into the room. "I am sorry to have made you wait." Cantor Rico came just behind him, and Sira rose to bow to her two seniors. Both men looked angry. Cathrin withdrew, her own face drooping in sad lines.

"Please, sit, both of you," the Magister said. "And eat, Cantrix Sira, or Cathrin will be after me."

"Forgive me, Magister, but I do not believe I can eat anything just now. My apologies to Cathrin." Sira sat down again and picked up the cup of water.

Mkel and Rico were both watching her closely. Psi sparkled in the room, but Sira kept her mind shielded, instinctively. It was the way she had controlled herself as a child. Before her Gift was molded and disciplined by stringent training, she had hidden her thoughts from her mother and her family, not understanding they could not hear her mind as she heard theirs.

Mkel seemed to sense her need for privacy. He spoke aloud. "Cantrix, now that your danger is past, I hope you will recover quickly from your awful experience." He smiled a little.

She nodded to him, and the poultice Maestro Nikei had pressed over her eyebrow pulled at her forehead, reminding her. "I am fine, Magister. Thank you."

Rico said, "We want to explain the events around the assassination of Magister Shen."

Sira transferred her attention to Rico. "I know Alks and Mike were working with—" her voice caught. She cleared her throat. "I know they were working with Wil. And Trude," she added, as if the name were an afterthought. Rico and Mkel exchanged a glance, and she knew she had not deceived them. "I do not know who actually shot Shen, or Rollie. Or me. It does not matter."

"You are quite right, Sira," Mkel agreed in a low voice. She had never seen him look so grim. "It does not matter who did it. What matters is who caused them to do it."

Sira put down her cup.

"Perhaps you were aware that there were tensions at Bariken," Mkel went on. "Rhia was actually ruling the House in all but name. Evidently that was not enough for her."

"Cantrix Sharn was concerned," Rico put in, "but there was little she could do. The tradition of inheritance makes it difficult to deal with an incompetent Magister. And nothing serious enough had happened before this to bring Bariken before the Magistral Committee."

"There is no doubt," Mkel said, "that Rhia arranged the assassination. Apparently she had expected to be Magistrix at Tarus, but the birth of a younger brother stood in her way."

"Rhia." Sira thought of the glossy-haired, elegant woman who had offered her the opportunity to go to Lamdon, an opportunity she had been thrilled to accept, feeding her own ambition. "I spoke with her. I felt no danger."

"I should think you would be angry, Cantrix," said Rico.

Sira had nothing to say to that. Maestra Lu's face glowed in her memory and in her broken heart. I should have known, she thought. My arrogance stopped me from knowing.

"You may rest assured that Rhia has been removed as Magistrix of Bariken, and will be placed under the jurisdiction of the Magistral Committee. Their judgment will be harsh. It may be that there will be a regent at Bariken until Trude's son by Shen is old enough to rule." Mkel paused, giving a heavy sigh. "Magret is working with Cantor Grigr for the time being. She can use your help, but not until you feel ready to go back."

Sira looked straight at Mkel. "I am sorry about Cantrix Magret, and I hope you will tell her so. But I cannot go back."

Mkel and Rico glanced at each other. Mkel said calmly, "Very well." Evidently the two men had discussed this possibility. "Perhaps you will rest here at Conservatory until you feel ready for another Cantoris."

Sira shook her head. "Forgive me, Magister," she said bleakly. "Rollie, who was my friend, died in the Pass. I almost did. Maestra Lu died trying to save my life, and right now I cannot imagine what it all means. I spent my youth trying to be the best at what I do, and then Rhia and—" The back of her throat was suddenly dry, and she swallowed with a small clicking sound. "—and Wil, and Trude, were content to destroy me for their own ends. What am I . . . what are all of us about, if we mean no more than that to the people we serve? I was trapped by my duty as much as by my ambition. I am ashamed and I am sad and I cannot be what they want me to be anymore."

It was a long speech, and the two men were silent for some time after Sira finished. She stared down at her hands, twined in her lap.

At length, it was Rico who spoke. "Cantrix Sira, we are as shocked as you by what happened. Conservatory Singers are to be cherished and protected. An isolated incident—"

"Excuse me, Cantor Rico," Sira interrupted. Her voice hardened. "Isolated or not, this incident is part of my life. I will try to understand it, but until I do, I will not be anyone's Cantrix. I will be my own person."

Rico looked helpless. Mkel said, "Sira. Give yourself time. We will wait for you."

His voice carried strong and skillful psi-inflections of empathy, and Sira had to close her mind against them. Her lips trembled, and she forced them to firm. "Thank you," she said. "But I will not change my mind." She rose, pretending composure, and bowed to her seniors with deep respect. Then, alone, she left the apartment.

Chapter Sixteen

Theo leaned back in one of the carved chairs in the Cantoris of Conservatory, feeling the tingle of his body as Maestro Nikei played his *filla* and used his psi to coax torn flesh and muscle to come together again. Nikei insisted on giving Theo precedence during Cantoris hours. It was not customary, but no one objected. Theo chuckled to learn that everyone at Conservatory regarded him as something of a hero, having saved Cantrix Sira from the Bariken murderers. Every day since his return, Theo had submitted to Nikei's ministrations, then stayed to watch as the Cantor treated other, less serious ailments.

He was walking now, carefully, but without too much pain. He joined Cantor Nikei on his way out of the Cantoris. "I have a question," he said.

Nikei nodded. "Of course, Singer."

"Don't you ever use the first mode for healing wounds?"

Nikei frowned a little. "I use the third, to prevent infections. Why would I use the first?"

Theo almost didn't answer, not wanting to offend the Cantor. But he was curious. "I often use it," he said diffidently, "to help the injured person relax. The healing seems to go faster. The fear that comes with a wound slows the mending, don't you think?"

Nikei pulled at his lip, considering. "I did not know itinerants practiced much healing."

Theo laughed, then pressed a hand to his still-sore belly. "We must. Or we lose too many of our customers!"

They strolled into the great room, and Maestro Nikei signaled to a waiting Housewoman for tea. "Perhaps fear is not an issue here at Conservatory," Theo said. "But outside, I have seen travelers so frightened by being hurt that they have to be restrained from doing themselves further injury."

"But what happens to hurt them, outside?"

Theo grinned. "Everything, Maestro Nikei! They fall off *hruss*, they cut themselves with their knives, they dent their heads on the branches of softwood trees, or they get blacktoe."

"Blacktoe?" Nikei frowned again.

If this was the Maestro's usual expression, Theo thought, it must cause some anxiety among his students. "Blacktoe," he told the Cantor. "When the feet get too cold, the ends of the toes turn dark. They must be warmed immediately, and slowly, or the traveler can lose them. The same for fingers. Blacktoe can kill a person if it's not caught early."

Nikei's frown smoothed away. "Ah, yes, I have seen this, but had not heard that name for it. I am very interested in what you say, Singer." Their tea arrived and they sipped at it. "Healing is the most difficult part of the Gift to develop. I had assumed—" He hesitated, and it was obvious to Theo that he chose his next words with delicacy. "I had assumed that those Singers who do not become–that is, who do not come to Conservatory—"

Theo grinned. "Rather the opposite," he said cheerfully. "Some of the best healers are itinerants. We learn it very early, out of need."

Nikei pulled at his lip again. "The first mode. For injuries. It is a new thought."

Theo savored a momentary sense of belonging. As he watched House members bowing deeply to Nikei, however, he was reminded of the great chasm that lay between them. At least Nikei conversed with him. He did not speak to any of the Housemen or women, only nodded acknowledgment to one or two. The Cantor was as aloof with his own House members as if the Glacier itself lay between them.

In a few more days, Theo was moving restlessly about the House and the nursery gardens. Still swathed in bandages under his tunic, he was sore, but his energy had returned in full. He needed something to do. Only after the evening meal, when he sometimes lingered with the students in the great room, telling them stories of outside, did he feel fully occupied.

Those evenings were lovely and long. Theo's position as one of the group that had rescued Sira gave him special privileges, and the students were allowed to stay in the great room an hour past their usual time, just to hear him talk. He told them of the southern Timberlands, and the Houses on the Frozen Sea, where tiny ships like floating *pukuru* dared the ice-clogged waters for fish that tasted fresh as sweet snow.

Once he told them the fable of the Ship, and the little ones listened wide-eyed, not knowing what was truth and what was invention.

"The Spirit of Stars," Theo recited, using the low tone that he knew made his youngest listeners shiver, "sent the Ship, like the greatest *pukuru* you can imagine, drawn by the six strongest and biggest *hruss* It had. Spirit knew the people would need plants and animals that did not grow on the Continent, and so the giant *pukuru* was packed full of fruit seeds and grain seeds and people seeds. When it landed on the Continent, it overturned, and all the seeds spilled out and began to grow. The upside-down *pukuru* became First House, and First Singer warmed it so the seeds could blossom and grow big and strong."

"But, Singer," a little boy asked, "what happened to the six big *hruss*?"

Theo inclined his head. "Do you know, that's a very good question." He pointed to the thick windows of the great room, where the darkness of the long night stretched beyond the glow of the *quiru*. "Have you ever seen the stars?"

The boy nodded. "On my way here, with my father," he said in a sad childish tone. He and his class were not yet adjusted, and Theo saw one of the older students touch the little boy's shoulder, and leave her hand there to support him.

"Did anyone show you the Six Stars?" Theo asked. The boy shook his head. "The Six Stars shine above the eastern horizon when you're outside at night. Those were the *hruss* that drew Spirit's big *pukuru*. When it overturned, to spill the seeds and to become First House, the *hruss* were freed. They raced up into the sky, and they still run there, across the sky each night, trying to get back to the Spirit of Stars."

The Housewomen came to fetch the little ones then, and Theo bid them good night. The older students smiled and nodded to him, several speaking aloud to wish him a good evening. Isbel, who Theo knew was Sira's closest friend, was the last to leave the great room, making sure he had everything he might want before she, too, retired.

The next morning, she teased him. "Tell me another story," she said as they walked from the great room after the morning meal.

He smiled down at her. "Do you want to hear about the Singer from Trevi who had to sleep in the stables because he wouldn't go near the *ubanyor*? Or the girl at Conservatory that Magister Mkel had to shut up in her room because she asked too many questions?"

Isbel giggled, and he smiled to see the dimples twinkle in her cheeks. "I do not ask too many questions! I am a serious student trying to learn more about the Continent!"

"A serious student?" Laughing, he bowed to her. "Then sing for me.

Here I am at Conservatory, and all the music I've heard has been the *quirunha*."

"I will, if you like. Tomorrow. It will cost you a story, though. And now I see Cantor Nikei watching us. He will scold me for keeping you too long."

"Wait a moment, Isbel! I want to ask you about Cantrix Sira. Is she well?"

Isbel's green eyes darkened, and her dimples disappeared. "I do not know, Singer. She has had a bad experience, and she will not open her mind to me."

"She won't?"

Isbel sighed. "She only speaks aloud. With all of us. She is far away from us, somehow, because of what happened to her in Ogre Pass."

Theo scowled. "By the Ship, that was a bad business!"

Isbel tilted her head and regarded him. "I have never heard that expression, Singer."

"No? They say it in the Southern Houses. What do you say when you want to swear?"

Isbel blushed, and smiled again, her mood as changeable as snow clouds over the mountains. "It is hard to swear when you do not speak aloud. But I know 'By the Six Stars,' and—" she lowered her voice—" and *ubanyit*!"

Theo grinned. "Is that your worst? It's a good thing you don't travel with itinerants!"

Isbel blushed again. Maestro Nikei was approaching, and she covered her mouth with her hand, but her eyes still sparkled with laughter as Nikei reached them.

They both bowed to the Cantor. Theo had to follow Nikei for his daily session in the Cantoris, and he left pretty Isbel smiling after him.

Theo met Sira again at last one morning in the nursery gardens. He was strolling among the flats of plants and seedlings that lay cosseted in yellow *quiru* light. He found her alone, bending over a tray of herbs to breathe in their fragrance. She turned with a flash of irritation when she heard him behind her.

She checked her reaction when she recognized him. She bowed slightly. "Hello, Singer. I am glad to see you recovering," she said gravely.

Theo flashed his lopsided grin. "I'm fine, thanks. Enjoying my convalescence." He was not quite as tall as she, but he thought she could not weigh half what he did. "And you, Cantrix Sira?" he asked. "Have you recovered?"

Her answer avoided his real question. "My wounds were not so serious as yours. They are almost healed." Absently, she traced her scarred eyebrow with a long forefinger. Its darkness would be forever marked by a slash of white.

"You know, Cantrix," Theo said in a light tone, "I've been an itinerant for three summers, and I've never had an experience like that one! Even when I accidentally came too close to the Watchers, they didn't try to kill me." He chuckled and shrugged. "Although they did shoot at me. But it takes time to heal . . . in many ways."

Sira turned to him, her back straight and the angles of her face hard. "Singer," she said harshly. "It is over. I do not think of it."

Theo lifted his eyebrows. "Good for you," he said mildly. He hooked a little ironwood bench forward with his foot and settled onto it, adjusting his bandages and resting his shoulders against the back. It occurred to him that perhaps he should leave her be, but an impulse, an intuition, drove him on. "So that means you're ready to go back?"

"No!" Sira said sharply, then stopped, visibly controlling herself.

Theo watched her tense face. "Another Cantoris, then? Probably a good idea. After all, as the saying goes, the *ferrel* builds more than one nest."

"My plans are not yet made, Singer." Sira bowed again, clearly meaning to end their conversation. "I am sorry you were injured helping me, and if I may help you in turn, please ask." She turned away with an air of finality.

"It seems to me, now that I think of it," Theo went on comfortably, as if she had not tried to dismiss him, "that I heard a rumor you refused another Cantoris."

Sira thumped her fist on a nearby table, making the seed flats jump. "I swear, a Singer cannot take a breath but what the whole Continent knows it!" Her flash of anger made the air around her glitter.

"Oh, I think your term is too general," Theo said. "It's just Cantors and Cantrixes whose every breath is of interest to Nevya."

Sira looked at him over her shoulder. "I do not understand."

Theo shook his head. "Sorry, Cantrix. Forget that."

Sira stood still for a moment, gazing out into the humid air of the nursery gardens. Then, as if she had forgotten all about Theo, she strode away, leaving him alone.

Sira was healing, although not in the way Mkel hoped she would. She had spent many hours in the nursery gardens, breathing in the damp earthy air and thinking, while the gardeners watched from a distance. She tried not to notice, but she was aware her story had spread throughout Conservatory. Everywhere she went the House members looked at her with sympathy. She doubted they would be sympathetic if they knew the whole story, the truth.

Stabbing Wil had been bad enough. But in her dreams she felt that flash of psi, over and over, that had destroyed Trude's mind. Often she woke, shaking in the dark, to wish hopelessly that Maestra Lu were there. Sira pondered all that had happened, and her resolve hardened like a pond at the end of summer as it gradually freezes from the top down.

Isbel came to her room one afternoon. *Sira. We should talk.*

Sira shook her head. "There is nothing to talk about."

Open to me, my friend.

"I cannot," Sira said. "I am no longer the person I was when I lived here."

"You are to me," Isbel said stoutly. "I want to help you find yourself again."

"That person is gone," Sira said. "We can never walk back in the same footsteps."

"That sounds like something the Singer Theo would say."

"Theo? Have you been talking to him?" Sira leaned wearily against a wall. "I think I have never met anyone with so much conversation."

"Yes. He is so funny. And he has such blue eyes, like a summer sky. We all like him."

Sira hardly heard her. "Isbel," she asked abruptly, "can you come and bathe?"

"Yes, of course. We can—"

"And do you have a sharp knife in your room?"

Isbel frowned. "I have the knife I use for cutting *filhata* strings. It was sharpened last week in the abattoir. But why?"

"Bring it, please," Sira said.

Isbel obediently went away to her room to fetch the knife, carrying it back carefully wrapped in a bit of leather. She followed Sira to the *ubanyix*. They walked together much as they had when they were students, the pretty plump girl and her tall, solemn friend.

In the *ubanyix*, the girls shed their tunics and trousers and immersed themselves in the warm water. Sira unbound her hair and ducked her head below the surface for a moment. When the thick mass of her hair was soaked, she knelt on the bottom of the tub with her back to Isbel. "Please cut it for me."

Isbel gave a gasp of dismay. "But Sira, why? Why cut your beautiful hair?" She held the knife awkwardly in her hand, as if she wished she had not brought it.

"Where I am going I do not want it," Sira said. She leaned back slightly, so that her hair hung directly in front of Isbel.

"But, Sira . . . Cantrix . . . where are you going?"

"Away. And I am not a Cantrix anymore, Isbel. I am just a Singer."

The odd tableau held for a long moment before Isbel, helpless before the force of Sira's determination, took the heavy wet hair in her hand. She began to cut, tentatively at first, and then, when Sira remonstrated, more strongly. Sira reached over her shoulder to catch the long strands as they fell. When it was finished, Sira put her hand to her head, marveling at the lightness of it. Her fingers slipped easily through her cropped locks, and she felt free.

Theo was almost sorry one morning to realize that there was no longer any pain or stiffness in his wound. He stretched his shoulders and arms, feeling soft and lazy from weeks of easy living. He had enjoyed every day of his recuperation, hearing the *quirunha* daily in the best Cantoris on the Continent, watching the single-minded discipline of the students. The students had come to treat him as one of their own, and he thought he would always look back on this time as one of the best of his life, a shining interval of community with these chosen ones.

He had not seen Sira at the *quirunha*, nor at any other House functions. He assumed she must be having her meals in her room. Since their encounter in the nursery gardens, he had heard nothing of her, so he was startled to find her at his door one morning.

He bowed courteously, trying to hide his surprise at her cropped hair.

"May I speak with you, Singer?" she asked.

"At any time, Cantrix. Could you call me Theo, do you think?"

"Will you call me Sira, then?"

He grinned at her. "Probably not. You're a Cantrix, after all."

"Perhaps I shall go on calling you Singer," Sira said, with a flash from her dark eyes. She stepped past him into his room.

Chuckling, Theo pulled forward the single chair for her to sit on, and seated himself on his cot. He waited for her to speak.

"I have questions for you," she said. Her young face was intent. The short hair, brushed away from her cheekbones, relieved the sharp angles of her face. Theo liked the way it looked.

"I prefer that no one know I have asked these questions," Sira went on.

"Go ahead," Theo answered cheerfully. "I'm as quiet as a *caeru* in a snowstorm."

Unsmiling, Sira said, "I want to know everything about being an itinerant Singer."

Theo found himself without words for once. He searched her face for her meaning, and she looked away, down at her linked hands. "Singer. Theo. You are the only one I can ask."

Theo sighed. "Cantrix Sira. The life of an itinerant is not easy. Constant exposure, loneliness, hard work. I don't want to brag—" he grinned, "—but we're a tough bunch."

"I will not be a Cantrix anymore. I want to choose my own way."

Theo said, "There is nothing I would like better than to give you whatever you need, Cantrix—I mean to say, Sira," he amended. "But I know this business. It would waste your Gift.

"You have something others would give a great deal to have, your Conservatory education. You have a place where you belong, people who care about everything you do."

"People who wish to control everything I do," Sira said bitterly.

"Believe me. You must not throw away these advantages. It would be wrong for me to teach you the itinerant's trade. And if I did, it would require practical lessons, not just talk."

"Take me with you, then, when you leave. I will be your apprentice."

"Sira. You belong here, not out there in the mountains and forests. I can't be the means of taking you away from those who need you. I can't bear that responsibility."

Sira sat still for a moment before she nodded acquiescence. She avoided his eyes as she said, "Thank you just the same." She stood and bowed. "I will consider further. And I appreciate your keeping our discussion private."

Theo stood, too, and moved to the door to open it. "Let me help you in some other way."

She shook her head. "I do not know what that would be, Singer." He held up an admonishing finger, and the ghost of a smile turned up her lips. "Theo."

He bowed. "Sira . . . give yourself time."

She did not answer, but walked away in silence. He watched her narrow back moving down the corridor. Such intensity, he thought. Perhaps that is what my Gift lacks.

*

Sira soon learned it was not easy to prepare all by herself. She had no metal, as Cantors and Cantrixes never had need of it, but she needed to obtain provisions and equipment, which were as essential as information. She had never cooked for herself. She had never saddled *hruss*. But, determined on her course, she visited the kitchens and the stables and the storehouse, begging supplies.

The Housemen and women knew her, of course, and the dramatic tale of her survival in Ogre Pass had spread throughout Conservatory. The people in charge of the things she wanted were inclined to be indulgent with her. They looked curiously at her short hair, but she was a full Cantrix, and they asked no questions. Slowly her small room began to fill with the things she needed–a knife, a cooking pot, a bowl and cup, some grain and dried meat, a small cache of softwood. She started to worry that everything would not fit into a saddlepack.

The problems of *hruss* and saddle plagued her the most. As inexperienced as she was in matters of trade, she knew these were valuable, and that such metal as there was often was spent on them. All she had of great value was her *filhata*, given to her by Conservatory before her first *quirunha*. It had been sent back to her from Bariken, and now she offered it to the man in charge of Conservatory's stables.

Erc was a paternal man. "Cantrix Sira, you don't need to part with your *filhata*. Magister Mkel would be glad to give you *hruss* and tack if you need to ride somewhere."

"No. I cannot ask him. And I do not wish you to ask him, please, Erc. I am not going on Conservatory business."

"What other business does a Cantrix have?"

"I do not think I need to explain," Sira said as sternly as she knew how.

Erc was abashed, and Sira regretted the necessity of being brusque. He said, "Of course, Cantrix. But we can lend you the *hruss* and saddle, and you will return it when you can."

"Thank you, Erc, but no. I much prefer to pay for it."

Erc's genial face creased with worry, but he pressed her no further. Awkwardly, he accepted her *filhata*, encased in its fine wrapping, and after showing her a saddle and saddlepack, took her to the stalls to choose a *hruss*. Sira did her best to look knowledgeable, but the *hruss* all looked the same to her. She accepted the first one Erc recommended, a comparatively small animal with shaggy chin and fetlocks.

"When will you want it ready, Cantrix?" he asked.

When she opened her mouth to answer, Sira realized that this was an important moment, the final step of her going. Her voice trembled ever so slightly. "Tomorrow morning, please."

Erc bowed deeply in acknowledgment. "It will be saddled and fed."

Sira bowed in return and set off for her room, empty saddlepack thrown over her shoulder. I will be ready, too, she told herself. Ready to live my own life.

Chapter Seventeen

Theo approached Magister Mkel at the morning meal. Cathrin was at Mkel's left, overseeing the meal from their table in the center of the great room. Most of the students, teachers, and visitors were present, crowding the room with more than three hundred people. Theo waited as a messenger spoke in a low tone to the Magister, who looked grave.

When the messenger departed, Theo bowed. "Good morning, Cathrin. Magister, I'm afraid I've enjoyed the hospitality of Conservatory long enough."

"Oh, please don't speak of leaving so soon, Singer," said Cathrin warmly. "I've enjoyed your stories so much."

"You're a patient listener," Theo said with a grin. "But I can't work up enough pain in my wound to justify this holiday any longer."

"Are you quite sure, Singer?" asked Mkel. He looked distracted, his eyes straying after the messenger as he wended his way through the tables. Theo followed his gaze, wondering what the news had been.

Cathrin touched her mate's hand. "Mkel. Be sure Nikei agrees the Singer is healed."

Theo turned back to her. "I will miss seeing your face at the center table every day." To Mkel he said, "If you know of a traveling party, Magister, I would be glad of the work."

"You will always be welcome here," Mkel said. "You have our gratitude."

"Thank you," said Theo. "But if I don't get back to work soon, I'll have no new stories for Cathrin when I see her next."

Cathrin laughed. Mkel said, "Just let Maestro Nikei examine your wound, Singer, to set Cathrin's mind at ease. Traveling parties are frequent here, as you have seen. I will recommend you to one."

"Thank you."

"You may wish to know, also," Mkel added, "that the Magistral Committee has ruled on the disposition of those involved in the attack on the Cantrix and the Magister of Bariken." Mkel leaned one elbow on the table as if too weary to sit upright. "Trude and Rhia," he said heavily, "were exposed in Forgotten Pass, a day's ride north of Lamdon. It was done three days ago. It must all be over now."

Theo nodded grim acknowledgment. Life on the Continent required fierce and swift justice. It was a brutal punishment, one that had been used as long as Nevyans could remember. In this case, Theo thought, being left to the elements, deliberately abandoned to the cold, was no less cruel a fate than the one the two women had planned for Sira.

"Has Cantrix Sira been told?" he asked.

"No," Mkel said. "That will be my next task."

There was nothing further to say about it. Theo bowed and left them, and made his way through the long tables to find a seat. He looked around at the now-familiar faces of the House members and wished he didn't have to strike out into the mountains with strangers once again. Isbel caught his eye and waved. He winked at her, enjoying her dimples as she giggled. Her classmates clustered around her, all except Sira. Once again, the young Cantrix was absent.

Theo finished his breakfast of fresh yeast bread and sliced fruit, then hurried to catch up with Isbel as she left the great room. She saw him following, and slowed her pace. Her auburn head just reached his shoulder as they walked on together.

"I hear you will be leaving us," she said, with a pout of regret.

"By the Six Stars, word travels around here as fast as a *caeru* can run!"

Isbel laughed, a merry chime that fell sweetly on the ear. Theo had to resist an urge to stroke her head as if she were a little girl. How he would miss the beautiful voices of these young Singers!

They walked on to where their paths diverged, while Theo wondered how to ask about Sira. At the turning of the hall, Isbel looked up at him. "I do not know where she is," she said, startling Theo. "I was not prying," she added, "but you are sending rather clearly."

Theo shook his head in helpless amusement, wishing he had Isbel's control. Then he wondered if she heard that, too. If she did, she kept it to herself. She put her hand lightly on his arm. "None of us knows where she is," she said. "It is kind of you to be concerned for her."

"Someone must know!" Theo exclaimed.

"Magister Mkel asked me," Isbel said, "and I assume he has asked others. If one of the students knew, we would all know. I fear she has found a way to leave."

"You can't mean . . . leave Conservatory?"

She dropped her hand and sighed. "Yes. And she cut her hair."

"I saw that, but . . . surely she didn't go alone!"

Isbel tilted her head. "Go where?"

The hall cleared of people as they talked, leaving them alone. Theo ran his hand over his own hair, freshly shorn by a Housewoman in the kitchens only the evening before.

"When I get ready to travel, I always cut my hair," he said. "The women itinerants all wear their hair short. Long hair is too hard to care for."

Isbel's eyes widened in alarm. "But would she—could she—do that?"

"Would she? I think so!" He spread his hands. "Could she? I don't know. Unfortunately, there's more to an itinerant's work than singing up *quiru*."

"She said I was not to call her Cantrix." Isbel's eyes filled with ready tears. "She has always been independent. But she is more dear to me than anyone in the world."

"It's my fault," Theo said miserably. "I refused to help her. I thought that would be and end to it." He rubbed his forehead in frustration. "I never thought she would go alone!"

"Singer, we must tell Magister Mkel."

"But what can he do?"

"He can find out who has left the House. I cannot believe she would want to be out in the mountains by herself again."

Back they went to the great room, but they found it empty. Isbel led Theo up to the Magister's apartment, where they were admitted by Cathrin. The Magister looked grave as Theo explained his last conversation with Sira.

Isbel broke in. "We must stop her!"

"I do not know how we can do that," Mkel said. "We cannot force her into a Cantoris."

"But she is in danger!" Isbel's voice rose.

Theo lifted his hand. "Isbel, I'll go after her. I promise."

Isbel fell silent, but her lips trembled, and she put her fingers over them.

"Do you know of anyone who has left in the last day, Magister?" Theo asked. Half of his mind hurried ahead, already dealing with the details of a hasty departure.

"I will ask the stableman," Mkel said. He looked suddenly aged, lines of care etching ever more deeply into his face. Cathrin hovered behind him. "This has been a bad business from beginning to end. I wish I had listened to Lu. She was against Sira's assignment from the first."

Theo stood. "I must take the blame for this." Mkel shook his head, but Theo said, "She asked me to tell her all about an itinerant's work, and I refused. I should have come to you."

"We could only have argued with her. She has a right to her own decisions."

"She's as stubborn as last winter's icicles, that's certain. But I will find her."

Cathrin said, "We must hire the Singer to go after her, Mkel. She can't know what it is she's doing." She gave Theo a pleading look. "At least bring her back so we can talk to her."

"I will try," he said. He hoped Mkel and Isbel would not catch his thought that it was a big Continent on which to find one girl, Gifted or not. His task looked enormous.

It took most of one day to prepare to leave, which Theo estimated put Sira two days ahead of him. Erc, the stableman, had dispatched two *hruss* the previous day, one for Sira, and one for an itinerant without a traveling party, an old Singer named Lorn who had told no one his destination. Theo could only guess at the direction they had taken.

Mkel, Nikei, and Isbel gathered to bid him farewell. It made him smile to see them grouped on the steps, as if he were a Cantor, to receive full ceremonies whenever he made a move. He stopped smiling when he saw the concern on their faces.

"Good luck, Singer," Magister Mkel said. "We thank you."

"Stay well," Maestro Nikei added.

"I hope you can find her," Isbel added.

Theo bowed. "I hope so, too. And you must try not to worry, Isbel. You have your Cantoris to think of."

She inclined her head, and the sun gleamed red on her hair. "So I do," she said. She would be Cantrix at Amric in a few short weeks.

Theo lifted his hand in farewell, and lifted his reins. Isbel watched him with her hands clasped under her chin. He winked at her, and received a small smile in answer. He was disappointed not to see her dimples.

They had decided the place to start would be Lamdon. Itinerants were required to register there. Mkel gave him a written message for Cantrix Sharn, which Theo had carefully stowed in his saddlepack, and which begged Sharn to persuade Sira to return to Conservatory. Theo doubted it would make a difference to Sira. But it would affect his reception at Lamdon.

He rode away from Conservatory alone, into the silence of the snowy mountains. Not much like a Cantor now, he reflected. No Cantor or Cantrix rides alone on the Continent.

He hoped that was true of Sira. Surely she would have this itinerant, whoever he was. Theo wished he could be sure where they had gone.

Lamdon was eight days' ride away. They would be lonely days, cold and worrisome ones. Theo only hoped Sira would not have already gone when he arrived.

He rounded the curve of the courtyard, and the walls of Conservatory disappeared behind the irontrees, leaving only its great roof visible. He looked back once, regretfully. In his head he heard the faint echo of Isbel sending, *Goodbye, Singer*.

Theo shook his head ruefully. He liked Isbel too well to be envious. But I would sing up a thousand *quiru*, he thought, to learn that skill.

Chapter Eighteen

Sira sat cross-legged across the campfire from Lorn, wondering how old he was. He seemed ancient to her, especially to be living the strenuous life of an itinerant. He had insisted on doing the *quiru* himself, and it wavered and faltered distressingly around them and their *hruss*. Last night she had wakened to find it almost dissipated. She had refreshed it with her own *filla* while Lorn slept on, unaware.

There had been no choice of traveling company. Lorn had been the only itinerant she could find who was not consulting with Magister Mkel or the Housekeeper about his departure, and now she understood why. Who would hire such a person?

It would only be a few days' ride to Lamdon, she told herself. There she would declare herself an itinerant, and try to find an apprenticeship with someone else. It should not be hard to avoid Cantrix Sharn, if she came into the House through the stables, and attracted no attention to herself. She had hoped to learn something about the work beyond *quiru* duties, but two days with the old itinerant Singer had made her doubt his ability to teach her anything.

Lorn reached forward with his gnarled hand and stirred up the remnants of the fire. "Not so easy, starting a fire with flint and stone, is it?" he said. Even his voice seemed old and frail. She wondered if he could sing anymore.

"I will try it again tomorrow," she said. "I need to learn."

"You'll get it," he said, and gave a wheezy laugh. "You'll learn to cook, too, or be awfully hungry. Hot food is important in the mountains."

Sira said nothing. Lorn's cooking had not been an inspiration, though she knew he was right about hot meals. Stars winked through the shaky *quiru*, and she decided to get into her bedfurs early, since she would certainly be up redoing the *quiru* before the night had passed. She thought that Cantors must not be the only Gifted ones in short supply, if this man was able to eke out a living as an itinerant Singer.

A long, wailing cry sounded through the hills, making Sira sit bolt upright. Lorn laughed again. "Don't worry. Just a *ferrel* hunting in the dark. The fire keeps them away from us. We'll build it up a little." He dropped some softwood on it, and it blazed higher.

Sira lay back down, but her skin prickled uneasily. The comforts of her room at Conservatory seemed very far off. She tried not to remember Theo's warnings. I am free, she told herself. I choose my own way.

She was glad she had not heard the *ferrel* cry when she had been alone in Ogre Pass.

She did not sleep until long after Lorn was snoring in his bedfurs. She renewed the *quiru* once he was asleep, and felt better seeing it strong above their campsite. The *ferrel* screamed again, making the *hruss* stamp and Sira shiver, but the fire burned steadily. She fell asleep at last under her warm furs, grateful not to be alone, even if Lorn was not an ideal companion.

The next day snow began to fall as the road led higher into the Mariks. Lorn said they would take the upper mountain route, going through Windy Pass to save several days, rather than travel east to the wider and more clement Ogre Pass. The softwood trees thinned out as they climbed, leaving only the huge ironwood trees and their network of thick, shallow suckers crisscrossing the trail. Lorn assured Sira they would be at the top of the pass before dark.

When night fell and the trail they followed had not yet opened into the narrow fissure that was Windy Pass, Sira began to suspect that Lorn had made a mistake. He was silent, and she did not ask, but she felt tension all around her.

She still could not start the fire by herself, try as she might. When it died out a third time, Lorn did it for her once again, but with none of the teasing there of the night before.

The next morning, Sira saddled her *hruss* without help. It groaned as if in pain as she drew up the cinch. Sira loosened it, thinking it must be too tight.

Lorn looked over at her, shaking his head. "You want to tighten that up. Pay no attention to the *hruss*. It thinks it wants the cinch loose, but it won't like that saddle ending up under its belly." He snickered. "And you'll have a faceful of snow!"

Sira turned back to the saddle and saw that now the cinch hung loosely from the beast's rib cage. As soon as she put her hand to it, the *hruss* took a deep breath and swelled out its ribs, tightening the cinch again. Sira laughed, and poked it gently in the belly. When it relaxed, the cinch swung free.

This time Sira pulled it firmly, then waited until the *hruss* had taken several breaths, to make sure the cinch was snug. She patted the animal, and went to get her saddlepack.

She had tried to cook breakfast, too. Her reward had been a bowlful of scorched grain. Lorn took a taste and frowned, eating cold dried meat with his tea instead. Sira, defiantly, ate every bite of her concoction. Now she could feel its weight in her stomach as she pulled herself up into her saddle.

When Lorn led the way out of their campsite, and turned into what seemed to be a road, Sira's sense of direction was offended. It didn't feel right to her, but she had made so many mistakes in their two days together that she hesitated to challenge the old man's choice. They rode for several hours in an increasingly heavy snowfall that obscured the trees and obliterated the outlines of the road.

"Doesn't usually snow so much about now," Lorn muttered, half to himself. "Usually get clear skies when the deep cold is starting."

Sira looked about uneasily. It had not been so many weeks since she had traversed Ogre Pass. These surroundings looked nothing like it. Could one pass be so different from another? The snow fell in curtains about them and the trees loomed close over their heads.

"Singer," she said, as respectfully as she could, "I think perhaps our direction is wrong."

He pulled up his *hruss*. "I don't understand it. We should have been in the Pass by now."

The *hruss's* fetlocks were heavy with unseasonally wet snow, which Sira supposed would freeze unpleasantly when darkness fell. Their path, which looked less and less like a road, had grown steep and treacherously slippery.

"We must go back," she said. "Retrace our steps until we strike familiar ground. We have missed the entrance to the Pass."

Lorn shrugged. "Might as well," he said. "Snow's getting thick."

Sira could not see the downslope to her right through the blinding snow, and it worried her. She had an impression of emptiness, that might mean a cliff or a talus slope, hidden by the storm. "Be careful!" she called over her shoulder to Lorn. She turned her *hruss* with difficulty in the close space between heavy rocks and trees on the uphill side and white blankets of falling snow on the other.

Sira had heard the expression "white weather" many times, but had never experienced it. The reality, she thought, was worse than the description. Sky, ground, rocks, and trees disappeared into pallid curtains of snow. She felt dizzy at the loss of perspective, only barely retaining her sense of up and down by watching her *hruss's* withers. The animal felt its way gingerly down the trail, and Sira felt every bunch and quiver of its muscles in her own legs and arms. A sudden squeal from the other *hruss* chilled her, as if a handful of wet snow had been dropped inside her furs. She heard Lorn make one short sound, a grunt or a curse.

"Lorn? Are you all right?" she called. She pulled up her *hruss* to listen. There was only the hiss of snow and the huffing of her mount. For a moment, panic tugged at her, a familiar feeling of being utterly alone in the wilderness. Then she heard Lorn's voice, shaky but audible.

"Sira, wait!"

She looked back, but could not see him or his *hruss*. Laboriously, she turned her own beast once again, and urged it gently back up the steep path. "Lorn!" she called again. Suddenly the *hruss* stopped, and Sira realized the other animal was down, sprawled in the snow at her own mount's feet.

The enveloping whiteness made it difficult to see anything. Sliding down from her saddle, Sira could just make out Lorn lying beside his fallen *hruss*. Snow trickled under her hood to wet her neck. She kept a hand on her *hruss's* neck to orient herself in the blank whiteness.

"Can you get up?" she asked.

Lorn's figure shifted a little. "It's my leg," he said weakly. "Afraid it's broken."

"And your *hruss*?"

"He severed his hamstring." There was a painful pause. "I cut his throat."

Sira's stomach lurched, but she nodded with respect for Lorn's quick and merciful action. "I will make a *quiru*."

She leaned back against her *hruss*, her mouth dry, her hand clutching at its mane as her boots slid on the icy ground. They would have to stay here until the snow let up enough to see properly. She had no experience with broken bones, and no confidence in her ability to deal with them. And how would they get down from here?

She pulled her *filla* from inside her tunic. Taking some snow into her mouth, she waited for it to melt. She squatted by the dead *hruss's* body across from Lorn. When her mouth was moist enough, she put the *filla* to her lips and played until a strong *quiru* blossomed around them. In its light, and the blessed relief from the white weather effect, she saw Lorn clearly.

His face was gray with pain, though he made no sound. He lay limply against the still-warm body of his *hruss*. Her own *hruss* sniffed at the dead one, shifting its feet nervously as it smelled the blood pooling under the poor beast's head.

Sira untied Lorn's bedfurs from the back of his saddle and spread them with difficulty, working them under him. Snow fell into the slender *quiru*, dampening her face as she tried to work. Everything would be wet with melted snow in an hour. The *quiru* would have to be kept very warm, and Lorn's leg would require whatever help she could muster. She wondered briefly how they could be found, so far from the traveled road, but thrust that worry aside. More immediate matters required all her concentration.

"Lorn, I will try to ease your pain. I do not know if I can do anything about the leg. Lie as still as possible and let your mind be open."

The old Singer nodded, gritting his teeth. Sira's earlier impatience with him dissolved in admiration for the unflinching way he accepted the accident and its consequences.

She began to sing, wordlessly, a simple melody in the first mode. His face smoothed and relaxed almost at once. She took up her *filla* and played in the second mode, with her eyes closed, trying to see the injured leg. Her psi encountered the chaos of broken bone and torn flesh, and collapsed, unable to go farther. She had almost no idea what to do.

The mountain *hruss* were heavy creatures, and it seemed Lorn's had fallen with its full weight on his leg. Sira put her *filla* back inside her tunic, and dug through Lorn's saddlepack until she found a large piece of softwood. She took a deep breath, put her hands on the crushed leg, and straightened it with one swift, strong movement.

Lorn gave a long, deep groan, but did not open his eyes. Sira bound the leg to the piece of wood with strips of leather cut from the injured man's saddle. She felt along it with her hands, hoping it was more or less straight. The bone, she thought, was in bits, one of them breaking through the skin. The pain must be ghastly.

"I am sorry, Singer," she muttered aloud. "All I can think to do is to try to get you down to the traveled road."

She sat back on her heels, wet and exhausted and afraid. Around her *quiru* the whiteness was as blank and forbidding as a solid cliff of ice. Lorn lay quietly against his dead *hruss*, and her own beast nudged at her anxiously. Sira felt as if she had been in this spot forever.

Thirst and hunger finally moved her to action. She worked her way to her saddlepack and untied it, laying it out on her bedfurs. The *hruss* whickered at her, and she patted its big shoulder. "Be easy," she said. "We will not be going anywhere today."

She cleared a spot of wet snow and set out softwood twigs and a little tinder, and began to try again with the flint and stone.

For the first time, she succeeded. She breathed a prayer of thanks as a curl of smoke, no less white than their surroundings, rose into the *quiru*. There was a chuckle from Lorn. "Finally got it?" he said through pale lips.

"Finally," she said. She was inordinately proud of her little fire crackling gently, melting snowflakes as they drifted into it.

"Can't fix my leg, can you, Cantrix?"

Sira looked sharply at the old man. She had told him nothing of her background. "I am just a Singer," she said lamely. "Like you."

Lorn ignored that. His voice was weak as he went on. "Conservatory doesn't teach that, I guess. It's bad, though."

"I am afraid it is bad," Sira answered. "But I am not a good judge. Without a *pukuru*, it will be difficult to carry you back to the main road."

Lorn's eyes fluttered, and Sira hung her head, feeling useless. What would she do now? Food, she decided, was the first thing. Then she would think, long and hard.

As she busied herself with *keftet* in her little cooking pot, Lorn roused again. "You'll have to go back without me."

Sira shook her head. "You could die here alone, and the pain would be terrible."

"I may die in any case."

There was a long silence. Sira made tea, and handed Lorn a cup. She stirred the grain and dried *caeru* meat over the fire, trying not to burn it this time, adding snow when it looked dry. At last she said, "I will make a sled and pull it behind my *hruss*."

Lorn managed another dry chuckle. "You can't even saddle your own *hruss*!"

"I can and I did," Sira reminded him. "When the weather clears, we will go down. Together."

It sounded simple enough, except that Sira had no idea where they were, or if she would recognized the road if she found it. But she could bear no more deaths on her conscience.

Lorn closed his eyes, submitting. He whispered, "Thanks, Cantrix."

"Just Singer," she said, but very quietly.

Chapter Nineteen

Snow continued to fall all night and most of the next day. When it finally began to taper off, it was already too late to make a start. Sira had sung for Lorn several times, when the pain began to rise again, and he accepted her help with gratitude. She cooked for him, too, inexpertly. They ate everything regardless of its quality. Between their two saddlepacks, they estimated they had food for about five days. But it was not food that worried Sira.

She fashioned a makeshift *pukuru* from Lorn's bedfurs, using the cinch, flank strap, and ties from his saddle as harness. She remembered the cushioned, bone-runnered *pukuru* that had carried Theo; hers would not be so comfortable. The deep snow would have to be Lorn's cushion until they found the road. Perhaps there she could find softwood trees to rig as runners.

The second morning in their precarious campsite dawned clear and cold. Now Sira could see the steep, treeless slope falling away to the east, as if they were on some winding mountain trail. It was certainly not one of the roads they had been seeking.

Lorn's face looked as gray as his hair, his eyes sunken and glazed. He barely touched the bowl of *keftet* she gave him.

Sira ate, and fed the *hruss*, then carefully turned it around on the narrow path. She struggled to fasten the clumsy runnerless sled to the back of her saddle. She knew little of knots, and had never tied anything but her hair when it was long. The leather was thick and unwieldy in her fingers, and rigid with cold. She fashioned an awkward sort of tether to attach to the bedfurs, splitting the other end with her knife, and tying the two pieces to either side of her saddle.

Mounting her *hruss*, and urging it into a gentle walk, Sira turned sideways to watch the improvised *pukuru* as it slid over the snow. She was afraid it would slide right under the *hruss's* hooves, or that it might come undone. They left the body of Lorn's *hruss* behind, though Sira contemplated butchering it for the meat. She decided she didn't need anything else to carry. They traveled for what seemed an impossibly long time, with Sira constantly looking backward until her neck and sides ached with twisting.

The path was treacherous, but the fine Conservatory *hruss* was surefooted. More than once Sira patted it gratefully on the withers. Once she had to stop and tighten the cinch, doing her best to make it comfortable for the animal but still safe. Lorn appeared to be asleep, so she mounted again, and they resumed their slow progress down the mountainside.

Softwood trees began to appear again, and the sky brightened. Sira could see why Lorn had thought the trail was a road. It widened and smoothed, little by little.

She wondered how she would ever learn all the roads and trails of the Continent, the way an itinerant must. She couldn't do it alone, that was certain. She would have to apprentice herself to someone. The independence she longed for seemed further away than ever.

At midday, Sira reined in her *hruss*, and got down to check the injured man. Lorn's color was no better, and he didn't rouse when she spoke to him. Rather than do battle with the flint and stone, she ate some cold dried meat and fed the *hruss* with a bit of grain from her hand.

Climbing back into the saddle, she set off again, stopping once in a while to adjust the sled or retie a strap. Through the long day they rode. Sira's back ached from the strain of guarding the *pukuru*. Her legs trembled with fatigue from bracing herself in the saddle.

At last the trail came out into a broad, more level stretch of packed snow that looked as if it might be a road. Sira stopped the *hruss*, shakily dismounting and leaning against the stirrup for a moment to let her muscles recover. She thought Lorn might recognize the road in the morning. Tonight they would camp here, and eat. Tomorrow they could decide their route.

Lorn still slept, even as she untied the sled and smoothed his bedfurs around him. She spoke to him, and touched his shoulder, but he did not respond. She even extended a gentle tendril of psi into his mind, but the waves of his thought were blank and unreadable.

Sira established a strong, warm *quiru* before dark fell. She struggled with the fire, almost giving up until she heard a *ferrel* scream in the distance. Then she tried one more time. The muscles of her wrists wearied of the effort, but she kept at it until a thin line of smoke curled from her little pile of tinder and softwood. She cooked *keftet* again and ate all of it quickly, though it was cold in the middle and burned underneath. The *hruss* nuzzled her shoulder and she realized she had forgotten to feed it.

"Sorry," she murmured, rising to dig grain out of her saddlepack. The *hruss* dipped its muzzle into the grain, and Sira spared a moment to worry about how flat the saddlepack was getting. The softwood was in shortest supply. It had never occurred to her to bring an axe, and she had no idea whether there would be deadfall to burn.

She bent over Lorn, but he lay ominously still and quiet, as he had all day. Sira did not know what else she could do for him. She turned back to the *hruss* and snuggled close to the animal's warmth for a moment. It turned its head to nose her shoulder. "I wish you could talk," she said. The *hruss* blew through its nostrils, and shook its shaggy mane. She laughed a little, weakly, and patted its broad head.

Finally she rolled into her own furs, first checking to see Lorn was well covered, and that the *quiru* would last the night. She slept, but fitfully, with dreams of great roads that led endlessly nowhere.

When the weak light of early morning woke her, a glance told her Lorn was no better. She knelt beside him, noting his poor color and irregular breathing. She knew, as surely as she had ever known anything, that the old Singer would wake no more.

She squatted there a long time, one hand on his shoulder. This was a man who had spent his life as a Singer in these mountains, yet had made a fatal error. She would do better, she swore to herself. Once she had learned this new craft, she would be the best, or not bother.

She could not leave Lorn while he still lived. They had no relationship, but she could not abandon him to die alone. She would do what she could. She tried not to think about what would happen next. Even a man at the point of death was some company. When his spirit left his body, she would be alone in the mountains once again.

In the late afternoon of that day, the old Singer took one last rattling breath, then was still. Sira, watching, knew he was dead. She prayed briefly for his passage beyond the stars. Then, with a pan from her saddlepack, she began to dig into the crusted snow beneath a nearby ironwood tree.

It took some time, and she was wet with perspiration when she had scooped out a hole big enough. She rolled Lorn, wrapped in his furs, into his makeshift grave, and stood looking down at him. It was over for him. Now she had to face her solitude, and decide what to do.

It was growing dark. She would renew her *quiru* for another night in this place. She had tried to judge her location. She could tell the east and west of it, but she had no way of knowing where she was in relation to any House except Conservatory, or even to a main road. Her education had been painstaking and intensive, but it had omitted the geography of the Continent; that was not something a Cantrix needed to know.

She was sure that west was the direction of Conservatory, Magister Mkel, and Isbel. There lay more arguments to persuade her from her decision. At Conservatory, she would have to confront her memories, and that seemed pointless. Nothing could make them go away. She shook her head even as she thought of it.

To the east lay mystery . . . other Houses, certainly Lamdon. Could she find them? There was risk in turning east, but she thought perhaps she could find Ogre Pass.

She reached for her *filla*. She had come this far. Fearful as she might be, she had no wish to turn back. In the morning, she would ride east.

Chapter Twenty

Theo was no stranger to lonely campsites. He always made his *quiru* early, and built a substantial fire for company. On this night, he couldn't help thinking of the warm atmosphere of Conservatory. His first night in the mountains stretched long and empty before him. He tried to pass some time before sleeping by whistling a tune he had heard one of the students play, putting it to his *filla*, thinking up words for it. But when he lay down in his bedfurs under the starred splendor of the mountain night, his solitude seemed more intense than ever. He closed his eyes with deliberation. It was past time he accepted being an outsider.

The season was beginning its shift into the deep cold of the year, when less snow would fall and the bite of the cold would grow sharper and sharper. Theo carried extra furs, purchased from the abattoir at Conservatory with the last bits of metal he owned. He would need more work soon to keep himself supplied. He smiled, remembering one of Isbel's fables, in which metal bits flew from the feet of the Six *Hruss* of the Spirit. Unfortunately, itinerant Singers had to work hard for those bits.

In the morning, he pulled on an extra layer of furs. He made an early start rather than have to renew the *quiru* just before leaving it. He saddled his *hruss*, and set out into the immense quiet of the mountains, his furs pulled close around him.

At midday his progress was interrupted. An inexplicable impulse came over him, urging him to leave the road, to turn up a lightly wooded slope to his left. He stopped the *hruss* and thought for a while, trying without success to identify his feeling. It was no more than a hunch, but at length, telling himself never to ignore the Gift, he reined his *hruss* around to climb the hill.

At the top he found a clear, flat place that had been a campsite fairly recently. There were the snowy ashes of a softwood fire and the rounded depression typically made by bedfurs. There was also an ominously shaped mound under an ironwood tree.

Theo's heart sank as he stared at the mound. Reluctantly, he slid down from his saddle and knelt beside it. The furs and leathers on the body were still visible, despite the evident care that had been taken to bury it under the snow. Bracing himself, Theo brushed away the snow. A hood was tied over the face. He hesitated for a long moment, not sure he wanted to know, knowing he must discover who was buried here. He undid the ties of the hood and pulled it back.

His heart pounded with relief. An elderly man, creased and weathered, with wispy graying hair, had been laid to his final rest here in the snow. It was not a face he recognized. Theo had no wish to disturb the body, but he had to learn as much as possible about anyone who died out here in the mountains.

Gently, he explored the furs and clothing, shaking his head sadly when he discovered a *filla,* still wrapped in soft leather, tucked inside the old man's tunic. He also found that one of the legs was badly broken, and inexpertly splinted. Crouching there, Theo wondered who this old Singer had been, and how he came to this isolated and inadequate grave. Where was the person who had laid him here? If the Singer had a traveler with him, there might well be another body in the vicinity.

Theo scanned the area carefully. Snow had filled in any footprints, but a second body should not be hard to see. He forced himself to search hard for that which he devoutly hoped not to find. At last, having made no more sad discoveries after a reasonable amount of time, Theo mounted and rode away from the campsite, whispering a quick prayer for the dead. He hoped he wouldn't need to say another one soon. He was all but certain this had been Sira's traveling companion. And now she was alone for a second time in the Marik Mountains.

Sira hadn't realized the season was changing until she felt the sting of the deeper cold through her furred gloves. The wet snowfall high in the mountains had confused her. She had ridden alone for one full day, heading due east, dreading the early dark and the long night alone.

The emptiness of the mountains was a tangible presence, every sound magnified, causing a thrill across her nerves. She made her camp at the first sign of dusk, raising a strong yellow *quiru* as the evening light shaded swiftly from violet to purple. Her *filla* sounded small and desolate under the looming peaks.

She struggled with the flint, but could get no spark to leap onto her little pile of softwood. The thought of a fireless campsite and cold food for the days ahead disheartened her, and she slumped onto her bedroll in despair. How have I reached this state once again? she asked herself. Why do I insist on having things exactly my way, and at such cost?

She looked around at her little campsite. Only her *quiru* looked right. She longed for the faint comfort of a cup of hot tea. She decided she was not stacking the softwood properly. Sighing, she took it apart and put it together again, and took out the flint.

Before she struck it, a sound fell upon her sensitive ears. She lifted her head, listening. A chill ran across her scalp as she grew certain that something, or someone, was approaching. It was not yet dark enough for a *tkir* to be hunting, but she wished with all her might she had gotten the fire going. Apprehensive, she stood and faced the direction of the sound.

She could see nothing, but she heard hoofbeats . . . a *hruss's* hoofbeats, softened by the snowpack. She closed her eyes and reached out with her mind, seeking the identity of the approaching rider.

Theo had pushed his *hruss* hard all day, but the canopy of cloudless sky was tinged with violet now, and if he didn't stop soon he would be risking the cold. Alone with his thoughts for many hours, his fears for Sira intensified. How would she know in what direction to travel? he fretted. How would she find the road that led into the Pass? He feared finding her body somewhere along the way, thrown from her *hruss*, injured by some wild animal, any of a hundred things. Even more he feared not finding her. Half-relieved, half-fearful, he pressed on.

The glow of a *quiru* up ahead, a slender finger of light shining like a beacon about a half hour's ride away, came as a surprise in the empty landscape. Theo hurried his *hruss* even faster, hope making his heart speed under his thick furs. The beast obediently stretched its long stride, its wide hooves making soft thuds on the snowpack. Theo patted its rough coat in appreciation.

Her campsite was tucked between two shallow folds of snowy ground. Theo saw her outlined in the light of the *quiru* as he approached, and he grinned broadly, celebrating his good fortune. He rode into her camp beaming, and was surprised and alarmed to see Sira, always so self-possessed, standing in a fireless *quiru* with tears running down her face, looking out into the dark. Waiting for him.

"Cantrix Sira!" he exclaimed. He swung one leg over the horn of his saddle and jumped down. "It's me. It's Theo!"

"I know," she said. She began to sob aloud, her face crumpling like a child's. "I could hear you." She meant, of course, his mind. He strode forward, and stood inches away from her. Every instinct told him to hold out his arms, comfort her, but this was a full Cantrix. Weeping.

"What is it?" he asked helplessly.

She shook her head, unable to speak. All at once he understood, with a flash of intuition almost as clear in his mind as her call for help many weeks before. She had rebelled against everything she knew to set out on this journey. She had watched a man die and she had buried him. She was alone in the dark for the second time in her short life. His arrival, at her lowest point, cut through her icy control. The long weeks of struggle demanded their price, and she had broken down completely.

He looked at the sobbing girl, so young to have seen so much, now lost and alone. With a wordless exclamation he offered to bridge the distance between them. He held out his arms.

Sira took the one step that was needed, moving into his embrace to weep against his shoulder for a very long time.

When she had finally cried herself out, all her fear and loneliness and disillusionment streaming out in waves, Sira was embarrassed at having displayed her feelings in such a way. But Theo, drying her face, settling her on her bedfurs, beginning preparations for a meal with pragmatic efficiency, commenced his usual flow of talk as if comforting crying girls was an everyday occurrence with him. Indeed, she thought, perhaps it was. She watched him start her fire with an easy flick of his wrist over the flint, and scoop snow into the pot for tea.

"I'm glad to have company out here," he said. "Two days alone is enough to think all your thoughts and be ready to talk about them. Now, some conversation, some *keftet*, some tea—that's the civilized way to spend an evening."

He looked up at her swollen eyes, the scarred eyebrow, and her tear-marked cheeks. "You're a wonderful sight for a lonely traveler," he said without irony.

Sira watched him where he squatted easily by the fire, slicing *caeru* strips into a second pot. Despite his size, he was light and quick in the cramped space of the campsite. She was afraid to try to speak with lips that felt puffy and shaky, so she sent to him, *Theo, I am glad to see you, too.*

His head snapped up. "I heard that!" He paused for a moment, then said, "Can you teach me to do it?"

"Perhaps," she said aloud, her voice still thick with tears. "If you receive easily" —she had to clear her throat before continuing— "you can probably send as well." She took the cup of tea he passed her, cupping her palms around its warmth. She shuddered with the last spasm of her bout of weeping, then sat quietly, waiting for her composure to return.

"You know, Theo," she told him. "We all heard minds spontaneously as children. I will try to think how to teach you."

Theo stirred the *keftet*, looking into the pot. She could see he was concentrating. His forehead gathered in deep lines.

"Do not force it," Sira said. "It simply feels like sending your thought away from you."

Theo tried again, though his eyes still narrowed with effort.

"Ready? I heard 'ready.'"

His lopsided grin was rueful. "It's a beginning, I guess. I was trying to tell you our meal is ready."

Good, she sent. *I am hungry.*

He winked at her, and his eyes were bright in the firelight. "Me, too," he said.

Chapter Twenty-one

Sira and Theo rode together down into Ogre Pass under a clearing sky, and made their next camp on the broad floor of the Pass between steep slopes. They faced northeast, toward where Lamdon lay, now at a distance of five days' ride. During the day they had experimented, with Theo sending to Sira, and she listening and reporting to him what she heard. Frequently, Theo laughed aloud at the result, Sira smiling in return. The *hruss's* long ears flicked back and forth between them, listening to their voices.

Sitting by the fire in the evening, Theo asked Sira to bring out her food supplies so they could measure what they had together. "It looks a meager pile," Sira said doubtfully.

There were two little cloth sacks of grain, and just a few packets of dried meat. "It's enough," Theo said. "If we don't take side trips, we should be able to eat three times a day until Lamdon." He kept the softwood, and stowed all the food supplies in Sira's saddlepack. "Take care of that," he admonished, grinning. "Empty bellies make cold company."

He did not try to persuade her to go back to Conservatory. He told her of Magister Mkel's concern and Isbel's fears. She nodded acknowledgment, but did not answer, and he let the matter rest. He had been hired to find her, not force her to return. If Magister Mkel felt otherwise, he would return the bits of metal Conservatory had paid him.

They went to sleep early, snug in their bedfurs. Theo watched Sira peacefully close her eyes, though she had told him how uneasy the sounds of the wilderness made her when she was alone. The night was windless and clear, and the smoke from the embers of their fire drifted in a narrow spiral high into the empty purple sky above the Pass. Theo had to admit that he, too, felt peaceful. It was nice to have company. Especially this company.

Theo woke with the sun bright in his eyes. The morning was quiet, but the *hruss* held their heads high, ears turned forward, staring at something beyond the sun-faded *quiru*.

Theo rolled over, and sat up. Squinting up into the light, he found a semicircle of men, conspicuously armed with bows and knives. They sat their *hruss* around the campsite, luminous ghosts in the glitter of sun on snow. His belly clenched in the sure recognition of trouble.

Sira lay in her bedroll, her face turned toward him, her eyes closed. Without stopping to think, he sent to her. *Wake up now, but move very slowly. Sira! Wake up now. Slowly.*

Sira opened her eyes at once and looked directly at him. She said nothing, and no reaction showed on her face. Deliberately, with no sudden movements, she pushed back her furs and sat up to face the riders ranged around their camp.

The scene held a moment in complete silence, until a *hruss* outside the *quiru* stamped impatiently, and one of those inside the envelope of light whickered.

"Sorry to disturb you, Singer," came a raspy voice. His accent was thick and guttural. "You will break camp now. One of us will give you a hand."

Theo slid barefoot out of his bedfurs and reached for his boots while Sira watched in a tense silence. He felt for his long knife where he had left it in one boot. He and Sira were only two against six, but he put his hand on the knife just the same, and measured the distance between himself and the leader.

"Chad will take the knife," the man rasped, pointing to one of the riders.

Theo straightened with the knife in his hand. The man closest to Sira drew his own knife and pointed it, almost casually, at her throat.

Theo sighed. He reversed the knife and held it out to the man called Chad, hilt first. Chad tucked it inside his own boot. Sira's knife, Theo remembered with regret, was in her saddlepack with the cooking things. Her *filla*, though, like his own, was safe inside her tunic.

She sent to Theo, *Who are they?*

He responded, *Watchers*. Even in the stress of the moment, he took pleasure in his growing ability to hear and send. He pulled his boots on one by one.

What next?

Careful, he sent back. He couldn't tell if she understood him, but surely she could guess. He was standing now, fully dressed and grim-faced.

"What do you want with us?" he asked the newcomers.

The raspy-voiced one nodded at Chad. "Saddle the *hruss*," he said, then to Theo, "We need you at Observatory, Singer. Your traveler can stay or come, as she wishes."

Chad dismounted and busied himself with *hruss* and tack. Sira set about dressing herself to ride, looking to Theo for guidance. He nodded to her, then turned back to the leader. Through a tight jaw, he said, "By what right do you abduct us?"

The Watcher was unmoved by Theo's ire. "By right of need," he said. He barked instructions to some of the others.

"We don't enjoy this, Singer. We have no choice." This was Chad, who was handing the reins to one of his own group, and rolling up Sira's and Theo's bedfurs to tie onto their *hruss*.

"You would leave me alone here, without *hruss*?" called Sira to the leader. Her deep voice rang across the campsite. Theo caught his breath. The Watchers had no idea what they had found. They assumed he was the Singer and Sira the traveler. He hoped Sira understood.

The leader took a closer look at her. He was short and squat of build, with hard, intelligent eyes. "We need *hruss* almost as much as we need Singers," he said. "But we need people at Observatory, too. Come with us. You would likely die out here in any case."

"Mount up, traveler," said Chad. "You too, Singer. We don't waste sunlight."

Theo moved toward his *hruss*. He caught Sira's eye and tried to send to her, *Do not*. She raised her scarred eyebrow in question, but kept silent as she walked to her own beast. They mounted, and settled into their saddles, but two of the strangers kept their reins. Chad picked up all the remaining equipment from the campsite, cooking pots, a packet of dried meat, a sack of grain, and stowed all of it on his own saddle.

Once again Theo tried, *Cantrix. Not tell.*

Sira's face was a frozen mask. *Do not tell them I am a Cantrix?*

Yes. Yes! he responded. A nod from her told him she had received the message.

I will not. She leaned back on the cantle of her saddle and folded her arms across her chest. She looked more angry than afraid. "I can guide my own *hruss*," she snapped at the man holding her reins.

"Soon enough," said the raspy-voiced one. "When we are out of the Pass." He clucked to his own animal, and led the party away from the campsite.

What will they do with us? Sira sent.

He did his best to answer. *They want me to work. To sing,* but he was fairly certain she could not get much of that. The group around them rode in heavy silence. As they rode south through the Pass, away from Lamdon, Theo inspected them as closely as he dared. Their furs were bulky and well-worn. Their *hruss* looked underfed. That they were a determined, even a desperate, group was clear. Theo held little hope for an escape.

The group traveled southeast across the Pass. Ahead, it seemed their direction would lead them straight into a mountainside. After two hours of riding, with Watchers still keeping Sira's and Theo's reins, they left the Pass through a litter of snow-capped boulders, climbing into a narrow snowy canyon. Their path had been invisible from the Pass itself. For another hour they traversed twisting, treacherous slopes where the firn, growing deeper every day, seemed almost to hang above their heads. The way was so steep that Sira had to hold on to her saddle horn at times to keep from sliding off. Theo watched their route, but could not see how he would ever remember it. It was nearly featureless, an unmarked way through a tangled landscape.

"Now you can have your reins," said the leader, whose name they had learned was Pol. "You could never find your way back alone from here." He fixed Theo with a stony stare. "Believe me, Singer. Too many men have died trying."

Theo mustered a cheerful grin. "Must be some House if men die trying to get away."

Unexpectedly, Pol gave a short bark of laughter. Sira glanced at him, then away.

When the party rode out onto a cramped, terrifying path that circled an immense cliff, Theo looked back over his shoulder to gaze in wonder at the vista below. The broad reaches of the Pass they had left hours before swept from the southwest to the northeast, seemingly almost beneath the *hruss's* feet. Beyond the Pass the Mariks rose in majestic, forbidding splendor. He understood how their abductors had found them. The smoke from their fire and the light of the *quiru* must have been beacons of invitation.

But hard as Theo tried, he was unable even now to trace how they had climbed to this spot. Their route was lost in a jumble of rocky cliffs and canyons.

He took the reins that Chad handed back to him and glanced ahead, where the *hruss* were strung out along the cliff path. He would have sworn the path ended in a cul-de-sac, but even as he watched, the lead rider turned right, as if straight into the bare rock of the cliff, and disappeared. Theo's heart sank. Pol, it seemed, was right.

When he arrived at the turning, he and his *hruss* had to squeeze through a narrow opening. The rock walls scraped his legs as he passed. Ahead was another steep path, winding further and further into a wilderness of rock and snow. They rode on for some time before the leader turned downhill into a broader and easier road across a mountain valley.

Theo found his shoulders tingling from the tension of the climb. He rubbed them to restore circulation as his *hruss* found easy footing on the descent.

It was almost dark when they approached the House. Pol raised one thick arm and pointed. "Observatory. Home."

Theo was astonished. The Watchers had made the trip out and back in one day. They had to have started very early, risking the pre-dawn darkness, riding without a Singer. Had anything gone wrong, their whole party would have been lost to the cold.

The House clung stubbornly to the southeastern slope of a narrow peak that towered over those around it. Observatory looked smaller than most of the Houses Theo knew, with an odd, circular addition high on its roof, like a knob or a bowl dropped upside down. Its *quiru* was pale around it, touching its roof and walls with faint illumination.

We will not sing, Sira sent to Theo. He heard her quite clearly. His only response was a shrug. These men had shown their willingness to let them both die.

I will not, in any case, she sent further. *They cannot force me*. He looked at her face, its narrow mouth set firm, and he hid a smile. She would not be an easy one to subdue, he thought with rueful pride. Cantrix Sira would surprise these Watchers.

They rode up to the House in purple twilight. No welcoming party greeted them. Sira looked down at the rough, slanting steps leading to the door, realizing they had once been straight, but had shifted and broken as the ground moved below them, and had not been repaired.

The House was cold, with dank, moldy corners and icy floors. Without ceremony, Sira and Theo were led to narrow, dark rooms furnished with only the simplest of cots and chairs. They were not treated roughly, but matter-of-factly, saddlepacks and bedfurs dropped on the floor, empty of all valuables. Sira's knife was gone, and all their food. Fortunately, no one had offered to search her. They could not suspect, she supposed, what she carried inside her tunic.

In Nevyan fashion, they were taken to bathe next, as if they were guests. Sira found the water in the *ubanyix* dark and tepid. Three other women were bathing. They looked at her in silent curiosity, and she turned her face away. She hid her *filla* in a fold of her tunic when she undressed, and endured a cold and unpleasant bath rather than reveal herself by warming it. She wondered how long it had been since the water had been changed. She took a perverse satisfaction in knowing that the other women must also be cold, but she shivered in angry misery as she dressed again in the same clothes she had been wearing.

Her dismal cubicle was at the end of a dark corridor, with empty rooms around it. She was grateful for that. In her own room, at least, she thought, she would have light and warmth. She brought out her *filla* and used it, softly, to brighten the air around her. The room grew warmer, but hardly more cheerful, as the increased light revealed creeping fungus in the corners of the ceiling, and beads of condensing moisture here and there on the walls. Sira sighed as she tucked her *filla* away.

They had apparently missed the evening meal, and no one offered them food or tea. There was nothing to do but go to bed. Sira piled her bedfurs over the ragged blanket on her cot and slid under the mound. The chill from the wall made the cot frigid, and she could not sleep until her body's warmth had heated it. She curled herself against the cold, waiting for warmth.

What this House needed, of course, was a strong, healthy *quiru*. A warm House *quiru*, established by a full Cantor or Cantrix, and maintained for some weeks with a daily *quirunha*. That would put an end to the molds and fungus and damp.

But I will not do it, Sira insisted into the darkness. Not for them.

Sira found her own way to the great room the next morning. She and Theo sat in silence with the rest of the community of Observatory, who were almost as silent as they were. The indifferent food, consisting almost entirely of meat, was eaten quickly and without ceremony.

They look ill, Sira sent to Theo.

His answer was jumbled, but she understood *Cold. Damp.*

She nodded, then caught Pol's eyes on her. *Careful. Pol watches us.*

He is not stupid, Theo responded, with surprising clarity.

Sira admired the quickness with which Theo's listening and sending were improving. What a talent, she thought, to have been wasted by not properly training it. She remembered young Zakri sending a ball spinning away from him, and she felt a sharp pang of sympathy. She looked around the gloomy room, seeing the reddened cheeks and noses of the House members here, and she grew angry again.

I would like to teach you more, she sent to Theo. *But they will find me out. And we must not sing for them or we will never get away.*

A hard cough from a child at one of the tables distracted her. She turned toward it, and found Pol's short, powerful figure in her line of vision as he came toward them. "If you have finished your meal, Singer," he said, standing before Theo with his arms folded.

Sira rose with Theo. Curious eyes followed them as they left the great room to follow Pol down a corridor, where he opened a heavy door.

"Our Cantoris," he said in his grating voice. He waved a hand into its shadows. Sira could just make out the dais in its center. "Here you will sing."

Theo put his head to one side and gazed down at Pol, an amused smile on his lips. "You must think you've captured a *ferrel*, Pol, when all you've got is a poor little *wezel* in your trap."

Pol's eyes narrowed in his heavy face as he looked up at his two captives. "I'm not so sure about that."

"I'm just an old mountain Singer," Theo went on in a bland tone. "I can't warm a whole House. You need to send to Conservatory for a real Cantor."

"I think perhaps Conservatory has sent us one," Pol rasped. He fixed his gaze on Sira.

Her neck prickled, and she felt her face warm. There was a long moment of tension, and Pol began to smile. She wondered how he had guessed. Perhaps he had understood that she and Theo were communicating without words. Or perhaps her voice had given her away. Indeed, thought Sira, he is not stupid. Only cruel.

She lifted her chin and looked down at him. "You will have nothing from me."

"Oh, I think we will," Pol said with offhand triumph. "By the Ship, I think we will! We'll have it sooner, or we'll have it later. But we'll have it." He closed the door of the Cantoris with a solid thud.

In the great room the next morning, Sira and Theo met Jon v'Arren, an itinerant Singer who had been struggling to keep Observatory warm by himself, with only his *filla* and his small travelers' *quiru*. Even indoors he was muffled in furs, a middle-aged, exhausted-looking man.

"Will you not try to help?" he asked Theo. "I've been here two weeks, and I can't get the place warm. I'm no Cantor, unfortunately."

"I'll try," said Theo, ignoring the look Sira gave him. "But where is their Cantor?"

"Their last one died. He had no Gifted one to train, apparently, so they got me."

"How did they find you?" Sira asked.

"I was with a party in Ogre Pass, and they attacked us. They may have killed someone. The man who hired me was a hunter, looking for *tkir*. He shot at them, and they shot back."

Sira saw Pol in a corner of the great room, and no one else close enough to overhear their conversation. "What about your travelers? Did they just leave them to die?"

"We were only three hours out from Bariken," Jon said. "They should have made it back. I hope." He shook his head. "These people are crazy. Do you know what they do here?"

Theo and Sira shook their heads.

"They watch the sky," Jon said.

"They truly do that? Still?" Theo asked.

"Every night. Two of them go to the top of the House and look though a limeglass roof."

"A pair," Sira said. "Like Cantors."

"Well, maybe. And even if I were able to establish a real House *quiru*, it would have to fade enough by dark so they could see the stars."

Sira, like all Nevyans, had heard the old fables of Observatory and the apocryphal stories of the Ship. They were children's tales. It was preposterous to think these people really waited here to be saved. "This is not sane," she murmured.

Jon gestured carelessly around the room. "I don't understand any of them. They don't even complain about the cold. Half of them are sick, and their babies die."

"Is there even a *filhata* in the House?" Sira asked. "A House *quiru* takes more than a *filla* to establish."

Jon looked at her with dawning hope. "Can you play a *filhata*? I've never even had one in my hands." He turned to Theo. "You? Are you a Cantor?"

Theo gave his lopsided grin. "I'm only an itinerant like yourself, my friend. I wouldn't know which end of a *filhata* to blow into."

Sira smiled, but Jon gazed at her intently. "You, then? Are you a Cantrix?"

Sira grew somber. "I was once," she admitted. "No more."

"Can you stop being a Cantrix once you have become one?"

"I did. And I will not sing."

"But you'll never get away, you know. You're stuck here, as I am. We may as well be comfortable, don't you think?"

"I am sorry," Sira said firmly. "I will not sing for them. And I will not stay. Pol has guessed what I am, but it makes no difference."

Jon heaved a gloomy sigh. "We're going to be cold, then. And you can't get away. They'll never let us go."

Sira was silent. I will not be used again, she thought. They cannot control me. There is no reason for me to sing here.

At midday, swallowing *keftet* that was short on grain, Sira looked around the great room for Jon.

"He's in the Cantoris," Theo murmured.

She nodded.

"He sings several times each day," Theo added. "And he's nearly worn out."

Are you going to sing?

Yes. Theo's eyes met hers. *They are cold.*

Sira did not object, nor did he try to persuade her to sing. Each of us has to deal with these Watchers in our own way, she thought.

She felt someone's eyes on her and glanced up to see Pol, at the center table, regarding her. The child with the cough hacked and hacked from one side of the room. Sira closed her mind to the sound, looking steadily back at Pol until at last he turned his eyes away. It was a small and bitter victory. Sira finished her tea and rose from her seat.

She heard the faint sound of Jon's and Theo's *filla* from the Cantoris. The House was slightly warmer and brighter as she walked back to her room. She was surprised, when she reached it, to find a carefully wrapped object, an unmistakable shape, lying on her cot. She folded back the stiff and moldy wrapping to disclose an old *filhata,* cracked and discolored.

It must belong to the House, she thought, and now there is no one left to play it. Its carvings were scratched and dented, and what remained of its strings hung untuned and out of condition from the pegs. She took it up. The instrument felt tragic, abandoned, as if it had a life of its own she could sense through her fingers. She wondered about those who had played it in times past, and whether anyone would ever play it again. At least, she thought, she could polish the body and restring it, without giving in to Pol. She could hardly resist it. Its cracked wood called to her. Its silent voice was more persuasive than any human's.

Theo found her tracing the carvings on the old *filhata* over and over again with her long fingers. When she saw him, she held it out.

"Someone left this on my cot."

He took it from her. "It's in terrible shape."

"I can repair it, if you will find some cloth and oil for polishing, and *caeru* gut for new stirngs." She paused. *But they will know I am working on it.*

He nodded.

Do you understand why I will not sing?

Theo smiled gently. *I do.* He added something else that she didn't catch. She looked at him, waiting, until he tried again. *Your own decision,* he finally managed. "They are ill, though," he added aloud. I have to do what I can."

Sira took the old *filhata* back into her lap. "That is their choice," she said. "They could rejoin the rest of the Houses, and have Cantors and Cantrixes. They could be healthy. I will not sing for fanatics."

Theo's crooked grin reassured her. "I'm not trying to persuade you, Cantrix."

"You must not call me that." She indicated the battered *filhata* on her knees. "But I could teach you on this," she offered.

Theo reached out to touch the instrument. "This was a long way to travel to find a teacher," he said, "but you have a willing student! I'll try to dig up what you need."

He left Sira's room and she sat on, holding the ancient *filhata*. She searched for its past with her fingers, like trying to recall a forgotten tune. How sad a place this was, this lonely and isolated House, cut off from the whole of its people by some wild and hopeless idea. The greatest tragedy of all was that the traditions of its Singers should have been allowed to die out.

She remembered the child coughing and coughing in the great room, but she hardened her resolve. If they wanted to be well, there were things they could do. They had no right to disrupt other people's lives, to imprison and use them. If she sang for them, she would only be supporting their delusion. She would not do it.

Never, she promised herself. I will never sing for these foolish people.

Chapter Twenty-two

Theo had some trouble getting what Sira needed to restring the *filhata*. Observatory apparently had no Housekeeper, and its various functions were only loosely organized. He found his way alone to the abattoir, a cold place at the back of the House, so dark he could hardly see inside. Three House-men labored there, doing their best to supply the House with meat and to cure the hides of the *caeru* brought to them by the hunters. They were using an odd smoky lamp, a device Theo had never seen in his life, to try to dispel the gloom. It reeked of rancid *caeru* fat, and its shaky flame guttered around a wick of rag.

Theo stepped just inside the door. "Hello. Want some help?"

They looked up in surprise. The oldest, a wrinkled skinny man of about eight summers, left his work and came forward. "You're the Singer, aren't you?" he asked.

"So I am." Theo entered the room, shivering at the chilly damp. In all Houses, the abattoir was the least pleasant of places, close to the outside for convenience, often littered with blood and refuse, but this was the worst Theo had seen. He doubted these men could see enough in the dim light to clean it properly. "Would you like the place a bit warmer, Houseman?"

The man squinted at him in bewilderment. A younger man came up behind him. "This place is never warm," he said.

"Colder than a *wezel's* nose in here," Theo agreed. He withdrew his *filla* from his tunic and showed it to them. They stepped back respectfully, and one of them pulled a stool forward for him. Theo sat on it, hoping it wasn't sticky with gore. It was too dark to tell.

The abattoir was an oppressive place to raise a *quiru*. The very air seemed greasy, and its dankness was heavy, resistant to Theo's psi. He felt as if he were pushing against it, like trying to force his way out of a snowbank. Finally he closed his eyes and pictured himself in the mountains. He imagined a campsite among the irontrees with the pale violet of twilight falling around it. He played a lively *Iridu* tune, and the heavy air began to lighten around him. Abruptly, and rather unmusically, he switched to *Aiodu*, the second mode, which he sometimes used when he wanted his *quiru* to last a long time. When he was finished, he opened his eyes, and saw the abattoir clearly for the first time.

It was small, but otherwise much like those of other Houses. Skinned *caeru* carcasses hung against one wall, and a pile of hides lay on a workbench. Others were pegged to dry, and the Housemen had been scraping these, their efforts considerably hindered by the cold. There was only one soaking vat, surrounded by piles of the ironwood bark used for tanning. Now the light of Theo's camp-style *quiru*, and the warmth that made the Housemen smile, revealed the work needing to be done.

"That's a nice bit of work, Singer," said the older man.

Theo stood. He felt something sticky catch at his trousers, but he disciplined himself not to look just now. He made an ironic bow. "Thanks."

The younger man was shedding his filthy tunic, reveling in the warmth. "You should do that in every room of Observatory."

Theo shook his head. "That would not be possible," he replied. "This one will diminish by evening, you know. I, or any other Singer, could spend every waking moment calling up *quiru*, and still not be able to warm the House. Probably collapse in the end, besides."

"You're welcome to play here any time," the older one said. "What can we do to bring you back?"

"Well, Theo said with a wink," there might be something." He went to the workbench, where coiled, split *caeru* gut was ranged in tidy rows. "I could certainly use some of this."

The Houseman followed him, and lifted the largest coil from the bench. "It's yours, Singer." He took a wood-handled *tkir* tooth from a peg on the wall, cut a long length of the gut cord with its sharp serrated edge, and handed it to Theo.

Theo took it and bowed again, though very little bowing seemed to be done here. He was on his way out of the abbatoir, now a considerably less dismal place than it had been, when the younger man called to him. "Singer?" Theo turned back at the door. "Could you warm my family's apartment, just once? My mate's never well, can't seem to get warm, ever."

Theo hesitated. "I'm sorry, Houseman," he said at last. "I wish I could. It would be unfair to warm one apartment and no others. I promise you, though, that I'm doing all I can."

The man's shoulders slumped in resignation, and Theo went out slowly, his own shoulders drooping under the weight of the need of these people. It was too much to hope that he could really make any difference in this House. He simply didn't know how.

The kitchens were neither so dark nor so cold as the abattoir had been. Theo found several Housemen and women working there, cutting chunks of *caeru* meat and dicing a tiny harvest of vegetables to fill a pot of *keftet*. Neither fruit nor nuts were in evidence, and the wooden tubs of grain were half empty. Even here, with softwood burning hot in the ovens, mold crept down the walls from the high ceiling.

Theo bowed to the woman who appeared to be in charge. "Housewoman," he said, "can you spare some clean rags and oil?"

She looked at him, her hands on her hips. Her gray hair was tied back neatly, though the tunic she wore looked as if her best efforts could never get it clean. She eyed Theo as if he were a small boy begging sweets.

"What are they for, Singer?" she asked crisply. "We have little to spare."

Theo tried to smile, but her stern expression daunted his effort. "Someone left me an old *filhata*," he said. "I thought I'd try to repair it."

"Can you play a *filhata*?" she asked. A glimmer of hope brightened her face. When he shook his head, she sighed deeply. "Than what point is there, Singer?"

There was a moment of silence, until Theo ventured another grin. "Now what would have happened, Housewoman, if the people had said that to First Singer? First Singer had to start somewhere, didn't he?"

The Housewoman looked suspicious, folding her arms tightly across her bosom.

"Don't you know that story?"

"What story?"

"Well," Theo began. He looked around him for someplace to sit. The other Housemen and women came closer, curious. Theo, despairing of a chair, leaned his hip against a table. "Well," he repeated. "You know that when the Spirit sent the great *pukuru* to the Continent—"

"You mean the Ship," put in the Housewoman firmly. "Spirit of Stars sent the Ship, with all the people and plant seeds."

Theo's grin widened. "The Ship, then. When Spirit sent the Ship, and it overturned and made First House, it started to get cold right away."

There were nods around him. They apparently knew this story, but they were clearly happy to suspend their work and listen to it again, told in a new voice.

"It started to get cold, and the people began to shiver. What were they going to do? They looked around them, outside the—the Ship, and they saw only irontrees. They got colder and colder, and First House got very dark when First Night came.

"It was during First Night that the wonder happened. First Singer began to sing to a little baby who was crying from the cold. First Singer hated to hear children cry, and he tried to make his lullaby a warm, sweet one to comfort this child.

"Now, if the mother of that child had told First Singer to be quiet, not to disturb her child, what might have happened? First Singer might never have seen that first glow that came from his warm lullaby. The people might have perished during First Night.

"But the mother didn't tell First Singer to leave them alone, and First Singer sang the warmest lullaby he could think of. First House grew warm and light, and the people survived."

The Housewoman gave an exasperated click of her tongue. "Singer, do you think you're going to work a wonder?"

Theo's smile faded, and he straightened. "I do not know," he said, sounding like Sira for a moment. "But if something great does not happen here, this House is going to perish."

The other workers moved uneasily, the mood broken. A young Housewoman sniffled and turned away. The Housewoman in charge, with a measuring glance at the others, moved to a drawer and took out a handful of cloths. "We're not going to perish," she said firmly. "But you might as well try to fix that old *filhata*. Mrie, fetch a bit of cooking oil for the Singer."

As the girl went to do as she was told, the Housewoman turned back to Theo. "No need to frighten the young ones," she said. "But it was a good story. You're no First Singer, I'm afraid. Still, we could do with a wonder."

"So we could." Theo took the oil and the cloths, and bowed to the Housewoman. She surprised him with a stiff bow of her own, something at which she obviously had little practice.

"Good luck," she said.

"Thank you." She turned back to her work. Theo was thoughtful as he carried the things back to Sira's room. Learning to play the *filhata*, he thought, would be wonder enough.

Sira and Theo worked on the *filhata* for three days before it was ready to play. Theo sharpened his own well-kept knife for Sira to use, and she cut the strings carefully from the *caeru* gut, saving the leftovers in a scrap of oiled cloth. She stretched the strings delicately from the body of the *filhata* to the pegs, then removed them to cut and cut again until they were just the right thickness. While she was cutting strings, Theo polished the marred surface of the *filhata* with oil, and tried to converse with Sira silently.

These cracks . . . carvings, he sent. Then something else that was a blur.

She looked over at his work. *The body is intact?* He nodded. *Good.*

It is hard to send without— His sending blurred again, and Sira shook her head, smiling a little. Theo sighed. Aloud he said, "It's like digging through a snowdrift. Why is my best sending only when I'm in trouble?"

Sira chuckled aloud, but she answered silently. *Emotion provides energy. The first sendings are always spontaneous. Receivings, too.*

"Doesn't frustration count as an emotion?" Theo asked aloud. He slapped his knee. "I have plenty of that!"

Send me a description of the filhata *now. Show me how it looks, what you are doing.*

Theo ran his fingers over the whorls and ridges of the carving. *The cracks are in the carved sections,* he sent. *The wood has dried and split. But the body is whole, and should resonate all right.*

Sira nodded with satisfaction, and took the instrument back into her own lap. She strung the strings more tightly now, twisting the pegs till the gut drew taut. She began to tune, patiently adjusting and readjusting strings at both ends, sometimes using the knife to trim a bit more.

At the end of the three days, she wrapped the instrument and placed it carefully on the single shelf in her room. Theo smiled with satisfaction. *Tomorrow?*

Yes. Your first lesson tomorrow. In perfect accord, they walked down the gloomy hallway to the great room for the evening meal, one dark head and one fair, one tall and thin and one powerfully built. They were friends now, Sira thought, truly friends. The Spirit of Stars had sent her an unexpected blessing, and she was grateful for it. It was the only light in the darkness of her imprisonment in this place.

The next day Theo worked with Jon in the Cantoris for an hour or more. He came to Sira's room after, looking tired and drawn.

Rest first, she sent to him.

He sat on the cot, leaning his shoulders against the wall. *This must be the driest wall in the whole House,* he sent. Sira laughed a little, but he did not laugh with her.

Sira grew quiet, catching a flash of Theo's feeling. It was troubling, and she wanted to shield her mind, but that was hardly fair. Their rapport was growing stronger each day. The people of Observatory were cold and ill, and she knew that troubled Theo.

She wondered if Theo thought she was being selfish, or perhaps cruel. As she thought that, he looked up at her. *No,* he sent. *I do not.*

Sira looked down at her hands, suddenly shy. She had not kept her thoughts low. She had forgotten his growing ability.

I think you are doing what you need to do, he went on. *And I am doing the same.*

She wished she could touch his hand. Aside from those moments in Ogre Pass, it seemed a summer since she had felt the touch of another human being. This thought she did keep low, though. She would not want the Singer to misunderstand. He had held her as she wept on that first night, but there was no need now. She was neither sad nor frightened.

For the first time in her life she wondered how the Cantors and Cantrixes bore the isolation that was their lot. Many worked in the Houses for six summers or more before being called home to Conservatory. All those years without a touch of a human hand seemed suddenly an enormous burden. She thought of Isbel, now on her way to Amric, and sighed.

What is it? Theo sent.

She shook off her mood. *It is nothing. Are you ready?*

Ready.

As Sira reached for the newly repaired *filhata* and placed it in Theo's hands, he sent, *I am grateful to you for teaching me.*

I am glad to have something to do. I am not used to inactivity.

Theo laughed. *You could sing, Singer.*

Sira made a face. *Do not make me regret that I taught you to send!* and he laughed again.

It was a new experience for Sira to be easy in the company of anyone but Isbel and perhaps Maestra Lu. But she and Theo had spent days together, practicing, talking, sharing their meals. In a way she felt as if he were filling the void created in her life by the loss of Maestra Lu. She took pleasure now in showing how to hold the *filhata*. With the briefest of touches she placed his left hand so, and showed him how to poise his right above the strings. She tried to look at him critically, as her teachers had done with her. He was her student now, her responsibility, though she was truly too young and inexperienced to teach. The unknowable Spirit had put them together in this way, and they could only try to do Its will.

A prickle of tears surprised Sira as Theo bent his blonde head and tried the strings of the ancient instrument. It seemed many summers ago that she had held a *filhata* for the very first time. It was hardly credible that it had been no more than two. As she adjusted Theo's hand position, Sira reflected that, in fact, she was only nineteen years old. She had barely four summers. But she felt as old as the very stones of Observatory.

Chapter Twenty-three

Sira sat alone at the morning meal listening to Jon and Theo working in the Cantoris, the sounds of their *filla* faint through the stone walls. They did their work early, so what *quiru* they were able to create would fade by night, in accordance with the requirements of the House. It was an unnecessary precaution; the *quiru* was never bright enough to fade the light of the stars.

Pol sat at the central table in the great room, his cold gaze fixed on Sira. She knew he was waiting for her to acquiesce, to follow her colleagues into the Cantoris. She tried not to think of the repaired *filhata* lying useless in her room. Stubbornly, she took a long time over her tea, letting him watch her sit idly, pointlessly at the long table.

The meals here left her hungry. She sometimes dreamed of the nursery fruit that was so abundant at Conservatory. Fruit would not grow at Observatory. Grain, yeast bread, and meat, with a paltry sprinkling of vegetables, were all Observatory's kitchens could produce.

At length, Theo and Jon joined her. Jon looked tired and reproachful, but Theo sat down beside her with a smile of greeting, cheerful as ever.

I am hungry, he sent. Sira reached for a bowl of the greasy *keftet*.

This is all there is, she sent. *And it has gone cold.* Jon had a bowl also, and was listlessly eating. Theo tried some, and made a face.

You should eat anyway, Sira sent to him.

If I eat my keftet, *will you teach me the* filhata?

Sira's mouth curved, and Jon looked up. "What's funny?"

"Nothing," she said, and stopped smiling. She pushed her bowl away. It was really not polite to be sending when Jon could not hear. The practice was good for Theo, though. She watched Jon as he slumped over his bowl. What exactly was the difference between them? Was Theo more Gifted, and Jon less? Or was it a matter of circumstance? Jon did not interest her at all as a student, while Theo seemed rich with untapped talent and special ability.

She rose from the table, compunction making her careful to keep her face impassive. *Meet me after your meal*, she sent to Theo.

He, too, showed nothing on his face. *I will be there soon.*

As she left the great room, she heard him telling Jon some joke, trying to bring a smile to the dour face. Her own smile returned. Theo was an unusual man, worthy of any instruction she could give him. She looked forward to seeing him learn.

The first lesson on the *filhata* was tuning. Sira showed Theo the middle, deepest string, and sang the C pitch for him, to which it must always be tuned. To be sure he understood, she spoke aloud. "You must memorize the C," she said. "Begin and end each day by singing the C until it is as automatic to you as your breath." She sang it again, and he sang it also.

"I believe I have already memorized it," he said.

"Have you? Do itinerants memorize it also?"

He shook his head, then grinned happily. "I can't speak for all itinerants. But since I was little I have always remembered all the pitches." He showed her by singing *Iridu*, the first mode, that began on the C pitch.

Wonderful, Theo, she sent. *Your Gift includes perfect pitch. You will be an easy student.*

Thank you, Maestra, he sent, with a little bow.

Sira's smile faded. *You must not call me that. I have not earned it.*

He raised his eyebrows, but made no further comment. He watched her fingers as she deftly turned the pegs in the neck of the *filhata*, then tried it himself. C was the middle string; from the top to the bottom, the pitches were E, B, F, down to the low C, then up to G, D, and A. Sira showed him the little exercise by which she had learned to check the tuning: C-G, D-A, E-B, F-C. Theo plucked it slowly, carefully, grinning like a small boy with a new toy. He did it again, and again. Sira gave him a new exercise, and he played that one, too, slowly at first, then faster.

After some time, they both sat back, satisfied. Sira had not noticed until that moment that her hands had been on Theo's guiding them, adjusting their position. His hair brushed her cheek as she leaned close to demonstrate the exercises. She had been too absorbed to notice. It had been exactly as if she were back at Conservatory, with all the Gifted ones with whom she had grown up. Now she felt shy again, realizing, but Theo's enthusiasm covered any embarrassment.

Play something for me, he sent. *Something hard!*

Sira smiled. *Something hard? I am somewhat out of practice, remember.*

But as she took the *filhata* in her hands, automatically checking the tuning once more, the feel of the carved wood and the strings under fingers recalled a melody she had played long ago. She had not held a *filhata* since Maestra Lu's death, and she found herself full of an emotion she had not yet expressed.

As she began her melody, she forgot where she was. The cold and dark and frustration and anger fell away from her, and she poured her soul into the music, as she used to do before her experiences had changed her life. The air in the little room grew warm and bright, and Theo's own psi floated with Sira's in an ecstatic moment of forgetfulness. She felt his mind there with hers, his strength and calm, and the closeness was a great comfort.

When it ended, they were quiet for some moments. Sira drew a deep breath, and Theo closed his eyes. And odd sound from just outside the room made him open them, and they looked at each other in surprise.

It came again, a mewling cry. It sounded like an infant.

Sira laid aside the *filhata* and went to the door.

The corridor outside her room had grown bright and warm with the overflow of heat from Sira's playing. Two women were seated on the floor, leaning against the outside wall of Sira's room, basking in the warmth. Each had a heavily-wrapped baby in her arms, infants with running noses and cheeks reddened with cold or fever—Sira was not sure she knew the difference.

The younger of the women, painfully thin, with wispy yellow hair, had her eyes closed. Her head lolled against the wall.

The other was trying to shush her child, the one who had cried. She turned her face up to Sira when the door opened. She looked dull and ill, but her face was defiant.

"Sorry to disturb you," said the woman. "But it's warmer here. My baby's sick."

The woman lifted the child to her shoulder, crooning. It was clear even to Sira that the mother was more ill than her baby. Sira shuddered slightly, as if in pain, and folded her arms around herself.

"It is all right," she said in a low voice. "You have not disturbed me."

As she returned to her room and closed the door, she reflected that she had not been truthful. The sight of them, sick and cold and hopeless, disturbed her deeply. She felt helpless. She felt trapped.

What is it? Theo sent.

There are two women out there, with their babies. They are sick, all of them. Sira lifted her shoulders in a helpless gesture.

Theo went to the door himself and looked out. After a moment he stepped into the corridor, softly closing the door behind him. Sira heard him murmur to the women, and their soft answers. There were shuffling sounds as they got up from the stone floor and moved away. When she went to the door and opened it again, they were gone, and Theo with them.

*

Not knowing where else to work, Theo led the sick women to the Cantoris. At least in the Cantoris, where he and Jon had labored with their *filla* that morning, there was some warmth and light. He did not bother with the dais, however, but asked the women to make themselves as comfortable as they could on the wooden benches.

The younger woman, with thin fair hair, was very ill indeed, Theo discovered. He took his *filla* from inside his tunic, and played in *Doryu*, the third mode. As he attuned his mind to hers, his own body began to ache with her fever. He experienced with her the effort it took for her to hold her baby. Her arms trembled with weakness, and he felt her great fear that she would die and leave her baby behind. It was painful, but he could not shield himself and still heal her.

He continued in the third mode, searching with his psi for the hottest spot in her body, the source of the illness. It was her throat, he thought, and probably the same for her baby. He played until he was exhausted, trying to cool her, switching to *Iridu* to try to soothe the pain of her throat and her muscles. He did the same for her child, and it was somewhat easier, as there was no wall of emotion to be breached.

The other woman was not so ill, but worn and tired from caring for her friend and for her own infant. Theo did what he could for her, and at length both women stretched out on the benches, drowsing, with their children beside them. Theo frowned down at them as he stood to stretch his stiff muscles.

"You're good at healing, Singer," came Pol's rough voice from the back of the Cantoris.

Theo looked up at him and shrugged. "I can only do so much."

"Why is that?" Pol challenged. Theo walked to the back of the room so his voice would not disturb the women.

He spoke softly, looking directly down into Pol's eyes. "Your House is in awful condition," he said. "It's cold, the food is bad, the walls are damp, so your people are sick."

It was Pol's turn to shrug. "What can I do about that?" he asked. "We brought you, and Singer Jon. Summers are better here. It's our destiny to suffer until the Ship comes."

Theo made a sound of pure disgust. Pol turned his small fierce eyes back to the women resting on the benches. "They understand that," he said. "They have always lived this way." He looked up at Theo again. "We have a song, you know, that used to say we will wait a hundred summers for the Ship. Now we sing that we will wait a thousand summers for the Ship."

"I have been to nearly every House on the Continent," Theo said. "No other House believes as you do. You're sacrificing your people for a foolish fable."

Pol pursed his lips, then said, "It's no fable. All Observatory knows it." He went to the doors of the Cantoris and stood there, looking out into the shadowy hall. "Shall I send someone to fetch these women?"

Theo nodded. "Yes. I'll wait."

"Others will want your help when they hear."

"I'll do what I can, but I am only one Singer."

Pol disappeared through the doors, and Theo went back to watch over the sleeping women. The older one was breathing easily, her baby resting quietly beside her. The younger woman, her wisps of pale hair awry, was sleeping, but her breath rattled in her chest, and her infant whimpered in its sleep. Theo picked up the baby, careful not to disturb its mother. He held the little one close to his chest. It was hot, its skin dry and marked with rashes.

"Poor little one," he murmured to it, putting his cheek to its fringe of hair. "I'm sorry, baby. Fables are not much good to you, are they?" As he waited, he sang bits of a lullaby he had heard long ago. He could not remember where he had learned it. In another lifetime, perhaps.

> LITTLE ONE, LOST ONE,
> SWEET ONE, SLEEPY ONE,
> THE SHIP WILL CARRY YOU HOME.

He held the baby until a Housewoman came and, smiling gently at him, took the infant into her own arms. Theo went slowly and wearily down the dark, cold corridors to his own room, and collapsed on his cot. He closed his eyes against the feeble light, and saw in his mind Pol's fierce unyielding gaze. Sira is right, he thought. These people are not sane.

Chapter Twenty-four

It became a ceremony at the morning meal for Sira to sit long over her tea while Pol rested his elbows on the table in the center of the great room and watched her. She did not look at him, but she felt the intensity of his gaze as he waited, willing her to give in. Sira had the advantage in this strange conflict, because she had nothing whatever to do, and Pol had more responsibilities than one man could reasonably carry. And so each morning she sat, stubbornly, staring at the carved wood of the table or looking out through the thick windows at the surrounding treeless peaks, until Pol was forced to leave the great room to resume his duties.

As Sira waited, she endured the inadequate efforts of Jon and Theo in the Cantoris across the hall. The air in Observatory brightened slowly as they worked. Her own inactivity stifled and irritated her, and she used those feelings to fuel her resentment and strengthen her resolve.

Sira? We are finished.

Guilt assailed her as she looked up to see Theo in the doorway. He had lost weight, and his shock of blonde hair seemed less vigorous. Her own hair was still short, but she knew her skin was dry. There were blotchy patches on her arms and legs.

Coming, she sent quickly, and got up. Several Housewomen and men were still moving about the great room, clearing the long tables.

"Singer?" said a Housewoman to Theo. "Can I get you some tea? Some food?"

"Thank you, Netta," he said, smiling at her. "I could take some tea to my room."

"I'll bring it right away," she said, and bustled off.

Do you know all their names? Sira sent.

I am learning them. Theo leaned wearily against the doorjamb.

I know hardly any.

He managed a smile for her, too. *Well, I am not a Cantor. Only an old itinerant.*

I do not understand.

Theo's smile faded. *I know. But itinerants live among the people, not separated.*

Do Cantors and Cantrixes not live among the people?

Theo shook his head. The Housewoman brought his tea, and he carried it in his hand as he and Sira moved down the corridor.

"I must speak aloud, Sira," he said. "I'm tired this morning. It's hard to send."

She nodded, and he went on to answer her question. "Everything in a Cantor's life separates him from the unGifted. He is taken from his family—"

"Not taken!"

Theo shrugged, and his smile was tired. "All right, given up by his family. He grows up at Conservatory, then goes to a Cantoris where he is never touched by a single person, where he is spoken to only by his title, where he never mates or has children . . ."

Sira drew breath to interrupt again, but thought better of it. Theo was saying something important. She pressed her lips together, and listened.

"Tell me, Cantrix," Theo said. "What friends did you have at Bariken?"

"My senior was my friend."

"No others?"

"Well, there was—" A painful pause ensued. "There was Rollie," Sira finished bitterly. "She was killed."

"Did you spend time with Rollie? Have tea together?"

"Only outside. She was a rider."

Theo nodded in sympathy. "This is the way with Cantors and Cantrixes. They have only themselves for company. They neither know nor understand the people they work with."

"Serve," Sira said flatly.

Theo ventured to touch her shoulder. "Yes, of course. Serve." He reached into his tunic and pulled out a bit of shining metal on a thong around his neck. "This belonged to my mother, and her father before that, and generations of Singers past remembering. They also served, and served well."

Sira did not know how to answer him. They reached her room, and she went in ahead of him. He slumped on her cot. *Itinerants*, he sent, *live with the people. Among them. And . . .*

Sira did not catch the last thought, and raised her eyebrows. He continued aloud, "And know them, what's important to them, what they care about."

Theo closed his eyes, and Sira watched him. His skin, too, suffered from the bad food and the constant cold of this place. Sira had not thought about how much she liked his appearance until this moment, as she saw that his brown cheeks were less smooth, the lines around his eyes and mouth deeper, and not so much from laughter now.

She put her hand on his, though he did not have the *filhata* in his hands. She liked touching him, feeling the hardness of his hands and arms, the warmth of his skin. She had not thought about that, either. *Rest,* she sent to him gently. *Rest, my friend. I will teach you later.*

He smiled without opening his eyes, and Sira drew a fur over his lap. She left the room, closing the door as softly as possible as she went out.

She had seen very little of Observatory. Suddenly, she felt impelled to see it all, to understand why Theo would allow himself to be used this way. Seized with purpose, she strode down the corridor. She would start, she thought, in the place that had been her favorite, both at Conservatory and at Bariken: the nursery gardens. She did not even know for sure where they were, but the release from inactivity felt good to her. She walked faster.

This House, she soon learned, was laid out much as other Houses. The gardens were in the back, protected between the two long wings of apartments and workrooms. Sira marveled at the phenomenon of a House, built untold centuries ago far above the other Houses of the Continent. She wondered if even the Watchers themselves understood its mysteries.

She peered into the nursery. The gardens of Observatory were not inviting. Sunshine filtered through the glass roof, but it was weak, diluted. There were shadows in the corners, and the plants languished in the cold. The miracle, Sira thought, was that Observatory had any vegetables at all. There was a faint scent of offal, and Sira suspected the waste drop was too close to the House. Perhaps they had no choice.

A gardener saw her and came forward. Sira did not even recognize his face. She withdrew quickly, feeling she had no place here.

She had no desire to see the abattoir, and as far as she knew, there was no manufactory at Observatory. There were only the kitchens and the family apartments to see. More slowly now, thoughtfully, Sira walked through the corridors, listening for sounds of family life. The halls were quieter than at Bariken, but she was sure Observatory housed considerably fewer people. She heard one or two children laughing, and at least one crying, before she reached the kitchens.

Several Housewomen were there, huddled together at a small table. The air was still warm from the preparation of the morning meal, but Sira saw that even the radiant heat from the ovens could not banish the ubiquitous mold that crept across the walls. She stopped in the doorway, struck by the attitude of the women.

One of them Sira recognized as the older woman who had been outside her apartment on the day of Theo's first lesson. She was weeping, silently and steadily. Two other Housewomen held her hands and leaned close to her, nodding rhythmically to her sobs, in the manner of an often-observed ritual. Helplessly, Sira watched them, struck with a sense of foreboding.

"Excuse me," she said.

A woman she had not noticed, gray-haired, aproned, came from behind some wooden tubs of grain. "Yes," she said, her hands on her hips. She had an air of being in charge.

"What has happened?" Sira asked, dreading and yet needing to know. "Why is this woman crying?"

The woman eyed her as if wondering whether she deserved an answer. At last she said, "Her friend has died, her friend Liva. And her baby with her."

Sira's heart sank like a stone cast into the Frozen Sea. She did not know the name, but she knew with a terrible certainty who Liva must have been. She remembered the two women sitting on the floor outside her apartment to take in the lavish excess of her *quiru*, apologizing for having disturbed her. O Spirit, she thought. I am so sorry.

The woman's weeping went on, silent, inexorable. The gray-haired Housewoman said without expression, "Do you want something?"

Sira looked at her in surprise. No title, no recognition. It was a strange feeling, and not a pleasant one. "I—I wanted to see—" She faltered. She had no business here. She had neither child nor friend to weep for.

Theo was right. She did not know these people, not their names, not their cares.

"I am sorry," she said at last. She bowed to the Housewoman, who stood stiff and unmoving before her. "Perhaps another time." Sira stepped backward through the doorway, away from the sight of routine, hopeless grief.

Sira did not tell Theo what she had seen. She tried to focus on his lesson. Theo was working in *Aiodu*, the second mode, striving to master the fingering. Sometimes Sira was impatient, seizing the *filhata* to demonstrate, her long fingers secure and precise on the strings. Today, though, she was methodical and tolerant.

You must release the wrist. Tight muscles inhibit other muscles.

Theo nodded. He put the *filhata* in his lap for a moment, and rubbed the back of his right hand. *Tired.*

Sira took his hand in hers and massaged the wrist. *You must stop when you feel this tension, here.* She pointed to the tendon in the back of his hand. *Begin again with your wrist in a better position.*

Theo turned his hand over and captured Sira's. *There is something bothering you.*

It was automatic for Sira to pull her hand away, but his felt comforting. She let the contact go on. *Did you know the young woman died? The one you treated last week?*

His eyes darkened to midnight blue. *I did. She and her baby were very ill.*

Do you think I could have saved them? If I had warmed the House?

Theo lifted one shoulder, expressively. Sira sighed and took her hand away, wrapping her arms around herself. So many deaths, she thought, to weigh on my conscience. She felt so old, so tired. *If I begin to sing here*, she sent to Theo, *I fear I will be trapped forever.*

Theo watched her, but kept his own counsel. When she looked into his face, she saw only patience and acceptance. *Do you not resent me?* she asked.

His crooked grin flashed at her. *Only because you can already play in* Aiodu *and I cannot. Now help me!*

Sira smiled a little, too, as he picked up the *filhata* and began again. But the feeling of ancient weariness did not leave her. How long could she go on like this? How many more deaths could she bear before she broke?

Chapter Twenty-five

"Theo has been a great help to us," said Pol, standing above Sira in the great room.

She stood so she could look down at him. For weeks she had sat here, idle, until he left the room. In all this time he had never before stopped to speak to her.

"Theo has more sympathy for fanatics than I," she answered.

Pol chuckled. "You're a stubborn woman. Do they teach you that at Conservatory?"

"At Conservatory, Gifted people are taught to serve the people of Nevya," Sira said. A flicker of doubt surprised her even as she said the words.

"You don't think Observatory is part of Nevya?"

Sira folded her arms, knowing as she did so that it was to bolster her courage in the face of strange emotions, not because Pol himself had disturbed her. "Observatory chooses to be separate. You attack innocent Nevyans and kidnap Singers. How are you part of Nevya?"

"We have a great duty," Pol said somberly. "We Watch. There is no one else to do it."

Sira felt the heat of indignant anger in her cheeks, and the air about her sparkled with energy as her breath came faster. "And so you add to your many offenses the sacrifice of your people to a foolish belief of many ages ago."

Pol's small eyes glittered in the light created by Sira's temper. He smiled thinly. "Will you come with me, Cantrix? I have something to show you." Sira pressed her lips together, about to refuse, but Pol held up a propitiating hand. "Indulge me this one time, please. There is reason why we believe. Proof."

"I will come," Sira said. "But you must not call me by a false title."

"As you wish." Pol led the way out of the great room with a purposeful step.

Sira had not been to the wing of apartments where most of the House members lived. She followed Pol down a long, dim corridor and up a staircase dimly illuminated by a grimy window. The unkempt state of the House made her shake her head. She heard voices, children crying, the sounds of family, but muted as if the very life of the House were ebbing away. At the very back of the House, Pol opened the door of a large apartment.

They walked through what were evidently Pol's own rooms. If he had a mate, or children, Sira was not aware of them. The apartment was filled with oddments, stacks of ledgers, what looked like a grain barrel, a stack of bows and fur-flighted arrows, even a saddle complete with saddlepack. Mold stained the walls, and the floors were frigid. At the far end of the room, Pol opened a door and stood aside for Sira to precede him.

This room was different. A long polished table stretched its length. The window was clean, so the clear mountain sunshine made the room light enough to read by. Pol held a chair for Sira and she sat, anger replaced by curiosity.

From a long cupboard that lined one wall, Pol slowly and carefully withdrew a fur-wrapped object and laid it gently on the table.

"This," he said with reverence, "is why we Watch."

He looked at her intently for a moment, making sure he had her full attention. Then, without taking his eyes from hers, he untied the thongs that held the wrapping in place. When they were loose, he laid them aside. Methodically, dramatically, he slid the fur covering from the object that lay on the table between them.

Sira gazed at it without understanding. At first she thought it might be a slab of stone, though knife-thin and polished, with marks carved into it. It was about the size of a *filhata*, and almost as dark as an *obis* knife. She realized after a moment that it reflected light exactly as bits of metal did, flashing and glinting as they were passed from hand to hand. Still, it took some time to sort out her visual impressions. When at last she understood, she put a hand to her throat.

"Is that . . . can that be metal? All of it?"

"It is," Pol said. He ran his thick hand reverently across its face. Sira followed his gesture, and saw that the marks were not carved into its surface but somehow set below, covered and yet not hidden by the surface, carved by some mysterious technique she could not guess at. It was a beautiful, a mystifying thing, and for a moment she was speechless.

"So much metal," she whispered at last. "More than I have seen in my whole life put together. What is it?"

"It's a picture of the stars from which we all come." Pol lifted the object so she could see the whorls and streams of light-points spilling across the darkly shining surface. His voice dropped low as he said, "This—this is from the Ship."

Sira stared at him in amazement. "But those are fables!"

"No, Cantrix. They are not. Look here, these six stars. They will come from there."

"Who? Who will come?"

"If we knew once who they were, we no longer remember. But they will come for us. To take us to a better, an easier world. To take us home."

Sira rested her arms on the table across from Pol, and gazed at him with sadness. "You believe this? This is why you all live here in isolation and suffering?" Sympathy softened her voice. "It is an illusion, Pol."

He pulled the artifact back to him and covered its shining surface. His face settled back into its customary remote expression. "It's no illusion. Even the Magistral Committee knows it, though they pretend they don't."

"Pol, I do not think the Magistral Committee indulges in pretense. It is more likely they understand what this great piece of metal is, and know better than to be slaves to a myth." Sira stood, and pushed her chair back from the table. "Allow us to leave Observatory," she said through a tight throat. "Nothing you have shown me justifies our being held prisoner."

Pol's voice was more hoarse than ever. "Leave, then. Try it."

"You know it would be impossible without a guide. We would starve before we found our way out of these mountains. We are as much in your control as if we were locked away."

He glared up at her. "We do what we have to do in this world. We need to Watch, and we need Singers. Watching is our destiny. Yours is to sing."

Sira was silent. The harsh truth of his words squeezed her soul. He was right. No matter where she went, her destiny pursued her. Perhaps freedom was an illusion for more than just Singers. But this—this sacrifice of generation after generation—this was madness.

Pol tied the wrappings over the artifact and stowed it with great care in its cupboard. As he closed the cupboard again, his thick hand rested on the wooden door for a moment. It is a devotion with him, Sira thought. He is sincere. He truly awaits this mythical Ship.

Her steps were heavy as she followed Pol out through his cluttered apartment. She saw no hope for her and Theo. And no hope at all for the people of Observatory.

Chapter Twenty-six

Jon v'Arren took a mate from Observatory a few months after Theo's *filhata* studies began. She was a thin, tired-looking woman with two children whose father had gone too far from the House on a hunting trip and been caught by the cold. Sira and Theo attended their brief ceremony in the great room, and Sira watched from a distance as Theo helped Jon move his few possessions to the family's apartment. At Theo's next *filhata* lesson, Sira was particularly silent, her lips pressed together in the way she had when she was unhappy.

I am better in Aiodu, *am I not?* Theo sent, trying to stir her from her dark mood.

She nodded absently. *And in* Doryu, *too.* She reached out automatically to adjust the position of his middle finger, so that it rested more securely on the C string. He played the scale in *Aiodu* again, then modulated to *Doryu* almost as smoothly as Sira herself. It was a passage he had practiced in private, to surprise her, but she only nodded again, and was silent.

Finally Theo put the instrument aside. *What is wrong?*

He felt her shield her mind at once. He sat still, waiting, watching her. Her face was thinner than ever, the white slash of her eyebrow like a flash of lightning above the thundercloud of her expression. Finally she turned her dark and troubled eyes to him.

She opened her mind again. *Theo. We should talk about your future.*

He grinned at her. She was as formal in their relationship as if they sat in a Conservatory practice room and not in a cramped room at Observatory as far from mannered society as they could be. *I am listening, Maestra.*

You must not call me that. I have told you. No smile brightened her features.

Theo touched her hand. Bit by bit she allowed more contact, but he tried not to hurry her. She seemed vulnerable to him, young and old at the same time, straining beneath her great Gift.

She let his hand rest on hers, but she dropped her eyes. *Since Jon has seen fit to take a mate*, she began—and Theo sensed clearly her underlying distaste—*I fear you will also wish to . . .* She shuddered a little, and Theo held her hand more tightly.

Sira, I will not do so, he assured her, and as he sent the thought, he knew it was no less than the truth. In his turn, he swiftly shielded his mind, realizing in a blinding flash why he would never take a mate from Observatory, or from any other House. He had not allowed himself to understand his feelings until this very moment.

Sira's eyes came up to his. *What is it?*

He released her hand. Keeping the private thought low, hidden as she had taught him, he sent, *It is nothing, Sira. Do not worry.*

He rose from her cot, and wrapped the old *filhata* to place it on the shelf over the bed. *Thank you for the lesson*, he sent formally, and bowed as he always did. Sira rose, too, standing only a few inches, but so very far, away from him. The sharp angles of her face glowed in the light their practice had created, and Theo's pulse quickened.

Suddenly he needed to be away from her, and quickly. He bowed again, and left her staring after him as he hurried out. He would bathe, he thought. The *ubanyor* was hardly his favorite place, but today it seemed just what he needed.

Theo warmed the *ubanyor* with a swift *Doryu* melody on his *filla*, glad that the tub was empty and he was alone. He was gratified, even in his black mood, to see steam rise at once from the water. Certainly, he thought, I am a better Singer than I was. That thought led him back to Sira, when his intention had been to stop thinking of her.

He sighed as he stepped down into the carved tub. His thick hair touched the water when he had immersed himself up to his shoulders. Its length surprised him. How long had they been here? He had not kept track, but it must be almost a year. Sira cut her hair often, keeping it cropped short as if she were ready to leave at a moment's notice. Theo had let his grow, usually tying it back with a bit of thong. Not since his childhood had it been so long.

He was resigned to a long stay at Observatory. Their imprisonment grieved him less than it did Sira. His studies gave him satisfaction, and his *filhata* skills grew quickly in the hours he spent with her, practicing, listening, working. He had not been outdoors in all that time.

What I need, he thought, is a trip through the mountains, a few nights under the stars to regain my balance. Maybe the hunters could take me, just for a few days.

He took up a rough, unscented bar of soap from a niche in the tub and soaped his hair savagely, knowing Pol would never allow him to leave Jon alone in the Cantoris.

"I must be the greatest fool on the Continent," he muttered savagely, "to fall in love with a Conservatory Cantrix!" The soap slipped from his hand, and he swore. "By the Six Stars," he exclaimed, as he searched for it under the water, "I hardly know what I am anymore!"

*

Left alone in her narrow room, Sira sat on the edge of her cot, her hands idle and empty in her lap. In her mind she allowed the image she had been suppressing to float to the surface.

It was Theo she saw. Theo with a mate, a family, children. A Theo who did not play the *filhata*, but only made small, camp-style *quiru* despite all their work together. This, Sira told herself, was what she feared.

The greatest sacrifice, for some Cantors and Cantrixes, was abstention from sex. Theo, who had grown up without the discipline of Conservatory, might not understand the need for chastity. As his teacher, she must explain it to him. At Conservatory, one of the men would have undertaken this lesson, just as one of the women took that responsibility for Sira and Isbel and the other girls. But here, at Observatory, Theo had only Sira for a teacher.

Sira's stomach fluttered. There was no point in postponing what needed to be done, however uncomfortable. Delay would not make this discussion any easier.

She closed her eyes and sent, *Theo, where are you? I need to speak with you.*

The answer was clear and immediate. *I am just leaving the* ubanyor. *I will be right there.*

Sira paced her little room, and the air sparkled and glistened around her. If only she could get out of this cursed House, she thought, see the stars and breathe the fresh, free air. I will never get used to being a prisoner, she thought. Never!

When Theo stood in her doorway, the sparks of her anger still glimmered in the room.

How can you bear this eternal confinement? she burst at him, not at all what she had meant to send.

He gave her his usual crooked smile. *Is this what you needed to say to me?*

Sira took a deep breath and released it. *No,* she sent more calmly. *It is not. I just—*

Her thoughts were confused. What had she really meant to say? Sex, yes . . . She needed to tell Theo about her fears and concerns, but he would never understand. He stood before her, blonde hair still damp and curling from the *ubanyor*, his familiar blue eyes ready as always to laugh at something.

Sira sat down abruptly on her cot. *I thought . . . I need to tell you why Cantors and Cantrixes abstain,* she began awkwardly.

Theo came and sat beside her. *But I know that, Sira.*

Her eyes came up to his. *But then I just realized,* she sent ingenuously, *that I have another reason for wanting you to abstain.*

He was still smiling, and he brushed her hair back from her cheek with the barest of touches. She did not pull back. *Tell me, Sira,* he prompted.

I do not want you to mate, she sent, as flat and clear a thought as a child's. *I want you to myself.*

Theo's grin broadened. *And so it will be.* His eyes shone like a summer sky.

Sira shook her head. The tears he had seen in her eyes only once before welled up. *No, you do not understand,* she sent. *I cannot mate, or . . .*

Theo laughed aloud. He took her hand in both of his. *Do you think I do not know that?*

Mating weakens the Gift, Sira sent. *Cantrixes and Cantors never mate while they have the responsibility of a Cantoris, never put their House in danger through personal weakness.*

"But, Sira," Theo whispered aloud. "You have no House. No Cantoris." He brought her hand to his cheek and held it there.

She shook her head. "It does not matter. I could never put my Gift at risk." She dropped her eyes. "Even though I have misused it in the worst possible way. My Gift is what I am."

"What do you mean, you have misused it?"

She turned her head aside. "I cannot speak of it."

"Not even to me?" Theo kissed the fingers he held. "I love you, Sira."

Sira's tears slipped own her cheeks, one at a time. "You should not love me. I used my psi as a weapon. I harmed someone. Trude, it was. I ruined her mind. I might as well have killed her."

"She was dead in any case," he said, his voice suddenly hard.

"What do you mean? She was alive, though I broke her mind with mine. I killed Wil v'Bariken with a knife, but I forced Trude into madness."

Theo's grip on her hand tightened. "The Magistral Committee exposed them, both Rhia and Trude, in Forgotten Pass," he said. "And they were right to do so. You should have no guilt where Trude is concerned. The decision to dispose of them was inevitable."

Sira was still for a long time, trying to comprehend what this news might mean to her. For so long she had carried the memory, Trude's mind breaking beneath her psi. She hardly knew how to put it down. Perhaps she could. Perhaps she could release it. She was not yet sure, but hope dried her tears, and years seemed to drop away from her.

"Theo," she said wonderingly, "I have nothing to offer you for your love."

He laughed again. "You have everything to offer me, everything I ever wanted! The training I was denied, the knowledge I craved—and your company."

But I cannot stay with you, Sira sent, too moved to speak aloud. *I love you as well, but I cannot stay here.*

Theo slowly, tentatively, drew her into his arms, so her head rested on his shoulder. *On the coast of the Frozen Sea they have a saying,* he sent. *"We cannot eat tomorrow's fish today."*

Sira wiped her cheeks with her hand. She felt his cheek press against her hair.

That means we must deal with each day's challenges as they come, he sent. *And so you and I will do together, Sira.* She nodded against his shoulder. *We will be more than friends. But we will never compromise the Gift.*

At that, she sat up and looked into his eyes. "How," she asked, "can you be so wise?"

Theo shook his head, and his smile returned. "This is not wisdom, Sira. I'm just a hard-headed old itinerant. We have to be practical in my business."

"But you are much more than an itinerant now, Theo. Much more."

He released her. "If I am, it is due to you." He stood and reached for the *filhata* on its shelf above the cot. "So perhaps we had better get back to work." He unwrapped the instrument and checked its tuning.

Sira smiled and smoothed her hair with her fingers. *Play that modulation for me once again, please,* she instructed, adjusting Theo's middle finger on the C. *From* Aiodu *to* Doryu. *It was quite good.*

Theo bent his head and began to play once more. Around him the air glowed and vibrated with his emotion. When he looked up at Sira for approval, she thought perhaps his eyes were a bit too bright, and she suspected her own were, too. If only, Sira thought, he did not look so thin.

Her doubts rose, and clouded her mind. *I am sorry. I cannot concentrate.*

He answered, *We will work later, then.*

She nodded, then stood and held out her hand. "Theo. Show me Observatory. Observatory as you see it."

He grinned up at her. "Now that's a fine idea," he said. "I will."

Chapter Twenty-seven

Theo led Sira through the dark halls of Observatory to the nursery gardens, where they stepped into a gloomy great space smelling of soil and the tang of growing things. A short gray-haired man hurried forward, wiping his hands on his trousers as he came, and greeting Theo with enthusiasm. "Singer, I'm glad to see you. We're happy to have one of your *quiru* any time you can manage."

Theo turned to Sira. "This is Ober, the gardenkeeper. Ober, meet Sira."

The man nodded to Sira, but his attention was for Theo. "Let me bring you a bench, Singer." He bustled to one corner, coming back with a small bench which he carried to the center of the space.

Theo followed him, taking his seat on the bench and pulling out his *filla*. "Sorry I couldn't be here before, Ober," he said. "So many people have been sick."

"Always are," Ober said. "But we're glad to have you here now. Every little bit helps."

Sira saw that three or four other gardeners were coming forward to listen. Theo was still for a moment, concentrating, and the men were respectfully silent. When Theo brought his *filla* to his lips and began a sprightly tune in *Iridu*, the air around him began to glow immediately. Sira closed her eyes and let her mind float with Theo's, following his musical thought and supporting his psi with her own. His technique was quite satisfactory. There was a swiftness, an economy, to his *quiru* that her greater finesse precluded.

She was thinking she might now explore *Lidya* and *Mu-Lidya* with Theo. She began planning which exercises might be best, but her thoughts broke off when she became aware, all at once, of the emotions of the men around her.

She was not accustomed to being open to such feelings. Being linked with Theo's psi left her without the refuge of her usual shielding. Had this been her own *quiru*, she would never have allowed it.

The gardeners were fully concentrated on Theo, following his melody, savoring the warmth and brightness of his *quiru*. Their rapt attention made their minds as clear as blue ice to Sira. This moment of music was restful for them, a respite from constant work and struggle. Their thoughts intruded on hers; this one was worried about mold on the grain crop; another one was grieving for some older woman, perhaps his mother, whose joints pained her unendingly in the cold; Ober himself was fearful for someone who had gone out to hunt that very morning, and had not yet returned.

Sira drew a shaky breath. Never had she felt these things while singing or playing. How could Theo bear it? She must make sure he learned to shield his mind when he performed the *quirunha*, or the distraction would affect his work.

The tune came to an end, and Theo put his *filla* in his lap and smiled at the men. Light now bloomed in this part of the nursery gardens, revealing the drooping grain, the sagging tops of the root vegetables, the black soil faithfully turned and tended. Sira looked up, and saw that the limeglass roof was kept as clean as possible, but Theo's *quiru* did not quite reach. It was warm and bright where she stood, and Sira had felt him stretch it as far as he could, perhaps a bit farther with her help. Still the corners and the furthest part of the gardens lay in misty gloom.

"Thank you, Singer," Ober said. Sira was glad not to feel his fear anymore, or the worries of the others. Their emotions tired her, made her feel as if she were carrying an obligation not her own. She was thoughtful as she followed Theo out of the nursery gardens.

You see their need, Theo sent.

More than that, she answered. *I felt it. That has not happened to me.*

It can be painful, was all Theo sent in return. They turned together toward the kitchens.

A young woman hurried up to them in the hallway. "Singer!" she cried, ignoring Sira. "There will be a revel! You must come to the great room, now!" She turned and ran off down the hall, too excited for simple walking.

"Lise, wait!" Theo called after her. "What do you mean, a revel? What is that?"

Lise turned back. "Don't you know? There was a sighting last night. The Watchers!"

Theo shook his head, and shrugged. Lise gestured down the hall. "There was a sighting, Singer. Now we celebrate! Come on, hurry. We don't want to miss anything."

Sira and Theo followed the girl, wondering. Hers was the happiest face they had seen in months. They encountered other members of the House streaming into the great room from the hall, all of them looking as if they had put on their best tunics and brushed and bound their hair. Even the children were washed and tidied. They looked, Sira thought, like a crowd at Conservatory going into the Cantoris. Something important must be happening.

Small cups of wine waited on the long tables. The company, growing quiet now, stood beside them, waiting for something. Everyone gazed at the center table, empty at the moment except for the winecups. The excitement in the air made Sira uncomfortable, and she shielded her mind to shut out its intensity.

Have you any idea what is happening? she sent to Theo

I can only guess. If I am right, it is beyond belief.

Pol made a sudden, dramatic appearance in the doorway to the great room. Two men flanked him. All three looked tired but triumphant, and Pol cast Sira a significant look as he strode to the center table. He picked up his winecup with much ceremony. The entire company did the same, holding the cups high. Even the children seemed to know what to do, with adults helping them so their wine would not spill.

"Revel!" Pol cried hoarsely. "The Watchers saw the lights last night, moving swiftly across the sky. The Ship comes closer!"

A cheer rose up, stunning Sira with its energy and jubilance. These dour people were transformed by . . . by what? *What actually happened?* she asked Theo in bewilderment.

They saw something, I would guess. Or they claimed to see something.

Pol believes it.

Theo nodded agreement as the two men came forward to give their testimony.

"It was like a star," one said, "only moving very fast in a straight line." There was not a sound in the great room as the people hung on his words. "It came from the west and disappeared into the east as we watched."

"And then," said the other, "it returned! It went in the opposite direction, very swiftly. It lasted only moments, but it was glorious."

Another cheer went up when the brief description was over. Sira had the distinct impression, even with her mind shielded, that this was all familiar. *They have done this before,* she sent to Theo.

Oh, yes. This is well-rehearsed. He narrowed his eyes for a moment, listening. *They are nevertheless sincere, I believe.*

Are you not shielded?

He grinned at her. *I am now. I think I know a camp story when I hear one, but the people believe this. They believe it absolutely.*

I know. Sira glanced around at the smiling faces, seeing the gardeners, who had brushed the dirt from their tunics, and Lise, at their table.

With a single motion the winecups were drained, even those of the children. A group of kitchen workers came out with plates of grain bread and small sweets. These were parceled out with care so each House member received an equal share. People strolled around the room greeting each other, slapping backs, laughing. The difference in their demeanor was more than Sira could take in.

She herself sat, though she did not touch the winecup before her. Theo watched her, and when she did not drink, he pushed his own cup away. Pol emerged from the crowd and came to stand across the table from them.

"You see," he said to Sira. "We have even more reason."

"Lights in the sky? The sky is full of lights, Pol."

"Not like these lights," he said complacently. "These are the signs they are coming."

"How often have you seen them?" Theo asked.

"They appear perhaps once every summer. Sometimes less. Sometimes more." Pol waved his arm grandly around him. "Can all these people be wrong?" His next words were drowned out by a song that rose spontaneously from the crowd.

> WE WILL WATCH FOR THE SHIP TO COME,
> TO COME AND CARRY US HOME.
> WE WILL WATCH UNTIL THE WATCHING IS OVER,
> A HUNDRED SUMMERS,
> A THOUSAND SUMMERS,
> FOR THE SHIP TO CARRY US HOME.

Like the lullaby, Sira sent to Theo. *And they are like children. They believe every word.*

Still we serve them, he sent. *Even if they are like children. Perhaps especially if they are like children.* He touched her hand beneath the table. *Unshield your mind for just a moment.*

Sira looked into Theo's eyes, which had gone as dark as twilight in the mountains, and she nodded slightly. Warily, she unshielded her mind. A tide of emotion swept over her, and she gripped his hand as the feelings of all the people in the great room swept over her.

There was joy, the more acute because of the pain which preceded it. There was triumph, as long-held beliefs seemed vindicated. There was grief, because some beloved person had gone beyond the stars and missed the occasion. And there was the most painful, the most poignant, of all emotions: a terrible, desperate hope, an emotion Sira herself had felt not long before.

She bore it for as long as she could before the shield of her mind sprang up, almost as a reflex. She gazed around her at the people of Observatory, and saw individuals, families, personalities. They no longer seemed nameless, faceless victims.

Theo, how do you tolerate it?

This is what life is.

She shook her head, as if to rid herself of all of it. *This is not my life. I could not bear to live with the noise of these thoughts.*

Theo squeezed her hand and released it. *I shield myself most of the time. But there are advantages to being open.*

She pushed back her chair and stood up. *They are pitiful.*

Theo shook his head. *They are no more pitiful than other people. Perhaps if they knew my feelings, they would pity me. Or even you.*

Sira looked down at him for a long moment before she turned and fled, unable to bear the scene anymore. She felt Theo's eyes following her as she hurried from the great room.

Chapter Twenty-eight

In the end, it was Theo who caused Sira to sing for Observatory.

Some weeks after the revel, a group of hunters who had left the House five hours before came galloping back with terrible news. One of their *hruss* had slipped on the cliff path and plunged into the great canyon. Its rider had been scraped from the saddle by an outcropping of rock, and was trapped, injured but alive, on a ledge overhanging the abyss. The hunters were desperate to save him, but it would not be easy. One rider had stayed with the injured man, talking to him over the edge of the cliff. The others had ridden back as swiftly as they dared.

Pol himself came in search of Theo, grating a few words of explanation.

"I will go, of course," Theo said, reaching for his furs even as he spoke. "But you will have to trust the Cantoris to the Singer Jon by himself."

Pol nodded. "If the Spirit allows, they can get Emil back up to the path before dark. Then you can all return tomorrow. In my judgment, we must take the risk."

Theo followed Pol out of the House and into the stables. His alarm over Emil was almost overridden by his relief at being outside. He had forgotten how good it felt to breathe clear cold mountain air, and to look up into the freedom of the wide sky. As a *hruss* was saddled, he tied back his long hair, and sent an explanation to Sira.

With good luck we will return tomorrow, he sent.

Be careful, Theo. Spirit of Stars go with you.

He sensed the shielding of her feelings, and through it, her anxiety. He would feel the same, if their positions were reversed. He would also not try to stop her from her duty.

The feel of the saddle under him and the reins in his hand was gratifying after months of confinement. He lifted his face to savor the sun, and sniffed the old familiar smell of snowpack.

Pol spoke a few words to the riders, and they were off. Theo was startled to sense Pol's envy, and he shielded his mind so as not to intrude on the man's private thoughts. It was curious to think that Pol would rather have ridden out on this frantic attempt to save a life than stay safely behind in the House. He does his duty as he sees it, Theo thought with reluctant admiration. Pol had very little freedom of his own.

The riders and Theo rode for two hours before they reached the narrow passage he remembered from his trip up to Observatory. His legs scraped rock once again as he and the *hruss* pressed through the crevice and came out onto the dizzying height of the cliff path. Here the riders slowed their pace. The rocks were rimed with ice, which had probably caused the accident. The path was no wider than a man's height, and the canyon gaped into bottomless darkness. Theo's heart thudded when he peered over the edge into the chasm.

"Now that is not a trip I'd like to make," he muttered.

The rider in front of him said grimly, "I'd think not, Singer. Hard to come back from."

At the site of the accident, the hunter who had stayed behind lay on his stomach keeping an eye on the injured man below. He had planted his toes behind a tongue of rock. His shoulders and head hung over the cliff edge.

The riders came up quietly behind him, and dismounted with care. Theo stole a moment, bracing himself with one hand on his *hruss's* withers, to look out on the vista of the Continent. Far below he could see the sweep of Ogre Pass from the Southern Timberlands to the northern Mariks. He drank in the view like a thirsty man, and for a moment, he understood Sira's craving to be away. It was hard to think of never traveling through the Pass again.

But now was not the time for contemplation. Gingerly, Theo made his way around the *hruss* to the edge of the precipice where the others were gathered. He was here to protect them from the cold, of course. But any extra hand might be useful.

"Emil stopped talking an hour ago," said the one who had stayed. "I'm afraid he's dead."

Theo closed his eyes and reached out with his psi. He found Emil's mind, blank and gray with pain. "He's not dead. He's unconscious," he reported with relief.

"How do you know that, Singer?" asked Baru, an older man with hard features.

"I can hear him," was all Theo said. He had no other way to explain. The men nodded as if he had said something wise, and he wished he had something really wise to offer. He leaned carefully forward to look down the steep drop.

The unconscious man was in danger of slipping off the ledge that had caught him. It was no more than a jagged outcropping in the wall of rock, and he must have come very near plunging all the way into the abyss.

"Only the Spirit could have put Emil on that shelf," muttered one of the hunters.

"We need to hurry," Theo said. "It's not long till nightfall."

Ropes had been brought out, but someone would have to be lowered to Emil, to help him up. There was little purchase on the slippery path. The men discussed the problem.

"We could tie ropes to one of the *hruss*," someone suggested.

Theo shook his head. "I don't think so. A *hruss* has already slipped. We don't want to lose another man along with this one."

The men nodded, accepting this. Theo glanced up at the sky, beginning to shade to violet. There was no time to waste. He looked around the group, assessing the men. "Baru and I are the heaviest. We should tie the rope around ourselves, and Stfan, who is so light, should go down."

Stfan was the youngest man present. His throat worked as he swallowed, but he didn't hesitate. He gave a stout nod.

"Good man," murmured Theo. "These others will help. We won't let you fall."

In moments, a harness had been fashioned for Emil, and another for Stfan. Theo checked Stfan's ropes himself, then rechecked them. He and Baru tied themselves securely into a web of rope, and braced themselves as Stfan put his legs over the edge of the cliff.

The last of the daylight glinted on the far wall of the chasm. The near side was already in darkness. Stfan looked back at Theo with eyes stark with fear.

Theo said, "We've got you, my friend." He and Baru began to pay out the rope.

Stfan used his legs to balance against the cliff as they gradually lowered him toward Emil's ledge. Theo and Baru checked with each other, each confirming the other had a firm grip, before they let the rope slip a few grudging inches through their hands.

Theo followed Stfan with his mind. Despite his fear, the youngster was determined to serve his House. He was prepared to die if he must. This is bravery, Theo thought. Facing fear, feeling it, going on anyway. He took a tighter grip on his section of the long rope.

With his mind open, he heard, *Be careful, Theo.*

Sira? he sent in amazement, even as his legs muscles trembled with effort. *Can you follow me so far?*

Maestra Lu could go even farther. When you return, I will tell you the story.

I can hardly wait.

The pressure on the rope suddenly eased, and Baru and Theo stood straight, flexing their knees. Stfan called up from below. "It's so dark. I'm afraid I won't tie the harness properly."

Theo edged to the rim to look down. It was true, the encroaching darkness had engulfed the ledge. He could barely make out the top of Stfan's head.

"Can't you do it by touch?" Baru called.

"I can try, but—" A wave of doubt swept from Stfan into Theo's mind.

"Wait," Theo said. He reached inside his furs for his *filla.* "Let me see how far I can extend a *quiru.* If I can make it long enough . . . Well, let me try."

Dark was coming quickly over the cliff path. The chasm had become a black void, making the *hruss* restive. Theo played quickly, without artistry, a simple *Iridu* melody.

The *quiru* sprang up faster than any he had ever created, strong and warm and deep. His psi stretched as far as it could, but he could not reach Stfan and Emil so far below. He wished he had the *filhata.* He could have done it, he thought, with the stringed instrument and his voice. He could have extended his *quiru* farther than ever before, but now . . . Perspiration broke out on his forehead as he struggled, pushing his psi with all his energy.

Never force, came Sira's calm voice in his mind. *Always release, like releasing your breath.*

Theo drew a deep breath, and tried to release his psi as he released the breath. It was better. The light spilled over the cliff edge, pouring like a glowing river down the wall of stone. But it was still not enough. Stfan stood in blackness with the helpless Emil at his feet.

I will help you, Sira sent. A moment later Theo felt his psi lift and strengthen. Sira's psi joined his, blended with his so he could not tell which was hers and which was not. He had never experienced such power. His *quiru* leaped outward, almost to the opposite wall of the chasm. It swelled upward into the night sky, and downward into the canyon, easily enveloping the two men below.

An appreciative murmur swirled around Theo. He sent to Sira, *Thank you, my dear.*

I am waiting for you, she answered, then released the thread of their contact.

Theo turned to the task of helping pull up Stfan, and then carefully, slowly, the injured Emil. It was only hours later, after he had made Emil as comfortable as he knew how, that he realized Sira had broken her own tabu. She had sung—vicariously, perhaps—but she had sung for the Watchers.

Chapter Twenty-nine

Sira put down the *filhata* after breaking her connection with Theo. "I see now," she whispered to the memory of Maestra Lu, "how you could reach so far. It was love that made it possible. Love, and fear."

She wrapped the *filhata* and restored it to its shelf. Her mind felt as sensitive as skin scraped raw on stone. Around her she sensed the thoughts and feelings of the House members, and she did not shrink from them. If Theo had the courage to face the barrage of thoughts coming from unGifted ones, so must she. She straightened her tunic, and stepped out of her room into the dark corridors of Observatory.

She went first to the *ubanyix*. Several women were in the tepid water, bathing in near-darkness and miserable cold. One of the strange little lamps smoked in one corner, but it did little to dispel the gloom, and it clouded the air with foul-smelling smoke. The women turned blank faces to her when she came in.

"Excuse me," she said. Their eyes on her were niether friendly nor unfriendly, but waiting. Of course they knew her only as Theo's traveler. "I would like to warm the water."

One of them snickered. "How are you going to do that, build a fire with the benches?"

"Of course not," Sira protested. "If we began that, the House would be gutted within days." The woman stared at her, and Sira realized belatedly that she had meant to make a joke. She shrugged, and reached inside her tunic for her *filla*. It would be best to simply begin. Let them understand about her in their own time.

She sat down on one of the benches and began to play a plaintive *Doryu* melody. The light grew gradually around her, an intensely warm circle that expanded slowly but steadily to fill the *ubanyix*. The water looked clearer in the light, and the entire room seemed to take shape out of the gloom, walls and benches and niches and shelves coming into focus.

One of the women exclaimed at the sudden warmth, and another stood up, naked and dripping. She pointed at Sira where she sat. "You're a Singer, too!"

They stared at each other, Sira and the women, for a tense moment. Then the one standing, her hair in sodden strands on her shoulders, burst out, "All this time you could have been warming this great cold pond, and you sat in your room listening to the Singer Theo play!"

Sira's heart clenched, and she hid behind the frozen mask of her features. This was how it must have seemed to them, that Theo came to her room to play, and she listened. They would not know, even Pol did not know for certain, what she was. And now, instead of gratitude for warming the *ubanyix*, she met anger and resentment. She received just what she would have given had she been in their place.

Her mask melted, and a laugh bubbled to her lips. "You are quite right, Housewoman," she said. "I have stayed in my room listening to the Singer, and now I am out of it. Make of it what you will!"

What a surprise she had for these people, she thought as she got to her feet. Not these poor, pitiful people, but these stubborn, spirited, hard-minded people. Perhaps she did not have to like them to admire them. And perhaps she did not have to agree with them to serve them.

She did not take time for a bath of her own. Instead, she hurried to her room to fetch the *filhata*. She unwrapped it, taking pleasure in the gleam of its restored wood and the nice tension of its gut strings. She tucked it under her arm in the old familiar way, and strode to the Cantoris.

She had avoided the Cantoris and its implications since her arrival. As she came into it now, it seemed little more than a high-ceilinged, empty space. It was neither elegantly spare, like that of Conservatory, nor ornately decorated, as it was at Bariken. Theo and Jon, it appeared, did not use the dais, but sat together on two carved chairs in the aisle between the benches. As Sira stepped up on the dais and took her seat, her boots left prints in the accumulated dust.

Her work with Theo had kept Sira in practice. Her fingers were sure and deft on the strings of the refurbished instrument. She tuned the C, and as a melody sprang into her mind, it was as if her last *quirunha* had been only yesterday instead of half a summer ago. If only there were a junior beside her, she thought, then smiled to herself. There would be, when Theo returned. He was almost ready. But this task she could handle alone.

She began in *Aiodu*, first just with the *filhata* and then, when her psi was clearly focused on the whole House—its apartments, its gardens, the kitchens, even the Watcher's bubble at the top—she began to sing. As she modulated to *Iridu*, the rise in pitch was accompanied by a steep rise in the temperature of the House. She forgot that Observatory's *quiru* was supposed to fade in the hours of darkness. She forgot she was a prisoner, and she almost forgot that Theo was working on a narrow path above a terrifying gorge. Sira lost herself in doing what she wa born and trained to do. Her concentration was absolute. And Observatory began to come alive.

One by one, then in small groups, Housemembers straggled to the Cantoris. The music was strange to them, but the glow and the warmth of the *quiru* was hypnotic, and they found their way down the corridors with eyes and mouths wide with wonder. The *quiru* billlowed out from the Cantoris, a wave of light and warmth and energy. The nursery gardens came alive, as if summer had burst upon them all at once. The abattoir brightened as if the suns had reached past the stone walls and right into its noisome interior.

Pol was among the first to come to the Cantoris. He stood in unabashed triumph at the back as Sira, his captive Cantrix, played the swiftest and strongest *quirunha* of her life.

In the mountains, two hours ride southeast from Observatory, Stfan looked up from where they all huddled on the path around Emil. "What's that?" he cried, his voice cracking like that of the boy he really was.

They all looked up to the peak which was Observatory's home. Theo grinned as he recognized the halo of light that bloomed on the far side of the mountain, a radiance like all those other beacons of warmth and safety, sister *quiru* that rose above the Continent where Cantors and Cantrixes served to protect their people.

"That, my friends," he said, "is Cantrix Sira v'Conservatory at work." He laughed, and slapped his thigh. "That is the result of a real *quirunha* performed by a Conservatory-trained Cantrix. No one will Watch at Observatory on this night!"

Sira finished her music, and looked up to see that the Cantoris had filled with people. Some stood, others sat on the benches. All but one stared at her in utter confusion. Unsmiling now, she stood and bowed to them all.

"I am Sira v'Conservatory," she announced. The resonance of the Cantoris answered her with a deep, satisfying echo. "I warn you that I will not stay at Observatory any longer than I must. But while I am here, I will serve."

Defiantly, though she knew it must be strange to them, and perhaps even offensive, she chanted the closing prayer of the *quirunha*.

> SMILE ON US,
> O SPIRIT OF STARS.
> SEND US THE SUMMER TO WARM THE WORLD,
> UNTIL THE SUNS WILL SHINE ALWAYS TOGETHER.

She tucked the *filhata* under her arm and stepped off the dais. The people watched her as she passed, and Sira, her mind still feeling exposed and raw, sensed a lightening of their worries. She sensed their hope, and its yearning intensity pained her. She pressed her lips together, and paced out of the Cantoris.

Pol caught up with her in the hall. "A marvelous *quirunha*, Cantrix." He cast her a sidelong glance, and matched her steps with his own.

Sira threw him a look. "Just Singer," she said firmly.

Pol chuckled. "You may choose your title as you wish. But please remember in the future that at Observatory we require darkness at night."

Sira stopped, thunderstruck at his arrogance. He stopped with her, and his eyes glittered savagely in the brilliance of her *quiru*. "I'm sure you can manage that," he added. His wooden features softened, almost a smile. "I doubt there's a more talented—*Singer*—on the Continent." He turned and marched away from her, wearing his satisfaction like a fur wrapped around him.

Sira took a deep breath. If she had expected gratitude, or compliments, they were evidently not forthcoming. Another laugh, bittersweet, burst from her. These people were more like herself than she had ever wanted to believe.

Baru knelt beside Theo, watching until the Singer sat back wearily to rest a moment. "Will he live?" Baru asked.

Theo sighed. "Wish I could say. I am doing all I can."

The other men slept, each snuggled close against the cliff face, as far from the edge of the precipice as possible. Stfan moaned in his sleep, and Theo turned to look at him. All was well, however, in the oversize *quiru* that still stretched along the path and down into the chasm.

Emil was badly hurt. Theo had spent most of the night trying desperately to stop the bleeding that threatened to steal his life despite all they had done. He felt Sira's presence, though she was silent. Indeed, he had no energy to spare for conversation.

Emil was bleeding inside his body as well as from lacerations of his belly and chest. He had been lucky not to plunge into the canyon with his *hruss*. He had likely bounced against the cliff more than once before landing on the ledge. There had been no need to play in the first mode, as Emil was still unconscious. It was *Aiodu* Theo used, reaching inside the torn tissues to nudge them together. If Emil wakened, the pain from his blood-filled belly would be intense.

Theo played a slow, searching melody as he followed the path of the bleeding. Here, he thought, must be the worst of it. He applied precise touches of psi to press on the source. And there, he told himself, there is another, and he did the same, the slow music and Sira's energy making him stronger, more accurate, more powerful than he had ever been.

It went on for hours, with Theo unaware of his own body, only of the torn one he was trying to mend. When at last he thought he had done all he could, he put down his *filla*, trembling with fatigue.

Sira spoke to him then, over the distance she had bridged with her *filhata*. *Well done, Singer*, she sent. *Emil is lucky to have you as his healer.*

Thank you. Theo felt the contact dissolve, and he looked around him for the first time in hours. The high mountain sun glimmered over the eastern peaks, and the sprawling *quiru* paled before its light. A faint color tinged the cheeks of the unconscious man, and Theo thought he might wake before long. The problem now was to transport him.

The path was too narrow for a *pukuru*, but Baru had fashioned a litter with *caeru* hides and softwood poles. They would carry Emil by hand back up the cliff path. The sun gleamed on the layer of ice that clung to the rocks. It would be a treacherous passage until they made it thorugh the crevice and into the broader road above the canyon. Stfan led the extra *hruss* on long tethers. If one of them slipped, he would have to let it go. Theo rode in front of him, keeping an eye on Emil and refusing to look down in the depths of the chasm. Baru and one of the riders walked slowly, with the litter slung between them, feeling their way cautiously, trying not to jar Emil. It was a silent and tense group of men.

When they were perhaps a quarter of an hour from the narrow opening, Emil began to wake from the stuporous sleep that had held him all night. He shifted and tossed in the litter, putting those who carried him at risk of slipping.

"Put him down gently," Theo called. They did so gingerly, mindful of their precarious footing. Theo dismounted and pulled out his *filla* once again. He knelt in an impossibly small space by the litter to play a melody in *Iridu*, to induce his patient to sleep. Emil's pain had begun to rise, and with it came delirium. Theo put his hand on the injured man's forehead, and the sensation of Emil's pain made him catch his own breath. He cast about for an idea.

Theo. Sira was with him again. *You need a sleep* cantrip.

I do not know one, Theo sent back, helplessly.

Then I will help you.

At this distance?

We must try, came her answer. *Be as open to me as you can. I will give you the* cantrip. *It will come from me, but you will be the instrument.*

Theo took a deep breath, set down his *filla*, and closed his eyes, putting himself in Sira's hands. He felt her psi, so strong, so steady, join with his own as if they were one person. Words came into his mind, and he sang them, as Sira's psi threaded through his own. His voice was neither so cultured nor so disciplined as Sira's, but the *cantrip* succeeded just the same. Emil's restlessness ceased, and he lay quiet and still. Only his breath showed that he still lived.

Somehow, Theo sent, *I must learn that skill.*

You have just done so, she answered.

Shortly afterward, the party was on its painstaking way once again, with Emil soundly sleeping in his litter. The *pukuru* was waiting for them beyond the cliff path, and when they had squeezed themselves and the *hruss* through the crevice, Baru hitched the sled to his own *hruss* and transferred Emil into it. He mounted, and looked back at Theo from his saddle. "I don't know how you did it, Singer," he said, "but you've saved this man's life. His family will be grateful, and so are we."

"Better thank the Spirit." Theo was too tired to smile. "I hardly know how it happened myself."

They were safe at Observatory two hours later, welcomed into a warm, brilliantly lighted House. They went to bathe in very hot water in the *ubanyor*. Mates and children greeted them excitedly, and the injured man was put to bed in his family apartment. Sira insisted that Theo eat and sleep, and she promised she would treat Emil's pain if he wakened.

I could not have stopped his bleeding, she sent to Theo in a private moment. *But I can ease his pain.*

I think you would be surprised at how much your healing skills have grown, Theo sent wearily. *But we can discuss that later.*

Sira gave him a narrow smile. *Indeed. Sleep now, dear. I will be here when you waken.*

In his fatigue, Theo pushed away the question that came to his mind. She would be here when he woke this time, but for how much longer? It was not a question he could deal with now, and he kept his thought low so as not to disturb Sira with it. He fell into his cot and slept for hours without moving and without dreams.

Chapter Thirty

What are you thinking of, Sira?
I am remembering Isbel. You met her, did you not?
Theo grinned across the table. They were at the evening meal, enjoy-ing the vegetable-laden *keftet* that now graced Observatory's tables. Sira delighted in seeing Theo's brown cheeks smooth again, his hair bouncing energetically around his shoulders. Her own hair she kept severely cropped, but she too was less gaunt, and her skin was healed, all patchiness gone.

Isbel with the dimples, who loved to tell stories, Theo sent. *She should be Cantrix of Amric now.*

So she should. For almost three years.

And what were you remembering?

Sira traced the grain in the ironwood of the table with her long forefin-ger. *Isbel's mother withdrew from her when her Gift made itself known. I never understood why that pained my friend so much, even when she had three summers. But now . . .* Sira lifted her head and looked around the great room. *Now I believe I do.*

The days of silent meals at Observatory had ended. Families sat to-gether, talking and laughing. Friends crossed the room to chat. Sira knew them now, their names, their histories. She had helped Theo heal many a small ailment and a few serious ones. She had eased the pain of the dying and the pangs of childbirth, and had learned from Theo to allow some feelings to penetrate her mental shields. If she did not love these people, she at least understood that they loved each other. And so she understood why Isbel had suffered for her mother's abandonment.

Together Sira and Theo left the great room. Many House members called out to Theo, and he answered every one, smiling. Annet, Jon's mate, said, "Good night, Cantrix Sira." Sira nodded to her with her customary gravity. One or two other House members bowed to her. Pol was in con-versation near the door. He looked up, and she met his gaze.

I am sure he thinks you are a gift straight from the Spirit, Theo sent.

She turned her eyes to Theo. The time was at hand when she must speak to him of her intentions. It would not be easy.

There is something else I am remembering, Sira sent. *A young boy, Gifted, but untrained. His mother was an itinerant who died young. His father refused to allow him—Zakri was his name—to be tested for Conservatory. He was deeply troubled when I met him, even desperate.*

This can be a cruel world, Theo sent. *Do you know what they say in the Southern Timberlands?*

She smiled, anticipating a proverb.

They say, Theo sent with a wink, *that a wezel with too many kits is feeding the ferrel.*

What does that mean?

It means you should not take on more tasks than you can reasonably accomplish.

But, Theo, the shortage of Singers is growing serious on the Continent.

Theo shook his head. *No. I think the shortage is of Cantors and Cantrixes. The Gift still appears. It has appeared here, at Observatory.*

Sira's eyebrows rose. *What do you mean?*

I think Lise's child—she is two—is Gifted. We will have a student.

Sira looked up swiftly. *But, Theo—she should go to Conservatory.*

Theo shook his head again. *I do not think so. Lise's child, and any other Gifted ones born to Observatory, should be trained at home. There must be a reason why the Gift appeared now, when you and I are here.*

Sira fell silent. Change was desperately needed on Nevya, and change was coming. She felt it as clearly as she and other Nevyans felt the coming of summer. Something profound and essential was in the making, and in some way on the Spirit could understand, she was part of it.

Theo smiled at her. *The way we treat the Gift must change. The cost must not be too high, or the Gift will be suppressed.*

Sira sighed. *And if the Gift is suppressed, the people pay the price.*

The summer was very near. From the aerie of Observatory, the people could already see the brightening of the sky that marked the beginning of the long-awaited warm season. Before long, the Visitor would appear, low on the horizon. When its warmth reached Nevya the snow would melt even here, at what felt to Sira like the top of the world. It seemed to intensify her sense of destiny, the destiny that pulled at her in a way she could neither define nor resist.

Theo took her hand when they were alone in the corridor. *You are very thoughtful tonight. Shall we walk, or do you prefer to be alone?*

Sira considered. *Let us walk in the gardens.*

Done, he sent, and pulled her after him in a half run that made her laugh as she tried to keep up. She pulled her hand away and slowed to a dignified pace when they encountered House members in the hall.

The *quiru* light in the nursery gardens had begun to dim just a little from its daytime brilliance. Sira and Theo held their *quirunha* very early, before the morning meal, to let it diminish before night fell, enough for the Watchers to see the night sky. There had been no more sightings by the rotating teams, and no revel, but the centuries-old tradition carried on as always. Here in the gardens the plants grew strong and high, and the effluvium of offal was replaced by the rich smell of compost and damp warm air. The gardeners smiled and called to the two Singers when they came in.

For some minutes they strolled arm in arm. Sometimes Sira pinched some dark dirt between her fingers, or Theo bent his face to a plant to breathe in its fragrance. Finally Sira indicated a bench under a sapling in one corner of the nursery, and they sat side by side.

Theo looked up at the tentative buds just beginning to show. *There may be fruit here one day.* He glanced at Sira, and the blue of his eyes darkened. *Or perhaps not.*

There will be fruit, Sira sent. *Because I think you want to stay here.*

And you do not.

Sira closed her eyes as if in pain. *My dearest dear,* she began, then felt Theo's hand on her shoulder.

I know, Sira. I know your thoughts and I believe I know your heart.

Sira opened her eyes to drink in Theo's face, the lines of laughter around his mouth, the vivid color of his eyes. She touched his hair, his face, his arm. For her it was a most demonstrative gesture, and it was his turn to close his eyes.

Theo, I cannot explain, but I have work to do. I hardly know how to begin it, or where, but it is of the greatest importance.

He caught her hand in his and pressed her fingers to his lips. When he opened his eyes, his usual smile was a ghost of itself. *Do you think Pol will let you go?*

He must. I have given Observatory their own Cantor.

Theo shook his head, but Sira insisted. *So I have, but only if you agree. A Cantor must serve willingly. He must choose the work, and the sacrifice.*

All my life I have wanted my own House, Theo sent, *but I never dreamed of my own Cantoris. I am not sure, even now, that it is possible.*

You are as Gifted a Cantor as any I have known, except Maestra Lu.

They looked at each other for a long time, knowing each other's joy, unable to avoid the pain that would come. Then Theo slowly, tenderly, put his hands on either side of Sira's face and kissed her fully on the lips. She did not pull back, though at the unaccustomed contact her stomach contracted strangely. His mouth was smooth and cool, and she tried to capture the moment in her memory, an indulgence that would not be soon repeated.

Come back to me, Sira. As soon as you can.

I will. I promise.

Theo flashed a sudden grin, merry and brave and steady. *I will serve you nursery fruit on your return!*

Sira found Pol in his apartments, and when she asked to speak with him, he led her through the varied clutter to the room with the long table on which he had shown her the artifact.

"I am going to leave Observatory when the summer is here," she told him without preamble. "Please arrange a guide for me, and when he has brought me to Ogre Pass he can return home."

Pol watched her through narrowed eyes. "I'm not going to let you do that," he rasped, with an air of finality.

"Your House has the Singer Theo now. I trained him for you. You owe this to me."

"My people have grown to like having a warm House. I don't know that the Singer Theo, fine though he is, can manage alone."

Sira stared at Pol. She felt no inclination to waste time arguing. "We will show you."

"The only way you can do that is for you to leave, Cantrix," Pol said heavily. "And I have told you, I will not allow it. I'm sorry," he added, surprisingly. "I see no choice."

The air around Sira began to sparkle dangerously, and her jaw grew tight with anger. She rose to leave, only looking back at Pol at the door. "I knew if I sang for you, you would think you had defeated me. You were wrong. I sang because of Theo, because his Gift is worth any sacrifice.

"You can never control me, Pol, any more than the Magistral Committee of Nevya could. You should seek a truce with the Committee. Your House members never need to live in the cold and dark again. You need a succession of Cantors and Cantrixes who are properly trained, and for that you need to rejoin the Nevyan community."

Pol, his face as hard as the cliffs around Observatory, folded his arms and said nothing.

The next morning Theo mounted the dais of the Cantoris alone. The sleepy House members who faithfully attended the early-morning ceremonies were already seated on the benches. Pol stood in back, as always. He stepped forward before Theo began.

"Where is Cantrix Sira?" he grated. The assembly looked back and forth, from him to Theo, curious and alarmed.

Theo felt their apprehension, and he grinned at them. Ignoring Pol, he said, "There is no need for concern." He bowed formally to the assembly, and took his seat as calmly as he had been doing each morning for months. He began in *Iridu*, modulated to *Aiodu*, and began to sing. Warmth and light swelled on the tide of his psi, and the room began to brighten, as always. The people smiled, comforted. As they had learned to do, they closed their eyes to listen.

Before the *quirunha* was finished, Pol offended all courtesy by stamping out of the Cantoris. Theo's concentration was so complete, so perfect, that he was unaware of Pol's departure. It had no effect on the *quirunha*.

When he stood to chant the final prayer, and bowed, receiving the answering bows of the people, Theo realized Pol was gone, and he smiled to himself. Let him look, he thought. Let him turn Observatory upside down. He will never find her.

For three days, Theo maintained the House *quiru* alone. Pol prowled the corridors, and asked questions of all the House members. He minutely examined the stables to see if *hruss* or tack were missing. All were accounted for. Even Sira's own saddle still hung on its ironwood peg, awaiting the day when she could use it again.

At evening of the third day, beside himself with rage and frustration, Pol pounded on Theo's door. Theo was practicing, but he laid the *filhata* aside, taking ample time to wrap it meticulously before opening the door.

"By the Six Stars, Singer, you will tell me where she is! Surely you would not let her try to find the Pass on her own?"

Theo grinned hugely. "Shall I sing for you, maybe a little something in the first mode, to help you relax? I do not think so much excitement can be good for you."

Pol controlled his temper with visible effort. His small eyes snapped with anger, but his rough voice was even. "Just tell me. I don't want her to die."

"She will not die. You have no need to fear for her."

"I sent a rider after her, all the way to the canyon. He didn't find her." Pol slumped against the doorjamb, and Theo took pity on him.

"Has the House been cold, Pol?" Pol shook his head. "Dark?" Another shake. "You are going to have to let her go."

Pol straightened and came into Theo's small room, looking around absently at its sparse furnishings. "It's true, Singer. The House has been as warm as ever. It has never been in better care." He folded his arms. "The Cantrix has given us a great deal. I want her to be safe."

Theo gestured to the door. "Come with me. I will show you where she is."

He led Pol down the corridors to the back of the House, where the abattoir doors opened onto the waste drop. A broad path lay within the reach of the House *quiru*, which was just beginning to fade for the hours of darkness. The two men stepped out onto the path, and Theo pointed down to the smaller mountain that bulked behind Observatory. A small circle of yellow light blossomed on a ledge of the mountain, perhaps an hour's ride away.

Pol looked at it and began to laugh, not his usual sardonic bark, but a rumble of mirth that took years from his appearance and infected Theo, too. Together they looked at Sira's camp *quiru* and laughed into the violet evening. Only when the House *quiru* began to noticeably diminish, and the cold to slip past it, did they step back in through the abattoir.

Theo sent to Sira, *You can come home now. All is well.*

Sira sent back, *I will. I will be there for your* quirunha *in the morning.*

Chapter Thirty-one

Sira did attend the *quirunha* the next day. She made her way down the slippery talus slope from her campsite in the first light of morning, and made the steeper climb up Observatory's peak just as the glow of the Visitor began to shine on the southern horizon. Sira walked into the Cantoris as Theo began with the ritual bow, and she and the other members of the assembly bowed in response.

Sira closed her eyes and listened to Theo. His technique was quite satisfactory, she thought. His voice was pleasant, lacking the polish that early training might have given it, but always true in pitch and inflection. His *quiru* had a strength and swiftness seldom equalled on the Continent. Observatory would be well served.

The House members had learned to recite the closing prayer. When it was over, the *quirunha* was complete. Sira stood where she was and spoke before Theo could leave the dais.

"Members of Observatory," she began. Surprised faces turned to her–

Theo's questioning, Pol's ironic, the people's curious. She walked forward, down the aisle between the benches.

Observatory had grown used to Sira's silence. She rarely spoke aloud in public. They moved uneasily in their seats, murmuring among themselves as she stepped up beside Theo.

"Forgive me for interrupting your *quirunha*," she said to Theo, and she included the assembly in her glance. "At Conservatory, where I trained, the day of departure from the House was the day on which a Singer became a full Cantor." Her voice rang through the Cantoris. Others heard her, and came in from the great room. The Cantoris was soon full, with people standing in the doorway and crowding the benches.

"Here at Observatory," Sira went on, "the ceremony is reversed. The Singer Theo has come to stay, and so it is on this day that I pronounce him to be a full Cantor. He has already proven himself. From this day, he is Cantor Theo v'Observatory, and as such, is to be accorded all the respect due his position and his title."

Sira turned and bowed to Theo. *Congratulations, Cantor.*

Thank you, Maestra, he sent with a wink. *And do not argue. You are* my *maestra.*

Sira stepped down then, away from the dais, leaving Cantor Theo to receive the congratulations and good wishes of his Hosue members. She watched from the doorway, where Pol joined her.

"I'm glad to see you back," he said.

"The summer is here," she told him. "There is a party in Ogre Pass. I want to go down to meet them."

He looked up at her, his intelligent ugly face resigned. "How do you know that?"

"I have seen their *quiru* these past two nights."

Pol nodded. "You're right. Our hunters spotted them yesterday." He bowed slightly. "I will arrange a guide. Your *hruss* is healthy, and your tack is ready."

"Have you considered my suggestion about renewing your ties to the Committee?"

"I have, Cantrix," he said. "I would appreciate your recommendation to them."

Sira measured Pol with a long look. She smiled a little, then bowed, deeply and formally. "It will be my honor," she said, "Magister Pol."

Pol laughed, but bowed stiffly to her in return. "Thank you, Cantrix Sira."

Sira looked back into the Cantoris, and saw Theo coming up the aisle. "When can I leave?" she asked, feeling a sudden bitter ache in her throat.

"Today," he answered, "if you wish."

"So I do," she responded softly. Pol turned away to make the arrangements, and Sira waited for Theo to join her. Together they walked slowly down the corridor to her room, and though they were in perfect accord, they neither touched nor conversed. Sira thought her chest would burst with her love, and she feared Theo must feel the same. Still in silence, they began to collect her few possessions.

It took no more than an hour for Sira to prepare. Morys, one of Observatory's riders, came by to announce that her *hruss* was saddled, and that he was ready to depart.

"I—" Sira began, then found she was unable to speak further. The purpose that had driven her these past days was suddenly drowned in a wave of grief. She hung her head in helpless misery, and Theo stepped forward.

"The Singer will be ready in half an hour," he told Morys. "We will meet you in the courtyard." The man nodded, and disappeared.

Heavily, Sira sat down on her cot. *This is so very hard.*

Theo sat next to her, but he did not touch her. *How can I ever thank you?*

You have already, in a thousand ways. She hardly dared lift her head for fear she would lose her composure. *I will miss you*, she sent, staring at her twined fingers.

I will be with you each moment, he answered. She took a trembling breath and looked into his eyes. His gaze was warm and reassuring.

There was nothing left to do, and after a time they rose to go to the courtyard. At the last moment, Theo pressed something small into Sira's hand. *For later.*

The *hruss* stood ready, its saddlepacks stuffed full of dried meat and grain. The two suns had begun their slow dance across the cloudless blue sky, and Sira stood in the courtyard with the reins in her hand to say fare-well to Observatory. She pushed back her furs to feel the mountain air chill her cheeks. The full warmth of summer would not reach the peak of Ob-servatory for some time yet.

She was surprised to find that Pol and a sizable contingent of House members had assembled on the steps, steps that were now smooth and straight and solid, to say goodbye to her.

She could think of nothing to say to them. She had been an unwilling guest in their House, yet she had worked hard and long for them. Several of the House members had tears in their eyes. Sira saw those tears, and accepted them as gifts.

Pol rasped, "Until you return, be well, Singer."

Sira bowed. At a signal from Pol, the House members retreated inside the double doors, leaving only Theo on the steps.

His smile was as bright as ever as he faced her, but she was as sure of his feelings as she was of the duty that was tearing her away from him. They stood for long moments in silence, the early suns glancing off the shrinking firn on the peaks around them. Then Theo, ever faithful, broke the mood. *Your guide is waiting.*

Sira nodded, and pulled herself up into the saddle.

I will be waiting, too, Theo added, and Sira turned her face away to hide the tears that slipped down her cheeks.

She was too late. He saw, and took a step forward, but she held up her narrow hand. *I cannot bear it.*

He stopped. *Sira, remember that I love you. Go with the Spirit.*

She wiped her cheeks with her hands, then turned back to Theo. *Goodbye, my dear friend.* Her face felt stiff and ugly with pain.

Theo's smile faded for just a moment, the blue of his eyes suspiciously bright, but he kept his control. *Be safe*, he sent. *And come back.*

I promise. She lifted her reins, and turned her *hruss*. She dared not look back as she rode out of the courtyard to join Morys, who waited among the trees. She felt Theo's presence, strong and calm, watching her go.

What am I doing? she asked herself, in a moment of panic.

You are doing what you need to do, Theo sent. He had read even her private thought.

Yes, my dearest dear, she sent back, comforted. Morys rode out to meet her, and led the way through the trees to the path down the mountain. *Goodbye, my Theo*, she sent.

Goodbye, my love, came the answer. She felt the warmth in his thought even after the contact was broken, and she was alone again.

Only then, when she could no longer hear him, did she look into her hand at his gift.

It was a fragment of metal strung on a thong, polished and imprinted with incomprehensible glyphs. It was Theo's necklace, which had been his mother's, and her father's before that. It was Theo's talisman, and now Sira's.

She placed the thong around her own neck, tucking the metal down inside her tunic over her heart. It was cold at first, then it grew warm against her skin. She pressed her fingers over it as she rode after Morys down the mountain. It seemed to vibrate with Theo's essence, from his soul to hers.

Thank you, she sent, sure he could not hear, but sending anyway. *Thank you.*

BOOK TWO:

SING THE WARMTH

Prologue

Sira watched as Theo modulated nimbly from *Aiodu* to *Doryu*. His hair had grown long, thick blond waves falling past his shoulders as he bent over the *filhata*. From time to time, he tossed his hair back with a quick movement, without disturbing the melody that flowed from the strings. Warmth billowed around them as he played, and the room brightened. He looked up once to assure the light was full and golden, the warmth secure, before he played a smooth cadence. He placed the flat of his hand on the strings and looked expectantly at Sira.

She sighed with pleasure, with pride, and with undeniable regret. He was ready.

Change was needed on Nevya, and change was coming. Sira felt it as clearly as she and all other Nevyans felt the long-awaited advent of summer. Something profound and essential was in the making, and in some way only the Spirit could comprehend, Sira and Theo were part of it, the two of them swept along as if by the waves of the Frozen Sea breaking against the rocky coast of the Continent.

Theo, she sent, then hesitated, wondering how to go on.

His eyes were as blue as hers were dark. When Nevya's wandering sun finally appeared to join its brother, the sky over the Continent would be that same blue, clear and intense, violet-tinged in the evenings. *What is it?* he asked. *Still not good enough?*

You know perfectly well how good it is. There is little more for me to teach you.

His crooked smile turned her heart, and the crinkle of his eyes made her breath catch in her throat. She might have stayed right here, singing beside Theo in the Cantoris, forever. But the force of the Gift drawing her away was too strong. She could not indulge herself any longer, and she saw in his face that he understood.

So, he sent. *We are at the end.*

Theo gazed at Sira's narrow face, her thin, strong lips. His eyes lingered on her eyebrow, scarred white by a *caeru* claw, and on her cropped hair. She kept it short, as if she were on the point of traveling at any moment. In truth, she had not left Observatory in four years.

I must find that boy, Zakri, she sent. *He is the next step.*

Well, you know the saying. He winked, trying to draw one of her rare smiles. *Even an* urbear *has a mate.*

Sira raised her eyebrows. *I suppose that applies, but I cannot guess its meaning.*

It only means no one is unique. Except, he teased, *perhaps the Cantrix Sira!*

Do not call me that! she sent, with spirit, but without rancor.

He laughed. However much she might protest, the title persisted, and with good reason. She had served Observatory as a full Cantrix. The House showed abundant evidence of her care, the people flourishing, the gardens growing, the children playing in health and security. Now, he knew, it was his turn. *You will be back.*

So I will. And I will think of you always.

He put his big hand on her long, narrow one for a precious moment. They rarely touched, and when they did, she always pulled away first.

I will be waiting for you, he sent.

Sira moved her hand, taking it from his to smooth her scarred eyebrow with her forefinger, a habitual gesture. She looked out through the thick window to the snowy peaks that hid Observatory from the rest of the Continent.

You will find the answers, he assured her.

She nodded. *With the help of the Spirit.*

Chapter One

Isbel spent a long time saying farewell to her home. She lingered in the practice rooms, stone-walled cubicles redolent of hours of *Doryu, Aiodu, Iridu*. She walked in the nursery gardens, remembering her friend Sira, who had disappeared without a trace in the Marik Mountains the year before. Isbel went to the *ubanyix*, too, and stroked the carved ironwood of the tub. She dipped her hand into the clear water and touched it to her cheeks, to blend with the tears there as she thought of Maestra Lu, her teacher, gone now with the Spirit beyond the stars.

Isbel's teachers and classmates had been all her family since the day she entered its doors as a frightened seven-year-old. Her mother, Mreen, had delivered her over to Conservatory, then gone back to her House, and died within the year.

The young Singers were gathered near the window of the great room, planning their last remarks to Isbel—the new Cantrix Isbel—just as she had done when others of her class left on their assignments. Cantrix Isbel. She would assume her title today. She hoped she was ready.

Isbel.

Isbel wiped her eyes with trembling hands, and smoothed her hair back into its binding. *Yes, Maestro Nikei. I am here.*

It is time.

Nikei's sending was gentle. The teachers knew how difficult it was for the young Singers to leave Conservatory, but Isbel doubted any of them could understand how truly bereft she felt. Still, this was her duty. Her personal feelings must be put aside as she took up her responsibilities in the House of Amric.

She straightened her shoulders and composed her face as best she could as she walked toward the great doors at the front of the House. She meant not to weep, but her eyes stung, and her lips trembled. Sira's ceremony had been cool and controlled. Arn, now Cantor of Perl, had smiled and waved. Jana, on her way to be Cantrix at Lamdon, had sobbed as she said her farewells. Isbel wanted very much to comport herself with dignity.

The people of Conservatory assembled in ranks on the wide steps facing the courtyard. Isbel pulled her *caeru* furs close around her face and fixed her gaze on the cobblestones as she passed through the crowd. She didn't lift them until she reached her traveling party.

One of Amric's riders stepped forward and bowed. He towered above Isbel, larger than life in his heavy furs. He led a shaggy *hruss* by the rein.

Isbel shrank back when she saw the size of the animal. She glanced around, a little panicked. Her mount was the smallest of all the party. She bit her lip, and took a step closer. She stretched her arm up, trying to reach the horn of the saddle, but she could not even graze it with her fingers.

The rider murmured, "Please forgive me, Cantrix," as he helped her to put her fur-booted foot into the wooden stirrup. Again he begged her pardon, and boosted her carefully up to the high-cantled saddle. Isbel realized, as she settled against the hard leather, that he was apologizing for touching her.

Until this moment she had not thought about what that meant. Her friends, her teachers—all of them touched and embraced as family. The Housemen and women of Conservatory did not touch Gifted ones, but the students hardly noticed that, occupied as they were with each other. At Amric, Isbel would have only her senior with whom she could be truly at ease, and he must be treated with the deepest respect. She would have to speak aloud almost constantly, as well. However would she become accustomed to it all?

Perched high on the mountain *hruss*, she gazed down past its broad head and drooping ears to Magister Nikei, Magister Mkel, and the remaining members of her class. The second-level students watched the events of the morning with composure, neither wonder-struck nor nervous. Their own ceremonies were still at least a summer away. The small class of first-level students observed everything with wide eyes. They had seen very few such rituals. They clung together like *caeru* pups on their first day out of the den.

The day was cloudy, and a bitter wind blew from the Mariks to nip at exposed skin. Isbel knew her ceremony must be short. The season of deep cold had Nevya firmly in its frigid grip.

Congratulations, Cantrix Isbel, Maestro Nikei sent. His use of her title began the ceremony, and the students joined in with enthusiasm.

Goodbye, Cantrix.

Good luck, Cantrix!

Cantrix Isbel, we will miss you.

The riders from Amric waited as their *hruss* shuffled their big hooves and puffed clouds of steam into the icy air. The riders could not hear this part of the ceremony, nor could the House members gathered with the Singers. Patiently, holding their furs around them, the unGifted watched in silence until the farewells from the Singers were over.

Two first-level students sobbed together as they tried to send to Isbel. They had not had long practice, and their sending was garbled.

Goodbye . . . Isbel, Cantrix, I mean . .

Isbel, we . . . we . . . with the Spirit! How often the little ones had clustered around her to hear her stories and songs as she tried to ease their homesickness and their longing for their mothers! And who, Isbel wondered, would tell them stories now?

Goodbye, Corin, she sent, flashing her dimples at them to make them smile. *Goodbye, Sith. Be well, and practice hard. I will think of you often.*

The silent messages ended all too soon. Little clouds of steamy breath hung before each face, a warning against staying out of doors too long. Magister Mkel cleared his throat, and concluded the ceremony.

"Cantrix Isbel," he said aloud. Threatening tears burned in Isbel's eyes. She knew the words that were coming. She blinked hard and squeezed her fingers together inside her new *caeru* fur gloves.

"Every Singer's true home is Conservatory," the Magister intoned. "Remember that we always wait for your return, by the will of the Spirit."

Isbel bowed to him, then clutched at the pommel of her saddle as she felt herself slip in her high seat. "Thank you," she whispered. There was more she had planned to say, but she no longer trusted her voice. She lifted her hand to the Magister and to all her House.

The House members bowed. The young Singers gazed up at her in silent intensity, each no doubt imagining their own turn, that day when they would start out as she was, to ride with a party of strangers to a strange House, and an unknown future.

Isbel swallowed, and set her lips so they would not tremble. She turned to the rider who held her reins. "I am ready." Her voice shook only a little, and though her chest hurt with holding back her tears, hold them back she did.

The tall rider handed the reins to her, and mounted his own *hruss*. Awkwardly, Isbel tried to imitate the way he held his reins, sat in his saddle. Never in her life had she ridden *hruss* by herself, nor even been out of doors since the last summer.

In a silence broken only by the huffing of the beasts and the clatter of their hooves against the cobblestones, the travelers rode out of the court-yard. At the last moment Isbel looked back over her shoulder at the faces of her friends and her teachers. The *hruss's* long strides made her sway in her saddle as it carried her away, down the snowy ride and around a stand of ironwood trees. Soon she could no longer see the people, but only the steep roofs of Conservatory outlined in the yellow glow of its *quiru*.

She sobbed twice, pressing her gloved hand to her mouth to muffle the sound. Then she drew a shuddering breath, and turned her face forward, toward Amric, her new House. She was an adult now, four summers old, more than twenty years. She was a full Cantrix, and she must behave accordingly. She prayed to the Spirit of Stars that she would be strong enough.

Kai v'Amric rode protectively close to the young Cantrix. He marveled that the power of the Cantoris should rest in such a small person. He watched her play her *filla* their first night out, when the party made their camp. The deft way she held the shining bit of carved ironwood to her lips, and the delicate melody she wove, seemed miraculous. He caught his breath as the *quiru* sprang up gracefully around her, warm and glowing in the early dark of the season.

How could it be, Kai wondered, that the Gift could be such a benefi-cent power in a person such as Cantrix Isbel, while in someone like that crazy boy at Amric it was like an enraged beast, lashing out at any provo-cation. That boy—Zakri, his name was—was an outcast. No one spoke to him. In fact, no one dared. He earned his keep by laboring among *hruss*, and anyone who valued his health knew enough to stay away from the stables when Zakri was there. The Housekeeper allowed him to stay at Amric only because he kept the night watch and promised not to bother anyone. Rumors abounded about his last House.

The Gift was a very different thing in this lovely girl, this brand-new Cantrix. Kai waited on her, bringing her tea and *keftet*, working the snow under her bedfurs to give her a smooth surface for sleeping. He bowed to her so often that she finally laughed, showing deep dimples in her pretty cheeks, and begged him to stop.

On the second day he knew she was saddle-sore. He waited for her to complain. He saw the awkward way she held her reins and moved in her saddle. He wanted to help her, to instruct her, but he knew better than to address a full Cantrix unless she spoke to him first.

Amric lay five days' ride to the northeast of Conservatory, six in bad weather. For Kai, this was an easy trip. The slow pace, the plentiful food, and the light duties of watching over Amric's new Cantrix made it almost a holiday. His older brothers, Rho and Tam, rode ahead with the guide, glancing back from time to time, but leaving him to his work without their usual teasing. The Cantrix's new Housewoman rode just behind them. So far she had not even spoken to her mistress, which was fine with Kai. He settled back into his saddle and grinned to himself.

"Is something funny?"

He straightened instantly. The young Cantrix's voice was light and musical, much as he would have expected. It was her red-brown hair and green eyes that surprised him.

"Oh, no . . . no, Cantrix. I was just thinking."

"Please tell me," she said. "And tell me what to call you." She had to look up at him from beneath the yellow-white *caeru* fur that circled her face. Kai's breath caught at her beauty, and something warm stirred in his belly.

A wave of shame swept him a moment later. One did not, could not, think such things about the Gifted. Well, itinerants, maybe, though he had never met one that raised such a thought in his mind. But this was a Cantrix, Conservatory-trained, inviolate, unreachable to the likes of an ordinary rider like himself. He said respectfully, "My name is Kai, Cantrix. I was just thinking what an easy ride this is."

She nodded to him, but her pretty lips formed a rueful pout. "Yet I was thinking how hard this saddle is, and wondering how you sit in it so easily." She shifted her weight, as if trying to find a position that didn't hurt.

"I ride almost every day. I'm a hunter," Kai said with pride. "I've hunted *caeru* more than two summers. Once my brothers and I" —he nodded toward his two brothers riding ahead of them—"we killed a *tkir*."

The Cantrix looked up at him once again, and Kai had to swallow as he looked into the clear green of her eyes. Like the first shoots of the softwood tree in summer, those eyes.

"What was it like?" she murmured.

"Oh, it's not a pleasant story, Cantrix," he said hastily, remembering the snarling attack of the *tkir* and the long scar his brother Rho still bore from its claws.

"I like all stories," the Cantrix said, and her dimples flashed. "I am a collector of stories."

Kai couldn't resist the dimples. He smiled down at her. "I will tell you, then, if you like." He moved his *hruss* a bit closer, careful that his leg should not inadvertently brush hers. "But I wouldn't think you'd want to hear about blood and arrows and such things."

"So I do," she said with a laugh, "if they are part of the story."

Kai grinned. "As you wish, then." He leaned back in his saddle and began his tale. At the most exciting moments the Cantrix turned her eyes up to him, and he found himself embellishing the account of the hunt to make her do it again and again. She was a patient and close listener, and he made the story last a long time. She smiled her thanks at the end.

He didn't hear her voice again that day until the camp was settled for the night. All the riders, and their young charge, were secure in their bedfurs, the *quiru* strong and warm around them and their *hruss*. Kai was almost asleep himself when he heard a slight sound.

He sat up to locate the source. He saw a small movement of the Cantrix's bedfurs, and he heard the sound again.

She was weeping, softly, trying to muffle the sound in her furs. Kai reached out his arm to comfort her, then drew it back, remembering. The glow of the *quiru* dimmed where she lay. Her unhappiness slowed the light, drew the warmth from the air, leaving an alarming little pocket of shadow around her.

Kai didn't know what to do. Who could comfort a Cantrix? He must neither touch her nor talk to her unless she spoke first. The tabu was as rigid as the trunk of an irontree.

Saddened, he lay down again. How lonely she must be! His baby sister would have been instantly swept up in the embrace of one of her big brothers, to cry against a shoulder until she felt better. This young Cantrix must weep alone in her bedfurs, with no one to offer solace.

Kai waited until the gentle sounds of her sobs ceased, then a little longer. When he sat up once more, the darkness was gone and she appeared to be asleep. He made certain her furs were tucked about her before he lay down again. He lay thinking, staring up at the cold dark sky beyond the light and warmth she had made. He watched the stars wheel above the *quiru* for a long time before he finally slept.

Chapter Two

The Houses on the Continent had been built so long ago that no one remembered their beginnings. Amric lay close to the Great Glacier, and the north wind continually blew the scent of ice and firn into its courtyard. Its thick stone walls seemed to have grown naturally out of the rocky landscape, looking as ancient as the fields of ice on which no creature walked but the *caeru* and the occasional *urbear* wandering east from the coast. Isbel found Amric cold and daunting. Its abundance of fur and leather and carved ironwood did not warm it for her. Even after she had been there for weeks, she yearned for the austerity of Conservatory, and for its company.

Her new senior was Cantor Ovan, a lean, pinched man of at least eight summers. He was remote at her welcoming ceremony, while Magister Edrus and the Housekeeper, Cael, were friendly and smiling. At her first *quirunha*, Cantor Ovan's black eyes burned at her, making her pitch tremble and her fingers slip once or twice on the strings of the *filhata*. She could barely follow his lead, and her voice wobbled in a fearful vibrato for several moments.

Ovan's own voice was reedy and harsh. His upper range, if he had ever had one, was gone. He played tortuously complex patterns on the *filhata*, as if to compensate for the ugliness of his singing. He had a habit of starting in *Aiodu*, then modulating abruptly into *Iridu* without warning or preparation. Their first *quirunha* was half over before Isbel could grasp his musical idea and follow him. His voice overbalanced hers, and there was nothing she could do about it.

Sira, she was sure, would have dominated even Cantor Ovan. She wished her friend were her to advise her, or even better, to play the *quirunha* in her place. Ignore him, she imagined Sira saying. Keep the accompaniment simple, let your voice spin. He is not the Singer you are.

But, Isbel thought sadly, I am not the Singer Sira is. And who knows where she is now?

She kept a respectful face turned to her senior, and did as she had been trained to do. Her first *quirunha* at Amric were not beautiful, but they did their work. The warmth and the light flowed out from the Cantoris, not as swiftly as she might have liked, but it enveloped the House, refreshing the *quiru*, keeping Amric safe for another day.

Cantoris hours were the hardest part of her new assignment. Every day, after the morning meal, Isbel took her seat on the dais next to her senior. Housemen and women, in their brightly-dyed tunics, lined up before them. Sometimes one or two of the Magister's people were there in their dark tunics, waiting their turn for healing. Isbel held her *filla* in tense fingers, breathing deeply to calm herself. Healing was hard enough without being frightened half to death.

She had reason to be nervous. Her first Cantoris hours had been disastrous.

A *hruss* had tripped on one of the great ironwood suckers that reached from tree to tree under the snow. The beast had fallen with all its great weight on its rider's leg, shattering the ankle. Ovan seemed unaffected by the ghastliness of broken bone and torn flesh. He played an *Iridu* melody and directed his psi into the mangled ankle without flinching. Isbel followed him as she had been taught, so that she might learn through observation, but the injured man's pain made her gasp and writhe in agony.

To her great shame, her senior abruptly ceased playing and turned his hard eyes on her. *Stop*, was all he sent. Isbel instantly closed her mind and her eyes.

The Housemen accompanying the rider set the leg under Ovan's direction, and the Cantor played again to heal the skin and muscle around the break. Isbel could not even watch.

When it was done, Ovan looked down his beaked nose at her, his lips compressed, nostrils pinched white. *Are they not teaching healing at Conservatory any longer?*

Yes, Cantor Ovan, they are. She ducked her head to avoid his eyes, and a lock of hair escaped its binding and fell untidily against her cheek.

It is not evident to me, Ovan went on. *Nor was it to that injured man.*

The House members standing before them watched curiously. Isbel felt their eyes on her, and her cheeks flamed. She longed to run right out of the Cantoris.

I—I need more practice, she sent.

You need more shielding.

I know, she answered miserably. *It is my weakness.*

He turned his back on her in a way that no one watching could have missed. When Isbel raised her head she saw the rider Kai watching from the back of the Cantoris, and she wished that he, of all people, had not been there to witness her humiliation. As soon as she could, she hurried from the Cantoris, her eyes on the floor. She avoided the great room, missing the mid-day meal rather than endure the glances of the House members.

Over the weeks since that first calamity, her healing had improved somewhat. If someone's pain or illness upset her, she hid it as best she could. Today a Housewoman with a bit of rag wrapped around her hand stepped up to the dais. Isbel watched as the woman undid the wrapping and held her burned hand out for Ovan to see. When he picked up his *filla*, his melody was uninspired, but the Housewoman closed her eyes and sighed, and Isbel thought his psi must be doing its work. She shielded herself carefully, and tried to follow, closing her own eyes, sending her psi after Ovan's as he soothed the blistered skin.

There was so little experience to be had in healing at Conservatory. Only the earaches and sore throats of the Singers gave the students practice. The youngest ones had always sought Isbel when they were sick, and until now she had believed herself adept with their complaints.

The ailments she saw now were far more upsetting. There were cuts and burns from the kitchen workers and the tanners. There had been something wrong with the breathing of a tiny baby, which brought tears to Isbel's eyes, but no idea of how to help. When she shielded herself, as she was supposed to, her psi seemed useless, aimless, unable to find the seat of the trouble. But she dared not repeat the experience of those first Cantoris hours, when Kai and the other House members had witnessed her humiliation.

The Housewoman with the burn bowed her thanks to Cantor Ovan and went back to the kitchen. A flushed, feverish Houseman stepped up in her place.

Ovan turned to Isbel. *Cantrix. Surely you can help this man? It is only a fever.*

She bit her lip. *I will try, Cantor Ovan.* Her breath came quickly as she looked down at the Houseman.

Her senior settled back in his carved chair, his *filla* idle in his lap. He gazed at her from beneath lowered eyelids.

Isbel took up her own *filla*. The man looked terribly ill, his skin ashen above his bright blue tunic. There was a slight movement behind him, and Isbel realized with dismay that the Magister, Edrus, had come into the Cantoris. He took a seat on one of the side benches.

Isbel closed her eyes, and put her *filla* to her lips. She cast about for a melody, anything, in order to begin.

She tried a tune in *Aiodu*, to carry her psi out and into the man's mind. Through her shielding, she could feel nothing of his discomfort. Ovan was following her, she knew, but if she could not feel the man's illness, how could she help him? For some moments she played, searching for a way, but finding none.

Bit by bit, she relaxed her shields, wary of her senior's criticism. Perhaps, if she opened herself just a little . . .

She felt herself, all at once, engulfed by the misery of the sick man. She felt his nausea and aches as acutely as if they were in her own body. She swallowed, and stopped. Opening her eyes, she said weakly, "This man needs to sit down."

Her senior arched a dark eyebrow, but a Housewoman nearby pushed a chair forward. Isbel saw the Magister watching, and quickly closed her eyes again, trying not to be distracted. A thrill of nerves fluttered under her breastbone. She had to brace herself to enter the Houseman's mind again. She tried to think only of him, tried not to give in to the illness itself. If her senior would just give her time, let her find a way . . .

She tried a different melody this time, in *Doryu*, as she had heard Maestro Nikei do for infections. She spun out her psi to search for the source of the man's fever. It was so difficult, so confusing. With the little Singers, the work had been straightforward: their ears hurt, or their teeth, and their young minds were clear and easy to read. This man was not Gifted, nor was his illness easily identified. How was she going to lower his fever if she could not find the source?

Hot, was all she could read from the man. He was hot, and weak. She tried to examine other parts of him, feeling with her own mind the sickness in his stomach, the trembling of his hands, the burning of his eyes against their lids. Isbel's melody faltered. She could not find what was wrong. All she could think of to do was to soothe and quiet him, as she had the children in the dormitory at Conservatory.

She played a soft air in *Iridu*, for sleep, one she had learned when she had only two summers. She used feathery touches of psi to try to cool the man's feverish mind, to make his limbs cease their trembling and his muscles relax. When she opened her eyes the man's head was tipped back against his chair, his eyes closed. He was asleep.

Isbel turned to Ovan. *It was all I could do, Cantor. I am sorry. I do not know what causes his illness.*

Ovan's black eyes flicked away from her. *Apparently not.* He signaled to two Housemen to help the man up. They put their shoulders under his arms and assisted him out of the Cantoris, his head lolling sleepily.

Isbel saw Magister Edrus leave also, and she sighed in relief. *Cantor Ovan, did you know what was wrong with him?*

He had already turned back to the waiting line of people. *A fever*, he sent in an offhand way. *Probably brought in from some other House. That is all.*

Isbel stared at his sharp-nosed profile. Was it possible that Cantor Ovan no more understood the Houseman's illness than she did? It was a rebellious idea, a disrespectful one, and she kept it very low, lest he hear it.

The lines of Ovan's face revealed nothing to her. It was beyond belief that her entire future was tied to this cold, unbending man. She was inextricably bound, with him, to the House they were both pledged to serve.

She turned back to the waiting Housemen and women, but she did not see them now. She saw the days and weeks and months of her life stretching out before her, building into long years of work and loneliness, of youth come and gone, of friends never seen again.

O Spirit, she wondered. How will I bear it?

Chapter Three

Kai lived with his family in a crowded apartment on the first level. Their rooms were too near the waste drop and the tannery, and too far from the great room, but they were big enough for the entire family to be together. Kai's older brothers and a younger sister were already hardworking House members like himself. His parents had two more boys still to raise, but they wanted all their children at home until they should mate and move into their own apartments.

"Kai," his brother Rho said. "Kai, I'm talking to you! Six Stars, where's your ears, Houseman?"

Kai had been staring blankly at the wall before him. He blinked and shook his head. "Sorry, Rho. What is it?"

"I asked if you want to come to the *ubanyor*. I'm ready now."

Kai rubbed his eyes hard to push away the thoughts that had distracted him. They were thoughts he shouldn't be thinking anyway. "I'm coming. Just a minute." He reached into an overfull cupboard for a fresh tunic and followed Rho out of the apartment, dodging the game of stone-and-bone his two youngest brothers had spread on the floor.

In the corridor, the smell of the tanning vats was heavy in the air. Rho sniffed and wrinkled his nose. "Smells strong," he said, and grinned. "They're working on the carcasses we brought in yesterday. We gave them plenty to do!"

"So we did," Kai answered. "The whole House must smell of it."

With their father and two other hunters, Rho and Tam and Kai had made a large kill just north of Deception Pass. Even their itinerant Singer's *hruss* had been heavily loaded with *caeru* when they rode home. There would be an abundance of meat for the tables in the great room, and the bones and pelts would keep many Housemen and women busy for some time.

Kai wondered if the odor of the tanning vats would reach the new Cantrix in her upper-level apartment. Perhaps she even knew of the hunting trip, and the riches they had brought back for their House. He tried to imagine her exclaiming over the size and value of their kill, her green eyes bright with admiration at his skill and courage. He couldn't picture it. More likely, he told himself, the Gifted gave no thought to the necessities of life beyond those they themselves provided. And in truth, why should they?

He looked around at the strong yellow light of the *quiru*. He knew when he stepped into the water of the *ubanyor* that it would be hot and soothing, and that it would be so because one of the Gifted–those untouchable, unapproachable creatures–had warmed it. They simply played one of their secret melodies on the little *filla* until the steam rose from the water and the leafy herbs swirled on its surface. Why should such a person—a person who could bring light to the darkness and heat to cold air and water—why should anyone with such power trouble themselves with questions of food or furs or tools?

The *ubanyor* was crowded with Housemen, and the brothers saw that even the Housekeeper Cael lounged at one end. Kai and Rho greeted several friends as they dropped their soiled clothing in an untidy pile and stood their boots against the wall. They lowered themselves with grunts of pleasure into the steamy water, and Rho ducked his head under its surface.

"Now this is living," he said, sputtering water from his mouth and nose. He reached into a carved niche for a cake of the smooth brown soap made in Amric's own abattoir.

Kai rubbed his face with wet hands and looked around the *ubanyor*. "By the spirit," he muttered to his brother. "Look who bathes with the Housemen!"

Rho followed Kai's nod to the other end of the great ironwood tub, and saw Cantor Ovan, his body slight and pale compared with their own husky ones, sitting apart from the other bathers. "So he does," said Rho in a low tone, "and so we have a nice hot bath today." He stretched his strong arms luxuriously. "I may spend the whole morning here."

But Kai turned away from the sight of the Cantor's narrow face and disdainful expression. His brother caught the movement and elbowed him. "What is it now, Kai? Have you taken a dislike to the Gifted?"

Kai shook his head. "Only that one," he muttered.

Rho leaned closer. "What is it?" he whispered. "Come on, tell me. What could a Cantor have done to Kai the hunter?"

Kai shook his head again. "Never mind." But Rho was having none of that. He prodded him again, laughing, insisting. Kai looked back at the Cantor, sitting alone and silent in the water, in the company but not of it.

"I attended the *quirunha*," he said quietly. "Her first *quirunha*. And Cantoris hours."

"Whose first? Oh, you mean the new Cantrix? The little one we brought here?"

"Who else, furbrain?" Kai laughed a little, but then his mouth tightened as he remembered. "He was cruel to her."

"How do you know?" Rho asked. "Are you Gifted, now, that you can hear them talk with their minds the way they do?"

Kai made a noise of disgust. "No! By the Spirit, I hear enough with my ears, and I see with my eyes. He made it as hard as he could for her, this poor girl just out of Conservatory."

Rho shook more water from his hair and leaned back against the edge of the tub. "Brother," he said weightily, as if he had much more than one summer above Kai's four. "That is not a girl you're talking about. That's a full Cantrix, Conservatory-trained. Such a person doesn't need Kai v'Amric to fight her battles."

Kai tipped back his head to drench his hair, kept short like that of all those who earned their living out of doors, and began to soap it furiously. "Maybe not," he muttered. "But I'm here if she does."

*

When Cantoris hours ended, and Isbel stood to leave, she saw that a Housewoman with a very young child waited beyond the ironwood benches. Cantor Ovan saw her too, and sighed. Isbel wished she could chide him as he so often chided her. It was not the Housewoman's fault that Cantoris hours had been long this morning. The woman came forward slowly, reluctantly. The child dragged its feet beside her.

Was she afraid? Isbel wondered. She looked into the woman's face, and the glowing face of her little daughter, and she knew immediately that it was not fear that slowed the woman's steps. It was grief.

"Cantor Ovan," the Housewoman said, with a careful bow.

"Yes?" he asked impatiently. "Who are you?"

Again Isbel wished she could admonish him. He did not even know his House members' names unless they lived on the upper level. The Housewoman, however, apparently saw nothing untoward. She caressed her child's hand in a nervous gesture, and avoided Ovan's eyes.

"I'm Brnwen, Cantor. Cantrix," she added, with a hasty bow in Isbel's direction.

Isbel gave her as warm a smile as she dared with her senior sitting so stiffly beside her. "Hello, Brnwen," she murmured. Brnwen seemed surprised by the greeting, and was still.

"What is it, Housewoman?" Cantor Ovan said. "We are very busy, you know."

"Oh," Brnwen said with a start. The look of suffering in her pale face intensified. "It's my daughter," she whispered.

"What is wrong with her?"

Brnwen looked up then, and the pain in her eyes made Isbel press a hand to her own breast in sympathy, though she knew even that small response would bring Ovan's criticism. There was a moment of tense silence before the woman blurted, "She's Gifted," in an ugly tone. It was as if the words had to be thrust out of her, forced out against great resistance.

Just so, Isbel thought, it must have been to give birth to the child, and now the mother must make a second great effort.

Cantor Ovan turned to the little girl and eyed her. "That is hardly something wrong, Housewoman. If it is true."

Brnwen dropped her head again, holding her daughter's hand so tightly the little girl whimpered.

"In any case, it will be for us to decide," Ovan went on. "Leave her here with us. We will need to test her."

Brnwen looked up, horrified. "Leave her? Oh, Cantor, please. Can't I stay? She was born only two years before last summer. She's never been away from me, even for a moment."

Ovan tutted sharply. "If she is Gifted, she will have to go away from you, will she not?"

Tears spilled over Brnwen's cheeks, and the child began to sob too. Ovan made an exasperated noise. "You see? How can we test her with this going on?"

"Excuse me, Cantor Ovan," Isbel interjected, rising quickly so he would not prevent her. "I believe I am rather good with children. I will test her, and I do not mind her mother's presence in the least."

Her senior looked at her narrowly, and Isbel thought he might object

simply on principle. But the sounds and aromas of the mid-day meal beginning in the great room wafted through the doors, and he nodded. "All right,"
he said aloud, then sent, *Are you sure you can test her? Be wary of her
mother's ambition. There must be no mistake.*

Isbel only nodded, keeping her thoughts pressed low. Behind her shielding
she was appalled that he would think this unhappy woman had brought her
daughter to them out of ambition. She looked at Brnwen's wet cheeks and
at the way she knelt to circle her daughter with her arm as she dried her
tears on the little girl's soft curls. The honor that would come to Brnwen
and her mate for producing a Gifted child would hardly allay the pain the
mother would feel when her child left her.

Children at Conservatory grew away from their parents. Each summer brought family visits, but the students dreaded them. By the time the
five years between summers had passed, parents and children were strangers
to each other. The students were accustomed by then to the intimacy of
sending their thoughts to other Gifted ones. Conversing aloud was a burden
and a hindrance. There was never anything to say, in any case. The visits
ended uncomfortably, bewildered parents standing apart from their children, the young Singers eager to say goodbye and return to their dormitory.

Brnwen was right to grieve. When her little one went to Conservatory,
she would no longer be Brnwen's daughter, but Nevya's. It was a terrible
sacrifice.

It was nevertheless a necessary one. Isbel stepped down from the dais
to stand close to the mother and daughter. Cantor Ovan left the Cantoris,
looking back over his shoulder as he walked down the aisle between the
benches. Isbel smiled reassuringly at Brnwen, and at the child, but she
waited for the doors to close behind her senior.

"Now, Brnwen," she said gently. "I know this is hard for you. If your
little one is Gifted . . . What is her name?"

"She's called Trisa," Brnwen said, rising, not releasing the child's hand.

"Ah. If your Trisa is truly Gifted, she may be feeling all your emotions,
your fear and your sadness." Isbel looked down at the child. Though her
rosy cheeks were still marked by tears, she looked back at Isbel with eyes
bright with curiosity. "Trisa is four, then?" Isbel asked.

Brnwen lifted her shoulders. "We always count summers. She was
born before last summer, so she has one."

"Five years between summers," Isbel said. "Last summer was two
years ago." She knelt by Trisa and gazed into her clear blue eyes. "Hello,
Trisa."

"Hello," the child answered in a high, sweet voice.

Isbel looked up at Brnwen. "I am going to talk to Trisa without speech.
If you will be patient for a moment . . . I am going to take her hand from
you. It helps in the testing if I can touch her, just her hand."

Brnwen's eyes filled with fresh tears. Her misery caused a physical
sensation in Isbel's own breast. Trisa began to sob again.

Isbel rose from her knees and sat down on the edge of the dais. She
waited quietly for Brnwen to regain control, and for Trisa, who had buried
her face in her mother's trouser leg, to stop crying. It took some minutes
for mother and daughter to compose themselves. Isbel sat still, trying to
shield herself, but intensely aware of their emotions.

At last Brnwen, with dragging steps, led the little girl to Isbel. She held out the tiny hand, releasing it at the last moment so her own fingers would not touch Isbel's.

Isbel held the child's fingertips with a gentle pressure, and Trisa gazed up at her with interest. Brnwen stepped back to sit on one of the benches, watching.

"Trisa," Isbel said. "Will you close your eyes, please?"

The girl looked at her mother and received a nod. She closed her eyes obediently, her long lashes lying against her cheeks like the thin shadows of softwood trees against the snow.

Trisa, Isbel sent. *Can you hear me?*

There was a blurred, but definite, response from the child.

If you can, Isbel went on, *please nod your head.* She sent a mental picture of a nod.

Trisa nodded her head—once, twice, three times—with her eyes still closed.

Thank you, Trisa, Isbel sent. *You may open your eyes now.*

The little girl opened her eyes to stare in wonder at Isbel. "Good," she piped. "I like it."

Brnwen came to stand behind her daughter. "She is Gifted, isn't she, Cantrix?"

"Yes. How did you know, Housewoman?"

Brnwen put her hands on the little curly head. "Whatever I feel, she feels. If I decide to go to the *ubanyix*, she waits by the door. If I'm tired, she wants to lie down."

"You have still some time before she is called, Brnwen," Isbel said. "You will see her every summer afterward, too, if you wish to go to Conservatory."

The Housewoman's eyes were bleak and knowing. Isbel knew she had given Brnwen little comfort, but there was none to offer. She watched them leave, the child reaching up to hold her mother's arm as if the four-year-old could soothe the adult. They moved as one person with two parts.

How sad, Isbel mused, that the Gift should be both a blessing and a curse. I cannot imagine life without it, and this Housewoman cannot imagine what it is to have it. Trisa will leave her, and make a new family at Conservatory. She will feel the pain of separation in her turn, when she leaves Conservatory to enter the Cantoris. It is hard, this life. But if we did not do our duty, what would happen to our people?

Isbel had little appetite for the mid-day meal. When she left the Cantoris she turned away from the great room, and walked, her head bowed, toward her own room.

In the distance she saw the hunter Kai, leaving the *ubanyor* with his brother, but she, a Cantrix, could hardly confide her sorrows in a mere Houseman. She was alone. She walked slowly up the staircase and into her apartment, with only the distant memories of her own mother, gone years ago beyond the stars, to keep her company.

Chapter Four

The long months dragged for Isbel as she settled into her routine at
Amric. It was strange to have rooms all to herself. She tried to create a
feeling of home in her apartment, placing her few possessions carefully on
tables and shelves, drawing a good chair up by the window that looked out
over the courtyard. She sat there to practice so she could watch the snow
fall or the pale sunlight sparkle on the tips of the ironwood trees. She yearned
for companionship.

Housekeeper Cael had made a special effort to make her rooms
attractive. Finely worked split leather panels hung on the walls, and the
floors and cot were thick with *caeru* furs. Isbel wondered if her senior
kept such things in his own rooms. He had never invited her to his apartment, and she knew nothing of his private habits. He disappeared each
evening immediately after the meal, giving her no chance to ask him
anything.

Isbel liked the leather hangings. Their firm surfaces gave the acoustics
of the room a nice ring, and she was fascinated by their workmanship.
Intricate patterns—shapes that looked natural but were not—had been
painstakingly tooled into them. She knew the House members of Amric
took special pride in anything they could make from leather.

When she was tired of practicing, or of simply gazing out the window,
she looked at the patterns in their hangings and wondered about the people
who had made them. She wished she could talk to them, ask them things,
hear their stories.

Only one event broke the monotony of those first months. There was a
story in it, but it was a frightening one. At an hour she could not have
measured, in the middle of one dark night, a Houseman came to her door,
looking pale and frightened.

"I'm sorry, Cantrix Isbel—so sorry to disturb you, but we can't wake
Cantor Ovan, and we need a Singer at the stables!" The man looked as if
he had been roused from his own bed, his hair standing every which way
and his tunic creased and rumpled.

"I will come, of course, Houseman," Isbel said. "I need just a moment
to dress."

He stepped back from the door hastily, as if afraid the Cantrix might
come out in her nightclothes. "Do you need your Housewoman?"

Isbel shook her head, and closed the door. Why could they not wake
Ovan? And why in the name of the Spirit did they need a Singer in the
middle of the night?

As she dressed, her heart pounded at the thought that someone might
be injured, and she would have to face some dreadful mess of blood and
pain. It was her duty, she reminded herself. She was their Cantrix.

With trembling fingers, she picked up her *filla* from its shelf and tucked
it inside her tunic. She took one deep breath and released it before opening
the door again.

The Houseman led her quickly down the staircase. The House was silent around them, and their boots whispered on the stone floor as they hurried down the corridor toward the stables. An odd moaning met them as they drew close, and Isbel tried to breathe steadily, promising herself she would be brave and strong.

When the door opened to the stables, Isbel saw at once why they needed a Singer. At first she felt only relief that there was no gross injury to deal with. But as she reached for her *filla* she realized how serious the situation could have been, and she trembled again.

"What happened?" she asked. Her voice sounded brittle in her ears.

The Housekeeper was on his knees beside a man who had collapsed on the floor. It was the man's continuous moaning, a kind of monotonous whimper, she had heard in the corridor.

"That *hruss* boy," Housekeeper Cael answered shortly. "Donel here upset him, and this is what happened!" He swept an arm about him to point out the trouble.

Isbel could hardly have missed it. The stables lay in a deep pocket of shadow, a dark and ugly gap in the *quiru*. It was cold in the room, and growing noticeably colder at every minute. The *hruss* in the loose boxes stamped nervously, making deep rumbling sounds in their throats. The Houseman with Isbel also shifted from foot to foot and rubbed his hands, not really cold yet, but fearful of it. Every Nevyan had a terror of the deep cold.

Isbel brought out her *filla* and played a swift and efficient melody in *Iridu*. It was not difficult to repair the *quiru*, to fill the darkness with warmth and light once again. But it was frightening to realize that such a rip in its fabric was possible.

When the stables were bright and warm once more, Isbel went to the Houskeeper, who still knelt by the groaning Donel. "What is the matter with the Houseman?"

Cael, usually a kind and cheerful man, was grim-faced, and his voice was angry. "I don't know," he said. "He was like this when we found him."

"It's that blasted boy!" cried the Houseman at the door. "We never should have let him come here!"

"The boy had to live somewhere," Cael said. "We could hardly send him out in the cold, could we? But he won't be able to stay now."

Isbel looked around, but she saw no one else. "Where is he?"

"He's probably up in his attic, and good riddance!" the Houseman said. "It's just like that one at Soren," he added darkly. "That one killed a man, stopped his heart, and the Committee never did a thing about it."

"What could they do?" Cael asked. "The boy at Soren ran right out of the House, and they didn't find him till the next morning. Not much you can do to punish a frozen corpse."

Isbel stared at Cael in horror. "Outside?" she breathed.

"Frozen to death at less than two summers," he snapped. "And that's what these itinerants get when they don't properly train their children!"

Isbel looked down at the man on the floor. His eyes were half-open, staring at nothing, and his face was pale and damp. She raised her *filla* once again, thrusting away her questions to concentrate, mustering her courage to try to help the man.

Donel's odd moaning went on and on, a wordless arrhythmic sound that ceased only when he took a breath. Isbel closed her eyes and began a slow tune in *Aiodu*. She extended a tentative fibril of psi, reaching for Donel's mind.

The darkness she found chilled her. Donel's consciousness had been thrust away, violently, in some way Isbel could not understand. His moaning was his attempt to touch the world, to stay in contact with what he knew. She cast about for a way to help him, but there was no physical injury to heal. His mind was beyond her reach.

She abandoned her melody and opened her eyes. "Housekeeper, I cannot help him," she said simply. "I think he will heal, in time, but just now there is nothing I can do."

"Do you think perhaps . . . your senior . . ." Cael's words trailed off. Isbel knew he was trying not to offend her.

She tried to speak composedly. "Perhaps, yes. We should certainly ask him."

"I pounded on his door," the Houseman said again. "There was no answer."

Cael frowned, and Isbel caught a flash of feeling from him, some deep worry he was trying to hide. He stood up, and she rose with him. "We'll need a litter," he told the Houseman. The Houseman hurried away.

"What about the boy, the boy who did this?" Isbel asked. "He must need help, too."

"His name is Zakri," Cael said. "He'll have to leave the House. I feel sorry for him, but he's completely out of control."

"But he must have a very strong Gift!" Isbel protested.

"It's no good, that Gift," Cael said in a flat voice. "Those itinerants should take better care of their children."

"I do not understand what you mean."

Cael made an abrupt gesture with his hand, as if to dismiss an entire group of Nevyans. "Itinerants!" he exclaimed. "We need some, obviously, but boys like this one—" He broke off, and folded his hands together. "Never mind, Cantrix Isbel. Itinerant Singers are no concern of yours, though they're a great concern to the Committee just now. I'm sorry we had to wake you. You'll be tired tomorrow, I'm afraid."

Isbel smiled at him. "I promise I will not, Housekeeper. I am glad to be of help. Please let me know how Donel fares, perhaps in a day or two."

"I will. Can you find your way back to your apartment?"

"So I can." She looked around her. "Do you not think I should at least talk to this boy—this Zakri?"

Cael shook his head. "Definitely not. It's not safe. This is not the first time he's made trouble. But it's the last time at Amric!"

They said good night, and Isbel went slowly back through the quiet House to her own rooms. Still she wondered about the boy. How terrible it must be, to bear a wild and untrained Gift, to be shunned and isolated. She wished there were something she could do for him.

After the incident in the stables long weeks passed without anything interesting happening. Isbel heard no more about Zakri. Cael told her Donel was beginning a slow recovery. Ovan never spoke of that night, and Isbel did not know whether the story had even reached his ears. Day after day, week after week passed with nothing to break the monotony of work and loneliness.

Isbel sat by the window in her apartment, practicing modulations from *Lidya* to *Mu-Lidya*. Sira's had been effortless, one mode mysteriously melting into the other, the lowered third of *Lidya* becoming the second degree of *Mu-Lidya* in the most natural way. Isbel played the transition over and over, searching for the fluid fingering she remembered. She barely heard the careful tapping on her door. She put the flat of her hand on the *filhata* strings to stop the tone, and listened to the knock. "Come in, Yula," she called, then instantly regretted it. Yula would think she had been listening to her mind. Spying.

Isbel's Housewoman was only slightly older than Isbel herself. Isbel was sure Cael had chosen her in hopes she would be good company for the new Cantrix. But Yula was horribly shy, her nervous fingers forever pulling on strands of her brown hair so they came loose from their binding and straggled across her blue tunic. And she was terrified of all Singers.

The girl opened the door, ducking her head and bowing nervously, making Isbel sigh. She could not think how to reassure her.

"Excuse me, Cantrix," Yula blurted hastily. "The Magister wants you." When she raised her head, her eyes were round with alarm. "The Housekeeper's with him, and Cantor Ovan!" She pinched her tunic with stubby fingers.

Isbel said mildly, "All right, Yula," and sighed again as the Housewoman hastily backed out of the room to stand fidgeting in the corridor.

It was an unusual summons, though Magister Edrus regularly attended the *quirunha*, and Cael often appeared at Cantoris hours. Rebelliously, Isbel reflected that the only unpleasant person at this gathering would be her senior. She pressed the thought far down where Ovan could not hear it, and smiled at her own foolishneess.

It was lovely simply to have a diversion. She took a *caeru* bristle brush to her hair to tuck it into a fresh binding, and smoothed her dark tunic over her trousers before going out to join her Housewoman.

Yula set off at a quick trot toward the Magister's wing. She made a comic sight, with errant strands of hair flying about, turning her head frequently to make sure her mistress was following. Isbel had to bite her lip to keep from giggling. She saw no reason to be fearful. Day after day she spoke to no one but her senior, her Housewoman, and occasionally the Housekeeper. She doubted she would be chastised for being lonely and bored!

Yula led the way down a long, broad staircase, then up another. They walked past widely-spaced doors through a corridor liberally draped with tooled leather hangings. The thick limeglass window midway down its length faced a different direction from the one in Isbel's rooms, affording a spectacular view of the expanse of the Great Glacier, an expanse of deep, silvery ice stretching off into the distance.

Yula stopped before a door at the very end of the corridor. She gave her mistress a hasty bow, and retreated, leaving Isbel to knock on the Magister's door herself.

The Magister's Houseman was not so shy as Yula. He was slight and gray-haired, and wore a tunic of a dignified dark red, befitting one who served on the upper level of the House. His bow was elegant. "Cantrix Isbel," he said smoothly. "Please come in. I hope you'll take some tea?"

Isbel stepped into a spacious and attractive room, full of light from a great window that filled most of one wall. The ironwood furnishings gleamed with polish, and furs were thick upon the stone floor. She imagined she could take her feet right out of her boots in this room, walk about barefoot, and still not feel the cold. There were numberous *obis*-carved objects scattered about on tables and shelves, and even more of the tooled leather panels.

Cantor Ovan sat beneath the window, cradling an ironwood cup in his thin hands. The Housekeeper stood beside him. The Magister rose when Isbel entered, and both he and Cael bowed. "Cantrix Isbel, I'm so glad you could join us."

Isbel bowed in return. Magister Edrus was rather young, his father having died early and passed the Magistership on to him. He smiled at her pleasantly. There was no tension in the room. Even Ovan looked reasonably content. With a flash of dimples, Isbel murmured her thanks to the Houseman for the cup of tea and the tidbit of nursery fruit he served her.

"We would have given you more warning, but an itinerant arrived only this morning with the news. I hope we haven't inconvenienced you." Housekeeper Cael spoke with just the right amount of respect for her station and solicitude for her youth.

Again, Isbel showed her dimples. "Of course not, Housekeeper." She could have added, It is a great treat simply to be in company! She cast her eyes to her lap and shielded her mind, knowing her senior would never approve of such exuberance.

Magister Edrus spoke. "We are expecting a visitor within the week. Cantrix Sharn, senior Cantrix of Lamdon, will be coming here, is in fact traveling to all the Houses."

Isbel raised her head. "Cantrix Sharn? That is a surprise!"

Edrus smiled. "A pleasant surprise, don't you think?"

Isbel felt her cheeks warm, and she had to resist the urge to press her palms to them. "Yes, of course, Magister. It is just that my friend, that is, Cantrix Sira said—Well, I would have thought Cantrix Sharn perhaps too frail for such a trip."

Sira had admired Sharn very much. On her ill-fated trip to Lamdon, Sharn had been kind to Sira, and impressed her with her perceptiveness. Only their old teacher, Maestra Lu, had exceeded Cantrix Sharn in Sira's estimation, and Isbel knew that was no small achievement. It had never been an easy thing to win Sira's admiration.

Edrus said, "It's true, Cantrix Sharn is not strong. But she's concerned about the shortage of Singers, as we all are, and she felt it necessary to make a tour of all the Houses. In any case, it's a great pleasure to have her among us, even for so grave a purpose."

"So it is, Magister," Isbel agreed politely.

Cael said, "The itinerant's message included you, Cantrix Isbel."

"Me? But I have never met Cantrix Sharn."

"She especially asked to see you."

"I wonder why," Isbel mused. "I am only a junior, after all. Nobody. I wonder what it can be?"

Cantor Ovan pursed his lips and interrupted her. "It is an honor for you, of course."

Isbel colored again, and looked at her senior guiltily, as if she had done something wrong. "Oh, yes, I know, Cantor Ovan," she said in a small voice. "I am—" She just stopped herself from saying, I am just curious. The Singer Theo had teased her about her curiosity. "I am looking forward to meeting her," she amended. "Of course."

Magister Edrus smiled warmly. "I'm sure you are. And so am I." He gestured to his Houseman to offer the tray of nursery fruits again. "Now tell me, Cantrix Isbel, how are you finding our House? I hope you'll tell us if there's anything you need."

Isbel tried to answer properly, while the greater part of her mind seethed with questions and anticipation. Cantrix Sharn v'Lamdon, coming here! It was a great event. Except for Cantor Ovan and one weepy four-year-old, Sharn would be the first Gifted person Isbel had seen since she had left Conservatory. They would talk perhaps, share their thoughts. And what business could Sharn have with Isbel, surely the most junior Cantrix on the Continent? Isbel could hardly wait to find out.

The senior Cantrix of the Magistral House of Lamdon arrived at Amric with the largest traveling party Isbel had ever seen. Twelve riders and no less than three itinerant Singers accompanied her. She herself did not ride *hruss*, but traveled in comfort in a softly padded *pukuru* drawn smoothly over the snow on bone runners. Upon her arrival she was helped from the sled and up Amric's broad steps with the greatest delicacy and respect. Her furs swathed her completely, so that during the welcoming ceremony her face was all but invisible. Only indoors, in the great room, did she put back her hood and show herself.

Isbel drew a delighted breath. Sharn was beautiful, with hair as white as the snow that fell on the Glacier, before it hardened into the firn, and with skin almost as pale. She reminded Isbel of an ancient song half remembered:

> . . . WHITE ON WHITE,
> SNOW ON SNOW,
> SNOW FALLS EVERMORE ON SNOW . . .

The lines of her cheeks seemed deeply tooled, as if by one of Amric's artisans, and she was as slight and thin as a child.

She was also, Isbel realized, very ill.

When Isbel was presented to her, Cantrix Sharn did something no one had done for many months. She came forward and embraced the younger Cantrix, laying her cold white fingers against Isbel's warm cheeks. *I am so glad to meet you at last. Your friend Sira spoke to me about you.*

Isbel's eyes filled with tears, both of gratitude for the physical contact, and of sorrow for her friend. *Thank you, Cantrix Sharn.*

Sharn nodded, as if she understood exactly what Isbel was thanking her for. Isbel saw why Sira had so admired the older Cantrix, and a quick warmth sprang up in her breast. This was indeed the sort of person to inspire devotion.

After I have rested, Sharn sent, her eyes on Isbel's as if no one else was in the room at that moment, *we will talk*.

While Sharn went on to greet Cantor Ovan, Isbel turned quickly to find the Housekeeper. He stood watchfully by the doors to the great room, and she hurried to him.

"Housekeeper," she said in a low tone. "The Cantrix is exhausted and ill. She must rest immediately."

The Housekeeper bowed to her without question. Moments later, Cantrix Sharn's party had dispersed, and the Cantrix and her own Housewoman were led straight to their apartment. Isbel watched these proceedings with gratified surprise. As she made her way to her own room, Cael returned and bowed to her again. "Cantrix Sharn would like to see you privately later on. Shall I suggest the *ubanyix*, Cantrix?"

Isbel inclined her head in agreement. Cantor Ovan was only a few steps away, and she felt a wave of irritation flood from him. She caught her lip between her teeth, suppressing a giggle. After all, did Cantor Ovan expect to bathe with Lamdon's senior Cantrix? It really was very childish of him to be resentful. And whatever was wrong with him that he could not shield his emotions better than that?

She sobered then, reflecting that Cantrix Sharn was far more than Lamdon's senior Cantrix. She was senior to all the Cantors and Cantrixes, indeed even the itinerant Singers, of the entire Continent. And she wanted to see Isbel, herself, and privately. Isbel hurried to the *ubanyix*, drawing her *filla* out of her tunic as she went. She would warm the water, check that there were fresh towels and cakes of soap, make sure all was at its best when Cantrix Sharn came to bathe.

The elderly Cantrix looked more frail than ever without the bulk of her furs and clothing. Only her eyes seemed vital, shining brightly from her pale and wrinkled face. She sighed with relief as she sank into the steaming water of the *ubanyix*.

I am not the traveler I once was, Isbel. It exhausts me.

I am sorry, Cantrix Sharn. Isbel was careful with her thoughts, pushing her curiosity aside. It was difficult. She loved a story, and there was one here, waiting to be told.

How are you finding your assignment to Amric?

It is going well enough, I suppose, Isbel sent cautiously. *I am not a great healer, I am afraid. But I think the* quirunha *are all right.*

Sharn smiled, and trailed her long white fingers in the water. *Healing is so very difficult. It takes a long time to learn. Be patient.*

I am patient, Cantrix, Isbel could not resist telling her. *My senior is not! It would seem I have not been much help to him.*

Sharn still smiled. *I remember Cantor Ovan from earlier days. Do not worry. I am sure he is pleased enough with you.*

Isbel let the subject drop. Her senior had certainly not indicated satisfaction with her in any way. But, then, it did not seem important at this moment. It was a joy to lie lazily in the hot water, talking with another Singer in almost as relaxed a fashion as she had once talked with her classmates at Conservatory.

I sat just so, in the ubanyix *at Lamdon,* Sharn sent, *with your good friend Cantrix Sira. Just after the last summer, that was. Almost three years ago. A remarkable Singer.*

Isbel sighed. *I miss her.*

Even more importantly, my dear, Sharn sent, putting her thin fingers on Isbel's plump ones, *Nevya misses her.*

Sharn leaned back against the carved edge of the tub. Her white hair trailed limply in the water and her scalp looked pale and vulnerable through its wetness. She closed her eyes, as if their conversation was almost too tiring.

Isbel felt her weariness, felt her own shoulders bowed down by the weight of concerns Sharn carried. The old Cantrix's eyes opened suddenly and looked directly into Isbel's. *Do you sense everyone's feelings at all times, Isbel? You must shield yourself from so much emotion.*

Isbel flushed. *I do try, Cantrix Sharn. It is hard at times.*

Of course it is. Sharn closed her eyes again. *But you must do it, or you will not be able to work.*

Isbel remembered Maestra Lu admonishing her on this same subject, though not so gently. She had told Sira about it, and Sira had looked puzzled, not understanding the need. Sira would never have been so weak. Her shielding never wavered. Her concentration and control were absolute.

Yes, Isbel, Sira was very strong. Sharn had followed her thought with much delicacy, and Isbel had no sense that her privacy had been violated. *Your Gift is different from your friend's, but no less precious.*

Has Lamdon given up hope for Sira? Isbel dreaded the answer.

We have lost three Singers. An itinerant named Jon, another named Theo, and Cantrix Sira. We have not given up hope, because we cannot. Nevya needs every Singer if we are to survive.

It was an answer, but not an answer. Isbel remembered the last time she had seen Sira, in the *ubanyix* at Conservatory. Sira had made Isbel cut her hair, and Isbel had wept as her friend's long dark tresses had fallen away. Sira had shed no tears, though she had been so unhappy.

If only, Isbel mused, I had argued with her, gone to Magister Mkel. Sira had been so bitter over Maestra Lu's death, and over her failure at Bariken . . .

Again Sharn followed her thought. *There was nothing you could have done, Isbel. You could not change what happened to your friend. You must grieve, and go on.*

It troubles me, Cantrix Sharn, that I have never known what happened to Sira. What was so terrible that she would leave the Cantoris forever? And risk her life in doing it?

Ah, Isbel . . . Sharn hesitated.

You are thinking I could not bear it. Sira thought that. She did not want me to have her memories, she said. But I loved her.

Yes, I understand. But what happened to Sira was so terrible, so tragic. She did not want you to carry the burden as she had to bear it.

I would rather know, Isbel answered.

Sharn smiled sadly. Aloud she said, "I will tell you, Isbel, but in words. Shield yourself."

Isbel nodded solemnly. She did shield herself, but there was pain just the same. A terrible thing had happened to her friend.

Choosing the most prosaic words, Sharn told her the story. An intrigue at the House of Bariken, with a plot on its Magister's life, had caught Sira in its web. She had very nearly been killed along with the rest of the Magister's party. Her great Gift and her iron will had saved her, but she had killed a man with a hunting knife, and sent a Gifted woman over the brink of sanity into mindlessness. The man's death had not troubled her, because he had meant to take Sira's life. It was the other tragedy, the obliteration of another's mind, the misuse of her Gift, that had haunted Sira most.

Isbel shivered in the warm water, thinking of the Houseman Donel injured by the wild boy Zakri. "Poor Sira," she murmured. "She would not even open her mind to me."

Sharn was silent for a long time, and their memories of Sira hung between them in the quiet of the *ubanyix*. At last Sharn stirred and began to rise from the water. Isbel jumped up to help, holding the elderly Cantrix's thin arm, reaching for towels to wrap around her.

We will talk privately again, my dear, Sharn sent wearily. *Now, please call my Housewoman. I must try to sleep.*

With a heavy heart and confused thoughts, Isbel did as Sharn asked. When the senior Cantrix was dressed and her hair rebound, she left the *ubanyix*, leaving Isbel to sit alone for a long time, wrapped in a towel, her damp hair hanging loosely on her shoulders. She bestirred herself only when Yula came looking for her. Other Housewomen were waiting outside, forbidden the *ubanyix* while Lamdon's senior Cantrix was using it.

Isbel tried to speak pleasantly to Yula, but she felt a great weight upon her. The evening's discussion would bring more worries, she was sure. And if Lamdon had stopped searching for Sira, she must do something, think of something. She could not—she would not—believe her friend was gone for always.

I will not let them forget, she promised herself. Until we know for sure, they must look for her, and so I will tell Cantrix Sharn.

In her heart, though, Isbel knew that it was an easy thing for a person to disappear on the Contintent. The dangers were many, and the Houses far apart. If Sira's body lay under the eternal snows somewhere in the Mariks, it might never be discovered in Isbel's lifetime. The thought of living with endless loneliness and vain hope was more than she could bear. Something, surely, must lighten the prospect of the years ahead of her. Isbel prayed fervently to the Spirit of Stars that it might be so.

Chapter Five

Trisa, in a bright green tunic, her curly hair neatly bound, stood on a thick rug in Magister Edrus's apartment and smiled up at Cantrix Sharn where she sat in an elaborately carved chair. Isbel thought they made a wonderful sight, the little Gifted child and the pale white-haired woman holding her hand. Brnwen stood stony-eyed behind her daughter, and Isbel felt her effort to control her emotions. Trisa's father looked stiff and uncomfortable, awed into silence by being in the Magister's private rooms. When Cantrix Sharn released Trisa's hand, the child's face clouded.

"More," she said, pouting. "Send more!"

Cantrix Sharn smiled down at her, then up at her mother. "There will be more–much more, Trisa, in your future," she said gently. The wave of Brnwen's sadness swept over Isbel, and she drew a sharp breath. Sharn glanced at her, and shook her head slightly. Isbel stared at the tips of her boots, ashamed of her weakness.

"Housewoman, Houseman," Sharn said, with a small formal bow to Brnwen and her mate. "Much honor is due you. Your little one is Gifted indeed, and precious to Nevya. The whole Continent offers you gratitude."

Isbel lifted her head as Brnwen's mate bowed and stuttered his thanks. Brnwen did not speak, and when Isbel looked at her, she turned her head away.

Sharn addressed Cantor Ovan next. "Are there no others?"

Ovan's lips were pressed so tightly together, it hardly seemed possible he could open them to speak. "No, Cantrix Sharn." His voice creaked with a sound like old leather cracking. "This child is the only Gifted one born to Amric for two summers."

Sharn's eyes were hooded and dark with worry, and Isbel sensed again the illness that weakened the old Singer. "At Bariken there were none at all," she said. "Nor at Perl. At Lamdon we have three, but two of those are children of itinerant parents who refuse to send them to Conservatory. Unless other Houses have fared better, once again the class at Conservatory will not be a full one."

"Can you not force the itinerants to turn over their children?" Edrus asked. Isbel saw Brnwen turn to the Magister with such an abrupt movement that her mate grasped her arm.

"The Committee wants to do just that," Sharn said. She passed her white hand over her forehead. "Endlessly they debate. Cantor Abram favors a ruling that will require all families to send their Gifted children to Conservatory regardless of their personal inclinations." She paused, and Isbel stepped to her side, knowing that Sharn's weakness nearly overwhelmed her. The senior Cantrix put out her hand. Isbel took it in hers, and stood close.

Cantor Ovan grated, "Surely something has to be done."

Cantrix Sharn agreed. "So it must. But if we force families to give up their Gifted children, they will begin to hide them, to deny the Gift."

"But that means madness!" Ovan cried.

"Madness for some, it is true," Sharn said softly. "But many itinerants manage to train their children rather well."

"But this business at Soren—" Edrus began, and his voice trailed away.

Sharn nodded. "Yes. I am very worried about what is happening at Soren. But there must be a reason why our itinerant Singers are breeding more Gifted children than our House members. It is more important to discover that reason than it is to make laws to force them. Despite all our efforts, it is a rare thing for itinerants to allow their children to go to Conservatory for training."

Isbel watched Ovan's angry features, knowing he was about to burst out with some remark. She felt a sudden wrench in her chest and a terrible tightness in her throat. All at once it seemed as if a great hand had gripped her lungs and was squeezing the breath out of them.

But it was not her pain. It was Sharn's she felt, and she knew it for a certainty when she knelt by the older Cantrix's chair and saw her mouth twist in agony.

Isbel looked about for Cael. "Housekeeper! The Cantrix is very ill. She needs to be taken to her bed at once."

Cael stepped forward, as if to assist Sharn to her feet. "No, she must be carried! A litter, please."

She turned back to Sharn. *How can I help you?*

Only . . . only to rest. Sharn's sending was so weak that Isbel could barely hear her.

I will stay with you, Isbel sent firmly, with as much reassurance as she could summon. Sharn's pain was like a fist within Isbel's breast, clenched so tightly she thought she could not draw breath without crying out. She shielded herself as strongly as she knew how, but it took several moments for her sense of the older woman's pain to ease. She kept Sharn's hand in her own as two burly Housemen were ushered into the Magister's apartments.

"Gently, please," Isbel whispered, as they lifted the Cantrix onto the litter.

"I'll be as careful as I can," one of them murmured in response. Isbel saw with a rush of gratitude that it was Kai, the tall hunter who had been kind to her on her journey to Amric. As she reached to smooth Cantrix Sharn's hair from her face, her fingers touched his briefly. His hand was warm and hard, and she found the strength of it comforting. She did not draw back as quickly as she might have.

Carefully the two Housemen bore Sharn's litter down the corridor. Isbel walked beside it, trying to appear calm. When Sharn's Housewoman received them, fussing and exclaiming over her mistress, Isbel went in to supervise the stricken woman's transfer from the litter to her bed.

One of the Housemen left immediately, but Kai lingered. "Isn't there something more I can do, Cantrix Isbel?"

She looked up at him, thinking how solid, how safe he looked, standing there in the doorway. "Yes, Houseman. Please ask one of the cooks for a very weak tea for the Cantrix."

He bowed. "I'll bring it myself," he said, and was quickly gone.

Sharn's Housewoman was offended. "I could've gotten the tea."

Isben shook her head. "The Cantrix needs you here. Let us see if we can make her comfortable, you and I together."

Somewhat mollified, the Housewoman smoothed the bedfurs beneath her mistress. She hurried to slide off her boots and cover her thin white feet with a *caeru* rug, turning it inside out so the warm fur was close against Sharn's skin.

Isbel knelt beside the bed, her hand on Sharn's. *Cantrix Sharn, you need to go to Conservatory, to Maestro Nikei. He is the greatest of all healers.*

Sharn's eyes did not open. *There is no time, my dear. Nevya's need is too pressing.*

Isbel sensed through her shielding how the pain in Sharn's chest eased slightly. Kai returned with the tea, and he cast a look of alarm at the old Cantrix lying so still on her bed, her frail body lost in the thick bedfurs. "What else can I do, Cantrix?" he whispered.

"You can find Yula and ask her to give you my *filhata* from my apartment," Isbel said. She had no real idea what she would with it when she had it, but she must do something, anything that might help. Kai bowed quickly and hurried away again.

"What are you going to do, Cantrix?" asked Sharn's Housewoman. The hope in her eyes was fresh pain for Isbel.

"I do not know," she answered. "Perhaps . . . just help your mistress to sleep."

The Housewoman nodded. "The healers at Lamdon do no good, either. They only ease her pain a little. And all I can do is pray."

"Pray, then, Housewoman," Isbel told her. "I will, too."

Kai was at the door again, slightly out of breath. Isbel was touched by his eagerness. She guessed he must be close to her own age, surely not more than a year or two older. "Thank you, Houseman," she said gravely as she accepted the *filhata*, still in its leather cover, from his hands. She took it out and tuned it softly. Drawing a stool up beside Sharn's bed, she sat with the instrument across her lap. She played the first melody she thought of, the old lullaby that little Sith and his playmates had loved at Conservatory. It was a simple thing, in *Iridu*, the first mode. She dared a mild *cantrip* for sleep as she played. It was presumption, of course, to use her psi in such a way on her senior, but there was so little she could think of to do.

A slight relaxation of Sharn's face rewarded her, the brow smoothing and the face less pale. The pain receded farther, and Isbel chased it away as gently, as gradually as she could. The words of the old song came easily to her lips.

> SING THE LIGHT,
> SING THE WARMTH,
> RECEIVE AND BECOME THE GIFT, O SINGERS,
> THE LIGHT AND THE WARMTH ARE IN YOU.

She was surprised by the thought that came from Sharn, an involuntary sending, like a sigh. *Sira.* Isbel caught a fleeting glimpse of memory, an image of a tall lean Singer with a *filhata* in her hands. *So long ago.*

Kai waited outside the door of the visiting Cantrix's apartment. The Housewoman had shooed him out as Cantrix Isbel began to sing, but he stood stubbornly in the corridor, hoping the young Cantrix might have further tasks for him. He listened to her voice through the closed door, a sound as sweet and clear as a rivulet flowing from the Glacier in summer. He thought he could stand and listen to it all the day long if they would let him.

A long time passed before Cantrix Isbel emerged from the room. Kai had been leaning against the wall, waiting with a hunter's patience. He straightened quickly, and bowed. "Cantrix Isbel. I hope the old Cantrix is better?"

Cantrix Isbel looked worn beyond her years, and at the same time small and vulnerable. She nodded, looking up at him with those clear green eyes. "She is somewhat better," she whispered wearily. "Thank you, Houseman. And thank you for your help. You have waited a long time."

"Kai, Cantrix," he said. "Please call me Kai."

She smiled a little at that, but she stumbled with fatigue as she started down the corridor. Instinctively, he put his hand under her arm, then drew it back with alarm. "I'm . . . I'm sorry, Cantrix, I just—" His voice trailed off as he looked down at her.

She shook her head. "It is all right, Kai. I am not offended. It is only . . . I am just so tired."

Kai thought how beautiful she was, with her red-brown hair and her curving cheeks. Her arm felt soft and fragile beneath her tunic. He wanted to hover over her, protect her. Instead, he stepped back and bowed. "Promise you'll call me if you want anything."

She looked up at him again. He thought he could drown in the summer green of her eyes. There were tears in them now, tears of fatigue and sadness. She pressed a shaking hand against her mouth, but it was too late to stop a sob, a childish hiccup.

"Cantrix!" Kai exclaimed. "Cantrix Isbel, don't!" And in the space of a heartbeat he found himself, Kai v'Amric the hunter, with a weeping girl trembling against his broad chest, a Gifted girl at that.

He looked swiftly up and down the corridor to make sure they were not observed. Then he simply put his arms around her and let her cry. Gifted or not, Cantrix or no. She needed this small comfort, and he would not deny her.

It was hours later, after the Cantrix had gained control of herself and departed with a shy apology, after the news had come that Cantrix Sharn was only marginally improved, that Kai truly thought about what had happened. His breach of the respect due to the Cantoris was so serious that he dared not even confide in his brothers. Suppose he had seriously compromised the Cantrix's Gift by touching her, holding her small body so firmly against him?

But what a delicious feeling it had been, the warmth and tenderness of her skin, the herb-scent that clung to her hair, as if she washed it every day in the *ubanyix*. He wondered if she did, and if she would taste of those herbs if he were to put his lips to her cheek . . . .

Kai fled his crowded family apartment and went to the nursery gardens. He thought if he spent some time alone, he could take himself in hand. This will never do, Houseman, he lectured himself firmly. Rho would say you had better seek a mate, and soon, and put an early end to such thoughts.

But even as he walked between the rows of plants, trailing his fingers against the tender leaves, he saw the young Cantrix's green eyes and smooth cheeks in his mind's eye, and he groaned aloud in an agony of doubt and confusion.

Chapter Six

The next day's *quirunha* took place in a mood of strain and worry. Kai, watching from the back of the Cantoris, saw that both Cantrix Isbel and her senior were subdued. Still, thank the Spirit, the light and warmth flowed out from the dais as surely as always. The Magister also looked distracted, and the assembled House members were gloomy. When the *quirunha* was complete, the ritual prayer was more solemn than usual.

SMILE ON US,
O SPIRIT OF STARS,
SEND US THE SUMMER TO WARM THE WORLD,
UNTIL THE SUNS WILL SHINE ALWAYS TOGETHER.

During the ceremonial bows Cantrix Isbel's eyes met Kai's, then quickly dropped away. Kai flushed with guilt and pleasure, and looked around to see if anyone had noticed. All eyes were on the dais, of course, and his returned there, watching Isbel tuck her *filhata* under her arm and step down neatly onto the floor. Her face was pale, her eyes shadowed. He wished he could stand closer, catch the scent of her hair once again.

It was ridiculous, of course. He set his jaw, and promised himself to banish such thoughts. I'm a hunter, he told himself, as he followed the crowd out of the Cantoris. I'm no soft Gifted boy to be mooning about in a Cantoris.

He strode through the House to the stables. There would be work he could do, active work with *hruss*, maybe mucking out stalls, something to use his muscles. He would feel more like himself if his arms and legs were tired and his mind relieved by the rolling sweat of his body.

The stableman chuckled as he assured him there was never any shortage of work. He put a wooden tub of tallow and a bit of rag into Kai's hands, and set him to soaping the high-cantled saddles that hung on wooden pegs in a neat row against one wall. Kai began the task with a will, rubbing the fine yellow tallow into the leather with such vigor that it foamed up around his cloth.

He was on his second saddle when he heard a new voice behind him. "That's good work, Houseman. We have some saddles that could use the same."

Kai looked over his shoulder to see the three itinerant Singers who had traveled with the Lamdon party. It was the shortest of them, a wiry smiling man, who had spoken.

Kai stood and wiped the sweat from his forehead with his arm. He bowed, not too deeply, because they were after all only itinerants, but politely, in respect for the Gift. "I'm Kai, Singers. Hunter for Amric. I'd be happy to lend you a hand if you need it."

"Greetings, Kai v'Amric," the Singers said. "I'm Iban v'Trevi." He gestured at his companions. "These two quiet ones are from Manrus. I think they were hatched on the ice cliffs. That's why they don't talk much."

There was a moment of laughter, and casual bows exchanged. Iban turned back to Kai. "We've been looking for something to do." His expression changed swiftly as he spoke, his brows drawing together and his mouth turning down. "We thought we'd be on the road by now. But Cantrix Sharn is too ill to travel."

Kai nodded. "So she is. Cantrix—that is, our Cantors are very concerned."

Iban's eyebrows made hopeful arches. "Can your Cantors help her? Maybe she's better this morning."

Kai shook his head. "I don't know, Singer. Our Cantrix Isbel—" Kai could not help feeling a special pleasure in saying her name. He turned his eyes down to the half-soaped saddle at his feet, afraid these Gifted ones might sense his secret. "Cantrix Isbel sang for her yesterday, but only to help her sleep, I think."

The other itinerants had found their tack and were spreading bits about on the floor, examining them for loose buckles or fraying stitches. Iban looked at them, then back at Kai. "Houseman, do you suppose . . ." He lowered his voice. "Could you speak to someone for me, someone in your House?"

Kai shrugged. "Probably no one you couldn't speak to yourself. But I'll do what I can."

"Perhaps you know your Housekeeper well, or . . . one of your Cantors?" Iban looked at Kai intently, and Kai felt a moment of anxiety that the Singer had in fact read his thoughts, though no itinerants he knew did that. The ones who traveled with the hunters spoke and listened like anybody else. Only the Conservatory-trained Singers were supposed to be able to hear the thoughts of others. It would be the worst of luck if this Singer Iban proved to be the exception!

Cautiously now, he answered, "It might be possible."

The Singer gestured toward the door, and Kai nodded. He wiped the yellow tallow from his fingers, indicating with a nod to the stableman that he would return to finish his job later. Together he and Iban walked out of the stables and down the long corridor toward the center of the House.

Beyond the glow of the *quiru* the day was bright and cold, with a fresh wind from the Glacier that carried away the stench of the waste drop. The warmth of the newly-refreshed *quiru* intensified the fragrance of the gardens. As they passed the door to thte tannery Iban sniffed. "I like the way your House smells."

"Not everyone likes the smell of leather curing."

Iban had to tip his head up to look at Kai. His gray eyes sparkled. "I do, though. It's a good, practical smell. I like the abundance of meat on your tables, too." He was smiling again, the lines of his face lifting as if he had not a care in the world. This Singer's moods were as changeable as cloud shapes in a summer sky. Every time you looked at the man, his face told some new story. What a one he would be to travel with!

Kai acknowledged the compliment with a bow. A clever fellow, he thought, quick with his words. He wondered what he wanted.

"Houseman," the Singer began, his smile fading once again and his brows lowering into straight lines of worry. "The thing is—without boasting—I have had some success as a healer."

"Yes?" Kay said, interested. "My brother Rho was healed by an itinerant once, of a nasty wound, too. We killed a *tkir* together, and the beast left Rho a great scar to remember him by."

Iban nodded, his face smoothing until there was no expression on it. "Sometimes," he murmured, "itinerants are better healers than Cantors."

Kai gave him a searching look. "You think you can help the old Cantrix?"

"It's possible. Do you know what's wrong with her?"

"Only what everyone is saying. She has pain in her chest, she's weak. Seems to me she's just old. Her skin is so white and thin, it's like looking through ice on a puddle. She must have at least twelve summers, wouldn't you think?"

Iban was silent for a moment as they walked on. He rubbed his chin, then tousled his ragged hair. "Your young Cantrix seems fond of Cantrix Sharn. I'd like to meet with her."

Kai was quiet in his turn. He didn't know how it was between the Conservatory-trained and those Singers who had not made their great sacrifice. For itinerant Singers, life and work were clearly very different than for those like Isbel whose entire lives were spent serving the great Houses. Had it been he, Kai, who had given up every freedom for such service, he would have resented the itinerants who plied the Mariks. They were independent, paid in real bits of metal for their work, making their own decisions . . . taking mates, having families. But then, Cantrix Isbel seemed so gentle, so quick with her dimpled smile, so kind. Perhaps she was not capable of a feeling like resentment or envy. In any case, she probably would not be angry with him for bringing the Singer Iban to her. And, he admitted to himself, it gave him a chance to speak to her.

At last he nodded. "I will take you to Cantrix Isbel. But be very careful with her," he warned. "She's tired and she's worried."

Iban answered with gravity. "I promise I will be respectful to your Cantrix."

Kai eyed him, wondering if he was being teased, but the Singer appeared perfectly sincere. Kai left him to wait in the great room while he went in search of Yula to carry a message to her mistress. Iban reclined in one of the window seats until Kai returned with Yula behind him, dragging her feet.

Yula bowed to the Singer, much deeper, Kai saw, than he himself had, deeper than was usual. She seemed to be nervous, picking at her tunic and twisting her hands. "Come this way, please, Singer," she whispered.

Iban rose from the window seat to follow her. She said nothing to Kai, and he had no choice but to watch their backs as the two of them walked away. The Singer was already at the door of the great room when he turned back. "Aren't you coming, Houseman?"

Kai jumped to his feet in joyous relief. "Oh, so I am, Singer." He was sure this time Iban hid a smile. Ah, well, he thought, it was worth a little embarrassment to see Cantrix Isbel again!

When Yula stood nervously outside her door, muttering that the hunter Kai begged her to meet with the Singer Iban, Isbel could not stanch the little burst of happiness that warmed her breast. These last days the House had seemed as bleak and dark as if the solitary sun hardly rose at all. Isbel had not found the strength to chide herself for her moments of weakness in the hunter's presence, although such physical contact went against all her training. In her whole life no one had ever held her in such a way, and she had been over and over the experience, wondering what it meant. To her great relief, the *quirunha* had been unaffected by the broken tabu. She kept the memory of it pressed very low so her senior could detect no trace of her offense. In truth, he seemed never to sense any of her feelings. She supposed he did not care.

Kai and the Singer were waiting in the Cantoris to meet with her, as was proper. The Singer Iban was as small and wiry as the hunter was tall and broad-chested. His gray eyes shone pleasantly from his thin brown face. "Thank you for seeing me, Cantrix Isbel," he said with a bow. His tone lacked the resonance of a Cantor's, but it was clear and well-focused. Isbel could imagine his voice carrying across snowbound valleys, calling up camp *quiru* for travelers.

"Is there something I can do for you, Singer?" she asked carefully. Her every nerve felt Kai's presence. He was so near that two strides of his long legs would bring him to her side. Her eyes burned with the effort of concentration, and every private thought was as securely shielded as she could make it.

"I hope so," the Singer said to her. "I would like to see Cantrix Sharn."

"Oh," Isbel said. She shook her head. "I am sorry, Singer, but she is too ill for visitors."

Iban's brows drew sharply together. She noticed how changeable his face was, his features moving and settling in a different expression each moment. "I know how ill she is, Cantrix," he said slowly. "You see, I have some skill as a healer, and I have eased my own mother when she suffered a similar ailment of the chest. I thought perhaps—"

Isbel lifted her head in quick hope. "Are you a good healer? Really? I am not strong at it, myself, and my senior—" she stopped herself. It would not do to admit to this stranger her doubts about Cantor Ovan's ability. Her cheeks flamed, and she dropped her eyes. "I am sorry. It is just that I would . . . I will do anything I can to help the Cantrix. She was so kind to Sira," she finished, in an almost inaudible whisper.

Kai heard the whisper, and wondered who Sira was. The scene before him was a strange one, the little Singer hardly taller than Cantrix Isbel herself, and making his odd claim. Cantors and Cantrixes, after all, were the ones with the real power, power over the light and the warmth, the mind and the body, even the water of the *ubanyor*. But Cantrix Isbel appeared to take the Signer Iban's proposal quite seriously.

"Yula!" she called.

Timid Yula put her head around the door. "Yes, Cantrix?"

"Please get Cantrix Sharn's Housewoman for me. Quickly!"

Yula vanished in an instant, and Isbel turned back to Iban. "I will stay with you," she said. "I must follow you, to be sure that—" She broke off, embarrassed at the implied suspicion.

The Singer forestalled her with a graceful inclination of his head. "Of course," he said. "You must be sure that I will not worsen matters for Cantrix Sharn." His gray eyes were clear and candid as he added, "I swear by the Six Stars I will use any skill I have only to help. If I can. And I will be glad to have you with me."

"Thank you, Singer," Isbel said simply.

It was not an easy thing to convince Sharn's Housewoman to allow an itinerant into the Cantrix's presence when she was so ill, but Isbel persisted. Once admitted, she and the Singer Iban sat close to the Cantrix's bed, and Isbel held Sharn's pale cold hand in her own. She was relieved to see that Iban was careful not to touch the Cantrix. Enough tabus were being broken already in these strange days.

The Singer drew out his *filla*, and Isbel looked at him in surprise. "Do you not use a *filhata*?" she whispered.

He shook his head. "Don't have one." His eyes remained open as he put the *filla* to his lips. The *Aiodu* melody he played was straightforward, slow and simple, without adornment.

It was strange for Isbel to follow a Singer whose training was so different from her own. This Singer who slipped so deftly into Sharn's mind was completely unshielded, and as Isbel followed him she felt once again the persistent pain that racked the old Cantrix. Her own chest ached, and she had to press her lips together to keep from groaning.

Singer Iban's psi went directly to the pain, quickly and fearlessly entering the very source, the center of it. Isbel had to follow quickly, or be left behind. There was no time to consider. She felt as if she were being pulled by *hruss* into an abyss, a dark chasm of suffering. It was terrifying, and she fought against the fear that she would be trapped, would never be able to climb out of that great blackness. She pressed down her doubts and gripped Sharn's hand, determined not to disturb the Singer's work.

It was abundantly clear form the start that Iban knew what he was doing. His psi, floating on the current of the simple second-mode melody, went to work immediately. Isbel was there with him, watching in amazement. At the very bottom of the abyss that so frightened her, in the exact center of the pain, there was a tiny passage, locked as though filled with ice, or with stone. With remarkable patience and persistence, Iban's psi nudged and tugged at the blockage, trying to clear it. Breathing deeply, Isbel stepped through her fear and began to help, following his example with great care. As she worked, she discovered to her surprise that both her pain and her fear abated, that the activity and the sense of purpose were greater than the sense of suffering. Bit by bit, together, she and the Singer cleared the tiny channel, and when it was open, the heart's blood flowed freely through it once again.

When it was over, Isbel looked wide-eyed at Iban, whispering in wonder, "You have healed her."

He shook his head. "No," he said softly. "There is too much damage, too many such constricted passages." He looked down at Cantrix Sharn, whose ice-pale cheeks bloomed now with a faint color. "But she will be well enough to return to Lamdon, at least."

"And she is free of pain," Isbel said. She released Sharn's hand at last, and flexed her fingers in her lap. "Thank you, Singer. From both of us, thank you."

Iban smiled, and his eyebrows lifted into high straight lines. "Thank you for your help."

"It was an honor," Isbel replied with complete sincerity. She looked up at Kai, who was waiting protectively near the door, and she smiled brilliantly at him. "She is so much better," she told him. "Please tell the Magister."

Kai bowed and hurried away. Isbel turned back to Iban. "How did you learn to do this?"

"All my training came from my father, who was an itinerant all his life."

"Why did you not go to Conservatory?"

Iban's face seemed to close, and he looked away from her. Isbel was certain she had offended him, and was immediately sorry. One of the frustrations of speaking aloud was that her true intent was not always understood.

"My family have bred Singers for a hundred summers," Iban said brusquely. "We have no need of Conservatory." He bowed and took his leave. He did not look back from the door.

Isbel gazed down at Cantrix Sharn, lying now in comfortable sleep, and she wondered. Remarkable things had been happeneing, and she had no way of understanding them. She wished her training had taught her more of the ways of the world, of the surprises that lay in store after the protracted years at Conservatory. She felt utterly unprepared for the curious twists and turns of her road.

She tucked the furs more tightly around the old Cantrix, then rose and went to the window to look out on the white landscape. Two more years until the summer, and then she could step out of doors, walk freely under the ironwood trees. By then, perhaps she would be resigned to this strange life, to the loneliness, to Ovan's moodiness. And in the summer, she promised herself, I will make them search for Sira. I will beg Cantrix Sharn, as soon as she is better. At the very least, they can do that for me.

Chapter Seven

The season of deep cold came and went, but Isbel hardly noticed. Her days within Amric's walls had not even the changing seasons to distinguish them, one from the other. The only variety in her life was that provided by the problems presented during Cantoris hours.

Isbel had learned something essential from Singer Iban, and she drew upon it whenever her senior allowed her to heal someone. She let herself be more and more open as the months passed. She risked Ovan's rebuke, but he seemed not to notice. She was especially grateful to be allowed to help with the children. She doubted Conservatory would have approved her methods, but in her isolation she had only trial and error for teacher.

There were three very sick children one day, all with the same illness. Their faces were hot and red, and the junior Cantrix could hear the rasp of their breathing from the dais. She felt their fever, felt the effort it took to draw breath, the weakness that made their little heads droop. As she closed her eyes, not even picking up her *filla* yet, an intuition flashed in her mind. She opened her eyes and turned to her senior. "I would like to take them to the *ubanyix*."

The Cantor was sitting slumped beside her, his head on his hand and his eyelids drooping. He gave her a halfhearted glance, then waved his hand in a dismissive gesture. There was no one else waiting, and Ovan stepped down from the dais and was gone from the Cantoris even before Isbel and the mothers, carrying their sick children, made their slow way to the door.

Isbel used her *filla* to warm the water in the *ubanyix,* prolonging her *Doryu* melody until steam curled from the surface. It was too hot to step into, but Isbel had the mothers sit at the edge of the tub, close to the water, with their little ones in their arms. The hot moistness roiled around them, and everyone's faces grew wet. Isbel played in *Doryu* again, then in *Iridu*, extending her psi in careful and precise touches, gently coaxing the children's tiny clogged airways to open. She worked with first one, then another, returning to each until she had done all she thought she could. It took a long time. Her lips on the *filla* trembled with fatigue, and her hands shook. The mothers were exhausted, too, but when Isbel put down her *filla* at last, the children were breathing freely, every one of them. The mothers looked at Isbel with tears of gratitude before they carried their babes away.

The stairs seemed impossibly steep and long as Isbel climbed to her rooms that day. Her feet felt heavy as stones. Yula came trotting after her to ask if she wanted food, but Isbel yearned only to collapse upon her cot and sleep until her strength returned.

She had just put her hand on the door of her apartment when an older child of perhaps two summers came running down the corridor. He stopped in front of Isbel, remembering at the last moment to bow, then held something out to her. "My father said to give you this," he blurted in a rush.

Isbel held out her hand, and the youngster, careful not to touch her fingers, dropped a little roll of split leather into it. "What is it?" she asked.

"It's to say thanks. For saving my little sister!" The child was already backing away down the corridor as if afraid Isbel might come after him. "We all thought she was going to die," he added matter-of-factly. He grinned once, and ducked his head again before turning to run down the stairs.

Inside her apartment, Isbel unrolled the thin leather. She took a delighted breath when she saw the beautiful tooled patterns that must have taken the craftsman months to complete. Wrapped inside the decorated panel of leather were small, slender pieces of ironwood that fit together to make a frame. It had been lovingly made. She ran her fingers over the curving design, sensing the care and patience that had gone into its creation. Tired though she was, she put the pieces together and stretched the little panel across them. The object was pure art, without utility. Isbel found it enchanting. When she went to her bed, she placed the gift on a table where she could see it as she drifted into sleep.

Shall I not bother to attend Cantoris hours anymore? Ovan's thought was as dark as his sullen face.

Isbel was at a loss. There was no mistaking the way the House members glanced in her direction, even forming their little line to her side of the dais, pointedly ignoring Ovan's. If she had imagined that when her healing improved her relationship with her senior would, also, she knew now it was not true.

Well, begin, then, he sent, in the nastiest way. *Heal them! It is what you want, is it not?*

She felt the beginning of tears, and dropped her head to hide them. What was she to do? All eyes were on her while Ovan taunted her, railed at her—in her mind, where no one else in the entire House could hear him.

You are now the great healer, are you not? Show us, then! This man here, with blacktoe, and that woman with the foulness on her skin!

At least I know their names, she thought. But she pressed that down. Ovan would only get angrier, torment her further. Nothing she did was enough. He would never be satisfied.

She lifted her *filla*, and tried to shut her senior's voice out of her mind. She must concentrate, do her best. Perhaps if she truly did heal these people, Ovan would be placated, would leave her alone. She saw no other way. But how long could she stand his hostility?

There were only a few weeks left now before the summer. Everyone spoke of it, looked forward to it. The children clamored to know when it would come, when they could add a summer to their age. Their parents laughed and counseled patience, but in truth, everyone was eager, anticipating the warm season of freedom.

Cantoris hours seemed endless. Isbel struggled to work while Ovan harassed her, and when she had healed the case of blacktoe, and soothed the Housewoman's blotchy skin, her senior was no happier. When the work was finished, she fairly ran from the Cantoris and into the great room, hoping that the mid-day meal might distract Ovan from her failings. Magister Edrus found her there, coming directly to the central table and bowing briefly before her.

Quietly, he said, "Cantrix Sharn has died."

Isbel's hands flew to her mouth. "O Spirit," she murmured, behind her fingers. Ovan was standing beside her, about to sit down.

Edrus included Ovan in his glance. "I'm sorry to have to bring such sad news. I will make a formal announcement after the *quirunha* tomorrow, but I thought you should know immediately." Isbel nodded. "Do you need your Housewoman?" Edrus asked sympathetically.

Isbel swallowed hard, and lowered her hands to lock them tightly together. Oh, Cantrix Sharn, she thought. I will miss you.

She looked at the bowl of *caeru* stew just set before her, and knew she could not eat. Abruptly she rose. "Please excuse me," she whispered to Edrus and to Ovan.

So you are not the great healer after all!

Ovan might as well have struck her with his hand. His sending was sharp-edged and violent. She had never felt such a blow in her life. The room spun around her, and she gripped the table edge for support.

We did help her, she protested. *Truly we did!*

Oh, yes? You allowed an itinerant into the mind of the senior Cantrix! What did you think would happen?

Isbel turned to him, stricken, her hand to her throat. The others at the table looked up, seeing their Cantor and Cantrix staring at each other, the Cantrix white and trembling, Cantor Ovan's sour features twisted with anger.

She was better, Cantor! Isbel sent desperately. *She said so! If you had only—*

He interrupted. *If I had? But you did not ask me, did you? You simply went ahead, took matters into your own hands, without caring about the risk!* Ovan's eyes glittered, and his lips pinched into colorless lines. *You are fortunate*, he pressed on, *that Lamdon does not know what you did. I have no doubt that you and that half-trained Singer hastened Sharn's death!*

Isbel gave a wordless cry. Every head in the great room turned to see what was happening at the center table. Isbel looked around at their shocked faces, then ran from the great room to stumble up the stairs, sobbing behind her hands.

At the door of the great room, Kai the hunter stood, eyes blazing at Cantor Ovan. Kai's fists clenched until they hurt. He could have struck the Cantor down without a thought if he had him alone, cornered him in the *ubanyor* or in the stables. But the senior Cantor sat down to his meal as if nothing had happened.

Kai gritted his teeth, and ran up the stairs after Isbel, fury lending wings to his feet. He at least could offer the poor girl some comfort. She had no one else.

Chapter Eight

The rocky peaks that loomed above the Pass still wore jagged caps of snow, but the narrow descending path the *hruss* followed was clear and dry. Morys, the guide from Observatory, rode ahead at a pace so deliberate that Sira, following behind, smiled through her pain. Certainly the Watchers had not been so solicitous of her comfort and safety when they forced her to ride up this difficult road. But that had been almost four years before, and they had not known what she was.

She twisted in her saddle to look behind her, but Observatory had already disappeared in the precipitous landscape. She could no longer hear Theo's farewells. The tenuous thread of their contact had broken some moments before. Still, she had not yet gone so far that it was impossible to turn back. She could call to Morys, change her mind, relieve the wrenching ache of separation.

She turned again in her saddle, facing forward. The two *hruss,* steady and unaware, pressed on. Sira would not change her mind. "Morys," she said. Her deep voice resounded from the rock walls around them.

The man turned in his own saddle. "Yes, Cantrix?"

Sira sighed a little. She had been unable to get them to drop the title. When she reached Lamdon, she vowed, she would see to it she was addressed only as Singer. She had relinquished any right to the title of Cantrix. But for now, she let it pass. "I am capable of a better pace than this," she said.

"Yes, Cantrix," he said again, and urged his *hruss* to a slightly faster walk.

The path seemed to end in an impenetrable wall of rock. Sira remembered the look of it from the other side, when she and Theo had ridden up this path as prisoners of Pol and his band of riders. The narrow passageway her *hruss* now pressed through, scraping her furred boots against solid rock, was no less daunting from this direction. The cliff path that waited on the other side of the passage was worse, narrow and uneven, with rock walls to the north, and a deep canyon yawning on the south side.

The drop was to Sira's left, and she tried to keep her gaze from it. She looked straight ahead, past the *hruss*'s flickering ears, concentrating on Morys and his mount as they led the way. At least now, in the summer, there was no rime of ice to make the *hruss* slip, though a bitter wind blew from the peaks, tossing the *hruss*'s manes and tails. For an hour the great shaggy beasts worked their way around the face of the cliff to the next narrow opening. When they had squeezed their way through that, Sira breathed a sigh of relief.

She could never have found her way alone from Observatory to Ogre Pass. The boulders she and Morys rode between were huge, some as high as three tall men standing on each other's shoulders. Morys knew exactly where to turn and circle and turn again, with the knowledge handed down to him by generations of Watchers. Sira would have starved if she had tried it on her own. The knowledge that this was so had been Pol's weapon, the threat that had kept her at Observatory, and Theo with her. Now she followed her guide with Pol's blessing, and Theo remained behind. His was a willing sacrifice, but that made it no easier to bear his absence.

They had not been the first kidnapped Singers at Observatory. But, thanks to the work she and Theo had done there, they should be the last. Theo would serve the people of Observatory magnificently. He would be lonely, perhaps as much as she was already. But he had become a fine Cantor, and Observatory could count itself fortunate to have him.

Sira and Morys stopped for a quick mid-day meal on a promontory of treeless rock that looked out over Ogre Pass. Here was a spectacle Sira also remembered well. The great Pass swept from the southwest to the northeast, cleaving the Continent in two. It was broad and deep, its floor as smooth as if it had been deliberately cleared. The trip from Observatory to the Pass and back again could just be managed in one long day, as she and Theo had discovered when Pol had seized them. Their first impression of the Watchers had been their willingness to risk their own lives for their cause.

Summer meant that travelers on the Continent would have a brief period of freedom. Only during these short weeks could a rider in the Nevyan mountains survive the hours of darkness unprotected. The Visitor trailed now above the skyline, adding its warmth to that of the sun. Here and there patches of unmelted snow dotted the ground, but the air was soft and clear, fragrant with the scent of the softwood shoots growing quickly under the light of the suns.

Sira looked far down into the Pass and spotted the traveling party she had sensed was searching for her. They were moving slowly to the southwest. She closed her eyes and extended her psi over the distance between them. Her reach was long, although it would never be as long as Maestra Lu's had been. She could only just touch each mind in the party. There seemed to be no one she knew. Cantrix Isbel of Amric might have urged Lamdon to send out the search party, or perhaps it had been Cantrix Sharn herself. By rights they should both have given up hope long ago, but Sira had faith in Isbel's friendship. Possibly Pol was right, as well; perhaps the Magistral Committee of Lamdon knew more about the Watchers than they admitted, and had reason to suspect her imprisonment by them.

In a few hours she and Morys would meet the party in the Pass. Sira would ride away with them, and Morys would return to Observatory alone. Sira could only guess at how painful the sight of him, riding back without her, would be for Theo.

A *quiru* trembled about the traveling party in the brisk breeze that blew through the Pass from the south. Sira tried to send to the Singer who had made the *quiru*, to warn him of their approach, but he was an itinerant, and could not hear her. She and Morys approached the campsite in silence until they were close enough for Morys to call out, "Greetings. Two more travelers here."

The people in the *quiru* did not hesitate to step out of it. In truth, they could have been comfortable without a *quiru* in the mild summer evening. The sky was just shading to the violet of the mountain dusk. Sira rode with her furs open, her hood pushed back. She lifted a hand in greeting, and she heard one of the travelers take a sharp breath. She lifted her scarred eyebrow, wondering which of them was so startled by her appearance.

There were four in the party. One still held his *filla* in his hand. Another was a woman, a rider by the look of her cropped hair and weathered skin. Next to her stood another rider, a man with hard black eyes. The fourth was an old man with hair as white as the snow on the high peaks. He was tall, as tall as Sira herself. She thought there was something familiar about him, but she did not know his name. Five *hruss* rested hipshot behind them, crowded into the circle of light despite the warmth of the evening.

"Cantrix Sira?" their Singer asked.

It was true, as Sira had thought. They had come searching for her.

She bowed from her saddle. Morys jumped down from his *hruss* and stepped forward. "This is Cantrix Sira. We've come from Observatory."

There was a moment of strained silence. The hard-eyed man stepped forward. "We're glad to see you, Cantrix," he said, and bowed. The others also bowed, and from the white-haired man Sira felt a distinct wave of relief. She was sure he was not Gifted, and that meant his emotion must be very strong for it to penetrate her shielding.

Of course, she reminded herself, her shields were not what they had once been. Theo had seen to that.

She dismounted, and a place was made for her in the *quiru*, her bedfurs unrolled, her saddlepack put within reach. She sat cross-legged and looked around at the party.

The itinerant Singer put his *filla* to his lips and played a brief melody to expand the *quiru* to encompass the two new *hruss*. The sky darkened swiftly to purple above the campsite, and the air sharpened.The white-haired man knelt stiffly in the middle of the camp to start a cooking fire, and the others began to introduce themselves.

"I'm Tani v'Lamdon, Cantrix," the woman rider said, putting her hand on her chest. She indicated the other rider. "This is Dom, rider for the senior Cantor at Lamdon. Cantor Abram, that would be."

Sira's head came up, and she fixed her gaze so fiercely on Tani that the woman took an involuntary step back. For the first time since they had arrived Sira spoke. "Cantrix Sharn?" Her voice rang in a breathless silence, and it appeared for a moment no one would answer.

"Died," said Dom. "She went beyond the stars a few weeks ago, Cantrix."

Sira breathed out slowly and dropped her head. She had been only a girl when Cantrix Sharn had received her in triumph at Lamdon. She remembered the soft, lined face and the gentle voice that belied Sharn's great strength and influence. There were so many deaths still to mourn. She shrank from thinking of what other news might await her.

The itinerant Singer waited for the moment to pass. When he introduced himself, his bow was perfect, neither too deep, because he was after all Gifted, nor too shallow, because she was a full Cantrix and he only a traveling Singer. "I'm Iban v'Trevi," he said in a light, clear voice. Sira nodded to him. He went on. "I was hoping the Singer Theo might be with you. The Committee thought you were together."

Sira dropped her eyes to her linked hands. Her throat constricted, and she dared not speak. Morys came to her rescue.

"The Singer Theo is now Cantor Theo v'Observatory," he announced with pride. "And a wonderful Cantor he is. Trained and presented by Cantrix Sira."

"How is that possible?" the Singer Iban asked. "And why would he?"

"It was his choice," Morys said with asperity. "Observatory isn't the outcast House you all would like it to be. It's a fine House, if a bit smaller than some, and now it has the finest Cantor on the Continent."

A smile overcame Sira's rush of sorrow. How Theo would laugh if he could hear Morys bragging about him. And how she would love to hear that laugh! The thought of his firm voice ringing out into the Cantoris of Observatory cheered her. She put her hand to her chest, where the bit of metal hung.

"I'm Morys, by the way," the guide added. "Morys v'Observatory."

The cooking fire began to crackle and dance. The white-haired man straightened with difficulty and turned toward Sira and Morys. Sira watched him, wondering why he seemed familiar. He was thin, looking like a softwood tree at the height of summer. He looked, in fact, a bit like herself. But he must be very old. Too old, surely, to be riding out into the mountains.

He bowed to her as the others had, but stiffly. "Cantrix Sira," he said, in a deep voice. "I'm Niel v'Arren."

It was Sira's turn to take a sharp breath. A silence stretched around the campsite. The other travelers watched as Sira slowly rose to her feet to face the old man. The flames from the fire made shadows that moved across both their faces, their angular, bony, thin faces. One was smooth and unlined, the other weathered and creased to the texture of ironwood, but the resemblance was unmistakable.

"I'm your father," Niel said at last. "I feared you dead twice. Now I thank the Spirit you're well."

Sira was at a loss. She had been seven when her parents delivered her over to Conservatory. They had visited her once after that, in her third summer. She had now five summers, by common reckoning. More accurately, she was twenty-three years old. She had not seen her father in ten years.

Not knowing what else to do, she bowed deeply. "I am sorry, Father. I did not know you. And I never expected–that is, I—"

Niel nodded, his face as grave and unreadable as Sira's own. "I thought I should be here," was all he said, and crouched again by the cooking fire.

Sira hesitated. "My—my mother is—"

Niel looked up at her. "Your mother is well. Busy with grandchildren."

Sira nodded. There must be many grandchildren. There had been so many brothers and sisters, and more after she left. She hardly remembered their names.

Her own childhood had not been like those of the children she came to know at Observatory. Her classmates at Conservatory, with her teachers, had been her family. The name of Maestra Lu, her master teacher, still caused her feelings of bereavement, but now, hearing that her own mother still lived and was well, she felt nothing more than a vague relief. She remembered being fond of her father when she was a small child, but the development of her Gift had set her apart, isolated her from the family. She sifted through her memories, trying to understand how her father came to be with this party of searchers.

Niel prepared the *keftet* with the quick ease of long practice, and soon all the party were seated on their bedfurs facing the little fire. Practiced travelers all, they ate every bit of the meat and grain, and washed their ironwood bowls with chunks of old snow from beyond the perimeter of the *quiru*. There was desultory talk, but no one seemed to know what to say to Sira, and she had little to say to them. Only when they were all preparing to roll into their bedfurs and sleep did she turn again to Niel v'Arren. To her father. "I would like to know why you are here."

He turned his solemn face to her. The shadows deepened on his craggy features, and his eyes were dark and determined. "I heard about what happened with your first assignment. Bariken. All the Continent knows the story."

Sira kept her face impassive, but under her breastbone a little flicker of emotion surprised her. "Yes," was all she said. She doubted he had heard the whole story.

"You refused to go back into the Cantoris."

"So I did."

Niel stared hard at her. "But Nevya needs you. All of you."

The flicker grew into a flame, and Sira recognized it as anger. She controlled her voice carefully. "Yes?"

"I didn't give up a child to Conservatory to have her turn her back on her duty."

"I see my duty differently than Conservatory does." Her gaze was level, no less determined than Niel's.

"Have you thought what this will do to your mother?"

"I do not understand you. Why should this decision harm my mother?"

"She isn't a young woman. She's become accustomed to certain comforts, and if you abandon the Cantoris, those will be taken away."

Sira shook her head. "I am sorry for both of you," she said. "I have disappointed you, and Conservatory, but I cannot help it. I have not abandoned Nevya. There is work I must do."

Niel turned his back and went to his own bedfurs.

Sira lay down and pulled her furs around her chin despite the abundant warmth of the *quiru* in the summer night. The air above her sparkled and glimmered with the force of her anger. She could sense, as clearly as though she were looking at him, the Singer Iban watching, but she could not quell her anger. If her own father, stranger though he was, had come all this way to try to force her to obey Conservatory's wishes, then certainly even more pressure would be brought to bear upon her. Yet Niel had not asked her a single question!

She calmed herself as best she could, mustering thoughts of Theo's face, his smiling eyes, longing to be able to pour out her thoughts to him. Then she concentrated on the image of young Zakri, whom she had come to find, and who symbolized the work she had to do. Before she slept, her first night in the Pass in more than four years, she looked up at the distant stars twinkling through the *quiru*. Her hand found its way again to the bit of strangely marked metal on its narrow thong. Theo had given it to her only that morning, a morning that now seemed long past, part of a different life. The metal grew warm in her hand, and it seemed as if Theo's hand were on hers as she held it. She sent a silent prayer to the Spirit of Stars for him, and for herself, and then she closed her eyes and slept.

Chapter Nine

Morys bowed low in farewell to Sira as the others stood watching in the pale light of early morning. It was an unusual formality for an Observatory Houseman, and he held the bow for a long moment. The sun was up, but the air was chilly and the Visitor had not yet made its appearance in the southeastern sky. Mist frothed at the level of the ground, making the band of *hruss* appear to be standing in cloud.

"Cantrix Sira," Morys said at last, "until the Ship comes, Observatory will always remember you in its prayers. You have given us back our home."

Sira watched him prepare and mount his *hruss*. She drew breath to speak one final message for Theo, but in the end she released it unused. There was nothing more to say. No one here needed to know of her friendship with Theo, or its nature, or indeed to know anything of her private thoughts. And Theo knew her thoughts already.

As Morys lifted his hand to her, Sira bowed briefly. "My thanks to you, Houseman." She spoke without inflection, but she had to turn away to hide her emotion as Morys rode away. Morys would eat his evening meal with Theo at the end of this day, while she made camp among strangers. She blinked her eyes to soothe their burning, and busied herself with her *hruss*.

"You will not be needing the mount we brought for you, I see," the Singer Iban said. He had brought her rolled bedfurs to her to be tied behind the cantle of her saddle. "I'm surprised they let you keep the *hruss*. If they're a small House, every beast must be important."

"It is my own," Sira said. "It is the same I rode when I arrived at Observatory. I paid for it with my own *filhata*."

"And so now you have no *filhata*," Iban said lightly. "Doubtless you'll be given another."

"I do not think so," she answered, and left it at that. She supposed her own *filhata* had been sold long ago. It was the one she had been given as a student and had used at Bariken, then later given to the stableman at Conservatory in payment for her *hruss*. *Filhata* were not easy to come by, and it had not been easy to let hers go, but it had been necessary.

There was little conversation as they broke camp and rode away. Sira did not look back as Morys disappeared from the Pass, but she saw Iban twist in his saddle to watch as the guide rode into the jumble of boulders that marked the road to Observatory.

"It will do you no good, Singer," she said to him. "Only Observatory riders can follow that road."

The Singer nodded, accepting her statement without argument, which she liked. Unnecessary talk irritated her, and especially today. They turned their *hruss* to the northeast, and Sira tried to breathe away the ache in her chest. She drew out the bit of metal at her neck to cradle it in her hand. It was the only metal she had ever owned in her life. It flashed when it caught the sun, a cheerful brightness that made her think of Theo's easy smile.

"Singer Iban?" It was Tani who spoke, the rider from Lamdon. "Coudl you ask the Cantrix something?"

Sira looked at the woman, arching her scarred eyebrow. "You may ask me yourself."

Tani smiled and bowed slightly. "Can you tell us what the Houseman meant when he said, 'until the Ship comes'?"

"So I can," Sira replied. "It is a strange thing." All faces turned to her. Even Niel urged his *hruss* closer to hear her answer. On the Continent few people knew anything of the Watchers except stories and rumors. "The Watchers believe that the Ship of legend will come to take them from Nevya to some other place, a warmer place. Home, they say, as in the old lullaby. Two of them watch every night, from the top of Observatory, for the Ship to come."

Iban chuckled. "I know that lullaby. We sing it to children." In his light voice, he sang:

> LITTLE ONE, LOST ONE,
> SLEEPY ONE, SMALL ONE,
> PILLOW YOUR HEAD,
> DREAM OF THE STARS,
> AND THE SHIP THAT CARRIES YOU HOME.

The day brightened as the two suns wheeled above the Pass, the Visitor trailing low against the skyline as if barely able to keep up. Sira felt a surprising sense of freedom as she breathed the open air under a clear sky, after being so long closed up within doors. She liked hearing Iban's song.

> LITTLE ONE, SWEET ONE,
> DROWSY ONE, LOST ONE,
> THE NIGHT IS LONG,
> THE SNOW IS COLD,
> BUT THE SHIP WILL CARRY YOU HOME.

"I like that, Singer," Tani said when he finished. "You should sing it for my little daughter sometime. My own voice is not so sweet!"

Laughter rippled briefly among the travelers, and then they settled in silence to ride through the long day. The broad floor of the Pass was feathered with softwood shoots that made the reaches glow a soft green. Intermittent patches of old snow gleamed among the seedlings, and the air had the scent of summer. Sira breathed and thought, and made her plans.

Lamdon, the capital House, lay three days' ride to the northeast. Theo had worked as an itinerant Singer for ten years, and had told Sira as much as he could of the locations of the Houses and the small and large passes that connected them through the Marik Mountains, but as she rode now through the greatest pass of all, she reflected on how much she had to learn. Every hill and stone and valley had a name to the itinerants, and those she would need to know. Every House had its own character, its own influence, and these she would have to study. The task of learning she had set herself was almost as great as the one she had pursued for so many years at Conservatory, and the most difficult part was that she could not undertake it alone. She must apprentice herself to someone, an itinerant Singer, someone willing to teach her. He would have to tolerate the resentment that would follow her, the Cantrix who had abandoned the Cantoris. Sira had no illusions about what awaited her at Lamdon. She gazed at the wiry figure of the Singer Iban as he rode ahead of her, and she traced her scarred eyebrow with her finger.

The days of their journey were long and filled with sunshine. They rode with furs thrown back and faces lifted to the fresh breeze. Dom and Tani talked quietly between themselves, and with the Singer Iban. Sira was silent for many hours at a time. She rode alone, thinking, gazing at the mountains. Niel was also silent. She often felt his eyes on her, but she could think of nothing to say to her father. He was no less a stranger to her than the others in the party.

Their last day in the Pass they rode late into the twilight, hoping to reach Lamdon before the mid-day meal of the next day. When their camp-site was finally selected, and *hruss* were being unsaddled, Singer Iban turned to Sira. "I would like to hear you play before the end of our journey. Would you call up the *quiru* tonight?"

"So I will, if you like," she agreed. "But you must call me only Singer, if you please."

He looked at her closely, the gray of his eyes catching the half-light, his eyebrows drawing quickly together as they so often did. Sira found his mobile face fascinating.

He bowed. "Singer, then. Will you sing?"

She bowed in return, and reached inside her tunic. Niel was already spreading her bedfurs, and she sat cross-legged on them, looking out into the violet evening. It seemed a shame to dull the colors of the twilight with the yellow light of a *quiru*, but she knew well how uneasy Nevyan travelers felt without the familiar haven of light around them. True and complete darkness terrified all Nevyans. Even at Observatory, where darkness was required at night so the two Watchers under their glass dome at the top of the House could Watch, some light of the day's *quiru* remained.

Sira played in *Aiodu*, a lilting melody she and Theo had created in the long hours they spent in her room at Observatory. Their tune, wafting into the open air, delighted her, and she modulated to *Lidya* to express her pleasure. To return to *Aiodu* she took a long time, slowing the melody, expanding its shape, transforming the lowered third degree of *Lidya* into the first degree of *Aiodu*, until her piece settled naturally into its final notes. The *quiru* swelled swiftly at first, then firmed into a column of light and gentle warmth around the people and the beasts.

Iban nodded and smiled, eyebrows dancing now. "Lovely, Singer Sira. And I wish you luck in renouncing your title. On all the Continent, only the Conservatory-trained play so."

Sira was silent as the meal was prepared, and though desultory chatter rose about her, she did not hear it. She listened instead, in her memory, to Theo playing his *filla* at Observatory. His modulations were as deft and sophisticated as her own. She had taught him herself, as far from Conservatory as a Singer could get, and she knew him to be as capable as any Cantor.

Her father stood before her now, a bowl of *keftet* in his hands. "You're a full Cantrix," he said in his deep voice. "You can never put that away."

She accepted the ironwood bowl and did not answer. How could she explain to him what she was only discovering herself? They looked into each other's faces, which were so like, and Sira reflected that she and he were alike in other ways, too. After several moments she shook her head and looked away. Niel turned abruptly, returning to the cooking fire, leaving Sira to try to finish her meal despite her ruined appetite. Neither spoke again for the remainder of the evening.

*

The largest of all the Houses on Nevya lay between folds of hills, dominating the landscape. Its *quiru* glowed brightly even in the summer light. Some sensitive Cantrix who heard their approach hastened to summon a sizable welcoming party. The Magister of Lamdon himself stood with a number of the Cantors and Cantrixes and members of the Magistral Committee, and many House members gathered below them on the broad steps. The afternoon suns shone on the brilliant red and blue and green sleeveless tunics of the Housemen and women. Sira, in the drab years at Observatory, had forgotten how bright colors could be, and how the House members at Lamdon went bare-armed, boasting of the warmth of their House.

Dom stepped forward to help her dismount, but Sira jumped down before he reached her. She faced the dignitaries, and a plump dark man began welcoming remarks with much formality.

"Cantrix Sira," he said, aloud so the Magister and all the company could hear. "I am Cantor Abram, senior Cantor of Lamdon. Nevya has waited for your return for a long time. I speak for all of us here in bidding you welcome home." He bowed, and sent, *Cantrix Sharn would have been delighted to see you safe. She thought of you often.*

Sira bowed in answer.

The Magister began a rather long speech of thanks to the riders who, he said at length, had rescued Cantrix Sira. Sira saw the amusement dancing on Iban's face at the use of her title. Much was made of Niel, the father of the missing Cantrix, who had left the safety of his House to go in search of his daughter. Conservatory also, the Magister said, would be greatly relieved at the news that the Cantrix was home.

Through all of this Sira stood in silence. The ceremony wound slowly on, seeming about to end several times, then gathering energy for one more speech, one more round of bows. It seemed hours before the travelers were at last allowed to step through the enormous double doors, to be led to rooms where they could doff their traveling clothes. The Housekeeper of Lamdon, with yet another deep bow, introduced Sira to a Housewoman who would serve her, and promised a special evening meal and entertainment in her honor.

Lamdon was too warm in these weeks of summer, flaunting its Singer power. On most days three Cantors sang the *quirunha*. There were eight of them assigned to Lamdon's Cantoris. Not only were the House members able to go about with their arms exposed, Sira observed, but they needed to, or they would cook like *caeru* meat over a slow fire. She hurried to shed her heavy furs, and when her Housewoman invited her to the *ubanyix*, she accepted with alacrity.

The bathing tub at Lamdon had to be the largest on the Continent. The last time Sira had seen it she had been a guest of Sharn, treasuring a moment of intimacy with the old Cantrix who had known Maestra Lu so well. Now several Housewomen were soaking at one end. One of them was washing a babe who squeaked happily as the water splashed over its head. Sira dropped her clothes onto a bench, and stepped down into the tub to slip beneath the lavishly scented water. Flower petals floated on the surface. Sira caught one in her fingers, marveling anew at the extravagance. The contrast with Observatory, even the renewed and stronger Observatory, was vivid and distressing. She reached into a niche for a fragrant bar of soap just as another woman, loosening the binding of her long hair, stepped down into the bath beside her.

We are glad to see you back, Cantrix, she sent.

Sira looked up and drew in a surprised breath. *Jana!*

The other Singer did not smile. *Cantrix, of course. Like yourself.*

Of course. I am sorry. It has just been so long . . .

It has been long indeed. Jana's hair fell free to spread about her in the water. *All our class have been full Cantors and Cantrixes for at least two years.*

And you were assigned to Lamdon, Sira sent. *Congratulations.*

The only one of our class, Jana responded.

Where are the others?

Jana went through the list, naming eleven other Houses, and the young Singers who had entered their Cantorises. Sira nodded, remembering each, their strengths, their weaknesses. She hoped they had had better luck than she.

Did you know Cantrix Sharn? she asked at last.

Jana shook her head. *She died just before I came. The whole Continent mourned her.*

Their Housewomen came into the *ubanyix*, carrying thick towels and fresh tunics. "Cantrix Jana," one said, "Cantor Abram has asked to see both you and Cantrix Sira."

"Coming, Oona." Jana swept up the wet strands of her hair and twisted them to squeeze out the water, then stood to step out of the tub. Sira marveled at how plump she appeared. Sira's own body was as lean as a *wezel*'s, her long arms and legs like the softwood saplings flourishing now in the Mariks. At Observatory there were none but babes who carried extra flesh. She had forgotten what it was to see rounded arms and bellies, soft thighs, generous breasts. When she stood, the water ran down her flanks and over her own breasts, which were barely larger than those of a well-muscled man.

Jana sent, *Let us talk later.*

Sira accepted a towel. *Do you know if Isbel is well?*

Jana nodded. Sira saw the two Housewomen exchange a glance, knowing the Cantrixes were communicating.

She is well, I believe, Jana sent. She made a wry face. *But I met her senior. It must be difficult working with him. He is not an easy man.*

A little quiver of premonition ran through Sira's belly. She frowned, wondering at it as she rubbed her cropped hair with the towel and handed it back. She put on a clean dark tunic, without sleeves, and a pair of too-short trousers and light boots. She was ready, but she had to wait several moments while the Housewomen helped bind Jana's long hair. She tried to concentrate, knowing how important this meeting with Cantor Abram would be. She must postpone thinking of Isbel, fragile, loyal Isbel. Isbel would never have survived the sort of disaster she herself had experienced.

I only wish, Sira thought, that Theo were here. It is very hard without him.

Chapter Ten

Lamdon's corridors were so long that Sira could hardly see from one end to the other, especially in the brilliance of the *quiru*. The staircases were broad and deep, and echoed with the cheerful voices of the House members. Cantrix Jana showed her into a large reception room that was abundantly decorated with nursery flowers, demonstrating Lamdon's Singer-wealth. Only in a House *quiru* of this intensity could these fragile blooms exist, delicate petals of red and pink and lavender clustered in exotic shapes that made Sira think somehow of music. The people of Observatory would have been open-mouthed with wonder.

Sira turned her gaze away from the flowers and onto Cantor Abram and the members of the Magistral Committee who flanked Magister Gowan around a long, polished table. More flowers, in an ornate *obis*-carved iron-wood bowl, rested in the center of the table.

Cantor Abram rose and bowed. "Please sit down, Cantrix Sira," he said, aloud for the benefit of the Committee and the Magister. Only the Magisters at Conservatory came from the ranks of the Gifted. It was the only Magistrate not conferred by birth.

As Sira took her seat she was aware that Cantor Abram was staring at her. She strengthened her shielding, and saw his eyes flicker in his plump face as he felt her do so. Had he actually been intruding on her thoughts? Cantrix Jana sat next to her, as a friend would sit close by, but Sira doubted very much that there was anyone, in all this gathering, who could truly be considered her friend.

All eight of the Cantors and Cantrixes of Lamdon were present, and the Housekeeper as well. Three or four other people, wearing dark but heavily-embroidered tunics, stood behind the Magister in formal ranks. Niel v'Arren sat in a prominent seat at the table, as befitted the parent of one of the Gifted.

Sira drew a slow breath, and linked her long fingers in her lap. My struggle, she thought, begins here.

Magister Gowan cleared his throat. "Cantrix Sira, I hope you're feeling refreshed?"

Sira bowed slightly in assent.

"Hmm, yes. Good. Well, the Committee—" The Magister, short and quite fat with soft white hands, indicated the other men and one woman sitting near him. "You know, of course, that Rhia and Trude v'Bariken were punished after their conspiracy against you and Magister Shen?" When Sira did not answer he said with distaste, "They were exposed."

A perceptible shiver ran around the room, though this could hardly be news. It had happened nearly five years before.

The Magister continued. "Now the Committee feels it's important to hear your story, to decide what steps must be taken as regards Observatory."

Sira arched her scarred eyebrow. "Steps?" she asked in a dry tone. Committee members exchanged glances.

"Certainly," the Magister replied. "You didn't think we would let them go unpunished?"

Sira pressed her lips together to keep from smiling at the absurdity of it. She took a moment to choose her words carefully. "I very much doubt you can take any . . . steps . . . regarding Observatory." It was mildly, even casually spoken, but it was a challenge, and she saw that every member of the Committee realized it at once.

An uncomfortable silence stretched around the long table. Sira felt Jana wriggling nervously beside her.

What is it, Jana? Sira sent.

Jana answered, *By the Spirit, Sira, this is the Magistral Committee! You must be courteous.*

Sira cast Jana a sideways glance, then looked back at Magister Gowan. "Forgive me if I speak bluntly. I am no longer used to formal meetings."

"Of course, of course. We were thinking, Cantrix—"

"Singer, please."

Magister Gowan looked blank. "I beg your pardon?"

"I prefer to be addressed as Singer. I have not been a Cantrix for some five years."

"But surely, now that you are rescued . . ."

Sira did smile this time. "I am not rescued, Magister."

He was speechless before this remark, and Jana sent again, *Sira, please!*

Sira did not answer her old classmate. Instead, she rose and stepped back from the table to look down from her height on the members of the Committee. She found them effete, soft and colorless, insubstantial. Did any one of them know what it was to be hungry, to be ill, to be desperate? They were accustomed to having and wielding power. Through the senior Cantor they worked with Conservatory to control the placement of Cantors and Cantrixes, thereby holding sway over all the Houses. No Magister dared cross the Committee and risk being short of Singers in his Cantoris. Obedience was more important to the Magistral Committee than capable leadership. Sira had seen that much when she was at Bariken, and Rhia, the conspirator, had paid a bitter price for it.

Still standing, Sira addressed the Magister. "It was not necessary, nor was it possible, to rescue me. It is—" She was about to say, "foolish," but she caught the insulting word before she spoke it. "It is pointless to speak of punishing the Watchers. You could not find them, nor would you have any power over them. Observatory allowed me to leave only because, in the end, I gave them what they wanted. I am glad that I did. I learned a great deal from the experience."

Sira was not used to speaking aloud at length. She fell silent for a moment, searching for the right words while her audience waited, watching her. She sensed that some were angry, others suspicious. None was surprised. Several kept their minds tightly shielded, and she wondered what trivial secrets they had to protect. She felt the tickle of Cantor Abram's probe again and flashed him a look. Jana had turned away from her, as if to deny their association.

At last Sira said, "I will not be a Cantrix again, Magister."

"Cantrix Sira!" Cantor Abram spoke this time, with sharp authority.

"The shortage of Singers is more grave than ever. Perhaps you do not know how small the newest Conservatory class is."

Sira bowed politely to him. "There may be a shortage of Cantors and Cantrixes. But it would be most interesting to know if there is actually a shortage of Singers."

Cantor Abram frowned. "I do not understand you," he said crossly.

"The class at Conservatory is small," Sira went on, "but are there Gifted children who are not being sent to Conservatory?"

"There are itinerants' children—" Cantor Abram began.

A Committee member put in, "We're taking steps to make sure they're sent in the future. Those families withholding Gifted children will suffer severe penalties."

Sira turned to him, and said flatly, "That would be an error."

"You don't know what's been happening!" the man burst out. The woman next to him put a hand on his arm.

Cantor Abram stood and faced Sira. "It is an error for a junior Cantrix to challenge a member of the Committee! You had better explain yourself."

Sira nodded, ignoring the use of the title. "Yes, Cantor Abram, I will try." She would have been much happier to send her explanation than having to express it aloud. But she had put considerable thought into how she would make this speech.

"Two years after my arrival at Observatory, conditions were much improved there, and a Gifted child was born. Before I left, two more children were born who Cantor Theo and I believe are also Gifted, though they were too young to test." Sira touched her eyebrow with her forefinger, remembering Theo with a chubby babe in his arms, his blond hair falling over the child's downy head. "You should know that the population of Observatory is very small, no more than half that of the Continent's smallest House."

Cantor Abram exclaimed, "With three Gifted children born between summers? That is considerably out of proportion!"

Sira went on. "Like our ironwood trees, which are all part of one great whole, the Gift is part of our whole people. If one of the ironwood trees is destroyed, by a landslide or by being taken by the Glacier, all those connected with it suffer, and some of them die. If an ironwood tree sends out its roots . . ." Sira extended her arm, seeing in her mind the network of thick suckers crossing back and forth above the ground. When the suckers took hold, they grew massive, rock-hard roots that penetrated the tundra over years of slow growth. The itinerants who traveled through the passes were careful of the suckers, knowing how important they were. But how often did any of this Committee travel through the mountains?

"If the ironwood extends its roots, but finds only stone, or ice, the treeling cannot take hold and flourish. So it is, I think, with the Gift."

She paused, looking around to see if someone, anyone, understood what she was trying to say. Cantor Abram's eyes were bright. The Committee members frowned and shook their heads at each other.

"If the Gift finds only suffering, isolation, disappointment, it does not flower," Sira finished. "If the Gift is punished when it shows itself, it will not appear."

"That makes no sense," the Magister said. "We don't punish the Gifted, we honor them. Privileges, special favors for their families, respect . . ."

"Do you think we honor the Gift by taking little children from their parents? By isolating the Gifted from friends, family, colleagues?"

Niel v'Arren stood up, scraping his chair against the floor. "We do our duty!" Sira felt his anger, and something else . . . perhaps some inner doubt he was trying not to admit. "We make our sacrifice for the good of all the people! Do you think it's easy, giving up a child?"

"How else would we survive, except through the service of our Cantors and Cantrixes?" the Magister asked.

Sira said, "I do not have answers yet. But my years at Observatory taught me many things. The most important was that there is more than one way to train the Gifted, to realize the full potential of a Singer."

One of the Cantors spoke. "There is only one way to train for the Cantoris, and that is Conservatory's way. It has been so for a hundred summers."

Sira dropped her eyes. She had known the resistance she would meet, but even so she felt weary, anxious and alone.

Cantor Abram spoke harshly. "I am sorry, Cantrix Sira, that you feel the way you do. But you are needed. I must insist—"

Sira raised her head swiftly to look into her senior's eyes, to stop him. She sent, *Please, do not order me. I have no wish to embarrass you.* It was easy to send to him strongly. His mind was wide open. He had been trying from the beginning to find a way into hers.

Cantor Abram closed his mouth, hard. They stared at one another for a long moment. *You do not understand the situation,* he sent.

I believe I do. That is why I am here.

"Cantrix Sira," Magister Gowan interjected. "What is it you want to do? Is there perhaps some compromise?"

"I am going in search of someone, one Zakri. I met him by chance when I was—" She stopped, the old horror springing up in her. Setting her jaw, she thrust the feeling aside. "When I was junior Cantrix at Bariken," she finished. "He represents all the problems we are having with the Gift. His mother was an itinerant Singer, and his father refused to send him to Conservatory, although I tried to persuade him."

"All Gifted children should be sent to Conservatory, without exception." This statement came from one of the Committee. "We must have control over it."

"And we must control the itinerants," someone else muttered.

"Your controls are ineffective," Sira said. "The Gift is disappearing from the Continent."

Cantor Abram's voice was heavy with sarcasm. "Do you think you alone will find the answers?"

Sira stared at him. If only, she thought, Cantrix Sharn were alive. She at least would have listened, would have thought before she spoke. Sira allowed this thought to be read by Cantor Abram's constant probing, and she saw his eyes narrow.

"With the help of the Spirit," she said aloud, "I will at least try."

She turned to leave the room, but Cantor Abram called out a question. "Who is Cantor Theo? I know of no Cantor by that name."

Sira stopped in the doorway to answer. "He is Cantor Theo v'Observatory, who was the itinerant Singer Theo."

"How is that possible?" demanded Cantor Abram.

In this, Sira knew, he had every right to ask. He was senior Cantor at Lamdon, and therefore senior to every Cantor and Cantrix on the Continent.

"Observatory's need was enormous," she replied. "I resisted them for more than a year, but they were hungry and freezing. Infants were dying, and their mothers too. In the end, I sang for Observatory. And I trained Theo. Cantor Theo."

"Your teaching an itinerant Singer a few tricks does not make him a full Cantor!"

Sira bowed deeply to the Senior Cantor, to assure him of her respect for his office. "In this case it does, Cantor Abram. There is nothing any one of us can do that Cantor Theo cannot. He is precious to the Watchers because he makes their House warm and bright, because he gives them hot water for the *ubanyix* and the *ubanyor*, because they can grow food in their nursery gardens. And he heals their sick, better than most of us do, in truth." She ignored Abram's bridling at that remark.

She bowed again, to the room at large. "I am sorry I cannot give what you want me to give. But I am doing what I believe I must."

She turned swiftly then, and left the room. An uproar of angry and astonished voices followed her as she paced down the hall to the stairs and to her room. She would make ready to depart as quickly as possible. Her welcome at Lamdon, she had no doubt, was worn out.

Chapter Eleven

Sira found the Singer Iban in the kitchens after searching for him in the great room, in the stables, in the halls. She felt eyes on her wherever she went, whispers behind her as she wandered Lamdon's corridors. She had not been here a full day, yet it seemed everyone in the House knew who she was.

The chattering kitchen Housewomen fell instantly silent when they saw Sira look around the door. She almost did not go in, but one of the women left the counter where she was stirring something in a large bowl, came forward and bowed, wiping her sticky hands on a bit of towel. "May we get you something, Cantrix?"

All other work stopped. In the silence Sira heard the crackling of soft-wood burning in the huge ovens lining the inner wall, where the warmth could spill into the House and gardens. "Just Singer, please," she said. She felt awkward, as she so often had at Observatory, uneasy with working Housemen and women. "Singer Sira," she repeated. "I am looking for the Singer Iban."

"Please come in, then," the woman said. "He's right here." There was a rustle of movement behind her, the scraping of a chair on the stone floor, and Singer Iban came into view.

He was also wiping his fingers as he bowed. "So I am," he said, his eyebrows drawing high on his forehead. His gray eyes were almost green in the light cast by the brilliant *quiru*, and he fairly radiated curiosity. "May I help you in some way . . . Singer?" He smiled.

Sira looked behind him, down the long room, and saw a number of people, perhaps a dozen, seated around a plain work table with cups and platters of food before them. Every face turned up to her, alive with curiosity. She took a step back toward the door. "I am sorry to interrupt your—" She could not think what to call the gathering. "Your conversation," she finally said. "But I would like to speak with you."

With an easy wave that reminded Sira of Theo, Singer Iban excused himself from the group. "You're not interrupting much," he said cheerfully. "Just House gossip and a little Lamdon wine. I'm sure what you have to say will be more interesting!"

He led her down the long corridor to the front of the House, where the doors of the great room and the Cantoris faced each other across the wide central hall. No one was about, and Sira feared the committee meeting was still going on upstairs. As Iban gestured her into the great room, she glanced up the staircase.

He gave her a quizzical glance. "I thought you were meeting with the Committee."

"So I was," Sira said shortly. "But I am finished with them."

Iban's eyebrows danced. "With the Committee, it's usually the other way around. I can hardly wait to hear this."

They pulled out chairs at one of the tables, and seated themselves, careful not to disturb the bowls and spoons laid ready for the evening meal. Through the windows, Sira saw full darkness beyond the *quiru*. Indoors the House was almost as bright as day. She had become accustomed to the near-darkness of night at Observatory, had found it soothing and peaceful once the House had grown warm enough to be comfortable. It would take days, she thought, for Lamdon to cool enough to suit her.

She abandoned the thought. Soon Lamdon's overheated, overbright atmosphere would not matter to her. "I need a master," she said bluntly. "I must apprentice myself to an itinerant, to learn the craft. Singer Iban, will you take me?"

Iban pursed his lips and whistled, a long, low sound. He leaned back in his chair and gazed at Sira for a long moment before he said, "I was certain they would have you back in the Cantoris within a week. I'm still not sure they won't. How is it that a Conservatory-trained Cantrix wants to work as an itinerant Singer?"

Sira supposed, if Iban was to be her master, it was only fair that he know everything. As she had earlier, she wished she could send her explanation, but she supposed Iban could not hear her thoughts. She spoke aloud, slowly, struggling again for words.

"I was Cantrix at Bariken," she said. "The first of my class to leave Conservatory."

"Yes," Iban answered. "We all know the story. You were the youngest full Cantrix in memory, and we know what happened to you. I'm sorry."

Sira made a dismissive gesture. "That is not important anymore. It only matters that I learned from it." She paused, and stroked her scarred eyebrow with her forefinger. "The Gift and its training are not the straightforward things I once believed them to be. It seems . . ." One of Theo's proverbs came to mind, and with it, a half-smile to Sira's lips. "It seems the *ferrel* builds more than one nest."

Iban grinned. "I know that proverb. It's from the southern Houses."

"I mean by it that I have learned there is more than one way to cultivate the Gift. I learned that the Gift can be trained outside Conservatory."

Iban chuckled, and Sira looked at him curiously, not knowing what he was laughing at. Then she realized, with a rush of embarrassment, that this would hardly be a revelation to an itinerant. He had obtained his training—how? Certainly without benefit of Conservatory.

"I am sorry," she said. "Of course, you—" She opened her hands, expressively, lacking words. Iban smiled without apparent resentment. "Of course you know that already. Please do not be offended, but my experience at Observatory shows that the full realization of the Gift beyond that . . . that usually demonstrated by itinerants . . ." It was not easy to say it all with tact, and Sira cleared her throat and pushed her fingers through her hair, struggling to find words. "It is possible without Conservatory. My concern is the Cantoris."

"Although you won't accept one again."

"I will not. What I need to do is more important."

"Are you so sure?"

"So I am." She shrugged. "I must be."

"What is it you want to do, then?"

She searched his face with her eyes, hoping to find acceptance there. "First, I want to see my friend Isbel, Cantrix Isbel v'Amric. Then I must find one Zakri, son of an itinerant. I will offer him the training I gave Theo. Zakri will be my demonstration to the Committee."

Iban's thoughts chased across his face, curiosity, doubt, interest.

"Will you take me?" Sira asked. "As apprentice?"

He considered, looking down at his tunic, smoothing the fabric. He was never still, this man. Sira pulled Theo's bit of metal from her tunic and held it in her hand as she waited.

At length, Iban sighed and spoke. "Trouble will follow you, Cantrix, like a *caeru* pup follows its dam."

"I know."

"There is more danger in your plan than you think," he went on. His mouth sagged, and Sira sensed he knew something he dared not tell her. She had no feeling of deception, though, only that he bore some knowledge that weighed upon him.

"But," he went on. "Your skill with the *filla* is worth a little trouble. I know your friend Cantrix Isbel. I'll tell you the story of our meeting on our first night out. After you call up the *quiru* so I can hear you play again!"

"I thank you, Singer," Sira said solemnly. Iban put out his hand to seal the agreement, then pulled it back as he remembered who and what she was.

Sira was relieved. She disliked being touched even more than she disliked speaking aloud. They rose, and bowed to each other. "In the morning, then," Iban said.

"I will be ready."

*

Iban and Sira departed without ceremony early the next day. Sira had said no farewells, and given no warning. The Visitor had not yet risen above the southeastern horizon, and the lone sun shone in the pale lavender of the morning sky. They left from the stables, something Sira had only done once before. Sira saddled her own *hruss* and tied her gear on by herself, then met Iban in the stableyard, where he was chatting with a Houseman.

"I asked him not to mention our going," he said to Sira as they turned their mounts to the north and rode away from Lamdon. "Not to lie, just not to mention it until he's asked. Thought that might be easier for you."

Sira nodded her thanks. She thought of Niel v'Arren and his anger, and of Cantor Abram's offended look. It was good to be away from them, to be on her way, breathing the cool morning air and feeling the movement of the *hruss* beneath her thighs. She did not look back at the great House behind her, but forward, past the beast's drooping ears, which flicked back and forth as it settled into its swinging gait.

Singer Iban, she soon realized, would take his position as her master seriously. As they rode, he called out the names of every large rock, every peak they could see. He pointed to distant cliffs and described the passes that wound below them. He made her repeat the names, and made her look back once in a while, to see their passage from a different perspective.

"Remember your road both ways," he said, "coming and going. Keep the picture firmly in your mind, because you never know how long it may be before you travel this way again."

"Do you earn many bits of metal this way?" Sira asked once.

Iban turned to wink at her. "Not one bit this trip," he said, making her blush. He laughed. "But sometimes I do. It depends on how far the trip is, and how many people. And on the metal."

"I do not know what you mean."

He reached into a little purse and brought forth several bits of metal which he cradled in his palm. They gleamed dully in the growing light. "Bits of metal come in different sizes," he said. "See, this one is a good deal larger than the others. I might take just that one for a whole trip, say between Perl and Filus."

He held the pieces out to Sira and spilled them carefully into her hand. They were irregularly shaped, lighter than *ferrel* feathers. As she gave them back, she told him, "I have seen a piece of metal that is bigger than all of those put together, many times bigger. As big almost as a *caeru* hide."

Iban's quick features spoke doubt as he looked at her. "How is that possible? Are you sure it wasn't something else?"

"I am very sure. At Observatory they are so poor they must make all their own tools and clothes, yet they have a huge piece of metal hidden away in an upper room. It is like a slab of stone except that it weighs almost nothing. It has marks on it, like this one." She pulled out Theo's necklace from her tunic and held it up. "Many more marks than this. Pol, the leader of Observatory, claims it shows the Six Stars. They think it proves the Ship is coming for them."

Iban still looked doubtful. "I can't imagine that much metal," he said.

"But I've seen lots of bits with marks on them. It's like the fable, you know, that says the bits come from the Ship."

"Where do you think they come from?"

Iban shook his head. "No idea. It's one of the mysteries. I leave such things to my betters." He tipped up his head to scan the sky. "Ah, there's the Visitor at last. We'll be putting off our furs, feeling the suns on our necks. Nothing like a summer day for riding in the Mariks!"

Sira smiled at the wiry Singer riding ahead of her. She appreciated his easy manner. The Spirit must have sent him to her. Short of having Theo at her side, there could hardly be a more pleasant companion for her journey. She turned her own face up to feel the Visitor's warmth on her cheeks. It would be three days to Amric, Iban had said. She would enjoy those days, she resolved, three simple days to refresh herself for the work ahead.

The *quirunha* at Amric was just over when a Houseman bowed before Cantrix Isbel. "Excuse me, Cantrix. There's someone in the great room who wants to see you."

Involuntarily, Isbel glanced at Cantor Ovan, and was relieved to see him in private conversation with Magister Edrus. The *quirunha* had been difficult, labored and slow. Isbel knew Ovan would be angry with her, but Edrus had forestalled his biting comments.

She asked, "Who is it, Houseman?"

The man shook his head. "Only an itinerant. But she insisted I tell you." He added quickly, "I can speak to the Housekeeper if you don't want to see her."

"No, no," Isbel said hastily. "I will see her." She tucked her *filhata* under her arm and started out of the Cantoris toward the great room. Her Housewoman, who faithfully attended all the *quirunha*, was nearby, and Isbel handed her the instrument.

"Be sure to wrap it carefully, Yula," she said, then hurried across the hall to the doors of the great room.

Tears sprang instantly to Isbel's eyes when she saw her visitor sitting in the window seat. With a wordless cry, she ran across the great room, and in joyous relief fell to her knees beside the traveler. Forgetting all propriety, she sent, *Sira! Sira, my dear, dear friend!*

Sira, too, abandoned restraint. She pulled Isbel into a hard embrace. *Isbel . . . how I have missed you!*

Other people in the great room stared as the tears of their junior Cantrix soaked the tunic of this tall, lean itinerant. Isbel sensed their curiosity, and it dimmed her joy. Someone was sure to tell Ovan, and she would be censured. Again.

She drew away from Sira's arms, wiping her eyes, smiling at the same time. *Sira, it is so good to see you . . . to . . . to see you alive!*

Sira bowed slightly, ironically. Isbel's tears started afresh as she took in her friend's scarred eyebrow, slashed through with white. She saw too the beginnings of lines in Sira's face, though Sira had no more summers than she. She had lived more, Isbel supposed, in the last two summers than most Cantrixes did in their whole lives. But she was smiling now, and Isbel treasured the moment, knowing how rare Sira's smiles were.

Come and bathe, she sent. *When did you arrive? And how? We have not heard that you were found! You must tell me everything!*

Sira chuckled, and despite the watching eyes, Isbel took her friend's hand under her arm. They were both full Cantrixes, after all. They at least were entitled to touch, even to embrace if they so wished.

They spent a long time in the *ubanyix* that day, so long that Isbel climbed out twice to warm the water. She hoped Sira did not notice that it took her rather longer than it should have, and she swore to herself she would be better in the future. For now she could hardly take her eyes from Sira's face. She delighted in sharing her thoughts, keeping her mind open for long periods at a time. She only had to keep certain thoughts separate, pressed down in a part of her mind where no one, not Ovan, not Sira, hardly even she herself, would recognize them.

For hours she and Sira lay in the warm water, idly toying with bars of soap, with the leaves of the herbs that floated around them. They shared their memories of the years they had been apart, and it was a relief to send every idea, every comment, never having to search for the words to speak! Isbel's forehead tingled with pleasure.

Are you sure you will never take up the Cantoris again? Isbel asked at last. *Absolutely sure? You are so strong, and our need is so great.*

Sira ran her fingers through her cropped hair, making it stand on end. Her dark eyes gleamed, and the bit of metal that hung from her neck shone wetly as she moved. *I know the need. There is something I must do about it, but it will take time, and I cannot do it in a Cantoris.*

But never? Never to play the filhata *again?*

Sira's mind was so open that Isbel could sense the longing that filled her at the mention of the *filhata. Yes, that will be hard,* was all she sent. There was another longing, too, that Isbel sensed but Sira did not mention. She supposed it was natural, now that they were both grown, to have secrets. She took no comfort in the idea, because she very much doubted Sira's secret could be as dangerous as her own.

But I will listen to you play tomorrow, Sira sent. She put her long hand on Isbel's plump one. *I look forward to it.*

Isbel made a slight face. *Our* quirunha *are not what they were at Conservatory.*

Sira laughed aloud. *You should have heard some of mine at Observatory! Maestra Lu would have been furious.*

Isbel laughed, too, at the picture Sira sent of swift, efficient *quirunha* in the dank halls of Observatory, but she knew just the same it was not true. Maestra Lu would not have been disappointed in Sira.

She watched as Sira stepped out of the tub and dried herself. She felt certain her friend knew what she was doing, and that it would be just, for herself and for her people. Isbel wished she could be as certain that her own course was the right one.

Chapter Twelve

It was easy for Isbel to follow Cantor Ovan's lead in their *quirunha*. His musical ideas were as predictable as they were scarce. The problem was not making music, however inferior, with her senior. The problem was with her Gift, and the flawed concentration that had plagued her ever since the news of Sharn's death.

Their two *filhata* sounded in tune, Ovan's *Aiodu* melody properly supported by her plucked harmony. Isbel instinctively smoothed the vibrato of her voice to try to blend with Ovan's dry tone. Still, the warmth that swelled from the dais came in a sluggish wave that Isbel knew would disappoint Sira. She closed her eyes, trying to urge her psi to a more effective intensity. She remembered how to do it, how it felt when it spun properly out and away, exciting the air around her into warmth. But somehow the harder she tried, the worse it was.

Quirunha were well attended at Amric, with Magister Edrus and Housekeeper Cael setting a daily example for all their House. Today, Sira and the Singer Iban also sat on the benches, listening, concentrating with the Cantors. Isbel felt a stab of panic. She would fail, Magister Edrus would suspect something was wrong. What would they do to her when they found out?

Her next breath, taken through the tension of her fear, was shallow and trembling, almost useless. Her voice faltered, and, to her horror, she missed a fingering, and played a discordant harmony. For one terrible moment she could not think what to play next, what note to sing. The progression made no sense. She feared she might burst into helpless tears right there on the dais, in front of her senior, her Magister, and Sira.

At that moment she felt the firm undercurrent of Sira's psi slip beneath hers, as if her friend had put out her hand to lift her up. Her own psi strengthened, freshened, swelled the *quiru* in the old manner. Her voice steadied, and her fingers found their place again. There was no time to wonder if Ovan would know, if he would detect that extra psi. The light radiated from the dais, glowing with gratifying strength and swiftness. Ovan's satisfaction and Sira's reassurance mingled with Isbel's relief. Ovan brought the music to an awkwardly prepared cadence, and Isbel's fingers trembled with strain as she lifted them from the strings.

She could pick out Sira's deep voice from the others as they chanted the ending prayer:

> SMILE ON US,
> O SPIRIT OF STARS,
> SEND US THE SUMMER TO WARM THE WORLD,
> UNTIL THE SUNS WILL SHINE ALWAYS TOGETHER.

Kai's voice was there, too. He had returned from his hunt last night, very late. Although Isbel had not spoken with him, she felt his presence in the House as some deep, sweet music played far away. She dared not think of him now, not with Sira here, not with Cantor Ovan still so open. She dared not listen for the timbre of his voice as it blended with the others. She bowed to the assembly and stepped down from the dais, her eyes averted. She did not know how she would explain why Sira had been obliged to help her. How would she excuse her weakness?

There was no time for discussion at the moment. She and Sira, along with Ovan, were swept along with the House members into the great room for the mid-day meal. They sat at the center table with Magister Edrus and his mate, the Housekeeper and various other residents of the upper floors. Sira tried to turn away, to join Iban at one of the lower tables, but Cael bowed and held a chair for her, and she had to accept out of courtesy.

When the meal began, and conversation rose around the room, Cantor Ovan fixed his black eyes on Sira. *Cantrix Sira. Are you on your way to Conservatory now you are back? To receive another assignment?*

The sharp angles of Sira's face revealed nothing. *No.*

Ovan's eyes narrowed. *Are you ill? In need of rest or healing?*

Isbel wanted to intercede for her friend, to speak up, but her shame and fear made her afraid to open her mind. Sira's gaze moved to her, her eyes widening in the old way that meant she was open, ready to listen. Isbel closed her own eyes, as if to say, I cannot. Sira hesitated a moment, then looked back to Ovan.

This was a new Sira. As a student, she had been impatient, candid, blunt to the point of tactlessness. But today, she was protecting her friend. Isbel wished she could send her gratitude.

I am not ill, Sira sent to Ovan. Her eyes were almost as dark as his, but they did not glitter as his did. Their light was warm and steady. She could still be blunt, though. The tone of her sending was unyielding. *I am apprentice to the Singer Iban, sitting there by the window. That is the work I will do.*

Ovan shook his head. *You are turning your back on the people who need you.* When Sira forebore to answer this, his face darkened. *Conservatory will be ashamed. Do they no longer teach loyalty and service there?* Again Sira sat in silence, making good work of her meal in the ready way of travelers.

Isbel toyed with the spoon beside her plate, but the spicy stewed meat that was Amric's pride had no appeal today. The three Singers sat in chilly silence as the talk of the unGifted swirled around them and Isbel's meal grew cold. At the end, they parted without courtesy.

Isbel drew Sira toward her own room with a hand under her arm. *You are being kind to me. I thank you.*

Sira pressed Isbel's hand against her side. *There is little enough kindness in your Cantoris. And I have learned from Theo that there are reasons for everything.*

Isbel smiled, remembering Theo and his teasing. *I am so glad you are friends, you two,* she sent. She held a picture of Theo's merry grin in her mind so they could share the memory.

Sira was preoccupied as they went into Isbel's spacious apartment. She sat down at a table strewn with oddments, and one by one she picked them up: brushes, a little packet of thick paper from Clare, the small framed leather panel. Isbel sat on her bed. She pulled the binding from her hair and shook it free, combing it with her fingers. She wondered how she could explain to Sira, and how Sira could understand, even now.

Sira sent, *Theo and I are more than friends.*

Isbel tensed, letting the long strands of her hair hide her face. Had Sira guessed?

But Theo and I . . . Sira paused delicately, and Isbel felt her eyes upon her. *We do not mate. We do nothing to compromise the Gift. But we do . . . love. He is with me in all things.*

Isbel's eyes stung, and her lip trembled like a child's. *Sira,* she sent miserably. *I have been so lonely. I have no one here.* She did not want to tell her friend of her wekaness, of the temptation that distracted her so that her psi was impaired. She longed for the two of them to be back at Conservatory, sharing the innocent secrets of their student days, with nothing to worry about but modulations and fingerings and phrasings.

Sira put her strong hand on Isbel's knee, and Isbel pushed back her hair and looked up through a blur of tears. *I am sorry, Isbel,* Sira sent. *I know what it is to be lonely.*

Isbel understood then that Sira would neither scold her nor press her for explanations. Sira's understanding brought even more tears. Isbel dropped her face in her hands and sobbed while her friend, her dear friend, only sat by her, steady in her support and affection.

Isbel swore to herself she would get control of the situation, that the lapse in this morning's *quirunha* would never happen again. When her tears were dried, she and Sira would bathe, and it would be as if nothing had happened, nothing had gone wrong. It would be as it had been at Conservatory, when Isbel was the understanding one, protecting Sira from the barbs and jibes of jealous classmates. Sira was back, and for the moment, at least, Isbel need not be lonely.

The second day of her stay at Amric, Sira was relieved that Isbel managed the *quirunha* without her help. She knew something was very wrong, just the same. Even in the openness of their sending, some small part of Isbel's mind was closed away, hidden from her. There was more, too, some flaw in Ovan's Gift that made the *quirunha* drag. It was not only that the music was indifferent. Had Ovan been strong enough, Isbel could have overcome her difficulties. There was too much pressure on her Gift, straining it to the breaking point. Ovan was concealing something, too.

But today, Isbel flashed her dimples as they shared the morning meal. The night before she had told a story, a colorful tale about a *tkir* brought down by Amric hunters. The hunters were three brothers, she said, and their family apartment boasted the only *tkir* hide in the House, a huge tawny thing that they walked on each day, sometimes feeling its layered fur against their bare feet. It had been good to hear one of Isbel's stories again.

As they rose from the table after their meal, Iban approached, bowing politely to them both. "May I speak to you, Cantrix Sira?"

"Singer," she corrected.

His eyebrows danced. "Singer. But everyone treats you as a Cantrix, you know. You sit at the center table, you're in a Cantrix's company . . ." He bowed again in Isbel's direction.

"In other words," Isbel said, with another twinkle of dimples in her rosy cheeks, "you act like a Cantrix, Sira!"

Sira smiled, happy to see Isbel joking after her misery of the day before.

"It is like one of Theo's sayings," Isbel went on. "'If it has neither arms nor legs, and breathes only water, you may as well call it a fish.'" Sira and Iban laughed, and a pretty color rose in Isbel's cheeks. People passing them on their way out of the great room smiled at the sight of their junior Cantrix laughing with her friends.

"Now, Theo–there is a true Cantor," Sira told them. "He sings in a Cantoris and he serves a House. I do neither thing."

Iban chuckled. "Perhaps I should call you apprentice, then. As I'm now your master."

Sira bowed, assenting. He went on, "I've had word of Zakri, the one you're looking for. It was Zakri v'Perl, wasn't it?"

"His father was from Perl."

"Your Zakri's now at Tarus, on the Frozen Sea," Iban said. "A traveling party just arrived from there, and their *hruss* were cared for by one Zakri v'Tarus."

"Not Singer Zakri?" Sira asked, frowning.

Iban shook his head. "They were definite about that. He's a stableman at Tarus, and a very strange Houseman they said he is."

"I am afraid he is more than strange," Isbel said. "He is dangerous. Why are you seeking him, Sira?"

"I met Zakri when he was quite young, no more than three summers. His mother was an itinerant who died. He wanted to go to Conservatory, I am sure of it, but his father refused. We argued about it, his father and I."

Iban added, "The riders from Tarus say he doesn't like people a bit. Spends all his time with *hruss*."

"*Hruss* have no emotions," Sira said.

"His Gift is out of control," Isbel warned. "I am not sure you can help him, Sira. You must be careful!"

Sira nodded, and touched Isbel's hand. To Iban she said, in a voice of command, "We must go to Tarus. As soon as possible."

Iban's eyebrows lifted. He said to Isbel, "You see how the apprentice orders the master!"

Isbel giggled, and Sira was abashed. "I am sorry, Singer Iban. I forgot."

Iban only grinned at her, and Sira smiled at the two of them, touched by the easy way they teased her. Friendship was a precious thing.

Isbel sent, *Must you leave so soon?*

Soon enough, Sira responded. *I will leave it to my master. I will come back, though. I promise.*

They went out of the great room together. They did not notice the young Housewoman with her curly-headed daughter in her lap, huddled in the window seat. But Trisa, five years old, murmured to her mother, "I could hear them, Mama, most of it anyway. It was about a Singer, a boy who didn't go to Conservatory. He had the Gift, too. If he didn't go, why do I have to?"

Chapter Thirteen

In the Cantoris early the next morning, Sira sat far from the dais, and neither Isbel nor Ovan appeared to notice her when they came in. Isbel stood to one side, her head bowed, waiting for Ovan to step up on the dais before she took her own seat. There were only two House members waiting for them. In summer, illnesses seemed to be fewer, as if no one wanted to waste the precious weeks of warmth by lying in bed. Sira remembered dealing mostly with bruises and scratches, as the children ran and played out of doors with an abandon not possible in other seasons. Sometimes they tripped over rocks or ironwood suckers, and, squalling with surprise and indignation, had to be picked up and carried indoors by their parents.

Still, the man who sagged in a chair before the dais was very ill. His eyes drooped, and he had to be supported by his mate, who bent over him to mop his sweaty forehead with a bit of cloth.

Ovan waved a languid hand at his junior. Isbel nodded obediently, and brought her *filla* to her lips, closing her eyes. Ovan folded his arms and watched her, his eyes widening slightly as he opened his mind to follow.

Sira had not been invited to join with the two Cantors. Custom demanded that she leave them to their work, but she cared nothing for that. She followed Isbel, too, but at a careful distance. Her eyes closed to shut out all distractions. She rested her elbow on the back of the bench, and her chin on her hand. To anyone else, it might have looked as if she were dozing, a tall, lean itinerant lounging in the back of the Cantoris. In truth, it required all her concentration to follow someone else's psi at a distance without the aid of music and without being detected.

Isbel played a traditional *Aiodu* melody often used for examinations. It was a tentative sound at first, the theme stretched into long, slow notes, sounded one at a time, with a breath after each one, as if the player was not sure what pitch came next. Bit by bit, as Isel's psi brushed the sick man's mind, the melodic line grew stronger. Her breaths were steadier, and the notes she played more decisive. Her psi was set free to search out the source of the illness.

Sira had to discipline herself not to pull back as Isbel slipped more deeply into the sick man's mind. It was not pleasant to feel his pain and nausea, but she had learned from Theo that a Singer must experience the illness to understand it. She must know where it hurt and how much. She must accept the sour taste in the mouth, the agony in the stomach, the burning in the blood. All of this was difficult for Sira.

Isbel, it seemed, did it without hesitation. Sira felt Isbel's awareness of the man's misery as she probed his mind and then his body for its cause.

But there was no distaste, none of the disgust Sira herself felt despite her good intentions.

To one side, holding himself even further from the process than Sira, was Cantor Ovan. Sira sensed that he was mystified by Isbel's skill. His resentment was a strong presence, and Sira had to press down her own reactions so he would not be aware of her. He must not find her trespassing. Surely he was more hindrance than help to Isbel as she worked! She could hardly be open to the sick man's mind, yet closed to her senior's.

Abruptly, unmusically, Isbel switched to *Iridu*. Sira listened in surprise. It had been a trick of Theo's to use *Iridu*, a mode commonly used for sleep, when he was working with illnesses or injuries. He said it relaxed the sufferer, making the process easier for all concerned. Indeed, it seemed that the Houseman breathed more deeply now, that his body relaxed. Where could Isbel have learned to do this?

Soon she modulated again, more gracefully this time, into *Doryu*, for infections. She concentrated her psi on a spot deep inside the man's body, a place for which Sira knew no name but where she could feel the heat and the pain. For some minutes Isbel's psi worked there, but what she was doing Sira could not tell. She knew Ovan could not, either, by the intensity of frustration she felt from him. She wished she dared intrude upon his mind, slap him for the poor support he gave his junior, but she held back.

Isbel ended her melody in the middle of a phrase. She sat back wearily, her eyes still closed. Sira felt her fatigue, and the lingering sensations of fever and nausea in her mind. The Houseman's mate helped him to his feet.

"Your mate must rest until he has been cool and without sickness for three days," Ovan said firmly to the Housewoman, as if he had been in charge throughout.

"Yes, Cantor," the woman said. But it was to Isbel she bowed, as best she could with her mate's weight on her arm. "Thank you, Cantrix Isbel," she said clearly. "We're grateful to you."

Ovan's black eyes narowed, and the air around him shimmered, an irregular convulsion of light that flared and flickered above the dais, and made Isbel cringe. He sent to her, *There was no need to waste time in* Iridu. *Where did you pick up such an idea?*

Isbel looked down at her *filla*, avoiding her senior's eyes. *I do not know, Cantor Ovan. The idea was there and—I just tried it. It seemed to help.*

Do not experiment during Cantoris hours, he responded. He gestured to the next House member to come forward. *Our responsibilities are too heavy to be playing games.*

Sira could bear it no longer. She rose from her seat in the back and walked with deliberate steps toward the dais. Casually, but as distinctly as she could, she sent, *Congratulations, Cantrix Isbel. You are a far better healer than most of us. When I see Maestro Nikei, I will congratulate him on his teaching.*

Ovan turned to her, and the air around him now glimmered yellow with fury. *Are you spying . . . Singer?* His sending had a nasty edge to it.

Sira feigned innocence. She saw that there were gaps in the light around him, and her eyebrow arched. *Why, Cantor, have I offended you?* She bowed to the two of them. *I was merely observing, of course. The House-man was so ill, and his color and posture were so much improved when he left. It was impressive.*

He was not half so ill as he would have us believe. Ovan turned to the Housewoman waiting before the dais. *If you will excuse us now, we have work to do.*

As Sira left the Cantoris, she heard the strain of the same *Aiodu* melody now coming from Ovan's *filla*. It was too fast, an impatient, irritating tempo. Sira gritted her teeth.

In search of Iban, she was just passing the great room when a small, high voice lisped, "Cantrix Sira!"

The girl who trotted to her had to tip her curly head far back to see Sira's face. The lisp came from two missing baby teeth. The child had clear blue eyes and an intense expression on her round face.

"Yes?" Sira said gravely. Placing her hands on her hips, she regarded the little girl, appreciating her courage. She rather thought her own appearance must be terrifying, all height and thinness and scarred face.

"My mama wants to talk to you," the child said. She reached a chubby hand up to seize Sira's, to pull her through the open doorway into the great room.

The mother was waiting just inside. She came forward quickly, saying, "Trisa! You mustn't touch the Cantrix!"

"I am only a Singer," Sira told her mildly, but Trisa had already dropped her hand.

The woman bowed. "We're told you're the Cantrix Sira who was lost and then found."

Sira nodded to her. "True enough. But I am no longer a Cantrix."

The woman frowned in confusion, and Sira said, "Never mind, Housewoman. What is your name?"

"I'm Brnwen. This is my daughter Trisa." The Housewoman put her hand on her child's shoulder in a gesture that was both caress and protection. Sira's shielding was still relaxed from the Cantoris, and she felt Brnwen's sadness as a cloud over the bright day.

"Trisa has the Gift," Brnwen told her.

"Ah. I see." Sira looked down into the girl's eyes. *Can you hear me?* The child nodded. *Can you send back to me?*

A tide of confused images and words flooded from Trisa. Sira had to hold up her hand to stop the deluge. It was no worse than her own sending had been before she joined her Conservatory class, but it was almost unintelligible. Sira walked to the window seat and sat down. Brnwen and Trisa followed, Brnwen to stand before her, Trisa to kneel on the cushion and stare up into Sira's face. "What happened to you?" she asked, pointing at the scarred eyebrow.

"Trisa!" Brnwen exclaimed.

"It is all right," Sira said. "All children are curious, and Gifted ones deserve special privileges, as they bear special burdens." She touched her brow with her forefinger. "A *caeru* claw made this mark," she told Trisa. "It was in Ogre Pass, a long time ago."

"Did it hurt?"

"So it did."

"Can I touch it?"

Brnwen caught Trisa's reaching hand. "I'm so sorry, Cantrix. She's very independent."

Trisa subsided onto the window seat, but her blue gaze searched Sira's face. "Why do you cut your hair?" she piped.

Brnwen said, "No more questions, Trisa. I'm sure the Cantrix has things to do."

Sira turned her attention to Brnwen. "Did you not wish to speak to me?"

Brnwen nodded, and Sira felt again the emotion that shadowed the woman's eyes and bowed her shoulders. She was young, not much older than Sira herself. Her face showed signs of suffering no less distinct than the scar on Sira's brow. "I hope you'll forgive me, Cantrix, but Trisa heard— that is, we didn't mean to pry, but—"

Sira waited while Brnwen strove to express herself, but her little daughter was less patient. "It's the boy!" Trisa burst out. "The boy who doesn't have to go."

"Go where?" Sira asked.

"Conservatory!" Trisa cried, with emphasis. "And I don't want to go either!"

A strained silence followed this declaration. Sira hardly knew what to say to this child, or to her unhappy mother. She could hardly tell them what she was only discovering herself. And yet, she could not let another child suffer what Zakri had suffered.

She turned her face to the window, looking out at the summer-green landscape beyond the *quiru*. A few Housewomen had taken their children out to feel the suns on their cheeks and breathe the sweet air. On just such a day, five years before, a younger Sira had played her *filla* in the courtyard at Bariken, and a girl no older than Trisa had danced under the two suns. That Sira had been sure of her society, confident of her role in it. Since then, the very foundations of her world had shifted.

Trisa's eyes darkened and grew solemn, sensing Sira's mood. Brnwen again put her hand on her daughter's small shoulder.

I understand what you are asking me, Sira sent to Trisa, holding the girl's eyes with hers. *But I have no answer for you yet. The search for an answer is why I am here, why I am back from Observatory, and why I have cut my hair.*

A spate of blurred words and images poured from the little girl, with an intense flood of fear and anger and confusion. Around her head shone a ghostly aureole of faint light, the beginnings of her power.

I cannot really understand you yet, Trisa. And if you do not go to Conservatory, you will never learn to send clearly, or learn to use your Gift to its fullest potential. Do you not want to sing, and play the filla *and the* filhata?

Sira sent an image of Trisa with a *filla* at ther lips, her eyes peacefully closed, her face calm. Trisa shook her head, hard, and put one chubby fist to her mouth as she began to sob. She whirled to hide her face against her mother's tunic. Brnwen clutched her, and her eyes filled, too. Sira felt utterly helpless. She shielded herself, because there was nothing more she could do to help. Brnwen's pain was like a wound that could never heal.

"Please, Cantrix," Brnwen said brokenly.

"I am truly sorry, Housewoman. In time, I hope there will be another way. For now, Conservatory is what there is for Trisa. I assure you, it is a wonderful place full of wise people."

"Like Cantor Ovan?" Brnwen whispered. Sira took a sharp breath. Brnwen's aim was fiercely accurate.

"There are all kinds of people there, as at any House," she said carefully. "And for Trisa, the alternative does not bear consideration. A Gifted child, untrained, will go mad. As she gets older, she will hear every thought, feel every emotion around her, if she is not taught to manage her Gift."

"The itinerants don't go," Brnwen said, louder now. Sira respected her spirit. She could surely name the source of Trisa's independence.

She said gently, "The itinerants teach their own children, when Gifted ones are born to them."

"I would take Trisa to the itinerants, if my mate would let me," Brnwen said.

"I do not know what you mean."

"The itinerants have their own ways," Brnwen said. "At Soren, you know."

"Do you mean the craftsmen there?"

Brnwen's eyes slid away from Sira's. "Not just that," she muttered.

"Then what?"

But Brnwen only shook her head. "We are not supposed to talk about it."

"I want you to teach me, Cantrix Sira," Trisa cried, jumping up from the window seat. "We'll go with you, Mama and me."

Sira gave her a half-smile, and bowed to her. "I am honored, Trisa. But I cannot take a little girl with me, even with her mama. I do not know for a certainty where I am going or what I will be doing." She pointed to her scarred eyebrow. "And sometimes there is danger."

"I'm not scared," Trisa said.

Sira rose. "I believe that. I see you are a very brave girl. You will not be afraid of Conservatory, then. I hope you will like it very much, as I did."

"But you left the Cantoris," Brnwen pointed out, her gaze as blue and frank as her daughter's.

Sira bowed with real respect. "You are astute, Brnwen. I admire your strength. If I could, I would explain to you. You have earned the right. But it is not possible."

She looked back at Trisa. *Go to Conservatory, Trisa. One day I will visit a Cantoris and hear Cantrix Trisa sing the* quirunha. *That will be a great day.*

As she left the great room, she felt their double gaze, stubborn and unpersuaded, scalding her back.

Chapter Fourteen

Housekeeper Cael surprised Sira after the mid-day meal with an offer to replenish her traveling supplies. Amric was neither as lavishly decorated nor as profligate with its wealth as Lamdon, but it lacked nothing in comfort or resources. Cael took Sira to the kitchens first, to exchange her old, cracked ironwood bowl for one that was almost new. The Housewoman who managed the kitchens also laid out a new spoon, a cup, and an array of dried *caeru* meat, dried fruits, and herbs for tea, all of which she wrapped into a neat bundle for Sira's saddlepack.

Next Cael led Sira to a large room situated in the hall near the *ubanyor* and *ubanyix*. The sharp fresh scent of clean laundry drifted out the door, and Sira sniffed it with pleasure. A Houseman was scrubbing towels against a stone slab, soap bubbling around his hands. Near him a Housewoman was folding linens and stowing them on the long shelves lining the room. Sira had never been in such a room, though she supposed every House must have one. She had never given any thought to where clean linens and towels came from, other than from her Housewoman's hands.

"I'm sure you could use fresh things," Cael said tactfully. "I'll leave you with Petra to make a selection."

Sira bowed to him. "You are considerate, Housekeeper, and you are right about my need. But as yet I have no metal with which to pay for these things."

Cael's bow was perfect, neither deep nor shallow. "Cantrix Isbel wants you provided with every comfort," he said. "And Magister Edrus knows your situation. The House of Amric would not want Cantrix Sira, or any other Cantrix, to leave its doors unprepared."

Sira spread her hands helplessly, but she was grateful for Isbel's kindness. Observatory had had little to spare for her when she departed, just one change of linens, one extra tunic. "I am in your debt," she told Cael. He gestured to the Housewoman, and left the room as Petra came forward to assist.

In the stables, the situation was the same. Sira's saddle was freshly cleaned, her tack restitched and tidy, and her *hruss*'s feet trimmed and oiled. Again, she bowed to the stableman and apologized for being unable to pay him. She received the same assurance of Amric's goodwill, finding that again Isbel had smoothed her path. She strolled back through the corridor to the House, thinking, and met Iban at the door.

"Ah, there's my apprentice," he said. "At last. Ready to ride, are you?"

"So I am. Do you wish to leave now?"

"The morning will be soon enough." Iban's eyebrows did their merry dance. "Unless my apprentice has other plans?"

"That is for my master to decide," Sira answered.

Iban chuckled. "Commendable obedience. In the morning, then. We might as well cadge one or two more excellent Amric meals before we leave. And a nice long bath as well."

They turned toward the *ubanyor* and *ubanyix*, Sira with her new possessions bundled under her arm. It would be nice to feel fresh new linens
against her skin. She could not recall the last time she had known such
luxury.

"Excuse me, Singers?"

They looked back to see a young man coming in the door behind them,
a big fellow with short-cropped curly hair and an open face. He bowed to
them. "Cantrix Isbel asked me to see that you have everything you need."

Iban bowed in return. "Thank you." He gestured to Sira. "This is my
new apprentice, the Singer Sira v'—" He paused. "Well. I guess she's Sira
v'Observatory."

Sira nodded to the man. Her scalp prickled as she looked at him, as if
someone were drawing a *ferrel* feather across her neck.

Iban went on, "Kai, isn't it? Well, Houseman, Amric has been generous and efficient. Your House deserves its fine reputation."

"Are you sure there's nothing more I can do?" Kai pressed. "Your
hruss are groomed?" Sira gazed at him, wondering why her Gift was warning
her about this fresh-faced young man.

"Our *hruss* are in fine condition," Iban replied. "You're a hunter, aren't
you? Not a stableman."

Kai stood a bit straighter. He was even taller than Sira, muscled and
proud. "My brothers and I are hunters, it's true. But I'm always happy to
do errands for Cantrix Isbel."

"And where is she now?" Sira asked. Her psi still vibrated with warning. She saw the shining of the hunter's eyes, the slight swell of his chest as
he spoke Isbel's name.

"I believe she has gone with her Housewoman to the *ubanyix*," he
said. "You could find her there."

"So I will," Sira answered. She saw Iban watching her from the corner
of his eye, his lips pursed in question, but she walked away from the two
men without apology. She would bathe with Isbel one more time, and she
would say nothing to her about this Kai. But Sira had a suspicion now of
what was wrong here at Amric, and why Isbel was struggling with her Gift.

Each Cantor or Cantrix had to meet this challenge in his or her own
way. Conservatory had been right in this, as in so many things. Sira remembered Maestra Lu's instruction on the subject, a stern and uncompromising
discussion, given once and then never again, as if once were enough to
dispose of the temptation and the sacrifice for a lifetime. Sira remembered
also the long line of examples set by the Cantors and Cantrixes she had
known, the ones who sang at Arren, where she was born, her teachers at
Conservatory, her senior at Bariken, and all those she had since met in her
travels. Only one she knew had failed this test, and her life had never been
the same after. Sira had no doubts what Isbel's course must be. She only
wished her friend's challenge did not come in such an appealing and eager
form as the young hunter she had just met.

Sira and Iban left Amric early on a bright morning. The Visitor rolled
above the horizon, and the light of the suns picked out the mountain peaks
in crisp green and soft distant purple. Isbel, standing alone on the steps of

Amric, made a small ceremony of farewell for them. She looked small and forlorn beneath the tall peaks of the roof. *Come back as soon as you can, my friend. You are always welcome.*

I will, I promise. Sira touched her heart with her hand. *I thank you for your generosity.*

Sira's saddle leather creaked beneath her and the *hruss* whuffed impatiently, energized by the fresh air. These were the familiar sounds of travel, and Sira was surprised by the eagerness she felt to be on the road.

Iban bowed to Isbel, and lifted his hand in farewell as he turned his *hruss*. Sira tugged at the left rein of her mount to turn its head, but she watched Isbel over her shoulder as they clattered away over the cobblestones.

Goodbye. Longing permeated Isbel's sending. *Be careful, Sira, please. Goodbye.*

Worry dimmed the beauty of the day for Sira. She tried to sweep it away, to convince herself that Isbel's training would carry her through, as her own had. It was hard to leave her to face her troubles alone. But her master was riding steadily away from Amric, and she followed him. It was time to go, to continue her search. She could only pray to the Spirit of Stars for strength for Isbel.

The only House on the Continent farther away from Tarus than Amric was Isenhope, at the mouth of Forgotten Pass. From Amric they would ride west through North Pass to Perl, then turn south through the mountains to Clare, in the heart of the Southern Timberlands, where the irontrees grew so thickly in places that *hruss* could not pass through, and the huge suckers crowded out even the softwood shoots of summer. From Clare they would have an easy trek to Tarus, but the entire trip, even in these warm days when they could ride long into the twilight, required at least fourteen days.

Iban said Amric had assured they could eat every one of those days. It was a good thing, he laughed, because although many liked to travel during these weeks of summer, having a Singer in each party was not a necessity. They would ask at Perl, and again at Clare, on the off chance of earning some metal as they made their way south. There were many people fearful of traveling without a Singer, despite the clement season.

Sira was content just to be riding through a new part of the Continent. As they went, she asked Iban the names of the peaks that speared the sky to the south. He pointed out smaller landmarkes for her to remember. Before they stopped to rest the night, they were already four hours' ride into North Pass, with icy breezes from the Great Glacier chilling their backs.

Iban watched as Sira wielded the flint and stone, starting the cookfire with considerably greater dexterity than the last time she had tried. As apprentice, she was also required to unsaddle the *hruss* and assemble the cooking pot, the bowls and spoons and *keftet* ingredients. At that point Iban took over, not wanting, as he said, to spoil Amric's fine meat and grain with a clumsy hand. He chuckled as he said it, and Sira yielded gladly.

She sat back against a rock she had learned was called a *caeru* rock, because of its smooth, mounded shape, and watched the suns set in a glory of lavender and pink streaks. First the Visitor rolled gradually down into the purple mountaintops to the northwest. The sun, bigger and brighter, sank slowly out of sight in the western sky. For long moments after they both disappeared their light lingered, giving shape to the shadowy trees and rocks around the campsite. Sira sighed in appreciation.

"No *quiru*, apprentice?" Iban asked over his shoulder. He was bent over the little fire, carefully stirring their meal.

"Do we need one?"

"Perhaps not. But it serves to keep the *ferrel* away, and the odd *tkir.* We are not far from the Glacier, remember, and those beasts love to hunt on the ice."

Sira reached inside her tunic for her *filla*. As there was no urgency, she played in *Lidya*, for pleasure, and the *quiru* came into being languidly, a leisurely and gradual brightening. Yellow light bloomed slowly, like one of Lamdon's exotic flowers opening its petals one by one. When it was finished, she saw Iban sitting still, listening, having pulled the pot out of the fire. He looked up as the last echoes of Sira's melody sounded from the trees and rocks around them.

"I've never heard anyone, itinerant or Cantor, play the way you do," he said. "I wonder that Conservatory didn't send you directly to Lamdon when you completed your studies."

Sira pondered the thought. Suppose she had been assigned to Lamdon? She would have been proud, no doubt unsufferably arrogant, at such an early fulfillment of her ambitions. She would never have suffered the shock of the attack on her in Ogre Pass. She would never have met Zakri, or begun to understand the problems inherent in the Gift. She would have enjoyed a long and illustrious career at the capital House, playing and singing for an erudite and insular audience. And she would never have met Theo.

She smiled at Iban. "I thank you. I suppose the Spirit of Stars had other plans for me."

"And for me as well." Iban pushed the pot back into the fire. "In the normal course of things, I would now be instructing an apprentice in the *filla*. What can I teach Singer Sira?"

Sira looked about her at the night shadows, and above her at the stars that appeared in small clusters to glimmer softly through the light of her *quiru*. "I hope you will teach me the Continent," she murmured. "All the big and small things I need toknow about being a traveling Singer. When I find Zakri, I need to be ready."

"What will you do when you find him?"

"I will teach him to be a Singer. He will be my example. My demonstration."

Iban's brows waggled a question. "Suppose your Zakri doesn't want to be a Singer?"

Sira stared at him in surprise. The possibility had never occurred to her. She remembered Zakri when she had met him at twelve or thirteen years old, when he had craved Conservatory so much that tears welled in his eyes. Zakri's Gift had gone unattended after the death of his mother, and when she had offered him her *filla* one day, a ball at his feet had rolled away, propelled by the strength of his emotions.

"He does want to be a Singer," she said. And after a doubtful pause, "He must."

Iban shrugged, handing her a bowl of *keftet*, and they turned their attention to the meal. Sira found it wonderful, both the ingredients and the satisfaction of her fresh-air appetite. "How do you make it so tender?"

"You must soak the dried meat before you cook the grain," Iban explained. He held up the pot to show her. "Soak it well, then stew the grain in the same water. "These—" On his palm he displayed some green leaves, and pointed to them. "These you cook with the grain, while these others you add at the last moment. And don't overcook!" he cautioned.

Sira nodded. "I will try it tomorrow," she said, and at his chuckle, she added, "with your permission, master."

His eyebrows all but disappeared under his fringe of hair. "We'll see, apprentice," he said, and laughed. "We'll see."

Chapter Fifteen

The days of travel from Amric to Tarus were long and pleasant. At Perl, Sira and Iban rested only one night, and picked up a small group of travelers there, three traders from Soren who carried sewn-leather cases of *obix*-carved ironwood implements for trading. The men had acquired long rolls of felted cloth at Perl which they packed in a *pukuru* drawn behind a spare *hruss*. At Clare they would barter for paper, and add that to the load in the sled. They were experienced travelers, but even in summer they preferred the reassurance of a *quiru* about them each night. They were in no great hurry. Gossip, news, and storytelling occupied their days as they waited contentedly for an itinerant Singer to come along and guide them House to House.

The three traders paid little attention to Iban's apprentice during their first day, but when Sira played her *filla* at their first campsite, they stopped what they were doing and listened with surprised attention. After the *quiru* had risen, strong and bright and tall, they pressed Sira with questions. When she shrugged and did not answer, they turned to Iban.

Sira's story was well known on the Continent. Even at Perl, when the stableman had learned her name, he told his Housekeeper, and soon Sira was asked to the Cantoris to see her old classmate, Cantor Arn v'Perl. Arn behaved grandly, pleased to feel superior to Sira at last. Now, when Iban admitted who she was to the traders, she became Cantrix Sira once again, and they would neither touch her nor speak to her from that time forward unless she spoke to them first. They were uncomfortable being served by her, and Sira had to allow Iban to hand them their *keftet* and tea. She insisted, though, on doing her share of campsite chores.

Sira had grown adept at the fire-starting, and even at using the little axe Iban carried in his saddlepack. In North Pass, which was little-traveled, there had been plenty of deadfall for their cooking fire, and they did not need the supply of softwood they carried with them. Sira made *keftet*, with Iban watching over her shoulder, and she scoured the ironwood groves for lingering patches of snow to melt for tea.

On their third day out from Perl, Iban pointed to a cluster of *caeru* rocks beneath two ironwood trees growing together from one root. The smaller tree leaned to the south, and the larger to the west. "There's the landmark for the road to Conservatory," he told Sira. "The path doesn't look like much here, but as you work your way west it opens up. Look back at it, too."

They rode a few more minutes, and Sira turned to look over the *hruss*'s rump. The landmark looked different from the new perspective, the leaning trees framing the cluster of rocks as if guarding them. "Remember that," Iban said. Sira nodded. She would remember.

She did not look back again, but her mind took that path to the west, traversing the Mariks to the courtyard of Conservatory. She saw herself going in the doors, passing under the ancient plaque:

> SING THE LIGHT,
> SING THE WARMTH,
> RECEIVE AND BECOME THE GIFT, O SINGERS,
> THE WARMTH AND THE LIGHT ARE IN YOU.

In Sira's imaginary visit, Maestra Lu was still there, and Isbel, and the others. Studies went on as they always had in those best of all days, when the future was assured, and no doubts marred the pattern of Cantoris life.

Sira released a long breath and returned to the present. The mountains, the deep open sky, and the fresh smell of new softwood trees invaded her senses.

Iban watched her, his mouth drawn into a drooping line. "Are you unhappy, apprentice?"

"No. I am only remembering my student days. They were good ones."

"They say every Cantrix awaits her return home to Conservatory. Is that true?"

Sira bowed her head, letting the swinging gait of the *hruss* soothe her. She breathed in and out, through the sadness in the center of her body, where her diaphragm curved up below her heart. "It is not true for me," she murmured after a moment. "Not anymore."

They rode on in silence, and Sira felt Iban's sympathy and concern. Indeed, the Spirit had sent her a fine master. She sent a prayer of thanks that it was so.

In the evenings the traders talked about their House, Soren, as the cooking fire burned to ashes and the stars wheeled slowly above them. The Gift was of concern to them, too, since *obis*-carving was their stock for trading. Sira knew little about this aspect of the Gift. She listened with interest as they spoke of the talent that led carvers to Soren to work with masters of the craft.

"May we see some of your wares?" Sira asked once. The leader of the group bowed, and hurried to untie one of his leather packs.

Many of the items were familiar. There were ironwood bowls, combs, pieces of saddle- and harness-making, and tools for curing leather, making clothes, and gardening. Sira did not touch them, fearing the trader would insist she keep anything she seemed to like.

When they had looked over the tools, the trader reached deep into the bottom of his pack and brought out a carefully wrapped pouch secured by a thong. He opened the pouch and laid out its treasures, one by one.

Sira murmured her admiration. In this inner cache were the delicate, the beautiful, the graceful objects she had sometimes seen in upper-floor apartments. They served little or no purpose except to give pleasure to the eye and to the fingers. Iban lifted one up on his palm, and held it out for her to see.

It was ostensibly a shallow bowl, though far too small and intricately carved to be useful. In its center Sira made out a woman's face, the upward sweep of her bound hair described by the natural grain of the wood. Incongruously, the carver had inserted a scrap of metal, no more than a bead, to shine above the woman's head like the Visitor itself. It was not a logical choice, but it was lovely, and Iban said so.

The trader smiled his agreement. "This was made by our very best *obis*-carver. It will bring a good price, perhaps from the Magister's mate at Clare, or from the Housekeeper."

"Who is the carver?" Sira asked.

"Cho v'Soren," was the answer. "When he was a child, I remember there was talk of his Gift, but when he was tested, he didn't pass. Better for us he didn't!" One of the other men frowned as if in warning to the speaker, and he hastily rewrapped the tiny bowl and stowed it in his pack. Sira looked on curiously, wondering what it was about Cho that should not be spoken. She sensed, as she had with Brnwen at Amric, that something was being hidden, though she had no inkling what it might be.

The talk turned to other subjects, but Sira was silent, thinking long about the Gift and its many faces. She had tested a child herself, at Observatory, and the results had been as clear and shining as stars in a cloudless night sky. She wondered about those children who were found not to have an intact Gift. Would they be sorry or glad? She herself would have been crushed, and her parents disappointed, but Brnwen and little Trisa would have been relieved. She supposed no one person could understand the complexity of the Gift and its forms.

Clare was not a large House, but its *quiru* stretched wide to include its manufactory, separated from the House by a short enclosed walkway. For as long as anyone could remember, Clare had produced both the parchment and the thick brown paper used on the Continent. As the travelers approached the House from the north, the sour odor of soaking softwood pulp reached their noses even before they could see the roofs and the halo of *quiru* light.

It was still a new experience for Sira to enter the Houses from the stables. There were people to meet and remember, stablemen, kitchen workers, Housemen and women who would arrange beds and baths and meals. Iban was greeted familiarly by all of them. Sira sighed helplessly as he spoke a dozen names, expecting her to recall them all. By the time a smiling Housewoman showed her to the *ubanyix*, her head ached with concentrating.

"I'm sorry, Singer," the woman said. "I didn't hear your name." Her name, at least, Sira remembered, was Almra, and she was short and plump.

"My name is Sira," she said. Almra's eyes were as round as her figure, and she turned them up to Sira suddenly, like a startled *caeru* dam away from its den.

"Not. . . not the Cantrix Sira, are you?" she asked.

Sira pressed her lips together. It was no use. She would either have to change her name or resign herself to this reaction. "Not any longer," she answered, but it did no good. At least the Housewoman did not run away, but she saw her wordlessly to the *ubanyix*. She set out towels and soap, then bowed and withdrew. Irritated, Sira threw her clothes in a pile and splashed into the tub. The water was too cool, and she had to climb out again to retrieve her *filla* from her crumpled tunic, and stand shivering as she played it. Her *Doryu* melody brought steam curling from the surface, and when she slipped back into the water it was deliciously hot.

When she had soaped her hair and rinsed it, and washed herself thoroughly, she leaned back to soak and float for a precious period of comfort and solitude. Soon three Housewomen came chattering and laughing into the *ubanyix*. They shed their tunics and trousers, and one Housewoman with her hair still in its binding put her bare toes in the water. "By the Six Stars! The water's wonderful!"

"Now why would that be?" another one asked. "No important visitors today, are there?"

The others hurried into the tub, groaning joyfully as they sank into the hot water. "Like my bedfurs when Anton's at home," one of them cried, and the others laughed.

Sira waited until the laughter quieted. "Is the *ubanyix* usually cold here at Clare?"

The three women turned to her, startled. "Where did you come from?" one of them demanded. "I didn't see you there!"

"I am sorry," Sira said with asperity. "I have been here some time. I warmed this water."

"Well, we thank you for that, Singer. For once we won't climb out with *ferrel* skin all over from the chill."

"But surely your junior Cantor warms the *ubanyix* and the *ubanyor* each day?"

"Oh, he tries," the woman said, bending her head forward to drop her long hair into the water. "That's our Cantor Iov. He's all right, but he's overworked. Cantrix Magret is not very well. Age, maybe, or maybe she's ill. They don't tell us simple Housewomen much." The others snickered at that.

Sira sat up very straight, water dripping from her lean shoulders. They fell silent at the fierceness of her attention. "Did you say Cantrix Magret? Magret v'Bariken?"

"V'Bariken she was. V'Clare now. Why, have you traveled to Bariken as well?"

But Sira, courtesy forgotten, had already climbed out of the tub and was toweling her hair and rummaging for her fresh linens.

"What's your name, Singer?" asked one of the women. "We haven't seen you before."

Sira turned, her clothes in her hands. "I am Sira v'Observatory." A shocked silence followed her announcement. "I need someone to take a message to Cantrix Magret. And quickly."

*

A Housewoman came to Sira where she waited in the great room, and bowed deeply. "Cantrix Sira, Cantrix Magret asks that you come to her apartment. She'll have refreshments for you there."

Sira followed her out of the great room, up a staircase and down a long corridor. The Housewoman knocked softly, then opened the door. Sira stepped through.

She had not seen Magret since she left Bariken for her fateful trip to Lamdon more than five years before. Magret's hair had gone as gray as old snow, and her once generous body had wasted until it was as thin as Sira's own. She did not rise from her chair, though she lifted her hand when she saw Sira. Only her voice, sweet and true, was as Sira remembered.

"My dear," she called softly when she saw her former junior. *It does my heart such good to see you. I thank the Spirit for it!*

Sira strode forward to kneel beside Magret's chair. She took the white hands in her own strong brown ones, and looked into the older woman's face. *I am glad to see you as well. I have never had the chance to say I am sorry for failing you. I could not go back into the Cantoris.*

Magret shook her head, and closed her eyes briefly as if in pain. *It was I who failed you, Sira. I will never forgive myself for what it cost you, and what it cost my House.*

This is wrong, Sira responded. *You could not possibly have known what Rhia and Wil were planning. Whatever Rhia may have been, she was not stupid. Nor was Wil.*

Magret opened her eyes and smiled again. *Perhaps you are right. I am surprised you do not blame me. I wish I could cease blaming myself.*

Sira squeezed Magret's hands until the older woman winced, and she eased her grip. *Please, Cantrix Magret, do not give them even this victory, that you should suffer for what they did. They are all gone now beyond the stars. And I did not know you had left Bariken!*

I could not stay there, Magret sent, *any more than you could return. When Trude's son by Magister Shen is of age, he will be Magister. Every time I saw him, it all came over me again. I could not work.* She gestured, and her Housewoman came forward with a tray of tea and fruit. *Come now, I have some time free. Tell me all about yourself . . . what I have not heard through gossip, that is!* Her eyes crinkled in the old cheerful way, but Sira knew she was not her old self, not at all. She looked aged, though Sira recalled she had only nine summers.

Are you ill, Cantrix Magret? she asked bluntly.

Magret shook her head. *I am just weary. I cannot seem to sleep, and I grow more and more tired every day.*

Is there no one to heal you?

Magret lifted one shoulder, as if to shrug with both would take too much energy. Sira drew a chair close, and put her hand on Magret's again, feeling the chill of her skin and the tremor of her fingers. *May I presume to offer you my help?*

Perhaps after we have had some tea, we can think about that, Magret sent. *Now tell me your news. I have not had a visitor in such a long time.*

And so Sira did, sending the story of the past five years in words and images, confiding in Magret her hopes for the future of Nevya. For a long time they sat together, until the tea grew cold and Magret's Housewoman came to spread a fur robe over her mistress's lap. Magret did not rise when it was time for the evening meal, but received it on a tray. Tonight it was a meal for two, and the Housewoman served it with tact and efficiency, not interrupting their silent communication. When the meal was over, Sira rose to go.

Must you go so soon, my dear? Magret asked. *Why not stay here with me?*

Sira looked about at the well-furnished apartment. It was certainly large enough, and there was a couch that looked almost of a size to accommodate her long legs. *Thank you. I will stay. And perhaps you will let me help you sleep.* She pulled her *filla* from her tunic and held it up in question.

Magret gave her weary nod, and spoke to her Housewoman, who hurried forward to help her to her bed. Aloud, Magret said, "It would be good to sleep well, just one night. My junior—" She stood, stumbling a little, and Sira added the support of her arm to that of the Housewoman. "Cantor Iov would like to help, but his healing skills are not strong. And when I do not sleep, I am little help to him."

"Why does Conservatory not send you someone to help?"

We must not speak of that. Something our Magister did or said angered the Committee. They will not allow him another Singer. It is very hard for Iov.

And for you, Sira sent.

Between them, Sira and the Housewoman made Magret comfortable. Sira sat near her bed and played in *Iridu*, a simple old melody. She wove a strong *cantrip* for sleep into it, directing it with strength and affection. There were dark places in Magret's mind, she found, rough places that were hard to soften and smooth. For long minutes she played, until at last the Cantrix's troubled features relaxed and her breath came deply and slowly. Sira sat back, exhausted and sad. She wished she could help Magret, who had been kind to her. She prayed to the Spirit of Stars to show her a way. Only when she was certain, by extending her thought into Magret's that the Cantrix was deeply asleep, did she go to her own rest.

Chapter Sixteen

The short weeks of summer were already beginning to fade as Singer Iban led Sira through the Southern Timberlands to Tarus. The path wound and twisted, searching out clear spaces where travelers and *hruss* could pass through the thick growths. Even then, huge suckers stretched between the ironwood trees, threatening to trip any careless *hruss* or human. The scanty patches of old snow they had been using for water disappeared, and Iban showed Sira where to look for tiny streams running from the

Glacier toward the sea. On their last day out, Sira was startled to find water falling from the sky onto her head and hands. When she looked up, drops of it, sweet and clean, splashed on her face and in her eyes.

"What is it?" she asked in wonder.

Iban laughed, and pushed back his furst to let the drops fall on his face. "Have you never seen rain?"

"I do not know what it is."

"Summer snow," he chuckled. "The Visitor turns all the snow into water, even the falling snow. Especially here, so close to the sea."

Shortly after they passed out of the rain, the light southerly breeze brought a salty fragrance. Sira's acute hearing caught an odd, distant roaring, as of a great wind. The trees around her were still, and the *hruss* seemed unconcerned. "Singer Iban," she said. "I hear something very strange."

His eyebrows flew up into his ragged hair. "Can you hear the sea already? I can't yet."

Sira sniffed at the new odors and listened hard to the rushing noises at the fringes of her hearing. Indeed, the Southern Timberlands were as strange as Theo had said. Although she had been born at Arren, she had left it so young that she remembered nothing of the coast.

That night they camped on a great bluff, and Sira stared for a long time at the expanse of water and ice stretching away to the south. It was even more vast than the Great Glacier, a heaving mass of green and white roiling into the distance until it met the edge of the sky. Great chunks of ice floated in it. Iban told her that when the summer was several weeks past, a good bit of the sea itself would be frozen solid.

"I haven't been to Manrus," he said, "but I hear that below the ice cliffs, people walk on the Frozen Sea just as the hunters walk on the Glacier. Even a *quiru* can't melt that ice."

Sira drew her furs close around her, feeling the chill of the changing season. Far into the night, she woke to see a strange grayness beyond their *quiru*, and though it was not raining, her furs and all their equipment were slick with damp when they rose in the morning. She tasted salt on her lips, and could hardly tear her eyes from the vista of moving sea and ice.

"Does it cover the whole world?" she asked Iban.

He looked out over the sea to the distant horizon. "No one knows that," he replied. "And I don't want to find out! These coastal Houses fish in little *kikyu* no bigger than a *pukuru*. They go bobbing about between hills of ice as they were *carwal* themselves. Me, I like keeping my feet on solid ground."

As they rode away, Sira stared over her right shoulder until her neck ached.

They went directly to the stables at Tarus when they arrived. A stableman greeted them, and opened the stable doors for their *hruss*. Sira looked around for Zakri, but she saw no one familiar. Iban knew hardly anyone at Tarus, having been there only once.

"You have business here, Singers?" the stableman asked in a friendly manner. "We don't get many travelers this far south, even in the summer.

And that's about over, it looks like." He helped Sira with her saddlepack, and she undid the cinches and lifted the saddle from her *hruss*'s steaming back.

"We're looking for somebody," Iban said. "We've heard there's a boy called Zakri here."

The stableman's smile faded, and he eyed Iban with a sudden wariness. "What would you want with him?"

Sira said, "Only to talk. I have been trying to find him."

"What's he done?"

Sira and Iban glanced at each other. "Done?" Iban asked.

"He came here by order of Lamdon. Kicked out of two other Houses." The stableman gave them a dark look. "But you know about that, don't you?"

"Better not to spread rumors," Iban said.

The stableman only grunted in response. He led their *hruss* to a loose box, and returned to hang the halters on a peg. "Come back after dark. He'll be here. I wish you luck with him, but you'd better watch yourself."

Sira said, "He is only a boy."

"A dangerous boy! He practically killed someone at Amric."

"I will be fine," Sira said firmly.

The Houseman gave a snort. "This is the first time that one's had anybody to visit him. He cares only for *hruss*. I never saw a man go so long without human company. Does his job, though, and you'll see how well the *hruss* look."

Iban shrugged, and the Houseman laughed, his cheery demeanor returning. "Come on," he said. "Almost time for the evening meal. The House-keeper will want to meet you."

Iban offered to come with Sira as she sought out Zakri for the first time, but she preferred to be alone for this initial meeting. She came back into the stables just as the rest of the House was settling in for the night. Beyond the *quiru* the dark was coming earlier each evening. As Sira walked from the House to the stables she saw the first stars begin to glisten through the limeglass windows.

The stables smelled richly of *hruss* and tack and fodder. The patient animals roamed in loose boxes or stood hipshot in stalls, sometimes whickering with their deep-throated sound, shaking their drooping ears. Tarus's stables were smaller than some, but clean-swept and tidy. Even the thick windows were clean, inside and out.

Sira looked into the tack room. Zakri was not there, but some task was in progress, with odd pieces of leather equipment and well-used rags piled on a bench next to a lidded ironwood jar of tallow. Sira sat on the bench, and stretched out her legs. She idly sifted through the little pile of tack, wondering if she could guess what needed doing.

She was turning a stiff braided leather nosepiece in her hands when the tallow jar leaped from the bench and cracked into two jagged pieces on the stone floor. Its thick yellow contents spilled in a pool around her boots. She gasped and jerked her feet away from it. When she looked up, she saw a furious face in the doorway.

"What do you think you're doing?" its owner demanded. He was of medium height, slender, with brown eyes that flashed in his pale face. "Put that down!"

Sira had no need to put the nosepiece down. She had no more than opened her hand when it flew from her, rising into the air and splashing into the muck of tallow at her feet.

"Now look!" the boy exclaimed. He whirled and disappeared as she stared after him, struck dumb.

It took several moments for Sira to recover herself. She had never seen such uncontrolled psi in her life, not even when her class was the newest and least-trained at Conservatory. There was no doubt in her mind that she had found Zakri.

She stepped over the puddle of tallow and hurried to the door of the tack room. "Zakri, wait, please," she called after him. He did not return. Frustrated, Sira turned back to the mess on the floor. The braided nosepiece had sunk into the pool of tallow along with the pieces of the ironwood jar. As she walked toward it, she felt a sticky pull. The fur of her boots was mired with the stuff, and she had left footprints across the floor from the bench to the door. She sighed, and shook her head. Not a good beginning.

She used a rag to clean up the tallow, trying to scoop it into a half-empty jar she found on a shelf. As she cleaned off her boots and the nosepiece, she sent gently, *Zakri. I am Sira. We have met before, at Bariken. Will you not come back and talk to me?*

There was no response. She reached out with her mind, and found him just outside the stables. She tried again. *Zakri, I am Singer Sira who was Cantrix at Bariken. I have come here to find you.*

Nothing. Sira put things back where she had found them. She waited a little longer, and then, with a sigh, gave up. Tomorrow, she told herself, she would try again. Or perhaps she could find Zakri in the great room, when he would not be startled. Once more she sent to him, just his name, but there was no answer. It was possible he could not hear her. But it seemed just as likely he would not listen.

Sira was becoming accustomed to the reactions of people when they heard her name. Even at Tarus, so far to the south, it was evident that the House members had heard exaggerated stories about her. She sensed no resentment that she had left the Cantoris, at least not among the Housemen and women. Housekeeper Aleen v'Tarus was another story.

Aleen started and her eyes widened when the stableman said Sira's and Iban's names. She called a Housewoman to show them to the baths and to sleeping rooms, but she backed away from them as quickly as she could, and hurried away. At the morning meal the next day, as they sat at one of the long tables, Sira felt eyes upon her from the center of the room. She sensed some strange emotion that she could not at first identify.

She looked past Iban to the Magister's table. The Magister was there, with his mate beside him, and Housekeeper Aleen and several others in the dark tunics of the upper levels. They were all talking, laughing, enjoying their meal in normal fashion, except for Magister Kenth. He glanced quickly away when Sira's gaze found him, and she understood then the emotion being broadcast so strongly. Magister Kenth v'Tarus was afraid of her.

"Singer Iban," Sira murmured. "What could there be between the Magister of Tarus and myself? Do you know?"

Iban's features came alive with curiosity. "Why? What's happening?"

"I am not intruding on anyone's thoughts," Sira hastened to assure him. "But the Magister is afraid of me. I am sure of it."

Iban pursed his lips as he thought it over. "You were Cantrix at Bariken. Who was it that . . .?" He paused, evidently not wishing to offend her.

Her lips twisted. "It was the Magister's mate, Rhia, and the House-keeper Wil. Also the former Cantrix Trude. They tried to kill me, not for myself, but because I was with Magister Shen's traveling party."

"Hmm. Well, I don't know a connection. I'll ask around."

Sira felt uncomfortable throughout the meal. She shielded herself carefully, but still felt the Magister's eyes on her. There was no sign of Zakri at the meal.

Sira and Iban idled away the day, Iban making friends with any who were willing, Sira fretting and pacing, eager to get on with her plans. When darkness fell, she went again to the stables. This time she waited until she was sure Zakri would already be there.

Before going into the tack room, she sent to him. *Zakri? It is Sira. May I come in?*

She sensed some response, some emotion felt dimly, as though filtered through the fog she had experienced on the bluff the morning before. The boy's psi was incredibly strong. It was unthinkable he could not hear her at all.

Sira took a hesitant step toward the door. *Zakri? Are you there? Can you hear me?*

Another moment passed. A third time she tried, sending her thoughts as strongly as when she was teaching Theo to hear. *Zakri! Can you hear—*

Her thought was cut off in midstream by his angry cry. "Stop that! Stop screaming at me!" he shouted. "Can't you leave me alone?"

She heard something fall from the wall inside the tack room. Zakri's anger burst over her, blinding her senses. She put her hand over her eyes instinctively, as if she could ward off the blow, and her strongest shielding sprang up, so that for several seconds she could neither hear nor send. The uncontrolled psi broke over her like a wave of the Frozen Sea, and until it subsided she felt she could hardly breathe. Minutes passed as she leaned against the wall, waiting for Zakri to calm down, and for her own heart to stop pounding.

When she could, she spoke aloud. "I want to help you. I have come a long way."

She sensed, from the other side of the wall, his effort to control his psi. At least nothing else fell or broke in the silence that followed. More time passed, while she waited as patiently as she could. Finally, the door to the tack room flew open to bang against the opposite wall. Zakri stood in the doorway, breathing hard, his eyes wide and blazing. Sira stared at him.

He could not, she thought, be more than seventeen. He looked as if he were still growing, with arms and legs too long for his body. His brown hair was fine, tied back in a thin tail like that of a *hruss*, and he wore the bright red-and-blue tunic of a working Houseman. He hissed, "Leave me alone!"

Before she could think of another plea, he rushed past her and out into the stables. She saw him hurry into one of the loose boxes and disappear behind the bulk of a *hruss*.

Sira had no intention of giving up, but she was trembling from the strain of resisting his angry psi. Such uncontrolled energy was especially dangerous to any Gifted ones who came within its range. She turned away to walk slowly back into the House. She needed to think of a way to deal with Zakri that would be safe for both of them.

Wearily, she made her way to her own room, and lay down on the cot. As she tried to sleep, she remembered the eager, vulnerable youngster she had met at Bariken so long ago. His problems were just beginning then. His father had promised Zakri would get the training he needed, but clearly it had not happened. Perhaps no itinerant could deal with the strength and wildness of his Gift. She wished she knew what had happened to him in the last five years.

She tossed on her cot for a long time that night, listening to the distant rush of the sea, punctuated occasionally by the crash of an ice floe against the rocky cliffs. After a long time, those same sounds lulled her into an uneasy sleep, in which she dreamed unexpectedly of Isbel and Kai. She woke several times to find her bedfurs tangled and her neck stiff. In the morning she rose, feeling as if she had not slept at all.

Chapter Seventeen

Zakri curried and brushed the Cantrix's *hruss* until it groaned with pleasure. Even its tail was silky soft when he was through. It was the only way he could think of to apologize. Tears wet his face, and more than once he leaned his forehead against the docile animal, sobbing out his grief and his anger.

How long had it been since he had been able to talk to anyone? His father had given up on him, and so had his brother. No itinerant Singer who valued his livelihood dared take him as apprentice. He had grown even worse in his isolation. It was harder and harder to control the lashings of his psi, those surges that leapt out from him like lightning in a summer sky. He shuddered, remembering the final humiliation that had sent him into this lonely life.

It had been at his home, at Perl. His father, Devid, was already furious with him, because the itinerant Singer who had been his master, the third to try him as apprentice, had made a hurried and unprofitable trip, with much muttering and shaking of his head, to return him to his father's hands. Devid made a public comment in the great room about this latest failure, and a flood of hurt and resentment and confusion burst from Zakri, right there in front of the House members. An entire table overturned, littering the floor with broken ironwood. *Keftet* and tea flew everywhere, splattering Housemen and women. Shocked faces had turned on Zakri and Devid both. A woman with a bleeding cheek went off for a bandage while her mate shouted at Devid to do something about his devil of a son. Devid had stamped away, leaving Zakri trying to apologize, trying to help clean the mess, eventually slinking away in misery. He had just over three summers then. He had been not quite fourteen years old.

Thank the spirit for *hruss*, or he might as well have died that same day. He dried his eyes on his sleeve, and swore for the hundredth time not to shed any more childish tears. He carried the *caeru* bristle brush and the ironwood curry comb back to the tack room and put them neatly on their shelf. His fingers lingered a moment on the comb, and his anger threatened to rise again. At least his father could have sent him to Soren! He could have learned to guide an *obis* knife with his psi. Perhaps someone there could have taught him to control his wild Gift, this cursed talent that had cost him everything.

But it was too late for any of that now. He needed only to be left alone.

He remembered Sira well from that summer after his mother's death. He remembered her standing in the Cantoris at Bariken, tall and straight and sure, demanding to know why he had not been sent to Conservatory. His father had been barely civil to the young Cantrix.

He remembered her playing, too, that magical, liquid sound she brought from the *filla*, and her agility on the strings of the *filhata*. He could not risk hurting such a person, nor could he bear to shame himself further in front of her.

Zakri went to the door of the stables to look up at the night sky and sniff the sharpening cold in the air. He wondered if it was too late in the season to travel without a *quiru*. He could run—again—find another House that would let him work with *hruss*, work at night when no one could bother him, and when he could bother no one else. He watched the dense icy fog roll slowly in from the sea. It was too late, but he was tempted to go anyway. Who would care if one crazy stableman from Tarus froze to death in the Timberlands?

Tears started up again, and he turned away from the door, blinking and stumbling. The *hruss* behind him were unaffected by his emotions, thank the Spirit. Even among the unGifted, his moods seemed to spill over onto those around him. Angry now, at himself and his father, at his memories, he seized an ironwood shovel and began to scrape at the floor of a stall.

He made too much racket to hear her approach. It was in his mind that he heard her, a gentle, almost a diffident call.

Zakri? Would you speak to me for just a moment? I am sorry I disturbed you last night.

Her sending was so clear, so precise, that he understood almost all of it. His forehead tingled, and the urge to respond in kind was almost irresistible. He bit his lip as the old envy surged over him. She would know, she would sense it, but he couldn't control it.

"I can't!" he called. "Go away!" As strong as his envy was his fear that he would hurt her in some way. He couldn't imagine anything worse.

From a distance, he felt her refusal to leave. She was as stubborn as a *hruss* refusing to leave its warm stable for the cold outside. His admiration swelled as he thought of the stories he had heard about her. He believed every word. He tried to close his mind to her.

Zakri. Will you not forgive me for upsetting you?

Fear made him furious. Hardly knowing he did it, he threw the shovel to the stone floor with a clang, making the *hruss* jump. He leapt to the door of the stables. The heavy tools on their pegs shivered with his emotion. If she came too close—it just wasn't safe.

"You have to go away!" he cried in desperation. His voice cracked, a harsh and ugly sound. "Leave me alone!"

The mist swirled outside, obscuring the cliffs and the sea. He wanted to immerse himself in it, lose himself, as the trees were even now disappearing in its gray folds.

She wouldn't give up, he could tell. Three nights now she had come here, tempting him. If only he could risk it, and let her try to help him . . . but she was Cantrix Sira, and far too important to put at risk for one ruined Gift and one miserable stableman. If he hurt her, what would they say about him then?

Zakri opened the stable door and dashed out into the fog.

Sira stepped cautiously into the stables, watching for things that could fall or fly through the air. Nothing was moving, and as she made her way past the stalls, listening, she began to worry. Where was he?

In one of the loose boxes, she recognized her *hruss*. Its coat was smooth and shining, its tail combed to silk. Even its drooping ears had been brushed. She gazed at it for a long moment. An angry, cruel boy would not take such pains over an animal. A sorrowing, lonely one would.

Sira searched the entire stables without finding Zakri. Her heart beat faster when she saw the door left open in back, especially when she saw that his furs, the silver-on-gray *urbear* furs worn by so many of the Tarus House members, still hung on the wall. She hurried to the door and looked out into the heavy fog that blanketed the ground. *Zakri! It is too cold for you.*

When she received no answer, she sent her thought out into the grayness, searching for him. He was there, certainly, but she could not tell where. She called his name aloud, once, then seized his furs from their peg and pulled them on. They were far too short, but they would protect her for the moment.

Gingerly, she stepped out into the mist. The stones of the stableyard were slippery with damp, and she could see only a short distance in front of her. She stretched out her arms like a blind woman, hoping not to run into a tree or a boulder. The *quiru* light made the fog muddy and strange, somehow more dense than if there had been no light at all. The cliff was not far off.

Zakri, where are you? She took a few more steps, cautiously, and stopped. The fog was cold, and she pulled the furs tighter. Soon, she supposed, this mist would hold crystals of ice, and even this short venture into the darkness would be perilous. Even now, with the furs around her, she felt the lethal fingers of the deep cold reach for her throat, for her lungs. *Zakri!*

Taking small blind steps, she reached the edge of the *quiru*. Beyond it the fog roiled and curled, obscuring the stars. The sea roared its unceasing song off to her left, and she was afraid to step out into the dark.

But Zakri must have. If a frightened boy could risk the darkness and the cold, how could she do less? Cautiously she stepped forward. The warmth drained away from her as she passed out of the *quiru* and into the grayness. She could see her feet, but nothing more. The sound of the sea filled her ears. *Zakri!*

Zakri wished he had seized his furs on his headlong rush into the cold and dark. He knew the terrain behind the House, so the fog only slowed him a bit, but the deepening cold numbed his fingers almost immediately. He crossed his arms and thrust his hands into his armpits, hunching his shoulders. Her call was clear and persistent. He leaned against an iron-wood tree, shivering. He would freeze to death, he told himself, before he would let her get close to him.

But a sudden sharp cry, wordless and in full voice, sent the blood racing in his body. He stood straight, trembling, his ears straining into the darkness. No more sending tickled in his mind, and he heard only the sounds of the sea with his ears. For many moments he stood, frozen in an agony of doubt.

His fears were realized. She had fallen, he was sure of it. She was so stubborn, so set on her own purpose, that she, who knew nothing of the ground out here, had followed him into the fog, and had fallen. O Spirit, what if she had slipped over the edge of the cliff?

He called out, "Cantrix!" He heard no answer, neither with his ears nor his mind. "Cantrix Sira!" he called again. Only the sea answered. "By the Six Stars," he swore, "if she is dead, I will throw myself over, too."

Cautiously, he stepped from behind his tree. The fog was so thick he had found his way mostly by feel. How would he find her in it? He could wander all night until he froze and still not know where she had fallen.

Experimentally, he took a few steps toward the House, still listening, but hearing nothing. He turned toward the cliff, but that was useless. There were a dozen places where a mistaken footstep would cast a person over to fall on the rocks or into the ice-laden water. He would have to search with his mind, open himself. He would have to risk everything.

When he was a little boy, Zakri had played games with his mother. As an itinerant, her skills had been limited, but the two of them had been close. They had played guessing and finding games without the others in the family knowing. In a way, that had made it worse for Zakri when she died. His mind had been open and exercised in a fashion few itinerants experienced. At this terrible moment, though, he was grateful.

He had to relax his mental shielding to try, and there was danger in that. He knelt where he was, oblivious now to the cold, and concentrated. He had not truly opened his mind in years. He feared it was a dam that would burst apart when he removed the first stone, that a horrifying flood of psi woud be released. But he saw no choice. He had to try.

Carefully, he began, letting his mind open little by little. He allowed his thoughts to run free, first one at a time, then several. He felt his lack of skill in the feelings and fears spilling out of him like streams of water from a melting snowbank. But he also felt Sira's presence, off to his right. She was alive.

Zakri, with a sense of surrender, allowed his mind to touch hers. Or perhaps it was her mind that found his. Either way, there was warmth in the contact. Her Gift was as powerful as his own unruly one, but perfect in its discipline. He turned his face in her direction. Though he was unable to send words, he sent his question, and received a laughing reply.

Indeed, I am unhurt, she sent. *I have not fallen, nor have I taken injury from your Gift.*

Zakri got to his feet and went to her, stepping carefully on the fog-slicked stones. She emerged from the mist, wearing his own *urbear* furs, looking as tall as a softwood treeling.

She smiled a little as she looked down at him. "I am sorry to have deceived you. I could think of no other way."

Tears welled afresh in Zakri's eyes. He looked down at his feet, away from the kindness in her face. He sobbed once, then pushed his knuckles against his mouth to stop the sound.

She didn't move away, or speak. Where others had wept, too, or railed at the discomfort he caused them, Cantrix Sira only waited for him to regain some control.

The cold was becoming intense. "We'd better get inside," he whispered. Sira followed as he led the way back into the light of the *quiru* and then into the fragrant warmth of the stables.

Sira took off his furs and put them around his shaking shoulders. They were still warm from her own body, and Zakri felt awe that she should share her warmth with him. He stared at his boots. "What do you want with me?" he asked hoarsely.

"I am going to teach you."

"No one can teach me. My Gift is ruined."

She closed the stable door and put her back to it, gazing at him. In his mind he heard clearly, *Your Gift is intact, Zakri, and so, thank the Spirit, are you.*

He brought his gaze up to hers. "You think you can make me into a Singer after all?"

Cantrix Sira smiled down at him, and he saw her scarred eyebrow for the first time. It had not been there when he met her at Bariken. *From now on you will send me your thoughts. You need the practice.*

Zakri shook his head. "It's not safe. When I open my mind, things happen."

It is perfectly safe with me. Begin now, please.

A little flame of hope began to burn in his breast. *I will try*, he sent hesitantly.

She nodded. *Good. Then I will see you tomorrow night.*

She bowed to him, and he stood amazed as she left the stables. O Spirit, he thought. What will happen to me now?

Chapter Eighteen

Sira was heavy-eyed and weary at the next morning's meal. Iban sat across from her, eyebrows dancing as he examined her face. "Not sleeping well, apprentice?" he asked.

"I hardly slept at all," Sira said. "But Zakri and I finally came to terms last night."

"He's like a *ferrel*, is he, only out in the dark?" Iban laughed. "Everyone at Tarus knows about him, though they never see him. They're just as pleased to have it that way."

"Are they?" Sira leaned her cheek on the heel of her hand, and stifled a yawn. "That is a very sad thing. Do they know he is only a boy?"

"They know he's a boy who's all trouble. But wonderful with *hruss*."

The *keftet* was excellent at Tarus, flavored with vegetables tart with brine and with the rich taste of fresh fish brought in by the fishermen in their little *kikyu*. Sira ate it with appreciation, despite her sleepiness. She hoped the Housekeeper would give them some dried fish when they left, and she said so. Iban's face creased in a swift frown, and Sira's psi prickled. "What is the matter?"

"I hardly know how to tell it," Iban said. "But the Housekeeper has made it clear to me that we have no invitation to stay long."

"They want us to leave already?"

"She didn't say exactly that. But there is something . . ." Iban shrugged and laughed. "The name of the great Cantrix Sira seems to hold no special powers here. Rather the opposite. It seems Magister Kenth is in haste to have you gone."

"How odd," Sira murmured. She looked over her shoulder at the Magister's table, but he was not there. The Housekeeper Aleen was, her head bent to listen to something the Magister's mate was saying. When she looked up, she caught Sira's eye and glanced quickly away. Too quickly, Sira thought. Why should that be?

"We cannot leave yet," she told Iban. "I have only begun to work with Zakri, and I do not think we can take him with us until he is in better control."

Iban made a mock bow. "I thank you for that, apprentice. From what I hear, the lad leaves smashed belongings and weeping faces wherever he goes."

"What can we do?"

"We can stall, saying we need a traveling party. We could offer metal for our keep, though that's not usually done."

"Can we not find out what the trouble is?"

Iban shook his head, looking out into the morning mist. "I've asked, but gotten no answer. I think you'd better hurry your teaching. We can't stay where they don't want us."

Sira rubbed her burning eyes. She felt so tired that deciding anything seemed impossible. "I will try. But some things come only in their own time. His Gift is much abused."

Iban regarded her with sympathy. "You know, apprentice," he said very softly, "if I could hear minds . . ."

She looked up at him under the arch of her eyebrow.

"It's just that if we knew what the trouble was, perhaps we could do something about it," he offered, watching for her reaction.

"I think you know I cannot do that," she sighed. "But I will begin teaching Zakri tonight, and we will simply have to stay here as long as we can. I suppose they would not throw us out?"

Iban chuckled. "No, probably not. But itinerants live by their reputations, and I certainly don't want mine spoiled."

Sira pushed back from the table and rose. "I think I must sleep, master. I will be seeing more of the stars than the sun in the next weeks."

Sira remembered Theo's tuition as a time of laughter and discovery, pleasure in his Gift as well as her own. Trying to harness Zakri's wild power was another matter entirely.

She went to him every night, and worked side by side with him in the stables as she began his instruction.

Send me the names of things, she began. They were on opposite sides of a *hruss*, Zakri with a curry comb, Sira with a brush. The *hruss* made its throaty noise, enjoying the attention. Sira held up a slender, pointed tool with a serrated edge. *What is this?*

Zakri's first response was a blur of mental noise that made Sira blink and rub her forehead. He looked at her over the back of the beast, quick tears forming in his eyes. "I'm sorry," he muttered. "I'm no good at it."

You will be. Focus your thought on the name of the thing, then tell me its purpose. She went on brushing out the long hair beneath the *hruss*'s chin, ready to shield herself.

It is a hoof pick, he sent.

She smiled across at him. *Good. It looks as if it is made from a* tkir *tooth.*

Without warning, an overwhelming image assaulted Sira. A huge *tkir*, tawny and speckled, leaped out of the darkness, great mouth open, jagged teeth dripping foully. The acrid stench of its body overpowered her senses, and terror of the beast's claws immobilized her. She cried out, and her shielding sprang up to protect her. For a moment she trembled with shock. When that passed, she still breathed hard. Perspiration trickled down her ribs. "By the Ship, Zakri! What was that?"

His tears did fall now, and several tools rolled from nearby shelves. Sira ducked, but one caught her a glancing blow on the shoulder.

"I told you!" he cried. "I'm no good at this!"

Sira stepped back from the *hruss*, trying to conceal how strongly the scene had affected her. It was not only the surprise of the event, but the incredible reality of it that stunned her. She ran both hands over her hair, then leaned against the side of the stall, collecting herself.

"I'm sorry, Cantrix," Zakri muttered miserably. He picked up the fallen tools, and turned back to bury his face in the *hruss*'s mane.

"Zakri, did you see that *tkir* yourself?"

He shook his head. "My father did, and he told us about it. It gave me awful dreams when I was little, and my mother would have to sit with me until I fell asleep again."

Despite Sira's shielding, the strength of Zakri's sadness clouded her mind, so the light around them wavered and dimmed. She put her head back against the wall and closed her eyes. This was not going to be easy.

When she had regained her equanimity, she said, "Now. We will start again from the beginning. It will be different for you than for others."

"It's hopeless!" he burst out.

Sira held up her narrow hand, and he dropped his head in shame. "Your Gift is incredible," she said quietly. "Its very strength is its greatest challenge. You must accept it for what it is, give thanks for it, then find a way to discipline it."

"You really think you can help me? Show me how, as my mother would have?"

Sira bent and picked up her brush again. She came back to the *hruss*, pressing down her private thoughts. She doubted even Zakri's mother could have coped with this wild talent. She only prayed that she herself would be strong enough. "I will show you as best I can. But in the end, you must be the one to take control of your Gift."

He nodded, looking at her with wet, miserable eyes, but setting his jaw as if preparing for a fight. He looked terribly young, younger even than his seventeen years. Sira had to quell an impulse to put her arms around him.

"You must remember, first," she said, "that I am no longer a Cantrix. I am only Singer."

"I will remember," he said solemnly.

"And now, we begin again," she said. Cautiously, she held up the brush in her hand, hoping it held no strong associations for him. *Send me the name of this.*

Chapter Nineteen

Isbel's voice felt full and flexible. Her sweet vibrato filled Amric's Cantoris with a beauty that made Ovan's tone even more colorless and harsh in comparison. Her fingers were strong and sure on the *filhata*, and her harmonizations exalted Ovan's drab melodies. But her psi, her Gift, was unpredictable. She would be there with Ovan, the *quiru* growing as they worked, expanding and intensifying, glimmering around the dais. Then it would be as if her feet had suddenly gone out from under her. Her psi would falter and weaken, and it seemed there was nothing to lean on, no support in her moment of difficulty.

Her senior was in a constant state of fury. Today was worse than ever, and after the chanting of the ending prayer, he turned on her. *Am I to do all of this by myself, then, Cantrix?*

His scorn was as painful to her as a blow. *I am sorry, Cantor Ovan.* She hung her head, contrite and frightened. Misery made her droop like a nursery flower needing water.

He towered over her. His face, pinched tight, made her shrink away from him. *See that you have pulled yourself together by Cantoris hours! I will try. I am so sorry.*

Sorry does not make quiru, *does it?* His step was heavy as he left the dais.

Kai was waiting for Isbel when she walked out of the Cantoris, though he kept a careful distance. The others around them, working House members and many of the upper class, nodded sympathetically to their young Cantrix; Cantor Ovan was not a popular man. Isbel and Kai walked away from the Cantoris with a little space around them, as if they two were in some way separate from everyone else, yet together. Still it seemed no one suspected.

"What happened?" Kai whispered, when they were far enough from the crush of people.

Isbel tucked her *filhata* under her arm and looked up at Kai with brimming eyes. Only Kai, she thought, cared how she felt. Only Kai cared for something other than how swift and strong her *quiru* could be. When he stood before her like this, so tall and strong and sweet, she thought she could not bear it. How could the Spirit have set her such a trial?

"It was as before," she answered him. "I simply could not do it. I could not keep up."

"He deliberately makes it hard for you!"

It was tempting to believe that. Isbel could have said, Yes, yes, he traps me, he confuses me, interferes with my psi. But she would always know it was not true. Her eyelids drooped, and she shook her head. "No, he does not, he could not. It is my own fault. My own weakness."

She walked on with a dragging step. The staircase was empty, and Kai followed her up, watching for other House members as he went. When they reached her apartment, he looked up and down the hall to make sure they were not observed, then reached for the door latch. Isbel held up her hand to forestall him.

"It is because of my love for you," she blurted. A sob caught in her throat. "I must choose, Kai. I must!"

Kai withdrew his hand from the door, and stood looking down at her. They did not touch, but the feeling between them was tangible, a bond that tightened and pulled. It seemed the more they resisted, the more it drew them together, like a wet leather thong that contracted as it dried.

"If you must, you must," Kai said. His voice was thick with longing. "You know I'll do whatever you ask. I'll abide by your decision."

"I know," she said faintly. "But it is a very hard decision."

He took a step away, and she put out her white hand as if to stop him leaving. "But what would I do without you?" she cried.

They stared at each other, there in the corridor, until the sound of voices told them someone was coming up the staircase. Kai touched his fingers to his mouth and then to Isbel's lips, and hurried away, first walking backward with his eyes on hers, then turning to run as the voices came closer. She slipped quickly through her door, and stood with her cheek pressed against the heavy wood as if it were Kai's broad chest. There, in solitude, she shed her tears.

After a time she dried her eyes. She wrapped her *filhata* and returned it to its shelf. She felt no appetite for the mid-day meal, but she had to gather her strength for Cantoris hours. They loomed before her like a threat, a punishment. They always seemed endless, with too many ill or injured people, and Ovan frowning beside her. Too often, just as she was about to identify some person's ailment, just as she was approaching its source, her senior would break in, spoiling the rapport. He flared at her with irritation and anger. Never, though, was he able to pick up where he had forced her to leave off. In such cases the ailing House member went away disappointed, feeling no better, and Isbel's sense of failure deepened.

She went to her cot and lay down with her hand over her eyes to shut out the *quiru* light. She had not slept well in so long. Could that be the problem? Surely she had not done anything so wrong that her Gift should be seriously impaired. It had been so little—a fleeting kiss, the pressure of his hand against her back, her waist. How could it be wrong, when his touch was so sweet, his hands so strong, his lips so warm? If she sent him away from her, she would have nothing. Her life would be utterly, irretrievably empty. She rolled over on her side and curled into a ball, trying to squeeze out the desperate feeling in her center.

A timid knock sounded on her door, and she sat up. Had he come back? Surely he would not dare, not now. Or could it be Ovan, come to chastise her? Carefully, she extended the thinnest tendril of thought to discover who had knocked. Her psi was greeted with a wordless burst of energy and concern. Trisa!

Isbel tried to smile as she opened the door for the little girl. *Hello, Trisa. Have you come to visit me?*

Trisa nodded, and tried to send something, but it was formless and unintelligible.

Try again, Isbel sent. *Tell me again.*

Trisa tried again. *Sad. Crying.*

Isbel took the child's hand and led her to the cot. *Trisa, you must not listen to other people's thoughts unless they send them to you. It is not polite.*

The child's round face fell, and her eyes filled with tears. "I'm sorry, Cantrix," she said. "I didn't mean to, but I could feel you. I don't want you to cry!"

Isbel hugged the little girl. Thank the Spirit, she thought, for one person in this House I can touch without guilt. "It is all right," she said. "I am glad to have you come to see me." She held Trisa until the girl stopped crying, then wiped her running nose with a handkerchief. "Even big people are unhappy sometimes," she said soothingly. "You must not worry."

"I hate Cantor Ovan," Trisa said stoutly.

Isbel laughed. "Now why should that be?"

"He's mean and ugly," Trisa answered, utterly without remorse. "And he smells funny."

Isbel looked at her in surprise. "What do you mean? How does he smell funny?"

"He smells like my father when he's been in the kitchens. Sweet, sort of, but bad sweet. Not good, like you." She snuggled back into Isbel's arms.

Isbel sighed. "Let us not worry about Cantor Ovan today. I have an idea, Trisa. I will tell you a story, but I will send the whole thing, and you have to listen very carefully. Then at the end, I will ask you questions, and you will send back to me. All right?"

Trisa glowed with pleasure, her cheeks pink once again. Her curls flew free of their binding as she bounced happily on Isbel's bed. She sent some babble of agreement, and Isbel laughed again. *Now*, she began. *I will tell you the story of the* ferrel *and the* wezel. *Ready?*

Trisa knelt close to Isbel, and Isbel closed her eyes at the delight of the warm little body against her own. She had been wrong, she reflected. There was at least one other joy in her life. Smiling, and curling one of Trisa's locks around her fingers, she began to tell her story.

Chapter Twenty

"The Housekeeper found us a traveling party yesterday."

Sira looked up from her *keftet*. Exhaustion made her feel dull and slow, and nagging dreams about Isbel had disturbed the little sleep she was able to get. "A traveling party?"

His face was alive with movement, dancing brows and quirky mouth. "Yes, a traveling party! We're supposed to be itinerant Singers, and that's how we earn our way. Perhaps you remember, apprentice?"

She rubbed her eyes. "Oh, yes, master. I do remember, now you remind me."

"I'm hard pressed to find a reason to refuse. Somehow Housekeeper Aleen doesn't find training Zakri the stableman to be an adequate answer."

"But it is the answer." Sira blinked tiredly. "Can you put this off?"

"I'm trying. But it will get harder and harder. How much time do you think you need?"

Sira shook her head. "We cannot hurry it. It would truly not be safe for you and Zakri to travel together yet." She looked out into the courtyard, where the heavy snow of the changing season was already falling. There was so much she did not yet know about traveling, much she had hoped to learn from Iban. "Perhaps," she said tentatively, "perhaps you should go without us. Perhaps Zakri and I must go alone."

Iban's eyebrows disappeared into his hair. "And lose my apprentice, when I have invested so much effort in her? I think not!"

Sira laughed despite her fatigue and worry. "Indeed, you are the kindest of all masters. I thank you, Singer Iban."

"If only we knew . . ." Iban murmured.

Sira understood what he meant, and her smile faded. "I wish we did," she agreed. "If we knew why they do not want us here, perhaps we could negotiate. But what can we do?"

"Well," Iban said. "If it were I who had the ability . . ." His eyes slid back to Sira and away again. "If I could hear thoughts, like some people . . ."

Sira wriggled her shoulders, trying to release their tension. The code of proper behavior ruled her life. What would Maestra Lu have done? Once, she recalled, Cantrix Sharn had all but admitted to her that she had listened to someone else's thoughts. In fact, it had been Rhia v'Bariken she had spied upon.

Iban looked sympathetic. "I'm sorry, but it's a strange thing. If they were open about it, telling us they were crowded, or short of *hruss* fodder—but they're not. It's subtle, a sort of pressure, as if they want us gone, but don't want to say so. Something's afoot."

"I suppose," Sira said, "that sometimes—if needs must—strong decisions have to be taken."

Iban nodded, suddenly brisk. "Exactly right! What a good idea, apprentice." He winked at her, and rose from the table, gathering up his bowl and cup to carry to the kitchen.

From the center of the room Sira could feel Aleen regarding them, watching Iban leave the great room, watching Sira still sitting with her tea. The woman was not Gifted, of course, but her worry was palpable to Sira, a little speck of darkness like a mote of dust in the snow-filtered sunshine. Yet it did not seem serious, or important. What could it be that would so worry the Magister and his Housekeeper, yet feel trivial to her psi?

She gazed around the room at the House members talking and laughing. Everything about Tarus seemed prosperous and healthy. She rubbed her neck ruefully. Somehow she would have to justify her trespass into the Magister's thoughts. Ah, well. She had already broken so many rules. What was one more?

It would have been easier with a *filhata*. Sira had to make do with her *filla*. In her narrow visitor's room, she sat on the bed with her long legs crossed and her *filla* ready. She reasoned that she needed to know what troubled Magister Kenth in order to continue with Zakri. If they were forced to leave now, anything might happen. Iban's shielding was not strong enough to withstand Zakri's errant psi. And she meant no harm to the House. Rather the opposite.

Despite her careful rationalization, it was hard for Sira to begin. She turned the *filla* in her hand for several moments, thinking how long she had had it, and how many hours she had spent with the instrument. Never had she expected to use it in such a way. She sighed, and put the shining ironwood to her lips to begin a melody in *Mu-Lidya*. If anyone heard her, they could assume she was entertaining herself. She hoped no one would, though, especially the Cantor and Cantrix who served Tarus. They were both considerably older than herself, and had shown no interest in her presence here.

Borne on the drift of her melody, Sira's psi reached easily through the House. As she searched for Magister Kenth, she heard the minds of workers in the kitchens and in the stables, the unencumbered thoughts of fishermen and gardeners. She intruded on none of them, needing only the lightest touch to know these were not the ones she sought. She played on, moving higher in the House, to the upper levels.

Here she encountered minds that were not so easy to hear. One was a man struggling with a column of numbers. Another was a woman concerned with some complicated House repair that had been going on for a long time. There were two glowing Gifted minds, in separate places. Sira identified and avoided them, and went on. She thought perhaps she would need to look in the nursery gardens, or the *ubanyor*. She was about to divert her psi when she touched something very odd.

It must be at the very top of the House, she thought, far from the great room and the Cantoris, away from any center of activity. It seemed to be a person, but the mind was a maelstrom, a tangle of dark and confused thoughts. Sira shied away, believing this was not her object, then came back to touch the troubled mind again, moved by both curiosity and sympathy.

It was no use. This was a mind destroyed, lost in its own twisted paths, its identity obscured by madness. Sira stopped playing and sat for some time, wondering, turning her *filla* in her fingers. The prompting of her psi told her she had found her answer. Hopeful that it was so, she tucked her instrument back inside her tunic, and went out into the corridor.

Tarus was a House full of life. Many apartment doors stood open, inviting visitors. Talk and laughter poured out into the hallways, and as Sira walked to the stairway, children dashed about her, some game leading them in and out of each other's homes. She smiled at them as she left the lower level and climbed the stairs to the upper one.

It was quieter in the upper corridor, the sounds coming from behind closed doors more subdued. The apartments were considerably larger, spaced farther apart. She walked to the staircase at the end of the wing, where a small window looked out over the roofs of the nursery gardens. The sea was just visible past the edge of the cliff, and the ice floes floating in it glistened white under the solitary sun.

Sira had to go down the stairs and cross the back of the House, past the entrance to the gardens, past the small tannery where the smell of the soaking vats reminded her of Amric. She bowed to two people who passed her, and walked on until she found another staircase.

The tingle of her psi drew her upstairs again, then onward, until she came upon another stair that led still higher. Guided by instinct, she looked behind a cupboard filled with dusty rolls of parchment, and found a door that opened easily onto a narrow and dark stairwell. She doubted many House members knew it was there, but the stairs were clean-swept. Someone was using them regularly. Sira climbed with a quick and sure step, her psi exultant, ready to release her when she drew close to her goal.

This third level of the House was close and dark, no more than a low-ceilinged attic. Sira could barely stand upright. It lacked both windows and decoration, and the *quiru* light glowed dully on hulking shapes of old furniture. In one corner, she saw a single closed door.

Sira approached the door and listened. There was an odd sound beyond it, a snuffling breath, an inarticulate murmur. Sira reached out with her thought, certain there was a person on the other side of the door, but touching that mind was like reaching into a dark hole without knowing what was in it. Hastily, she withdrew the contact. She put her hand on the latch and pulled the door open.

For a long moment she stared at the miserable creature inside. It was a horror of long tangled hair, blotchy skin, and wild eyes. It hardly seemed human.

Mystified, Sira stepped into a little cramped room outfitted with a cot, a noisome chamber pot such as little children used, and a bare table. The odor in the room was almost unbearable. Sira was sure its occupant had not seen the *ubanyix* in a very long time.

Ubanyix was the right choice, though. It was a woman who huddled on the cot, her lips moving in a toneless babble and her fingers raking at her hair. Sira gazed at her for a long moment. She felt a strange, brief nausea, and then she felt rage.

She knew this woman, or who this woman had been. She was supposed to be dead, exposed in the Marik Mountains by order of the Magistral Committee. She was Rhia v'Bariken, formerly the mate of Magister Shen v'Bariken, briefly Magistrix of Bariken. She had conspired to kill her mate, his riders, and the young Cantrix who traveled with them. Sira.

Sira backed quickly out of the room and slammed the door behind her. The air around her sparked with her fury, and she let it burn as she made her way back through the dark attic. She took the narrow staircase and then the main staircase, two steps at a time, and made her way with long strides to the great room.

A startled Housewoman responded to her demand to see the Housekeeper as if Sira were a full Cantrix in Tarus's own Cantoris. Only a few moments passed before Aleen, pale and clearly frightened, bowed before her. The air around Sira still glittered ominously.

"I will see Magister Kenth," Sira snapped, in a voice that rang across the room. "Now."

The Housekeeper bowed again. "Yes, of course, Cantrix. This way, please. I—I think he is free." She hurried ahead, as if afraid she might be singed by the energy radiating from Sira.

Sira followed, her lips pressed tight. Aleen cringed before her anger, but Sira was not seeing her. She was seeing again that awful scene in the mountains, five years before, and her friend Rollie dying with the others in the snow.

Magister Kenth was blond and rather young, probably no more than six summers. His skin was pale and smooth, and he turned even paler when the Housekeeper burst into his apartment with the briefest of knocks. Sira came behind her, swathed in the sparks excited by her anger. To his credit, Kenth did not shrink from her. He put aside a thick ledger, and stood to bow her to a chair. She declined with a shake of the head.

He squared his shoulders, and drew one deep, audible breath. "She's my sister," he said.

Then Sira remembered, could see Rollie's face as she looked across a *hruss*'s back and told Sira that Rhia had expected to be Magistrix at Tarus until the birth of a younger brother forced her out. Tarus! How could she have forgotten? Rollie was from Tarus, had gone to Bariken with Rhia when Rhia mated with Shen. Sira's anger evaporated bit by bit, like the morning fog burning away from the rocky coastline.

Now she did accept a chair, wearily settling into it. The air around her calmed as the sparks of her anger blinked out. "I see," she said. "I had forgotten the connection."

Kenth sat, too, and signaled for Aleen to leave the room, which she hastened to do. "I'm sorry, Cantrix, for what Rhia did. In a way, I'm to blame for it, all of it. And I couldn't let her die that way."

Sira traced her eyebrow with her finger. She felt exhausted, burdened with her knowledge and her memories. She thought of the ruined human being in the attic room. "She is all but dead, anyway."

Kenth's eyes were dark with grief and guilt. "I know. I think probably she would have preferred the death in the snow. But she was my sister. Everything that happened was because of me, because of my birth."

"No, Magister. How can you take responsibility for being born?"

"I thought I could. Should."

"I do not see how you managed this."

"It was not easy, but there are always itinerants in need of metal. And there are plenty who care nothing for the laws of the Committee. I found one such, and he followed when the Committee sent my sister and that other woman into Forgotten Pass."

"What happened to the other one? To Trude?"

Kenth was clearly reluctant to tell it, but Sira, having come so far, intended to have the whole story. She stared at him in silence until, resigned, he began to speak again.

"The itinerant Singer I hired had to wait until the Committee's riders had left the Pass. When he could go to the women, they had already spent a night in the cold. Rhia—my sister—had used the other woman's body, and her furs, as a shelter. There was enough warmth that way, at least until . . ." Kenth faltered, but pressed on like one making a confession. "At least until the other one froze to death. Rhia was half-dead herself by then."

Sira spoke harshly. "She never stopped using people to her own ends, even then."

Kenth had no answer for that. "I brought her here, and hid her in that corner at the top of the House. In only a few weeks she became what she is now—mindless, useless."

They sat together in silence then, each remembering the woman Rhia had been. At length Sira sighed, and rose.

"Will you report me to the Committee?" Kenth asked.

Sira met his eyes. "I see no purpose in it. Enough suffering has come from all of this."

Kenth stood, and bowed to her. "I'm very grateful for your understanding."

"I am not sure I do understand. But I will not report you."

"I thank you for that. My House is at your disposal for as long as you wish, Cantrix."

"That may be quite some time," Sira warned him. "You have a stableman, Zakri, who is Gifted and needs training. He is my reason for coming here."

"I will tell my Housekeeper to give you what you need. I only wish I could in some way make up to you for what my sister did."

"Your hospitality will be sufficient," Sira said. "I will be grateful, too, if you will extend it to my master, Singer Iban."

"So I will."

Sira smiled faintly at the young Magister. "I have a friend who would say, 'The drifts are deep in this one.'" She bowed. "But I think your House is well served by its Magister. I wish you well."

Kenth's pale cheeks colored, making him look very young indeed. "I thank you, Cantrix. Nothing else matters so much to me. I'm still learning what it all means, I'm afraid."

"So are we all, Magister," Sira said, and she left him alone.

Chapter Twenty-one

The snows had begun in earnest when the rider from Conservatory appeared one afternoon at Amric. He and an itinerant Singer were making the traditional rounds of all the northern Houses, while another pair would be going to the southern ones. Conservatory was calling together its next class.

"How many?" was the question on everyone's lips as the rider spoke with the Cantor, his junior Cantrix, and the Magister.

Isbel knew Gram v'Conservatory from her student days. He was lined and lean, with a face burned dark from years of traveling on the Continent. He knew Conservatory's business as well as any Cantor. He smiled warmly at Isbel and bowed low. She suffered a pang of nostalgia for the naive girl Gram had known. She bowed in return, but her answering smile was sad. Those days were past now, and the subject at hand was a serious one.

Gram frowned as he held out his brown fingers to add up the new class. "One is coming from Manrus, and one from Perl; two from Isenhope–twins."

A murmur of delight came from the little group at this good news, but it faded as Gram continued his count. "None from Lamdon, none from Bariken or Tarus. One from Filus, one from Trevi, none from either Arren or Soren. Your own little one, and three from Conservatory."

"Ten only," Isbel said. Trisa's would be one of the smallest classes in many summers.

Cantor Ovan grumbled, "The Committee must do something! How many Gifted children are being withheld, I wonder?"

Gram knew nothing of that. Magister Edrus put in mildly, "We need itinerant Singers, too, Cantor Ovan," but Ovan's mouth turned down even further. His dark features looked to Isbel as if they might fold in upon themselves. She thought it remarkable that a mouth so pinched could ever open enough to sing. She carefully pressed her thought low, and twisted her hands in her lap.

At the edges of her mind she felt Kai's absence from the House, an emptiness which only he could fill. The Cantoris was the greatest part of that emptiness, a void pulling her farther and farther away. It felt like a chasm yawning before her, which she would topple into if he did not hold her back. She would disappear forever into that gaping void, be consumed by it, her last choice gone from her for always.

She startled from her black reverie when Gram asked, "Who will be bringing the child—Trisa, is it?—to Conservatory? Her parents?"

"Yes," said the Magister. "We'll arrange for an itinerant to accompany them." Isbel's heart contracted at the pain coming to Brnwen, and to herself.

"Is it not interesting," Ovan said grimly, "that there are always plenty of itinerants, but never enough Cantors?"

All eyes turned to his black ones, but no one had a response. Isbel remembered Sira saying, "If the Gift is punished, it will not appear." She wondered about that. Three from Conservatory, none from Bariken or Tarus or Lamdon. Poor little Trisa! And poor, sad Brnwen. There was no surcease for the suffering that was coming to them.

It was a hard farewell. Trisa cried, and Isbel could hardly bear her sadness. She wept, too, as Ovan stood frowning, his mouth pressed tight. The parting ceremony was brief, a swift intense pain like the cut of a sharp knife. Isbel thought she would sob aloud from the ache in her throat as the *hruss* carried Trisa away, and she had to retreat inside the doors of Amric.

Ovan turned on her the moment the doors closed. *Discipline yourself! This is something to celebrate, and you have spoiled it with your foolishness!*

Isbel turned her brimming eyes to her senior. She sensed the Magister and Cael watching, and she bit her lip hard. The pain at least helped her to control her tears.

We will begin Cantoris hours now, Ovan sent, stepping past her toward the Cantoris.

Cantor Ovan, it is so early. Could I not have just a moment to—

Ovan swung around, narrowly missing stepping on Cael's foot. *Now!* His thought was a slash, a whip of psi that made Isbel stumble back and close her eyes.

She put a shaking hand to her forehead. Cael frowned. "Are you all right, Cantrix?"

"She is perfectly well," Ovan snapped. "Please do not interfere, Housekeeper. It is a senior's duty to discipline a junior."

Cael set his jaw, but he backed away from Isbel. One did not argue with a senior Cantor.

Isbel drew a ragged breath. She felt her tears drying on her cheeks as she went across the hall and into the Cantoris. As she passed Ovan, she caught a strange, sweet odor about him—as Trisa had said, "bad sweet". She wiped her cheeks as she stepped up on the dais, and looked down at the wetness on her fingers. What was the use of it all? There seemed to be nothing in the world but pain and bereavement, loneliness and suffering. No matter how hard she worked, how she strove to please, she found nothing to look forward to.

When she reached inside her tunic for her *filla*, it felt as heavy as stone in her fingers.

*

The season of heavy snow closed over Nevya. During Kai's hunting trip it seemed the sky was forever white. When he turned his face upward, fat soft flakes or tiny icy ones coated his eyebrows and eyelashes.

Kai and his brothers had been hard put to locate the *caeru* in the deepening drifts. They finally uncovered a den by digging through a fresh snowbank. They found a pack of four, a male and three females. One of the females was heavy with pups, and the hunters let her go scrabbling away over the snow. The others they killed cleanly, their arrows as swift and accurate as they could make them. They cut the throats to protect the meat. The livers and hearts of freshly-killed *caeru* were special treats reserved for hunters. Their Singer cooked them on the spot, and Kai and Rho and Tam ate them seared brown on the outside and red and rich on the inside. They remembered to thank the spirits of the *caeru* for giving them strength. Rho held out a bit to the Singer, grinning, with fresh meat juice dripping down his chin. The Singer laughingly refused.

By the time the kill was gutted and skinned, and the hunters turned for home, they had been away from the House five days. They rode into the courtyard at Amric just as the evening meal was being served, but it was long over by the time the *caeru* carcasses had been hung in the abattoir and the tired *hruss* stabled and fed. When one of the cooks offered them a hot bowl of *keftet* and a platter of nutbread, the men gratefully accepted. They sat at the long table in the kitchens, bragging and laughing. Tam was planning to mate soon with one of the kitchen Housewomen, and he teased her out of one small cup of wine for each of them, while the cook pretended not to notice.

They all went to the *ubanyor* and bathed, growing quieter, feeling their fatigue. When at last they were toweled dry and dressed, even Kai longed for his bed.

She was waiting in the corridor, in the shadows behind the door that stood open to the empty *ubanyix*. Kai was walking with Rho, too tired now even to talk. She whispered his name as they passed. Rho heard, and winked at Kai. "Someone wants you, little brother," he said with a chuckle. "Didn't know you'd found a girl!"

Kai could find no words to answer, and his brother laughed as he hurried on after Tam. If he knew who it was waiting behind that door, Kai reflected, he wouldn't think it funny. He would be shocked as perhaps nothing else on the Continent could shock him.

Awkwardly, Kai waited until the men turned a corner, then stepped into the shadows where she waited. His exhaustion evaporated in a heartbeat as he felt her breath against his neck. Her hair was still damp from the *ubanyor*. He couldn't resist bending to taste its fragrance, and the smooth skin of her forehead was just beneath his lips.

He couldn't have stopped himself then if the senior Cantor of Lamdon had been standing at his shoulder. She was so small and soft, so delectably close, there in the rectangle of darkness cast by the open door of the *ubanyix*. He couldn't bear it.

"Isbel," he murmured, his voice little more than a groan. "Oh, Isbel, please!" and she was in his arms, her lips pressed to his and the swell of her breasts maddeningly warm and pliant against his chest. He lifted her right off her feet and into his hard embrace.

Not until they reached her room did he see that her eyes were swollen, their green gone dark with weeping. She tried to explain, to tell him that Trisa had been taken away sobbing just that afternoon; that there had been no one to talk to to confide in, to cry with; that she had had to go on with Cantoris hours as if nothing had happened. Kai hardly heard her words over the loud demands of his body. They were too insistent to deny, and soon her own need rose to meet his.

Kai was not Gifted, but he felt nevertheless as if he and Isbel melded into one person, body and mind. She knew his every thought and desire without his speaking, and he knew there would never be a more intense experience than this night. She was the Continent for him, the whole world, every mountain pass and peak. All the stars and both suns she offered to him as if he were the master of the universe.

Not until much, much later did he understand the events that had precipitated her crisis. By then it was too late for reason to save them. They had chosen.

Chapter Twenty-two

Why do I have to play scales? Zakri demanded of Sira. *Teach me a tune, a real one!*

No. To be able to work in the modes, to understand their structure, you must practice them just like this.

It is boring.

That may be. Now do it again. Listen for the intonation so that the lowered thirds in Iridu *and* Lidya *are clear.*

No Conservatory student could pass into the second level before mastering this exercise. When Sira had given it to Theo, he had perfected it by himself before his next lesson. Now, sitting in the tack room of Tarus's stables, she had to guide Zakri as if he were a stubborn *hruss*. *Iridu*, modulate to *Doryu*, to *Aiodu*, to *Lidya*, and finally to *Mu-Lidya*. Correct the intonation, the lowered second and fifth degrees of *Mu-Lidya*. Release the center to sustain the breath, even out the tempo. Again. And again.

At last she allowed Zakri to put down his *filla*. The *hruss* in the loose box had crowded forward, hanging their broad heads over the half-wall to watch the humans.

Zakri pointed the *filla* at them. "Silly beasts. You'd rather hear a song, wouldn't you?"

Sira almost chided him for speaking aloud, but decided to let it go this time. He was making progress, despite his complaints. His sending and listening were strong and clear. On the *filla*, the same that had been his mother's, his tone was true, if not as full as Sira might like. His mother, before her death, must have made a start on his training.

The next step was to acquire a *filhata*. Zakri had quickly learned the C, though unlike Theo, he lacked perfect pitch. They began and ended every lesson, just as at Conservatory, by singing the C to which the middle string of the *filhata* must be tuned. Sira was a little concerned about her own skill with that instrument. She had not touched one since leaving Observatory.

Working through the night and sleeping in the daytime made her feel sluggish and irritable, but there was no choice in the matter. She often lay awake and exhausted on her cot, and when she did sleep, she dreamed of Theo in the Cantoris at Observatory, and of the days she had spent teaching him. He seemed so real in her dreams, so close, she could almost put out her hand to touch his hair or his strong fingers on the strings. At other times, she dreamed of Isbel, and those dreams troubled her, jarring her awake with a jolt of anxiety.

I will teach you a tune now, she sent to Zakri, as much to banish her worries as to please her student.

But I remember one, he sent back, grinning at her. He put the *filla* to his lips and launched into a jaunty melody Sira had never heard before.

You must have practiced that! Is it your own?

My mother taught it to me. Zakri's brown eyes clouded, and Sira braced herself, but he kept his control.

It is a charming melody, she told him. *You must teach it to me.*

He smiled again, his slender cheeks curving in a way that reminded her of Isbel's dimples. Sira looked at him with fondness. He had grown taller, and he stood straighter now. Nothing had broken or fallen around him in weeks, nor had he shed the helpless tears that had so plagued him. In truth, he was better in every way. *Perhaps it is time to cut your hair*, she sent.

He laughed aloud and put a hand to the silky tail of hair that hung down his back. *Are we leaving, then?*

Possibly. Sira smiled at his enthusiasm. *First Iban must approve.*

But he is away from the House. Zakri's disappointment clouded the air in the tack room. Sira lifted one long, admonishing forefinger, and he quickly brightened it again, without ever touching his *filla*. For the thousandth time, the strength of his Gift astonished her.

Yes, she answered. *A traveling party was headed to Trevi, and he took it for the chance to see his parents and his sisters. But I expect him back soon.*

Let us go to meet him! Zakri jumped up to do a dancing turn in the cramped tack room, his ebullience returning with this new idea.

We can wait, Sira sent mildly, though she liked his flashes of gaiety. He seemed young again at such times. She could almost have danced with him, but she must beware of relaxing her guard. His Gift could still startle, even injure. *Let us cut your hair, though, and perhaps you should speak to the stableman.*

Zakri swept her a bow. *So I will, Maestra!*

Do not call me that! Zakri's dance ended abruptly. *Where did you learn it?*

I have heard you use it, I think. It is a teacher, is it not? Have I made a mistake? His eyes began to darken once more, and Sira shook her head and held up her hand.

It is not important. It means master teacher, and I am not that.

To me you are. He stood before her, slim and soft-faced in his youth, but no less stubborn than she herself.

She stood and faced him, her hands on her hips, a wry smile on her lips. *I thank you for the honor, but I have not earned that title. Nor will I ever earn it now, I suppose. Please do not use it again.* She reached to a shelf for a sharp knife used for splitting leather, and for a stone to hone it on. *Now sit here. I will cut your hair for you.*

Zakri sat down on the bench. As she untied the string that held his fine long hair, and lifted the strands in her fingers, he sent, *Please do not make me look like Iban. His hair looks like an* urbear *chewed it off!*

This made Sira laugh, but she did take care. She sliced off the length of his hair first, dropping the soft locks on the bench in a little silken tassle. Then she cut the hair around his face and at his crown to the length of her thumb. When she was done, it lay against his skull like the downy fur of a newborn *caeru* pup. When he turned his face up to her, his eyes shining beneath the soft brown halo of his hair, Sira was surprised by a rush of maternal affection. She caught her breath at the power of it.

Her shields sprang up immediately, hiding the feeling. She released her breath, and sent only, *Do not worry, Zakri. You look nothing at all like Iban.*

Zakri was keeping secrets of his own. He hid even from Sira the true extent of his Gift. She had said he must take control of it himself. He struggled with it, trying to discipline and restrain it, channel it into usable forms. Still, despite Sira's power and her own strong Gift, he heard things from her mind that she did not mean him to hear.

When they worked together, her psi lifting and directing his own, showing him how to apply his energies to those tiniest particles of the air around them, he became aware of her hidden thoughts. He needed her help, especially at first, to focus his abundant energy, to avoid throwing brushes or sailing bits of tack across the room when he was trying only to create *quiru*. On his own, experimenting in his attic room, he still had difficulties. Most of his few possessions had flown across the floor more than once. But when they were joined, Sira's psi twined with his, he sensed that other, Theo, ever present in her thoughts. He was neither shocked nor disturbed. The revelation made her seem more human, more vulnerable, less overwhelming in her discipline.

With Iban it was different. When the three of them left Tarus at last, generously supplied and outfitted by Magister Kenth, Iban cheerfully assisted Sira in Zakri's ongoing training. *Quiru* called up with Iban were swift and economical, as straightforward as the Singer himself. With Iban it was not difficult to obey the precepts of courtesy, and when the music stopped and their psi subsided, he knew no more of the man than had they simply taken a walk together.

Zakri was both fearful and excited when he learned they were on their way to Conservatory. The heavy snows had come and gone, and they rode in icy sunshine over deep snowpack, the broad hooves of the *hruss* almost soundless on its surface. Iban kept a cheerful countenance as Sira and Zakri conversed silently.

"I am sorry, master," Sira said on their first night out in the Timberlands. The stars were incredible, Zakri thought, beyond numbering in the purple mantle of the night. "If Zakri speaks aloud too much now, he will lose the ability he has developed."

Zakri heard her send, *Can you hear this, Singer Iban?* When he showed no sign of having heard, her face remained politely impassive. "Of course we will speak aloud with you whenever you wish it."

Singer Iban nodded and made some light remark, his strange eyebrows flying up and down. But Zakri wondered if it did not hurt him, just the same.

Zakri wondered many things, especially how Sira expected to wrest a *filhata* from Conservatory. She had confessed to owning not one bit of metal. She heard this idle thought of his, and she raised the warning finger, reminding him to discipline his mind. He sighed at the familiar gesture, and she smiled a little and relented. *I have to rely on old associations. And to convince someone—perhaps Magister Mkel—that what we are doing is beneficial to all Nevya.*

Zakri doubted whether anyone could be convinced of that, including himself, but he kept this thought very low, and Sira did not appear to hear it. *What happened to your own* filhata?

I bought my hruss *with it. It was all I owned of value.*

It had never occurred to Zakri that a full Cantrix would have no metal to spend. He still wondered whether it was possible to obtain a *filhata* for someone like himself, but he could only trust that Sira would find a way. He was glad to give himself up to the glory of riding through the snowbound countryside, and to the joy of having companions.

Everything about traveling appealed to Zakri. The *hruss,* his special responsibility, delighted in eating up the distance with their swinging steps. Their coats stiffened and rose to thicken their padding against the deep cold. At night their mouths hung open as they tried to cool themselves in the *quiru* warmth. They could have left the heat for the frigid darkness beyond the light, of course, but the silly things couldn't bear to be far from the humans, so they huffed and panted through the long nights. Zakri patted and soothed them, and they nuzzled him, almost trampling his feet as they pushed close.

Keftet had never tasted so good as it did when cooked in a campsite under the broad sky. This Zakri said aloud, and Sira told him that her own first efforts at camp cooking had been all but inedible. "Like eating burned stones."

"Singer Iban's *keftet* is wonderful," Zakri said.

Iban bowed from where he knelt by the little fire, measuring the herbs he used to make tea. "I thank you, Singer Zakri."

Zakri's cheeks warmed, and he ducked his head. "I am not yet a real Singer."

Sira smiled. "I think you must be, if our master says so."

"So I do," Iban asserted. "You lack only experience, and that you're getting now."

Zakri felt bubbles of joy rise in his throat, like the white foam on the stones of the beach below Tarus. He smiled at Sira and at Iban, and Iban suddenly laughed aloud. "By the Spirit, Zakri, you look as if both the suns just rose behind your head!"

Zakri looked around him and saw that his surge of happiness had enveloped him in a fiery corona of light. He shot Sira a guilty look, but she only lifted her teacup to him.

"You are entitled to be proud," she said. "And this, tonight, must be your ceremony. Congratulations, Singer Zakri."

"Thank you, thank you both." Zakri's heart felt too full for his chest to contain it. The air around him shimmered with a giddy brilliance.

But remember, Sira sent privately, not revealing by so much as the flicker of an eyelash that she was sending. *You have another title still to earn, and that one will be far more difficult.*

Zakri carefully controlled his own face. He looked down at the cooling tea in his cup. *I remember.* But even her note of warning could not dim his happiness. Singer Zakri. He had not thought it possible. No song he had ever heard could sound sweeter than that title.

Chapter Twenty-three

The glitter of deep snow and the vivid icy blue of the sky were spectacular, when the travelers dared glimpses of the beauty around them. They rode muffled and swathed, their furs pulled well forward over their faces. Sira began to long for some smell other than the tang of *caeru* fur, but the fresh air, when she let it inside her hood, burned her nose and lungs with cold. Her saddle leather creaked stiffly beneath her, and the ironwood trees groaned and cracked above her head. Iban said, "That sound reminds you're in deep cold season—as if you could forget."

Twice already Iban had spoken sternly to Zakri for exposing his face to play his *filla*. "No, do it this way," he had said, allowing only the very end of his own *filla* out of the warmth of his hood. "Make sure your furs are roomy enough that you can play inside them. Otherwise, you can lose some skin where it hurts you the most." He tapped his lips with a barely exposed finger. "Keep your sleeves pulled down, too, just your fingertips out. The biggest mistake an itinerant can make is to underestimate the cold. Worse than getting lost."

To Sira he said, "No elaborate melodies in this season. Quick *quiru* are important."

"Yes, master," she answered respectfully.

In her mind she heard *No fancy stuff!* and Zakri's mental laugh.

Pay attention, she sent to him. *These lessons could save your life one day.*

The cold slowed their progress. The journey took half again as long as it might have in easier weather. The sun rose late and set early, and seemed to shed no warmth at all once they had wended their way north through the Timberlands and climbed into the Mariks. Every day Iban had some lesson for Zakri, or for both of them. Though the trip was long, the time passed easily. The days were full of learning, and the evenings they spent in *filla* practice, singing, and storytelling. When at last they turned east at the landmark of trees and rock, toward Conservatory, Sira almost regretted seeing this journey come to an end.

They made their last camp well before the sun sank past the mountain peaks to the west. Iban was confident they would reach Conservatory the next day. Sira knew the time had come to speak to her master, but she was reluctant.

She watched with pleasure as Zakri's strong, bright *quiru* swelled around them. She did not tell him, but she had never seen *quiru* so intense as those he called up in their mountain campsites. They all pushed back their furs in relief, glad to feel fresh air against their cheeks. Zakri hurried to pull the saddles of the *hruss*, to let the beasts cool while Iban unpacked the cooking things. Sira struck flint and stone over a tiny pile of softwood from her saddlepack, and it blazed immediately into a cheery yellow flame. "You see, master. I got it the first time."

Iban grinned down at her. "That's an odd small thing for a Cantrix to be proud of!"

"I worked hard to learn it."

Now if only the great Cantrix could cook! Zakri sent.

I can cook, you rascal! Only you and Iban do it so much better.

Zakri knelt beside Iban at the fire, dropping more softwood twigs on it. "I'll make the *keftet*, master."

Iban handed him the much-scarred and seasoned ironwood pot and a long spoon. "You think you remember everything?"

"So I do." Zakri scooped a handful of clean snow into the pot and balanced it on two stones close to the fire. His fingers were deft as he sliced *caeru* meat into the pot to soak. Sira's stomach grumbled as she watched him add the grain to the melted snow water, letting it soften before he sprinkled in the bits of green and yellow herbs and flakes of Tarus's dried fish for flavor. He stirred everything after each step.

You take a long time over it, Sira complained.

Cooking is an art. It needs patience, he answered. *Like your stomach.*

I would like to see such patience with your scales!

Zakri's cheeks curved with laughter, but he kept his eyes on the *keftet*. *Scales do not fill empty bellies.*

"Smells good," Iban said, sniffing the aroma that rose from the cooking pot. "Makes me hungry. Let's finish up Tarus's fine fruitbread, too."

Sira sat cross-legged, idle, and watched as the men served the meal. They were all silent as they savored Zakri's *keftet*. It was moist and spicy and wonderfully hot.

"Excellent," Iban murmured. "Singer Zakri, you're a worthy student."

"Since our master makes us eat it all, it might as well taste good," Zakri said, with a sidelong glance at Sira.

She arched her white-slashed eyebrow. *I will be happy to let you prepare all meals.*

Oh, I thank you! he responded in mock relief. Sira's lips twitched as she returned to her meal.

They made a long evening of it, with a feeling of celebration over journey's end. Iban sang a silly song he had picked up on his trip to Trevi:

> IF A CANTOR CAN'T AND A SINGER SINGS
> AND A *FERREL* FLIES ON FEATHERED WINGS
> THEN A *WEZEL* WON'T WITH AN *URBEAR* BONE
> BUT A *CAERU* CAN IF YOU LEAVE HIM ALONE!

They all laughed, and Iban confessed he had cleaned up the words of the song a bit for Sira's sake. Zakri played the *filla* for them, first the old melody of his mother's and then, to tease Sira, the scale exercise she made him play so often. Even when he was only playing the modulation exercise, *Iridu, Aiodu,* right through the modes to *Mu-Lidya*, the air around him glowed brighter than the rest of the *quiru*. At the end of the evening Sira sang the old lullaby Isbel loved. Her fingers danced on her lap, remembering the feel of the *filhata* strings.

> LITTLE ONE, LOST ONE,
> SLEEPY ONE, SMALL ONE,
> PILLOW YOUR HEAD,
> DREAM OF THE STARS,
> AND THE SHIP THAT CARRIES YOU HOME.
> LITTLE ONE, SWEET ONE,
> DROWSY ONE, LOST ONE,
> THE NIGHT IS LONG,
> THE SNOW IS COLD,
> BUT THE SHIP WILL CARRY YOU HOME.

"What does it mean?" Zakri asked when she was finished.

Sira shrugged one shoulder. "I do not think it means anything."

"The Watchers do, though," Iban put in.

"So they do." She looked out into the night, where the softwood trees drooped under the frozen weight of snow on their branches. "The Watchers believe in the Ship. They send two of their House members to the roof of Observatory every night, and they watch for the Ship to fly to Nevya like some sort of *ferrel* of the stars. They sing a song that says they will wait a thousand summers for it to come."

Zakri's eyes gleamed in the firelight. "Why should they put faith in such a fable?"

"Once in a great while, perhaps once a summer, they see strange lights in the sky, and they think that means the Ship is coming for them. And then—" She broke off, remembering. The others waited, and only the sound of the *hruss*'s raspy breathing and the crackle of the fire filled the campsite. Sira made a wry face. "The leader of Observatory, Pol, is a strange man. Nothing matters to him but his House and its beliefs. He showed me a huge piece of metal once, a bigger piece than any you can imagine. As big as a *caeru* hide, and smooth as still water! He claims it is a map of the stars, and that it shows where the Ship will someday carry his people."

"What do you think it was?" Zakri asked.

"I cannot explain it."

After a time they went out of the *quiru* to relieve themselves, in twos as Iban had taught them. First Iban and Zakri went together, then Iban went with Sira, politely turning his head to give her privacy. The distant roar of a *tkir* rumbled out of the darkness as they came back into the light. Zakri's eyes flashed white, and Sira moved closer to him.

Iban had not heard the story of Zakri's nightmares. "The *tkir* hate this season," he said in a low tone, as if the animal might hear him. "All the little animals stay safely in their dens—except us!" He winked at Sira. "Did anyone bring a throwing knife? Just in case?"

Zakri listened in silence, the air around him calm.

Iban still teased. "*Tkir* won't bother you in your *quiru*. Nor will *urbear*, usually. But I do remember a time—just out of Forgotten Pass, it was—" He kept his eye on Zakri, but Zakri had dropped his gaze to the embers of the fire. "A *tkir* hunting on the glacier, desperately hungry . . ."

Iban spun his story out for several minutes, but Zakri did not react. Sira relaxed, and after a time Iban chuckled and gave it up. "I see you're a fearless man, Singer Zakri." He bent to unroll his bedfurs, and Sira decided the time had come to speak.

She had just drawn breath when a deep growl sounded around them, much closer than before. This time it was Iban whose eyes widened and flashed in the *quiru* light. He jumped to his feet and peered out into the darkness. The growl came again, lower and louder, with a threatening snap at the end of it.

"What in the name of all the Houses—?" Iban began.

Zakri, who had not moved, fell back suddenly onto his bedfurs, laughing up at the stars. Even Sira laughed aloud, and Iban stared at both of them, his curse cut short. "How did you—Zakri, you whelp of a *caeru*, did you make that sound?"

Zakri gulped back his laughter. "So I did, master. I am sorry, but it was too good a chance to let pass!"

Iban sat down again, shaking his head. "You caught me out, and that's the truth! I've never heard a human make such a noise."

"I can make many of them," Zakri said. He whuffed deep in his throat, exactly the sound a *hruss* would make when hungry or lonely. Then he imitated the *ferrel*'s cry, which made the *hruss* throw up their heads and stamp. He quieted them with a crooning murmur.

Iban chuckled as he lay down on his furs. "Never a dull moment with Singer Zakri around!" He propped himself on one elbow and looked across the fire to where Sira sat still smiling at Zakri's joke. "I'll miss this," he said casually.

Sira's brow lifted. "Master?"

Iban said lightly, "Your apprenticeship is complete."

Sira could not speak for a moment, moved by the depth of his wisdom and perception. When she could, she answered in a low voice, "I am sorry to end it."

"But it is time, Singer, and past time. I have little left to teach you." For once Iban's brows were level. "I have learned as much from you, Cantrix, as you from me."

Sira inclined her head to him with deep respect. Iban had known already what she had not yet found words to tell him. She wished she knew how to properly thank him. For a year they had traveled together, worked together. She would miss his changeable face and his constancy. She could only say, "I am certain we will meet again."

Iban smiled. "I'll be at your service. But there is one more lesson I must offer you."

She waited. Iban spoke with care. "There's something happening on the Continent, something to do with itinerants. I've heard only rumors, but

I want you to know, to be prepared."

Zakri sat up suddenly. "My father!" he whispered. "That was what my father was going to tell me."

Iban frowned. "What do you mean?"

"My father said that when I completed my apprenticeship, he would tell me something important. But I never completed it!"

"You have now," Sira reminded him, and he smiled.

Iban nodded. "It's something about Soren," he said, "but I don't know exactly what. Some House members seem to know, and a lot of itinerants, though not all."

"Know what?" Sira asked. "I do not understand."

"I'm sorry," Iban said. "I don't, either. But a lot of itinerants are traveling to Soren, more than they need for their trade. They're keeping it very quiet, especially from anyone with connections to the Committee. I just thought you should know."

"Thank you," Sira said. She lay down on her furs, and looked up at the night sky through the brilliance of Zakri's *quiru*. Her psi prickled, telling her Iban's warning was important. She wondered how long she would have to wait before she knew why.

Chapter Twenty-four

The courtyard of Conservatory was empty when Sira and Iban and Zakri rode into it. No greeting party stood on the broad steps. Sira had not expected one, yet she looked up at the blank windows of the House and felt a pang over something missing, something lost. They dismounted and led their *hruss* around the side of the House to the stables at the back. The stableman, Erc, greeted Iban as sooon as he pushed back his furs.

"Singer Iban! It's a pleasure to see you once more." They exchanged the shallow bows of old acquaintance. Sira and Zakri also put their hoods back, and Erc's demeanor turned formal. He bowed deeply. "Cantrix Sira. Welcome home to Conservatory."

The correction of her title was on her lips, but Erc went on before she could speak. "I see you still ride the same *hruss* that carried you away from here. It looks in remarkable condition."

Sira nodded to Zakri. "This is Singer Zakri. He is very good with *hruss*."

Erc bowed to Zakri. "Singer," he said, and Zakri blushed and bowed. Sira feared she saw a glimmer in the air around him, but no one else seemed to notice. Erc added, "This beast looks fresh as a foal. That's good work, Singer. Cantrix Sira, no one knew you were coming! I'm sure a welcome would have been arranged! You go ahead now and find the Housekeeper, and I'll take care of these *hruss*."

"I will help you, Houseman," Zakri offered. "If you will just show me where."

Zakri and Erc turned into the stalls together while Sira and Iban went on into the House.

Almost five years had passed since Sira had walked the halls of Conservatory. She looked around her at the spare beauty of the corridors, the unadorned arches of the doorways, the smooth worn stone of the floors. As she led Iban toward the great room the sounds of music floated from the student wing, notes both sublime and sour, scales and fingering exercises and fragments of melody. Sira's eyes suddenly stung. Had she been Zakri, she thought, she would be surrounded by a gloomy haze.

But she was not Zakri. She was a travel-hardened and experienced woman of twenty-four. She blinked her eyes hard, and kept her head up and her back straight.

She had not changed so much, perhaps. A Housewoman recognized her as she came into the great room, and bowed deeply before hurrying away in search of theHousekeeper. Sira went to the window seat and looked out through the thick, wavy windows at the familiar scene. Snow blanketed the trees around the House. The weak sunlight was faded to nothing by the strength of Conservatory's *quiru*. Sira sat down, thinking of Gifted children clustering here after meals and before bed. There was no place on the Continent like Conservatory. It was full of music, of the Gift, of the dedication and labor of the Singers. What possible substitute could there be for such a place? Yet something must change, or there would be no more Gifted ones to fill these halls.

It was not the Housekeeper, but Magister Mkel himself who came to greet her. "Sira," he said aloud. "Welcome home." His voice was less resonant, less deep than she remembered.

She rose quickly to bow to him. "I am glad to be here." She introduced Iban.

"It's an honor, Magister," Iban said. To Sira he added, "I'll leave you alone now." The Housekeeper had come behind the Magister, and Iban, with a wink to Sira, followed him out.

"Let us go to my apartment," Mkel said. "Cathrin will be delighted to see you."

Sira followed the Magister's familiar gray-headed figure, slightly stooped now, up the wide stairs. Her feet fitted perfectly in the centers of the treads, the stone worn hollow by generations of Singers' feet. Strains of music followed her, haunted her like ghosts from her own past, and she was just as glad to reach the Magister's apartment, to go in and close the door.

"Well, Sira," Cathrin exclaimed. They had agreed, it seemed, on how to address her. "How wonderful to see you!"

She brought a chair forward, and bustled about bringing a tray of fruit and tea, very much in the same way she had when Sira was last there. But there were differences now. Sira felt a chill, as if she had brought the deep cold with her into this cheerful room.

Sira and the Magister sat near the largest window, just as they had during their last, painful interview. How hard it had been to refuse the pleas of both Magister Mkel and Cantor Rico v'Lamdon! They had used their psi to persuade her to return to the Cantoris, and she had almost given in beneath their pressure.

But now Mkel only smiled pleasantly as Cathrin withdrew. "Tell me about yourself," he said. "You have been a long time at Tarus, I hear."

"So I have. I have been working with—that is, teaching a young Singer, Zakri v'Perl."

Mkel's expression did not change, but Sira had the sense that his features stiffened, froze into place. His eyes were cold, and she wanted to squirm in her chair like a first-level student.

"Zakri was the son of an itinerant who died, Magister," she said hurriedly. "He never received his training, yet his Gift is great, the strongest I have seen. For years no one could work with him because of its wildness."

The Magister let a moment pass. "I feel sorry that the boy's life has been so hard. If only he had been sent to Conservatory at the proper time, if his family had seen their duty, he need not have suffered so."

They were the words Sira had used herself with Zakri's father years before. She took a deep breath. "So I thought myself, Magister, when I first met him. His family refused, and there was little a young boy could do. But now I see another way. I would like you to meet Zakri, to understand for yourself how strong his Gift is."

Another moment of silence passed. Sira concentrated on her breathing as she waited for an answer. At length, Mkel said, "Nevya needs itinerants, of course, Sira. But it needs Cantors more. I wonder if you realize how desperate our shortage is." He spoke as if the issue were no longer of concern to her, as if she had no part in it.

"So I do, Magister," she said. "That is why I am here."

He only gazed at her, waiting in his turn. She moistened her lips. "At Observatory, there was a Singer." She shielded herself carefully. She knew how perceptive Mkel could be. "Theo is his name. I think you met him."

He nodded briefly, and Sira rushed on. "There was also a *filhata*, but they had neither Cantor nor Cantrix. Theo and another itinerant were trying to maintain the *quiru* with only a *filla*. It was hopeless, and exhausting. But Theo was so strong and capable. I taught him to play the *filhata*. I was trapped there, and the people were cold." She paused for breath.

"That is quite interesting," Mkel said. "But Observatory could rejoin Nevya. It is their choice to remain outside the Magistral Committee's jurisdiction. They live as outlaws, when they could be a part of our community, their needs met with properly trained Cantors."

"But Theo is properly trained!" Sira insisted. "His *quiru*, Magister—"

"Everyone is partial to their own students, Sira. But only Conservatory produces Cantors and Cantrixes."

Sira felt as if she had missed a turning and walked straight into a wall. "The shortage—"

"If Observatory were to come within the law, and send their Gifted children for training, perhaps that would ease the shortage."

Sira had thought Mkel was her best hope for understanding. He had always been a sympathetic, if stern, leader, and he had taken a great interest in her work. At this moment she felt keenly her drop in status.

"Magister," she said in a low, intense voice. "Have you not wondered why fewer of the Gifted are being born to the Houses?" He did not answer, and she pressed on. "It seems the cost is too high. Isolation, loneliness, sacrifice, await every Cantor and Cantrix. Cantrix Isbel—"

"Cantrix Isbel?" Mkel interrupted. "What do you know about Cantrix Isbel?"

A dizzying moment of premonition swept Sira, and she had to grip the arms of her chair until it passed. "Why—I only know how unhappy, how lonely, she is. Her senior—"

"Cantor Ovan is a hard-working and dedicated Singer."

"He is mean and nasty to Isbel," Sira said. She felt the heat of temper in her cheeks. "He is a terrible healer, and he blames her for it."

"Cantrix Isbel," Mkel said, stressing the title, "will one day be senior herself, and then she will understand."

"But she has nothing now," Sira protested. Her temper cooled as she thought of Isbel's sadness, Zakri's need, her own losses, and the pressure of destiny that drove her on. "She is without friendship, without even the satisfaction that her work could bring. But Cantor Theo—" Mkel's eyes narrowed, but he only pressed his lips tightly together. She hurried on. "Cantor Theo has a rich and rewarding life. He is loved and respected, and he knows his House members each by name. He is the best healer I have ever seen, because he allows himself to feel what his people feel. He is overworked, of course, because he is alone, but—"

Mkel began to speak, but Sira held up a swift and commanding hand. It was evident she had nothing to lose here. She spoke with the authority of experience and the impatience of necessity. "Three Gifted children have been born since Theo began to serve in Observatory's Cantoris. Three. To a House that is no more than one-third the size of Conservatory."

"That proves nothing."

"I think it does." Sira sat straight in her chair now, sure of herself. "I think we will perish if we do not explore other ways of training the Gift. We are killing it."

"Ridiculous," Mkel declared. They were at an impasse.

"I hoped to persuade you to give me a *filhata*," Sira said wearily.

"*Filhata* are for Cantors and Cantrixes. You gave up your title. You turned your back on your duty."

"I know. I am sorry, Magister, that I have disappointed you. But I have work to do."

"What do you want? Would you destroy Conservatory, your home, your background?"

She rose from her chair and went to the window to lean her forehead against the cool glass. She looked down into the courtyard where she had last seen her beloved Maestra Lu. The sense of loneliness, of isolation, chilled her breast and tightened her throat. She let her emotion rise unshielded, hoping Mkel was open enough to sense it. But, she reflected, before Theo had taught her to allow the feelings of others to affect her, she would not have been able to do so. It was unlikely Mkel would understand.

She straightened, and shook her head. "No, Magister Mkel, I would never wish to destroy Conservatory. For me, it was the perfect way to develop my Gift. I was happy here." She turned to face him. "I was more than happy here—I was fully alive. But things are changing on the Continent, and I would offer an alternative for the Gifted for whom Conservatory is not the perfect path. Another way to acquire training, to learn the skills vital to Nevya's survival. The Gift is showing us that it is necessary, that we must—diversify—if it is to stay with us."

Mkel appeared unmoved. Sira bowed deeply to him. "I wish you well," she said in farewell. "I have the greatest respect for you and for your work. I only wish I could believe, as you do, in the one way, the only way."

She left the apartment, and Mkel neither rose nor spoke as he watched her go. As she made her way to the stables, Sira thought of Pol, every bit as sure of himself as Mkel. She had had the greatest difficulty in persuading Pol of anything, and she had less hope of changing Mkel's mind. She had no idea where to turn next. How could she complete Zakri's training without a *filhata*? Could she have come so far only to fail in the end?

Chapter Twenty-five

Zakri knelt on the floor of the tack room and Erc leaned over his shoulder to point out a burst seam in Sira's saddle. "This'll cause your *hruss* a nasty sore spot."

"So it will," Zakri agreed. "If I can borrow a needle, I will fix it now."

Erc handed him a small coil of split *caeru* gut and a smooth bone needle. "I'd soak that gut first, though," he advised. "Then when it dries, it'll hold tight."

"Thanks, Houseman. I will do that." Zakri did not tell Erc that he knew these things quite well already. There was joy in sharing the work. He did not want to say or do anything to spoil it. He concentrated, too, so no telltale shimmer would spring up around him to alarm the stableman. I am just like a lonely *hruss*, Zakri reflected, too long shut out of the stables and let in at last to the light and the company.

When he had set a length of leather to soak in a jar, he turned to lathering the saddles with tallow. Erc helped, opening out the folds of the felt blankets they used as saddle pads, brushing them until they were smooth and almost as fresh as when they were new. "I'll hang these to air," he offered.

"Thanks." Zakri wiped down the excess tallow from the saddles and wrung it out of his cloth, back into the jar Erc had given him. The *hruss* in their stalls munched noisily with their heads deep in the mangers. Zakri stood and looked about him. "Your stables are as orderly as any I have seen," he told Erc. "Larger than most, are they not?"

"So I've been told," Erc responded. "Though I've never seen any others. I've never put my foot outside Conservatory, for all I send so many travelers on their way. Would you like to see the rest?"

"So I would." Zakri followed the stableman as he led the way up a short ladder to the loft, which was stacked with sacks of grain and dried softwood leaves for *hruss* fodder, its walls neatly lined with rolls of cured leather. This storage loft was at least half again as large as the one Zakri knew at Tarus.

They went down another ladder to a second tack room, which Tarus did not possess. It was hung with saddles, bridles, and halters, some in various stages of repair, and ironwood jars of tallow and oil stood ready on shelves. A half-finished saddle rested on a wooden brace, and Erc shrugged modestly when Zakri admired the work, although he did admit to tooling the leather himself.

"There's one more room." A narrow door opened onto a small room at the back that was not much more than a closet, too small for more than one person inside. Zakri stood in the doorway to look at the saddlepacks, bedfurs, and oddments of tack and supplies crowded into the space. "We're always ready to supply any of our House members or our Singers who might need to travel," Erc said. "And let me show you this." He squeezed past Zakri and reached to a top shelf to bring down a neatly wrapped bundle.

"What is that?"

"Just look." Erc brought the parcel out of the closet and laid it gently on the workbench. He drew back its leather wrappings slowly, fold by fold. "When Cantrix Sira left here a summer ago, all upset she was by the doings at Bariken, she wanted a *hruss* but she had not a bit of metal to her name. I would have given her the beast, or loaned it, but she insisted on paying for it."

He opened the last fold of leather to reveal a gleaming, beautifully carved *filhata*, its patterns of leaves and curving branches catching the *quiru* light. It shone with oil that must have been often applied. "This was her own," Erc said, "that she received before her first *quirunha*."

Zakri delicately stroked the ironwood of the instrument, and touched the strings that hung slack and untuned from their pegs. "It is beautiful," he murmured.

"Made at Soren," Erc said, "and bought by Conservatory especially for her." He began to rewrap the *filhata* in its nest of soft leather, smiling at his memories. "She didn't know a thing about traveling, or about *hruss*. She just took the first one I suggested, and gave me this. She wouldn't hear of anything else."

"That sounds like her," Zakri said with a laugh. "As stubborn as last winter's icicles."

Erc had just finished rewrapping the *filhata* when Sira came back into the stables. When she found them in the second tack room, her face revealed nothing, but Zakri felt her distress as distinctly as if she had been openly weeping. His own enjoyment of the afternoon drained away instantly, and he struggled to suppress his feelings. This was no time to see that warning finger lift, that scarred eyebrow arch.

Sira nodded to Erc. "Please excuse me. I must speak with Singer Zakri."

"Of course, Cantrix." Erc bowed, and said, "I'll just tend to an errand." He left the wrapped *filhata* on the workbench, and climbed up the ladder to the loft.

I am sorry, Sira sent to Zakri. *There is a problem.*

She avoided his eyes, and Zakri felt a surge of sympathy. He had never seen his teacher less than completely confident, sure of herself, clear in her direction. She was vulnerable at this moment, and it made her seem younger than he had thought her to be. He looked closely at her for the first time in many months. *What is it? Can I not help?*

She leaned wearily against the wall of the tack room, looking every bit the worn and weathered itinerant, but Zakri remembered that she was only a summer older than himself. The lines in her face were put there by the cold, by the wind and the sun, and now by unhappiness.

Zakri, I have failed you, she sent.

How could that be? I owe you everything! he answered in a rush.

But I want to teach you the filhata, *and now I cannot.*

Zakri was immediately awash in guilt. *It is me, is it not? Because they know about me, and my problems.* Before he could catch himself, the air in the tack room began to darken. He took a deep breath and focused his psi, and it brightened again.

His effort was not lost on Sira. She managed a small smile. *It is not about you. It is all about me, and what I have done. And what I have not done.* She ran her fingers through her hair and rubbed her eyes. *I am so tired, I can scarcely think.*

Zakri sent, *It does not matter. We will just go on as we have been. We will find a traveling party, earn some metal, and I will practice very hard on the* filla.

We need to do more than that, Zakri. Your Gift needs more than that. But I do not know what to do next.

Why is the filhata *so important?* he asked. *I bet I can do a House* quiru *without one!* He closed his eyes and concentrated again, and the air in the tack room brightened still further, growing uncomfortably warm. The effort beaded his forehead with perspiration, but when he opened his eyes, the room was brilliant with light.

Sira was smiling, and shaking her head. *Yes, your Gift is powerful. But to maintain a House* quiru *that way, or even with only your* filla, *would exhaust you. I have seen this before.*

Zakri nodded. He knew Theo's story. He wiped the perspiration from his face, and sent, *It could be that there will never be a House for me to warm in any case. Who is going to want the two of us—a half-trained itinerant and a rebel Cantrix—in a Cantoris?*

Sira sighed. *I do not know. But I feel it. There will be a need, and you must be ready. The Gift is demanding it.*

Then the Gift had better show us a way! It is like a master that orders our every move!

Sira nodded acknowledgment of that truth. She straightened and looked around at the overly bright room. *You have made it as warm as Lamdon in here. Come, let us at least go to the kitchens and get something—* She broke off. *What is that?*

Zakri followed the direction of her pointing finger. When he saw what she was looking at he began to laugh, and her white-scarred eyebrow arched high, making him laugh harder. The sound brought Erc hurrying back down the ladder into the tack room, to see Sira staring at the workbench where her own *filhata* lay in its wrappings.

"Why, Cantrix Sira," the stableman said. "Don't you remember your own *filhata* that you left with me all this time?"

Sira moved to the workbench and put her hand on the fine leather. Zakri stopped laughing, but he could not suppress a chuckle, and a grin so enormous it almost hurt his cheeks.

She unwrapped the *filhata*, slowly, and he felt the emotions pour through her as clearly as if she had sent them to him. In those moments he knew her love for her teacher, her pride in her first *quirunha*, her anticipation when she went off to Bariken. He felt the crushing disillusionment that had driven her out onto the Continent in search of meaning for her life and her Gift. While she was so open, he also knew the weight of her fears, and his own heart ached.

With the *filhata* in her hands, Sira turned to Erc, her dark eyes shining with tears. "Houseman," she said. "I had thought this long sold to pay the cost of my *hruss*."

"I would never sell your *filhata*, Cantrix Sira," Erc asserted. "I knew one day you would be back for it."

And so the Gift used him as well, Zakri sent.

Sira nodded as her long fingers found the tuning pegs and began to twist them. Then, abruptly, she turned back to the workbench and put the *filhata* down. "It is no longer mine."

"But it is," Erc protested. "I've only waited for you to come back and claim it."

"But I cannot pay you for it."

"That's no matter to me."

"It is true, nevertheless," Sira said firmly. "This must be done right. But we will find a way. We will earn the metal, Singer Zakri and I, and we will be back for the *filhata*." She smiled at Erc, a full smile such as Zakri had never seen on her face. She stood very straight, her entire bearing changed, lightened, charged with energy once again. "I am more grateful to you than I can say, Erc. You do great credit to your House."

He bowed low, and Sira bowed in return. She left the tack room with a lingering glance to the *filhata*, and strode away, weariness and fears forgotten. Zakri followed her out, glancing back from the doorway to see Erc rewrapping the instrument with care.

"We may be back sooner than you think," Zakri said to him. "When Singer Sira sets her mind to a thing, it is as good as done."

As he set the bundled *filhata* back on its high shelf, Erc nodded to Zakri. "She's not the only one, I think."

Zakri laughed, and went to catch up with Sira, leaving the stableman standing alone in his overheated, overbright tack room.

Zakri found Iban soaking in the *ubanyor*. He dropped his own clothes on the floor and splashed down into the tub. Iban protested and threw up his hands as flying drops of water covered him and everything else in the vicinity. Zakri laughed and sank deep under the surface, coming up sputtering to look about him. How plain and severe everything was here! It was as if decoration might distract the House members or the students from the serious work they all did. The tub was generous in size, but devoid of any carving or ornament. The water was gloriously warm, though. Zakri ducked his head under the water, came up for air, and submerged again.

"Singer Zakri, if you don't take time to breathe, we'll be planting you in the waste drop!" Iban cried.

Zakri squeezed a bar of soap in his wet hands to make it fly across the water. Iban laughed, but when he caught the soap he refused to give it back. "If you make a mess in here, the Housekeeper will be after both of us."

"I will not," Zakri promised. "May I please have the soap back, master? I have two weeks' worth of dirt in my skin!"

"No more tricks, then," Iban warned, holding the bar on his palm. "I just want a peaceful bath. And tell me what's ahead for you and Singer Sira. Did she get what she came for?"

"She did not," Zakri told him as he took the soap. He watched Iban's eyebrows dance in surprise. "They refused her. We have to earn metal!" he added blithely.

Iban's brows made a straight line. "That could be tricky. Not many traveling parties will want to hire a Cantrix as itinerant, no matter how capable. It's not the way people like to think of the Conservatory-trained."

Zakri paused in the energetic washing of his hair, and peered out at Iban from between soapy fingers. "Would you perhaps have a suggestion for us, master?"

Iban tuggged at his own fringe of wet hair. "Could be. But it won't be what Singer Sira planned, I expect."

Zakri resumed lathering his hair, trying to be patient. Iban frowned, then lifted his brows. His eyes began to twinkle. "Let's take on a party together, you and I," he suggested.

Zakri grinned. "Would you take me? Truly?"

"I would truly take you, Singer Zakri. You're a very capable Singer. You're maybe a little unpredictable, but I think we could manage."

Zakri crowed, "It's a wonderful idea, Singer Iban! I would love to earn the metal we need, and present it to Singer Sira. She has done so much for me. How much do you think we can earn in one trip? Five bits, six? To share?"

Iban chuckled. "We'll have to see. Let me find out who's going where, and how big a party, then we'll negotiate. Your job will be to arrange things with Singer Sira."

A moment's doubt assailed Zakri. "That might not be so easy." He considered the problem. "She should rest. It has been a long time since she had a rest."

"I'm sure it's true, and I wish you luck persuading her," Iban said dryly. "I'll talk to you at this evening's meal."

Iban climbed out of the tub and dried himself, grimacing at the wet spots on the floor left by Zakri's splashing. Zakri remained in the water after Iban left, soaping his hands until they were as clean as a baby's, scrubbing his face until it stung. Lying back and raising his legs out of the water, he examined his dripping feet. If they grew any more, he thought, they would be as big as *hruss* feet. He was eighteen now, and almost as tall as Sira. Probably he was done growing, but if he could only manage another inch or two, he would reach her height. He grinned at the thought. It would be nice to look down at people!

Dried and dressed in fresh clothes, Zakri wandered out of the *ubanyor* and down the long corridor. It was odd having nothing to do. Of course, he could be practicing, but maybe just this once he would put it off a bit. He reached the turning of the hall where it opened onto the great room and the Cantoris. He meant to go into the great room, but the sounds of music from farther down the corridor drew him past it to the practice rooms where students worked behind closed doors. He heard the scales he himself had learned only this year, bits of songs, one or two Singers doing the vocalise he was still waiting to learn.

Outside one of the rooms he stopped. There was no music here. What he heard was sobbing, the sound of a child crying her heart out. Her pain seized Zakri like a hand, stopping his progress, drawing him to her.

For a moment he stood helplessly outside the door, not knowing what to do, but not able to leave the child without responding in some way. He lifted his hand to knock, but it seemed the wrong choice. Finally he sent to her, risking offense. *What is it? What is the matter? I am Singer Zakri. Can I help you?*

The sobbing stopped abruptly. The door to the practice room opened, and a little girl with tumbled curly hair and cheeks blotched with crying looked up at him. Her lips trembled, and she put a pudgy hand to them. *You are the boy!* she sent. *You are the one!* Her blue eyes were round with amazement, their lashes sparkling with tears.

Zakri knelt and looked into her face. *I do not know what you mean. What boy am I? And who are you?*

I am Trisa, she responded, and her lips quivered again. *And you are the boy who did not have to come here! Did they find out about you? Did they make you come after all?*

Zakri shook his head. *No, Trisa, I traveled here with Singer Sira. When I was young like you, I wanted to come here very much.*

I do not like it here. She dropped her gaze to her feet. *I miss my mama so much. I like the music, but . . . I miss . . .* She began to weep again, and without stopping to think, Zakri put his arm around the child. Her small body was warm and fragile, and he stroked her unruly hair and let her soak his tunic with her tears.

"What are you doing?" The voice behind him was sharp with anger, and something else. "Do you not know better than to touch one of the Gifted, even a child?"

Zakri drew back from the little girl and turned, still on his knees, to see a frowning woman in a dark brown tunic, her hands braced on her hips.

"I am—I am sorry," he said. "I did not mean . . . she was crying."

Trisa, the woman sent, without shielding herself, *go back into the practice room.*

The child's tears stopped instantly. She pushed out her lower lip and looked up at the woman with a fierce light in her eyes. *Where is your* filla? the teacher demanded.

Trisa's chin rose high and her cheeks flamed. She stepped back very slowly to let the woman see into the practice room, and pointed with her chubby finger to the floor. Zakri saw the *filla* lying where she had flung it, and he sucked in an audible breath.

I hate it! Trisa sent. Tiny sparks of anger flew about her face. *And I hate this place!*

Zakri winced and threw a glance over his shoulder at the woman. Her face was dark. As she opened her mouth to speak, Zakri reached out with his psi and rolled the *filla*, ever so gently, toward Trisa. *Pick it up*, he sent to her. *Please! You should not drop it, ever.*

Trisa looked up at him for a moment, and the woman behind him. Then she bent and picked up her *filla*. *Thank you, Singer Zakri*, she sent. She went back into the practice room and slammed the door with as much force as her small body could muster. The sound reverberated in the corridor. *But I will not practice!* came clearly from behind the closed door.

Slowly, Zakri got up from his knees. "I apologize, Cantrix," he said again.

She stared at him, openmouthed. "Who are you? How did you do that?"

Zakri shrugged. "I am Zakri . . . Singer Zakri," he amended. "Sometimes I am able to move things." *And sometimes I cannot help it!* But he shielded that thought.

The teacher crossed her arms and shook her head disapprovingly. "I do not think such demonstrations are good for the children. Itinerants should not be in this wing, in any case. This is the student wing."

"I heard her crying."

"Many of the students cry in their first year. They are lonely, and they are working hard. They get over it."

Zakri looked at the woman closely now. She was not young, and she looked tired and worried. He clearly heard her thinking that the rest of Trisa's class had stopped crying for their mothers, and that she feared Trisa would never adjust. He knew he should shield himself, and not trespass, but it was so much easier to gather information in this way.

"I hope she does," he said mildly. He bowed, hiding his expression.

"I will go in to her now," the woman said dismissively.

He bowed again as she followed Trisa into the practice room. In a few moments he heard the halting sounds of a *filla*, badly played. He listened for a bit, then walked away. He would have to ask Sira how this child might have known who he was. He would not soon forget her heartbreaking sobs, nor her stubborn spirit. Trisa. Yes, he would have to ask Sira about Trisa.

Chapter Twenty-six

After much argument, Erc was persuaded to set a price for the *filhata*. He asked only four bits of metal, but Sira knew the *filhata* to be worth far more. She insisted the price be a fair one. In the end, they agreed upon eight bits.

It was hard for Sira to let Zakri go off with Iban to earn it, while she remained behind at Conservatory. She bid them farewell, and welcome when they returned, and otherwise made herself as useful to Erc as she could, to earn her keep. She avoided Magister Mkel and the Cantors and Cantrixes. She kept away from the student wing, from the great room, and from the Cantoris. She ate her meals in the kitchens, in Erc's company, and she bathed late, when most House members were in bed. It was a strange time, being in Conservatory but not part of it.

The weeks passed slowly. When Iban and Zakri returned to Conservatory, the three reunited like a family coming together. Zakri seemed bigger each time Sira saw him, and he grew brown and strong with the constant travel. They resumed his *filla* lessons each time he came back. Sira polished and refined his technique, working on his fingering and his tone. When he was away she slept long hours, more than she ever had in her life. She dreamed often of Theo, and when she woke it seemed as if they had really been together, and had only just parted at the moment of waking. She missed his presence at those times with a physical ache, assuaged only by taking up some heavy chore in the stables.

It was while Zakri and Iban were on their last journey together that the rumors from Amric reached Sira's ears. Two kitchen workers, gossiping together, whispered their news, assuming none of the Gifted were about. Sira, finishing her mid-day meal at the table, froze in her place and listened. Her heart turned over at what she heard.

She left the kitchens to pace the halls, fretting, worrying. For the first time since coming to Conservatory she felt caged and useless. She could only thank the Spirit that Zakri and Iban were expected the next day.

Already six bits of metal rested in the leather pouch Erc kept tucked into a drawer in his workbench. Each time Zakri and Sira had turned over a little more of the agreed-upon price, Erc offered the *filhata* to them, but Sira firmly declined. This trip, however, should bring the last of it. Sira lay wakeful through the long hours of the night, and the next morning, she cast her mind out past the stable doors a hundred times, listening for the travelers' return.

It was almost night before they rode up to the House, the Singers and their travelers weary and hungry, their *hruss* wet with falling snow, fetlocks and long ears clotted with ice. Sira had heard their approach half an hour before, and she and Erc were waiting. They led the animals into the stables while the traveling party made for the great room. Zakri and Iban, tired though they were, stayed in the stalls, brushing and rubbing the *hruss* with towels until all the beasts were clean and comfortable. Sira felt Zakri's looks at her, sensing her anxiety and impatience.

At last the chores were done. Zakri and Iban wanted to eat something before going to the *ubanyor*. In the kitchens Sira spoke aloud, for Iban's sake, but softly. "I heard something yesterday about the Cantoris at Amric. I do not know what is happening, but it is said the *quiru* there is weak, and fading badly at night."

"And Cantrix Isbel?" Iban asked.

"I do not know. But I must go there, and quickly. I do not understand, if there is a problem, why Conservatory is not taking action."

Zakri spoke even more quietly, and they both leaned closer to hear him. "I do not think they have anyone to spare."

Sira stared at him. "How do you know that?"

"I hear things. When we have been here at Conservatory, and when we went to Lamdon the trip before last."

Iban's eyebrows rose high on his forehead. "I didn't hear anything. How did you?"

Zakri looked down at the bowl of *keftet* he was working his way through.

Sira sighed. "You should not listen to others' thoughts unless invited." The tips of Zakri's ears grew pink. He put a huge spoonful of grain and *caeru* meat in his mouth and chewed it, looking up at Sira with his cheeks bulging and his eyes round and innocent. She shook a finger at him in exasperation. "Perhaps in this case," she muttered, "it is as well you did. But you must not make a habit of it."

The men went on with their meal as Sira waited, drumming her fingers on the table and arranging and rearranging her long legs. When at last they were finished, Zakri reached into his pocket to pull out four shining bits of metal.

He held them out on his palm, where they flashed in the *quiru* light. "There you are, Singer Sira. The full price, with a little left over."

She held out her own hand and Zakri poured the metal into it. He was grimy and tired, his hair matted and his eyes reddened from the glare of sun on snow, but smile was wide and white in his sunburned face. "I thank you, Singer Zakri," Sira said. "A job well done." She nodded to Iban. "And I thank you, as well. Your help has been beyond price."

"And so what will you do now?" Iban asked.

Sira stroked her scarred eyebrow. "We must go to Amric. Zakri can begin his *filhata* studies as we travel."

"I wish you good luck, then," Iban said. "I hope all is well with Cantrix Isbel."

Sira nodded, but she felt very little hope. If Zakri was right, the shortage of Singers was more urgent than she had guessed, certainly more serious than Conservatory and Lamdon would admit. She wished she could fly to Amric like a *ferrel*, erasing the days of riding that lay between her and Isbel. She looked down at her hands, flexing and curling her fingers. She would very soon hold the *filhata* in them again. It would be a comfort.

Iban bid them farewell with so many reminders of his instructions that Zakri was laughing and shaking his head as they rode away. Sira flashed him a look.

Now I suppose you will say, he sent, *that you must not laugh too much in the deep cold, or your lungs will freeze!*

Sira looked back to lift her hand to Iban and Erc where they stood in the stableyard, then turned forward to gaze up at the white peaks rising into folds of gray cloud. She rehearsed Iban's instructions: two days west to the turning of the road, then three or four days' ride north to Perl, depending upon the weather. From Perl, three days through North Pass to Amric, again contingent upon the weather. It was likely to be to be snowing in the Pass. The deep cold was beginning to release its rigid grasp on the Continent, and the snows of the next season were already falling in the lower elevations. There would be powder, and swirling snow about them as they rode.

The precious *filhata* was tied securely to Sira's saddle, cushioned by her bedfurs. She reached behind her to reassure herself it was really there. *Your lessons begin tonight,* she sent.

He grinned at her. *My lessons have never ceased since I first laid eyes on you, Singer Sira. Tonight they only grow harder.*

Never mind that. You just remember your C, because tonight we tune. She leaned back against the high cantle and recalled Theo's first lesson. If Zakri could learn as quickly as Theo, he would be a competent Cantor before the next deep cold season. She shielded this thought, remembering how hard Theo had practiced, how diligently he had applied himself to every problem. It would not be fair to compare the two. Theo had been a grown man, disciplined and experienced. Zakri would have to find his own way, and learn at his own speed.

Despite Zakri's jokes about Iban's nagging, he was meticulous in his chores as they made their camp that night. The cold was easing, but nevertheless Zakri played his *filla* with only the end visible from his hood. The music came effortlessly from the circle of *caeru* fur. He indulged in one or two embellishments, but his *quiru* was swift and economical. Sira built and lighted the campfire, and Zakri cooked their evening meal from the supplies paid for with one of their bits of metal. Then, in the long evening, when their *quiru* light was the only bright spot in the blank white landscape, Zakri began to study the *filhata*.

He had grown so much, in every direction it seemed, that his fingers were as long as Sira's own, and all the strings of the *filhata* were an easy reach, regardless of mode. By the second night of their journey, he played the tuning exercise with a facility that had taken him weeks to acquire on the *filla*. C - G, D - A, E - B, F - C. Sira adjusted the position of his fingers, and tapped his wrist to show him where to release the muscles, where to increase the angle. He played the exercise again, and then, before she could comment, he rearranged it, turning the fifths upside down, plucking the C string in a little ostinato, adding rhythm.

She laughed, and leaned back against her bedfurs. *You have been playing this instrument behind my back!*

He grinned. His fine hair was charged by rubbing against his furs all day, and it rose in a tousled nimbus around his head, like a small *quiru* just for his face. His eyes shone with pleasure. *I have not. But it feels as if I have.*

Then try this one. She took the instrument from him and dictated, playing a new exercise once quickly, then very slowly, articulating each note before handing the *filhata* back. He played it awkwardly at first, then more with more fluency. His fingers moved naturally upon the strings, as if indeed he had worked this way before. *Try the same exercise in* Doryu.

He closed his eyes for a moment, thinking, then played the exercise in the new mode without error. *Why is the* filhata *so much easier than the* filla?

It is not, she answered, *except perhaps for you. But be careful of overconfidence. It requires much practice and concentration. And you must learn to use your voice with it.* A little abashed, she shielded the rush of affection that filled her heart. *We will try your voice tomorrow.*

When Zakri's fingers grew sore from pressing the strings, Sira took the *filhata* into her own lap and played melodies remembered from long-ago hours in the practice room. Her fingers had lost their protective calluses, and she grimaced when, like Zakri's, they began to hurt too much to continue. Reluctantly, she wrapped the *filhata* and stored it carefully among the saddle packs. *We should be able to turn north tomorrow.*

Yes. The two leaning trees are about three hours' ride away, Zakri sent. She raised her eyebrows, and he gave her a sly smile. *Iban and I took a party to Perl.*

Tomorrow, then, we turn north. Tomorrow night we will play again, and try your voice.

They rolled themselves into their bedfurs, and Sira lay looking up at

Zakri's strong *quiru*. She was proud of him, but she worried whether she pushed him too hard. For the thousandth time, she asked the Spirit of Stars to guide her, to ensure that she chose the right path. She had Zakri's immense Gift in her hands now. It was too late for doubts.

Their journey took them nine days. They worked on the *filhata* for an hour in the mornings before setting out, and twice as long in the evenings. Before long, their fingers grew less sensitive as pads of callus formed on the tips. Zakri's voice was easy to work with. If Sira had not been so worried about Isbel, she could have enjoyed their days of riding through the snowy landscape during the hours of light, filling the hours of darkness with music. But dreams of Amric, lying and dark and cold, plagued Sira. A sense of urgency made her fidget in her saddle and turn many times each night in her bedfurs.

On their last morning before reaching Amric, somthing kept her from leaving their campsite. She sat for a long time with the *filhata* in her lap, reaching ahead as far as she could with her psi. Something was happening at Amric.

Isbel's heart pounded as she stepped up on the dais and sat next to her senior, holding her *filhata* before her like a shield. The *quiru* looked dim and drab to her frightened eyes, and Cantor Ovan's fierce gaze pierced her soul.

If you fail today, he sent, *I will denounce you to the Magister.*

She had no answer, but only bowed her head, checking her tuning with trembling fingers. As much as she resented Ovan, he was right. The House *quiru* was failing, and she was at fault.

She had faced the truth. She had told Kai that what had been between them must never happen again. Night after night, she longed for him, weeping tears of sorrow, but she kept her word. She had accepted her duty, and given him up. Yet still her Gift would not respond.

Spirit of Stars, she prayed, help me. I have not enough strength to do this alone.

Ovan began, his lead even less musical than usual. Isbel followed obediently, knowing he must be as frightened as she. Lives depended on them, and the faces looking up to the dais were pale and uneasy. For weeks, Ovan had essentially accomplished the *quirunha* alone, though the House members did not yet know that. Such an effort would exhaust a more competent Cantor than he. He looked tired, and Isbel felt guilt about that as well.

Ovan began a melody, an old and familiar one, many times tried and trustworthy. Isbel joined him. Her voice felt fuller and easier than ever. If only her Gift would flow as easily as her voice, this could be a successful *quirunha*.

She tried. She concentrated, and sent her psi out with her voice. She tried not to force, but to release. She searched for the memory of how that had always felt, before everything had changed. She strove to open herself, to hold nothing back, to offer her Gift as it was meant to be offered, all save that one small corner of herself, that one hidden part she dared not expose.

Perspiration dampened her neck, and trickled between her breasts. She took deep breaths as she sang, and her voice swelled to dominate Ovan's, but her psi was almost useless. She yearned to feel the warmth sweep out from her. What she felt instead was Ovan's anger and fear, and her own fright rose in a moment of blinding panic. She grew suddenly dizzy, and her fingers and her voice faltered. Her eyes flew open as she tried to orient herself in the spin of the world around her. She was sure she was about to faint, right there on the dais in front of everyone, and she feared what Kai, standing in the back of the room, might do.

Then, somehow, the shaky thread of her psi steadied. It took on strength and substance. Her dizziness fell away, and she found herself borne up by the music, her psi expanding to a stream, to a river of power. It must be the music. The music was better now . . .

But no, it was not the music. She recognized the psi that flowed beneath her own. She knew that resonance very well. Sira was there, somewhere. Sira was with her.

The House grew warm and bright, and the listeners in the Cantoris smiled in relief. The music went on, with Ovan leading Isbel to every corner of the House, strenghtening, energizing the *quiru* to last through the hours of darkness until the next *quirunha*. She followed him effortlessly now, her psi floating and free, untroubled, borne up on Sira's great Gift. Only the tears that glistened on her cheeks gave away her feelings. Before Ovan could see them, she dried them on her sleeve.

SMILE ON US,
O SPIRIT OF STARS,
SEND US THE SUMMER TO WARM THE WORLD,
UNTIL THE SUNS WILL SHINE ALWAYS TOGETHER.

The ending prayer was recited with more than customary fervor. Ovan stepped down from the dais with neither a glance nor a word to Isbel. Contrasted with his angry attacks of the previous weeks, his silence was almost flattering. Isbel faltered as she stepped down from the dais, and she had to support herself with one hand. She felt lightheaded, and her stomach was queasy. Perhaps, she thought, she was ill, and that had been her problem all along.

She dared not send her thanks to Sira now, lest Ovan hear her. Sira seemed very far away, perhaps too far to hear her in any case. Her own reach was not so long. Her friend was not yet in the House, Isbel was certain. Isbel tucked her *filhata* under her arm, and hurried to the refuge of her apartment. Sira would be here soon. All would be well after all.

Chapter Twenty-seven

What is happening to her? Zakri asked.

Sira sat cross-legged, exhausted, the *filhata* still in her lap. Reaching so far had taken all her energy. Zakri had followed her, their psi wound together like the twining suckers of an ironwood grove. Snow fell steadily and silently around them, thick flakes that melted instantly when they floated into the *quiru* light. *I do not know*, Sira responded, *but I fear for her.*

Zakri stood and began to break camp. She sat where she was, regathering her strength.

They had camped in a little hollow of land beneath a huge boulder, in the middle of a ring of great trees. It was a lovely spot, but Sira thought it was not the beauty of the place, but the Gift that had brought her here. She ached for Isbel. Today, Isbel would be all right, but Sira dreaded what she would find when they reached Amric.

Their days in North Pass had been easy despite the continual snow. Zakri's aptitude for the *filhata* delighted Sira, and his voice had proved sweet and clear. More depth and resonance would come with maturity. The hard physical work he had always done made his breathing easy. She had showed him the source of the voice's power with one touch of a finger midway between his breastbone and his belly, and his swift comprehension astounded her.

I wonder, Singer Zakri, she sent once after a long and productive lesson. *We struggled so hard with the* filla. *I do not know why the* filhata *and the voice are so much easier for you.*

He grinned. *Better ask the Gift.* He went off humming to settle the *hruss* for the night.

It was as good an answer as any. Who could ever fully understand the Gift? Its complexities were as tangled as the patterns of life on the Continent, and it revealed itself to each Singer in its own time, in its own way. Those who bore the Gift were as much in awe of its power as those who did not.

Now, on the day they would arrive at Amric, Sira had been caught in Isbel's struggle. It was time now to face, with Isbel, the source of the trouble.

Reluctantly, Sira opened her eyes and got to her feet.

We can go whenever you are ready, Zakri sent. He waited just inside the *quiru*'s edge with the reins of both *hruss* in his hand.

They mounted and rode away from the campsite, leaving the empty *quiru* glowing softly behind a curtain of falling snow. Sira pulled her hood forward to keep the snow from her eyes. In silence, they rode from the northern mouth of the pass down the long, gentle slope that led to Amric. The descent took more than four hours. The *hruss* set their broad hooves with care in the slippery powder, and they wore mantles of snow on their rumps and withers by the time they rode into the courtyard. Sira and Zakri pushed back their hoods and looked up at the House. Isbel, muffled in thick yellow-white furs, stood all alone on the steps, waiting for them.

Housekeeper Cael had Sira's things carried directly to Isbel's apartment, saying the Cantrix wished Sira to be her own guest. He installed Zakri in an itinerant's room. Zakri reported gleefully that it was right next to the kitchens. Sira was grateful for Amric's hospitality. They would need it.

I thank you with all my heart, Isbel sent to her when at last they were alone in her rooms. *I do not understand why my Gift is failing, but it is getting worse.*

Sira shed her furs with relief, and rubbed her itchy face with her fingers. *There is no need to thank me. But I am fearful for you.*

Isbel avoided her eyes. *I have made a great mistake,* she confessed. *But I will not make it again.*

Sira looked down at her friend, and reached to tuck a strand of Isbel's hair into the thick coil that shone against her dark tunic. They were the same age, she and Isbel, but she felt infinitely older. *Perhaps it will be all right, Isbel. You are not the first Singer in Nevya's history to . . . to make this particular mistake.*

Isbel looked up, and Sira frowned at the hollowness of her eyes. *You are being kind to me,* Isbel sent. *But you did not give in to this temptation. You were strong enough. I was not.*

I did not have to work with Cantor Ovan.

And I do, Isbel responded. *I still do. I must somehow find my Gift again.*

Isbel said nothing about Kai, but Sira put a hand to her own breast, feeling the ache of Isbel's loss. *You will recover in time,* she sent gently, and hoped it was true.

Isbel's Housewoman knocked on the outer door of the apartment before she put her head around the door. "Would the Cantrixes like something to eat?" Yula asked in a tentative voice. "Or would you prefer to bathe first?"

"A bath, I think," Sira said. She sent to Isbel, *Let us talk, about everything. Let us have no secrets. Together we can get through this time.*

Isbel tried to smile, but her lips trembled. Sira commanded, "Yula, see that the *ubanyix* is empty for us. We need privacy."

Yula's eyes grew round, and her mouth fell open. She disappeared without an answer.

Isbel sent, *Now you have frightened her.*

Sorry. But she is easily frightened, is she not? She and Isbel walked slowly on their way to the *ubanyix,* giving Yula time to herd out any Housewomen who might be there. Several people passed them, bowing to Isbel, staring from the corners of their eyes at Sira.

Sira was glad to shed her tunic and trousers, dropping them at her feet. The water felt delicious, and she slid beneath its surface, eager for its warmth to soothe her travel-weary muscles. She looked up as Isbel, slower than she, folded her own clothes neatly on a shelf, and turned to the bath.

Sira caught back the exclamation tha rose to her lips. Reflexively, her shielding sprang up. In shock, she closed her eyes.

Unaware, Isbel stepped down into the water, and leaned her head back against the scrolled edge of the tub. *I have been so tired. I have wondered if perhaps I am ill.*

Sira opened her eyes. *If you are, I will do what I can to help.*

I just do not know. Isbel pulled her hair out of its binding, and it fell around her in deep glossy waves. Her face had grown thinner, and her eyes were enormous, darkly green in the light of the *quiru.* Sira marveled at her friend's innocence. Despite everything, Isbel did not understand. She lacked Sira's experience of living with ordinary House members. Isbel was like one of Lamdon's nursery flowers, delicate and fragile. Sira feared that when she understood what had happened to her, she would crumble like one of those flowers left lying in the cold.

They took a long time in the bath. Sira was not eager for the moment of revelation. Isbel washed her hair and Sira helped her bind it again. Her own short locks were already dry by the time they walked together back to Isbel's rooms. Yula was waiting for them, bowing nervously behind a tray of tea and nutbread. The moment the two Singers were seated, she escaped, leaving them to their meal.

Sira ate with the healthy appetite of the itinerant, and drank two cups of tea. Isbel took a slice of nutbread, but Sira saw her taste it only once. *Are you not eating well, my friend?*

Isbel set down the bread. *At times I have good appetite. But lately I am sometimes not able to eat at all. I think it is just that I am so unhappy.*

Sira pushed the tray of food aside, and went to kneel beside Isbel. She took her friend's white hand between her own two brown ones.

Isbel, I have seen this . . . illness . . . before, at Observatory. I can help you feel better, but I cannot restore your Gift.

Isbel sat very still. Only her eyes moved, following Sira's. She did not appear to breathe. With all the gentleness she could muster, Sira went on. *My dear friend. You are with child.*

When Isbel did not react, she sent again, *You are pregnant.*

Sira was poised ready to put her arms around Isbel, to steady her, or hold her if she grew faint, but it was not necessary. A light began to grow in Isbel's eyes, and a healthy color to bloom in her cheeks. Her breast moved with a sudden deep breath, and her other hand came up to grip Sira's.

"Are you sure?" she asked aloud.

Sira pulled one hand free to touch the swell of Isbel's stomach where it arched under her tunic. She spoke aloud, as Isbel had, knowing Isbel's days of sending and listening would be coming to an end. "I saw you in the *ubanyix.* I am only surprised you did not yet see it yourself."

Isbel dimpled. "I have been so unhappy, Sira, that I saw nothing but my misery. But now—it is out of my control, is it not? There is nothing more I can do!"

Sira stood, releasing Isbel's hands. She went back to her chair and sat gazing at Isbel's glowing face. It was true. There was nothing now to be done. Had it been she . . . But Isbel seemed only relieved. And what of the Cantoris?

"Kai will be delighted, and Cantor Ovan will be furious," Isbel murmured. Her dimples faded. "Conservatory will have to send another Singer."

"It may be that Conservatory has no other Singer to send," Sira told her.

Isbel's eyes met hers, and they both understood in an instant what that would mean. A great weariness washed over Sira. She closed her eyes, and shielded her feelings from Isbel. I will deal with this somehow, she thought. Somehow. But, O Spirit . . . is there no end to it?

Zakri followed the House members into Amric's Cantoris the next morning. He took his seat among the working Housemen and women, his blue tunic blending with the crowd of red and green and blue around him. On the forward benches he saw the somber colors of the ruling class, Magister Edrus and his mate seated with their children, Housekeeper Cael on the opposite side of the aisle. Everyone rose as Cantrix Isbel and Cantor Ovan came in, and stepped up onto the dais. They bowed to the assembly, and the House members bowed in return, sitting when the Singers did.

Cantor Ovan's voice was ugly. It grated on the ear and had almost no resonance despite the ample size and good hard surfaces of the Cantoris. His musical ideas weren't much better, his melodies unimaginative, his rhythms unpredictable. Singer Iban made better music on his *filla* than this dried-up stick of a Cantor made with voice and *filhata* both.

But Cantrix Isbel—now there was a voice. Zakri liked its pretty vibrato and the lovely ring it had in the high register. She was limited, of course, by having to blend with her senior. Zakri would have liked to hear her sing all by herself. He wished he could shut out Ovan's abrasive tone and hear only Isbel.

He followed at a respectful distance as the *quirunha* progressed, and he recognized the other presence as soon as it appeared. It was such a strong and distinctive Gift that it was beyond comprehension that Cantor Ovan did not know it was there. She was not even in the room, yet her presence was a powerful undercurrent to the stream of energy flowing out from the dais, borne by the music, powered by the Gift.

Zakri held back carefully so as not to be detected. He listened, and observed, and he saw that it was Sira, and Sira working virtually alone, who performed the *quirunha*. Isbel was almost a passive presence in the synergy of music and psi. Ovan's strength was ragged, unreliable, with such gaps and weaknesses that only Sira's strength could have compensated. And despite everything, the room grew brighter, and the warmth reached to every corner of the House, the nursery gardens, the stables, and the tannery. The snow on the roof of the House began to melt and run, dripping onto the cobblestones outside. Zakri saw how carefully Sira worked, how she hid behind Isbel, protecting her. Poor Isbel! It must be awful for her to be forced to work with such a one as Ovan.

When the *quirunha* was complete, and the assembly rose to chant the ending prayer, Zakri saw the gleam of tears in Cantrix Isbel's eyes, and he felt the strength of her gratitude.

He sent to Sira, *Well done!*

She did not answer. He knew she wanted to avoid detection, but he doubted Ovan would hear in any case. He did not appear at all sensitive.

Cantrix Isbel looked better today. Her color was higher, her eyes less hollow. She looked around the Cantoris as if searching for someone, and he followed her gaze.

In the farthest corner stood a tall man, perhaps two summers older than Zakri himself. He had an open face, and he wore his hair short, curling around his ears. His eyes and Cantrix Isbel's met above the heads of the assembly.

Zakri was sure Sira would not know if he eavesdropped. Shamelessly, he opened his mind to hear the communication between Isbel and this man. There was nothing to hear. They were not sending to one another, though their eyes spoke as clearly as if they had been.

Zakri shielded himself once again. Something was afoot here. A Cantrix and, by the look of him, a Houseman. He could ask Sira, but probably she would not tell him anything. He would just have to find out for himself. Amric was proving to be a very interesting place!

Chapter Twenty-eight

As Isbel's body bloomed and grew, her Gift withered. She looked and sounded better than ever, but her psi was distracted, diluted by the work of her body. She could hear still, but increasingly her sending was weak. Sira found it harder and harder to sustain her in the *quirunha* at any distance. Secluded in Isbel's apartment, she bent over her *filhata* as she worked, and the perspiration ran down her body. She grew tired, taking hours to recover after each *quirunha*. It seemed, too, that the harder she worked, the less Ovan did.

On a day when the snow fell so heavily that it blotted out the pale sunlight, the *quirunha* began with a fragmented melody from Cantor Ovan, and Isbel took it up on her own *filhata* immediately, hardly waiting for Ovan to finish his first exposition. She filled out the music with harmony and a steady rhythm. But Ovan's psi was as weak as the winter sunlight, and Sira was left virtually alone. She asked the Spirit for strength, and extended her psi as strongly as she could, no longer trying to disguise what she was doing. The *quirunha* mattered more.

She struggled. The gardens and the tannery seemed almost beyond her reach. She concentrated until her forehead burned with the effort. Her psi pulled strength from every part of her being, but still it was not enough.

As she reached toward the tannery, her fingers beginning to tire on the *filhata* strings, she was surprised to find the air there already bright and warm. In the nursery gardens it was the same. As her *quiru* swelled, it seemed to meet other *quiru* coming in from the outer edges of the House, sister circles of heat and light that rolled to meet her. She drew a deep, relieved breath, and her face relaxed. She let her psi contract, and she listened from a distance as Ovan and Isbel concluded the *quirunha*. When they were finished, she broke the contact and leaned back in her chair, utterly spent.

Good work, Singer! she heard.

And good work from you, Singer Zakri. I thank you for your help.

His sending was full of energy. *It was my great pleasure! Let us do it again tomorrow!*

Sira smiled in spite of her weariness. Yes, she thought, they could do it again tomorrow, if they did it together. But it would be better to face the scandal now, and declare it. There would be less strain if she were to step openly onto the dais and serve as Cantrix. There was risk in it, risk to them all, but less than there would be in maintaining this deception. And there was no way to protect Isbel from the storm of accusation that loomed ahead. Sira could only hope that when the storm broke, Kai could shelter his beloved from its fierceness.

They gathered in Isbel's apartment at Sira's request. She looked around at them, wishing she could find a different answer in their faces, but knowing nothing could change what must happen now. Kai hovered over Isbel while Zakri hung back, watching everything with wide eyes. Isbel sat near the window, her heair glowing a lovely near-red in the combined light of the *quiru* and the winter sun. Her cheeks curved and dimpled once again, and her eyes were bright when she turned them up to Kai.

Kai alone was completely delighted with Isbel's pregnancy. For him it meant a reprieve from suffering, and he was blithely indifferent about the loss to the Cantoris. "Let Conservatory send someone else," he said to Sira. "We didn't intend this, but the Spirit has sent us a babe, and there's nothing to be done now but be mated properly."

"Houseman, have you thought how your House will react to such a mating? Isbel is Cantrix here!"

The hunter stood straight, his head up and his jawline hard. "It doesn't matter now. What would you have me do? Turn away from my child, or its mother? I won't, no matter how they all carry on!"

Sira sighed and ran her fingers through her hair. She felt drained in body and mind,

The new life growing under Isbel's heart, sent by the Spirit or not, had determined Sira's path. She saw only one way out of their troubles, but she was loath to follow it.

"Can we not go on this way for a bit longer?" Isbel asked.

Sira felt a pressure in her chest. Isbel did not understand the effort required to perform the *quirunha* at such a distance without being detected. And she did not want to tell her, to add to her feelings of guilt. It would not ease her own burden to add to Isbel's. She answered as mildly as she could. "For a bit longer we can go on. But soon . . ."

Kai laughed. "Soon everyone will be able to see for themselves!"

Isbel said, "But why, Kai? I bathe in private, and wear my tunics loosely." She caressed the swell of her belly.

The ancient gesture, made by one of the gifted, a full Cantrix, made Sira squirm in her chair. Even though it was Isbel, her beloved friend, she could not deny the shock she felt at the sight of it, the sense of wrongness— and of waste.

"Isbel," she said. "Have you not seen the women of the House close to term, how they strain their tunics? You are approaching your last weeks, and you will not be able to hide it."

"And besides," Kai said, "we're only putting off what must be done. My family will make room for us. And when the Magister and the Housekeeper get used to the idea, they'll see to it we have an apartment of our own, like other new families. I work hard for my House, and it's my right to have my own home."

Sira doubted it would be so easy, but she held her peace. In her mind she heard, *Amric will be famous for this all over the Continent!*

Zakri had been lounging near a table where Yula had placed refreshments. Every time Sira looked at him, his mouth was full. She cast him a helpless glance now as she rose and answered Kai. "Perhaps you are right, Houseman. But I think perhaps it is best if I talk to Magister Edrus first. I will try to explain."

Isbel said, "I must do that myself, Sira. When I am ready."

And then you had better be ready too, Singer Sira!

Sira shot Zakri another glance. She could see by the sparkle in his eye and the cheerful creasing of his cheeks that he was enjoying himself. She could not see the humor, but still, Zakri was right. When Isbel revealed her secret, Sira would be forced to step into the Cantoris herself, to serve with Cantor Ovan.

Isbel left her seat and followed Sira to the door. She whispered, "I am so sorry. I know I have caused great trouble for you." She embraced Sira, her cheek smooth and warm, her round, taut belly pressing against Sira's hip. Sira held her tightly for a moment, and kissed her lightly on the forehead. Unexpected tears welled under Sira's eyelids and she closed her eyes to suppress them. *Be careful, my friend,* she sent.

Isbel nodded, and went back to Kai, waiting for her by the window. They stood a little apart from each other. Kai never touched Isbel in Sira's presence, but still, she fought a feeling of revulsion. She was aware of the irony that she, the great rebel, had such difficulty accepting the very human thing that had happened here. Magister Mkel would be amused, she supposed. Zakri came to stand beside her, and she knew that her feelings were open to him. It was obscurely comforting to know that at least someone understood her, though it changed nothing.

As they left Isbel's apartment, she sent, *Someone must tell Magister Mkel as soon as Isbel has made her announcement. Perhaps there is something they can do.*

What I heard was clear, Zakri answered. His eyes had gone dark and he was no longer smiling. *At Lamdon, they said there are no Cantors to spare unless they send someone away from Conservatory. Even there they are short of staff. The youngest class is suffering from it.*

Sira lifted her hands in despair. *It falls to me, then.*

Zakri bowed to her. *Yes, Cantrix Sira. It falls to you.*

Isbel went alone to Magister Edrus. Sira and Kai watched her go, a small figure walking away from them down the corridor, then they went into the apartment to wait. Sira sat looking out into the blankness of the snow-filled landscape, willing herself to stay away, not to listen as Isbel made her confession. She could not bring herself to speak to Kai. He too was silent, pacing the apartment like a *tkir* on the prowl.

More than an hour passed. The tension grew in layers, like the snow drifting outside. Sira gripped her hands together until they hurt, and Kai occasionally groaned from the pressure. A second hour was almost gone when Sira heard, *Sira! You had better go to Isbel!* Zakri, in the urgency of the moment, forgot both their titles.

In a flash Sira was on her feet, striding from Isbel's apartment. Kai followed closely, asking, "What's happened? What is it?" but she had no time to answer him. She cast her mind ahead, to find out what had alarmed Zakri.

Even as she heard Cantor Ovan berating Isbel, she reached Magister Edrus's door and threw it open. Zakri, running from the other direction, entered close behind her.

Isbel was crouched on the floor. Ovan's fury assailed her mind, an assault such as only one of the Gifted could make upon another. It was cruel beyond belief, a mental screaming that rang inside Sira's own skull. Sira knelt beside Isbel, and added her shielding to Isbel's weak defenses. *Leave her alone!* she flared at Ovan. *There is no good to be had from this!*

Little whore! His sending was like a shout. *Slut! You are worthless, a traitor, you should never have been allowed into my Cantoris! I will see you exposed in North Pass and forgotten! You—*

Zakri joined Isbel and Sira, and they combined their energies to form a wall of psi to shut out Ovan's ravings. Isbel fell to one side, and sobbed brokenly where she lay. Sira looked up at Ovan's pinched face, the lips and nostrils white against the darkness of his skin. He was shaking so, she wondered how he could stand. Magister Edrus bent over a table, his face in his hands. He would have heard nothing of Ovan's attack.

Sira spoke aloud. "Cantor Ovan, I know you are frightened and tired. But there is no excuse for such brutality toward your colleague, however grave her error."

Edrus looked up. "What is happening here?" His gaze found Isbel collapsed on the floor. "Cantrix Isbel! There is no need for this. You mustn't . . . Cantrix Sira, she says she is—" He trembled, too, his hands unsteady as he pushed himself to his feet. "What will happen to my House? What will we do now?"

Sira left Isbel in Zakri's and Kai's care, and came to stand before Edrus. "We will see that no harm comes to your House. We have been doing that, in truth, Singer Zakri and I."

Ovan's eyes flashed. "What do you mean by that? Who is this young man, and how dare you say such a thing?"

Sira held up a commanding hand. "Let us be calm. Anger and accusations are pointless. The important thing is the Cantoris, and the security of the House."

Magister Edrus indicated a chair for Sira. Before she took it, she turned to where Zakri was helping Isbel to her feet, either ignoring the tabu, or not caring. Kai was on Isbel's other side, a protective arm around her.

Zakri, Sira sent, *please help Isbel to her apartment. Explain to Kai what has happened, and I will see you there as soon as I can.*

Zakri looked at Ovan as he answered, and his eyes were darker than she had ever seen them. *I will. But I wish you luck with him.* Zakri made no attempt to shield his sending, and Ovan fairly ground his teeth as he heard him.

Zakri and Kai drew Isbel, now sobbing weakly, out the door, and closed it behind them. Sira sat down then, as did the Magister. She rested her hands on the table, palms up. "This is a tragic circumstance, Magister, but it is not the first time it has happened on the Continent."

He nodded heavily. "Of course you're right. But I have my House to think of. And I'm fond of Cantrix Isbel, and so is my mate." His eyes slid involuntarily to Ovan. "She brought something to our Cantoris that we're going to miss."

"Did you tell her that?"

"I had no chance. Cantor Ovan was—understandably, I know—very upset."

Ovan stepped up to the table and banged his fist on it. "Upset?" he grated. "I am devastated, and Conservatory will be equally so. I must say, Sira—" His emphasis on her name, without any title, was a deliberate insult. "There must have been something seriously wrong with your class, that two of you have failed so miserably. Conservatory will have to answer for that! And now we must ask them for yet another Singer to replace these incompetents!"

Sira's breath came quickly as she strove to control her own anger. "It is most interesting, Cantor Ovan," she said evenly, "to hear you speak of incompetence."

Ovan sucked in a breath, and his face grew so dark she thought he might collapse at their feet. "How dare you, you—"

Edrus drew himself up. "Yes, Cantor Ovan, we will ask Conservatory for another Singer. But I fear they have none to give us. Can you manage alone for a time?"

Sira watched Ovan, her scarred eyebrow lifted in a challenging arch. His bravado faded before her regard, and his face seemed to fall in upon itself as if some inner support were collapsing. He looked, all at once, like an aged and frightened man. "It . . . it would be difficult, Magister," he faltedred. He sank into a chair. "It is hard for any Cantor to work alone, and Cantrix Isbel has been unable to fully support me for some time now. I thought, naturally, it was her youth, or perhaps . . ." His voice trailed off.

Magister Edrus turned his gaze to Sira. He folded his hands before him, and waited.

"I see you already know what we must do," she said. Her back was to Cantor Ovan, and she did not include him as she spoke. "I will help in your Cantoris, as your Cantor's junior. I ask only that I be allowed to go on with Singer Zakri's training while I am here, and that you send your request to Conservatory as soon as possible."

"That is generous of you," Edurs replied. He turned to Ovan, and said with much meaning, "Are we agreed, then?"

There was only a moment of hesitation before Cantor Ovan gave one reluctant nod. Sira rose and bowed to Magister Edrus. There was nothing more to be said.

Only when they were in the corridor outside the apartment did Ovan send to Sira. *You have not heard the last of this. Your slut of a friend will pay for what she has done, and the price will be high.*

Sira met his black gaze. *Shall I speak of your own weakness, then? Or shall we try to work together, we two, for the good of your House?*

With a derisive grunt, the Cantor turned away and hurried down the hall. Sira followed at a slower pace. This would be even harder than she had thought. She dreaded the *quirunha* she and Ovan would perform together, the Cantoris hours they would share. Being junior to such a Singer, joined with his mind, would be an odious thing. Thank the Spirit, she thought, for Zakri.

Chapter Twenty-nine

It felt strange to Sira to bow before an assembly once again. She had been absent from the dais a long time. Cantor Ovan gave the House members no explanation of her presence, and behind the benches reserved for the ruling members of the House, men and women in colored tunics shifted in their seats and whispered to each other.

Ovan stated a melody in *Iridu*, a simple thing, safe and dull. Sira's *filhata* felt heavy and warm in her hands. She held back at first, harmonizing Ovan's tune, watching him from beneath lowered eyelids.

Then she modulated, shifting to *Aiodu* before Ovan understood her intent. The new mode made dissonance of his melody, and his voice faltered, searching. Sira let her own voice rise above his, transforming the melody in *Aiodu*, reshaping it into something more graceful, and more interesting. She widened its range beyond the capabilities of Ovan's voice. Her psi leaped ahead of his as well, and the *quiru* flared dramatically out from the dais, an abundance, an extravagance of warmth spilling into every corner of the House.

Sira disliked being joined with Ovan. His mind was flawed and distorted by anger and fear. She cared nothing for that. Her own anger was a powerful force she barely restrained. Since the day before, Isbel had cowered in terror and pain in her apartment. Sira spared no energy on sympathy for the Cantor, as he had spared none for Isbel.

When they were finished, Ovan's eyes glittered, and his mind closed like a fist. Sira stood tall and looked down at him. She bowed deeply, once, as to a senior, but then jumped down from the dais and preceded him out of the Cantoris, spurning protocol.

Zakri caught up with her in the corridor. *Quick work. You must be in a hurry.*

The less time I spend joined with that man's mind the better. They reached Isbel's rooms and went in, finding Yula in the center of the room with a tray in her hands.

"Oh, Cantrix Sira," she said, paling but standing her ground for once. She held up the full tray for Sira to see. "Cantrix Isbel hasn't eaten a thing since yesterday morning!"

"I see that, Yula. I will go in to her now."

Zakri relieved Yula of the tray and took it to the table. The Housewoman backed out of the apartment, muttering to herself, and Sira quietly opened the bedroom door.

Isbel lay on her side on her cot, her knees drawn up, her trousers rucked around her ankles. She clutched the bedfurs to her throat, and her eyes were tightly closed.

"Isbel?" Sira whispered. Isbel opened her eyes, and they were too brilliant, glistening in the renewed light of the *quiru*. Sira stepped closer. "Are you all right?"

Isbel said in a feverish way, "He is screaming at me still. He will not leave me alone."

"But that is not possible, truly." Sira spoke in as soothing a tone as she could. "He has been doing the *quirunha*. We did it together. And now he is at the mid-day meal."

"But I hear him," Isbel said. "Over and over. I cannot hear anything else, not the music, not your sending. He tells me I have betrayed my House, he calls me names." Her eyes flew open, and she stared at a point past Sira's head. "He says my Gift is ruined."

"His own Gift is not much better. Has he always been so weak?"

Isbel only went on staring at nothing. Sira smoothed the furs over her, tucking them around her bare feet, then slipped out of the bedroom, drawing the door softly closed behind her.

Zakri looked up from finishing the last of the *keftet* Yula had brought for her mistress. He licked his fingers and wiped them on his trousers. *We must get her away from this House.*

There is no place for her to go, Sira answered sadly. *Who will take her in now?* She sat down across from Zakri, easing herself gently into the chair as if her bones hurt.

But she is right, he sent. *Cantor Ovan is still at it.*

How is that possible?

He is better at anger than at quiru.. *The moment the* quirunha *was over it began again.*

Zakri made no apology for eavesdropping, and Sira did not chide him. She rubbed her eyes with her fingers. *We cannot shield her at every moment.*

Zakri thought for a moment, then rose from the table. *I can distract him, at least. I will go to the great room, to have my mid-day meal.* Sira eyed the now-empty tray. Zakri grinned. *I can manage a few more bites. I will draw Ovan's attention to me. We have not spoken at all, and he will be surprised when I send to him. I doubt he is so strong he can attack two of us.*

I will stay with Isbel for a bit, Sira sent. *Then I must speak to the Magister. And we must hold Cantoris hours sometime today.*

As Zakri left the apartment, Kai appeared in the doorway. His expression was grim, and Zakri gave him a sympathetic glance as they passed each other.

"What is happening, Houseman?" Sira asked.

"My family has refused us. They say I've hurt my House, and they'll have nothing to do with me. The Housekeeper won't talk to me. I don't know what we're going to do."

Sira clasped her hands before her and rested her forehead on them. She felt trapped. There was only one place on the entire Continent where she felt sure of her welcome, and that was all but impossible to reach.

If they could only hold on until summer . . . she suddenly longed for Theo as acutely as she had the first day after their separation. If they could manage until summer, she and Zakri and Isbel, and if she could reach Theo from Ogre Pass, someone would come for them. Observatory needed people, needed House members. They would not care that one was a disgraced Cantrix.

Sira raised her head. "I have a thought, Houseman. I will talk to the Magister once again. Go in to Isbel now, and keep her company. I will be back after Cantoris hours, and after I have seen Magister Edrus." She stood and leaned on her hands, looking into Kai's face. "I know a place," she told him, "but it is far away, and we cannot go yet."

"Where is it?"

"Have you heard of Observatory?"

His eyes widened. "Only in fables. They tell us it's just a story."

"So I thought." She straightened. "But it is real enough. The problem is to find it."

Kai stared at her in confusion. She only gave him a tired nod. She would have to explain later. She picked up her *filhata* and tucked it under her arm. Perhaps there would be a way. She could only hope so.

"The *quirunha* this morning was wonderful," Magister Edrus said. He looked as if he had not slept since the revelations of the day before. "I am grateful." He held the door for her and she went into his apartment, bowing briefly as she passed him.

"We must protect your House, of course." She laid her *filhata* on a low table. "I will hold Cantoris hours, too, Magister, but I wanted to talk to you first."

Edrus indicated a chair, but Sira shook her head. She needed to move, to pace as she talked. The idea that had come to her brought a brief surge of energy that thrust away the weariness of the last hours. "You need me here, and I need something as well. There may be a way to get through this without harm to your House, but we will need to work together."

Edrus sank into a chair, his shoulders slumped. "I blame myself for this disaster. I should have foreseen it."

Sira ceased pacing to stare at him. He said, "I know Cantor Ovan was having some sort of trouble. His work was suffering, but I thought . . ." His voice trembled, and he swallowed. "I thought Cantrix Isbel could manage. I see now how unfair that was, too much for one so young and inexperienced."

"You have not held your Magistership for very long, have you?" Sira asked.

"That is no excuse."

"I do not believe you need one."

"You are kind. You know, Cantrix Isbel is—she became, in any case—such a fine healer. I thought she would heal whatever was wrong in my Cantoris."

"She has always had empathy," Sira said. "It makes for strong healing, but it also makes the Singer vulnerable." She resumed pacing, short strides to the window and back again. "Your House members will probably be disappointed in my own healing," she added with a humorless laugh. "But I will do my best."

She came to stand before Edrus once again. "You need me in your Cantoris. Cantor Ovan is barely capable even of assisting in the *quirunha*. What I need is to continue training Singer Zakri, and also to make provision for Isbel and her babe. I propose that your House allow me to do both things in exchange for my service, until the summer comes."

"It's little enough." Edrus spoke slowly, thinking. "You know that Cantor Ovan will say you're simply doing your duty."

"He will not be wrong. But I ask your indulgence just the same."

"You shall have it."

Sira bowed. "I thank you. I think also we must notify Conservatory. I hope that by summer they will be able to send you a Singer, and I can take Isbel away, to a place where she can live and raise her child in peace."

"Where would that be?" Edrus asked. "Her position seems a most untenable one. For myself, I would gladly have her here, but I can't protect her from Cantor Ovan's anger, or from the resentment of other House members."

Sira greed. "It would never be a comfortable situation, though it has been done before. But I hope to take her to the House which is home to me. To Observatory."

Amazement chased all weariness from Edrus's face. "Surely you don't—you can't mean—truly? All my life I've believed such a place to exist only in stories."

Sira turned to look out the window. The snow had stopped, and the sky was a clear, blazing blue. The landmarks around the House were folded away under blankets of white. Ice crystals caught the sun and dazzled her eyes. She yearned to be away from all this, riding off among the pristine hills. She took a resigned breath and turned her back on the beauty beyond the glass. "Observatory is hidden in the mountains southeast of Ogre Pass. It is impossible to find without a guide. They have kept to themselves for a hundred summers, only coming down from their mountain when they are desperate. They need people—House members—more than anything. It could even be that Isbel's Gift will return to her there, if the Spirit wills."

"Let it be so, then," Edrus said. "But I should tell you there is pressure from the Magistral Committee because I allow you to stay here."

"Will they withhold a Singer from you because of me?"

Edrus shurgged. "So they say. But I can hardly let my House freeze because of that. Surely now they will see things differently."

"Conservatory should have dealt with Ovan before this. Magister Mkel was not ignorant of the problems."

"Conservatory has its own difficulties," Edrus observed. They regarded each other for a moment, in perfect accord.

"I am much relieved," Sira said.

"And so am I." The Magister stood and bowed formally to his new Cantrix. It was all the welcoming ceremony there would be. Sira picked up her *filhata* and tucked it under her arm before she bowed in return. She went out of the apartment with a firm step, down the broad stairs to hold her first Cantoris hours at Amric.

Since when does an itinerant presume to send to a full Cantor?

Ovan stared at Zakri over the heads of the House members in the great room. His eyes blazed in his dark face.

Zakri gave him a wicked grin. *Since yesterday. Since Cantrix Isbel needed my help.*

She is no concern of yours! Ovan turned his face away, as if to speak to someone.

Zakri sent very strongly, *All the Gifted concern me, Cantor Ovan. Even you. Actually, now that I think of it, especially you!*

Ovan froze, his mouth open, his chest heaving as if he gasped for breath. He turned a suspicious gaze back to Zakri.

I know what troubles you,, Zakri sent, very clearly.

Ovan stood, scraping his chair noisily on the floor. *Nothing troubles me except upstart itinerants with no respect for their betters!* He tried to shield his mind, but it was a weak and unstable barrier that bothered Zakri not at all. *Leave me alone!* Ovan sent, stumbling out of the great room.

Zakri sat where he was, but he did not release the contact. He stayed with Ovan as the older man hurried to his apartment. Only when Ovan was inside his rooms, the door shut tight behind him, did Zakri get to his feet. Concentrating, following Ovan with his mind, he hardly knew where his body was. He stubbed his toe on a table leg and jostled a Housewoman as he made his way out of the great room into the corridor.

Ovan's need was so overwhelming that he was hardly shielded at all, and he no longer recognized Zakri's presence in his mind. Through Ovan's eyes, Zakri watched the Cantor's shaking hands reach to open a cupboard, to take out an ironwood jar with a carved stopper.

With sharp strength, Zakri sent, *Even now, Cantor Ovan? Before Cantoris hours?*

Ovan started violently, and Zakri seized his chance. He made a supreme effort, lashing out with his psi, using Ovan's own psi as a weapon—a whip, or a club. Before Ovan threw up his shields in desperation, Zakri saw the jar of wine fly up to shatter against the cupboard door, splattering the wall and the floor with red. Ovan succeeded in breaking the contact then, pulling free with a tremendous effort.

Zakri, suddenly weak, leaned against the wall outside the great room. He laughed silently as he waited for his strength to return. The very side of his Gift that had caused him so much trouble had been a useful tool just now. Exhaustion was a small price to pay. He had in his hands just the weapon he needed, the information that could protect Isbel and assist Sira. He gave no thought to the unethical way he had acquired it. The stakes in this game were too high for such distinctions.

Feeling much better, he straightened, and hummed a cheerful tune as he watched people file out of the great room, until Sira came along.

Come and observe, she sent. *I would like you to try to follow during the healing.*

Zakri hid his grin with a bow. *Yes, Cantrix. I will try my best.*

Chapter Thirty

Isbel huddled beneath her bedfurs, alone in her room. Ovan no longer tormented her, but still she heard his accusing voice sounding in her head. The names he had called her were both vicious and accurate. They whirled unendingly in her mind. Slut. Harlot. Whore. And the worst, the one that was most true and most shameful. She was a traitor, a traitor to her House and a traitor to her calling. The pain that now racked her seemed a fitting punishment. She welcomed it, gave herself up to it without protest.

She bore the torment dumbly, until the claws of pain tore so deeply into her belly that consciousness receded. When she cried out, it was a gasping scream that brought Kai and Yula hurrying to her bedside. She opened her eyes, when the pain subsided a bit, to see their frantic faces above her.

"Quick, Yula," Kai cried. "Find Cantrix Sira!"

Isbel tried to push a refusal past her lips, but the claws rent her once again. Her awareness turned inward, and the world faded away from her. Pain was her universe, and she needed all her energy merely to comprehend it. She had earned it, she deserved it. Whore. Traitor. She could do nothing now but accede to the agony, welcome it. It was her redemption.

When Kai tried to take her hands, she thrust him away, and returned to her fate, her punishment, her sentence of pain.

Zakri watched, biting his lip, as Sira ran her hands over Isbel's tortured body. The *filla* lay on the bed between them. Kai and Yula waited in the outer room, but Zakri knew they suffered with Isbel. Sira knelt, her eyes closed and brows drawn hard together, her hands moving. Zakri held back, afraid and repelled. A musky odor filled his nostrils.

Sira's eyes opened suddenly. *Follow me*, she commanded. *This is bad. I will need you.*

She reached for the *filla*, and closed her eyes once more. Obediently, Zakri knelt beside her, putting aside his reluctance. He shut his own eyes and let his psi spin out to join Sira's.

Before she began, she sent, *I am sorry you have no experience, but there is no help for it. It shocks you, but you must try to ignore that.*

He sensed her own unease, and he resolved to be unaffected by anything he might find. *I am with you.* He followed as she began her *Aiodu* melody.

Aiodu was for examinations. That much he had already learned. Its clarity, the simplicity of its progressions, was to help the Singer to see, to understand what was happening behind the barrier of the flesh. With Sira leading, their joined psi found the curled form of the infant in Isbel's womb, and felt the strain as the womb contracted around it.

Isbel's pain was beyond anything Zakdi had known before, and he gasped before he could catch himself. He realized at the same moment that the *filla* had ceased playing, and the contact was broken.

He opened his eyes. Sira was still on her knees, her hands covering her face. The *filla* lay at her elbow.

What is the matter? he asked.

She raised her head. *I am not the healer I should be. When I feel Isbel's pain, it is like a door slammed in my face.*

Zakri stared at her. *But she needs us!*

Isbel groaned between compressed lips. Sweat matted her hair and wet her tunic. Sira nodded, looking at her. *I will try again.*

Zakri saw that her fingers trembled as she lifted the *filla*.

Cantrix Sira, he sent. She stopped, looking at him. Amazed by his own daring, he held out his hand. *I will do it,* he sent. *I can do it, if you show me.*

Slowly, Sira lowered the *filla*. She hesitated a moment, then handed it to Zakri. When he put it to his lips, it was still warm where her own had touched it.

He began with *Aiodu,* but then, moved by some instinct, he modulated to *Lidya.* With Sira's psi guiding his, he carried them both back into Isbel's body.

The babe was buffeted and squeezed by the contractions. Pain was the background, the field upon which all events were taking place. It came in waves of red darkness that rocked them both as they broke over Isbel. Zakri felt Sira falter, but she held on, supporting him, guiding him.

He had no way to interpret what he found. He knew the infant was there, felt its tiny heartbeat speed frantically under the force of each contraction. He knew the wetness, and the dark, and many details that meant nothing to him. Pulling Sira with him, he withdrew, ending the music and opening his eyes.

Isbel rested for a moment, her knees drawn up to her swollen belly. Without thinking what he did, Zakri stroked one of her bare feet, rubbing it lightly from ankle to toe. It was cold as ice under his hand.

Sira sent, *We must turn the babe.*

Zakri froze with Isbel's foot under his palm. *Why?*

It cannot come out in that position. She showed him with her hands. *We must turn it, so. But very carefully, or we hurt the mother.*

I do not see how she could take further pain.

Sira shuddered. *I am sorry,* she sent, shaking her head. *This is my weakness.*

Zakri took Isbel's other foot in his hand, gently rubbing it. She moaned as another contraction began, and he released the foot. *Ease her pain first,* he sent to Sira. *Then I will do it.* He pushed aside his own fear, and his revulsion. He told himself he could feel things later, think about them later. Now was a time to act.

O Spirit, he prayed. Do not let me make one of my mistakes. Not here. Not today.

Sira was awed by Zakri's dexterity and power as he moved the babe, ever so smoothly. He coaxed its little head down, and its tiny legs curled upward. Isbel's torment went on unabated. She had retreated, withdrawn into her suffering as if she had chosen it for herself.

Sira had assisted several women to give birth at Observatory, but never had she seen a reaction like Isbel's. The laboring women had embraced her help, were relieved by it, eager to ease their pain. It must be my own weakness, she thought, my ineffectiveness. She wished she could take Isbel's pain into her own body.

The babe was in position now. The labor went on. Kai paced the outer room, and Yula came in and out, her fear of the Gifted forgotten as she pressed cool cloths to her mistress's forehad and combed her wet hair back with her fingers. Sira and Zakri waited, watching.

There is something amiss still, Sira sent. *There should be a flood of waters before the birth. They seem often to ease the passage.*

Zakri nodded. *This I have seen with* hruss. He picked up the *filla* and played a straightforward tune in *Aidou*. He extended a small, sharp blade of power, almost as simply as putting out a finger, and the membrane that held the waters broke open. Sira marveled at the sheer kinetic strength of his psi.

Yula had been waiting for this moment. She leapt forward, crowing with satisfaction as she padded Isbel with towels. "There we are, there we are," she cried. "We're almost done now." She nodded to the two Singers as she mopped Isbel's wet face. "Soon now, the babe will be here soon."

But still the birth did not come. For what seemed an age, the pains went on. Sira had to leave for a time, to go to the Cantoris and perform the *quirunha* once again. When she returned, Zakri was playing a fragment of *Iridu* over and over. He looked as pale as Isbel, his fine hair hanging in wet tendrils around his face. Sira knelt beside him, closed her eyes, and followed.

She trembled at what she found, and wondered that Zakri had the strength to stay where he was. The contractions were powerful now, and Isbel should have been past pain, consumed with the effort of thrusting her child into the world.

But Isbel seemed locked in her misery, mated to it. Her heart beat weakly, and with a frightening unevenness. She lay passive, not so much a part of the birthing as a victim of it. The baby's swift heartbeat came more faintly now. Yula crouched beside Isbel's head, crooning and pleading with her mistress.

As Sira watched, Zakri exerted a gentle force, and the infant began to move. Sira only supported him. She knew he was working by instinct, neither of them knowing what else to do. It was terrifyingly clear that if they did nothing, both Isbel and the child would be lost.

Zakri pushed and pulled by turns. It seemed most effective when he waited for a contraction. He took deep, noisy breaths, and endlessly repeated the little *Iridu* phrase, over and over and over until it seemed to have gone on forever. When at last the babe emerged to Yula's waiting hands and tearful cries, Zakri collapsed to the stone floor, and Sira had to lift him up in her arms as Yula lifted up the newborn infant.

I am all right, Zakri sent. *See to Isbel!*

Sira picked up the dropped *filla* and turned back to the bed with a dragging fear.

Yula was holding the babe, now wrapped and clean, to its mother, but Isbel was too weak to take it. Her eyelids fluttered and her face was pale and gleaming, ice on a stone. "Poor little thing," she whispered, so faintly Sira barely heard her. "She does not cry."

"It is all right," Sira said. "The child is fine. You must rest now, gather your strength."

Yula held the babe close to her own breast and turned to leave.

"Wait," Isbel murmured, her voice a little louder now. Yula came back, and put the infant down, close to its mother's face. Isbel pressed her trembling white lips to its forehead, then fell back on her pillow.

"Take the child to its father," Sira said to Yula. Zakri, who had been busy with the afterbirth, pulled himself to his feet and followed the Housewoman out. He closed the door softly behind them.

"Now rest, my friend," Sira said quietly. Fear choked her, and she swallowed hard.

Isbel shook her head, almost imperceptibly. "I have only a moment," she whispered.

"No, dear heart." Sira's throat tightened.

Isbel's eyelids lifted, fluttering. "Yes." Her voice was as light as a breeze through softwood leaves, a ghost of a voice. She moved her fingers, and Sira took them in hers and pressed them to her own cheek. She was startled to find her face wet with tears.

"Tell Kai," Isbel breathed, "to care for her. To love her."

Sira could no longer speak. She sent instead, *Isbel, do not leave us!*

I cannot help it. Isbel's sending was suddenly clear and lucid, as if it were coming from a bright and open place. There was still pain in her body, Sira realized, but it was only an echo, a memory. *The poor babe,* Isbel sent. *Tell Kai her name is Mreen. Poor motherless Mreen . . .*

Sira bent to kiss Isbel's cold cheek. *No, Isbel, no! How can we bear this? Try, please!*

But it was too late.

Sira feared Kai's reaction, but she saw when she came out to him that he already knew Isbel was gone. He stood by the window, looking out over the frozen landscape as if he were watching her leave. The babe he cradled tenderly against his chest, a morsel of Isbel left behind for him. He pressed his cheek to the little head. His jaw was tight, and there were no tears.

"Isbel says—said—the child's name is Mreen," Sira murmured, with infinite sadness.

Kai nodded, his gaze not leaving the window. "Mreen she shall be." He rocked his daughter in his arms. "It was her grandmother's name."

Yula, sobbing aloud, went back into the bedroom to do the things that must be done. Sira fell into a chair near Zakri and put out her hand to him. *You saved the little one.*

Zakri's eyes were red. *I wish . . .Isbel . . .*

You cannot heal someone against her will.

They sat in silence for several minutes before Sira sighed and rose. *I must tell Magister Edrus. And I must hold Cantoris hours.*

I will help you, Cantrix. Zakri gave her a bleak look. *I doubt Ovan will be much use. But I will sit in the Cantoris and support you, and no one need know.*

Gratefully, Sira clasped his arm. They took a last look at Kai, and the infant Mreen, before they went out, side by side, to carry on with the work of the House.

Chapter Thirty-one

Magister Edrus asked Zakri to escort his courier to Conservatory. "There are no other itinerants here," he said, with an air of apology. "Cantrix Sira feels, and I agree, that Conservatory should be informed of what has happened as soon as possible."

Zakri bowed. "I'm happy to help, Magister."

Delighted would have been a better word, though Zakri felt some compunction about that. He missed Isbel, and he often thought of her when he stepped into the Cantoris, or into the apartment which had been hers, and where Sira now resided. But Sira was inconsolable. Outside, the sun shone relentlessly on the snowy hills, but Sira did not see it. For weeks, her world had been shadowed by grief. She never spoke of Isbel, but her sorrow spilled into Zakri's mind as they worked together. Zakri was relieved at the chance to be away, to be outside again, to breathe cold fresh air and the scent of *hruss* and tack. He would miss almost two weeks of *filhata* practice, but perhaps he could bring back some good news to ease Sira's mind.

The courier, Berk, was a huge man who frequently said his hair had gone gray in the service of his House. He rode the largest *hruss* in Amric's stables, and still his legs hung far down on either side of the beast's broad body. Tucked inside his tunic was a leather-wrapped roll of thick paper, inscribed by Magister Edrus himself. Together Berk and Zakri rode away from Amric into a brilliant blue and white land, the sun shining unobstructed from a clear sky. By nightfall, at their first campsite, the sunlight glancing off the snowpack had made their faces tender and red, and they were glad of the tiny ironwood jar of salve that Housekeeper Cael had sent with them.

Berk knew countless stories to enliven their evening campfires. In his youth he had been a rider for Amric, often traveling with Magister Edrus's father. Although a son of the working classes, his reliability and discretion had brought him to his Magister's attention, and more important duties had come his way. Now he wore the dark tunic of the upper levels.

"My mate thinks the whole family should move up the stairs," he chuckled one night. "Especially all of her grandchildren! But my daughters and their mates are content where they are. And we see the children often enough, if you ask me! They make such a noise, a man can't think a thought."

Zakri was fascinated. His own family life had ended so early he hardly remembered it. Though Berk's words sounded like complaints, Zakri felt clearly the affection that underlay them, especially when the big man was talking about his grandchildren.

"Six!" he boomed. "Six of the little rascals, and never a clean nose among them! My mate spends all her time running down the stairs to look after them. Morning, noon, and night she's somewhere else. A man might as well live alone." He laughed as he said it.

Zakri smiled. "So you're happy to get away from time to time," he said slyly.

Berk winked at him. "And happy to get home again."

The courier talked for hours on their journey. By the time they arrived at Perl, Zakri's head was full of House politics and Continent history. When he asked Berk about Observatory, the older man looked grave. "Most don't know it's really there. The Magistral Committee likes it that way. But every once in a while Observatory riders swoop down from their mountain to kidnap someone or steal *hruss*. Although now I think of it, I haven't heard any stories since last summer, or maybe the last two summers. It could be the Committee is hushing up the rumors."

"But why should it be a secret?"

Berk shrugged. "None of us has any idea. They say it's because Observatory upsets the balance, breaks the rules, but I don't know. They have some strange beliefs. Or maybe it's just the way people are, like a *caeru* litter that pushes the runt out in the snow. Every group likes someone to look down on."

At Perl, Zakri was gratified to be addressed as Singer, and treated as someone of importance. The stableman was surprised by his insistence on caring for their *hruss* himself, but when he saw Zakri knew his work, he gave him a free hand. They stayed for only a night before riding off toward Conservatory.

"That Cantor Arn is a one," Berk said, their first night out from Perl.

"Why do you say that?" Zakri asked.

"He said to his Magister, in my presence, that Cantrix Sira got what she deserved. He said she always thought she was better than the rest of them." He looked up at Zakri. "Sorry. Maybe I shouldn't have told you."

But Zakri was laughing. "You can be sure she was the best of her class, and that she knew it. She is the greatest Singer on the Continent, and no mistake about it."

Berk finished the last of the *keftet* Zakri had prepared, smacking his lips with pleasure. "You're a fine cook, Singer." Then, after a pause, "Do you think Cantrix Sira will stay at Amric, then, in our Cantoris?"

"No." Zakri hesitated before going on, wondering what he could say. He did not like to dissemble with a man like Berk. "I cannot speak for Cantrix Sira, but I can tell you there is even more important work to be done on the Continent than singing in a Cantoris. And she is the only one to do it."

Berk surprised him by saying, "It's been a long time since anything on the Continent has changed. Change is necessary sometimes." He scrubbed out his ironwood bowl with a handful of snow, and laughed aloud. "It hurts, though, and the old ones don't like it!"

Zakri mulled that over for a long time before he fell asleep that night, while his strong, steady *quiru* glowed above him in the half-darkness of the snowy mountains. Change is necessary, but it hurts. It had hurt him, yet look what he had gained. He had his calling, his friends, his teacher. He thought of Isbel, and all she had lost, and he prayed to the Spirit that her passage beyond the stars had been a swift one.

*

Berk kept Zakri with him when he met with Magister Mkel at Conservatory. Mkel's mate served them tea and dried fruit before Mkel opened the leather wrapping and took out the roll of paper. There was a long silence as he read the message, then read it a second time. His face was aged and sorrowful, and Cathrin stood protectively behind him.

"This is terrible news," he said heavily.

Berk inclined his head in acknowledgment. Zakri sat still, listening to the flood of thoughts pouring from Mkel. Mkel obviously did not know he could hear him, and Zakri felt it best to keep that secret for the time being. There might be something here that would aid Sira.

"Cantrix Sira is working with Cantor Ovan," Mkel said, shaking his head over the idea. Cathrin put her hand on his shoulder. Zakri heard the Magister thinking that Sira was back where she belonged at last, and if there was anything good about this tragedy, it was that she would be forced to serve as she had been trained to do.

"Well, Magister," Berk said. "Cantrix Sira is working in the Cantoris, yes. As to Cantor Ovan . . . ahem . . . he hasn't been well."

Mkel looked up in question. "Magister Edrus says nothing about that." Zakri heard Mkel's thought: It was true about Ovan, then.

Berk leaned a little forward, in a confidential manner. "Actually, Magister Mkel," the courier began. His delicacy made Zakri hide a smile. Berk was such a big man that his nicety of manner became even more pronounced. "As it happens, Singer Zakri here has been of some help to Cantrix Sira."

Mkel flushed a sudden dark red, and looked at Zakri. *I had no idea, Singer.*

Zakri bowed where he sat. *I understand, Magister. We have not met, you and I. I am Cantrix Sira's student.*

Mkel frowned, but his thoughts were shielded now, and Zakri could hear only his spoken words. "And so Cantrix Sira continues to challenge Conservatory's authority."

Berk said quietly, firmly, "To us at Amric, she is a gift straight from the Spirit."

"The Committee will be furious," Mkel said. "They have enough problems without the Gifted taking matters into their own hands."

"Magister Mkel," Berk said solemnly, "imagine what might have happened had she not."

"But where will be be if others behave in like fashion? We're having enough trouble with the itinerants at Soren!"

"What trouble?" Zakri asked.

"It's not all the itinerants," Mkel said, without explanation. "But enough to worry us. I imagine the Committee will soon make a ruling that will force all parents of Gifted children to be sent here for training. I don't know what else we can do."

He heaved a sigh, and stood. "Your Magister has requested a Singer for his Cantoris. I will write to him, and you will carry the letter, if you please. In perhaps a year and a half, by next summer surely, one or two of our third-level students should be ready for assignment. There is no one now to spare. We have already sent two Singers who were teaching here to help at Bariken and at Manrus. Our first-level class is seriously short-handed because of it."

Zakri and Berk had both risen when the Magister did. "I don't blame your Magister for allowing Sira to work in his Cantoris," Mkel added. "I can see he had no choice."

Zakri felt a sudden flare of anger. *Perhaps you should blame yourself! If you knew Cantor Ovan was incompetent—*

Mkel stared at him. *You know nothing about these things.*

The air around Zakri had begun to glimmer. He shielded himself quickly, and concentrated on regaining control.

Berk was bowing his farewell. Mkel sent to Zakri, *Do not think we will let Sira dictate to us how we use our resources. I cannot stop her from teaching you. But Conservatory recognizes only Cantors trained here, trained properly. Remember that.*

I will remember, Magister. Zakri cast his eyes modestly down to his boots. *No one understands better than I what a poor substitute I am for a full Cantor. I only help because I am needed, and I use my Gift— my small Gift—as I can.*

Mkel's mouth tightened, and he did not answer. Zakri struggled with renewed fury. He did not want to embarrass Sira by losing control in front of the Magister of Conservatory. But would Mkel rather Sira had to work alone?

He took a steadying breath. He must trust that the Spirit had its own plans for them. They would follow the path it laid out. He avoided Mkel's eyes as they left the apartment. No wonder Sira did not want Conservatory running her life! These people were like *carwal* cast up on the beach at Tarus–hidebound, dry and inflexible. Sira would show them all.

Come to think of it, so would he.

Thus their mission was quickly accomplished at Conservatory. After only one night's rest they were ready to return to Amric. Zakri felt some urgency, knowing Sira was working all but alone in the Cantoris, though Ovan continued to appear on the dais. It would take some time, Sira said, for the Cantor to repair the damage to his Gift. She had spared no pressure on Ovan, and he had sworn, if they told no one of his lapse, that he would discipline himself.

Before the dawn had fully broken behind the mountains to the east, Zakri had the *hruss* saddled and ready. He met Berk in the kitchens, where they begged a bowl of *keftet* from one of the Housewomen. They ate standing up, and drank two cups of tea each. The Housewoman had heard their news. Indeed, judging from the talk in the *ubanyor* the night before, it seemed all the House members had. She gave them a fat packet of nutbread and fruit for their saddlepacks.

"We're just heartbroken for the young Cantrix," she said. "We hate to lose one of ours."

Zakri was touched by the familial way in which she spoke of the Singers. Singers here were cherished, nurtured until the time of their leaving. The separation had to be a great shock.

When the travelers could see through the House *quiru* that light streaked the sky with violet and pink, they went to the stables. There was no one to see them off. As Berk led his mount through the outer door, Zakri took the reins of his own beast and turned to follow.

"Please, Singer Zakri." A small voice spoke behind him, musical and very young. "Please take me with you."

Zakri whirled to see a tiny figure, swathed in furs, standing inside the stall. She put back her hood to show her curly hair. "Trisa!" Zakri breathed.

"Yes. I want to go home. I want to go with you."

"O Spirit," Zakri groaned.

Berk's gray head appeared around the stable door. "Problem, Singer? I thought you were right behind—" He stared at the little girl. "Who's this, then?"

She had to tip her head far back to see Berk's face. "I am Trisa. I want to go home, with you. Home to my mother."

Zakri dropped his *hruss*'s reins and went to kneel beside the child. She had grown since he had last seen her, but her face was still round, her eyes stretched wide as she looked at him. *Please, Singer Zakri. It is terrible here.*

Zakri cast Berk a despairing look, then said, "Trisa, we cannot take you away. This is where you belong."

"But we are all very sad," she replied. Her eyes swam with tears. "We have only one teacher for our whole class. We are not learning as fast as we should—everyone is saying so—and I am so lonely. Please, Singer. Please, Houseman."

Berk looked down at her with great sympathy. "I'm sorry, little one," he said quietly. "Singer Zakri is quite right. You belong here."

Trisa began to cry, making Zakri's heart ache. Her unhappiness was almost as uncontrolled as his own emotions had been a scant three years before. He remembered the motherless babe at Amric, and felt as if his heart would break in two. It took all his strength to turn away from Trisa. *I am so very sorry,* he sent, trying to penetrate her misery. *There is nothing I can do.* He pushed down the thought that maybe Sira could help this child, could undertake the training of her Gift as she had his. It was not a decision for him to make.

He felt the girl's tearful gaze on his back as he led his *hruss* out of the stable. It seemed unbearably cruel to ride away and leave her crying, all alone. He wept tears of his own as he mounted, and he saw that Berk was affected, too.

I will not stay! she sent after him. *I mean it, Singer Zakri! They cannot make me!*

"This is a one, Berk," Zakri said. "She is still after me. I wish we could take her home."

"It's a terrible shame."

They were a dismal pair as they rode away. Zakri was grateful Trisa did not send more pleas after him. He did not think he could have borne it. As it was, he lagged behind Berk, as if to leave Trisa more slowly was kinder than to rush away.

They did not make good time that morning. It seemed to Zakri that Trisa held him back, as if her little hand were pulling at his furs. His *hruss* dragged its feet in response to his mood. Berk said nothing, but he had to stop his own *hruss* several times to wait for Zakri. At mid-day they stopped briefly to have a cold meal, unwrapping the Housewoman's packet of bread and fruit, supplementing that with strips of dried *caeru* meat from their saddlepacks. They were just mounting *hruss* again when Zakri heard it.

Singer Zakri!

He threw up his head. There was no one near, of course, and he had heard no other *hruss*. "Just a minute, Berk. She is still sending to me, and I do not know how that can be."

Berk grunted with surprise. He settled his bulk into his saddle and held his reins, watching Zakri.

Singer Zakri, can you hear me?

I can. But where are you?

The answer came faintly, but clearly. *I am following you, but I cannot keep up as I have no* hruss.

"By the Six Stars!" Zakri swore. "Berk, she has done it now."

"What? Where is she?" Berk asked in alarm.

Zakri looked back the way they had come. "She is somewhere back there, on foot. We have to go back for her, or she will die of the cold." He saw no choice. He could hardly leave the girl behind in the mountains. He gave Berk a helpless glance.

The gray-haired courier clucked his exasperation. "We'll have a time explaining this one. She's got a mind of her own, doesn't she? I have a granddaughter just like that!"

"What do you think I should do?"

Berk shrugged his shoulders, a massive gesture under his furs. "What can you do, Singer? Take her home to her mother! Truth to tell, Amric's got so much trouble already we'll hardly notice another scandal."

"But Conservatory will be furious!"

"They've had their chance with this one," Berk said stoutly. "She's been there two years, and she's miserable. Let her go home."

Together, they turned their *hruss*. *Trisa, we are coming. Stay where you are.*

Thank you, Singer Zakri.

Zkari and Berk made much better time on the return trip. Some three hours later they came upon Trisa sitting on an ironwood sucker, waiting. The sun had already started its descent into the west, and she was shivering badly inside her thick furs. Zakri reached his hand down and pulled her up behind him, and the docile *hruss* turned about to walk over the same road for the third time that day.

Thank you, Singer Zakri, Trisa sent, as casually as if he had done her a simple favor.

You are fortunate I could hear you. You could have frozen to death. Do you realize that?

Yes, Singer Zakri, she answered demurely. He felt her happy wriggle behind him as she settled onto the saddle skirts.

I do not know what is going to happen to you.

I do not care. If you take me back to Conservatory I will run away again.

Zakri shook his head, worried, but Trisa put her arms around him and snuggled into his warmth. As they rode, he was startled to find the image of his mother floating up from the past, an image he had thought long gone. He sighed again. It could be a cruel world for children.

He patted Trisa's gloved hands where they were locked around him, and he felt her cheek press against his back. Sira would certainly have something to say about this. And he was not looking forward to hearing it. Not one little bit.

Chapter Thirty-two

Zakri and Berk skirted the courtyard of Amric and rode around to the stables. Trisa sat small and silent behind Zakri on his *hruss*. Berk had said that under the circumstances, the less attention they drew to themselves, the better it would be.

She had been smiling and happy all through the trip. At Perl, Zakri located an itinerant bound for Conservatory, and Berk sent a carefully worded message, wrapped in *caeru* leather, informing Magister Mkel that Trisa was in their care. She had left a note behind on her cot in the dormitory, but Berk thought that would hardly be adequate. "Your teacher will think you've frozen to death by now," he told her.

Tris had looked up at him with the stubborn light in her eyes Zakri had come to recognize. "They will not care," she said.

Berk shook his grizzled head. "You're quite wrong. They will make themselves ill with worry." But she was unrepentant.

Trisa looked young to Zakri for her nine years. Her hands were as smooth and plump as a baby's, with short stubby fingers, and her eyes were round and clear. When she spoke aloud, she still lisped, though her sending was clear and precise. When he asked her to play the *filla* for him, she declined.

I am no good at it, she sent. *My teacher made me practice and practice, but I was no better.* She added, with faint resignation, *Maybe I am not meant to be a Singer.*

She was fascinated by Zakri's playing, though, and listened raptly as he raised their *quiru* each night. *Do you play the* filhata *too?* she asked him.

So I do. But not very well yet. Cantrix Sira is teaching me.

She nodded, her curls bouncing against her furs. *I think if she will teach me the* filla, *maybe I can learn it. I have trouble with* Doryu, *and with* Lidya, *the fingerings.* She held up her short-fingered hands and looked at them as if they had a life of their own. *My class was ten students, and only one teacher. She did not like me. I felt all her feelings, when she was angry and when she was afraid. It bothered her.*

How were your classmates?

Trisa shrugged. *We were not a good class, that is what they told us. It was hard there, and lonely. You would not like it, Singer Zakri.*

Zakri smiled at her. *We will never know about that.*

Now they were home, and Trisa had grown quiet and solemn, no doubt thinking of the scenes she would face. Berk went directly to Magister Edrus with the letter from Conservatory, and Zakri led Trisa up the back stairs to Sira's apartment. Sira had heard them as they aproached the House,and she was standing in her open doorway, waiting. She glared down at Trisa, and then at Zakri, her mouth set in a hard line. *What have you done?*

Excuse me, Cantrix Sira, Trisa sent before Zakri could respond. *It was not Singer Zakri's fault. It was mine.* She bowed very low, a sadly adult gesture from one so small. *I am sorry to cause trouble, but I will not go back. No one can make me, not even*—she looked up daringly—*not even you.*

Sira lifted her eyebrow, but she stepped back, and they passed into the apartment. Trisa stood in the center of the room, and she and Sira stared at each other for a long moment. Zakri hung back, wishing he had stayed in the stables with the *hruss* until this confrontation was over. He shielded his mind for once. This was a conversation he had no wish to hear.

It was enough to watch their faces. Trisa's lower lip pushed out in a little pink semicircle, and ragged sparks rose around her head. Sira's features were drawn, but her control, as always, was absolute. At the end, she nodded once, sharply, to Trisa, then turned her back to them both, walking slowly to the window. She leaned on the casement, and gazed out in silence on the white mountains.

Trisa asked aloud, "Can I see my mother now?"

The inevitable protest erupted a few days later in the form of a loud and angry courier from Conservatory. Magister Edrus sat in his apartment, wearily surveying the group assembled around his table.

Sira and Zakri sat together, with Berk standing behind them. Brnwen sat nearby, trembling, and Trisa leaned against her, one arm circling her mother's neck. Cantor Ovan glowered from one end of the table. At the other end Conservatory's messenger, a man named Vlad, twitched and shifted in his chair. Singer Iban had brought Vlad to Amric. Iban lounged just inside the door, still in his traveling clothes.

Vlad was shouting. "This is outrageous! There has never been such an offense! The child comes back now, with me, and there will be no more argument!"

Magister Edrus tried to speak, but Vlad ignored him. Ovan's harsh voice joined his. "The scandal! Amric will never recover from it!" and, "Lamdon will never allow this!"

Trisa and Brnwen were both pale, but Trisa shook her head. "No," she repeated, her voice small in the tumult. "I will only run away again. No."

Edrus held up his hand, but Vlad and Ovan persisted until Sira's ears rang from the din. "You will not—we will see to it you do not! You are going back where you belong! Amric will be punished severely if—" Edrus dropped his hand, despairing of stemming the tirade.

Sira, at the end of her endurance, used her deep voice like a knife to cut through the noise. "Enough!"

Ovan's mouth snapped shut when she turned her eyes on him. Vlad was silenced by sheer surprise. Sira leaned forward, her forearms on the table, and looked at each of them, one by one. "This is very difficult for Magister Edrus. All these events have been beyond his control. Trisa has made a decision, and it should be evident to everyone that she cannot be forced to rescind it." Vlad opend his mouth to speak, but Sira held up a commanding finger. "There is nothing you can do, Vlad, and you must tell Magister Mkel this."

"You have no right—" sputtered the courier.

Sira inclined her head to him. "That may be true. I am no longer sure how right is conferred. But I have talked with Trisa, and I can tell you beyond any doubt that her education is not proceeding well. Possibly it is not proceeding at all. I will try to teach her myself, as that is what she wants. I will keep Conservatory informed, if you wish, about her progress."

Vlad's face was ugly with frustration and anger. "The Magistral Committee—" he began.

Sira lost her temper. She slapped the table in front of her with the flat of her hand. Vlad and Ovan both jumped, and Brnwen gave a nervous squeak.

"The Committee has even less control of the Gift than Conservatory does!" Sira snapped. "Can you not see that Nevya is in serious trouble? You—that is, we, all of us—cannot go on abusing the Gift and expect it to survive! Here is this child who has spent two years at Conservatory in utter misery, and what do we have to show for that? Nothing! She hardly knows more than she did when she left. Something must change, and now, or we perish!"

Trisa's color returned with a flood of pink to her cheeks. Brnwen still looked white and shaken. Iban's eyebrows danced, and Zakri sat with his hand over his mouth, his eyes bright above his fingers. Ovan and Vlad scowled at each other, Vlad obviously expecting assistance from Amric's senior Cantor, and Ovan afraid to offer it. Thank the Spirit for giving her the weapon to hold over him!

Sira folded her arms, gripping her elbows with her hands, amazed at the depth of her own anger. The air around her was brilliant with it, but she made no attempt to quell the effect. Let them see her strength, her power. Let them fear her!

The silence stretched on, charged with tension like the uneasy quiet that follows a storm. Edrus let it last some moments before he spoke. "Although I would never have foreseen my House in this position," he began, choosing his words with care, "it appears we must allow these drifts to carry us where they may. Nothing in my experience has prepared me to make these decisions, but then, perhaps nothing could." He nodded toward Sira. "I intend to encourage Cantrix Sira in her work here, as she sees fit to pursue it. I will so inform Magister Mkel."

"This is open rebellion," Vlad opined. "Amric is no better than Soren, with its itinerants! The Committee will see you punished. You need Cantors, do you not? And when you ask, you will be refused!"

Sira gave a bitter laugh. Zakri grinned, and Iban watched them both with twinkling eyes. Vlad's face reddened.

"It is most interesting to me to hear you speak of rebellion," Sira said. "I have never ceased working, all my life, to nurture the Gift and guard the well-being of my people." She sat back in her chair, her anger fading into fatigue. "I have been shot with an arrow and kept prisoner for years at Observatory. I trained a full Cantor there, and I helped keep Amric warm when there was no one else to do it. For all these services, Conservatory calls me traitor."

She pushed away from the table and stood. "So be it," she declared. Her voice sounded flat in her ears. "If Conservatory cannot see what must be done, you may all give thanks to the Spirit that someone does."

She strode from the apartment. Vlad's voice rose again as she shut the door, and she heard Edrus try to answer, but she no longer cared. She would waste no more of her energy on their wrangling. There was real work to do.

Chapter Thirty-three

The five years of winter on the Continent dragged slowly to their end. Little by little, the air felt warmer to travelers riding through the mountains and the Southern Timberlands. Those in the Houses paused often by the limeglass windows to look out at the sky, searching for signs of the Visitor. The snows that fell were soft, big flakes collecting in loose drifts that formed and re-formed outside Amric's walls, making graceful shapes like waves of the Frozen Sea caught at their peak. Children began to ask when they would have another summer to boast of, and their parents smiled and promised soon, soon.

When the reticent Visitor showed its face at last, a pale small disc rolling along the eastern horizon, its mild warmth joined with the sun to bring on the thaw and the budding of softwood shoots. Sira's heart began to warm too, beginning to heal. She had labored long and hard at Amric, but Conservatory was sending a Singer at last.

Her students, Zakri and Trisa, flanked her as she stood with Magister Edrus and his mate, the Housekeeper Cael, Cantor Ovan, and a number of House members on the steps of Amric to receive their new Cantor. Just so had Sira begun at Bariken, and Isbel at Amric. This Singer's name was Gavn, and he looked hardly older than Trisa when he put back his hood and bowed to them all.

Could I ever have been that young? Sira wondered.

O Spirit, was Zakri's reaction to the sight of him.

Magister Edrus welcomed Cantor Gavn aloud, and Cantor Ovan sent a few words. Sira also sent her greetings.

Are you . . . are you the Cantrix Sira? he asked. When she nodded, he bowed again to her, very low, making Ovan mutter to himself. Zakri put his head to one side and pursed his lips, and Sira was afraid he would laugh aloud.

When the ceremonies were completed, and they all trooped indoors, Sira sent to Zakri, *Stay with him, and watch.* Zakri would understand that she meant for him to watch Ovan's behavior. They had worrried about it, and Cantor Gavn's appearance was not reassuring. His face was soft and smooth, unformed by experience, vulnerable as a child's. He had to have at least four summers, but he looked as if he had less than three.

Sira's own six summers felt like ten. She could hardly wait to be away, to put her grief and her loneliness behind her. She drew out Theo's bit of metal from her tunic, and held it up in the *quiru* light to study its strange markings. They were so like those on Observatory's large piece of metal, meaningless to her, to all of them, but still compelling. Now they seemed to call to her, to pull her back to Observatory.

Trisa interrupted her thoughts, bowing politely. Conservatory manners had made their imprint on her, and Sira was glad. Trisa was now nine years old, and she behaved very much like all the Conservatory-trained, with formal courtesy and mature bearing. Sira wished she knew some way to inspire similar manners in Zakri.

"Cantrix Sira, will we have lessons today?" Trisa spoke aloud, as was proper until Sira opened her mind. Zakri observed no such niceties.

Sira dropped her necklace back inside her tunic. *Yes. At least for a time. Then we need to talk, you and I, and I need to speak to your parents.*

Thank you, Cantrix. Trisa showed no curiosity. Dobutless she already had a good idea what Sira was planning. Even now she carefully dropped her eyes, shielding her mind, but she was sure to have sensed the brightening of Sira's mood, the growing lightness of her heart. She would have guessed Sira was preparing to leave.

Well, good, Sira thought. That will make it easier to explain.

In the apartment, Trisa took up the *filhata* and played through the tuning exercise and the first mode, slowly, but accurately. Sira nodded approval. Since her return, Trisa's skills had grown in great leaps, as if doors that had been locked to her were now flung open. Her hands were small, but nimble. Sira had spent hours coaching her fingerings on the *filla* until they were second nature, just as Maestra Lu had done with her years before. Trisa had mastered all the modes on the *filla* at last, and had made a good beginning with the *filhata*. It would be difficult for her until her fingers lengthened a bit, but she had reached second-level standards, as she should have done with her Conservatory class. The problem was what to do with her now.

For a time Sira listened, adjusted Trisa's hand position, then listened again. She made her straighten her back and lower her shoulders. It was as all lessons were, and more than once Trisa sighed with effort as she began an exercise a second or a third time. At the end of an hour Sira leaned back in her chair. *Very good, Trisa. That is enough for now. Have you spoken to your mother?*

Yes, Cantrix, she is waiting outside.

All this time? With your father?

Trisa shook her head, and pushed out her lower lip. Sira had come to know the look well. *My father will not come here. He is still angry.*

Sira understood. The honors and privileges accorded the family of one of the Gifted must have been hard to relinquish. She wondered how things stood now between Brnwen, who had wept with joy when Trisa came home to Amric, and her mate. Sira remembered Niel v'Arren's face when he had told her, his daughter, that she must return to the Cantoris. Her refusal had made him angry, too, despite everything that had happened to her.

Call your mother in, please, she told Trisa. She got up and went to stand by the window, rubbing the muscles in the back of her neck. She could not see the Visitor from this perspective, but she knew it was there. Soon, she told herself, as everyone said to the children.

Brnwen followed Trisa into the apartment, bowing shyly to Sira and seating herself only when Sira waved her to a chair. As usual, Trisa stood protectively by her mother, a hand on her shoulder. Did she try to protect her in their own apartment as well? Sira wondered. The last years could not have been easy ones for the family.

She sat down in a chair near Brnwen's. "Now that Amric has another Cantor, I will be leaving this House. But Trisa needs to continue her studies."

Brnwen's eyes were wide, waiting. Trisa looked utterly calm.

"Perhaps Trisa already knows what I am going to say," Sira suggested. Trisa's smile was all innocence. Sira watched them both, and a smile of her own began deep inside. "I am going to a House that is far from here, and isolated. It is a House that needs members and is not inclined to be critical in the way that Houses on the Continent might be."

"Cantrix Sira," Trisa lisped. "My mother and I would like very much to go with you."

"Do you already know, then?"

"Yes!" Trisa exclaimed. "We have talked about it. Singer Zakri told me about Observatory, and about your friend who is Cantor there. Singer Zakri wants to go, and I do too."

Brnwen said softly, "Cantrix, I'm a hard worker. I think maybe they'll be glad to have me there. I'm good with fur and leather, because my father was a tanner." She indicated the panels that hung on the walls of the apartment. "I did the tooling on some of these."

"And what of your mate?"

Brnwen dropped her eyes. "He thinks we should have sent Trisa back. We've had terrible arguments, and now . . . ." When her eyes came up, they glistened with tears. "I'm going to release him. He wants to mate with someone else."

Sira took a long breath, and released it slowly. How hard the Gift had been on these people! Trisa patted her mother's shoulder, and Brnwen put up her hand to touch her daughter's.

Sira said, "I am glad to have you go with me. Observatory is not an easy House," she warned. "But we will all be together, and Trisa's training will go on. That is most important."

"There is something else, Cantrix Sira," Trisa said. Her eyes were a clear and shining blue, untroubled by the complex tangles they were all trying to work through.

"What else, Trisa?"

"It is Mreen, the baby."

Sira drew another deliberate breath, and she wrapped her arms around herself, around the pain she still carried with her, the ache of loss. "Isbel's Mreen," she murmured.

"Yes. Mreen has the Gift, too. We have to take her with us."

Shame flooded Sira. She had given no thought to the child, ever, in all this time. She had indulged her own grief, without concern for any other. She asked quietly, "Who has been caring for the babe?"

Brnwen spoke up, made bold by the subject. "Her father has. Kai. And I have, Cantrix. I couldn't nurse her, but I could do everything else, and I think we might . . . Well, it's possible that . . ." She looked away, not finishing her thought, but Sira could guess well enough what it was. Kai and Brnwen were close enough in age, and both would soon be free.

"So, Trisa, have you arranged all of this as well?" Sira asked.

Trisa was smiling, bubbling with enthusiasm over her plans. "Oh, yes, Cantrix. Kai will go as well. And you will teach Mreen when she is old enough, just like you teach me. And I," she added with pride, "will teach her to listen and send. I will be her classmate!"

Sira stood and went back to the window. She felt the Gift like a hand on her shoulder. Pushing or pulling? she wondered.

"When will we leave?" Brnwen asked.

Sira looked up into the hills, where she thought she could see a faint spot of green, far up where the first melt revealed softwood shoots beginning to sprout. The sky was clear and blue and inviting. "Soon," she said. "Very soon."

Cantor Gavn was not a great deal younger than Zakri, but he had no experience at all of life beyond Conservatory's walls. He would have no way to resist Ovan's bullying. Zakri, sitting in the back of the Cantoris, observed their first *quirunha* closely, following so near it was a wonder Cantor Ovan did not detect his presence.

Zakri saw Sira sitting at the front of the Cantoris with Magister Edrus. He was sure she saw, as he did, that Gavn's psi was clear and well-directed, if not yet powerful. There was a freshness in his voice that was lost in the grate of Ovan's. Giving up his vice had no more improved Ovan's music than his temper, and his psi was still shaky and unreliable. The *quirunha* took too long. Cantor Gavn's unformed features drooped with dismay and confusion when he stood with everyone else to chant the ending prayer. Zakri heard him thinking that he had never taken part in such a weak *quirunha*, and he had no idea what might be wrong. Conservatory, despite everything, had not warned him.

SEND US THE SUMMER TO WARM THE WORLD,
UNTIL THE SUNS WILL SHINE ALWAYS TOGETHER.

Zakri knew then what he must do. The knowledge rolled over him like a warm wind from the south, as sure as the coming summer. He did not like it, but he did not try to resist it.

Seeing that Ovan sent nothing to Cantor Gavn after the closing prayer, Zakri sent, *Nicely done, Cantor Gavn. You will be a credit to the . . . to our House.*

Gavn looked out from the dais, searching for the sender. Zakri raised a hand to identify himself. When he caught the boy's eyes, he winked at him despite the shadow of resignation that darkened his mood. Might as well have a good beginning.

Sira sent some modest compliment then, and Gavn was distracted. Ovan, however, had heard, and he sneered in Zakri's direction. *There will be no further need for you in this Cantoris, Singer,* he sent. *We now have two proper Cantors, full Conservatory-trained Cantors.*

Zakri looked at Sira, and saw her staring at Ovan. Her lips were pressed tightly together, and her dark eyes were narrow. Zakri sent to her, *Never mind! I know what must be done here.*

She turned her gaze to him. He added, *Could we meet with the Magister, you and I?* He smiled, ruefully, and watched her scarred eyebrow arch as she waited for an explanation. *I will tell you both together,* he sent.

She nodded briefly, and bent her head to speak to Magister Edrus. She and Edrus went out together, other people stepping back to make way for them. Zakri followed, shouldering his way through the crowd. No one stepped aside for him, or even noticed him particularly. Few in the House knew the work he had been doing as he sat in the Cantoris, his eyes closed, supporting Sira in the *quirunha* while Ovan sat on the dais next to her, the full Cantor Ovan, whose Gift was all but useless.

Well, he thought, perhaps all that will change. Or perhaps not. Either way, he saw his duty now, and he was prepared to accept it.

Magister Edrus had already assessed the situation. As he and Sira sat down with Zakri at the long table, he said, "Cantor Gavn won't be able to handle Cantor Ovan either, will he?"

Zakri laughed. "Are you sure you do not have the Gift, Magister? Seems to me you hear minds fairly well!"

Edrus smiled, but he shook his head. "I only read faces, and yours tells me everything. And now—I suppose you're here to tell me what to do about it."

Zakri leaned forward, his hands flat on the table. "Yes, Magister, actually I am."

Sira regarded Zakri with wonder. He looked harder, suddenly, and older. He had taken charge of this meeting. She did not know whether to be amused or proud. She settled back in her chair and folded her arms, waiting.

"Cantor Ovan is not to be trusted," Zakri said bluntly. "I will be fair, and admit that he may not intend it, but he is no man to have a young and inexperienced junior. There is no way you could know this, Magister, but Conservatory should have."

"I wish I had understood it sooner," Edrus said. "Cantrix Isbel might have had a chance."

"I think Cantor Gavn will have a better chance," Zakri said, "if I stay in your House to help him."

Sira suddenly sat very straight, and looked into Zakri's eyes. A refusal was on her lips, but he sent to her, *There is no other way. I am ready.*

Edrus looked to Sira. "Do you agree? I know Singer Zakri has been studying the *filhata,* but is he ready for the Cantoris?"

Sira looked again at Zakri, measuring the change in him. He was a man, a strong Singer with a purpose of his own. She wanted to touch his hand, his fine brown hair that he kept short, like hers, ready to travel. She wished she could stop this, change this somehow, but she feared Zakri was right. She could see no other way, either. Perhaps it was time for him, his own time. He could not remain a student all his life.

"Magister," she said slowly, "you know that it is Singer Zakri who has assisted me in your Cantoris for many months. Cantor Ovan sits on the dais, but it is Zakri who warms your House. There is no reason he cannot support Cantor Gavn in the same way."

Edrus frowned. "How shall I manage this? The Magistral Committee is already watching my House as if we were fomenting treason here! All I want, as you both know, is to keep my House members safe."

"Never mind," Zakri said lightly. "I will go on doing what I have been doing. No one needs to know."

"No," Sira said firmly. "They should know exactly what you are and what you have done. You have earned your proper title."

"Cantor Ovan will never stand for it," Edrus argued.

"I will take care of Cantor Ovan," Sira answered. She rose from the table. *Zakri. Are you quite sure?*

He grinned at her. His lips trembled and his eyes glistened, but nothing lifted from the table or smashed to the floor. The *quiru* light around him was steady. He was in perfect control.

I am ready, he answered. *It is time.*

Chapter Thirty-four

Cantor Ovan faced Sira across the empty Cantoris. His eyes glittered across the room. His anger and fear had built into an emotional maelstrom that swelled and beat against her.

By what right do you threaten me? he demanded.

Sira stood with her hands braced on her hips. *By right of necessity,* she answered him. Pol had said something similar to her, long ago. By right of need, he had told her. She had been forced to accept it then, and Ovan was going to accept it now.

What is the necessity? Ovan began to breathe hard, as if he knew what was coming, as if he could keep it away with his fury.

Do you not know how we have sustained your quirunha *all this time?* Sira sent. *You have been lucky, lucky in Cantrix Isbel, and in me. And now you are lucky to have Zakri.*

Ovan's face grew darker, and a pulse beat in his forehead. Sira felt a flicker of something like sympathy despite her dislike of the man. His Gift had been irretrievably flawed by years of abuse, and it was a terrible loss, the worse because he had brought it on himself.

Are you saying I am no longer capable of warming my House?

Your people might have frozen without me, she answered bluntly. *And I could not have managed so long without Zakri's help. Between us we have kept your* quiru *strong. But I am leaving your House now.*

Ovan straightened a bit, and Sira saw a flash of hope in his face. She shook her head. *I am convinced that to leave you alone with Cantor Gavn would be a catastrophe. You must be objective in this, Cantor Ovan. The safety of your people is at stake.*

That is a lie!

Again Sira shook her head. *It is not, and you know it. I had hoped your Gift would return in strength, but it has not, and I cannot help you.*

Ovan's mouth opened, but no sound emerged. *Why are you doing this to me?* His frustration and resentment were ugly, filling Sira's mind with darkness, with immense sorrow and helplessness. She pictured Isbel in her last hours, racked with pain, and she stiffened her neck. The brief feeling of pity faded, and the air around her began to shimmer with steady light.

You have done this to yourself, she sent. *For the good of your House, there will be no more. Singer Zakri will become Cantor Zakri this very morning, on this very dais, and you will be senior to two Cantors. If not, I will tell Magister Edrus exactly what your offense was, and you will be disgraced.*

You cannot do this! I will not stand for it! Ovan raised his fist and stepped forward, as if he would physically strike her.

The choice is no longer yours. Sira did not move, but faced him squarely.

He took another step, leaning toward her with his body curled, his hands white-knuckled. Around him the *quiru* light was uneven, glimmering in places, shadowed in others. It shifted as he moved. He spoke aloud, a hiss that resounded in the empty room. "You take too much on yourself! You are nobody, nothing. You failed in your own Cantoris, and I will not let you put an upstart itinerant into mine! He has not earned the title of Cantor. I will never call him by it!"

Sira was enveloped now in a brilliant corona that faded the *quiru* to nothingness. She extended it, letting her temper flare, and the light widened until it reached halfway across the Cantoris. Ovan sucked in an audible breath.

Sira regarded her adversary through narrowed eyes, and her chin lifted. "You do not understand, Ovan," she said in a low tone. "You should have faced this long ago. Now it has been decided for you. Do not test me. I will do exactly as I say."

Ovan stumbled closer, bruising his leg on a bench, then kicking it out of his way. It banged against the one in front of it, and loud echoes bounced from the high ceiling. He loomed so close now that Sira could smell the sharp odor of his fear, and the light of her anger reflected in his eyes. It seemed he might actually strike her.

The air around her glinted like starlight, a dangerous flame that could burn or freeze. Her psi lashed out at Ovan's, a whip of energy that snapped just short of doing real injury to his mind. She felt the softness of his Gift, the weakness, like the center of a rotten fruit. It was poorly shielded, and it lacked resilience. Her psi jolted his and withdrew, a clear and terrible warning.

He cringed and threw his hands up to cover his face. "What are you doing? Stop!"

"Consider it a demonstration," Sira said, her tone dropping ever lower. "I have shown you your weakness. This House and these people are not safe in your care."

"You have no respect for my title! You could have destroyed my mind, doing that!"

"Yes," Sira answered coldly. "But I did not. You say I have failed in my Cantoris, yet I have sustained yours for a year. My Gift is intact. I know exactly what it will do when I use it."

Ovan backed away then, stumbling again. His eyes had gone dull. "You will ruin me."

"I may save you." Sira relaxed her shoulders and hands, and drew a cooling breath. The brightness around her subsided. She turned away from Ovan to look up at the dais, where Zakri would receive his title within the hour.

It was no easy task that he faced, but Zakri's life had never been easy. He had the strength and the courage he needed. Now would be his opportunity to grow. She hoped he would find satisfaction here, in this Cantoris. Only the Spirit could guide him now.

She looked over her shoulder at Ovan, slumped now on a bench, pale and beaten. *Cantor Ovan, Zakri is a fine Singer, and so Cantor Gavn will be, in time. They will be your juniors, and will show you every respect. Your Gift may even return, if you take care. Meanwhile, your House and your position will be secure.*

He sent, *You have no idea how hard it is, working alone, day in and day out, forever.*

She sighed, a deep sigh that came from the bottom of her soul. *You are mistaken, Cantor Ovan. I have always known. From the very beginning, I have always known.*

Chapter Thirty-five

Softwood saplings grew everywhere, leaping for the sun like pale green arrows loosed into the night-darkness of the ancient ironwoods. Sira's lungs filled with the essence of summer, the sweet tang of softwood leaves that would forever after remind her of this journey. There were seven in their traveling party. For six days they had ridden southeast at a deliberate pace, enjoying the suns of summer.

Singer Iban and Houseman Berk were there to see them all safely to the Pass. Tiny Mreen traveled in a soft fur carrier, either tied to Kai's back or slung about Brnwen's shoulders. Their evening *quiru* were mostly for appearances. The air was balmy and warm enough to be safe without them. They had heard a solitary *tkir* bellow, but it was far away.

It had not been as difficult as Sira thought it might be to say farewell to Zakri, Cantor Zakri v'Amric. With Isbel's *filhata* tucked under his arm, he had smiled from the steps of the House as they made their parting ceremony. Cantor Ovan stood as if made of stone, and Cantor Gavn watched with stunned surprise, hardly knowing what further shocks awaited him. The general mood had been one of celebration and pride; only Lamdon had more than two Cantors, after all! If there were some ominously shaken heads, that could not be helped. Houseman Berk had a great deal of influence among his House members, and he had been quick to acclaim their new Cantor. Sira had no doubt Cantor Zakri's *quirunha* would be well-attended.

She had not yet felt Mreen's Gift, but she accepted Trisa's judgment in the matter. Trisa would know. She was surprised, though, to find herself charmed by the baby. Mreen's eyes, bright and curious, were as green as her mother's had been. Her hair, though now the rosy color of summer dawn, promised to be as rich a red-brown as Isbel's. She was cheerful and smiling, and Sira had not once heard her so much as whimper. And why should she? Kai, Brnwen, or Trisa leapt to do whatever Mreen needed or wanted to have done! Thank the Spirit the child would not have to mourn her mother, as Isbel had grieved for hers, all alone.

They rode down into the Pass in the same place Sira had so many years before, where Theo had caught up with her in her lonely *quiru*. This time the road was clear, the snow melted, leaving only worn gray patches in the shadows of boulders or ironwood trees. There had been any number of fat *caeru* scampering away from the travelers into the forest. They could have stopped at Bariken, but saw no reason to do so. Now they made their camp in the Pass, waiting.

When it was dark, and their *quiru* shone still and golden above them in the purple night, Sira unwrapped her *filhata*, and sat cross-legged by the cooking fire. As she took the instrument in her hands she thought of Zakri's hands upon it, and a pang made her close her eyes. Isbel would be glad to have Zakri inherit her *filhata*. But her own would always remind her of him.

Trisa came to kneel close by, ready to follow, to help if she was able. The others in their party were silent, Mreen asleep with her pink lips parted, her plump cheek buried in Kai's shoulder, Brnwen and Berk and Iban relaxing on their bedfurs. The stars were just beginning their night's watch.

There was a melody Theo loved, which Sira had played for him early in their days at Observatory. It was a long, winding air that modulated from *Lidya* to *Mu-Lidya* and back again. It had no particular function. It was purely musical, and they had relished its shape and structure. Sira played it now, slowly, lingering on each note, not using her voice but only the rich sound of the strings resounding through the darkness.

She stretched her psi far out away from her in a long, sinuous fibril. It reached up and up, past the huge boulders that hid the path, past the treacherous cliff road they would soon have to traverse. It floated across the rocky valley beyond the chasm and farther up, to the mountain peak where Observatory perched high above any other House on the Continent.

It was a long way, a very long way. Sira took care not to rush, not to push. She had waited five long years to be here again, and she could not fail. When she knew she was there, she searched only moments before finding him.

Theo.

His answer was immediate, a joyous outpouring of feeling like the flaring of a solitary star in the wide sky. *Sira, is it you?*

Yes. I am here, in the Pass.

Dear heart! Someone will come for you tomorrow.

Theo . . . Sira's fingers moved automatically, supporting the slender thread of psi that connected them. It took tremendous strength to sustain it, but she was loath to let it go, after so long. It was pure gossamer, the faintest touch, this contact between them. She had sometimes feared she would never feel it again. *Theo . . . soon, now.*

Very soon. I will be waiting. I have been waiting.

Just a little longer. She released the thread. She let the melody drift to its cadence, and she lifted her fingers from the strings and opened her eys.

Trisa was watching her, open-mouthed in wonder at the length of her reach. *Did it work? So far away?*

Sira smiled, then laughed, stretching her tired fingers and running them through her hair. "Oh, yes, Trisa," she said, so that everyone could hear. "Oh, yes, it worked very well. Someone is coming tomorrow, coming to guide us. To take us home."

From her carrier, the infant Mreen's green eyes regarded her in solemn silence.

Trisa had imagined Observatory to be huge, a massive pile of stone on top of a mountain they would have to climb, struggling over rocks and crevasses. She was disappointed in her first glimpse of it. They rode up a narrow path that had only a gentle rise. The cliff road was the scary part, but they had left that behind two hours before. Now she saw that the ancient stone walls of the House were bounded on two sides by walls of rock. It looked small, almost cramped in comparison to the Houses she knew.

Its *quiru*, though, shone as brightly in the sunshine as any other, and in the courtyard they found a formal welcome, just as they might have done at Conservatory or at Amric. People crowded the steps of the House, people in tunics of every color.

Trisa sensed the general surprise at the size of their party. A thickset man with bushy gray hair stepped forward. He bowed to Sira, but awkwardly, as if he was not really used to it.

"Welcome back, Cantrix Sira," he said in a raspy voice. His accent was odd, like that of the guide Morys who had come down to the Pass for them. "I see you have brought new House members to Observatory. We're glad to have them."

"Thank you, Magister Pol." Sira's greeting brought a chuckle from the gray-haired man, but Trisa did not know why.

Several House members came down the steps to help the travelers dismount. One Housewoman held out her arms for Mreen, and cooed with delight as the baby reached up fat hands to pat her face. Pol and one other remained on the steps, and Trisa forgot everything else as she stared at the man who stood beside the Magister.

He was not quite as tall as Cantrix Sira. He had heavy shoulders and long, curling blond hair tied neatly at his nape. His eyes were the bluest Trisa had ever seen, so bright she could see their color from where she stood in the courtayrd. He smiled at them all, but she knew from the way his eyes sought Cantrix Sira's that this must be Theo. The warmth of feeling between them was as real to Trisa as if it were coming from her own breast. She heard Cantrix Sira send, *Theo, my dear,* and she shielded her mind quickly to give them privacy. Just the same, their feelings were so strong she could hardly have kept from sensing them.

Sira walked up the steps to stand in front of Theo. For a long moment they looked only at one another, as if there were no one else in the world. They did not touch, but it seemed to Trisa's dazzled eyes that they were surrounded by a light of their own, as if their feelings for each other raised a private and intense *quiru* about the two of them.

Suddenly Trisa realized that around her people were talking and laughing, introducing themselves, handing over saddlepacks and bedfurs. She had thought, watching Sira and Theo, that the whole world was as silent and rapt as they.

When she looked back at them now, she saw Theo presenting three youngsters to Sira. He said aloud, "Your students, Maestra."

Sira laughed, the second time Trisa had heard her laugh in as many days. "I bring two with me as well, Cantor Theo." She turned to beckon to Trisa.

Trisa hurried up the steps and bowed low. "I am pleased to meet you, Cantor Theo."

"I am delighted to meet you, Trisa." His voice was deep and clear. His eyes crinkled charmingly as he smiled. Trisa thought she had never seen such a lovely man. "It seems we will have our own school here, does it not?" he said.

"It is my privilege to be part of it," Trisa answered carefully. Cantor Theo laughed, and the cheerfulness of his nature invested the entire courtyard with magic. All around them the people seemed happy, and healthy, and attractive in some mysterious way. There would be a school here, with five students, and no one of them—or any of their parents—shedding tears. It was wondrous beyond anything Trisa had hoped for.

Her grin was so big it hurt her cheeks. *I like your House,* she sent, breaching courtesy, carried away by pelasure at the warmth of their welcome and her delight in her new teacher.

I am very glad, Cantor Theo responded.

Sira smiled broadly, too, looking happier than Trisa had ever seen her. Mreen was carried forward, and Theo took her into his arms.

Isbel's daughter, Sira sent. There passed between Theo and Sira a moment of such intense emotion that Trisa had to shield herself once again.

Pol spoke loudly, interrupting everyone. "All right, into the great room before the cook has my head! She claims she has something special to celebrate the Cantrix's return!"

Trisa hung back, watching as her mother lifted Mreen out of Theo's arms, and then, with Kai, followed the people in through the double doors. The *hruss* disappeared with a couple of Housemen, and soon no one was left on the steps but herself, Cantrix Sira, and Cantor Theo.

It was Theo who turned and held out a big hand to her. She put her own into it. *Will you not come in now, Trisa?* he asked. *I think you are home.*

She saw tears of joy sparkle in Sira's eyes. Her own eyes stung. Two tears slid past her smile, but it did not matter. *Oh, yes, Cantor Theo*, she sent. *We are home.*

Side by side, the three of them went up the steps and into Observatory.

BOOK THREE:

RECEIVE THE GIFT

Prologue

Mreen's small fingers danced across the stops of her *filla*, and her *Aiodu* melody bubbled up to resonate merrily against the stone walls. Sira listened and watched, her chin propped on one long, narrow hand, her elbow on the ironwood table between them. She did not interrupt until Mreen began to embellish her tune.

No, no, Mreen, Sira sent then. *You must stay in the mode, or make a modulation to the next.*

Mreen's eyes flashed green. *Why, Cantrix Sira?* She put down the *filla*, and kicked her short legs against the chair. *Why must I?*

Sira regarded her gravely. Mreen was redheaded, dimpled, and plump. She was, in fact, very like her mother. But Isbel had never been as wilful as her daughter, except once.

It is unmusical, Sira sent to her. *It jars the ear.*

Not on my ear! Mreen responded. Tiny sparks, born of her temper, appeared in the air around her. They glinted on her hair, and lifted little tendrils of it to waft around her face.

Sira raised one long forefinger. All of her students knew that warning finger very well. Mreen's pink lip pouted, but the disturbance in her tiny *quiru* subsided at once.

When you are a full Cantrix, and have mastered your art, Sira sent, *you will undoubtedly forget all I have said and embellish however you like. But for now, please follow my instruction. When you play in Aiodu, you must not leap to Doryu without preparation. I will show you.*

Sira lifted her own *filla*, *obis*-carved at the House of Soren just as Mreen's had been. She repeated the notes and rhythms of Mreen's melody exactly, but after the first statement her modulation to *Doryu* was smooth and sweet, like a tidbit of dried fruit melting on the tongue. Mreen caught her breath at the beauty of it.

Sira stopped playing and gazed at her student with an arch of her scarred eyebrow. This, too, was familiar to her students.

Mreen, not yet five years old, squirmed and giggled. *All right, Cantrix Sira.* She dimpled as she picked up her own instrument. *I will try.*

Sira rested her chin on her hand again, and listened. She could almost see her old friend Isbel standing behind her daughter, a hazy familiar figure, an apparition of memory reaching out to stroke the childish curls. A wave of remembered grief swept Sira, and she shook her head sharply to banish both the image and the emotion.

Abruptly, Mreen stopped playing. Her eyes glistened with welling tears; like the needles of the ironwood trees curling in on themselves in the deep cold season, they turned dark, a black-green for which there was no name.

Oh, Mreen, Sira sent swiftly. *It was not you. I—I thought of something, that is all.*

I know what you thought. The tears, shining faintly yellow in the light of the *quiru*, spilled over Mreen's smooth cheeks.

Do you?

The little girl dashed away the tears with her fingers. *I always know. I see the pictures.*

Sira looked down at her *filla,* turning it in her fingers. Sometimes she hardly knew what to say to this child, who even now was two years younger than the youngest student ever to attend Conservatory. Mreen's Gift was so intense that she went about Observatory wrapped in a little cloud of light that only faded when she lay down on her cot to sleep. Her moods brought sparks flying about her, or small shadows shifting through the light. And she was silent, always.

Gifted students never spoke aloud in Sira's presence, in order to practice their sending and listening, to sharpen their skills. With their families, and with other House members, they chattered as volubly as other children. But Mreen did not speak at all, not to her Gifted friends, not to her teachers, not even to her unGifted father and stepmother. She had never cried as a baby, nor made any of the usual infant sounds. She was utterly and entirely a creature of the Gift.

Who is the lady? Mreen asked. *The one you saw? Why does she make you sad?*

Sira gently wiped the last tear from Mreen's face. It hurt to know that Mreen could see the image in her mind, yet not recognize it. Sira took the child's small hand in her own.

She was your mother, Mreen, she sent gently. *She loved you very much.*

The little girl sat still for a long time, looking down at her hand in Sira's. When she raised her eyes, the look in them made Sira's scalp prickle under her short-cropped hair.

I thought so, Mreen sent. *I have seen her.*

How could you have seen her?

Mreen turned her little hand over and pressed it into Sira's. *Cantrix Sira . . . when I touch things, certain things . . . I know about them, about the other people who touched them.*

Sira watched the little girl's eyes. There seemed to be an old, old woman behind them.

Kai, my father, that is . . . gave me my mother's brushes. When I hold them in my hand, I can see her.

Perhaps you only imagine that, Mreen. It would be natural.

Mreen shook her head firmly, her red curls bouncing, and she let go of Sira's hand. *No, Cantrix Sira. I can see her. She had red hair, like me!*

That is right, Mreen. She was beautiful.

Was she your friend?

Sira nodded, and sighed.

Was she a Singer, Cantrix Sira?

Sira hesitated. This was the hard part, and she had hoped not to have to touch upon it for some time yet. The child was so precocious—there were no rules to follow in teaching her.

Your mother was a full Cantrix. Cantrix Isbel v'Amric.

Mreen was still for a moment, thinking. When she looked back at Sira, the old woman looked out again from behind the childish features.

But Cantrixes do not have babies.

That is right, Mreen. But to your mother—Sira remembered Isbel, caressing the swell of her stomach, smiling up at Kai. *To your mother, you were more important than being a Cantrix.*

Mreen's pink lips pursed. *I think I am too young to understand.*

That is a wise observation.

They sat in silence for a time, each with their own thoughts. Sira asked, *Will you play once more?*

Mreen dimpled, and reached for her *filla. So I will. I will modulate!*

Sira smiled a little as she sat back to listen, but her heart ached. A strange and heavy Gift had been laid upon the child. As Mreen began her melody, Sira reflected that there was only one place where Mreen could realize her full potential. She needed the structure, the discipline, and the safety of a House entirely devoted to the Gift and to the Gifted. She needed Conservatory.

It would not be easy to send Mreen away, to let others take charge of her training, of the molding and direction of her Gift. Her father and her stepmother would miss her terribly, and so, Sira knew, would she herself. But like every Cantor and Cantrix on the Continent, Sira was accustomed to sacrifice. She would not shirk this one. She would do what she must.

Chapter One

The snow of the deep cold season lay thickly on the peaks and valleys around Amric. Ironwood trees drooped under its weight and the road leading away from the House was blankly white, undisturbed by any footstep of man or *hruss*. When Cantor Zakri v'Amric looked out through the rippled lime-glass window of his private apartment, cold sunlight sparkling on the snowpack dazzled his eyes. The wide vivid sky infected him with restiveness, with longing to be outside. He had worked in Amric's Cantoris for three solid years. He had not been outside its walls since the day Cantrix Sira had left the House in his care and departed for Observatory. Not since his early childhood had he spent so long a time in one place.

Idly, Zakri stretched out a lazy fibril of his thought and tweaked one of the ironwood branches overhanging the courtyard, just to see a cascade of glittering snow fall from it. He chuckled, leaning into the window to watch the little pile of white snow drop to the cleanswept gray of the cobblestones. At least he could still do it. Three years of Cantoris discipline had not dulled his special talent!

The *quirunha* had been performed an hour before, and the warmth and light of the House *quiru* enveloped even the edges of the courtyard, spilling over onto the snow beyond. Cantor Ovan and Cantor Gavn, Zakri's senior and junior respectively, had flanked him on the dais in the Cantoris as they did each day. Amric's *quiru* was one of the strongest and warmest on the Continent, behind only those of Lamdon and Conservatory, making Magister Edrus justifiably proud of his three Cantors.

Zakri sighed again, and turned away from the window to brush and retie his long hair. He patted his tunic to make sure his *filla* was there before he went out of his apartment and down the broad carved staircase to return to the Cantoris. Cantor Gavn was already seated, and a short line of people in brightly dyed tunics waited in front of him.

Not many today, Cantor Zakri, Gavn sent.

Zakri stepped up on the dais and sat down next to his junior. Indeed, their duties would be light. *You could handle this all by yourself,* he sent to Gavn with a wink.

Gavn's answering smile was shy. He was only slightly younger than Zakri, but his Conservatory upbringing made him seem tender and unformed. Even his features were babyish, his mouth full and soft, his cheeks smooth. Zakri shielded the thought, sure that Gavn would not appreciate it. Gavn had four summers, after all, and would have five before long, Spirit willing. He had to be at least twenty-two years old.

Zakri was not sure of his own age; his parents, like so many itinerants and working people, had measured their children's ages only in summers. With five years between summers, the system was no more than a general one, and there was great variety in its accuracy.

I could handle these, I think, Gavn sent now, *but they would only ask for you in any case!*

Zakri's mouth curled in amusement. *If they only knew!* he responded. *Perhaps I should stay away and let them find out what you can do.* He turned to nod to the small group of waiting people. The first stepped forward, and Zakri took his *filla* out of his tunic, ready to begin.

He had barely opened his mouth to ask the Houseman what was troubling him when a clatter of *hruss* hooves sounded from the courtyard, and a hoarse voice called from the steps. Every head in the Cantoris turned. Gavn murmured aloud, "Travelers!"

The Housemen and women chattered excitedly to each other, and turned about, torn between their turn at Cantoris hours and wanting to see who had come. Very few travelers had been seen at Amric during the past months, and in recent weeks, none at all. A new face at the evening meal, bearing fresh news and gossip, would be welcome.

Housekeeper Cael burst into the Cantoris, hurrying up the aisle between the ironwood benches. His face was pale, his expression grim. As Zakri rose to meet him, he felt a chill of premonition creep across his shoulders.

Cael bowed very briefly. Zakri nodded in return. "Housekeeper?" he said.

"Cantor Zakri, you are needed in the great room," Cael murmured.

Without hesitating, knowing in his bones that something grave was happening, Zakri tucked his *filla* back into his tunic and stepped down from the dais. To Gavn he sent, *You will have to care for these people alone, after all.*

Yes, Cantor Zakri, Gavn responded. *Shall I join you then?*

Good idea. As Zakri followed Cael out of the Cantoris, he heard Gavn speaking to the House members in a soothing and assured voice. He did not sound a bit shy.

The double doors to the great room were closed. Cael opened one of them for Zakri to slip through, then shut it firmly again, forestalling several curious House members who lingered in the hall, trying to see inside.

The great room was empty except for two men, heavily swathed in traveling furs, collapsed into one of the deep window seats. One looked up at Zakri with desperate eyes. The other sprawled in the seat with his legs dangling to the floor. He did not move at all.

Zakri's steps slowed as he approached them, and his premonition solidified into dread. A tiny seed of fear and anger was born just under his heart. He knew already whose face he would see when he pulled back the *caeru* fur hood of the unconscious man. And he knew the man was beyond any help he could give.

He tried just the same. He got out his *filla* and played, searching frantically for a spark, for any glimmer of life in his old friend and master, but there was none to be found. He played on. His psi probed and prodded, but there was no consciousness to awaken, no pulse, however weak, to encourage. The people of Amric believed Zakri to be the greatest healer on the Continent. But there was nothing he could do for the Singer Iban.

Iban had been his mentor and his master. Any healing Zakri knew he had learned from Iban. But Iban was gone now, gone with the Spirit beyond the stars.

"What happened?" he demanded of Iban's companion. The man slumped beside his dead comrade, his face sagging with fatigue and fright. "Who are you?" Zakri snapped.

The man turned pale eyes to Zakri, then looked swiftly away. "I'm Clive v'Trevi. Iban's sister's mate. We were coming to you . . . you're Cantor Zakri, aren't you?"

He looked up to see Zakri's nod. "We were coming to you, to tell you—" He broke off, looking up at Cael, then, fearfully, at Zakri. "Iban wanted to see you."

"But what happened?" Zakri repeated. He spoke harshly, out of grief and shock and anger. The air around him shifted and darkened, as if his emotions were a cloud before the sun. He took a sharp breath, concentrating on his control, and the light returned. This was no time for an undisciplined display. It would do no honor to Iban's memory to lose control of his Gift.

"I don't know," Clive muttered. "We were hurrying, traveling as fast as we could in the deep cold . . . and then last night, just after the *quiru* was up, he cried out, like he'd seen something or heard something . . . and then no more." He shivered in evident horror. "I couldn't wake him up, not then nor since. As soon as morning came, I just followed the road here. I was so afraid—"

Clive v'Trevi hung his head, and Zakri and those around him were silent. They were Nevyans, and they understood perfectly. Of course he had been afraid. He was no Singer, who could call up a *quiru* whenever he needed it. Had Clive not reached Amric before dark, his own death would have been as certain as Iban's.

"Where were you riding from?"

This was a new voice, a deep and commanding one. Clive's eyes darted up in search of the speaker. He hesitated a long time, and the hard spot of cold under Zakri's heart spread wider, filling the space between his ribs.

"Soren," Clive finally whispered. Zakri looked up at Berk, who had asked the question. The Gifted Cantor and the unGifted courier stared at each other until Berk made a gesture with his big hand.

Zakri turned back to Iban's body, directing the Housemen to transport it to his own rooms. In the background he heard Berk speaking to the Magister as he and Cantor Gavn came into the great room. Cael led Clive away, and Zakri heard Berk telling him to be in the Magister's apartment within the hour. There would be little rest for Clive v'Trevi, at least not until all the truth of the disastrous journey were known.

Gavn came to Zakri and stood before him, biting his full lower lip. *Are you all right, Cantor?*

Zakri shook his head. *Something terrible has happened.*

What is it? Who was that man?

That was my master.

Gavn sucked in a noisy breath, and his blue eyes were wide and shocked. *Not the Singer Iban! From your itinerant days?*

My itinerant days, thought Zakri. They had not lasted long, but they had changed him forever, changed everything. For a moment he missed them with a longing so fierce that he saw Gavn step back suddenly, and knew he had not shielded himself enough. *I am sorry*, he sent. *It is just that, without Iban, I would certainly not be here today. Or perhaps anywhere!*

The two Cantors walked slowly out of the great room, and started up the wide staircase to the upper level of the House.

Can I do anything to help? Gavn asked.

I do not know yet.

Too many Singers had died in recent years. No Nevyan Singer's death would ever be lightly dismissed, but in this case, Zakri swore to himself, he would have answers . . . or else. What else, he could not have said at that moment. But the coldness under his heart wound itself into a frigid knot of fury. He felt it when he breathed, when he moved. It demanded release. It demanded revenge.

"The rumors from Soren have been around for a long time," Berk said heavily. His body dwarfed the carved ironwood chair he sat in, and his long legs barely fit beneath the table in the Magister's apartment. Berk's grizzled hair and beard were always neatly combed, but despite his years of service to the upper levels of the House, he retained the weather-beaten, travel-hardened look of a rider, as he had been in his youth.

"For too long," Zakri said. "It is time something was done."

Magister Edrus leaned forward. "But what will you do, Cantor Zakri?" he asked. "If you and Berk go riding into Soren, you risk your own safety."

Zakri shrugged. He was spending a good deal of his energy simply controlling his psi, so as not to darken and disturb the *quiru* light in the room. He felt Gavn staring at him.

Edrus pressed him. "What injury did you find in Singer Iban?"

Zakri took a shaky breath. "I found no injury at all, Magister," he said slowly. "No injury to his body, that is."

Berk turned in Clive's direction. The smaller man cowered in misery at one end of the table. "Houseman! Are you sure you heard nothing last night, no *hruss* or men behind you?"

Clive's eyes flickered nervously from side to side. He shook his head. Zakri saw that his hands trembled, and that he grasped his elbows to stop them.

Berk looked at Zakri, his eyebrows up and his lips pursed beneath his beard. Zakri knew what that look meant.

Carefully, as Berk and the Magister discussed possible actions to take, Zakri extended his psi, reaching ever so cautiously into Clive's mind. He had to be very subtle. If Cantor Gavn, so painstakingly trained in discretion at Conservatory, were to catch him trespassing, he would never understand. And Cantrix Sira would have objected. Or perhaps she would not, if she had seen Singer Iban lying dead in the great room, his mobile features stilled forever. The thought made Zakri set his jaw. Trying to keep his face impassive, he strengthened his touch, delving more boldly into Clive's thoughts.

It was little use. Clive had no Gift at all. Zakri read only a confusion of fear, clouded by fatigue from his sleepless night and frantic ride from last night's campsite. Zakri withdrew his psi, and gave Berk a small shake of his head. Gavn's eyes were on him again, and he shielded himself carefully.

"I want to go home, to Trevi," Clive whined. "I've told you all I know! How can I know what's wrong at Soren? I'm no itinerant!"

Berk turned an unsympathetic face to the man. "It's too bad you're not," he growled. "We've not seen an itinerant here for weeks. There's no one to escort you."

Clive averted his eyes again. Zakri watched him with narrowed eyes. He sensed something, some slight deception, some hidden fear.

"Clive," Zakri said slowly. "You said Singer Iban went to Soren with goods from Trevi." Clive nodded. "What were the goods, what was he carrying?"

Clive looked out the window, at the floor, anywhere but at the three other men. "It was just food and cloth. We make felted cloth at Trevi, you know, and we grow the oaten grain no one else does, so they wanted . . . they sent . . ." His voice trailed off, and Zakri clenched a fist in irritation.

"What?" Berk pressed. "They sent what?"

"They sent us an itinerant."

The three Amric men stared at the traveler in amazement.

"They had nothing else?" Magister Edrus blurted.

Clive blinked. "Nothing else we wanted, I guess."

"Has this happened before?" Magister Edrus wanted to know.

"Once or twice. They've sent an itinerant for our Magister to use for a trip or two, and we sent him back loaded up with supplies. Only this time . . ."

"Yes?"

"They said they needed the grain quickly, and since Singer Iban was at home, and the Magister wanted the itinerant for something else, Iban and I took the shipment to Soren." He blinked again, looking either innocent or stupid.

"Something happened at Soren. That's what we need to know," Berk said firmly.

A silence stretched around the room. The Amric men waited while Clive shifted and squirmed in his seat. The scent of fear grew sharp around him, but Zakri and the others did not relent.

Clive perspired freely now, though he had shed his heavy *caeru* furs. "I don't know what you want!"

Zakri stared at him. "I think you do."

"But if I—"

"Yes?"

"Do you know what they're doing to people there?" Clive burst out in a panic. "I have a family, children . . . ."

"Singer Iban had a family!" Zakri rapped, and the air around him glimmered angrily. "And friends!"

Clive sagged in his chair, his chin on his chest. More moments of silence passed. Zakri gritted his teeth until his jaw ached. At length Clive looked up.

"There was a man . . . he used to be a Singer, an itinerant. Karl v'Perl." Clive struggled for courage. "He sits at meals in the great room at Soren, like—like a warning. A threat. His mind is gone. He—" Clive shuddered. "He drools. And he shakes. He—he soils himself. His mate has to do everything for him."

Cantor Gavn sucked in a shocked breath.

Clive cast him a look, then stammered on. ""When they took Iban up the stairs, up to Cho's rooms . . ."

"Cho?" asked Magister Edrus.

"Cho is an *obis*-carver, or he was. But something has happened to the Magister at Soren, and Cho seems to be in charge. He sits at the center table."

"What about their Cantors?"

Clive shook his head, pale and beaten looking. "I never saw them," he whispered. "The place is full of Singers, but they're all itinerants. They took Iban up to Cho, and when he came back, he wouldn't tell me anything. He said it was better I didn't know. We left in a hurry, sneaked away, really, just before dawn."

"We must report to Lamdon," Magister Edrus said to Berk and to Zakri. "They need to know what's happening, take some sort of action." He turned back to Clive. "It's true there are no itinerants in the House. We can't send you home at the moment."

Clive nodded. "It was the same at Trevi. No itinerants."

Berk thumped the table with one big fist. "That's their weapon. Control the itinerant Singers and you control the Continent."

Edrus nodded. "The people are trapped. Prisoners in their own Houses."

Zakri's voice shook when he spoke. "Iban refused to join them," he said bitterly, "and so they killed him. By the Six Stars! They will pay for this."

Clive held up a shaking hand. "Cantor Zakri, be careful! You don't know . . . you didn't see that man, that awful man, slobbering and mindless. She has to feed him, has to hold his head and . . . put the spoon in his mouth . . . . it's awful!"

Zakri shoved back his chair and stood. "They will pay for that, too." He nodded to Gavn. "Magister, Gavn and Ovan can manage for a time without me. I must go to to Soren. I must see what is happening for myself, and find out what happened to Iban."

Magister Edrus regarded him for several moments. "I suppose, Cantor Gavn, that you and Cantor Ovan can handle the Cantoris?"

Gavn's round, smooth chin stuck out. "Of course, Magister."

Good for you! Zakri sent to him.

Gavn sent back, *I hope.*

Berk stood up, and looked down at Zakri from his great height. "I'm coming with you."

"It may not be safe," Zakri warned.

Berk chuckled. "Less for you than for me, Cantor," he said. "And you and I are old road comrades, in any case."

"So we are," Zakri said. He rose, keeping his expression blank. His face felt as stiff as a piece of *caeru* leather left in the cold. He wanted to weep, or storm about in a tantrum as he would have before Cantrix Sira and Singer Iban had taught him to harness his wild Gift. He took a deep, slow breath, and bowed deeply to Magister Edrus, and to his junior.

"By your leave, then, Magister." He nodded to Berk. "And thank you, Berk. We will ride in the morning."

He strode from the room. In his mind, he heard, *Good luck, Cantor Zakri. Take care.*

And you, Cantor Gavn.

All will be well until you return.

Zakri felt a sudden homesickness that he would not have credited earlier in the day. But there was no time for doubts now. The task at hand was too important.

Chapter Two

Sira watched from the dais as Observatory's House members took their seats. Anyone who could be spared from their duties was present today in the Cantoris. Theo sat on the nearest bench with the students clustered around him. He had cut his blond hair for the coming journey, and it curled vigorously around his ears. It made him look younger than his eight summers. Mreen knelt beside him on the bench to have a good view. Her small round face was solemn in its nimbus of light. The other student Singers, Yve and Jule and Arry, fidgeted on Theo's left, their short legs dangling, their fingers in their mouths or their noses. They were even younger than Mreen, and had hardly begun their studies. At Theo's insistence, they spent most of their time with their families still. Sira made no argument; Theo's instincts were unerring. And they were being proved right once again; another Gifted babe had been born at Observatory, assisted into the world with Theo's help. There had not been such an abundance of the Gift on the Continent in a hundred summers.

Magister Pol leaned against the back wall of the Cantoris, his powerful arms folded across his chest. His blunt features were impassive, but Sira sensed his mood clearly. Indeed, this was a great day, and Pol was right to feel pride in his House, and his Cantoris; next to Sira on the dais, now tuning the precious and ancient *filhata*, was Sira's and Theo's very first student, Trisa. Today she would perform her first *quirunha*, with Sira as her senior. Her mother and stepfather, seated with the assembly, watched her every movement as she adjusted the central C and tuned the other strings to it.

Only the Spirit, Sira thought, could have wrought such change as Observatory had seen in the past two summers. The House glowed with light and warmth; its nursery gardens thrived, as did its people. Their clothes were simple and their tools either well-worn or make-do, but the people were healthy, and safe from the cold.

It was time. The Singers on the dais stood, and the assembly stood with them. They bowed formally. Trisa sat on her stool, the *filhata* across her lap. She closed her eyes, took a deep breath, and began to pluck the strings of the *filhata*. She played a melody in *Iridu* that she had practiced over and over in the past months, so often that at one time she cried out that she never wanted to hear it again! But Sira had been taught by her own teachers to begin with the familiar and expand upon it, and so she taught Trisa and Mreen. She knew that today, with her nerves charged and everyone watching, Trisa would be grateful for the hours she had spent on this particular piece.

Trisa's work was not the changeable, virtuosic music Mreen would one day play. She was consistent and steady, very like Theo himself. Her fingers were nimble, and her voice, when she began to sing, floated nicely on the breath, without tension or pressure. Her transition to *Aiodu* was perhaps a little rushed, but that was to be expected. Sira joined in when the new mode was established, enriching the texture of the music with a counterpoint on her own instrument, supporting the melodic line with her dark, even voice. After today, it would be Sira leading, or Theo, and Trisa following. But this, by tradition, was Trisa's *quirunha*, and she must demonstrate her ability to direct it.

The light and warmth swelled from the dais, a wave of energy that broke only on the barrier of deep cold beyond the House. Theo's psi was joined to theirs, but he stayed behind, beneath, there only to encourage Trisa should she falter.

Sira could no longer count the *quirunha* she and Theo had peformed together. She often felt they were as one person, she and Theo, two halves that were whole only when their psi was joined. She had healed her wounds, here at Observatory with Theo; and she dreaded being alone again, even for a short time.

The *quiru* was secure, the *quirunha* complete. Trisa stilled her *filhata* with the palm of her hand laid flat on the strings, and waited for a moment, eyes still closed, listening to the last notes fade against the high ceiling. When she opened her eyes, she looked first to her teacher.

Well done, Singer Trisa, Sira sent. *Your first modulation was a bit hurried, but all in all, a fine* quirunha. She stood and bowed formally to the new Singer.

For years Trisa had been working toward this moment. She bowed in return, carefully proper, but her eyes shone and her smile stretched so wide Sira thought it must hurt. She turned out into the Cantoris to find her mother. Brnwen's cheeks were wet, and she leaned happily toward Kai, her mate, whispering to him as she watched her daughter accept the bows of the Housemen and women.

Everyone present chanted together:

SMILE ON US,
O SPIRIT OF STARS,
SEND US THE SUMMER TO WARM THE WORLD,
UNTIL THE SUNS WILL SHINE ALWAYS TOGETHER.

The moment the formal prayer was finished, Trisa leaped off the dais, fourteen-year-old dignity forgotten, and danced up the aisle to her parents. Sira saw, though, that although the girl chattered excitedly to Brnwen, they did not touch. That discipline, at least, she had absorbed at Conservatory. She would not be a full Cantrix for some time yet—there was still much for her to learn—but she was officially Singer Trisa from this moment. There were formalities associated with her new title, and Sira approved of her observance of them. It set a good example.

Theo came to Sira as she stepped down from the dais. *Congratulations*, he sent.

And to you, she answered. The people swirled around them, the parents of Yve and Arry and Jule coming to fetch them, bowing respectfully to Sira and Theo. Only Mreen stood alone, a tiny figure encircled by light.

Theo nodded toward the new Singer where she stood surrounded by well-wishers. He grinned at Sira. *Well, it seems the two of you will manage perfectly without me.*

Sira touched his hand very lightly, a brief and fleeting contact. She felt an urge to smooth back his thick curls, a thing she would never dream of actually doing. *We will manage,* she told him, *but never perfectly. We will miss you greatly.*

Then I had better hurry back. He winked at Mreen. *But this one is in a terrific hurry, are you not, little one?*

So I am, Cantor Theo!

Theo chuckled. *The* ferrel *chick can hardly wait to tumble from its mother's nest.*

The three of them turned to go up the aisle. Kai waited a few steps away, and Mreen went to him, reaching up to take his hand. Kai looked down at his little daughter with a sad pride. He was not troubled by the faint glow that always surrounded her; it was her silence that disturbed him, although he had stopped asking about it. Mreen was all he had left of Isbel, and now Mreen would leave him, too, very probably never to return. Sira thanked the Spirit that he had Brnwen and Trisa to comfort him.

And Mreen—Mreen would have Conservatory. Sira was surprised to feel a tiny flame of envy flicker in her heart. Despite all that had happened, she still missed it. At her farewell ceremony—how long ago? Three summers?—Magister Mkel had said that every Singer's true home was Conservatory. Perhaps, she thought, in her deepest heart she believed him.

Pol stepped forward to meet them. His bow was stiff and awkward still, but most definitely a bow. "Congratulations, Cantrix Sira," he said gruffly, "and Cantor Theo. A fine debut for your student. A fine day for Observatory."

Theo bowed too, in the elegant way of a big man who is also graceful. "So it is," he said. "Your Cantoris is multiplying like a softwood grove in the summer, Pol!"

"Just don't forget that it still needs you, Cantor Theo," Pol growled.

Theo's eyes were on Sira as he spoke. "I will not forget." His eyes were the deep blue of summer, the rare and precious summer when both suns rose to wheel across Nevya's skies. "This is my home."

When Theo spoke the word, home, Sira felt a whisper of premonition tickle in her mind. She bit her lip. She knew better than to ignore the call of her Gift. But what could this be, this slight breath of warning? What did it mean? Surely, before summer came, they would both be here again, together. Home.

All the supplies necessary for travel were laid out on the floor and on the long workbench in Observatory's stables. Morys, the guide, pointed them out to Theo, who handled each one, making sure everything was in good repair and sturdy enough for the long journey. Mreen stood on tiptoe beside him, trying to see what was on the workbench. There were two saddles only, since Mreen would ride behind Theo. The saddlepacks were clean and ready to be filled with grain and dried meat and herbs for the *keftet.* There was an ironwood cooking pot, much dented and black with many summers of use, but whole; and carved ironwood cups, bowls and spoons, three of each. A bundle of softwood, gathered from the slopes of Observatory's mountain and then dried and cut into lengths for the cookfire, filled the room with a summery fragrance. Yellow-white bedfurs had been neatly rolled and tied. And, at the end of the table, a tiny *caeru*-leather pouch, set aside especially for this journey.

Morys pointed to the pouch. Theo picked it up and poured its contents into his hand.

"We've been saving that," Morys said proudly, as if it had come from his own cupboards. "Not much metal at Observatory, but this should be enough for supplies to get us home."

Mreen reached out her hand, and Theo dropped one of the bits into her palm. It shone, catching the light, and Mreen gasped.

What is this, Cantor Theo? she sent with intensity.

It is only a bit of metal, Mreen, he answered. *It is what I used to be paid, when I was an itinerant Singer. It has been quite some time since I saw any.*

She stared at the metal for long moments. As she looked at the metal, her eyes grew glazed and glassy. Theo frowned and stepped closer.

I see . . . I see so many hands, she sent. *Hands, and then more hands . . .* The light around her dimmed and rippled. Theo touched her shoulder, then knelt beside her. Her small body was tense, her face strained and white. She seemed to be struggling with some idea, some concept, too big for her.

So many hands, and . . . something . . . .

What is it, Mreen? Theo asked. Her hand, holding the bit of metal, trembled now. Gently, he uncurled her fingers and took the metal away. Her eyes focused again, and her color returned, but her little *quiru* was still faded.

What a strange thing, she sent to him. *I do not understand what I saw, Cantor Theo!*

Theo smiled at her, and she leaned against his shoulder. *I do not know, Mreen. I do not see the pictures as you do.*

She stared at him. *But you have been a Singer all your life! Why am I different?*

You will have to ask the Spirit that one, Theo sent, and he chuckled. *I have eight summers, but I have few answers!*

Mreen smiled suddenly, making her dimples flash. *You are so old, Cantor Theo!*

Indeed.

What does it feel like to be so old?

Theo laughed aloud. *Like one of those ironwood trees down the mountain,* he told her. *Tall and broad and hard, and like I can see a long way.*

Then I am like a softwood tree?

A good comparison. You are certainly soft! He tousled her red hair, and she giggled without making a sound.

How many summers do I have, Cantor Theo?

Theo got to his feet and looked down at her. He was almost as tall as Sira herself, and Mreen had to tip her head far back to see into his face.

You are an unusual case, Mreen. You were born just before the summer, so you already have one, but it hardly counts!

And how long until I have two?

Until the Visitor comes.

How long until the Visitor comes?

One more year. Five years between summers, remember?

I remember that! It is easy! Much easier than remembering how to modulate from Aiodu *to* Doryu!

So it is, Mreen, so it is. Theo turned back to Morys and their preparations. When he chanced to look down again, he saw Mreen's eyes fixed upon the little leather pouch, and her curiosity was like a fire burning under a cooking pot, bright and hot.

Cantor Theo, she sent. *Where does the metal come from?*

I do not have the answer to that, either.

"I don't see the point of this," Pol rasped, but he stood back, holding the door, and Sira bowed slightly and stepped in to his apartment. Theo followed behind, with Mreen at his side.

The room was large, dominated by a long, polished table and a number of chairs arranged around it. Pol ran his House differently from any Magister Sira had known. In his rooms, all sorts of work took place. Cupboards lined the walls, and here and there some unfinished task waited, an open ledger book or a stack of arrows needing furring. Otherwise the apartment was austere and bare. In truth, there were very few objects anywhere at Observatory that were anything but functional. Sira thought of the lovely bits of *obis*-carving she had seen in her travels. Perhaps when Theo returned, he might bring just one example, some small bit of art like those from Soren, where the *obis*-carvers lived and worked. Not for herself alone, but for the House members to appreciate.

The three Singers sat at one end of the table, and Pol, still standing, regarded Mreen intently. She looked back at him with a clear and innocent gaze, the air around her faintly but clearly brighter than the rest of the room.

"Don't talk, do you?" Pol said abruptly.

Mreen shook her head slowly. Sira saw Theo put his fingers over his lips to hide a smile. "But you want to see our metal?" Pol went on. "Do you understand what it is?"

Mreen shook her head again.

"When we told her of it, she asked to touch it," Sira said, "to try to understand. In the stables, she held a bit of metal in her hand—"

"Metal generously provided by you for our journey," Theo put in.

Pol waved his hand rather grandly. "Observatory is proud to send one of our Gifted children to Conservatory."

Theo grinned. "Even the Glacier itself can change direction," he murmured.

Pol shot him a hard look. "It will not hurt the Houses of the Continent to be reminded of what we have here," he said. He stuck out his chin as if he faced the Magister of Lamdon himself. "It has been many summers since the Committee has had real news of Observatory."

May I see it now? Mreen sent.

Sira lifted her scarred eyebrow at Pol. "Mreen is ready." she said. Years before, a lifetime of experience before, as it seemed, she had seen this treasured artifact, once and once only. She had been unable to understand its nature. Pol, of course, believed he understood it perfectly. He was fanatic about it, in fact. Sira resisted such unsupported beliefs. Indeed, despite her years at Observatory, she resisted virtually all of their philosophy, but she admitted to a vague hope that Mreen's odd ability might dispel this one mystery.

Pol moved deliberately, in the manner of performing a ritual. He walked to a tall cupboard at the end of the room and opened it. It was empty except for one long, slender, heavily wrapped object, which he bore with much care to the table. He laid it on the polished wood and carefully, layer by layer, put back the folds of soft leather.

Sira became aware of Theo's tension beside her, and realized that he had never seen this. It had perhaps not been laid open to the light since Pol had shown it to her to settle their argument years before.

They had never resolved the argument. Nor were they likely to do so, Sira thought. But she caught her breath again as the smooth, shining surface of the great metal slab was revealed.

Incredible . . . . Theo's sending was almost involuntary. He bent far forward, to touch with one finger the black, glazed piece that lay before them. Its markings were strangely carved into it, shining up from below the surface as if from below some thick, dark, but translucent ice. Its edges were uneven, looking almost torn, but smoothly surfaced, as if they had melted away. *I have never seen anything like it. Surely such a large piece cannot be metal!*

But what else could it be? Sira asked. Theo shook his head. Pol stood over the artifact, triumphant in the silence. *He believes it is evidence, proof of their beliefs,* Sira added. *He says it is the reason they Watch.*

Mreen left her chair, and came closer to the object. She put her hands on the edge of the table, to lift herself up enough to see clearly. She waited for the space of a heartbeat, then reached out one small hand to lay it on the shining surface of the strange thing. She squeezed her eyes shut. Sira closed her own eyes and followed her.

I am here with you, Mreen, she sent reassuringly. *Right here.*

I am fine, Cantrix Sira. I—

Mreen broke off, and Sira felt as if in herself the trembling of Mreen's hand on the metal, the waves of sensation that came through her fingers and into her mind. There was an impression of spinning, and of speed, a feeling so intense that Sira gripped the arms of her own chair to keep from falling. Everything around her—around Mreen—was a deep, empty blackness, with pinpoints of light—stars, perhaps?—in strange and unfamiliar patterns. It was profoundly beautiful, spacious and peaceful until, with a suddenness that snatched Sira's breath from her lungs, terror filled the emptiness, and there was a flood of fear and grief. The speed became a dreadful thing, an overwhelming sensation of falling, of impending impact, as if she had tumbled from the cliff road and were plunging into the chasm below.

It was all Sira could do to stay with Mreen, to keep from closing her own mind, until she felt Theo's hand on her own, and realized that they were together, the three of them. The sensation of falling grew worse, more frightening, and Sira did not know where it would lead.

It was Theo who broke the spell. Sharply, he sent, *That is enough, Mreen. Lift your hand from the metal.* She obeyed. The vision, the impression, faded instantly.

The three Gifted ones stared at one another, and Pol's small, hard eyes watched them until he could bear it no more. He burst out, "What happened?"

Neither Sira nor Mreen could find words for what they had experienced. Theo spoke, haltingly. "It would be difficult to describe. I am not so sensitive as Cantrix Sira, or Mreen, but there was an impression of blackness, and speed . . . and points of light, little flames, or stars. Then a falling, as if from one of these great cliffs around us. And fear. Terrible fear."

Pol gave a short, sharp laugh that grated on Sira's nerves. "The Ship!" he cried.

Sira looked up at him, shaking her head. "I do not know," she said slowly. "Perhaps. But it was not a pleasant thing."

Theo went to stand behind Mreen, who looked up at him with solemn eyes. *Were you afraid, little one?* he asked gently.

She shook her head. *No, Cantor Theo. But someone was. Very afraid. But you do not know who?*

No. The picture is . . . sort of faded. Dim. It was—I think it was too long ago. It is too old. She looked up at the object on the table, and took a quick step backward.

Sira stood. "Thank you, Magister," she said.

Pol bowed, and went to the door behind them. "You can tell them at Conservatory," he said to Theo. "And they can tell Lamdon. Tell them it is still here."

"I will, if you like," Theo answered doubtfully. "But I am not sure even now what it is."

"They know," Pol said with assurance. "They have always known!"

Chapter Three

"It is wicked," Zakri told Berk, as they made their first camp in the Mariks east of Amric, "how good it feels to be out in the open again."

Berk laughed. "Please, Cantor Zakri, make your *quiru* before you indulge in your feelings! It's mightily cold in these mountains today."

Zakri pulled his *filla* from his tunic, but he stole one more moment to look out into the gathering twilight. Nevya's sky darkened swiftly to violet, presaging the purple of the long night. As he watched, a lone star began to beckon in the south. Conservatory's star, the itinerants called it. Iban had pointed it out to him on their first trip together. When Conservatory's star begins to shine, he had said, you'd better have your *filla* in your hand or it'll be too late.

I remember, Zakri called silently after his master's departed spirit. I remember. When he put his *filla* to his lips he played an itinerant's melody, a brief and simple melody Iban would have approved, and the *quiru* sprang up swiftly around them.

Berk chuckled, "That's more like it." Even the *hruss* shifted their feet and gave throaty growls as the circle of light swelled around them. "*Hruss* don't like the dark anymore than I do!"

"Silly beasts," Zakri said, "and they were born to it!" But he tucked away his *filla* and went to pull off their saddles and set out their feed. He patted the shaggy broad heads and tugged their drooping ears, making them whuff and push their heads into his chest, asking for more. He gave each of them one last rub. "Later, you foolish things. I would like my own meal!"

Berk had already put flint to stone, and a little cooking fire crackled invitingly in the center of the *quiru*. Zakri pulled the cooking pot and *keftet* makings from his saddlepack.

"I can do that," Berk said, reaching for the pot. "You're Cantor Zakri now, after all."

Zakri laughed, and pushed back his *caeru* hood. "You see this?" he said. He passed his hand over his head. Only wisps of fine hair met his fingers at the back of his neck. "I am an itinerant once again, shorn hair and all. Singer Zakri!" He began to slice the dried *caeru* meat while Berk melted some snow in the pot to soak it. Zakri added, "In truth, if we go to Soren I had best be simply Singer. It may not be healthy to be a Cantor in that company."

"If you're going to be Singer, you'd better do something about the way you talk," Berk told him.

Zakri protested, "What about the way I talk? I was raised with itinerants!"

"Yes, but you've come to sound just like Cantor Ovan and Cantor Gavn. Like all the Conservatory-trained. Like you'd rather be sending than speaking aloud."

Zakri stirred the *caeru* meat in the pot and found it soft enough. He dropped in the grain and the spicy herbs, again as Iban had taught him. "I did not realize," he began, and then stopped, surprised. "I didn't realize that. I have not . . . I mean, I haven't thought about it."

"That's better," Berk said. "But you'd better practice."

Zakri sat back on his heels to look up through the glow of his *quiru* into the wide starry sky. The ironwood trees groaned as the deep cold settled over them, and the wind sighed through the branches. It was easy to believe himself an itinerant once again. If he had not been so grieved over Iban's death, he could have enjoyed the respite from the pressures of the Cantoris, of caring for the sick, of knowing that each day, no matter his inclination, the work must go on.

The two men ate their *keftet* as experienced travelers, leaving no scrap of meat or grain behind. They brewed and drank tea, then went together out of the *quiru* to relieve themselves before rolling into their bedfurs. Berk banked the little fire, and it glowed softly within the brighter light of the *quiru*. Zakri lay awake watching it for a long time, relishing the freedom of the mountains and the stars.

It seemed only yesterday, yet a lifetime ago, that he had traveled with Iban. Iban had been patient, funny, strict . . . the perfect master for a boy who had had no master for too long. Zakri's two teachers—Sira and Iban—had helped him to discipline and harness his untamed Gift. It was hard to accept that Singer Iban would no longer come riding up to Amric, would no longer tease Zakri the Cantor about Zakri the itinerant Singer. The days of their journeys together seemed shining and perfect now in memory.

Yes, Zakri thought, there was much to be said for the itinerant life, but it had not been his to choose. The Gift had always had him in its grasp, and the Gift would not be denied. Even Iban had known that.

The journey to Soren from Amric took eight days of riding. Berk and Zakri pressed the pace, but the *hruss* needed more and more rest as they labored toward the southeast. Zakri had not ridden in three years, and his thighs and backside ached on the second and third day, but the saddlesoreness disappeared as they rode on. They saw *caeru* grown thin and wary from the long years of winter. They came upon tracks of *tkir*, and were thankful not to see the beast itself. A *ferrel* scream disturbed their sleep once or twice, but otherwise the nights were peaceful. Several wild *hruss* raised their heads from foraging as they passed. Zakri called to them in a low tone, but these beasts were not accustomed to people, and their liquid dark eyes rolled as they made their throaty growls and flicked their ears nervously back and forth. Zakri laughed. *Hruss* raised in stables could hardly bear to be out of the sight of humans. If a Singer did not make his *quiru* big enough, the *hruss* would trample the travelers rather than be left outside the light.

Since Berk had decided they should avoid Ogre Pass, and Bariken as well, they took the most direct possible route south. They saw no other people during the journey. Zakri had never actually been to Soren, but Iban had described all the Houses and the landmarks and roads that led to them. As part of his apprenticeship, Zakri had carefully committed them to memory.

As they rode down into the Southern Timberlands, the air softened and grew warmer. Ironwood suckers, thick and numerous, crisscrossed the open country beneath the snowpack. In places softwood trees still stood in little groves here and there, but they were black and shriveled by the cold. Mists clouded the ground in the early morning hours, and they often broke camp with wisps of fog swirling around the thick legs of the *hruss*.

There was no danger of missing the last turn to Soren. Zakri had never seen such a well-traveled road. The snowpack was trampled and dirty, and *hruss* prints and the marks of *pukuru* runners were everywhere.

"Busy place," was Berk's comment.

Zakri grunted agreement. He was concentrating, keeping his mind open, listening for anything that might give him a clue, or a warning. They rode two more hours before they saw the glow of a *quiru* shining among the hills. Then one last rise, and the House lay before them, a great ancient sprawl of stone and ironwood cupped in a shallow valley.

Soren's walls were weathered to the soft blue-gray of the morning mists. Its unswept courtyard was as trampled and dirty as the road leading down to it, and its circle of light was dimmer, more ragged than any House *quiru* Zakri had ever seen. The chill of presentiment prickled his skin again. He could well believe that Soren's Cantor and Cantrix were already lost.

"Look at that," he said to Berk. "Their nursery gardens must be in terrible shape. I do not—I mean, I don't see how they can grow anything in a *quiru* like that."

Berk muttered, "It looks bad." They rode into the courtyard, and waited for a moment before the steps, but no one came to open the doors. They dismounted and turned to lead their *hruss* to the back of the House. Zakri kept his mind open, listening, but he heard only muddled echoes, half formed and unfocused. It was like peering into cloud, seeing only shapes and shadows. Berk raised questioning eyebrows at him.

He shook his head. "Nothing. Not even their Cantors."

A stableman, feeding grain to several *hruss* in loose boxes, looked up with a frown when they appeared at the stable door. "Not more beasts to feed!" was his greeting. "How does Cho think I can manage that?"

Berk glared at the man with snow-reddened eyes. "Is that your welcome? We have been traveling eight days! Since when does any House on the Continent treat travelers so?"

The stableman, who was about Berk's own age, put his hands on his hips and stared at them both. "This House is full of nothing but travelers," he said. "Problem is, they come, but they don't go. Look at this crowd!" He waved his hand at the stables around them, where *hruss* looked curiously out of every stall, their long ears turning back and forth. In truth, Zakri had never seen so many *hruss* in one place before.

He held the reins of both their beasts in his hand as he stepped up to face the stableman. "Look, Houseman," he said. "This is Berk v'Amric. He's courier for Magister Edrus, and I'm his Singer! You'd better fetch somebody to take him up the stairs, and do it quick."

The man smiled nastily at Zakri. "You think Singers are special here?" he said. "You'll see before long." He gestured to the stalls. "Well, I'm not turning you away, in any case. If you can squeeze your beasts into one of the stalls, you're welcome to. Tack room is over there—" he pointed, "—and kitchens the other direction. Although I hope you're not too hungry. Nothing much but meat on our tables these days."

The stableman went back inside, and they heard him calling for someone. "Better do this the usual way," Berk said. "I'll go up alone."

Zakri nodded. "Yes, Houseman," he said mildly. "I'll no doubt meet you in the kitchens, or the *ubanyor*."

They parted, Berk to go in search of his escort to the upper levels, and Zakri to unsaddle and curry the *hruss*. He debated simply leaving them outside the stables, knowing they wouldn't leave the circle of light. But the state of the *quiru* gave him no confidence. He found a stall with only one beast, and crowded his two in with it. The tack room was also full, crammed to the rafters with bridles and ropes, stacks of bows and furred arrows, empty saddlepacks. Zakri shook his head, looking at the clutter. It must be true. Soren was overflowing with itinerant Singers.

Alone, Zakri wandered in the direction of the kitchens. Soren, by long tradition a House dedicated to *obis*-carvers, was richly adorned with objects, some useful and others only decorative. They lined every wall, and filled every corner. Open shelves were laden with bowls, vases, boxes, and implements. Closed cupboards, Zakri was sure, held even more. He stopped to examine some of the things, impressed by their intricacy, and in some, true beauty. Occasionally the mark of the *obis*-knife, the metal blade wielded with psi, could still be seen on the ironwood. More commonly the psi-carving was so smooth and skilled that the ironwood, which would yield to a bone or stone implement only when used with great strength, seemed to have been smoothed with a miraculous hand, as if it were no harder to shape than the gray clay found in summer above the cliffs of Arren.

What was bizarre about the House was its *quiru*. It was quite warm in places, then utterly frigid in random spots, as if it had gaps, rifts in it. It was like the water of the *ubanyor* or *ubanyix*, improperly heated by some careless junior Cantor, with icy currents left flowing beneath a warm surface. And the House itself appeared untidy, as if its care was as random as the warmth of its *quiru*. Zakri guarded his mind, hiding his surprise, as he walked on to the kitchens. He felt like a *caeru* pup that had stumbled into an *urbear* den, and he meant to watch his step at every moment.

"Well, here's another new face!" The woman who spoke was wrinkled and cross-looking. "And where did they get you from, Houseman?"

Zakri bowed to her, and to the three or four Housewomen laboring at the sinks and the ovens. Their glances were cursory, but he smiled politely at them. "I have—I've come from Amric," he said. "I'm Singer Zakri," he added, and bowed again to the whole group.

The woman snorted. "Another one! Well, you're probably hungry and thirsty. I'm Mura, and these are my kitchens, so you'll not be helping yourself without permission."

Zakri smiled as winningly as he knew how, and bowed again to Mura. "I wouldn't think of it," he murmured sweetly.

"Hmm." Mura's sour expression did not improve. "Sook!" she called.

A young girl hurried forward, wiping her hands on a bit of towel. Her hair, bound back with a strip of soft *caeru* leather, was as black as the stone of the ovens, but glossy as ice. She had great dark eyes that slanted upward at the corners. She nodded to Zakri, and smiled, the first friendly gesture he had received at Soren.

Mura pointed to a long scarred table. "Sook will find you a bite and you can have a sip of wine, since you've just arrived. Sit over there."

Zakri did as he was bid, but he said quickly to Sook, "I'd rather just have tea." The girl turned to the huge fireplace and reached for a large kettle resting on the hob.

Mura snorted again. "What itinerant refuses wine when it's offered?"

Of course, no itinerant Zakri knew would refuse, but he could hardly tell her that. "We—we're not much for wine at Amric," he said. He hoped Amric was so distant that these women knew nothing at all about it. "But you're very generous, Housewoman," he added. "It's good to be sitting down in a nice warm kitchen."

"Just don't sit too long," Mura snapped. "We've work to do." She turned her back to him and took up a great knife carved from ironwood. She was cutting a hunk of cured *caeru* meat into chunks with rapid, sure slices with the knife.

Sook smiled again at Zakri as she brought him nutbread and a small knife, and a bowl of quickly heated *keftet*. She poured the tea into a finely carved teacup, so thin it was almost translucent. She set the kettle near his hand. He watched her work, admiring her long eyes.

"Sook," he mused. "Now that's a name I've never heard."

"It's a traditional name here," she answered as she handed him a spoon. "It was my grandmother's, and her grandmother's, summers past remembering."

"It's lovely." Zakri took a spoonful of the *keftet*. He and Berk had eaten better in their campsites. As the stableman had said, there was too much meat and not enough grain. The bit of fish that flavored it was welcome, though. He had not tasted fish since his days at Arren. He drank two cups of tea, quickly, then stood and carried his dishes to where Sook was scrubbing pots at the sink, her small hands red with water and strong soap.

"I thank you," he said.

She took the dishes from his hands before he could put them down. As she did so, her wet fingers brushed his hands. Before he could catch himself, he flinched away from her touch. The carved teacup slipped between them, and fell toward the floor. It would no doubt have shattered into a dozen pieces. Reflexively, Zakri's psi flicked out, a quick tap of energy that lifted the cup back into Sook's fingers. Her eyes went wide, and she looked from him to the cup, unsure of what had happened. She opened her mouth, but he shook his head slightly, and she closed it again.

He must be more careful. He had not realized how accustomed he had become to the discipline of the Cantoris. When had anyone except his own Houseman last touched him? It must be almost a summer ago.

He smiled at Sook, and she smiled back, but warily. He cursed himself as he left the kitchens to go in search of the *ubanyor*. Surely, he scolded himself, you can manage yourself better than this. One would think he was a wild boy again!

Soren was indeed full of itinerant Singers. When Zakri found the *ubanyor*, its big tub was half-full of them, lounging about in the water, laughing and joking. From the *ubanyix* down the hall, similar laughter sounded in the higher registers. He stripped, dropping his soiled tunic and trousers in a corner, and slipped under the water with a groan of pleasure. At least, with so many Singers about, the water was decently warm. His skin tingled with it, and he ducked under the surface to soak his hair.

A heavy man slid over next to him, making the ironwood of the tub creak as he moved. "You're the courier's Singer, hmm?"

Zakri looked out from under the lather he was rubbing into his scalp. "So I am," he said. "Zakri v'Amric."

The man was dark, and looked to have eight or nine summers. The arm he rested on the edge of the tub was thick and covered in black hair. He pointed vaguely upward with his chin, at the upper levels of the House. "I'd drop the Amric part of that, if I were you. Cho won't like it."

Another man came closer on Zakri's other side. "It's true, Singer. We're all v'Soren, now. All of us." He gestured around the *ubanyor*. "Every man in here is an itinerant."

Zakri leaned back to rinse the soap from his hair. He scrubbed his face with his fingers to give himself time to think.

When he took his hands away, he contrived as innocent a look as he could. "Amric is a long way from Soren," he said.

"So that means you haven't heard?"

"Heard what?"

The second man peered at Zakri. His red hair was faded, and his complexion roughened by sun and weather. His face and body were narrow as a *wezel's*. "You'd best come talk to Cho."

"Cho?" Zakri kept his mind blank and empty, just in case, but he felt no tickle of probing psi. More than likely, these itinerants could not hear his thoughts.

"Cho. He's the one in charge here."

"But what about your Magister?"

The man's eyes became mere slits, and he stood, dripping water on Zakri. "I'll take you to Cho. He'll explain how things are."

The first man put a heavy hand on Zakri's shoulder, and Zakri whirled. Water flew from his hair as he shrank from the touch, and his bare skin scraped against the ironwood of the tub. The man cried out, "By the Spirit, Zakri! I didn't mean to scare you! Listen, all Singers are safe here. It's elsewhere you have to worry."

Zakri drew a deep breath. "Sorry, Singer. I—I've been on the road a while. I'm jumpy."

The heavy man nodded, as if he understood perfectly. "Sure you are. That close to the Glacier . . . *tkir*, even *urbear*, I hear."

Zakri grinned as casually as he could. "*Urbear* come off the Glacier once in a while," he agreed. "It's the *tkir* that scare me."

"Down here we have mostly *carwal*, and they hardly move out of the water." The man patted his belly. "My mate tells me I look just like one!" he laughed.

The red-haired man climbed out of the tub, and gestured to Zakri. "If you're ready," he said as he reached for a towel from a lopsided stack. "We can get in to see Cho before the evening meal."

Zakri followed, and accepted a towel to dry himself.

The dark man lifted a hand in farewell to Zakri. "See you in the great room," he said. "By the way, I'm Shiro, and that's Klas. I was born right here at Soren, so you can come to me if you have questions."

"Good to meet you, Singer Shiro." Zakri bowed shallowly above his towel.

"You can drop the Singer," Klas laughed. "There's so many of us here, it's hard to find somebody who isn't one!"

Zakri dried as quickly as he could. He had to dress in his soiled clothes, with only a change of linen from his pack. He followed Klas down a long corridor and up a staircase. As they went, he listened. There was a great deal of psi about, but none trained as his own had been, at least none that he could detect. Where on the Continent, he wondered, were the Cantor and Cantrix of Soren?

Chapter Four

Zakri shouldered his saddlepack and hurried after Klas. The older man scurried down the corridor like a *wezel* fleeing from hunters. His pale eyes darted back from time to time to make sure Zakri was following. The patchy *quiru* made irregular shadows, and Zakri's shoulders prickled each time he walked through a little pocket of darkness. To leave them unrepaired offended all his instincts. It disturbed him to think that there might be no one in the entire House who could do it. How did the House members live with such a *quiru*?

Only once did he see a bit of intact *quiru* light, evenly bright from stone floor to ironwood ceiling. It was just beneath the main staircase, a narrow hall leading toward the back of the House. He fell behind Klas as he peered into it, trying to discern the origin of the light. Klas already had one foot on the stairs when he saw that Zakri had stopped. He flapped his hand in the direction of the hall.

"Carvery," he said, then hurried on. Zakri had to leap the stairs two at a time to catch up with him.

The banister of the staircase felt strange under his hand. When he looked down at it, his progress slowed yet again. There were banisters on every staircase on the Continent, of course, but this one was beautiful, *obis*-carved into a design of whorls and spirals that seemed almost to move, to writhe under his fingers. Its pattern drew his hand upward as if the carver's Gift still haunted the ironwood. When he reached the top, his fingers lifted from it with reluctance. His guide appeared not to notice, neither the beauty of that piece nor of any of the others that met their eyes at every turn.

Klas scuttled on to the very end of the upper hallway. More laden shelves and cupboards lined the walls, but Zakri had to pass them with no more than a brief glance. Klas was already bobbing his head to several men squatting over a game of stone-and-bone. A woman leaned in bored fashion near a door, watching the throw of the game pieces. All of them, the men and the woman, wore the leather tunics and cropped hair of itinerants. They looked Zakri up and down in a moment of idle curiosity, then turned back to their game.

"So who's winning?" Zakri asked. No one answered.

Klas pointed at Zakri with his red-stubbled chin, and said, "We need to see Cho. This one just came today."

The woman straightened to push open the door. "Take him in, then," she said. She eyed Zakri briefly as he passed, then turned away. He was only one more Singer in a House full of Singers, hardly worth her interest.

Zakri had been in more than one Magisterial apartment, and the room he and Klas entered was exactly that. It was spacious, with elegant and generously proportioned furnishings, everything gracefully carved in what he already thought of as Soren fashion. A long table dominated the room, with chairs drawn up to it in formal ranks.

But there was no Magister here. The thin dark man pacing past the window wore the dark tunic of the upper levels, but it was an affectation. It did not suit him. A man and a woman, also dressed in somber colors, sat at the table. The woman had a large account book before her, her arms curled around it as if to protect her responsibility. The man held a *ferrel*-quill pen in his hand, poised above a sheet of Clare's paper. They watched the man pace with hooded eyes and drawn faces. When the dark man whirled to see who had entered, both of them stiffened.

Berk glowered from one end of the table. He had not yet bathed. His gray hair was coming out of its binding, his beard was matted, and he scowled indiscriminately at everyone in the room.

Klas cleared his throat. "Cho, here's an itinerant who just rode in today. Thought you'd want to meet him . . . ." His voice trailed away as the man's eyes, long, dark eyes like those of the girl Sook, fixed upon him. Klas stiffened like the others, and Zakri heard the click of his throat as he tried to swallow.

When Cho's eyes shifted to Zakri they narrowed. Instinctively, Zakri shielded his mind, and not a moment too soon.

At first it was only an intrusion, much like being prodded with a rude finger. But when the finger met resistance, the psi became a knife that thrust and sliced at Zakri's mind without regard for any harm it might do. It was clumsy, and it was obvious, but it was also powerful, and very, very dangerous. Zakri struggled to keep his face innocent as he closed his mind against it.

Cho's eyes flickered. Zakri tried to disguise his shields behind a cloud of muffled thoughts like those he heard around him. The effort sent perspiration trickling down his ribs under his tunic. He made his eyes round, and he produced a foolish smile as he bowed.

"Are you the one I thank for the nice hot bath?" he asked.

The flicker left Cho's eyes, leaving them the flat black of charred ironwood. "No," he said. "I have better things to do than warm the *ubanyor*. Who are you?" His voice was light, the pitch rather high, without resonance or inflection.

Klas put his hand on Zakri's shoulder, and Zakri held himself still, suppressing his discomfort at the touch.

"This is Zakri," Klas said.

"My itinerant," Berk growled. His eyes met Zakri's briefly, and then turned back to Cho. "We'll be on our way first light tomorrow," he said.

Cho leaned against the window casing. He tipped his head tipped back to look down his thin, hooked nose. He wore an *obis* knife strapped around his waist in a finely tooled scabbard. His black hair was long, braided into a plait that hung over his shoulder almost to his waist. He drew it through his fingers, again and again, as he regarded the newcomers. "And what if your—" he emphasized the possessive, a slight smile curling his lips. "If your itinerant would rather not?"

"It's hardly his choice, is it?" Berk snapped. "My Magister hired him. He's been paid."

Zakri tried to look as guileless as possible. "That's right," he said brightly. "Magister Edrus keeps me very busy at Amric, actually. If it's not travelers, it's hunting parties. I never have to go looking for work."

Cho straightened, and tossed the braid back over his shoulder. "Well, it's time their precious Cantors and Cantrixes did some of that work! Real work. Let them get their own hands dirty." He strolled to the chair at the center of the table and sat, leaning to one side with his arm draped lazily over the high carved back. "Young Zakri is welcome to join us here," he said to the room at large. "We'll have plenty of work for him, if work is what he wants."

Berk sat back heavily against his own chair, and glared at Cho.

"Um, well," Zakri stammered. "Um—Houseman Cho—Singer Cho?"

"Not Singer," Cho said, very quietly. "Carver." He took his arm from the chair back and leaned forward, angling his body menacingly across the table at Berk. "I wasn't good enough for Conservatory, you see," he went on. "My Gift was only good enough for the carvery!" Louder, he added, "And good enough to gather every itinerant on the Continent into my service!"

Berk still stared, his arms folded. Zakri cleared his throat.

"Well, then, Carver . . . Cho. You see, I really need to get Houseman Berk, here, back to Amric. How else will he go? And my family, you know . . . they'll be expecting me." He shrugged, and shuffled his feet like a boy of three summers.

"Ah." Cho's black eyes measured Zakri, up and down. Klas, standing beside him, drew a sharp breath and took a sudden step back, as if trying to get out of the way. Again, and without warning, Zakri felt the bludgeon of Cho's psi, the crude attack against his shields. He had never felt a mind like it. There was an animal essence about it, a brute aggressive force like that of a hunting beast. Even in the early days, when his own psi had been out of control, Zakri felt certain it had never been so ugly, so—vulgar, was the word that came to his mind. At another time, he could have laughed at himself, the upstart itinerant who had become Cantor! Was he now as refined as any Conservatory-trained Singer? But Cho was trying to force him to reveal who and what he was, and such an invasion of uncontrolled psi could be lethal. Turning it aside took all his attention.

Thank the Spirit, Sira's instruction had been thorough. Zakri thickened the fog in the forepart of his mind, and hid behind it. It was difficult. The trickle of perspiration became a flood, but he held his silly grin in place, and endured. Behind him he heard Klas groan slightly, and he knew the itinerant felt the effects of Cho's psi. He remembered well the nauseating sensation inadequate shielding could cause, and he marveled at the strength of Cho's mind.

Then, suddenly, it seemed that his disguised shields had done their job. Cho lost interest all at once. He glanced around the room at the others, then back at Zakri. "If you know what's good for you," Cho said lazily, his lip-curling smile returning. "You'll stay right here. This is where it's going to happen."

"Um . . . what would that be, that's going to happen?"

"Never mind!" Berk ordered. He stood suddenly, towering over everyone in the room. The two at the table, the unGifted ones, had watched everything in tense silence, and Zakri was sharply aware, through his shields, of their fear. Berk stamped to the door and pulled it open. "Let's go, Singer," he said.

Zakri turned obediently to the doorway. The heavy door, as if it had taken on life of its own, flew abruptly from Berk's hand and slammed into its frame with a bang that echoed in the high-ceilinged room. Zakri whirled to look at Cho.

Cho still held his negligent pose, but his effort had brought beads of sweat to his forehead. "That's a taste, Houseman," he sneered. "No one leaves until I permit it."

Berk said deliberately, "Would that be the room, or the House?"

Cho said, "Both," and laughed.

Zakri said innocently to Berk, "Houseman, I don't understand. What's happening here?"

Berk lifted his hand, palm up, toward Cho. It was an elegant, very upper-level gesture. "Perhaps, Carver, you'd like to explain to Zakri," he said. "And while you're at it, you can tell him what's going to happen when Lamdon gets word of all this!" This time he succeeded in making his exit. Klas stood pale and sweating by the door, looking longingly at it as it closed behind Berk.

Zakri turned slowly to face Cho once more. The cold knot of anger under his breastbone had drawn painfully tight. His Gift raged within him, and he concentrated on his control as he never had before. His back felt as stiff and unyielding as Glacier ice.

"You won't be leaving here just now," Cho said. His tone was casual. "If I let you go, it spoils the effect."

"Effect?"

Cho's lips lifted, just the outer corners. The Housewoman at the table began, "Cho . . ." but he silenced her with a hand.

"All the itinerants have banded together," he said, "right here at Soren. This is a new day for Nevya, a new day for Singers. We have more of the Gift under this roof than any House on the Continent—even Conservatory!"

Zakri looked about him, keeping his eyes wide and his expression naive. He could not resist. "Then why is the *quiru* such a mess?" he asked.

The Housewoman's eyes slid up to his face, then away. The Houseman sat with his shoulders rigid, his gaze locked on the paper before him. There was a small thump behind Zakri as Klas stepped right against the wall, as far away as he could get.

Cho stood and leaned forward, fists on the table, eyes black and cold. "Do you see anyone freezing?" he hissed. "Anyone suffering? There is more than one way, more than Conservatory's way, to keep a House warm! We'll teach it to you." He waved a hand at the door. "Now go. Klas will find you a room. Might as well be comfortable. You'll be here a while."

"But . . ." Zakri began.

The blow of psi came again, but Zakri was prepared this time. He turned it away with a parry of his own, a reactive feint of energy. He stopped short of actually striking at the other man's mind, but just the same Cho frowned, sensing the resistance. Zakri smiled and shrugged, as if it was little matter to him if he stayed or not, and as if he had not felt Cho's psi at all.

Cho raised his long arm and pointed at the door. Klas hastened to throw it open and make his escape.

Zakri followed, but he looked back over his shoulder to see Cho snatch the account book from the Housewoman's hands with unnecessary roughness. The Houseman slumped over his piece of paper, his pen idle in his hand.

Zakri reached back with his psi and tugged at the chair behind Cho just as the carver was about to resume his seat. The heavy chair crashed satisfyingly against the floor, and a spate of curses rang out as Zakri closed the door. The players squatting in the corridor raised their heads at the noise. Zakri grinned cheerfully down at them. "Did you hear something?" he asked brightly. They looked from his foolish grin to the closed door, but they kept a prudent silence.

By the time Zakri reached the staircase, though, the pleasure of his small prank faded. As he followed Klas downstairs he had to repress a shower of sparks that bloomed about him like little rebellious flowers.

Klas showed him to a room already crowded with three other itinerants and their possessions. Before he left, Klas asked, "Didn't you feel that, feel Cho's psi? It just about knocked me over, and it wasn't even me he was after!"

Zakri turned away the question with one of his own. "Why would you want to work for a man like that? What is . . . what's the point?"

Klas shrugged, and his pale eyes shifted from side to side. "It's because we're tired of being used, of having nothing. Why should the Cantors and Cantrixes have all the privileges? We're Gifted, too!"

Zakri stared at him, wanting to argue, to dispute such idiocy. He sensed the other's resentment, but it seemed compounded as much of fear and confusion as real indignation. He reflected that any discussion with such a person would be pointless, and would only arouse suspicion. He answered Klas's shrug with one of his own, and another boyish grin, and carried his pack into the overcrowded room.

Cho sat in the Magister's seat at the evening meal, at the center of the great room, with several itinerant Singers about him. The Singers were noisy, talking and laughing, all but one. That one sat limply in his carved chair, his head lolling against the shoulder of the woman next to him. His mouth was slack, his hands useless on the table. A woman spooned *keftet* into his mouth. Most of it fell back out, and patiently she scooped it up and tried again, over and over. Zakri remembered Clive's horror as he described this man, the drooling mindless man that was Cho's example. Clive had not exaggerated. The man's empty eyes made Zakri's skin crawl.

Cho leaned against the arm of his chair, toying with his braid, looking about the room and eating little. Several upper-level House members, in their dark tunics, sat at a corner table. The working Housemen and women clustered near them, avoiding the tables dominated by Singers. Zakri would rather have sat with the Housemen, but he was squeezed between Klas's wiry frame and Shiro's large one. Berk was at the corner table.

Berk raised his brows, but Zakri shook his head. Tomorrow he would find a safer time. Tonight, he dared not open his mind to listen to others' thoughts. Cho's psi was too dangerous, and it was possible that there might be others willing, and able, to misuse the Gift as he did.

Shiro elbowed Zakri and pointed with his spoon to a quiet group near the windows, perhaps eight men and women. They looked somber, even grim, but with none of the sinister intensity of Cho. "Those are the other carvers," he said, through a mouthful of *keftet*. "They keep to themselves, even now."

Zakri said, "I would—I'd sure like to see the carvery."

Shiro made a grandiose gesture. "I could show you—after the morning meal. Been there a hundred times." He dug his spoon into his bowl again, shaking his head. "Right now it's the warmest place in the House."

"Better watch what you say," Klas muttered. "He hears more every day."

Shiro scraped the spoon against the bowl, gathering every bit of grain that was left. "Ship! I didn't say anything everybody doesn't already know," he complained.

"Just warning our young friend here," Klas said.

Zakri finished his *keftet* and pushed his bowl away. It was Sook who saw, and came to his table to take it from him.

"More *keftet*, Singer?" she asked.

He shook his head, and she smiled down at him as she picked up the bowl. Shiro asked loudly, "No bread tonight, Housewoman?"

"Not tonight," she answered, and turned to leave.

Shiro shocked Zakri by reaching out to pinch the girl's arm between a meaty thumb and forefinger. She snatched her arm away with a little gasp. Zakri was sure the pinch had hurt.

"Are you sure, little Sook? Just a bite of bread for one of the Gifted?"

Her face flushed, and she rubbed at her arm with her free hand. With asperity she said, "No bread for the Gifted or the unGifted!" As she spoke she moved back, putting distance between herself and Shiro. The Singers at the next table noticed the exchange, and one of them reached over and tweaked her tunic, just above her slender hips.

"So, why not, little Housewoman?" that one cried, and laughed when she jumped.

"You explain it, why don't you?" she snapped. "The grain hardly grows anymore!"

"Ship and stars, she's a nice little piece!" Shiro said, and he reached for her arm again.

Zakri took a deep breath to control his seething temper, but somehow one small fibril of psi escaped him. It nipped out, just one lash of energy that collided with Shiro's teacup and flipped it, spilling steaming tea into his lap. Shiro cried out in pain and leaped to his feet to hold his hot trousers away from his skin. The Singers hooted with joy at this new target, pointing and calling out insults. Sook seized her opportunity and fled the great room.

Zakri dared not speak. He thrust back his chair and stalked away from the table, struggling to manage the energy that welled from him like a fountain, cold and hot at the same time. Berk followed, and caught up with him in the corridor beyond the kitchens.

Zakri relaxed somewhat when they were alone, but the air around him glimmered.

"They may not let us go, in truth," Berk told him quietly. They walked with a casual manner toward the stables, as if going to check on their *hruss*, but they kept a sharp eye.

"When we are ready, we will go," Zakri answered through tight lips. "But I want to know exactly what is happening here first. Will you be safe, Berk?"

"I'm more worried about you," Berk said. "No one's saying much, but the Gift has been used in some terrible ways in this House. And to top it all off, there is a Gifted child, ready and wishing to go to Conservatory. Cho has refused to allow it."

"But that is outrageous! How can he stop it?"

Berk's face was bleak. Zakri was sure the big man was no less angry than he. "Everyone in this House is terrified of Cho. Did you see the man in the great room, at the center table?"

"I did."

"It's revolting."

"He has already tried his psi on me," Zakri said. "But I can handle it."

"Are you sure?"

Zakri rubbed his hand over the soft wisps of his brown hair. His shoulders prickled again, and he took a deep breath and released. "I will be all right, Berk. Let us pretend that we are resigned to staying for a time. But it will be a short time!"

"Be on your guard at every moment, Cantor Zakri."

"I will, Berk. By the Spirit, I will!"

Chapter Five

Zakri, having been for some time used to sleeping alone, spent a poor night listening to the chatter and then the snores of the three itinerant Singers whose room he had to share. He gave up trying to sleep eventually, and left his bed long before the morning meal to wander the corridors of Soren, feeling the sting of the cold floor even through his fur boots. After a time, the sounds and smells of cooking drew him to the kitchens. At Amric, his Houseman brought tea to Cantor Zakri before he was even awake. No such luxury for an itinerant, and most certainly not at Soren! Cautiously, he put his head around the kitchen door, wary of Mura's sharp tongue.

Mura was frowning over a younger Housewoman as she stirred the *caeru* stew that bubbled on the huge stove. Sook, her cheeks pink with the heat of the cookfire, was slicing loaves of hot nutbread at the table, stopping occasionally to blow on her fingertips. The scarlet of her tunic made her the brightest spot in the room, and Zakri smiled to see her. Behind her, the big kettle steamed gently on the hob. It was a shame, he thought, that those who dwelled in the upper levels of the House—any House-should so rarely come upon this charming scene.

He waited to call to Sook until Mura had turned away to one of the grain barrels in a corner, and even then he kept his voice low.

"Sook! Good morning to you. What's the chance of some tea?"

She looked up and smiled, then put her finger to her lips. "Sshh! Mura will scold you!" She glanced at Mura's back, and then sidelong back at Zakri, her dark eyes gleaming in the firelight. "Wait there," she murmured.

Zakri hastily withdrew, and lounged against the wall by the kitchen door. Only a few moments passed before Sook slipped out with one of the beautifully carved teacups in her hand, and a little slice of fragrant nutbread on a scrap of cloth.

"You're an early riser, Zakri," she said. She held out her offering. Tendrils of black hair clung to her damp cheeks, and she brushed them back after he took the teacup from her hand.

"So I am," he agreed. "I thank you for the tea, Sook. It is—it's always good to have a friend among the cooks!"

She laughed, and opened her mouth to speak, but a cry from the kitchen forestalled her. Quickly, she pulled the door open and looked back inside. "Oh, no—Eun has burned herself!"

Zakri followed her back into the kitchen. Eun, a woman of perhaps eight or nine summers, stood over the sink, closing her eyes tightly, grimacing with pain. The burn had left a broad stripe against her palm, already blistering, and Zakri knew it must be viciously painful.

Mura poured cool water over the burn, her hands gentle and careful, all the while cursing steadily under her breath. Zakri forgot everything but the injury, stepping up beside the burned woman and leaning over her to see clearly.

"This cannot wait until Cantoris hours," he said with authority. Mura and Sook both looked at him strangely. Suddenly remembering, he shook his head. "What I mean is, she won't be able to stand the pain," he amended. "Someone should call your Cantor or Cantrix now."

The women glanced at each other, then back at him without responding. He knew without their saying it there would be no Cantor to treat this burn. Eun sobbed, "It's not fair."

There was risk in this, but the healer in Zakri could not turn away. He handed his teacup and nutbread back to Sook, and reached into his tunic for his *filla*.

"Well, now, Housewoman," he said lightly. "Just between us, don't you think itinerants are the best healers anyway?"

Mura snapped, "So Cho would say! In any case, it's all we have, and in abundance."

"Oh, do be cautious, Mura!" cried Eun, fearful even in her distress.

Sook cast Zakri a grateful glance, and led Eun to a chair. The woman leaned back against it, holding out her burned palm as if it might hurt less if it were further away. Zakri knelt beside her, and played a quick fragment of melody in *Doryu*, soothing the heat of the burn, easing the pressure beneath it that made the skin blister. The palm was a sensitive place, he well knew. It was the seat of feeling and the root of touch. Iban had taught him that.

He modulated to *Iridu* to help Eun relax, something else Iban had taught him. He did not hurry, but played for several minutes while the other Housewomen stood by, listening. Sook kept a sympathetic hand on Eun's shoulder, but her eyes never left Zakri's face. Mura leaned against the ironwood table, creasing her apron with her fingers. She, too, watched Zakri closely, her wrinkles deepening and her eyes bright and quick as a *ferrel's*.

When Zakri stopped playing and laid his *filla* down, Mura handed him a clean strip of felted cloth for a bandage. He wrapped it around the burned hand, securing it with a bit of quill Mura fetched from a drawer. Eun opened her eyes then, but their lids drooped, and she yawned. "She should rest now," Zakri said. "She will sleep for a little. That would be good."

"I'll take her to her apartment," Sook offered. Zakri nodded agreement. Mura still observed him with fierce attention.

Another of the Housewomen came to help. "Take her arm, Nori," Sook said. Together, careful of the bandaged hand, they lifted Eun to her feet, and supported her between them. Slowly, they made their way out of the kitchen.

Mura eyed Zakri in speculative silence. He could only give her his best grin and a helpless gesture with his two hands. "Better put me to work, Housewoman!" he said. "I am—I'm more used to the stables, but I'm willing."

"I wonder about that, Singer," she said.

"About what?" he asked. He got to his feet, picking up his *filla* to tuck it away in his tunic, and sipped at the tea that had grown cold as he worked.

"I wonder about you and the stables," Mura said flatly.

He looked up and met her eyes, and his smile faded. Mura's was an intelligent face, a face made hard by experience, and by suffering. He had no wish to lie to her. "It is true about the stables," he said, "I assure you of that. I have worked many hours with *hruss*."

"Not many itinerants play the way you do, though I grant you they're sometimes fine healers. Who taught you?"

"The Singer Iban taught me, for one," Zakri ventured.

Mura caught her breath and bit her lip. She looked about to speak, but then turned quickly away as if to stop herself. She hesitated, her back to Zakri. Then abruptly she pointed at the loaves of nutbread on the table. "If you want to help, you can get started on those," she muttered. She did not turn back again.

It felt strange to Zakri to be loitering about with nothing to do at midday. He helped Sook and Mura in the kitchen, and then he bathed, but still he felt restless and idle as the traditional hour for the *quirunha* approached. Curious, he wandered toward the Cantoris.

The doors to the Cantoris stood open, but the room was empty. One or two people in bright tunics passed Zakri as they came to and from the great room. They looked at him without curiosity. Only the Housemen and women seemed to have much to do. He peeked in past the double doors of the great room, and saw that the tables were being laid for the mid-day meal, just as in any other House on the Continent.

An itinerant Singer wandered down the corridor and went into the Cantoris alone, his *filla* in his hand. Another Singer, a stocky woman in leather trousers, took up a position just outside the great room. A third, a man not much older than himself, went to stand in the great room among the tables. A Houseman working there quickly disappeared, glancing at Zakri as he hurried away toward the kitchens.

Each of the Singers began to play his own *filla* in the mode and the melody of his choice, as if to call up the small *quiru* of traveling parties. They made no effort to coordinate the music. They played at will, each in his own fashion. Zakri watched and listened in amazement.

From the corridors, from the *ubanyor* and *ubanyix*, from the staircase, from the upper levels, he heard the jangling discord of a dozen *filla*. Circles of light and warmth grew, touched, and blended together where they overlapped. The colors were oddly disparate, and the shapes of the *quiru* were strange, some circular and wide, others tall and slender. Some were ragged, like those made by apprentices still learning the craft. The result of these efforts was a patchwork of varied light throughout the House. It reminded Zakri of a snowfield dappled with shadow.

He had never seen a more infuriating and wasteful exercise. Berk came out of the *ubanyor*, and they stood together in the corridor watching the bits of *quiru* bloom. Berk was openmouthed with surprise. Zakri was fuming.

He thought his anger would burst from his chest in a scalding fountain. The Gift was poured out in this place as if it were no more than the contents of a chamber pot dumped into the waste drop! Where were Soren's Cantor and Cantrix? Who would accept this excuse for a *quirunha* if it was not necessary?

A thought came to him suddenly, and he tried to check his anger. This was the moment to listen, surely. Every Singer in the House was occupied, trying to cobble together a House *quiru*. Could Cho detect one mind open and vulnerable among so many? Zakri hoped not.

He signaled to Berk, a lift of his hand and quirk of his eyebrow, then moved to a chair in the hallway. He sat in it, vaguely aware of the intricacy of its carved arms and back, no doubt the life's work of some long-gone carver. He leaned back against it, and closed his eyes while Berk stood nearby, keeping watch.

The mental noise was almost unbearable as Zakri opened his mind. He relaxed his shields gradually, bit by bit. With each barrier that he lowered, more of the clamor poured in. Not since his early days, before Sira had taught him the skill of effective shielding, had he allowed such invasion. He was no longer accustomed to it. He gripped the arms of the chair as he opened himself further. His stomach turned as he reeled under a flood tide of thoughts and feelings and fears.

For several moments he simply let it all wash over him. It did not get easier to bear, but he began to be able to distinguish some of what he heard. The Gifted minds of the Singers, although unfocused, were like eddies in the torrent, set apart from the unGifted minds. There were others, which Zakri guessed must be the carvers, whose Gifts were different, yet clearly delineated from the unGifted. There was one dark, strong force, some distance away. It had a shape, looming, fearsome. There was a space of silence around it, a chasm of fear between it and all the others. Zakri knew it to be Cho. He skirted it carefully as he searched through the flood.

Then, at last, he found what he was seeking. He heard her through the noise, through the distraction. She was far from him, he guessed at the very top of the House, and her mind was dim with fatigue and despair, but she was alive.

Cantrix Elnor? Zakri sent very carefully. *Can you hear me?*

He sensed her sudden attention, and the intensity of her fear.

She answered after a cautious interval. *I can hear you. Who are you?*

It is safer for both of us if I do not tell you that, Zakri answered, trying to send clearly without being detected.

Where are you?

I am here, he responded simply. *In the House.*

Can you help me? Can you get help?

I am going to try. I wanted to know if you were here, if you were safe.

Cantrix Elnor's thoughts came again, very clearly. *I am here, but not safe. My senior is dead. Killed.*

The horror of her flat statement made Zakri's throat close, but there was no time for sympathy. *Do you know where your Magister is? And his family?*

They went to Lamdon, but never returned. I can only hope that they reached it.

Zakri felt Berk move closer, warning him. He sent hastily, *I will send to you again soon. Be patient. Be careful.*

And you. Be watchful at every moment. They hate all who come from Conservatory.

Zakri had not come from Conservatory, of course, but it was far too complicated to explain to her now. He doubted Cho and the itinerants would appreciate the difference in any case. He broke the contact with Cantrix Elnor, and threw up his shields with immense relief.

When he opened his eyes, Berk was standing as close to him as he could without actually touching him. The Singers had ceased playing, and the odd, fragmented *quiru*, warm and bright in spots, shady and cold in others, was as complete as it was going to get. Zakri rose, shaky with nerves and still feeling a faint nausea. He watched the Singers put away their instruments and amble by twos and threes into the great room for the mid-day meal. He was too tired at the moment to be angry, but Berk was not.

"Preposterous," he growled. "Cho has filled the House with fools!"

"Better keep that thought to yourself," Zakri whispered. "Come on, let us go to the stables, and I will tell you what I heard."

Before they got far, however, Sook came running after them. "Zakri," she said, almost but not quite bowing. "Mura asks if you would come to the carvery for a moment."

Zakri met Berk's eyes, and hesitated. Sook said softly, "It's all right. It's safe there." Her dark eyes flashed about her, from one side to the other, making certain no one else had heard.

The two men turned to follow her. House members and Singers streamed past them into the great room. Sook fell in behind the crowd. When no one was watching, she turned right, down the corridor beneath the staircase, instead of left to the great room.

It was pleasant to walk into the even brightness and warmth of the carvery. The fragrance of newly cut ironwood wafted from the open door, a clean, pungent odor. Zakri sniffed appreciatively at this new scent. Only a psi-Gifted *obis* carver, equipped with an *obis* knife, could actually cut into and through the rock-hard wood of the ancient trees. Even the suckers by which the great trees propagated, and which stretched in tangled patterns all over the Continent, were as hard as the knives themselves.

The *obis* knives were what Zakri saw first when he entered the carvery. They hung in gleaming rows within easy reach of the carvers, meticulously clean, shining with rendered and purified *caeru* oil. They were dark and mysterious, sharp, flexible, virtually unbreakable. Their ironwood handles were almost as black as the precious metal of the knives.

Eight carvers sat idle at their workbenches as Sook led Zakri and Berk into the carvery. Half-finished pieces rested before each, but no one was working now. Mura stood with her hand on the shoulder of a young man who looked very like her. He was strongly built, with long black hair bound neatly behind his head. One of the other carvers got up to close the door.

"Zakri," Mura said. "This is my son, Yul. The carvers have something to say to you."

Zakri bowed slightly. He felt Berk's wary presence behind him. It was like having a big boulder at his back, solid and immovable. Zakri was glad he was there.

Yul bowed to them, and gestured to the group around him. "We want to know if my mother is right. She has guessed you're not interested in joining Cho, and we've been hoping, expecting someone, from somewhere, to come. We're taking a terrible risk in asking, but Sook thinks you can be trusted. Is that true?"

Berk gave a low rumble in his throat, a warning sound. Zakri heard him, and flicked him a look of assent. He opened his mind again, briefly, to scan the room.

It was interesting, touching these minds. Zakri had begun his life with itinerants, and then had spent his youth in seclusion, his own Gift dangerously out of control. Very late, when he already had almost four summers, he had been taught to hear and send safely by Cantrix Sira, and since then he had listened to the highly disciplined thoughts of the Conservatory-trained on a daily basis. But these Gifted men and women, the *obis*-carvers, were different. They were not able to send and listen, as Cantors and Cantrixes were. Their minds were clear and practical, disciplined in another way. Their application of the Gift, the intensity with which they had to focus their psi to carve the unforgiving ironwood, gave their minds a sharpness, a definition, that had great appeal to Zakri. And at this moment, more to the point, he sensed no deception or sinister intent. He doubted they would have been capable of hiding any.

He nodded now to Yul. "I was an itinerant," he said, including all the carvers in his glance. "But I do other work now, for Amric." He sensed Berk's approval, his relief that he did not reveal everything. He intended to use absolute caution in this House, lest some questing mind guess his true status. But he felt confidence here. He liked these artisans.

Sook smiled brilliantly at Zakri. He supposed it to be hope that made her dark eyes glow. Mura gave a sharp little sound of satisfaction, but she had another question. "Him?" she asked shortly, pointing a work-hardened finger at Berk.

Berk chuckled. "I'm a courier for Amric, Housewoman," he said. "I have been so for seven summers. I've grown these gray hairs in the service of my House and my Magister. I would hardly change my course this far along."

"That's good enough for me," she said.

"Well, then, Houseman," said Yul slowly, "and Singer," inclining his head to Zakri. "You've seen how it is here, I think."

"We have," Berk said.

"We've had no choice in these matters. Our Magister and his family went off to consult with Lamdon when it first began, and they never returned." Yul's eyes glittered in the bright light of the carvery as he looked back and forth between them. "But their itinerants did," he said in a flat voice. "Their Singers came back only four days after they left the House."

The carvers watched in painful silence as horror crept over Zakri's and Berk's faces. Four days. Lamdon was at least eight days' ride from Soren, more probably ten or twelve, with a large traveling party. There was no hope for Soren's Magister.

"There were children?" he whispered.

Yul's eyes were bleak as he answered. "Two little ones," he said. "The Magister's mate was afraid to leave them behind."

"Has no one tried to resist?" Berk asked, his voice a mere scrape in the deepest register. Zakri knew how this story would affect the courier. Berk loved his grandchildren with a fierceness that was sometimes comical; at this moment it was tragic.

Another carver stood and spoke. "Yes," he said bitterly. "This is—was—a fine House, a brave House. But everyone who confronted Cho either died or ended up like that Singer at the center table in the great room, mindless, helpless. Even our senior Cantor is dead, although everyone pretends it was just age, or sickness. The itinerants stand between Cho and the rest of the House, and even those Singers who would rather be free are afraid to oppose him. His reach is long, and his power is growing."

Sook put in nervously, "We'd better get to the meal, or someone will get suspicious."

Mura moved quickly to the door. "We'll talk again. We just wanted you to know." She slipped out into the corridor.

Berk followed, with Sook behind him. Zakri looked around at the carvers once more, recording their faces in his memory. It would be good to know their allies in this business.

He wished Sira were with him. Her strength and courage would be an enormous asset to them all. He and Berk could hardly save the situation alone. Yul, and Mura, and Sook—they would all be helpful. But they were dealing with a Gift gone bad, its genius perverted. Anyone who opposed it would put himself in the greatest danger.

Well, with the help of the Spirit, Zakri thought, I will try to imagine what Sira would have done . . . and then do it. But I wish she were here!

Chapter Six

Mreen had been driving her parents wild, going again and again to Observatory's thick windows during the endless days of white weather, pressing her face to the glass, trying to see through the snow that fell so thickly the sky was indistinguishable from the ground. White weather preceded the change of seasons. When it was over, milder temperatures settled over the Continent. Half a year would pass before the Visitor rolled up over the eastern horizon, adding its feeble warmth to the sun's to bring the summer, but by that time, Mreen would already have begun her new life as a first-level student at Conservatory.

The white weather passed in its time, and the long-awaited day of Mreen's journey was at hand. The night before the departure, Theo and Sira walked in the nursery gardens. They breathed the steamy rich air and felt the fronds of growing things brushing at their cheeks and hands. Other House members strolled past, leaving the Cantor and Cantrix alone. Sira sometimes stroked a leaf or a bud, using her right hand, the one without calluses, to feel the textures on her fingertips.

I have had the same dream three times, she sent.

Tell me.

All dreams were significant, and they respected them. But any that came more than once were a call from the Gift, and received special attention.

It is odd, she sent. *In the dream, I see a tiny* quiru. *It is small, but very bright, and all by itself out in the open, as if on the Glacier, or . . . I do not know where, really, but alone. And there is a* tkir—*I think it is a* tkir—*approaching the* quiru, *and not afraid of it as they are supposed to be. There is no fire, no people . . . just the glow of the* quiru *shining above the snow. The* tkir *circles the light, around and around, and somehow I know it wants to put out the light, to jump on it, to smother it. The beast, whatever it is, makes a terrible sound, like growling, but not a natural noise, and it tenses, ready to spring. I am too far away, and I cannot do anything, but it seems important that the* quiru *hold. Then, just before the beast actually leaps, I waken.*

And what do you think it means?

She traced her scarred eyebrow with her forefinger. *It seems a warning.* The angles of her face were sharply drawn, her eyes fierce with concentration. *Be on your guard, Theo. Beware of everything, and especially . . . .*

I know, he sent back. *Especially Mreen.*

She touched his shoulder with her palm, briefly. For them, it was an intimate gesture. *Especially Mreen,* she agreed. *The little* quiru—*the light—it could be Mreen. But why should she be in any danger?*

I wish you could come with us, Theo sent.

Sira had not traveled outside the walls of the House for three years, yet her hair was cropped as short as any itinerant's, shorter even than Theo's was now. He had always seen it as a symbol of her restlessness, her feeling of never truly belonging.

It is too soon, she answered him. *Trisa is far too young to manage the Cantoris alone.*

I know. Theo was less shy of physical contact than she. He reached for her hand and caught it between his. *I will be on my guard. I promise you.*

She returned the pressure of his hand for a moment before pulling her own away. Theo gave her the lopsided smile that made merry creases around his eyes. It was an expression she loved, and she had to return it despite her worry. Their minds were one. Their least thought, their most intimate concern, lay always open to the other.

She had often wondered if the unGifted, who mated and then lived in physical closeness all their lives, could ever comprehend the intense communion there was between herself and Theo. She loved him as she loved the Gift, with reverence, joy, and gratitude. When he was gone, she knew she would feel as if part of her very being were missing; and this was the only thought she shielded from him.

Go with the Spirit, my dear, she sent. *And come back swiftly.*

Mreen and Morys and Theo mounted their two *hruss* on a gray and cloudy morning. The beasts were laden and outfitted as if by Lamdon itself; Pol had spared nothing that might enhance the reputation of his House. Kai found no words to bid his little daughter farewell; he knelt and embraced her, his cheeks wet and his mouth twisted. His pain was such that the Gifted ones around him had to strengthen their shields. Brnwen, too, kissing her stepdaughter goodbye, wept openly. Mreen's own eyes were red and swollen with tears and with indignant surprise that, after waiting so long, and so impatiently, she should now grieve at leaving her parents.

It will pass, Mreen, Sira sent to her. *You will always miss them, but the pain will pass.*

Kai and Brnwen stood in misery on the steps, with Trisa beside them sending her silent goodbyes to her stepsister. Theo and Sira had made their farewells; Theo nodded to Morys that he was ready. He wanted to go quickly, and not prolong the scene. Pol stood proudly on the top step, nodding and smiling as if he had caused it all to happen.

Theo bowed, lifted his hand, and turned his *hruss* away from the House. Mreen clutched his waist, hiding her face against his back, wetting his furs with tears as they rode after Morys.

It had been a long time since Theo had been on the road that led to Conservatory, and he was amazed again at its tortuousness, at the sheerness of the cliffs that loomed to the north, at the towering boulders that obstructed the way and promised to confound any who tried to find the way to Observatory—or from it—on their own.

Mreen clung to him, a speck of warmth and silence behind him. Once they started down the canyon road, where the chasm gaped to their left and the icy rocks made the *hruss* step slowly, she took one look into the dark void and hid her face once more against his back. She sent nothing during the slow hours of riding, until the *hruss* squeezed through a narrow slit in the cliff, and the path opened out onto a valley of sparse irontrees. The trees, smaller than those lower on the Continent, leaned to the north, their roots dry and crooked against the rocky ground.

Mreen, Theo sent gently. *We have left the cliff road.*

Her grip loosened as she lifted her head and looked around at their surroundings. Over his shoulder, he saw her faint glow brighten, and he smiled. She was as changeable as light itself, a sprite of energy, of emotion. Conservatory would have their hands full with this Gift!

Morys called over his shoulder, "Was your little one afraid? It's a scary road, all right."

Mreen cuddled against Theo's back again. *I just thought about Conservatory,* she sent happily. *I told myself I could only go to Conservatory if I could ride down that road!*

Theo laughed. "She will make a fine traveler, Morys."

Around them the day was as gray as old snow, the clouds hanging heavily above their heads and the rimed rocks dull and dark. The brilliance of the sky in the deep cold season was gone, but Theo knew that to be a good thing. The sun in a clear sky could make tender skin flame. He himself had not been out on the roads since first going to Observatory—how long ago? Could it possibly be eight years? Indeed, he would soon have nine summers!

He threw back his head and breathed deeply of the fresh air. The peaks of Observatory's mountains loomed above them in tumbled spikes of rock and snow, higher than any of those on the Continent. It was no wonder Observatory had been isolated for so long. It was not only their beliefs, watching for the Ship, that separated them from the rest of Nevya; whoever had chosen the site for their House, summers past remembering, must have intended them to be separate, different. But now, with the sending of Mreen to Conservatory, a connection would be made. Observatory would be part of Nevya despite their differences. The Gift willed it so.

Morys wanted to be down in Ogre Pass before the end of the daylight. They ate a quick mid-day meal in the saddle, handing bits of nutbread and dried *caeru* strips back and forth, taking snow in their mouths to quench their thirst. Once or twice they stopped to relieve themselves, but otherwise they pressed on. Theo looked back during one of these brief rests, and saw that the road they had traversed was already invisible. Giant rocks were scattered everywhere, as if by the hand of the Spirit itself, to disguise the way.

When they could just see the Pass through breaks in the landscape, Theo heard Sira faintly in his mind.

Theo?

Yes, he answered, as strongly as he could. His reach was not nearly so great as hers. *All is well. We are in the Pass.*

And Mreen?

Fine.

He could not understand her last message, but he caught the sense of it. He wished he could have heard it more clearly; he would not hear her voice again for a long time. He sent back to her as strongly as he was able, and could only hope that perhaps she could hear though he no longer could. Then Morys was leading them down the last slope, and pointing to a campsite, a level spot protected by a stand of giant trees, encircled by their suckers. The Pass stretched before them, its road wide and clear as if scraped out with a gigantic *obis* knife, running from the northwest to the southeast. They dismounted, and Theo lifted Mreen down. She stretched her arms over her head and did a little dance of freedom, then dashed about the campsite with all the energy of a five-year-old who has been restrained for too many hours.

Morys laughed. "Doesn't say much, does she?"

Theo was taking out his *filla* to call up his first camp *quiru* in years. "She does not say anything, my friend," he answered. "Not a word."

Morys stared at the child. "I'd heard that, but I thought it was exaggerated—you know, stories about the Gifted." He began unsaddling *hruss*. "Why doesn't she speak, Cantor Theo?"

Theo turned his *filla* absently in his hand, and looked to the northeast, over the snowy reaches of the Pass. "We are not exactly certain. Perhaps it is because her stepsister sent to her since her babyhood, or perhaps it is simply her nature."

"Does she always have that light around her like that?"

Theo looked over at Mreen, who was plunging her fingers into the snow and scattering it around her in a pale shower. "Yes, Morys, she does." He laughed, filled with pleasure at the calm evening and the carefree play of the child. "She will never be cold, that one!"

"Lucky," Morys said.

Theo hoped he was right.

Mreen was fascinated by the darkness outside the *quiru*. Theo took her out once to relieve herself, then had to insist that she hurry back into the safety of the light and warmth.

I want to look at the stars! she protested.

You can see them from the quiru, he answered. *It is not safe to stay outside in the cold.*

Why? I do not feel cold!

You could feel it, though, very soon, and by the time you felt it, it might be too late.

Why?

For answer, Theo scooped up the squirming girl and carried her back to her bedfurs, dropping her in a giggling pile. Morys was laughing, but Theo looked somber.

Mreen, he sent.

She looked up at him, giggles subsiding, her eyes suddenly round, the deep green of ironwood needles. *Yes, Cantor Theo.*

Riding on the Continent is a very serious thing. When it comes to the cold, and the danger, you must no longer be a child. Your Gift is precious, and it is your duty to protect it.

Mreen pointed to the saddle they had ridden during the long day. *I know,* she answered. *There are many pictures with that.*

Are there? Theo knelt beside her, helping her off with her bulky furs, tucking her into her bed for the night.

Yes. I know people can die of the cold, and of other things.

It is true, Mreen. It is our lifework—we Singers—to try to keep that from happening.

I will remember.

Mreen yawned and snuggled into the yellow-white depths of her bedfurs. Morys had already banked the fire, and rolled into his own bed. The two *hruss*, grumbling in their throats, stood hipshot, broad heads hanging low, to rest the night. Theo went to his own bedfurs, and sat down to pull off his boots.

Mreen's eyes were already closed, her thick auburn lashes making delicate half-circles on her plump cheeks. *Cantor Theo.*

Yes, Mreen?

Mreen sighed, almost asleep. *Cantrix Sira sends good night.*

Theo looked up. He had heard nothing, not so much as a tickle in his mind. He stared at Mreen, and tried hard to push down the thought that he would have preferred to hear Sira's voice himself. If his Gift was not strong enough, there was nothing to be done about it.

He looked up at his *quiru* and found it steady and strong in the vast darkness. The embers of the fire glowed dully under the banked softwood. All was well.

He rolled himself into his furs, and pulled them up under his chin. Before he slept, the deep and rewarding sleep that came after a day in the open, he gave thanks to the Spirit, with passionate sincerity, for his Gift and its training.

Chapter Seven

Far into the night hours, Zakri started up suddenly from an uneasy sleep. A rhythmic sound had invaded his dreams, and it persisted when he was fully awake, a light tapping at the door of his room that paused and then came again. As the other occupants of his room slept on, Zakri extended a cautious fibril of psi to find who came knocking at such an hour. When he recognized her, he hurried to the door, wearing only his trousers.

Sook stood in the hall, her eyes wide and glistening in the *quiru* light. Her black hair hung in long tangles, as if she too had just risen from her bed. "Oh, Singer, thank the Spirit it's you!" she whispered. "Could you please come, please? And hurry!"

Zakri answered without hesitating. "Of course." As a Cantor, he was used to calls that came in the middle of the night. He stepped back into the crowded room to retrieve his tunic and boots. He pulled them on in the hallway and tucked his *filla* into his tunic while Sook shifted from foot to foot beside him.

"What has happened?" Zakri asked as he followed her quick steps down the corridor. He kept his voice low, and his thoughts as well. Shielding his mind every waking moment was tiring him; even as he tried to sleep, he must stay half-alert, on guard.

"It's Nori," she said breathlessly. She led him around a corner and down a long corridor to the back of the House, where large family apartments flanked the nursery gardens and the carvery. "She's bleeding . . . "

Her eyes were enormous, tear-washed and frightened. "We don't know what it is, and she won't say anything . . ."

They did not have far to go. The apartment was near the *ubanyor*. Sook opened the door without knocking, and went in with Zakri close behind. Several strained faces turned up to them. Zakri recognized Mura, but he had no time to speak to her before Sook seized his hand.

With a strength that surprised him, she tugged him into another room, an inner bedroom. It was small and dim, furnished with a cot and a chair, and a carved table cluttered with a young woman's small possessions—brushes, hair bindings, quill pens in an ironwood jar. Nori lay on the narrow bed with her knees drawn up, bedfurs clutched tightly to her breast. Her eyelids and her lips were clenched and pale. She was surely no older than Sook; Zakri doubted she had four summers, but pain aged her, making deep furrows in her smooth skin.

Zakri had to lower his shields to assess the girl's agony, the wrenching spasms that made her moan wretchedly. He scanned her body with his psi, briefly, his *filla* still in his hand, before he knelt beside the bed. He spoke quietly to Sook.

"Have you attended childbirths?"

Sook protested, "This can't be a childbirth, Singer!" Her eyes flashed in the half-darkness. "Nori's not mated!"

"She is having a miscarriage, nevertheless," Zakri said, completely forgetting to watch his speech patterns. "We will need towels, a sharp knife, and water, and if you are too upset to help her, then you must find an older woman who has some experience."

"No! I'll do it!"

She put her head outside the bedroom door to ask for the supplies, and was back almost immediately, hovering over Zakri, touching Nori's hand and forehead.

Zakri played in *Lidya* first, to relax the suffering girl. Her fear and the tension it caused made her pains worse. He had helped several Housewomen at Amric to give birth. The powerful natural process usually needed little assistance, but laboring women were grateful for his soothing melodies and for his special talent, the gentle touches of psi here and there that gently urged the babes on their way. But there was nothing Zakri could do for Nori's babe; he knew as soon as he touched her with his psi that her child was dead before it was formed.

Mura brought clean towels and a heavy pitcher brimming with water. "What is it?" she whispered to Sook. She took a sharp small knife from a pocket. "What's wrong with Nori?"

"The Singer says it's a miscarriage," Sook said. She took the towels from Mura, and Mura set the pitcher at the foot of the bed. Zakri went on with his melody, aware of Sook lifting the fur that covered her friend, placing a pad of towels beneath her. She replaced the blanket, then knelt beside Zakri. He sensed her gaze on him, felt the pressure of her trust and hope.

Nori's body needed to shed its burden, and because of that Zakri dared not stop her bleeding completely. He was worried about the risk of her losing too much blood, growing too weak. He tried not to think of the tragic circumstances of Cantrix Isbel's giving birth to her babe; surely this girl need not suffer the same fate as Mreen's mother.

Moments passed as the *Lidya* melody flowed on; Zakri transformed the lowered third of *Lidya* into the second degree of *Mu-Lidya*, a subtle variation. Nori's tight fists relaxed, and her eyelids smoothed and fluttered slightly. A sighing breath escaped her. Only then did Zakri modulate to *Aiodu*, the second mode, to sweep her body once again with his psi.

He hoped no one was listening at this moment. His mind must be fully open. This was Iban's legacy, this understanding that to sense the precise functioning of Nori's body, to touch her thoughts, to feel what had gone wrong and to find what he might be able to put right—to do all these things, the Singer's mind must not be shielded. He must feel the sufferer's pain and misery in himself. It was the flaw in Conservatory's rigid training, the weakness that made Cantors and Cantrixes superficial healers. It still plagued Sira's healing.

Zakri touched Nori's mind now, gently, searching for a cause. She was unGifted, of course, but her feelings were very strong. She was so frightened, and hurt. Zakri's melody died as he sucked in a sudden breath. The sharp hiss made Mura and Sook jump.

In Nori's mind was an unspeakable deed, a vile image. Zakri had to put down his *filla*, and pull away from the awful picture in her mind.

Nori knew exactly what had happened to her, and the understanding of it made her afraid to speak, even to her friends and her family.

Zakri knew that her body and her babe had been deliberately hurt. The life that had taken root in her had been extinguished, pinched out as deliberately and carelessly as one might pinch out an annoying ember that fell from a campfire. With his carver's psi, he had severed the cord that nourished the growing babe in her womb. No doubt he had convinced her he could kill her just as easily—and perhaps he could.

Zakri reeled under the shock of it, the violence, the enormity of the evil that inspired it. He lost the iron grip he kept on his Gift, and behind him a brush and a quill rolled from the table. The empty chair scraped noisily on the floor as if someone had pushed it. Sook gasped, and Mura exclaimed.

Zakri leaned forward, pressing his forehead into his hands, striving for control.

O Spirit! he thought. How is it possible for the Gift to be used in such a way?

In his mind he heard a flashing warning. *Be careful, friend. He will hear you.*

Zakri closed his mind sharply, suddenly, and sat back on his heels. He trembled, and perspiration stung his eyes when he opened them. Sook was staring at him.

"What is it?" she begged. "Singer! What is it?"

Zakri shook his head back and forth, slowly. "It was he," he said wearily. "Cho did this."

He had already been angry over Iban's death, but now he was filled with a deep revulsion as well. Not only was Cho dangerously powerful, but he must be a man without remorse, without even the semblance of control. What sane person could have done such a thing? Everyone in this House was in peril. Zakri felt the knot in his breast turn to stone.

Are you all right, Singer?

It was the same voice that had warned him, the same person who had heard him in his shock. *I am all right,* he sent back. *Were you following? Yes.*

Can he hear us?

There was a pause before the imprisoned Cantrix answered, and her sending when it came was careful and wary. *It seems he hears very strong thoughts, although he is not able to understand more subtle ones. But he is easily angered, and very dangerous, especially for us . . . and probably for you. Beware any mention of Conservatory.*

There was no time to explain everything now, to reveal the truth. Clearly, Cantrix Elnor believed Zakri to have come from her own tradition; and in a way, of course, he had. He only sent, *Thank you,* before he broke the contact.

The girl on the cot moaned as a fresh spasm began, and Zakri picked up his *filla* again and resumed his melody to ease her. Sook replaced the blood-soaked towels with fresh ones. Mura came with broth, and when Nori was able to drink, they spooned a bit into her mouth. The night passed slowly. Morning found them all exhausted, but Nori was stronger, her burden shed, the bleeding stopped.

Before she fell into a healing sleep, Nori clutched Mura's hand. She made a pitiful sight. Her eyes were red and swollen, her hair tangled around her. With a sob, she said, "You have to know—I thought he meant to make me his mate. I believed him!"

Mura tried to shush her, putting her rough hand against her cheek, but Nori shook her head. "No, Mura, it's true! Cho . . . I thought he cared about me, that he—" She sobbed again, and her voice rose. "But when I told him about the babe—"

Mura smoothed Nori's hair. "There," she murmured, "it doesn't matter, and he isn't worth it. It doesn't matter. There will be other babes for you. Sleep, now."

Sook wept, too, silently, but Zakri sensed her tears were more from anger than sorrow. When they left the bedroom, she seized his arm with sharp strength, and her eyes blazed.

"Singer," she said in a tense whisper. "I thank you for healing Nori. We have to do something about Cho!"

"I must find Berk," Zakri said. "We will go to Lamdon at once. They will take action."

Mura, who had been consoling Nori's family, spoke from behind him. "Cho won't let you leave," she said. "No Singer is allowed to leave this House except under his orders."

Telltale sparks flew around Zakri, and he quelled them quickly. He was at risk of letting these brave women learn his secret, and in this House, knowledge was dangerous.

"We need a distraction," he muttered. "Some noisy event to keep Cho occupied."

Sook stared at him for a long moment, her eyes brilliant in her weary face. "When can you be ready, Singer Zakri?"

"Sook!" Mura cried. "What are you thinking?"

Sook began to gather the long strands of her hair into a fresh binding. "I'm thinking of the carvery, and the carvers. They can be very noisy sometimes."

Before Zakri could answer, the door to the apartment was abruptly opened from the outside. The three of them were caught by surprise, off guard. The members of Nori's family clung together.

Cho himself had opened the door. He stood now in the doorway, his long arms braced on the frame, the thin braid of his hair swinging gently against his chest. His narrow eyes fastened on Zakri. "What business could you have in this apartment, Singer?" he asked lightly.

Mura stepped forward. "One of my kitchen girls was taken ill in the night," she said. "Nori. This Singer was about, so I called on him to help."

"Why, whatever could be the matter with our little Nori?" Cho asked. He stepped inside the apartment. One of the itinerants from upstairs followed close behind, not speaking, watching Cho's every movement. Cho's glance took in Nori's family, then turned to the closed door to the bedroom. "Is she in there?" He took a step toward it. "I'll just see if she's feeling better."

"She's asleep," Mura said hastily.

Cho chuckled, a sinister, light sound. "I won't disturb her a bit."

As Cho moved toward the bedroom, Sook moved, as if to intercept him. Zakri caught her eye and shook his head. Her eyes flashed, but she stopped, and stood with her hands on her hips, watching Cho open the bedroom door.

Zakri closed his eyes. Controlling his temper was taking a great deal of his energy, and he was following Cho with his mind at a careful distance, ready to act if Cho threatened Nori any further. He listened as the man bent over the sleeping girl. Tension made Zakri's shoulders hard, his neck stiff. He breathed deeply, trying to release it. He felt a gaze on him, and he opened his eyes to see Cho's man staring at him. Still he watched over the sleeping Nori with his Gift, his physical eyes open but unfocused. He followed as Cho touched her body with his own, cruder psi, then withdrew it.

Cho smiled as he came out of the bedroom. "Nori looks fine to me," he said. "When she wakes up, you can tell her I was here, and that I'm sorry she had a bad night. No doubt that will make her feel better."

Mura looked murderous, and Sook stood beside her, her chin lifted, her eyes glittering.

Cho laughed, a sound like the slither of claws on stone. "Oh, yes, I look out for all my House members," he said lightly. He tipped his head to one side and his eyes moved over Sook, up and down. "All of them," he repeated. "Remember that, won't you?"

Cho's man pulled the door closed behind them as they left. Zakri released his breath in a rush, and Sook gave a little sound of relief. Mura stood in the center of the room, her arms folded tightly. "I could poison that man!" she hissed.

"Be careful, Housewoman," Zakri told her. "It is possible he could hear that thought."

"Yes, I know," she answered. "But at this moment I hardly care. No one is safe here!"

"That is perfectly true," Zakri agreed wearily. "But we will do what we can." His eyes burned with fatigue. It was time for the morning meal, but he only wanted his bed.

"Well, Sook," Mura said, "we'd better get to work."

"But you must be exhausted!" Zakri said. "I am—I'm worn out!"

"Well, you did all the work, Singer." Sook patted his shoulder. "We only helped."

"Yes, go to your bed," Mura urged him. She didn't smile, but the wrinkles of her face were a little softer as she looked at him. "When you waken, come to the kitchens. We'll save you some *keftet*."

Zakri bowed slightly in thanks, and raised a hand in farewell to the other House members before he left the apartment.

He was in the hall when he heard footsteps behind him. He looked over his shoulder to see that Mura had followed him out, and he waited for her to catch up.

"Singer," she murmured, "you should have been a carver. Did you never think of it?"

"I—I beg your pardon?"

Her eyes were sharp as she looked up at him. "I saw what happened, there in Nori's room. I saw the things move, the brush and so forth, the chair. Your psi is strong, isn't it?"

Zakri ducked his head and laughed, trying to look as if he had been caught out. "Well, sometimes it is, yes. I try to control it, but—" He lifted one shoulder, and spread his hands. "It gets away from me."

"Hmm." Mura looked at him one more time, hard. Zakri knew she had no Gift, but he felt as if her eyes saw to his very center. He averted his own.

"Well," Mura said. "Have a good rest, Singer."

"Thank you, thanks, Mura. I—I'll see you later." He bowed to her and hurried off down the corridor. He must be more careful! Mura saw far more than was good for her. He did not want either Mura or Sook to be endangered by knowing his secret.

Chapter Eight

Zakri and Berk made surreptitious preparations. They filled their saddlepacks with generous provisions from Mura's stores, everything she could spare, and Zakri made sure their *hruss* were clean and well-fed, ready to ride. Sook promised them a signal. Zakri fretted about her safety, but she cast him a sidelong look from her wonderful eyes and assured him she could take care of herself.

"It's you who has to be careful, Singer Zakri," she said. "And I . . . we'll be waiting for you to come back!"

She put her small, warm hand on his. He controlled his impulse to pull away, as much not to hurt her feelings as to hide his secret. He admired her spirit. Any House could be proud of such a member.

They waited three days. Then, at the mid-day meal, Berk found a badly cracked cup at his place, one that would clearly leak if tea were poured in it. He lifted it up and said loudly, "This is broken!"

Sook was hovering nearby, watchful. "Oh, I'm sorry, Houseman," she exclaimed. "Let me get you another!" She hurried out of the great room, wending her way deftly between the long tables. Zakri heard the exchange from his usual seat between Klas and Shiro, and he saw Berk's nod in his direction.

It was the agreed-upon sign. Berk rose and left. Zakri sat on, pretending to take part in the conversation around him. The carvers and Sook had planned well. Only a very few minutes passed before the uproar began.

Shouts and crashes rolled from the corridor behind the stairs, and a flood of psi came with them, a wave of it that Zakri was sure would deafen anyone who tried to listen through it. He threw up his own shields before it could reach him.

Cho cursed. He and his henchmen leaped up from the center table and hurried toward the carvery. Zakri and several other Singers followed them out, but once they reached the corridor, Zakri turned in the opposite direction, only glancing behind him to be certain no one noticed. The noise increased, a din of raised voices and the slam of ironwood against stone. The racket followed him as he made haste down the hall.

He saw the stableman running toward him, drawn by the commotion, and he ducked into the linen room until the man passed. Then Zakri fled, his boots quiet on the stone, to the stables.

"By the Spirit!" Berk muttered. "What are they doing in there?" He was hastily saddling his *hruss*. He had already saddled Zakri's, and it waited patiently beside him, all saddlepacks tied on, bedfurs secured with their thongs. The stable doors stood open to the morning.

"I believe they are fighting, Houseman," Zakri answered with a grin.

"Over what?"

"Why, what do men fight over?" Zakri responded. He put his foot in the wooden stirrup and swung quickly up into the saddle. "They fight over women, do they not?"

He tried not to think of Sook in the middle of the melee, of Sook drawing Cho's attention to herself. At least, he thought, she was not Gifted. Cho's interest in her should be short-lived. All of them—Mura, Sook, Yul, and Zakri—were counting on it.

Berk settled into his own saddle, and they urged their beasts out of the stable. *Hruss* rarely galloped, or indeed moved at any pace faster than a heavy, swinging trot. It took some time to work them up even to that. Zakri watched nervously over his shoulder as they rode around the House to the front, where the road ran up the slope.

They still heard the shouting from the carvery. Zakri wished desperately to know what was happening, but he dared not open his mind. The carvers had planned a barrage of their special psi. He felt it beyond his shields, a storm of it beating against the barricade. It would be foolhardy to allow that bedlam to touch him, and it should effectively cover their escape.

He sincerely hoped it gave Cho a stinker of a headache.

Sook shrank against the wall of the carvery, beaten back by the turmoil around her. She knew there was more in the air than shouts and banging, but she was deaf to it, and glad to be so.

When Cho came in, the carvers, who had divided themselves into two groups beforehand, bellowed and shook fists at each other. One daring pair shoved each other back and forth, making the workbenches rock. The two Singers who always accompanied Cho turned sickly pale. One staggered, wth his hands over his sweating face. Sook knew the psi randomly thrown about the room was too much for him. One carver's psi could not have done it; but their concerted efforts created a strong enough wave to affect a Singer.

Cho thrust up his long arm, his black eyes snapping. "Stop!"

Sook wasn't sure it was enough time. Yul caught her eye, and she shook her head. Zakri and the courier needed more, a little longer. They would barely be out of the courtyard yet.

Yul took her cue. He picked up a half-carved chunk of ironwood and held it over his head with a yell, as if he were about to throw it, and someone immediately howled back at him. The din worsened. The black *obis* knives rattled on their hooks, and half-carved pieces on the worktables danced under the force of the kinesthetic psi flashing around the room.

The other Singer felt the effect now, hunching his shoulders and lurching to the door. House members clustered there, peering in, trying to see what was happening. In his disorientation the Singer could not get past them.

Cho stepped to the middle of the room, both arms lifted above his head, palms outward. He turned his dark gaze on Yul, and Sook held her breath.

The ironwood dropped suddenly from Yul's hands, and the carver pitched forward to the stone floor, nerveless. All noise ceased abruptly as the carvers stared at their fallen comrade. The sudden silence made Sook's ears ring. A moment passed before she could hear the gentle clicking the *obis* knives made as they swung back and forth, bumping against each other. She cried out, and ran to kneel by Yul.

"So," Cho said in a soft, insinuating tone. He pointed at Sook. "Is this the cause?"

One of the other carvers stepped forward, fearful, but holding his ground. "There aren't enough of them anymore," he said stoutly, following the line Sook and Mura had invented. "Girls, I mean! This House is full of men. There are hardly any women, and this one was promised to me!"

Sook bent her head as if in embarrassment. They had planned this carefully, hoping to trivialize the incident in Cho's mind. They hadn't thought Cho would actually attack a fellow carver—she could hardly believe even now that he had. She thought of the drooling man at the center table in the great room and she shuddered.

Two of the other carvers offered comments, weakly, trying to keep up the pretense of argument. The sight of Yul sprawled on the floor restrained them. Sook knew the courage required to face up to Cho, and she prayed she would have it, too.

Cho's eyes, assessing her, were stone-hard. "Ah—you again," he said. "You're Nori's friend. Sook, isn't it? You'd better come with me. Looks like you're the one to answer for my meal being interrupted."

Someone had run to fetch Mura from the kitchen, and she came rushing in now to crouch beside her son. She threw a vicious glance up at Cho.

"If he doesn't recover," she hissed, "you'd better watch what you eat, Carver!"

Several of the carvers gasped at her daring, but Cho laughed. "So I will, Housewoman!" he exclaimed. "So I will! But don't worry. He'll recover. It was just the tiniest slap, a warning. Next time perhaps he'll heed me when I speak!"

Indeed, Yul's eyes were already opening, and his ashen face began to color again. Sook chafed his wrists while Mura gently stroked his temples. Yul turned his hand to grip Sook's, and she breathed a sigh of relief; he was telling her he was all right. She gave Mura the smallest nod of reassurance.

Cho stooped to say in her ear, "I think you and I will have a little talk upstairs."

Sook shivered with a sudden chill. She cringed as Cho took her arm just above the elbow. He was strong, and his grip hurt when she tried to pull away.

"Let her be," Mura snapped.

Cho only laughed again. "Mind your son, there, Housewoman. I'm just going to get an explanation from our little troublemaker, here."

Sook had to get to her feet, or be dragged up bodily. She stood up, and when she wrenched her arm from Cho's long fingers she knew she would have a nasty bruise by evening. His eyes were glittering, half-shut, as he leaned over her.

"Don't ever do that again," he whispered, so close to her face that his breath stirred the loose tendrils of her hair. "Do you think only the Gifted are vulnerable to me?"

The room was deadly silent now. Even the *obis* knives hung still on their hooks; no psi buffeted the air. All eyes were on Cho and Sook. Cho was far taller, and he gripped her chin and tipped her head back, forcing her to look into his eyes. She wished she dared spit in his face. She felt small and alone—who would stand against him if he wanted to harm her?

Zakri and Berk were surely far enough away by now, she thought. She let her gaze drop. "Just leave me alone," she said in a small voice. "Please. I didn't mean to cause any trouble."

Cho hesitated. Then he snorted derisively and released her. "My friends," he said, addressing them all. "We have more important things to do than fight over women." He chuckled as he turned to the man who had spoken before. "Don't worry, Carver. There will be plenty of these to go around before we're done."

He lifted his hand to his two itinerants, now recovered, and went to the open door. The Singer Shiro met him there.

"Cho!" he cried. "They're gone! The Singer Zakri and his courier! *Hruss*, tack, everything, gone!"

Sook's heart thumped suddenly in her breast, and she kept her eyes down.

Very slowly, Cho turned back from the door. Sook held her breath as his fur-booted feet came to stand before her once again.

"What have you done, little Sook?" he said, his voice no more than a whisper. "You think you can play grown-up games? Do you want to play with me?"

He seized her arm again, only this time there was no pulling away. He held it tightly, at the same time deliberately pressing the back of his hard hand into the softness of her breast. Sook looked up at him, and a wave of revulsion swept her, stronger than her fear. He laughed, and she knew he had felt it, read it from her. Her skin prickled as she realized that he liked it.

"Cho!" Mura spoke up boldly, but Sook heard the tremor in her voice. "It's my fault—it was my idea!" the older woman insisted.

"It doesn't matter." Cho didn't even turn his head as he answered. "Little Sook here will help me understand. She'll be telling me all about it!" He propelled Sook toward the door.

One of his itinerants stepped forward, saying uneasily, "Cho, don't you think—couldn't you—"

Cho paused for the barest moment. His eyes narrowed and his chin rose as he looked down his nose at the man. He didn't speak.

The itinerant stumbled back, and fell hard to his knees. His fellow Singer jumped to his side, catching him before he could collapse all the way. Without aid, he would surely have struck his head against the side of the workbench. Cho thrust Sook forward then, through the door, past the watching, silent House members. She cast a last look over her shoulder at the itinerant. He was unconscious, his body limp, his features slack.

Mura ran after them, crying, "Cho! Let her go!"

She caught up with them in the corridor, and took hold of Cho's sleeve. He stopped once more. With a jerk that Sook felt, too, he pulled his arm free of Mura's hand.

"Woman," he said flatly, "if you ever touch me again, I'll kill that halfwit son of yours."

Mura stepped back, haltingly, turning helpless eyes to Sook. Sook turned her face away to hide her own terror. "It's all right, Mura," she heard herself say. "I'll be all right." Some part of her marveled. Where did the courage come from? It was for Zakri, that was the answer. She had done it for Zakri.

Cho dragged her up the broad staircase and down the long corridor to the Magister's apartment. Several itinerants in the hall watched dumbly as he pulled her inside, and kicked the door shut behind them.

In the Timberlands that night, in the mouth of Ogre Pass, Zakri woke trembling and sweating in his bedfurs, driven from sleep by an awful dream. He had seen an *urbear* dragging Sook off across the Great Glacier. She screamed for his help, and he tried to run to her, feet dragging in the heavy snow, but he could not reach her.

Sira had taught him that the dreams of the Gifted are never to be ignored. But what could he do about this one? O Spirit, he prayed, watch over Sook. Keep her safe until I can return.

Chapter Nine

In the eight years that had passed since Theo's last visit to Conservatory, Magister Mkel seemed to have aged four summers. Theo bowed low to him, hiding his concern at Mkel's appearance. He knew that Mkel's shielding would shut out all but the strongest emotions. Just the same, Theo had no wish to offend.

Mreen and Theo had come directly to the Magister's apartment on their arrival, leaving Morys to stable the *hruss*. Mreen, suddenly bashful, hid herself behind Theo as he greeted Mkel and his mate, Cathrin.

Mkel's gray hair had grown white, and so thin that his scalp showed through. The skin of his face sagged, and was darkened in patches as if he, whose duties rarely allowed for travel outside his House, had been riding in the cold and sun. Cathrin was still plump and pink-cheeked, her white hair thick and beautifully bound. She stood close to her mate, one hand on the back of his chair as if she could support him through its ironwood.

"Magister Mkel," Theo said formally, speaking aloud for Cathrin's sake. "Observatory sends you greetings, and a student for Conservatory."

Mreen peeked around Theo's leg, showing only one green eye and a tumble of hair mussed into an auburn cloud by her *caeru* hood.

Cathrin smiled down at her. "Welcome to our House, dear. Won't you say hello?"

Mreen vanished immediately behind Theo, her small hands clutching at his trousers, her face buried in the furs he still wore.

Mkel spoke slowly, as if he did not quite understand. "Observatory sends a student?" His voice was cracked and hoarse, and Theo was certain he must be ill. But this was Conservatory! Surely someone here could heal him.

Theo bowed once again. "It is true, Magister." He stepped aside so that Mreen was visible, and he urged her forward with a gentle hand. The *quiru* at Conservatory was bright, but still Mreen's little halo shone distinctly, darkling now in places because of her shyness. Cathrin took a small sharp breath.

"My goodness," she murmured. "What is this, Singer?"

Mreen tipped her round face up to Theo. *Why does she call you Singer?* she demanded. *Does she not know you are a Cantor?*

When I was last here, I was only Singer, Theo sent back to her.

Mkel said, "Cantor? What does she mean?"

"Who?" Cathrin asked.

"It is this child, Cathrin," Mkel told her. "She wants us to call Theo Cantor."

Cathrin held up her hands, confused. "Please," she complained. "Will one of you tell me what's happening? Surely the child doesn't already send?"

Mreen did not release her grip on Theo, but her usual ebullience was returning, and her eyes shone brightly up at the old couple. *Theo is Cantor,* she sent firmly, and very clearly, as if perhaps Mkel could not hear so well.

He has been Cantor Theo v'Observatory these five years! Did you not know?

The heavy lines of Mkel's face lifted, and Theo recognized a bit of the spirit and good nature he remembered.

Mkel said, "No, child, I did not know." He leaned forward in his chair to meet Mreen's eyes. "I do not know you, either. What is your name?"

Mreen frowned up at Theo. *Cantor Theo, can he not send?*

Before Theo could respond, Mkel sent, *Of course I can! But my mate, Cathrin, is not Gifted. Can you not speak?*

Mreen shook her head. *No.*

"Excuse me, Magister," Theo hastened to say. "And Cathrin. I had better explain. It is rather complicated."

"So it must be," Cathrin said. "Well, it's been a long time since I heard one of your stories, Singer . . . Theo! Oh, I hardly know what to call you." She bustled about, bringing chairs forward, signalling to a Housewoman to bring refreshments. "At least sit down, and have something to drink and to eat."

The Housewoman brought a tray with tidbits of nuts encased in dried fruit, and Cathrin held it out to Mreen. "Do try something, child," she said with a smile. "And don't worry—we're going to work it all out."

Mreen happily seized a sweet morsel, and wriggled up into a chair to sit crosslegged, munching. When Theo was also settled with a cup of tea in his hand, Cathrin herself sat down. Mkel watched Mreen throughout all the preparations, his eyebrows rising as her little cloud of light brightened and shifted with her mood. Wisps of curly hair wafted about her face.

"I have never seen such a one," he murmured.

Theo said gently, "Magister Mkel . . . this is Mreen. She is Isbel's daughter."

Cathrin put her hand to her breast, and then to her cheek. Mreen saw her, and caught her mood. The light around her darkened, and a shadow seemed to float through it, crossing her face. Cathrin bit her lip, and reached for the tray of fruit again. "Never mind, child," she said. "It is past." The little girl dimpled at Cathrin as she took another sweet.

"Mreen came to Observatory with Cantrix Sira last summer," Theo went on. "I know you have reservations about what we have done there, Magister," with a polite nod, "but we have done what we must. I am not Conservatory-trained, though I would have liked to be; but I serve now as Cantor in Observatory's Cantoris, and we—Sira and I—are teaching four other Gifted children there."

"So many!" Cathrin breathed.

"Indeed. And one, Trisa, has already performed her first *quirunha*."

Mkel leaned on one arm of his chair, chin cupped in his hand, and regarded Mreen. Theo kept his mind respectfully shielded, but his shields were not what Mkel's were, and the older man's emotions seeped through. Sadness, regret, and self-reproach had been dragging at Mkel for a long time. They had aged him, worn him down like the waves of the Frozen Sea wear away the rocks of the coast.

"Theo—Cantor Theo," he said slowly. Theo knew what a great effort it was for Mkel to use the title. All his precepts, all the discipline by which he had lived his life, were challenged by it. Theo sensed his attempt to find a footing, to choose a path that would reconcile his past and this present.

All the ground beneath him must seem to be shifting and crumbling like talus at the foot of a cliff.

Theo said quietly, "At least at Observatory I am Cantor Theo."

"Of course," Mkel answered. He straightened in his chair. "And so you should be here. Cantor Theo, I failed Cantrix Isbel. I can never forget it. I failed Cantrix Sira, as well. I am hard put to understand why Observatory should have so much of the Gift and the Houses of the Continent so little."

"It is what we are all trying to understand," Theo said tactfully.

"But Sira seems to know—she was so sure!"

"Sira has insights only the Gift can explain," Theo murmured. He wished he could say more to ease Mkel's self-reproach, but, he thought ruefully, the insights were mostly Sira's.

Mreen had eaten her fill of sweets. She knelt in the big chair, diffidence forgotten, and gazed intensely at Mkel. *Why do you have a mate, and the other Gifted do not?*

It is tradition, he answered her. *The Magister of Conservatory takes a mate, because he has no Cantoris of his own, and because his mate acts as mother to all the children who come here to study.*

Theo was impressed by the immediacy and directness of the answer, but Mreen seemed to take it quite for granted. *And so I will never have a mate?*

Do you wish to be a full Cantrix, and play the filhata *on the dais, to perform the* quirunha?

The little girl squirmed, and her halo of light glittered joyously. *So I do! Oh, so I do!*

Mkel smiled once more, but Theo felt his weariness like a stone in his mind. Mkel's shoulders were bowed by the weight of it, his body tired by what his mind could not push away.

Cathrin leaned toward Mreen. "Are you full now, dear? Would you like to bathe?"

Mreen nodded.

"Can you not answer me, Mreen?" Cathrin asked, not yet understanding.

Mreen shook her head, very deliberately.

Cathrin's eyes filled with bright tears. "Oh, Theo," she said softly. "She can't talk at all? Not a word?"

"No," he responded. "She has never spoken aloud in her life, or cried, or laughed."

The tears spilled over Cathrin's pink cheeks, and Mreen jumped down from her chair and ran to stand beside her. She patted Cathrin's hand, then looked over her shoulder at Theo.

Cantor Theo, she sent, *please tell the lady not to be sad, because I am not. Tell her about my Gift, and tell her not to cry!*

"Cathrin," Theo said, "Mreen sends that she is not unhappy, nor should you be. Her Gift is very strong, and that is why she is here. She wanted this very much, to come here to study."

"Will she sing?" Mkel asked.

"We think not. But, as you see . . . ." Theo had to grin at Mreen's small figure and its nimbus of light that now glowed with sympathy as she gazed up at Cathrin. "She has no difficulty making *quiru*."

Cathrin, the mate of the Magister of Conservatory, held a unique position on Nevya. She was the one unGifted person on the Continent whose life was surrounded and saturated by the Gift. She gave a pragmatic sigh now, and held out her hand to Mreen.

"Wait for just a moment, Cathrin," Mkel said. With difficulty, he stood and shuffled to a cabinet nearby. The others watched and waited as he dug in it, reaching far to the back for something. In a moment he returned to his chair, sitting down with a grunt, as if the effort had tired him further. He held a leather-wrapped object in his hand, something small and narrow.

Mreen? he sent, smiling a little at the child. *Will you come here to me?*

Mreen glanced up at Cathrin and then gently freed her hand and walked slowly to Mkel.

Mkel held out the little package. *I would like you to have this, child,* he sent. He leaned back wearily in his chair to watch her unwrap the folds of soft *caeru* hide.

A *filla* lay inside. It was small, inset with tiny bits of metal at each stop. It was worn to shiny smoothness by generations of fingers. Mreen wrapped her fingers around it and lifted it. She closed her eyes, and Theo held his breath.

After a moment, she opened her eyes and looked hard at Mkel. *It is a very old* filla, she sent to him.

Indeed it is, Mreen, he answered. *I would like you to have it.*

She looked to Theo as if for permission. He could only lift one shoulder. *Mreen, I believe this is between you and Magister Mkel.*

She turned back to Mkel and dimpled. *Thank you,* she sent simply. *I like it much better than my own. I will send mine back to Observatory, and I will play this one!*

Mkel smiled. *It has not been played in a very long time,* he sent. *Not since I became Magister of Conservatory.*

But why do you not play?

Mkel leaned his head tiredly against the back of his chair. *I am a Magister instead of a Singer,* he answered. He closed his eyes, and Theo looked at Mreen and put his finger to his lips. Mreen trotted to the door and took Cathrin's hand.

"Well, that's nice, isn't it," Cathrin said. "And now you'll bathe, and then we'll go to the dormitory, where there are nine other children just like you."

Mreen looked over her shoulder again. *Just like me, Cantor Theo?*

He winked at her. *There is no one just like you, Mreen.*

Will I see you again?

Of course. I promise.

Mkel opened his eyes to watch them leave, and when the door had closed behind them, he gave a heavy sigh.

"Are there only nine in the newest class, then, Magister?" Theo asked.

"Only nine. Ten, now, with your little one. We have been very worried . . . some think we should force all itinerants, by law, to send their children here for training. Had this been done before, you might have come to Conservatory as a child."

"But how could the itinerants be forced?"

"Lamdon could take away their privileges, their freedom, even deny them their homes. As you know, itinerants are always welcome in all the Houses, fed and given beds as they need them. I hate the idea of denying them that. But I do not know what will happen to us all if the Gift does not return to us."

"Magister Mkel, Sira and I both believe that the Gift flourishes at Observatory because of the welcome it receives. You remember Trisa, do you not?"

"Yes, I remember her very well. She ran away from us, and Amric refused to send her back. They have paid a high price for that."

Theo rubbed the back of his neck, suddenly feeling very tired himself. He had not yet bathed. His muscles ached, and he was hungry. "Do you know, Magister Mkel, Trisa is doing very well at Observatory. Her first *quirunha* was not brilliant, but it was nothing to be ashamed of. The three others are all showing every indication of a good strong Gift—"

"But they speak, surely?"

Theo laughed. "Indeed they do! They have to be reminded often to keep their lips closed and their minds open!" He sobered as he looked at the door through which Mreen had passed. "It is only Mreen who is this way," he said softly. "Her Gift is so unusual, it must have some special purpose. We are convinced only Conservatory can prepare her properly."

"Cantor Theo," Mkel said slowly. "How is Sira? In truth?"

Theo smiled at the older man, and opened his mind so that Mkel would understand fully. *Sira is well, and happy,* he sent. *She sends you her best regards.*

Has she forgiven me, then?

I am certain she would say there is nothing to forgive.

Mkel passed his hand over his eyes, a gesture so weary that Theo wanted to touch the man's hand, to clasp his shoulder as Cathrin did. He shielded his feelings of sympathy.

There is much for which I need forgiveness, I am afraid, Mkel sent. *She asked me for help, tried to explain . . . I should have listened to her, heard her out. But it cannot be undone now. All I can do . . .* He, too, looked at the doorway where Mreen, wrapped in her cloud of light, had gone hand in hand with Cathrin. *I will do my best for the child. Isbel's child.*

That will be a great deal, Magister.

Perhaps.

A silence stretched between them, and Theo waited. After some moments, Mkel shook himself. "Now," he said aloud, striving for a matter-of-fact tone. "You must bathe, and eat. I am sure you are tired."

"So I am," Theo agreed. The Magister's Houseman came forward, and Theo bowed to Mkel and took his leave.

The Houseman led him down the stairs to the *ubanyor*, and as he always had, Theo admired Conservatory's spare elegance, its polished archways, its high ceilings and broad unadorned corridors. Strains of music floated through the House from the student wing. Theo smiled, remembering the envy those sounds had caused for him years before. Even now he knew he could never be one of the elite, one of the Conservatory-trained Cantors with their refined techniques and sophisticated musicality; but his Gift was fully realized, thanks to Sira, and he had no need to be jealous any longer.

As he sank into the hot water of the *ubanyor*, feeling the warmth caress his tired muscles, it came to him that Conservatory might be ready at last to hear Sira's message. It would mean change. Many would resist. But Mreen's very existence was powerful evidence that there could be another way, perhaps a better way.

Probably, he thought, Sira should have made this journey with Mreen, and he should have remained behind.

He stretched under the water, and dropped his head back to soak his hair. On the benches of the *ubanyor* were piles of thick towels, and sweet-smelling bars of soap filled the niches in the carved tub. Fresh linens waited, left by the Houseman, and a meal was even now being warmed for him in the kitchen.

It had been Sira's decision to stay at Observatory. She could have been the one to make this trip, certainly. He chuckled. At this moment, luxuriating in the comforts of Conservatory, he was glad she had not.

Chapter Ten

Zakri and Berk rode as far into the twilight as they dared. They pushed their *hruss* until the beasts grumbled, but they kept them at the quick pace. It was their second night out from Soren, and they were well into Ogre Pass, their road now flat and broad, the familiar steep mountainsides rising to the east and west of them. Only when the men had begun to shiver dangerously did they stop to make their camp.

Zakri sat his *hruss*, and kept his *filla* inside his hood as he played, not letting his face or more than the tips of his fingers be exposed to the frigid evening air until the *quiru* bloomed about them and its warmth crept in through their furs.

Berk put back his hood to feel the heat on his grizzled cheeks, and took a grateful sniff of fresh air. He dismounted, grunting as he stretched stiff muscles. "It's almost too much for these old bones," he growled. "Any colder and they wouldn't move at all. But I doubt anyone from Soren would dare ride this late!"

"We took a bit of a chance," Zakri said. To the east he saw Conservatory's star glinting above the horizon. "But Iban taught me a trick or two about quick *quiru*. And I believe you are right—no one will come after us now."

He looked up through the *quiru*. Shreds of flat cloud, luminescent in the reflected light of the snowpack, crept across the sky. "How long till the summer, do you think?" he mused.

Berk squatted, laying out softwood for the cookfire. He chuckled. "Are you going to be like the children, Cantor?" he said. "Asking how long? How long?"

Zakri laughed down at him. "So I am," he said. "How long?"

Berk struck the flint and stone and sat back on his heels as the fire began to crackle. He squinted up into the night. "Let's see," he mused.

"The deep cold passed a quarter of a year ago. That leaves half a year, so it should be a quarter of a year more before the Visitor shows up."

"Not soon enough," Zakri commented, soberly now.

"No," Berk agreed, "not for Soren." He sliced dried *caeru* meat into the cooking pot, and threw in a double handful of snow. "By then they'll have nothing to eat but meat."

"Yet the itinerants think they can keep the nursery gardens going on their own, with those overlapped *quiru* they waste so much energy on!"

Berk eyed Zakri. "That makes you angrier than anything else, I think."

Zakri shook himself, and let out a gusty breath. "No, not really. But it is insane—they keep their Cantrix locked in an attic! What is the point of that?"

"The point is that Cho fears her. You were able to shield yourself from his psi, and she might be strong enough to resist him, too. He's surrounded himself with people he can control."

"And gotten rid of any others."

"Yes."

"But I still do not know what he did to Iban. Or how he made it happen!" Zakri went to his *hruss*, as he had so often in his youth, for comfort. He leaned his forehead against the rough long hair, and pulled at the beast's ears. It rumbled, and nudged him with its broad head.

Berk went on stirring the *keftet*, adding the green and yellow herbs, crumbling in bits of the salted fish Mura had sent along as a treat. Zakri unsaddled the *hruss*, and as he waited for the meal to be ready, he curried them both thoroughly, tired though he was. He had pushed aside his worry about Sook all day, but now, with the idleness of the night, it rose in him again. He dreaded his dreams.

"Come and eat, Cantor," Berk said. Zakri obeyed, coming to sit close to the fire, his rolled bedfurs at his back. Berk handed him a full bowl and a spoon, and they both made quick work of the meal, eating every scrap, following the *keftet* with strong tea. When they were finished, their bowls scrubbed out, they sat watching the cookfire burn down, and listening to the vast silence around them. The quiet was punctuated once by the long scream of a hunting *ferrel*. Zakri lifted his head when he heard it.

"That is strange," he said.

"What is?"

"Iban told me animals rarely hunt near the Pass. Too many humans travel through it, too often, and scare them off."

Berk snorted. "Cho's seen to that. No one's doing much traveling these days."

The silence stretched again, until Zakri asked, "What do you think Lamdon will do about it, Berk? What can they do?"

Berk stood up to unroll his bedfurs, looming over Zakri like one of the irontrees on the ridge above them. "I think it's a job for the senior Cantor," he said heavily, "though I doubt, in these times, they'll be able to pry him out of his nice warm House."

"By the Ship, Berk, one would think you did not approve of Lamdon!"

"I've been a courier a long time, Cantor Zakri—a lifetime, as my bones are telling me tonight. And I've seen a lot. Sometimes I think Lamdon treats the Continent, and the Houses, like they were pieces in a game of knuckle and bone!"

His bedfurs were ready, but Berk stood looking out into the purple night as it folded over the frosty white landscape.

"You know, there's an old story . . . it's not as if our Cho v'Soren was the first Gifted ever to go bad.

"Summers and summers ago, before my own father was even born, or his father . . . there was a Cantrix at Perl. The story goes that she was listening to everything around her, eavesdropping on the thoughts of anyone she pleased, and she got hold of some information—she found out the Housekeeper there was selling this and that for bits of metal, things that weren't his, and then there were other things, some secret of her senior's he didn't want known. Generally, she just caused a lot of trouble for everyone.

"In the end, the senior Cantor of Lamdon went to Perl and confronted her, disciplined her. He faced her right in her own Cantoris, and they had it out, psi and all. That's the part that people remember, the two of them going at it in the Cantoris, and things falling around them, the *quiru* disturbed and the other Gifted in the House hardly able to think for the noise."

"What happened to the Cantrix?"

Berk shrugged. "I expect she settled down and did her job! It used to be that the senior Cantor was a powerful presence on the Continent."

"But not now?"

"Well, now the Gift is in such short supply . . . everything seems different. Not since Cantrix Sharn made her tour of the Houses a few years ago have we seen any Cantor leave Lamdon's courtyard, to say nothing of the senior."

Zakri smoothed out his own bedfurs, and sat to pull off his heavy boots, sighing with pleasure as he wiggled his bare toes in the fresh air. "You know, Berk, it could be that even the senior Cantor is no match for Cho. His is a weird Gift, a dark one, as if it is turned inside out, the opposite of what the Gift is meant to be. We use the Gift to build, or to create—but his talent is for destruction." Zakri leaned back on his elbows and stared up into the stars. "My own Gift could have been like that, if not for Cantrix Sira."

"But you would never have used it in that way," Berk said with confidence.

"No," Zakri said. He rolled into his bedfurs, and pillowed his head on his arm, looking up at the distant stars. "No, that would not be in my nature." Very softly, he added, "But I might have used it on myself."

"We at Amric thank the Spirit you did not, Cantor," Berk said warmly.

Zakri smiled at him, touched by the affection in his voice, and even more by Berk's faith. "Better thank Cantrix Sira, while you are at it."

"So I will, when I see her!"

Berk lay down in the soft pile of his furs, and drew them around him. Silence fell across the campsite, broken only by the panting of the *hruss* and the occasional rustle of a breeze through the tops of the irontrees. It was a precious moment of peace that Zakri treasured before he fell asleep. It did not last. His dreams were terrible, fearful ones, with Sook suffering at the center of them. He woke in a sweat, tangled in his furs and breathing hard. But there was nothing at all he could do.

*

Zakri had made his earlier visit to Lamdon as Iban's apprentice, and had been stunned by the profligate way in which they spent their Singer energies, the warmth which caused the House members to wear thin sleeveless tunics and the lightest of boots, and the short-lived nursery flowers that were cut from their stems and set to languish briefly in *obis*-carved vases.

On this visit, the Housekeeper greeted him warily. He was no longer an itinerant, yet no one outside of Amric recognized him as full Cantor. The Housekeeper struggled delicately with the problem of his status. She assigned him a Houseman, and gave him a room reserved for visiting Cantors, but she avoided using his title. Her bows were equivocal, neither deep nor shallow. Zakri repressed a smile at the ambivalence in her expression.

The senior Cantor of Lamdon had no such doubts.

"Amric's courier tells me I must address you as Cantor," he said. They met for the first time in the Committee chamber, as the other Cantors and Committee members were gathering. Abram's bow to Zakri implied both disdain and disapproval. He spoke aloud, as well, which Zakri knew was intended to be a deliberate insult. Abram demanded, "Why should the House of Amric need three Cantors, and one of them an itinerant? I fail to see it."

"Do you, Cantor Abram?" Zakri blinked innocently and leaned toward the older man. Abram was plump and dark, and considerably shorter. Zakri gave his sweetest smile. "Shall I explain it to you, then? It is really quite a simple thing . . ."

Abram bristled like a *wezel* in the cold, but his response was interrupted by the arrival of Lamdon's Magister and his entourage of Housemen and women. Everyone around the long table rose and bowed. Berk winked at Zakri from his place near the Committee members, and Zakri grinned and gave him a cheerful wave. He knew Abram was watching him, but he was surprised when he felt the exploratory tickle in his mind. The senior Cantor was listening to his thoughts! It was unbelievably rude, an utter breach of courtesy. It was, in fact, the same offense Zakri himself practiced whenever he deemed it necessary.

Zakri turned the probe aside. He had no doubt his shields were equal to those of any Conservatory-trained Singer. Sira had seen to that. But he wished he dared stretch out a playful finger of psi, perhaps tweak one of the flowers out of the elaborate arrangement in the center of the table, or flick all the *ferrel* quill pens onto the floor. Sira would have heard his thought, and raised her long forefinger, warning him to discipline himself. The image made him chuckle, and Abram frowned harder.

"Are we amusing you?"

Zakri looked into the Cantor's eyes, and saw the anger and resentment that festered there. With insight born of his own miserable youth, he understood that Abram's feelings arose from his fear, and he felt a twinge of sympathy. "I remembered something funny, Cantor Abram," he murmured. "Nothing more."

"I find nothing amusing in the present crisis," Abram snapped.

"No, of course not," Zakri said mildly. He glanced across the table, where Berk was shaking his head. Zakri lifted a deprecating shoulder, and sat down in his chair with his hands folded before him, the very picture of a dignified and mature Cantor. Abram sat next to him, across from the Magister.

All of Lamdon's eight Singers were present, six Cantors and one Cantrix. The Committee members were also present. Magister Gowan gave a formal greeting, and the Cantors and Committee members sat down, with their Housemen and women standing behind them.

Zakri had never seen so fat a man as Magister Gowan, nor one so pale. Skin, hair, shining fingernails—he was white all over. His long hair was twisted into an intricate binding, and the skin of his neck spilled over the collar of his tunic to lie in folds against the black fabric. His eyes were the color of blue ice. They were almost lost in the thick flesh of his face.

"The courier from Amric," the Magister began, "tells me there is a situation at Soren that must be addressed." He nodded to Berk. "Apparently a number of itinerants have gathered there, and are causing a good deal of mischief."

Zakri abruptly unfolded his hands. "Mischief?" he repeated in amazement.

"It can hardly be more than that, can it?" Cantor Abram asked. He waved a dismissive hand. "They are only itinerants, after all."

Zakri drew breath to speak again, but Berk, sensing an explosion, forestalled him. He said, "You understand, Magister Gowan, that Cho is not an itinerant. He was a carver, who very nearly qualified for Conservatory . . ."

"Yes, yes, I remember that, Berk," the Magister interrupted him. As he nodded his head, the flesh of his neck rippled. "Cantor Abram," he went on, "I do think we'll have to send a party to Soren. Sort this out as quickly as possible."

Abram shifted uneasily in his chair. He opened his mouth, but then closed it again without speaking.

"Beware, Magister," Berk said bluntly. "Cho's a dangerous man, and he's surrounded himself with itinerants who—"

"You needn't worry," Gowan said. "No doubt we can handle one rebellious carver."

Zakri could restrain himself no longer. "You do not realize that Cho has killed several people, and rendered at least one mindless? That he imprisons the Cantrix of Soren in an attic?"

Magister Gowan's pale eyes flicked toward Zakri and then to Abram. "I'm sure the senior Cantor will have the situation well in hand before the summer comes. Won't you, Cantor?"

Abram's dark eyes moved to the Magister, to Zakri, and away again. His voice trembled as he answered the Magister, "Of course." There were nods of approval around the group.

Zakri sent urgently, *Cantor Abram, anyone who confronts Cho must have strong shielding! You must be on your guard every moment. His Gift is crude but powerful, and he—*

Abram stiffened in his chair, and his face darkened.

"Cantor Zakri," he snarled, with a nasty inflection on the title. "Were you not taught that you do not send to your seniors unless invited?" He held up his hands, and his voice rose to shrillness. "This is what comes of allowing half-trained Singers to step into the Cantoris! We must take steps, see that this sort of corruption does not happen again."

"Cantor—" Berk began, but Abram ignored him.

"I urge the members of the Committee to take note, and when the present crisis is past, to seriously consider passing the laws we have proposed. That will settle the problem of the Gift and its training once and for all. Cantor Zakri, here—" again the emphasis on the title—"might possibly have become a very fine Cantor if he had had proper training. Conservatory training."

Zakri sighed and rolled his eyes. He stood up slowly, and put his fists on the table, leaning forward to look down at Abram.

"Zakri!" Berk implored, without effect.

"With all respect, Cantor—" Zakri spoke the title lazily, drawing it out. "You know nothing of me or my work, or the need of the Cantoris I serve. More to the point, you are completely ignorant of what is happening at Soren, and how serious it is!"

Abram leaped to his feet. "Be silent!" he hissed. "I am the senior Cantor of Nevya! How dare you speak to me so?" He turned to the group at large. "Do you see? Do you see the kind of thing we have to deal with? There is no respect anymore, no discipline!"

Berk stood, too, and looked across the table from his great height. "Cantor Abram, Magister Gowan," he said. "Whatever you may think of our arrangements at Amric, Cantor Zakri's right. What's happening at Soren is bad, for the House members there, and for all of us. They've gathered every itinerant on the Continent, willingly or unwillingly. Those they couldn't persuade to join them they've killed. Singer Iban was one of those. "

Abram snapped, "Itinerants! Their shields are a mess, their control is sloppy. Have no doubt, Berk, we will send someone fully—" He glared at Zakri. "Fully qualified."

Zakri folded his arms, and closed his mouth firmly. *And are you sure your shields are better, Cantor Abram?* he sent.

Of course they are, the Cantor answered.

Zakri's chin rose. *Then shield this.* His psi whipped out, a quick slash that separated the binding restraining Abram's long hair. Abram gasped, feeling it snap apart. He reached back for it, but too late. His hair tumbled freely down his back, and the ruined binding fell to the floor.

How dare you? he sent. His psi fluttered at Zakri, as if to answer in kind.

Zakri parried it effortlessly. *Do you see, Cantor Abram? When you go to meet Cho, you had better be ready!*

He broke the contact, and became aware that around him angry voices were raised, fists thumping on the table and chairs scraping as men leaned forward to shout at him and at each other. Berk was begging for calm, for rational thought. No one listened.

Zakri cast one scornful glance around the table, at the well-fed and elegant people who sat in judgment on the business of the Continent. Cantor Abram was trying to retie his hair, snapping at his Houseman who was struggling to help him with the broken binding. Magister Gowan was barking commands that no one heard.

Zakri gave a short laugh. He would have better luck with the cooks at Soren, he thought. He turned his back and strode out of the Committee chamber. Only the faint, flashing glitter of the air showed where he had been standing. Soon it, too, faded.

Chapter Eleven

Mreen's nimbus sparkled in the morning sunlight, setting her apart from her classmates. She glowed like a small sun among stars. Her hands expressed her every thought, and her eyes danced with them, making her a vivid, if silent, figure. The children around her were noisier, filling gaps in their sending with spoken words.

Mreen felt Theo's gaze and turned to look across the great room, to find him where he sat with the Magister and Cathrin at the center table. *Is it today, Cantor Theo?*

It is, Mreen.

The light around her dimmed. She nodded solemnly.

I will miss you.

And I will miss you, Theo answered. He smiled at her. *We all will.*

But Cantrix Sira is waiting for you. And Yve and Jule and Arry.

Yes. So they are. Theo winked at Mreen, then rose from the table. "Cathrin," he said with a bow, "and Magister Mkel. It is time once again to say farewell. I thank you for your hospitality these past days."

Cathrin had to help Mkel struggle to his feet. The Housekeeper came to his aid, as well. Theo felt a painful twinge of premonition as he watched the Magister straighten, leaning heavily on the back of his chair. Mkel gestured to the Housekeeper, who in turn signalled a Houseman waiting by the doors of the great room.

"Cantor Theo," Mkel said. "It has been a pleasure having you here again, even for so brief a visit. And now, there are some things we would like you to carry to Observatory for us." The Houseman stepped forward to lay several neatly wrapped packages on the table before Theo.

Cathrin smiled warmly at him, and rested her hand on one of the bundles. "Here are some seeds, and root cuttings from our own gardens," she said. "They're for plants you may not have at Observatory. And there are a few small things—clothes, and one or two toys, and three *filla*—for the children. For the Gifted ones you and Cantrix Sira are teaching."

It was like a benediction. In a way, it was Conservatory's formal blessing of Observatory's tiny school. Theo was overwhelmed with emotion. He thought of what these gifts would signify to Sira, the joy they would bring her, and he could have glowed like Mreen. He bowed again, deeply. "On behalf of my House, I thank you."

The Housekeeper added, "When you come again, Cantor, if you will bring a *pukuru*, we will send other things, the bigger things you need, rolls of cloth and cooking pots. Perhaps you could bring a list."

Mkel said, "In the meantime, with your permission . . . " He held out a small pouch for Theo to accept. "We understand how remote Observatory is, and how difficult it must be for your House members to buy what they need."

"Magister Mkel . . . this is very generous of you," Theo said. He lifted the little leather bag in his palm, appreciating its weight. "Magister Pol will be grateful."

What is that, Cantor Theo?

Mreen had crossed the great room and come to stand beside him. She gazed with intensity at the leather pouch. Theo put the bag in her hand.

Mreen's eyes went wide. She did not open the bag at first, but she stared up at Theo. *Oh,* she sent, *it is metal. Many little pieces!*

Yes, Mreen. This bag holds bits of metal for Observatory, to buy things like spoons and brushes, or perhaps a strong pukuru *to haul things up the mountain.*

Mreen opened the pouch and peered inside. She plunged in her hand, and pulled out a shining black oblong that glittered in her small palm. She gave the bag back to Theo, and examined the bit of metal, turning it over, tracing with her finger the mysterious marks that lay beneath its surface.

Theo smiled at Mkel and Cathrin. "Magister Mkel, you are most considerate, and Sira will be touched. There are many things—"

"Why, Theo, what is the matter with the child?" Cathrin exclaimed.

Theo looked down at Mreen to see that her eyes were glassy, fastened on some faraway point. The bit of metal was clutched in her fist, and the fist pressed to her cheek.

Mreen? Theo sent. *Mreen, what is it? What do you see?*

Now a small hand, Mreen's free hand, crept into his. *Theo, the pictures are wonderful! The hands, and the stars, and the wind . . . It is beautiful.*

It is not frightening this time?

Mreen sighed, and blinked, and turned her face up to Theo. *The piece is too small,* she sent pragmatically. *The big piece shows me more pictures.*

Mkel was staring at the two of them. *The big piece?*

Theo said aloud, for Cathrin's sake, "Observatory has a very strange object, stowed away in a cupboard."

Mkel and Cathrin exchanged a glance. Mkel's expression was guarded as he looked back at Theo. *We will not speak of it aloud,* he sent carefully.

Theo stared at Mkel. He remembered Pol's words, on that day in his apartment when he had unwrapped the metal slab to show them. They know, Pol had said, they have always known.

"But—" Theo began aloud, and then caught himself. *But why?* he finished.

Tell me first why the child knows of it, Mkel sent carefully. *What does she mean when she talks of pictures?*

Theo squeezed Mreen's hand. *Mreen, can you explain to the Magister?*

Mreen bit her lip, looking across the table at Magister Mkel. Around them, the morning meal went on, lively talk amid the clatter of ironwood dishes and cups. Cathrin stood close behind Mkel, forced to wait until he had the opportunity to explain to her what had happened. The Housekeeper also stood helplessly watching. Morys had come up beside him.

Magister, I will show you, Mreen sent. She surprised everyone by ducking under the long table. She wriggled between the chairs, and Theo chuckled to see her emerge on the other side like a *caeru* pup darting among irontree suckers. Having found the quickest path to his side, she now stood very close to Mkel, holding out the bit of metal on her palm.

If I concentrate, I see pictures, she sent, looking up at him with solemn eyes. *Would you like to see them?*

Mkel smiled. He sat down, his eyes on Mreen's earnest face, and he nodded. *Yes, Mreen, with your permission I will follow you.*

You should close your eyes, Mreen instructed. Mkel obeyed. Mreen closed her hand over the metal, and put her other hand on Mkel's. Her eyelids wavered, half covering her eyes. Her expression grew distant. For some moments the two of them, the old man and the tiny girl, were isolated in silence, as Theo and Cathrin and the others watched and waited. After a time, Mkel opened his eyes and blinked as if to clear his vision. Mreen gave his hand a little pat before she bent down to thread her way back under the table.

When she reappeared next to Theo, she returned the bit of metal to him. *Thank you, Cantor Theo.* Blithely, she waved at Mkel and Cathrin, and scampered back across the great room to the table where her classmates sat finishing their meal.

Cathrin could bear it no longer. "Mkel, what is it? What was happening?"

Her mate shook his head heavily. "I hardly know how to tell you, my dear." He reached to take her hand, and held it as he spoke. "I have never seen such a Gift, nor heard of one."

"Mreen sees pictures, Cathrin," Theo said quietly. "Certain objects, when she touches them, seem to speak to her of those who have touched them before."

Morys, who knew of this phenomenon, swelled with pride at the rare talent Observatory had produced. The Housekeeper stood in silent amazement.

"Did you see the pictures, then, Mkel?"

Mkel sighed. "I did," he answered. "But only because she showed them to me."

Magister, Theo sent. *Is it true that Lamdon knows of the big piece of metal?*

Mkel looked up at him thoughtfully. *It is something of an open secret, Cantor Theo. No one speaks of it, and some no longer believe in it.* He shrugged. *We do not know what it is, and we would not want other Houses to follow Observatory's strange customs . . . and so we have relegated it to one of those stories with no ending. Mostly because no one knows the ending.*

Slowly, Mkel rose. "Do you know, Cantor Theo," he said aloud, "I hope you have done the right thing, bringing Mreen to Conservatory. We are delighted to have her among us, but I wonder whether we know any more about how to train her Gift than you or Cantrix Sira."

"I think her Gift will find its own way," Theo said.

"If the Spirit wills. But I wonder if Sira herself should not be teaching her."

"Sira thought she needed Conservatory."

Mkel sighed and said sadly, "It would be best if she had both."

Cathrin looked across the great room. Mreen glowed among her friends, a tiny, smiling, haloed sprite. "Poor little thing," she murmured. "I'm afraid for her."

Premonition tingled in Theo once again. O Spirit, he prayed, keep her safe. Watch over Isbel's child.

It was all he could do. Even if he spent every moment guarding Mreen, he could not shield her from the strength, and the import, of her birthright.

The Gift had them all in its grasp, and they could only go where it sent them.

Chapter Twelve

"We can ride north, through Forgotten Pass," Zakri suggested. "In this season, it should not be too cold, should it?"

He and Berk strolled together through Lamdon's long, hot corridors toward the stables. They planned to leave early the next morning, at first light. Zakri was sure he could wheedle some bread and fruit from the kitchen to take along, so they would not have to wait for the morning meal to be served in the great room.

"Forgotten Pass is always cold," Berk answered. "But it will do. Windy Pass is easier, but it takes longer. I'd like to get home before my grandchildren grow up!"

They had decided to go straight to Amric. Zakri missed his Cantoris, and Berk wanted to report to Magister Edrus. Zakri wanted to put the whole mess of Soren behind him; he tried to believe that because they had turned the situation over to Lamdon, to authority, that he could be finished with Cho v'Soren and his rebels.

But he still had no answers about Iban. And, worse, Sook still worried his dreams. In his latest, she had been calling to him, crying out for help. She teetered on the brink of a precipice, with no one to catch her. He tried to go to her, slipping and skidding across slick ice, but found Cho standing in his way, a thin dark figure growing taller as he approached. Zakri woke in a fiery sweat of fury and frustration, his legs aching from straining against his bedfurs.

When they reached the stables, Zakri led the way in, turning left toward the loose box where they had left their *hruss*.

The stables were alive with noise and bustle. Stablemen and Housemen called orders and questions to each other, and handed gear back and forth, bridles and harness and saddlepacks. In one corner several Housemen were packing a large *pukuru*.

Six *hruss* were being curried and fitted with saddles, and a seventh with harness for the *pukuru*. An enormous pile of bedfurs blocked the door, with the Housekeeper herself frowning over the stack. Pointing to one of the bedfurs, she made a Housewoman pull it out and unroll it to check its thickness. Then she gave instructions as the woman redid the roll and tied it.

Two of Lamdon's Singers stood against the far wall, watching the proceedings. Their faces were carefully blank, but even without hearing their thoughts, Zakri felt their unease. They were both young. Cantrix Jana,

Zakri knew, had been a classmate of Sira's, and Cantor Izak appeared to be no more than a summer older than she. Zakri himself was even younger, but he considered himself aged by experience.

Zakri and Berk sidled past the clutter and made their way to the loose box. Berk pulled open its half gate and Zakri went in to pull the *hruss'* ears and stroke their shaggy necks. He picked up their feet, one by one, to inspect their hooves. While he occupied his hands, he listened.

Izak, do you know anything about traveling? I do not even know how to get there! This was Cantrix Jana, standing with her hands folded tightly together. Her features were rigid, as if carved of ice. Izak affected a fierce look of concentration as he surveyed the preparations.

We will have four experienced travelers with us. He answered bravely, but Zakri knew it took effort.

But no itinerants? Not even one?

Jana, there is not one in the House—it is as the Singer from Amric said. All the itinerants have been gathered at Soren.

But what will we be able to do, you and I?

We will have to do as Cantor Abram says—reason with them, but shield ourselves carefully. Strongly. We will have Magister Gowan's courier with us, and he is experienced in this sort of negotiation. The main thing is to get their Cantrix back in the Cantoris where she belongs, and to help her establish the quiru.

Jana fell silent, watching the bedfurs and packs being tied to the saddles. The *hruss* were put in their stalls, the saddles laid in a neat row before them, ready for the morning.

Zakri whispered to Berk, "They are sending their youngest and least experienced Cantors," he said. "And both are scared to death."

"So they should be," Berk muttered. He leaned on the stable door, ostensibly supervising Zakri's work, but casting a skeptical eye on the hubbub behind him.

Zakri said softly, "Ship and Stars! It is like offering newborn *caeru* up for the *ferrel* to find. They will not last a day at Soren."

Berk said, "It's your decision, Cantor. I'm only the courier here."

Zakri leaned wearily against the nearest *hruss*, and closed his eyes for a moment. He thought of his Cantoris, of Cantor Gavn coping with Cantor Ovan. He thought of his dream of Sook begging for help. And always, underlying everything, was the vivid image of Iban, dead in his arms. There was really no choice in the matter.

"We will have to follow them," he said. "Amric will have to wait a bit longer."

"It will still be there," Berk said calmly. "Although my mate won't recognize me when I finally make it home."

Zakri managed a tired chuckle. "Are you sure she has noticed your absence?"

Berk laughed. "You make a good point, Cantor Zakri. In any case, the Spirit has me by the ear, and it hurts too much to tug it free."

"Let us keep our plans to ourselves, though," Zakri said. "I doubt Lamdon's courier wants us along. Although—" he was quiet for a moment, listening again. "Although I have no doubt that a certain Cantor and Cantrix would be much relieved to have our company."

"Perhaps you could ease their minds a bit, just tell them we're not far behind."

Zakri thought about that for a moment. He picked up the curry comb, and began working tangles out of his *hruss'* thick coat, and as he did so he dared a stronger probe. Gently, so as not to be detected, he tested the minds of the two Singers, just a brief touching that gave him a sense of their natures, their characters. He flattered himself that even the great Cantrix Sira—had she been able to bring herself to try it—could not have done it more smoothly.

He shook his head. "I think it is best I do not," he said. "They are both—naive, I think is the best word. They are unused to keeping secrets, and even less to having to shield themselves at every moment. They are frightened, but perhaps that will save them."

"Maybe," Berk said. He looked over his shoulder at the young man and woman standing stiff and silent amid the commotion. "But maybe not."

Zakri and Berk watched the elaborate farewell ceremony for Cantrix Jana and Cantor Izak from the window seats in the great room. They would make their own departure, without formalities, once Lamdon's party was well away.

The Magister's white hair shone brilliantly in the morning sun. Clouds waited on the western horizon, and Zakri knew they would stretch across the sky by noon. He was glad. He doubted anyone had warned Jana and Izak they should protect their faces and their hands. Their skin was soft and pale as only the skin of those who spent all their lives within doors could be. Four riders waited behind Jana and Izak. An extra *hruss* was harnessed to the large *pukuru*, and the bone runners of the sled pressed deeply into the snow, weighed down by the heavy load.

As the Magister and the senior Cantor gave speeches, Zakri watched how Cantrix Jana shrank into her furs, hiding her fear, and how Cantor Izak sat straight, imitating courage if not able to feel it. Zakri admired his nerve. It could not be easy for Izak, as it had not been for his own junior, Gavn, to face uncertainty after years of Conservatory, where every step was planned, every decision dictated by tradition.

The ceremony went on too long, wasting daylight, making Zakri fidget. He wanted to do something to hurry things along, tweak a *hruss* tail or tug on a rein.

"Never mind, Cantor," Berk muttered. "One more day won't make that much difference."

Zakri didn't answer, but he knew their progress would be limited by the speed of Lamdon's party. The *pukuru* alone would force the party to a slower pace.

He sighed, restraining himself. It would be so easy to spank the nearest *hruss*, just a light slap of psi to hurry things along, get them all moving. But then, he supposed it would be like trying to hurry the Glacier in its slow progress. He said only, "I hope you are right, Berk."

*

It was harder even than they had expected to match their pace to that of the Lamdon party. The first night, they almost rode right into Lamdon's camp. With still an hour of light left, Jana and Izak and their Housemen had made camp right in the middle of the broad road that was Ogre Pass. Someone had created an enormous *quiru*, the largest Zakri had ever seen out of doors. Its light extended far beyond the perimeter of their camp, almost reaching from one side of the Pass to the other, and stretched up past the irontrees on the slope, its outer edge paling from yellow to a faint green against the early twilight. A large cooking fire blazed, tended by one of the Housemen. Only the size of the *quiru* warned Berk and Zakri off. They saw it above the irontrees, and backtracked until they were certain their own modest *quiru* would not be visible.

"At this rate, it will be summer before we get there," Zakri fumed.

Berk chuckled. "Perhaps we should just ride right up and join them."

Zakri bit his lip, thinking. "Do you think perhaps we should?"

Berk shook his head. "No. I think a party of that size will have Cho and his Singers on the attack all too soon. They will lose the opportunity to negotiate, and you and I will be easy targets." He gave a hard laugh as he pulled softwood out of his saddlepack. "I doubt we're Cho's favorite people just now!"

The night seemed interminable. They had been forced to stop at least an hour too early, and they could not break camp until Lamdon left theirs. It felt to Zakri like mid-morning when he finally mounted his *hruss*. Until then there was nothing to do but watch. He sat on a huge irontree sucker, his back against the trunk of its parent tree. He was shielded by enormous boughs that drooped under their burden of snow. The Lamdon travelers rolled and stowed their bedfurs, laboriously refilled their saddlepacks, which they had for some reason completely emptied the night before, and at length, at last, saddled their *hruss* and departed. Zakri tried to listen, but at such a distance, he heard only fragments of thought. Sira, he knew, could have heard everything. She could have sent to them as well, as effortlessly as if they were in the next room. He grinned, thinking how good Sira was at eavesdropping, when she had had so little practice. It was he who was the expert!

The trip south to Soren took half again as long as Zakri and Berk had spent riding north. Their *hruss* grew lethargic, ambling through Ogre Pass, resting too long at night. Snow fell, the fat slow flakes of late winter, and the heavy clouds only parted in the early mornings. The landscape was a dull, monotonous gray. Zakri was anxious about Sook, and worried about his Cantoris, but mostly he was bored and restive. He itched for action, and he managed to blame Cho for the tedium of this slow journey. In his mind, he planned a hundred maneuvers against his enemy, but every scenario he devised ended the same way: his own strength against Cho's. Even in his imagination, he shied away from that. He had serious doubts about his ability to deal with Cho alone. He had even less confidence in that of Cantrix Jana or Cantor Izak.

On the night before they would finally leave the Pass, Zakri asked Berk, "Do you think they will find the right turning to Soren?"

"So I do," was Berk's answer. "I know Bran—he's Lamdon's courier. I'm sure this slow pace is not his choice! He's traveled as much as I have—we're of an age, I think."

"And what age would that be, Berk?" Zakri asked.

Berk combed his beard with his fingers and looked past the *quiru*, where the irontrees loomed behind veils of drifting snowflakes. "I served our Magister's father for five summers," he said thoughtfully. "I've served his son for two. I was almost five summers when I became courier for Amric—and I believe all of that gives me twelve summers." He raised his eyebrows and laughed aloud. "That makes me sixty years old, give or take a year! Six Stars, but that's a great number!"

"Berk, I will ask the Spirit to make me just like you when I have twelve summers," Zakri said sincerely. "You are all that is fine and strong in a Houseman."

Berk inclined his head. "You're kind. But it's easy to serve the House of Amric."

"That is true," Zakri agreed. "It is a fine House, with a fine Magister. It will be good to go home again."

A silence fell between them as they each thought of Amric and their own concerns there. Zakri had surprised himself by speaking the truth—he had come to regard Amric as home. He had been without a home for too many years; then, when Sira had come for him, home had been wherever she and Iban were. But now, truly, he felt he belonged at Amric. Odd that he should come to understand that only when he was at such a distance from it.

In his bedfurs that night, Zakri prayed to the Spirit that he might go home again, once it was all over, Cho defeated, Sook safe, Iban avenged. In the back of his mind, behind a door he dared not open, there lurked a fear as dark as the shadowed trees around their camp. If Cho were to win, then he, Zakri, would be the defeated one. That would mean his death. He had hoped to hand this duty over to Lamdon, but the Spirit had other plans. There was no choice but to follow this through to the end.

Soon they would reach Soren. Even the Lamdon party could not stretch out the last bit of road past two days. The two Cantors from Lamdon would ride right into the heart of danger, and Cantor Zakri v'Amric would be as close behind them as he dared.

Chapter Thirteen

Zakri and Berk watched from behind a towering boulder on the hill above Soren as the Lamdon travelers took up a position in front of the house, just beyond its cobbled courtyard. Izak and Jana played their *filla* together, seated side by side on stools, as formally as if they were in their own Cantoris. Their *quiru* bloomed high and wide, its light spilling over the cobblestones and the trampled snow beyond, a circle that shone brilliantly against the grayness of late winter. It was as unblemished and steady as the walls of Conservatory itself, and the ragged *quiru* that was all Soren had wavered and trembled, abashed by its neighbor's perfection.

The Lamdon Housemen busied themselves with bedfurs and cooking pots and saddlepacks. They unloaded rugs to set them on. Even a small table emerged from the *pukuru*. When all these things were arranged in the *quiru* there was still room to spare. The campsite looked like the inside of an upper-level apartment.

The courier Bran bowed to the two Singers and walked slowly across the courtyard to the double doors of Soren. They opened immediately to admit him.

Zakri could hear nothing. He was too far away. But he and Berk could see faces in Soren's windows, faces that changed as the House members took turns peering out at the great *quiru* and the people inside it.

"I'd have thought Bran was wiser than that," Berk grumbled.

"Yes, I wish they had done something different. They still do not understand," Zakri answered gloomily. He pulled his furs tighter against the cold. "All that display only makes Cho's point."

The hour of the *quirunha* came while they huddled beneath the great rock. Soren's *quiru* grew marginally brighter, but no less ragged. Cantor Izak and Cantrix Jana sat stiffly on their stools. Their own sphere of light glowed with unwavering warmth around them.

"I think we had better get closer," Zakri said. "I doubt I can do anything at this distance. I fear that—"

The double doors to Soren opened once again. Bran came out and crossed to the *quiru*, where he bowed once again, and spoke to the Singers. Cantor Izak rose and stepped out of the *quiru* then, his back very straight. He crossed the courtyard with the courier at his heels. Cantrix Jana stood to watch them go. When the doors closed behind Izak she stayed where she was, a solitary figure in the yellow circle of light.

Zakri and Berk mounted their *hruss* and hurried down the last distance into the valley. As he rode, Zakri stretched his mind outward, trying to hear something, anything. The difficulty of it surprised him. He had suffered terribly from the random thoughts and feelings of others, and had worked hard building shields to protect himself. Now when he needed to be open, his every instinct rebelled. He felt exposed and vulnerable, but he persisted, refusing to let his shields spring up. The lack of them was a sensation of chill against his forehead, as if he had forgotten to pull his hood around his face. As they rode closer, fragments of thought reached him, but nothing from Cantor Izak, nor from Cho's brutish Gift. Perhaps he had been wrong, and Lamdon truly did know how to negotiate with a rebellious carver!

"Do you see those trees, just to the north of their camp?" Zakri asked. "That might be close enough."

Berk grunted assent, and they turned their *hruss*.

The Southern Timberlands were named for their thickly-forested hills. Away from the traveled road, the irontrees grew in tangled, impenetrable groves. Suckers swelled in great woody coils above the ground, too high for the *hruss* to step over. They were forced to turn and backtrack again and again.

It took too long, but they finally reached the spot Zakri had chosen. He dismounted and leaned against the trunk of the nearest irontree to close his eyes and concentrate. He cast about, sampling the fragments of thought that reached him, but with caution. Cantrix Elnor had said Cho was capable of hearing thoughts if they were very strong. Behind him Berk stood quietly, holding the reins.

Zakri whispered, "Cantrix Elnor is still there, she is sending to Izak! He is answering her, but I am afraid—it is too loud—Izak is careless—" He fell silent, straining to hear.

"What is it?" Berk asked softly.

"I do not know. It broke off." Zakri straightened, his eyes fixed on the House as if he could see through its stone walls. Sook was in there, somewhere.

The doors opened, and Cantor Izak walked away across the courtyard, his steps deliberate, neither quick nor slow. He was alone. Jana came to the edge of their *quiru* to meet him, and he lifted his hand to her as he approached. There was something in his hand, some small object that flashed briefly in the sun. Behind him, a tall, dark figure appeared in the doorway, flanked by two shorter ones.

Zakri threw up his shields immediately, and expanded them, trying to put them between Izak and that dark figure. He drew an enormous breath and clenched his fists, throwing all the strength he had into an extended barrier, knowing it would be thin and fragile, but hoping at least to dilute what was coming, to weaken it. He tried with all his might, reaching past the limit of his power . . .

Izak fell at the edge of the cobblestones, just short of the Lamdon *quiru*. He crumpled as if the impulses that connected mind and body simply ceased to be, all at once. His body lay sprawled in an ungainly position, his legs at a ghastly angle, and he did not move.

Zakri heard the cries of Cantrix Elnor in his mind, *Cantor! Cantor Izak, are you all right? O Spirit . . .*

Jana sent, too. *Izak! Izak! Send something . . . oh, who will help us?*

Zakri ran. His boots slipped in the snow as he raced toward the Lamdon *quiru*, propelled by Jana's desperation. He felt, at the edges of his mind, the darkness that was Cho, and he drew in his shields, thickening and strengthening them, shutting out the calls of the other Singers.

He parried battering strikes from Cho even as he ran toward the camp. Jana reeled and fell to her knees, clutching her head between her hands. Zakri called out aloud to her, "Shield yourself! Cantrix, close your mind, or he will injure you!"

The ashen face she turned to him was distorted with fear and shock. She recognized him, though. He felt her shields go up in the thin, brittle barrier of the Conservatory-trained. Cho's waves of energy skittered away from it like drops of water on a hot stove.

"Yes! Keep it up!" Zakri called. He ran to Izak, and knelt beside him.

Between the open doors of Soren, Cho raised his long arms, his hands in claws, his face dark and furious. The two itinerants beside him each took a step back, forced away by his rage.

Behind Zakri Jana cried out. Her sobs made Zakri grit his teeth. Cho's eyes glittered from the shadows of the House, and Zakri let the cold flame of his own anger burn high. The distance across the courtyard seemed to shrink to nothing as he gathered his resources for a furious, reckless wave of psi. Cho staggered slightly under its impact, and Zakri grinned fiercely, showing his teeth. For the moment, he did not feel like

Cantor Zakri; he felt like Zakri the hunter, like a *tkir* with his blood high and his prey in sight.

He was tempted to throw caution aside, to indulge in the savage joy of open battle. He could strike again, could try for the weakness in Cho's defenses, without regard for the consequences. It would be a relief to pit his own strength against the carver's without a thought for what might come later. His psi flexed within him, eager for release.

It was the sound of Jana crying, a woman's tears, that held him back. Sook might be weeping, also, in that cursed House.

Cho's kinetic abilities were stronger even than Zakri's. A lifetime of wielding an *obis* knife had honed them, and he was unrestrained by empathy. His response to Zakri's attack was a vicious swamping of psi that cut off even Jana's sobs. Zakri was saved from Izak's fate only by those shields he had worked so hard to develop.

Zakri felt as if he and Cho were two *hruss* butting their heads together, kicking with their hooves, biting, striving for domination. Neither would go down. The struggle could drain away the last drop of life from both combatants if one did not surrender.

Abruptly, as if he realized exactly that, Cho ceased his attack.

Zakri, trembling, sat back on his heels by the fallen Cantor's head. His tunic was soaked with sweat under his furs. How close, he wondered, had he been to breaking? In his fury, he had lost his sense of vulnerability. He was appalled at the risk he had been ready to take.

Cho recovered quickly. His itinerants had disappeared, unable to bear the proximity of the psi battle, but Cho leaned casually against the doorjamb, fingering his narrow braid. He contrived to look as if their struggle had been only an amusement, something to while away a dull afternoon.

"Singer," he called. "Welcome back." His high-pitched voice carried clearly across the courtyard.

Zakri thought irrelevantly that Cho might have made a good Singer after all. It would have been better for them all if he had. He bent to lift Izak's body from the cobblestones.

"Leave him there!" Cho commanded. His psi, dark and ominous, began to gather again, like thunderheads rising, threatening a storm.

Zakri paused with his hands under Izak's shoulders. "If I leave him, he will die in the cold," he snapped at Cho. "How will that help your cause?"

"He is dead anyway," Cho said in an offhanded manner.

Cantrix Jana gasped, and sent, *Izak! Izak?*

Zakri looked down at the unconscious Cantor. The breath still moved in his chest, and a pulse throbbed in his forehead. He still held the little object in his hand, and Zakri saw now that it was a bit of carving, a small ironwood panel of some kind. "He is not dead," Zakri told Cho.

But when Zakri tried to lift Izak, Cho attacked again, and he needed all his energy, mental and physical, to protect himself. He lowered Izak gently to the cobblestones. Even then, because his strength was divided, Zakri felt shaky and sick from the effects of Cho's psi. He turned to face the carver one more time.

Taking a deep breath, Zakri concentrated everything he had, or hoped he had, into one blow, a sharply focused blast of psi that would have devasted any Singer. Cho dropped his offensive, and there was a sudden, shocking, mental silence. Zakri felt dizzy with exhaustion, and took satisfaction in assuring himself Cho felt the same. They were at an impasse.

"I will not leave him here," he said when some of his strength returned.

Cho laughed, and lifted his narrow head to look down his nose. "I always leave an example behind me," he snarled. "That way the next one thinks twice before crossing me."

Izak groaned, and moved slightly, but from his mind there was nothing. Zakri got slowly to his feet and went into the *quiru* to stand before Cantrix Jana. Her eyes were wide with fear, but she met his gaze steadily.

We must do this together, he sent. *Together we can make a shield strong enough, I think, and then I will bring Izak here, where he will at least be warm.*

He cast a quick glance at the sky. Twilight was not far off, and the deep cold right behind it. Even now Izak was in danger of freezing. Zakri knew all too well what would happen if he lay too long on those icy stones.

Tell me what to do, Jana sent.

Join your shields with mine, he told her. *Follow me closely, and we will combine our strength.*

He meant only that they should combine their psi, but when he returned to Izak's side, and bent to lift the fallen Singer, the Cantrix followed him, putting her hands under Izak's shoulders to help support his weight.

Cho stood with his head tilted back against the doorjamb, as if nothing that happened were of any concern to him. But when they lifted Izak between them, the cutting edge of his psi sliced at them. It was a different attack from the brute, undirected blows they had felt before. It was as precise a strike, Zakri was sure, as Cho was capable of. It was as lethal as the highly honed blade of an *obis*-knife.

Jana sucked in her breath, but she held. *I am here,* she sent to Zakri, and he felt the polished discipline of Conservatory in her effort. Her skills were born of years of training and unrelenting practice. Despite her fear, for herself and for Izak, the refined precision of her shielding, added to his own, made them doubly strong. And, thank the Spirit, Cho was weakened and tired. They turned aside the attack, and together they raised Izak upright. The injured Singer's feet shuffled and stumbled, seeking purchase on the cold stones. He gripped the bit of ironwood tightly, mindlessly. It seemed only the muscles of that hand were fully in his control.

Supporting the Cantor between them, they backed away from the courtyard and over the much-trampled snow to the camp. Inside the *quiru* the Housemen hovered about them, unwilling to touch one of the Gifted, but not wanting Izak to fall again. Zakri and Jana stretched the Cantor on a pallet of bedfurs, where he lay with his head falling back, his legs nerveless. He was safe, at least for the moment. Zakri looked back at the House.

Cho called, "He will not thank you. He will wish you had left him to die!"

Jana had been bending over Izak, covering him, pillowing his head. Now she came to stand beside Zakri. *What does that man want? And what has he done to Izak?*

Cho turned and stalked into the hall behind him. He did not touch the great double doors, but they slammed shut behind him with a great crash that made everyone jump.

He did that, Zakri sent to Jana. *He did that to Izak's mind.*

O Spirit, she sent shakily. *Will he recover? He will not die, will he?*

Zakri wished he could reassure her. *I do not know, Cantrix. I will do what I can, and you must, too. But I do not know.*

Damn Cantor Abram! she exclaimed unexpectedly.

Zakri raised his eyebrows, looking down at her.

He sent us because he was afraid to come himself. I know it as surely as I know anything. If Izak does not recover, I will denounce him!

Is that such a strong punishment? Zakri asked.

Jana went back to Izak's pallet and knelt beside him. *For a Cantor, it is the only punishment,* she sent slowly. *And for the senior Cantor of Lamdon . . . well, perhaps not. But it is all we have.*

Zakri sank down on Izak's other side, and pulled his *filla* out of his tunic. *For now, let us see if we can help Cantor Izak.*

Jana brought out her own *filla* and prepared to follow Zakri. Exhausted as he was, he smiled at her.

I think your senior Cantor would be surprised by the courage of his junior Cantrix.

She answered with a lift of her chin. *I thank you. I know he would be surprised by Amric's Cantor! I can hardly wait to tell him.*

Berk joined the Lamdon camp before dark. He turned their two *hruss* in with the other beasts just as the last light was fading to the west, the sky shading from violet to purple. The Housemen cooked and served a generous meal of *keftet*, dried fruit, nutbread, and tea, while the House members of Soren crowded the windows to watch. Zakri and Jana worked over Izak for an hour, then rested, ate, and worked again.

Dark came, and with it the bite of cold beyond the *quiru*. Zakri and Jana lay down on their bedfurs, too exhausted to do more. The Housemen were preparing to sleep when a sound from the House brought them all to their feet.

The big doors opened, which was in itself a shocking thing in the hours of the night. There was a moment of suspense before Bran, the courier, stumbled into their sight, staggering as if he had been pushed.

No doubt, Zakri thought, he had been pushed. No Nevyan fully in his right mind willingly leaves House or *quiru* after dark. The courier caught his balance, and looked back at the House as if hoping for a change of heart.

"Bran!" Berk called. "We're here, man!"

Bran whirled to see that the camp *quiru* was intact, and he hurried across the courtyard to rush into its warmth and light.

"Thank the Spirit!" he breathed as he stepped inside. "They would have left me out here to die!"

He looked down at Izak, who lay pale and unmoving as if his spirit had already gone beyond the stars. Bran recognized Zakri, and bowed briefly. "Is he dead?" he blurted.

Zakri and Jana exchanged a glance.

"He is not dead," Jana said, "but he would have been had Cantor Zakri not been here. He extended his own shields, risking himself, and because of that, Cantor Izak may recover the full use of his mind. Without Cantor Zakri's aid, Cantor Izak would surely have died, and most probably I would too."

The Housemen and Bran looked at each other, wide-eyed. The deaths of their Singers meant the deaths of them all. Bran rubbed his eyes as he collapsed on a nearby stool.

"I could not persuade them," he said wearily. "There were no negotiations, only a list of demands."

"What are they? Who gave them to you?" Jana asked.

"They want food, clothes, other supplies—even metal. They want higher pay for itinerants, more privileges. As for who made the demands—" His face was bleak as he looked up at the group. "They have no Magister. This carver, this Cho—he acts as Magister, and claims their own Magister came to Lamdon. Of course we never saw him there. And Cho says he now speaks for every itinerant on the Continent."

"We've already told you all of this," Berk said roughly. "Why did it take Cantor Izak being hurt to make the Committee listen?"

Bran shook his head and shrugged. A Houseman began stoking up the cookfire to make tea, and Bran watched him for a moment before he spoke.

"Our Magister has never been outside the doors of Lamdon in his life, nor has our senior Cantor, since he came there. They—to be honest, I, too—had no idea that such evil was possible, that anyone would use the Gift this way."

"And why, why would he do it?" Jana cried.

"Cho was tested for Conservatory, years ago," Zakri told her. "He failed his testing, and I believe he has never forgotten. He has gathered other malcontents around him, Singers who are willing to hurt anyone in their path."

"I wonder that he failed," Jana said slowly. "His Gift must be very strong."

"Strength is not the only criterion, though, is it?" Zakri had never been tested except during Sira's rigorous training of him. "There is the question of discipline, of control, of character. Someone must have sensed Cho would never make a Cantor. But such power–by the Ship! Surely it could have been channeled somehow."

"And now what? How do we fight him?"

It was the question no one wanted to ask. No one had an answer.

The cookfire blazed, and tea was made. When Bran had been served a restorative cup, each of them took one, and they sat on into the night, watching the stars, waiting for the dawn. Sometime mid-night, Jana lay down to sleep while Zakri kept watch over Izak.

Berk lay down as well, and the Housemen rolled into their bedfurs. Only Bran sat up with Zakri, too agitated by the events of the day, and his own failure, to sleep. When the others had closed their eyes, Zakri asked him quietly, "Did you see a girl in the House, a young woman with dark eyes and black hair? Her name is Sook."

Bran turned slowly to look at Zakri. "Is she a friend of yours, Cantor?"

Zakri's mouth dried. "So she is," he said roughly.

Bran sighed. "He keeps her in his apartment," he said heavily. He did not explain who he meant, but Zakri understood all too well. "I saw her once."

"Is she all right?"

"I don't know," was the answer. "She never spoke."

"Did you hear any word of Cantrix Elnor?"

The courier shook his head.

There was nothing more to say. Bran bent forward, his elbows on his knees, his face in his hands. He didn't look up to see the flashes around Cantor Zakri, the fury that sparked and burned in the air. Zakri sat on through the night, close by the injured man, his hands clenched into fists and his mouth a bitter line.

Chapter Fourteen

Mreen and her class listened as Maestro Nikei played a short study in the third mode, *Doryu*. It was only an exercise, but Nikei's technique was limpid, perfect; he played as if support and intonation and tempo were as effortless as the breath he took to begin. Mreen wriggled in her chair with the sheer pleasure of it. The teacher played it twice through, then each of the students attempted it in their turn.

Mreen barely waited for the boy next to her to finish before she put her own *filla* to her lips. The pattern was as clear in her mind as if she had always known it. The notes swirled in precise and graceful shapes, organized by the rhythm into a sharply defined pattern. She repeated the exercise exactly. Maestro Nikei smiled at her when she was done, but he spoke only to the others, pointing out their errors, asking them to try again.

Mreen's nimbus clouded about her, and she kicked her feet against the legs of her chair until the teacher turned to her.

Mreen, why are you angry?

I played the study perfectly!

Nikei folded his arms and regarded her calmly. *Yes, you did.*

But you did not say so!

Why should I point out what you already know?

Mreen's mouth opened in surprise. Someone giggled and she snapped her mouth shut and glared at him. *Be quiet, Palo,* she sent. *You cannot even play the first mode studies yet!*

Palo wailed, "That's not fair! Maestro—"

Nikei sighed. *Palo, please do not speak aloud in class. Send your thoughts.*

But she—the boy began.

The teacher held up his hand. *Enough,* he sent sternly. *Mreen, please go to the third practice room, with your filla, and wait for me there.*

Mreen was indignant. *Why?* She jumped to her feet, and stood looking up at Nikei with her hands on her hips.

He was not a tall man, but she was small. Nikei looked down at her, his lips pursed, making deep grooves in his face. Mreen was sure he had at least twelve summers, maybe thirteen. His hair was gray, and the skin around his eyes and mouth was wrinkled and thin. But his voice, and his music, were as fresh as new snow.

Mreen, he sent clearly, *do as I ask. Now.*

All the children could feel Nikei's temper rising, though no telltale shimmers appeared around him. His control, of course, was absolute. Mreen hung her head in humiliation as she left the classroom. Her feet dragged as she wandered down the hall to the practice room. Behind her she heard Palo trying the *Doryu* study once again, missing half the notes and making a mess of the rhythm. Mreen stamped her foot in frustration. She gave the practice room door an angry bang when she went in.

She stood with her back to the wall, her *filla* dangling in her fingers. They were all so slow, so stupid! It was boring, boring! waiting for everyone else to catch up.

She nursed those thoughts, building up a good case of temper, planning revenges on Palo she knew she would never complete. After a time that, too, got boring. She turned around and around in the practice room, looking for something to do.

There was nothing, of course. The practice rooms were small and bare, cubicles furnished with just one stool, meant for only one thing. Time passed. The tedium made Mreen yawn, but she could not even lie down, unless she lay on the cold stone floor. At last she sat on the stool. The only diversion she had was her *filla*.

The *Doryu* exercise was as clear to her as if it was painted on the bare wall of the practice room. Its simplicity made it perfect. How could the others not see? The scale shaped itself if you only played the right rhythm, and the lowered fourth degree melted down to the third in the most logical, natural way.

She played it again. It reminded her of a similar study in *Aiodu*. They could be combined, she thought, if she allowed the fourth degree of *Doryu* to become the seventh of *Aiodu*—oh, yes! And then, if you added quarter-tones to fill in the interval . . .

The little practice room was bright as summer sunshine when Maestro Nikei came looking for her at last. Mreen had forgotten all about pouting.

Listen, Maestro Nikei, she sent, the moment he appeared. *Listen to this, this works, do you not think?*

He leaned against the wall, and she played her new creation for him. He nodded when she finished. *Try the cadence again*, he sent. *Retard the ending, like this . . .* He demonstrated on his own instrument, and then listened as she imitated.

Yes, that is better, Mreen agreed. She dimpled and swung her short legs. *I like this better than class. Could we not just work together, you and I?*

Nikei kept her waiting for a response while he tucked his *filla* away, then folded his arms, gazing down at her. *You must think, Mreen.*

Mreen sat very still. *You are angry with me.*

No, I am not angry, but I want you to think about what you came here to do.

I came here to learn to be a Singer!

Yes, and so did your classmates. They are slower than you, and they knew less when they arrived, but they want to be Singers just as you do. You must not impede their studies.

Mreen pondered that. She thought of Palo, and Emle, and the twins who had cried for their mother for weeks after they arrived at Conservatory. She thought of the first-level students too, Corin and Sith who would soon go into their own Cantorises, and who had known her own mother, her real mother, when she was a first-level student here and they had been third-level, like herself. Thoughts of her mother led her to Sira, and Theo, and she began to see the pattern. It was a design, and it had shape, like the *Doryu* study, with a rhythm defined by Nevya's seasons, by its history, and by the Gift. This pattern was too great, too complex, for her to hold in her mind all at once, but she saw it was there. And she knew, looking up at Nikei, that he was helping her to see it.

Nikei followed her thoughts. *Yes. You are part of a great tradition. Some are quick, and some are not, but we all serve together. We each make our sacrifices for the Gift—yours is to be patient.*

She sighed, and looked down at her *filla. I am sorry, Maestro Nikei.* She looked around at the brilliance of the light in the practice room. Palo would never make such warmth, and she felt sorry for him. She stood and bowed to her teacher. *I will remember. May I come back to class, now? Please.*

It took Zakri and Berk eight days of travel to reach Conservatory with Cantrix Jana and Cantor Izak. Their pace was slow, because Izak had to ride in the *pukuru*, well-padded with bedfurs. They jettisoned all unnecessary supplies, leaving them lying outside Soren's courtyard. They were hardly out of sight over the hill before the House members came running out to retrieve everything for use in the House.

Izak had not regained enough strength to ride *hruss*, but he was improving. Zakri and Jana worked over him every night and every morning, trying to repair the bonds broken by Cho's attack. Little by little, the sparks that joined his mind and his body grew in brightness and strength. Zakri feared for his Gift, but he was alive, and for brief periods he could stand and move about, with help. He had not spoken, nor would he release the bit of carving from Soren. When anyone tried to take it from him, he whimpered and pulled away. In the end, they thought it best to let him keep it.

Unheralded, they rode into Conservatory's courtyard. One of the Housemen pounded on the doors, and the Housekeeper of Conservatory came out onto the steps.

"Cantrix Jana!" he exclaimed, appalled. "We had no—why, what is all this?"

Jana dismounted with the help of one of the Housemen, and trudged up the steps. "This is Cantor Zakri v'Amric," she said, with a gesture. "And in that *pukuru* is Cantor Izak, badly hurt. We have come directly from Soren."

The Housekeeper paled, and stared at Zakri. Then, without a word, he whirled and hurried into the House.

Several Housemen and women came to take charge of the *hruss*, and to bring a litter for Izak. They moved him into it, and carried him indoors. Everyone else followed, and the Housekeeper led them upstairs. Zakri looked back to see the litter set gently down in a room just beneath the foot of the staircase.

The Housekeeper had summoned the Singers of Conservatory. They were already gathered in Magister Mkel's apartment, a circle of grim faces around the big table.

They were all new faces to Zakri. Maestro Nikei, Maestra Lisvet, Maestra Magret, the others. He struggled to keep their names straight. It seemed Conservatory was full of gray-haired Singers. He knew they must think him very strange; he was introduced as Cantor Zakri, yet none of these people, the people who trained Nevya's Cantors, had ever met him.

Bran hastened to explain what had happened. "You know of the problems at Soren, I'm sure," he said to Magister Mkel. "Cantor Abram sent Cantrix Jana and Cantor Izak and myself to negotiate with this Carver Cho, try to bring him to some understanding." He shrugged eloquently. "There's no use talking to that one. He's got a House full of frightened people, and a bunch of itinerants who do everything he tells them."

"But what does he want?" asked Maestro Nikei. "What will satisfy him?"

"He says he wants equality," Bran said flatly. "For all the Gifted. I think he wants power, and Spirit knows he's got plenty of that. I'm sure he likes things just the way they are."

"And the carvers?" Magister Mkel asked. His appearance concerned Zakri; he was gray of skin and his hands trembled where they rested on the table. "Do they want the same?"

Bran shook his head. "I don't know about the carvers," he said. "I didn't see them."

"Did Cantor Izak?"

"No," Bran answered. "We were together. We met with Cho, but he laughed at everything we had to say. It was—I'm afraid Cantor Izak had no patience. He was angry. I don't blame him for that. Cho was insulting. It was a nasty argument, all about duty, and responsibility to the people, and the Committee—Cantor Izak said everything Cantor Abram and Magister Gowan told him to say. Then he told Cho he could see why he had not been admitted to Conservatory. He said if he'd had a decent Gift he'd have been a Cantor like himself, and as it was, he'd have to let the fully Gifted rule the Continent. Then he walked out. He just turned his back and left. I liked his spirit! But Cho followed him. I didn't know—" Bran gulped and spread his hands. "I didn't know what he could do."

The Housekeeper raised one more question. "If Cantor Izak never went to the carvery, where did he get that piece of carving he's holding so tightly in his hand?"

"Cho gave it to him—threw it at him, more like," Bran replied. "Cho said, 'Look at what my Gift can do! Where would you be without that?' and tossed that bit at Cantor Izak. I don't know why he kept it."

"He will not let it go," Zakri put in. "Of course, for the moment, his mind is not whole—Cho is capable of terrible violence, especially to the Gifted. But for Cantor Izak—perhaps it feels to him as if, keeping that bit of carving, he can understand what has happened to him."

"What is it?" the Housekeeper asked.

"It is a panel for a *filhata*," Jana said miserably. "The section that fronts the soundboard. He has not let it leave his hand since it happened."

Zakri looked at her with sympathy. She had been blaming herself, ever since the confrontation at Soren, for not going into the House with Izak. She believed she could have helped him to keep his temper. Zakri was certain it would have made no difference.

Magister Mkel looked around the room, into each face. "How can we risk any more Singers? We have so few to spare. And yet, Cantrix Elnor is trapped, and Soren's House members are being held hostage. I hardly know where to turn next."

A heavy silence settled over the room. Zakri had held a vain hope that here, at Conservatory, he would find the weapon they needed to deal with Cho. Now it seemed they were no further ahead than they had been. O Spirit, he thought, what are we to do?

There was no knock, or any audible footstep outside the Magister's apartment, but the door swung open, making a small click in the stillness. Every head turned.

A small child, no more than five or six, stood alone in the doorway. She was wrapped in a halo of light that made her red hair shine, and that moved with her as she stepped into the room. Her eyes, the color of softwood leaves in summer, were glazed, round and unfocused.

Four years had passed since Zakri had seen her, but he guessed immediately who she was, even before Cathrin exclaimed, "Mreen!"

Mreen? Zakri sent.

Her eyes seemed to look at him through a thick fog. *Are you Cantor Zakri?*

Yes, I am.

You play my mother's filhata?

Yes.

We must go after Cantor Theo, she sent. *He is too far away for me to call him, but we will need him.* Her childish features were drawn, making her look like a caricature of a very old person. Her hands were clasped tightly around a bit of carved ironwood held before her.

Zakri crossed the room quickly to kneel beside her. He felt the stares of the Conservatory Singers, marveling at this strange Cantor and the little haloed girl.

Mreen, what is it? Why do we need Cantor Theo?

She put out her hand to him, and he took it in his own. Her fingers were small and soft, but they gripped his hand with a strength she should not have had. He found himself awash in images, a flood of ghostly scenes that flowed through his mind with frightening power. He did not see how her child's mind could bear them.

Do you see? she sent, begging with her eyes.

I see them. He released her hand, and stood to address Magister Mkel. "It would be best," he said aloud, "if we speak privately."

Mkel looked about as if for counsel, and Nikei bent toward him. Without compunction, Zakri listened as Nikei sent to Mkel, *I do not know what the child sees, but as you know, hers is a strange Gift. It would be better to work this out without the audience of these Lamdon folk!*

Mkel nodded, and gave his mate a subtle sign with his hand. She squeezed his shoulder, then urged everyone but the Singers out of the room. "Come to the great room," she said comfortably. "You'll feel better for some refreshment, and then a bath. We have such nice hot water here, because our students practice on it!"

With evident reluctance, the Housemen and the two couriers followed Cathrin, Berk with a lifted hand to Zakri. The three teachers remained behind with Zakri, Jana, and little Mreen.

Mreen put the carving on the table, then clambered into the chair nearest Zakri. Her hand found his once again, but no nightmare visions came with it this time. He wondered why she had sought him out, in particular.

You are the one, she sent, her eyes clear now, looking up at him. *You knew my mother, and you can help me.*

Help you do what, Mreen?

Help me call Cantor Theo, and Cantrix Sira.

Mkel and the others watched them in amazement. *Mreen,* sent Mkel. *Will you tell us why you came here today?*

Mreen's round eyes were solemn, her little nimbus steady and bright. *I heard the man, the sick man, calling.*

Jana and Zakri exchanged a glance. *Do you mean Cantor Izak, child?* Jana sent.

Mreen nodded. *Yes, Cantor Izak. He was calling, and I went to find him.*

I did not hear him calling, Jana sent, shaking her head.

But I did, Mreen assured her. *And I found him, and he gave me that.* She pointed her short finger at the carving lying now on the table. *And when I touched it—* she shuddered, and Zakri held her hand tighter.

She saw things—pictures of battle, very like the one we have already experienced at Soren, Zakri sent to them all.

Mreen nodded. *And the man—Cantor Izak—sent me to Zakri. Zakri knew my mother!* she added, and Magister Mkel smiled a little at her. She went on, *And Zakri, I mean, Cantor Zakri, will help me. We need them. We need them now.*

How do you know that, Mreen? asked Magister Mkel.

She looked back at the little carved ironwood panel before her, but she did not touch it. *That told me,* she sent, slowly, almost dazedly. Her face was round and plump, meant for smiles and dimples, but now solemn. Her eyes narrowed, with an expression as old as the mountains themselves. *That is for a* filhata, she sent to Mkel, *but if the carver is not stopped, there will be no more* filhata, *no more Gift, no more Singers. We need Theo, and Sira. And Zakri.* Her eyes glazed again, and her body went slack in her chair. *And me,* she finished. Zakri gripped her hand, hard.

"Mreen!" Nikei said sharply.

Mreen shivered, once, and then her eyes focused on her teacher's face. *Yes, Maestro Nikei.*

"Let it go now, Mreen," he said, firmly, but gently. "Clear your mind." To the others he sent, *It is too much for her. Too strong—*

But she is right, Zakri sent. *She has had a vision, and she is right. We will need Theo, and Sira. I must go after them.*

You have to take me, too, Mreen told him. *Because you cannot reach so far, and I can.*

Zakri took a deep breath. *So I will, then, Mreen, with your teachers' permission.*

Cantor Zakri . . . is there no other way? Nikei asked. *She is so young!*

I know of no other way, he answered. He looked down at the tiny girl, radiant in her baby *quiru,* and he marveled at how much she looked like her mother, and how strong and strange her Gift must be.

Tears stood in Jana's eyes, and Mkel looked as if he could hardly hold up his head from weariness. Nikei frowned deeply, his arms folded across his chest. But Mreen smiled now, looking up at Zakri. She released his hand and scrambled down from the big chair.

All right, she sent calmly. *I must go back to practicing now.*

They all watched her small figure go tripping out of the apartment. Mkel asked generally, *Can we be certain she will be safe?* No one had an answer.

Chapter Fifteen

Sook's one respite from confinement was her daily visit to the *ubanyix.* It was a relief to walk the corridors, even though Bree, one of Cho's itinerants, was with her at every step. The House members she encountered were too frightened to speak to her. Bree stared defiantly at everyone they met, as if daring them to approach. When they reached the *ubanyix* she said briefly, "Wait here," and Sook had to stand in the hall while three other women were banished from their bath. They passed her on their way out, and their glances were sympathetic, without resentment. "Now," Bree ordered, and Sook followed her inside.

"O Spirit, it's good to be away from that room!" Sook exclaimed.

The itinerant sat on the bench with her legs crossed, her arms folded. Sook looked out at the vast, empty ironwood tub as she drew off her boots and tunic and trousers, and she sighed. "I don't see why I can't have company, at least to bathe."

"It's your own fault," Bree said sullenly. "You think I like being your serving woman?"

"My fault?" Sook asked. She gave the binding of her hair a sharp tug, and her scalp stung. "Am I locking my own door then? Turning away everyone who wants to talk to me?"

"You're a troublemaker, just like he says! Believe me, I'd be just as happy to see you go back to the kitchens where you belong."

Sook piled her soiled linens on the bench that encircled the room. Fresh ones, cleaned and folded, were waiting, laid out for her by Mura. Naked, she stood facing Bree with her hands on her hips, her hair falling in a black curtain to her waist. "I have an idea, Singer," she said. "Why don't you and all those other itinerants go back to your own business, get out and earn a living? Then he won't have any power over me, or anyone else!"

Bree shifted her weight, and turned her eyes away. "Cho wants what's best for all of us."

"Does he indeed! Living as prisoners in a House that gets colder every day? We have no visitors and no metal. We're running out of paper and cloth. There's hardly a speck of fruit or vegetables from the nursery gardens because they're too cold to grow. It won't be long before we're down to nothing but meat on the table!"

"Cho will see to all of that," Bree said.

"When the Glacier melts!" Sook retorted, and turned her back.

"Get on with your bath," Bree answered. "I want to get back upstairs."

"So you can stand around outside his door waiting for something to do?"

"It's better than this," Bree muttered.

Sook ignored that, and stepped down into the big tub. The water was tepid and looked greasy in the dim light of the tattered *quiru*. She gritted her teeth and immersed herself anyway. It took more than just warming the water every day to have a fresh tub to bathe in! How would these lazy Singers feel if the kitchens cooked their food in filthy water?

She was reaching for a bar of soap when the door to the *ubanyix* swung open, slowly and cautiously. Mura and Eun looked around it, then stepped inside, bringing Bree swiftly to her feet. She stood in front of them, barring their way.

"Not now," she said. "No one comes in here now."

Sook bit her lip, but Mura winked at her. Eun held a napkin-covered cup out to Bree.

"What's this?" the Singer demanded.

"Just a bit of a treat," Mura murmured. Her sweet tone made Sook want to giggle. Eun pulled aside the cloth, and Bree sniffed the brimming cup, not letting it touch her lips.

Bree eyed Mura suspiciously. "You told Cho we had no more wine. I heard you!"

"We certainly don't have enough to go around," Mura told her. "I thought you might enjoy this last bit of it. If you don't want it . . . "

Bree hesitated, her eyes sliding to Sook. Sook held her breath and looked down at the dark water.

"Don't worry," Eun put in timorously. "We won't tell anyone! We'd be in more trouble than you would. Just let us bathe with Sook this once. She's had no company for weeks!"

Bree gave them a sour smile. "She's got Cho for company," she said. Mura snorted derisively, and Bree chuckled a bit herself. She reached for the winecup. "All right," she said, "just this once. But if Cho finds out, we'll all be sorry!"

Mura and Eun hurried to shed their clothes and step down into the tub. Mura gave a grunt of disgust when the lukewarm water lapped her thighs.

"Singer Bree!" she called. "Couldn't you do something about this bath? It's as cold as glacier water in summer!"

Bree set the cup down carefully, and came to the edge of the tub, stooping to dip her fingers into the water. She snickered. "It's refreshing, don't you think, Cook?"

"Ship and Stars! I don't know what good it is having Singers underfoot everywhere when we can't at least have a hot bath!" Mura snapped, sounding much more like herself. Sook smiled behind her hand. Mura's temper was perhaps the one thing in the House that hadn't cooled.

Bree pulled a battered *filla* out of her tunic, and held it up. "Suppose I heat the water for you," she said, "what will you do for me?"

Eun was indignant. "We already do for all of you!" she protested. "It's not easy making meals with nothing but meat and ancient dried fruit and no grain to speak of! What else would you have us do?"

"I have a taste for some bread, but if there's no grain, I guess that's out."

Mura said impatiently, "*Keftet* without grain is not to my taste, either, but that's all we'll have to eat before long. Tell that to your Cho!"

Eun sucked in her breath. "Mura, be careful!"

Bree laughed. "Oh, yes, Mura, be careful! Or you'll end up like Sook here, a prisoner of her own big ideas."

"Singer Bree," Sook said quickly. "No one needs to know any of this."

Bree rolled her eyes, but she brought her *filla* up. She played a *Doryu* melody to the end, then began again at the beginning. Three times she played it through.

Sook had heard Singers and Cantors do their work all her life, but she had never listened critically, never analyzed what they did. Now she was struck by the thought that Bree's playing was a simple matter of the same melody, with the same rhythm, over and over again. The water began to get warmer, which meant it was fulfilling its purpose. But the melody seemed meaningless. Before she met Singer Zakri, she would not have noticed such a thing.

When Zakri played, the music changed every time. His melodies were living things, growing, developing, building lives of their own. They were more than just patterns of notes. They touched something deep inside a person, even a simple cook like herself. Or perhaps, she thought, it was just because he was Zakri, and nothing he did was ordinary.

Sook doubted the pool of warmer water reached much past her end of the tub. Maybe when all the Singers bathed together . . . she remembered with longing the hot baths that Cantrix Elnor provided, steaming water that made her muscles limp and her cheeks hot, that caused beads of moisture to roll down her face. She was sure Singer Zakri could do the same. How wonderful it would be to be really warm again! Baths these days were more penance than pleasure. Still, the water was nicer than it had been. She said, "We thank you, Singer."

Bree grunted and went back to her bench and the waiting winecup. Sook began to wash her hair to make the bath last longer. Mura took a cake of soap from the nearest niche and slid closer. Under cover of lathering and scrubbing, she asked softly, "Sook—are you all right then? He hasn't—"

Sook looked up at her from beneath a cloud of foam. "No," she whispered back. "He hasn't. I don't think that's what he wants from me. Nori still—well, Nori comes to see him, and she's willing." She made a face. "I'm certainly not!"

"What does he want, then? Why does he keep you?"

Sook rinsed her hair, and wrung the water out of it. She wrapped it in a loose thick coil on her shoulders, glancing up to be certain that Bree was enjoying her wine and paying little attention. She kept her voice low. "I think it's about Zakri—Singer Zakri," she told them. "Cho knows I caused that ruckus in the carvery just so Zakri and his friend could get away."

"Right enough," Mura muttered. "But why keep you locked up?"

Sook rubbed the chilled skin of her shoulders. The water was still not really comfortable, but she was loath to leave it. Life as a prisoner was sometimes frightening, but mostly it was tedious, with nothing to do but stare out the window at the white peaks and forests of the Timberlands, or listen through the closed bedroom door as Cho and his itinerants talked and talked, endlessly, pointlessly.

"I think," she said slowly, "that Cho is afraid of Singer Zakri. He's afraid Zakri will come back, and he won't be able to fight him. And he thinks Zakri cares about me!" She pictured Zakri's sweet face and slender figure, and she smiled fiercely. "He's right, too!"

"Oh, Sook, be careful," Eun said. "Don't tell him that!"

Sook shook her head. "I don't tell him anything. But I heard him talking, after that Cantor was here—the one from Lamdon. I heard Zakri's name. And I know—" She splashed her small fist into the water. "I know Zakri will come back! Then we'll . . ."

"That's enough," Bree called from her bench. "Surely you're clean by now!"

"Just a bit longer," Eun begged.

Bree set the emptied winecup on the bench, where it teetered and then clattered to the floor. She grabbed for it. "No, now!" she called. "Cho will wonder where you've got to. I don't need him angry at me."

"I'm coming," Sook said.

"Sook!" Mura said. Her round face showed real concern, and there was urgency in her voice. "Listen, I think Singer Zakri—I wouldn't want you to be disappointed if—"

"Let's go!" Bree said again, stumbling slightly as she got to her feet.

Sook stood, too, dripping and shivering, but she still smiled at the thought of Zakri. She breathed, "He's coming back, Mura, I know he is! And I'll be waiting for him when he does."

Bree came to the edge of the tub and threw a towel to Sook, cutting off Mura's answer. Sook was shuddering at the cold air on her wet skin, and she dried herself quickly. She dressed in fresh clothes, and Eun helped her bind her hair. Bree hurried her out without giving her a chance to say goodbye.

Mura looked grim, staring after her. There was something she had wanted to say, something else she needed to tell her. Sook could only wonder what it might have been.

Cho was leaning into the window casement, his back to the door. Two of his itinerants sat at the long table with their legs stretched out, empty teacups in front of them. When Bree and Sook came in, Cho turned his head just enough to show them a thin smile. "So there you are at last, little Sook."

Sook took a step toward her room, and Cho's eyes narrowed, looking past her at Bree.

"Bree?" he said slowly, his smile growing wider. "Have you been up to something?"

"No—no," Bree stammered. "Just the *ubanyix*."

Cho straightened, and fixed her with his black-ash eyes. Bree stepped backward until her heels met the door. "Gone a long time, weren't you?" Cho asked. He pulled the thin plait of his hair through his fingers, over and over, and took a slow, almost languid step toward them.

Sook heard Bree groan, ever so slightly, and she knew Cho was doing it again, that strange and cruel thing he did to the Gifted. Whatever it was, it turned them sick and pale. It had sent more than one of them racing for the chamber pot, to bend over it heaving and gagging. She put herself between Bree and Cho, and lifted her head to meet his eyes.

"I like a long bath, Carver," she said. "What would you have her do . . . leave me all alone in the *ubanyix*? Where I might actually enjoy myself for a few moments?" She tossed her head, and started past him toward the bedroom which had been her cage for weeks.

Cho seized her arm. He pulled her close and leaned over her to put the point of his long, curved nose against her hair. "Mmm," he said. "Doesn't little Sook smell nice?"

She tried to pull away, but his grip was as hard as the ironwood he used to carve. Behind her, the door to the apartment clicked, and she knew Bree had made her escape.

Cho's thin body pressed against hers. Her cheek chafed against his tunic, and she smelled the scented oil normally reserved to the ruling classes, an upper-level tang that was as alien to her as the Magister's apartment had been before her imprisonment here. She turned her head as far away as she could.

Cho laughed. He slipped his hand around her waist and held her fast against him. With his other hand he lifted his long braid of hair and tickled her face with it, drawing it back and forth across her eyes, her cheek, her lips. She twisted her head from side to side, but she could not escape it. He squeezed her tighter and put his mouth close to her ear.

"Wouldn't you like to know me better, Sook?" he whispered.

She shuddered at the feel of his breath against her skin, and she put all her strength into a shove, her fists against his chest, her legs braced. She fell back away from him, staggering against the edge of the table as he suddenly let go.

"Leave me alone!" she cried. Behind her the chairs of the two Singers scraped as they stood up to move uncertainly away.

Cho gave a sharp gesture with his head. The itinerants hurried from the apartment, the door closing sharply behind them. Sook backed around the table, stumbling again as her foot caught on a chair left in her path.

His smile was mocking, a twist of dark, narrow lips. "And where are you off to?" His icy tone chilled her very bones.

She did her best to glare back, to warm herself with fury. "Your tricks don't work on me, Carver," she said. "I'm not Gifted in the least!"

"Well, small one," he said. "You may not be Gifted, but you have your own fine qualities." He moved around the table. "Those black eyes, for instance . . ."

Sook cast a longing glance at the door, but she knew there were only enemies beyond it, Gifted enemies who were vulnerable to Cho, and who would do anything to avoid his attacks.

Cho reached her. She felt the wall at her back and his long arms on either side of her, pinning her. His long-nosed face was too close, descending on hers like a *ferrel* swooping down on a defenseless *caeru* pup.

"So my tricks, as you call them, don't bother you?" he murmured. His lips hovered over hers, and when she tried to evade him, his arm prevented her.

She thought of Zakri, so fair and clever, and so strong. She prayed for strength. Then she closed her eyes as if in acquiescence.

As Cho bent to her, Sook dropped. She went straight down between his outstretched arms, crouching and then wriggling quickly away. As she went, she snatched the *obis* knife from its scabbard at his belt.

She reached the door to her bedroom, and she held up her prize in her fist. "If you come near me again," she declared, proud of the ring of her voice, "I'll stick this between your ribs!"

She panted with exertion, and with triumph. Cho laughed, and narrowed his eyes.

To Sook's dismay, the *obis* knife leaped from her hand and skittered across the floor. It felt as if he had slapped it from her fingers. There had been nothing she could do. Helplessly, trying to conceal her fear, she pressed her back against the door and waited.

Cho bent to pick up the knife. He dangled it in his fingers and smirked at her. "Never mind, little Sook," he said softly. "Rape is not my idea of fun. Not now, anyway. I have more use for you . . . intact, as it might be!" He thrust the knife back into its scabbard. "You just remember . . . Gifted or unGifted . . . I have all the power here."

He walked around the table and opened the bedroom door. "Except," he added softly, "except perhaps for the power of those eyes!" He traced them with his finger, and she shivered.

She pulled away and slipped through the door. Cho smiled at her as he shut it. She heard him shoot the bolt, and she hurried to her cot to collapse, weak with relief and anger and fear.

"Damn him," she whispered. "Damn him!" She rolled over to pull the furs around her, to shut out the cold of the air, to shake off the chill of her fear. "Just wait until Zakri returns!"

Chapter Sixteen

Mreen behaved as if the trip to Ogre Pass were a holiday, with nothing more serious to think about than which *hruss* she would ride. She took turns riding behind Jana or Zakri, keeping up a stream of mental chatter for hours on end. Sometimes, leaning against their backs with her cheek buried in their furs, she would fall suddenly asleep, lulled by the *hruss'* swinging gait, comfortable on the wide saddle skirts. She would waken suddenly, and resume her merry conversation where she had left off. In the evenings, she practiced her *filla* under Jana's watchful eye. Then she played, climbing on irontree suckers, packing snow into interesting shapes, climbing into her bedfurs upside down and pretending she couldn't find her way out.

Zakri, watching her, felt old and careworn. His concern for Sook was never far from his mind, and he had added several other worries since leaving Soren, not the least of which was Mreen's safety.

Berk, however, was Mreen's fast friend from the beginning. On their first night out from Conservatory, Berk and Mreen struggled for a way to communicate.

"This isn't fair," rumbled the huge man. He was kneeling by the fire, looking down at the tiny girl. "You can understand me, but I don't have an idea what you're thinking!"

Mreen dimpled up at him, her halo twinkling. Berk was trying to bank the cookfire while Mreen teased him for more softwood to burn. She had delighted, as he cooked their evening *keftet*, in being the one to feed twigs into the fire, clapping her hands in glee as they caught the flames and blazed up under the pot.

Now she snatched a twig from the bundle in Berk's saddlepack. *More fire,* she sent. Berk pretended to shake his head, no. Mreen made claws of her hands, and exposed her little white teeth in a pretend growl. *The* tkir *might get us!* she sent.

"What? What's that?" Berk demanded. He wrested the stick from her, and held the pack at arm's length, far out of her reach. She danced around him, grimacing silently and pouncing upon him with her make-believe claws. He obliged her by falling backward into the snow, making a supine mountain that she immediately leaped upon with her soundless laugh.

"She is a *tkir*," murmured Jana. "You are about to be devoured, Houseman."

Mreen dug her hands into Berk's furs and pretended to bite him. He yelped in falsetto. "Ouch! ouch! I'm being eaten! Someone, please, build up the fire!"

Triumphantly, Mreen scrambled across him and retrieved her softwood twig. She plunged it into the banked fire and watched it blaze up, whirling to smile wickedly at Berk where he still lay in the snow. *There!* she sent dramatically. *I have frightened away the* tkir*!*

"The beast is gone now," Jana said under her breath.

"Thanks," Berk said to Mreen. "But it's too late for me. I have terrible bites all over!"

Do not worry, Mreen sent. *Just lie still! I will heal you.*

She reached into her tunic for her *filla. Now close your eyes.*

Jana was about to relay this, but Mreen ran her palm over Berk's eyelids and he obediently closed them. She sat crosslegged beside his head and played a short *Iridu* melody. *There,* she sent.

"You are quite well now," Jana told Berk. He opened his eyes and sat up.

"Thank you, Singer," he said to Mreen, bowing. She bowed, too, flashing her dimples.

Zakri sat in silence, watching. Jana caught his eye. *Are you all right, Cantor?* she asked.

He nodded to her. *I am,* he answered. *Only worried by what is to come.*

Jana held his gaze for a moment. Zakri noticed she was considerably thinner than she had been when he first saw her at Lamdon, and he reflected that she must be fearful too, for different reasons. She would be concerned about Izak, of course . . . and then there was Observatory.

Are you anxious, Cantrix? he asked.

She nodded, smiling a little. *So I am,* she responded. *It is foolish . . . but all I know of Observatory is what the legends say . . . and it is all frightening.*

What do they say?

She gave an embarrassed shrug. *Oh, it is so silly. It cannot be true!*

Tell me.

Jana looked across the fire. Mreen was waving her hands about and making faces, trying to tell Berk something. Berk was laughing aloud, Mreen silently.

There is an old song, Jana began.

Sing it, then.

She thought for a moment. When she began the song, it was with an air of apology, and she kept her voice low:

> BEWARE THE WATCHERS! YOU CANNOT SEE THEM.
> THEY DESCEND FROM THEIR MOUNTAIN,
> THEY PLUNGE FROM THEIR CLIFFS,
> THEY HIDE BEHIND BOULDERS TO SEIZE THE UNWARY.
> THEY DISDAIN THE COLD AND THE CRIES OF THEIR VICTIMS,
> THEY SEIZE ALL THE SINGERS AND EAT ALL THE REST.
> BEWARE THE WATCHERS! YOU CANNOT SEE THEM.
> WATCH FOR THE WATCHERS!
> FOR THEY ARE WATCHING YOU.

Zakri chuckled. *Sira would say it is all imagination,* he sent. But Jana was not looking at him. Mreen had come to stand by his shoulder.

It is not all imagination, Mreen sent, staring at Jana with wide eyes. *They do Watch, you know.*

Of course, Mreen, Zakri answered. *But the Watchers do not eat people.*

They did once, Mreen sent. Jana shivered.

Mreen! Zakri protested.

Her eyes turned to him. They were very dark, and something ancient looked out from their depths. *Cantor Zakri, it is true. When there was nothing else. People died, and there was no other way to make the* keftet. She lifted her hands expressively. She looked like a tiny old woman at that moment, her mouth turned down, her nimbus shaded. *But that was a hundred summers ago.*

Jana sent, *How can you know such a story, Mreen?*

It is not a story, the child answered. *I saw it when I picked up an old cookpot, thrown away on the waste drop.* She smiled suddenly. *It had a hole burned right through it,* she sent brightly, as if that were the most interesting part. *My whole hand went in! And then I saw the pictures.*

Berk was sitting on his own bedfurs now, pulling off his boots. "That's a pleasant song for bedtime, Cantrix," he said wryly. "Don't you know some more?"

"So I do, Houseman," Jana smiled. "And I will sing one for you. But first, I think, a certain Conservatory student should make ready for her bed."

Mreen sent, *No!* and scuttled backward to hide behind Berk.

"I understood that well enough," he boomed. "Be off with you, and no more nonsense! I'm quite out of patience with you, little one!" But no one believed that, least of all Mreen.

Sira heard Mreen's call just as she was stripping off her boots, ready for bed. She froze with one boot in her hand, listening. The child could not possibly be any closer than Ogre Pass, yet the call sounded clearly, if faintly, in her mind.

Wait, she answered, standing with one foot bare, reaching for her *filhata* on its shelf. *Wait, Mreen!* She tasted fear in her mouth as she tore the leather wrappings from the instrument. Theo had returned days before, and they had been trying to accustom themselves to Observatory without Mreen's small haloed figure in their class, in the halls. She could not imagine a circumstance that would have brought Mreen to the Pass, certainly none that was auspicious.

Without bothering to tune the strings, and with her unbooted foot feeling the chill of the stone floor, she launched into a simple air in *Lidya*, one her fingers could play automatically, that needed no concentration. She opened her mind as completely as possible.

Mreen? What is it? Are you all right? Why are you there? Her psi spun out urgently over the long distance. She reached down Observatory's mountain, skimming above the cliff road and the boulder-strewn slopes, stretching a fibril that grew ever thinner as it extended to its utmost limits, to touch at last the mind of her student. Her former student, who should at this moment be safe within Conservatory's walls!

Mreen had no *filhata* of course, would not have earned one for years yet. Still, her thoughts were as clear to Sira as if they were in the same room, face to face, as if she had leaned close to press her forehead directly to Sira's, a thing children sometimes did when they were learning to hear and send. *We are in the Pass,* she sent. *Cantor Zakri and I. And Cantrix Jana.*

But why? Why did you leave Conservatory?

They needed me, came the simple answer. *For this.*

Mreen, what is happening?

There was a pause. Sira played the *Lidya* melody, over and over, her fingers finding the right strings, the right rhythm. She sensed Theo come into her room to lean against the wall, his arms folded, supporting her extended psi with his own strength. She did not feel the ache of the cold in her bare foot. Her eyes were closed, her mind as focused as she could make it, and Theo listened through her.

Cantor Zakri says to tell you it is Soren, and the Singers there. People are hurt, and people need help, and . . . Another pause, while

Sira's fingers played on and on, repeating the familiar patterns. In the silence, the distance between herself and Mreen seemed insurmountably long and empty.

Then the child's sending came again, a small, crystalline, delicate voice, all the voice Mreen had. *Cantor Zakri says he needs you, and Cantor Theo too. Cantrix Jana will go up to Observatory. Cantor Zakri says, send Morys.*

The request had far-reaching implications. Mreen could hardly be expected to understand, but Zakri would know. Sira opened her eyes and met Theo's. He gave her his crooked grin. *I would never argue with that child,* he sent, shrugging.

We will be there tomorrow, then, Sira sent. Her back had begun to ache, and her fingers to tire. *Tell Zakri—* The image of Zakri was clear between Mreen and herself, and Sira felt a rush of pleasure at the thought of seeing him again. And to be riding once more on the roads of the Continent . . . *Tell Cantor Zakri we will be there tomorrow.*

She broke off her melody, and the contact with Mreen. She straightened her back, holding her *filhata* upright on her knee, and flexed her arms and her weary fingers.

Do you have any idea what is happening? Theo asked.

She shook her head slowly. *I must think, try to remember. It is so odd—Jana, Cantrix Jana, was assigned to Lamdon. I cannot think what brings her here.*

But Mreen is well. Theo pulled up a stool to sit close to Sira.

Of course he knew her worry for Mreen, the frightening dreams she had. He knew all her thoughts and fears. She smiled a little, appreciating his calm, and the immediate way in which he had sensed her need and come to her when Mreen had called. *She seems perfectly well.*

Theo took the *filhata* from Sira and wrapped it again in its leather covering. She watched him, but she was thinking of Soren. *What is it?* he asked.

It is Soren—did you hear her mention Soren? Where the carvery is . . . I remember a rumor, something Singer Iban told me.

Singer Iban? He was your apprentice master.

She smiled again. *So he was, and a very fine one. His eyebrows dance on his forehead like* ferrel *wings—you would like him.*

And about Soren?

Sira narrowed her eyes and rubbed her temples with her long fingers, trying to remember. *He said—there was something about the itinerants, and they were gathering at Soren . . .* She spread her hands in a helpless gesture. *I simply cannot remember, or else he never told me more.*

We had better see Pol, Theo sent, always practical.

He will not like this, she answered, making a wry face.

Theo laughed aloud. *No, Pol does not like surprises! But as they say, even the ironwood bends if the wind blows hard enough.*

Hm. I thought it might have been the one about the Glacier changing its course, she answered. The tension eased in her, and she became aware of the bite of the cold in her bare foot. She bent to put her boot on again.

You think you know me! Theo teased. *But I promise you, I have any number of proverbs you have not yet heard.*

Sira looked up at him, savoring the crinkling around his eyes, the twinkle that so often caused her to thank the Spirit for creating him. *You seem to be pleased enough about this . . . whatever it is.*

It has been a long time since we had an adventure, he answered. *And together, at that.*

She arched her scarred eyebrow. *You will meet Zakri at last.*

He winked at her. *Ah, the troublemaker. In the thick of it once again!*

So he is, she answered thoughtfully. *So he is.*

Chapter Seventeen

The halls of Observatory were hushed and dark when Sira and Theo emerged from her room. The two Watchers of the night had already made their brief ceremony and climbed the narrow stairs to the limeglass bubble at the top of the House, to spend the hours of darkness searching the stars for a sign of the Ship.

Sira called to Trisa as she and Theo went up the staircase. *Trisa, are you asleep?*

The answer was drowsy, but immediate. *No, Cantrix Sira.*

Could you dress, please, and meet Cantor Theo and me in Magister Pol's rooms?

There was only a slight hesitation, a swell of surprise and curiosity quickly shielded, before Trisa answered. *Yes. I will hurry.*

Moments later, she came flying up the stairs, still tugging her tunic down over her trousers, her unbound curls tumbling around her shoulders. She caught up with them as Pol opened his door to their knock.

An open ledger and inkpot on the table behind Pol showed he had been working. A flickering and odorous lamp, necessary in Observatory's dim nighttime *quiru*, cast a narrow circle of hazy light over columns of figures. He lifted his bushy gray eyebrows at his visitors, and his rough voice was hoarser even than usual. "Cantrix Sira? Cantor Theo?"

Theo said, "We need a word with you, Magister."

Pol's hard eyes swept them. "I can guess this will be no pleasant surprise," he rasped.

Theo grinned without remorse. "Sorry," he said. Sira flashed him a look, registering the distinct lack of sincerity in his tone. He blinked innocently at her.

Pol took a step back to usher them into the gloom of his apartment. He had to clear chairs for them to sit in, moving bridles and torn saddlepacks to a corner, pushing back a stack of papers that teetered at one end of the table.

"You look busy," Theo commented.

"It's been a long winter," Pol said. "I have to keep close track, because everything's running low. But in the summer—" He reached to the center of the table for the precious pouch Theo and Morys had carried from Conservatory. He held it up for them to see. "This summer, we're going to make an expedition to the Continent. I'm going to go myself!"

Theo saw Sira's astonished look, and he felt no little surprise himself. "Have you ever been to another House, Magister?"

"No living Observatory member has," Pol said shortly. "No one. But Conservatory has made it possible now." He nodded brusquely to Sira. "You made it possible, through the little girl." He tossed the pouch in his hand once, nodding at the solid clinking of the metal bits, before returning it to its place of honor.

Sira inclined her head, accepting the tribute without comment, but Theo sensed her deep feeling at the sight of the little leather bag. He knew the gifts from Conservatory meant more to Sira even than to Pol. When she had unwrapped the three small *filla* meant for Jules and Yves and Arry, her eyes had grown bright, the stern lines of her features easing. She had picked the little instruments up, one by one, sliding her fingers over the their intricate *obis*-carved surfaces. She had held each of them in her hand, staring at it for long moments as if it had something special to say to her, some message from her past, from Magister Mkel or from Conservatory itself, something only her sensitive fingers could understand.

Trisa looked from Pol to Sira to Theo, making an intense effort to control her curiosity. She neither sent nor spoke, but she wrapped her arms around herself and bounced in her chair, up and down, back and forth. Her lips were pressed tightly together, holding back the questions that bubbled up inside her. She looked, Theo thought, exactly like a kettle about to boil.

Sira had not yet spoken. She sat down for only a moment before she got up again and went to the window, leaning against the frame to gaze out into the night. There was little enough to see beyond the faded glow of the *quiru* except the jagged peaks that surrounded Observatory. They rose like apparitions against the dark sky, reflecting starlight from their snowy flanks.

"Trisa," Theo said softly, "could you brighten the *quiru*, do you think, just here in Magister Pol's apartment?"

Trisa quickly unwrapped her arms and reached inside her tunic for her *filla*. Theo nodded approval at her being prepared. It would have been an easy thing to leave it in her room, forgotten in some other tunic or pocket. He hoped his other students would learn from her example. She played a short *Aiodu* melody, quickly increasing the light and the warmth to a daytime level. She played just enough, gracefully but not dramatically, which might have been considered excess. The room brightened, its corners and high ceiling fully lighted, but Theo had perfect faith that beyond its walls, the *quiru* would be unaffected. Sira turned from the window and regarded Trisa gravely.

She sent to Theo, *Our young protege is a model of discipline and skill. Observatory will surely be safe in her hands for one day.*

All you have to do, he sent back dryly, *is convince Pol of that.*

So I do. She broke her silence then. "Magister, the girl we sent to Conservatory—Mreen—is down in Ogre Pass."

Pol folded his arms and grunted. He regarded her from beneath his heavy brows.

"There is a great crisis on the Continent," she went on, looking from Pol's frown to Trisa's eager face. "One of Lamdon's own Cantrixes is also in the Pass, with Mreen. She is waiting to be escorted here, in exchange for Theo and me."

Trisa's eyes went wide, and her fingers whitened where they gripped her *filla*.

Pol growled, "Are there no other Singers, that they need the ones from my Cantoris?"

Theo leaned forward to answer. "They need me, because the crisis concerns the itinerants. I was an itinerant Singer for three summers, as were all of my family for generations past remembering. I know the itinerants and their business. There is some sort of rebellion, an uprising, and it sounds serious."

"It is hard to understand exactly," Sira added, "because our information came through Mreen, and she does not really comprehend all of it. But the only way they could reach us was through Mreen."

"They? Who? Who is with her?"

"I told you about Zakri, who is now Cantor at Amric."

"I know him!" Trisa burst out, her first words since coming into the room.

Sira nodded to her. "Yes. The situation must be grave, because he has left his Cantoris to come for us. He would not have done that if it were not necessary. He is a strong Singer, with a great Gift, but only Mreen and I can send over the distance between Observatory and Ogre Pass."

Pol measured Theo with a cold glance, then Sira. "Why both of you? They're asking a lot of my House!"

Sira said, "Zakri knows my strengths. If he says I am needed, you may be certain it is so."

There was a short silence. Pol rose to pace the long room while Trisa watched openmouthed. Her nervousness and her excitement made her shiver in her chair, and she hugged herself again, trying to be still. Theo caught her eye and winked.

From the opposite end of the room, Pol barked, "Do I have any choice in this matter?"

Theo pushed away from the table and went to stand next to Sira. "Magister Pol, your House will be safe. Singer Trisa is perfectly capable of performing the *quirunha* alone for one day. And on the second day, Spirit willing, the other Cantrix will arrive to act as her senior."

"Observatory is rejoining the Houses of Nevya," Sira said slowly. "It is a great work, a noble accomplishment. You are part of the community of the Continent now."

"This is a high price to pay for it," Pol grumbled.

"But not to pay it," Theo said, "would be unthinkable."

"My father would have turned them away in a heartbeat," Pol mused.

Sira stared hard at him, her scarred eyebrow arched high. "Your father," she said, "was content to rule a cold House and hungry people. But under your leadership, Observatory flourishes, and the Gift fills it with life. You are a very different man."

Pol stood a little straighter. A light kindled in his small, shrewd eyes as Sira spoke. He did not exactly smile, in fact Theo could not remember ever seeing him smile, but the set of his shoulders and the lift of his head spoke of his pride. He nodded to Trisa. "Singer? Do you agree with all this?"

Trisa looked to Sira and to Theo, and then answered with grave dignity, her trepidation well hidden. "If my teachers say I am capable, then I am." But she sent privately to Sira, *Who is it that is coming?*

Sira smiled a little at her student. *She is Cantrix Jana, a classmate of mine. Do not worry, Trisa. We are confident of your skills.*

Trisa turned back to Pol. "A Singer serves where she is asked," she said.

"Commendable, I'm sure," Pol growled. "So, when does all this trading take place?"

"We must wake Morys," Theo said. "And fill our saddlepacks. We will ride at dawn."

It was possible, of course, to make the trip to Ogre Pass and back in one very long day. The riders from Observatory had done it when they first brought Sira and Theo to the House as prisoners. But it was far riskier to leave the House when it was still dark, to ride down the cliff road in the uncertain light of early morning. And it would be hard enough, Sira knew, for Jana to have to ride that terrifying path above the chasm. She wanted her to have the advantage of full day when she did it.

She herself had no qualms about the road. At the bottom of the mountain, in the Pass, were Zakri and Mreen, and her heart was light, soaring on the knowledge that soon, very soon, she would see them both.

The sun was high, its light filtered through thin clouds, when Morys led Sira and Theo around the concealing jumble of great rocks at the end of Observatory's road. They rode their *hruss* out into the open and paused on a lip of stone overlooking the Pass. Sira felt a beating at the base of her throat as she looked down to find the *quiru* perhaps a half hour's ride away. Its strong yellow envelope glowed vividly against the snow, reaching as high as the tops of the towering irontrees. The figures of the travelers were motes of darkness moving within its light.

There was still a twisting, complex path to negotiate as they made their final descent into the Pass. Sira wanted to urge her *hruss* forward, coax it to into its lumbering trot, but she restrained herself. She stayed behind Morys, but she felt the muscles of her thighs strain forward, as if she could move them all faster with her own efforts. The travelers heard them coming, and they stood waiting, peering out of the *quiru* at the approaching riders.

Sira was the first to dismount. She tossed her reins to Morys and paced impatiently into the *quiru*, putting back her hood as she went.

It was Jana who bowed to her first. *It is good to see you again, Cantrix,* she sent.

Sira bowed in return. *And you, Cantrix. I thank you for your sacrifice.*

It is an honor. Jana smiled, and Sira was surprised to see how she had changed. She was thinner, and her face had grown brown, yet she somehow looked happier than the last time they had met. There was a brightness, an aliveness, to her face.

Jana stepped back, and Zakri came forward.

Sira's breath caught at the sight of him. He had grown taller, and his shoulders and chest had filled out. His hair was as fine as ever, cut short now to curl about his ears and neck. His eyes, the clear soft brown she remembered so well, glowed with pleasure.

He bowed as formally as Jana, but his sending was different. *Cantrix Sira,* he sent. And with mischievous humor, *Maestra.*

She had started to bow, but interrupted it to send, *You must not call me that! I have told you before.*

His eyes twinkled as he straightened. *You are as changeless as these mountains!*

She had to smile, a full smile of joy at seeing him so tall and straight and strong. Her throat was tight, and she doubted she could have spoken aloud. *You, Cantor Zakri, are much changed. You are . . .*

Bigger? he finished for her.

She shook her head. *That, too, of course, but . . . you are different. Older.*

He laughed. *I have almost five summers!*

It is so good to see you. I have— Sira caught herself. She dropped her eyes to the snow, powerless to disguise the emotion that moved her. She had to control it, to stop herself from touching him, putting her hand on his cheek or stroking his hair. She composed her face before she looked back at him. *I have thought of you often, Cantor Zakri.*

He grinned, answering, *And I of you, Maestra.*

Before she could remonstrate again over the title, Theo was beside her, Mreen already hugged tightly in his arms. He and Zakri bowed to each other.

Cantor Theo, this is Zakri—Cantor Zakri.

Zakri was carefully respectful. *It is an honor to meet you, Cantor.*

Theo shook his head, chuckling. *No need to be formal. I am just an old itinerant with a new job. In fact, you and I have a lot in common. We are two leaves from the same tree!*

Zakri laughed at that. *Does she let you call her Maestra?*

Not a chance.

Sira turned to greet Mreen. She did touch the child, just a light pat of her hand. Zakri and Theo, like old friends, went to the cookfire to assemble a meal. Morys and the huge Houseman Berk, who Sira remembered from her days at Amric, had the *hruss* well in hand, and Mreen danced around them, underfoot, a sunny nuisance.

Sira turned again to Jana. *Can you tell me what is happening?*

Jana nodded, and gestured to two rolled bedfurs they could sit on. *It is bad,* she sent. They sat side by side, watching the activity. *There is a carver at Soren—*

Is his name Cho?

It is.

Sira nodded, remembering a little bowl, breathtaking in its delicacy. She had admired it, years before, when Iban had been her master. And Iban had warned her then.

Jana sent, *Cho has gathered every itinerant on the Continent into his service, and those who would not join him he has coerced, or killed.*

Their Cantor? or Cantrix?

Jana could only lift her hands helplessly.

Zakri, with his usual lack of regard for convention, had been listening. He came to kneel beside Sira, looking into her face.

Cantrix Sira, he sent gently. *The Singer Iban—our master—is one of the dead.*

Sira had to close her eyes, and her mind, to hide her pain. Not Iban, surely. Iban dead? It did not seem possible that someone so full of life, so generous, so merry and good, should be gone. She pressed her hand to her breast. *What happened?*

This Cho is very strong, and untroubled by conscience. I do not yet know how he did it, but he killed Iban. And he holds the entire House of Soren hostage to his search for power.

Sira opened her eyes, looking into Zakri's and finding strength and courage, the courage they would need. *And this is why you came for us.*

He nodded.

Have you told Theo?

Zakri nodded again. *This will not be easy,* he sent. *Cho tested for Conservatory, but failed. He has never forgotten it. He hates Conservatory, and his Gift is out of control.*

Sira put her chin in her hand, and thought for a long time about Iban, and about the Gift. Once again she felt the tides of change swirling about her, tugging at her. But she did not fully understand, did not recognize the pattern, even when Jana told her how ill Magister Mkel had seemed when she was at Conservatory, how weak and pale and vague he had been. Sira asked worried questions, about Mkel, about Cho, but still she did not see the road that was opening up before her. She knew the Gift was pulling her, but she did not know where it led. It did not matter, of course. She did not need to understand. She would follow regardless.

Chapter Eighteen

Shouts and slamming doors and running footsteps outside Sook's prison brought her to her feet. She jumped up from the window seat and went to press her ear to the door. Loud voices called, and Cho and one or two others answered, but she couldn't make out the words over the noise of chairs scraping across the stone floor. She strained to hear.

She was sure no one new had come to Soren; she would have seen them. Her window looked out over the courtyard, right above the great double doors at the front of the House, and she had little to do these days but gaze out over the snowy landscape, passing long dull hours in solitude. In recent days there had been no movement at all in the courtyard, not even hunters riding past with their itinerant escorts. Sook welcomed any diversion.

The outer door to the apartment shut with force, and a crash followed, making Sook pull back and rub her ear. Silence followed. She waited for a breathless moment, straining her ears, before she tried her door. It was unlocked. She pulled it partly open to peek out. "Bree?" she called softly. There was no answer. She opened the door wide and stepped out of her bedroom.

The big central room had been abandoned. Teacups and pens and paper cluttered the long table, and the chairs were pulled out every which way. An ironwood pedestal, overturned by the banging of the door, had pitched a carved vase to the floor, smashing it. Sook picked her way through the shards to the outer door. It was also unlocked. She took a tentative step into the hall.

The Singers usually camped outside Cho's apartment were charging away down the corridor, forgetting all about her. They surprised her by turning right at the end of the hall, not left, down the stairs. Sook followed, hanging back so she could duck into a doorway if they stopped. Her feet were soundless in her furred boots, and her breath came quickly.

Around that corner, she knew, a staircase was set into the connecting corridor. It was a narrow set of steps leading to the attics where the carvers stored their finished work. But in a dormer room on that floor, the itinerants had locked their other, more important prisoner: Cantrix Elnor. She had not been seen outside her room for months. Some House members feared that, like her senior, she was dead. Mura prepared trays every day, to be carried to the Cantrix by one of Cho's men, but she had no way of knowing who really ate from them; she knew only that they returned empty.

Sook reached the corner in time to see a clamoring knot of people pouring down the staircase and into the corridor. It was not Cho at the center of the group, but someone else, someone shorter. Sook couldn't see. Was it—could it be Cantrix Elnor? That would mean at least she was alive!

Sook shrank back into the meager shelter of a doorway, but no one was looking in her direction. There was nothing gentle in the way the itinerants were hauling their captive about, the whole lot of them yelling and cursing as they dragged whoever it was downstairs. Sook couldn't believe that even the itinerants would treat Cantrix Elnor so. They descended the staircase in noisy disorder. Sook ran to bend over the banister and peer into the lower corridor.

The din below her diminished, then abruptly dwindled to nothing. A crowd of House members collected in hushed dread as the band marched their captive into the carvery. A voice cried, "You bastard! What gives you the right?" There was a crack of flesh against flesh.

Nori was at the foot of the stairs, staring after the itinerants, her hands pressed to her mouth and her eyes wide.

"Nori!" Sook hissed. "What is it? What's happened?"

Nori's eyes turned up to her, filled with tears. "It's Yul . . . he was in the attic, where Cantrix Elnor . . . He shouldn't have gone there! It wouldn't have done any good!"

"What about Yul? What do you mean?" But Nori only buried her face in her hands.

Sook's neck prickled under the coil of her hair. She crept down the stairs, a tread at a time, until she could see the carvery door. No one noticed her, neither Singer nor Houseman. All eyes were on the end of the corridor, all ears straining.

Just as Sook reached the bottom of the staircase, Mura came running from the kitchens, her hands wringing a towel. Her eyes flicked over Sook, but she didn't stop. She pushed her way through the people. "Let me by! Let me through!" she cried.

Sook sidled through the crush to follow Mura. When people recognized her, they pulled back, as if she were dangerous. She understood it. There would be some penalty for her brief freedom, but she didn't care. She caught up with Mura, and they reached the door together.

The carvery was brilliant with light and hot with tension. Yul was just getting to his feet with the aid of two other carvers. He touched his swollen lips with his fingers. The mark of a hand showed clearly on his face, imprinted in red. When he took his hand away, he reached above his head to the row of *obis* knives, and snatched one from its hook. He pointed it, black and gleaming, across the room.

Cho leaned against a workbench on the opposite side of the carvery. His plait lay across his shoulder, and his own knife remained in its scabbard. His companions fell back, wary of the sickening psi that was sure to come.

"Yul! Don't!" Mura cried. Her voice echoed against the high ceiling amid the soft jangle of the swinging *obis* knives.

Her son lifted his free hand to acknowledge her, but his eyes never left Cho. The long, slender blade of the *obis* knife trembled in his hand, catching the light. Yul held it before him with the blade out, his forefinger braced against the choil as if he were about to make the first cut into some raw chunk of ironwood. Only the Gift, wielded with the *obis* blade, could separate the fibers of the irontrees, force their unyielding bonds apart. It was the special province of the carvers to do that work, and they served long apprenticeships learning their craft. They had a discipline and tradition all their own.

But this knife was pointed at a man's heart. Cho stood with one hip against the workbench, his arms loosely folded. "Do you think you can do it, Carver?" he said lightly.

Yul's lips drew back from his teeth. His face was so suffused with anger that Sook hardly recognized him. "We've had enough of you!" he shouted. The veins in his throat stood out in ropes, painful to see. "Singers loafing around the House, gardens half dead, darkness, cold!" He gestured about him with the knife, and the carvers near him stepped hastily away.

"Yul!" Mura cried again.

Cho flashed her a brief cool glance. "Ah, the cook," he said. "You should have taught your son obedience when you had the chance, Housewoman." His thin body in the dark tunic snapped suddenly straight, looking like a blade itself. "It didn't work, anyway, did it, boy?" He gestured around him to the people watching. "You didn't get away with it, did you? Maybe these honest Housemen and women like their freedom after all!"

"Get away with what?" begged Mura.

Yul looked to his mother, looked around at all the faces in the carvery and crowded into the corridor beyond it. "Cantrix Elnor is alive!" he exclaimed. "I heard her voice, and I tried to get her out of there! She's shut up like an animal, like—"

One of the other carvers stepped up to Yul again, cautiously touching his arm. "Yul, be careful! There's no point—"

Yul shook him off. He said, "It's time to fight back." He shifted the knife in his hand, the nib pointing up, the haft in his fist. "Though I never thought to use my Gift in such a way."

Cho sneered at him. "You and your sacred Gift! What good is it if you don't control your own destiny?" Languidly, he lifted his braid and dropped it back over his shoulder. Then, very slowly, he unfolded his arms and opened them, spread them wide like the black wings of a *ferrel* gliding on the wind. He exposed his chest to Yul, both invitation and challenge. Sook felt as if the stone floor were dropping away beneath her.

The knife in Yul's hand quivered with the strength of his psi gathering around it. It seemed to take on a life of its own, vibrating, glowing faintly. Mura moaned her son's name.

Yul pulled his arm back. With a graceful motion, he threw the knife directly at Cho.

Someone in the hallway shrieked. Sook knew without turning her head that it was Nori. The knife flew toward Cho, aimed with psi, thrown with muscle. It sang through the air, describing a precise arc. For one splendid moment it seemed to the House members it would succeed, that it would reach its target and free them from the tyranny destroying them.

But as they watched, the path of the knife changed. The arc became an angle. The knife lifted high, hilt trailing, then descended, blade down, whistling as it fell. Its sharp point struck the floor. The blade sank a thumb's length into the stone. The haft quivered for long seconds.

In the following silence, Sook heard the faint ring of the *obis* blade shuddering against the stone. "As I thought," Cho said. "You couldn't do it." He lowered his arms without haste.

"Someone will!" Yul said. He made no attempt to get away, but stood stalwart, empty hands hanging, facing his fate. He knew, and so did everyone there, what was coming. A tear sparkled briefly in his eye and was gone, blinked away as he thrust up his chin and waited.

Mura trembled as Cho looked down his nose at Yul, and began to narrow his eyes.

The Singer Bree cried out from behind him. "Cho! It's not necessary!"

His head snapped around, and he glared coldly at her. "It is," he hissed. "Or shall I waste time defending myself whenever one of these *hruss* decides to challenge me?"

Bree faltered, swaying on her feet.

Cho swept the crowd with his eyes. "Anyone else?" Only Mura moved, one step into the carvery. That didn't concern him. "Good," he said clearly. "You'll all remember this."

Mura cried, "No!" Nori sobbed from the hallway. Those were the only sounds as Cho's eyelids lowered until his eyes were only slits of darkness. Yul sank to his knees, then slumped to the floor, his eyes rolling back, his mouth open.

Mura's scream turned Sook's stomach to ice. Mura ran to bend over her fallen son, with Sook close behind her. They knelt beside Yul on the stone floor. They chafed his wrists and rubbed his cheeks, called to him, cradled him in their arms, but it did no good.

Mura turned her wet and livid face up to the other carvers. "Get him!" she shouted. "All of you, at once, you could do it! He's killed Yul! He's killed my son!"

The carvers gazed at her in mute misery. One woman wept, the others huddled together in fear and revulsion and shame.

Cho laughed aloud. "You see, Bree?" he called. "None of these will try me again."

Mura jumped to her feet. "I will!" she shrieked. "Give me a knife, someone! His cursed Gift is nothing to me!"

Sook's eyes were on Mura, and she didn't see Cho come for her. She felt her arm twisted savagely, and she was jerked to her feet with a painful wrenching of her shoulder.

"And is this girl nothing to you?" Cho's voice was as sharp and light as a knife edge. He had Sook's arm tight in his hand. "Do you want to attack me now?" he taunted Mura, leaning over her so that drops of his spittle struck her cheek. He gave Sook a shake that jarred her teeth and loosened the binding of her hair, spilling her long tresses over her shoulders.

"Let me go!" she cried, and despite the pain in her arm, she tried to pull away. He wrapped his other arm around her, holding her like he might a sack of grain. She kicked and struggled, but she was too small and too light. When she gave it up, panting, she saw Bree bent to her knees, clutching her head, and she knew the Singer had tried to interfere.

Cho backed out of the carvery, dragging Sook. The people in the corridor stepped on each other's feet in their haste to get away from him. Sook's toes could not reach the ground, and now her ribs and stomach hurt with the pressure of his arm. She could barely breathe. When he finally set her feet on a stair, two treads above his own, she gasped for air and sagged against the banister. A drop of blood fell out of her sleeve to the floor, leaving a small pitiful mark.

Cho held out his hand to Nori, and she came to take it, her head lowered, looking sidelong at the people she passed. "I always repay loyalty," Cho murmured, smiling.

Sook stared in speechless horror. Nori—Nori had betrayed Yul!

The people in the corridor gasped, and one or two made sounds of disgust. Nori's head dropped lower yet, but she let Cho draw her up the stairs nonetheless, and he prodded Sook to make her precede them. Slowly, pressing her fingers to her bleeding arm, she climbed the steps. The most eager of Cho's followers came after them, resuming their posts at the door as Cho thrust Sook into the apartment, and he and Nori followed.

He took Nori into his own bedroom, the large one. Just before closing the door, he cast Sook a thin smile. The feral gleam in his eyes made her shrink against the wall.

He said, "Your turn will come, little Sook."

He shut the door between them, and Sook turned with dragging feet to her own room. Before she closed her door, she heard Nori cry out. She knew Cho had hurt her, taking his pleasure, if pleasure it was, without regard for her pain.

Sook shut her own door sharply, and leaned her forehead against it, sick with fear and grief. My turn, she thought. If my turn comes, I'll kill him. I swear it!

She went to the window to look out over the snowbound hills. She wished with all her might for Zakri to come.

Chapter Nineteen

"Between us, we are strong enough to defeat him," Zakri said, aloud for Berk's benefit. "The trick will be to get to him without one of us being hurt."

"Can we not simply go in, and force him to leave?" Sira asked. She looked to Berk. "Surely we have the authority?"

Berk was just shedding his furs, and combing out his hair and beard with his fingers. He shook his head. "Cho doesn't recognize authority," he said. He eased himself down with a groan to rest his back against an arching ironwood sucker. It had been a long day of riding, pushing south through Ogre Pass. In the late afternoon they had turned into the road to the southeast. The way led through irontree groves so thickly grown the branches sometimes meshed above their heads into a canopy of dark green needles.

"You know, these gray hairs of mine are reminders to you all that my bones are old!" Berk grumbled.

Mreen scrambled up from feeding softwood twigs to Theo's cookfire and trotted to Berk. She bent over him, looking into his eyes and patting his grizzled cheeks with her small hands. *Cantor Theo,* she sent, *please tell Berk I will heal his bones for him.*

"Mreen says she will work on those old bones," Theo said, grinning at the courier.

Berk grunted, trying to shift into a more comfortable position. "She must be some healer, if she can make old bones young!"

He has to sit still, Mreen sent. *And Cantor Theo, you have to tell me what mode to use!*

Theo chuckled. "This could be interesting, Berk. You have to hold still, and she does not know which mode to use, so it could take a while!"

"Being still sounds fine to me," the big man rumbled. "I can use the rest." He tapped Mreen gently under her chin with a thick finger. "Take as long as you like, little one." He leaned his head back against the great root and closed his eyes.

Mreen, I suggest Lidya, Theo sent. *Your patient is more tired than ill.*

Theo went on with the *keftet* preparation while Mreen played a *Lidya* melody on her *filla*. The notes were clear and dry in the violet evening, fading to nothing almost before the ear could catch them.

Sira nodded approval. *Your fingerings are much improved.*

Mreen's nimbus glowed, and she hopped from one foot to the other, as full of energy as Berk was drained. *Oh, yes!* she bubbled. *Cantor Nikei is very strict.*

So I remember.

Mreen danced to the cookfire and knelt beside Theo once again. *Cantor Theo, will you ask Berk if he is better?*

Theo did. Berk opened his eyes, then closed one in a wink at Mreen. "Much better, child, thank you. Now you just do that every night, and this old carcass might make it through the journey." The travelers laughed. The *hruss* lifted their heads, long ears following the voices.

As Theo put the finishing touches on their meal, Zakri warned Sira, "You must not underestimate Cho's strength. His Gift is crude, but his psi is like a kick from a *hruss*. It can do a lot of damage. He can ruin an unshielded mind. It is better if we combine our shields, as Jana and I did when he attacked Izak."

"And his own shields?" she asked.

Zakri held up his hands, palms out. "Do carvers even learn to shield? We do not know."

"And if we attack him? Then what happens to his mind?"

"I have given that no thought," Zakri answered. "I am not likely to care, either!"

Sira's lips pressed together, and she dropped her eyes. Zakri saw Theo give her a sharp look before he pulled the *keftet* from the fire, ready to spoon it into their bowls. Mreen stuck her finger into the pot and licked a dollop of *keftet*, smacking her lips. Theo tousled her hair. "What Singers does Cho have around him?" he asked.

"I know hardly any names," Zakri told him. "There is a man named Klas, and one named Shiro. Those are all I met, though the House is crowded with Singers. I was only one among many. I know several of the House members, though . . . the cooks."

"So I am not the only one who is changeless," Sira observed.

Zakri laughed and saluted with his carved spoon. "I promise, Cantrix Sira, my appetite is only that of a healthy grown man!"

"Indeed," she said. "We will see."

"My father knew Klas v'Soren," Theo said as he handed them their bowls. "Called him a thief and a sneak, not to put too fine a point on it. He traveled with him once, and warned me never to make the same mistake. Singer Klas came poorly supplied, so he helped himself out of my father's saddlepacks—then took more than his share of the metal at the trip's end."

"Not a strong Singer, though, I think," Zakri said.

"Probably not, or he would not have been a thief," Theo agreed. He came to sit crosslegged on his furs next to Sira.

They were all quiet for a moment, enjoying the excellent *keftet*. It was fragrant with Observatory's spices and rich with good grain. Zakri could have smacked his lips like Mreen. He eyed the pot to see if there was more.

"What I would like to know," Theo went on after a time, "is why so many Singers follow someone like Cho? Klas I can understand, but the rest of them—I knew many a fine itinerant, honest and hardworking men and women. Where are they all?"

Zakri swallowed a large mouthful before he could answer. "I suspect there are a number of them who have second thoughts about the whole thing, but Cho wastes no time in punishing anyone who challenges him. His talent is for controlling the Gifted. They are all terrified."

"And the House members?"

Berk put his spoon down and looked around at each of them. "You have to understand, before we go into this situation, that Soren's House members are helpless," he said. "Their Magister's gone, with all his family. Their Cantor's dead, and by now their Cantrix could be. They're dependent on the itinerants for their warmth, such as it is. Cho has them trapped."

"There is a Gifted child at Soren, ready and willing to go to Conservatory," Zakri added. "But Cho will not allow it."

Sira's eyes flashed darkly at that, a look Zakri remembered well. "How could things have gone so far?" she demanded. "Has the Committee done nothing?"

Zakri shrugged. "Lamdon did not know until we told them Singers from all over the Continent were disappearing. Iban was trying to reach Amric to warn me, I believe. He almost made it. He came so close."

Sira laid her bowl aside, her meal unfinished, and turned her gaze beyond the *quiru* as if she were at that moment wishing Iban safe passage beyond the stars. Watching her, Zakri felt the pain of their master's loss once again, renewed by the freshness of Sira's grief.

Theo felt it too. *We will set it right, Sira. I promise.*

Spirit willing, Sira answered. She met Theo's eyes, her face open and vulnerable in a way Zakri had rarely seen. He was surprised to see Theo touch Sira's knee, and to see that she did not pull away, but even laid her fingertips briefly against his hand.

Would the Spirit dare will anything Cantrix Sira does not? Theo sent.

That made Zakri laugh, startling Berk. "I am sorry, Berk," he chortled. "It is this Cantor Theo and his jokes. I will make him speak them aloud from now on."

Berk smiled wearily. "I'm half asleep anyway, and no decent audience." He bowed to Theo. "Cantor Theo, if you could save me a joke for tomorrow, I'd appreciate it."

Theo made a deprecating gesture. "Your Cantor Zakri is too easily amused."

Zakri smiled at Sira. "So I have heard, and often." He won a slight smile from her in return, though her eyes were shadowed.

Theo collected the *keftet* bowls, frowning over the bits Sira had left in hers, and stepped to the edge of the camp to scrub them out with chunks of snow. Sira took Mreen outside the *quiru*. They came back quickly, shivering. Despite Mreen's protests, Sira made her sit still while she undid the binding of her hair and helped her pull off her boots and her trousers. In just her tunic, Mreen quickly wriggled down into her bedfurs. Zakri saw Sira touch the little girl's cheek with the backs of her fingers.

Sleep well, child, she sent.

One song first? Mreen begged.

Zakri joined in. *Yes, Cantrix Sira! One song, please!*

Sira shot him a look. *You are still listening to every conversation around you!*

He gave her his most winning smile. *It has been a most useful habit.*

She sighed in mock exasperation, but she sat back on her heels at the edge of Mreen's bedfurs and thought for a moment. *One song, then*, she sent to Mreen. *A very old one.*

Mreen dimpled and snuggled deep into her furs. The layers of the *caeru* pelt, yellow on the outside, creamy white in the soft depths, tangled with her red hair, encircling her sleepy face. Zakri's heart warmed at the sight. He could understand, just now, the look Sira sometimes turned on him. Occasionally he caught her watching him, her angular features softer than usual, her eyes brighter. She always averted her glance if their eyes met, and the expression on her face was a mystery to him. He felt a bit sad, thinking of it. He closed his eyes to listen to her sing, and to sense the gentle cantrip for sleep she wove into the lullaby.

> LITTLE ONE, LOST ONE,
> SLEEPY ONE, SMALL ONE,
> PILLOW YOUR HEAD,
> DREAM OF THE STARS,
> AND THE SHIP THAT CARRIES YOU HOME.
> LITTLE ONE, SWEET ONE,
> DROWSY ONE, LOST ONE,
> THE NIGHT IS LONG,
> THE SNOW IS COLD,
> BUT THE SHIP WILL CARRY YOU HOME.

Mreen's drooping lashes made delicate shadows on her cheeks. Berk murmured, so as not to wake her, "Lovely. It's good to hear you sing again, Cantrix. We've missed you at Amric."

Sira inclined her head to him. "You are kind, Berk. I thank you."

Mreen's eyes opened again, resisting. *More*, she sent sleepily. *One more song.*

Zakri chuckled. *I will sing you one. I am no Cantrix Sira, but I sing a little!*

Sira smiled at him. "It would give me pleasure to hear you. It has been some time."

"There is a song my mother taught me," Zakri told Mreen. "My mother was a Singer like yours. Not a Cantrix, though—an itinerant Singer."

Mreen's green eyes opened wide, thinking about this. *Is she dead, too, like mine?*

Zakri gazed at her across the banked fire. He saw her mother in her eyes, laughing Isbel of the beautiful voice and auburn hair. *Yes*, he answered, and he sent Mreen a picture of his own mother, as best he could remember her. She gave a little nod of understanding. "Now, I will sing this song, but then you must go to sleep. Promise?"

She nodded, heavy eyelids struggling against the effects of Sira's cantrip. Zakri turned his own eyes up to the stars blanketing the night sky above their *quiru*. It had been a long, long time since he had thought of his mother.

> THE *CAERU* HAS PUPS, AND THE *FERREL* HAS FLEDGLINGS,
> THE *HRUSS* HAS ITS FOAL, AND THE *WEZEL* ITS KITS.
> THE *CARWAL* HAS WHELPS, THE *TKIR* HAVE THEIR CATLINGS
> AND I, MY SWEET DARLING, HAVE YOU.

THE *URBEAR* HAS CUBS THAT PLAY ON THE GLACIER,
THE *TKIR* LETS ITS BABES RUN WILD IN THE SNOW,
BUT THE CHILD OF MY HEART TUMBLES HERE ON THE FLOOR,
WAITING FOR SUMMER, WAITING TO GROW.

Sira, still kneeling on the edge of Mreen's bedfurs, looked up at Zakri. H was shocked to see tears in her eyes. *I am sorry, Cantrix,* he began.

She shook her head. *No, Zakri, do not be. It is a beautiful song, and a beautiful thought. I only thought of your mother . . . it touched me.*

Mreen was sound asleep at last. The whole camp was quiet, ready for the night. Sira got up and went to her own bedfurs. The men made a quick trip out of the *quiru,* and Zakri made a last round of the *hruss,* making certain they were settled in. Their heads hung low to the trampled snow, but their ears swiveled back and forth, following the sounds the people made.

When they were all in their bedfurs, Zakri leaned on his elbow, looking across the coals of the cookfire. *Cantrix Sira, why did that old children's song upset you?*

It did not upset me, she sent firmly. *I was moved. That is all.*

But something upset you, earlier. I saw it.

Sira sat up in her bedfurs, tracing her scarred eyebrow with her finger. Theo sat up as well, watching her.

You were talking about carvers, and whether they learn to shield. Zakri nodded. She put her arms around her upraised knees and leaned her chin on them. *Long ago, I hurt someone, and I am loath to do it again. Perhaps I cannot do it again. I fear this whole crisis comes about because of the way we treat the Gift, measuring it, testing it as if it were an absolute. For this carver, only Conservatory could have satisfied his ambitions. Theo felt much the same, but his parents would not allow it . . . they insisted he follow in their traditions. If there were more choices for the Gifted, other paths for them to follow, this tragedy might have been averted.*

Theo put in, *Remember, Sira, the irontree sucker cannot force the treeling to take root.*

Sira shook her head. *I remember the proverb, but . . .* She shrugged.

Zakri laughed quietly. *I do not get it either,* he sent.

Theo sent, *Cho is responsible for what he has become. You are certainly not, Sira, nor even, I think, the Committee or Conservatory.*

She hugged her knees tighter. *Just the same, I am fearful for the Gift. Will they listen, now, when we tell them about Observatory? That we have so many, while the Houses of the Continent have so few? And what awful things will we have to do at Soren?*

At the least, Theo assured her, *we will save the little one there. One task at a time.*

Sira took a deep breath, rubbing her eyes as if to banish her dark thoughts. *Why, Theo, no proverb for that?*

Too tired, my dear. He yawned to prove it. They both lay down, pulling their bedfurs close about them.

Zakri followed their example, but for some time he lay staring up at the stars past the *quiru,* thinking. He was fearful for Mreen, for himself, for these others. But he was very glad to be here, to be with Sira and with Theo. He was grateful for the choice.

Chapter Twenty

Sook, standing alone at her window, saw the travelers crest the ridge above the House. They trooped down toward Soren in a colorful wave of *hruss*, some carrying riders, two laden only with bulging packs, two with loaded *pukuru* sliding behind them over the snow. She pressed herself against the window and counted them. Twelve people, and sixteen *hruss*! Never had she seen so many riders at one time. With trembling fingers, she brushed and rebound her hair, her eyes never leaving the scene. Surely this meant Zakri was here at last!

Perhaps Zakri could even see her, standing in her narrow window. She clasped her hands beneath her chin and watched the *quiru* bloom about the traveling party, just beyond the courtyard. It towered against the gray sky, a wide column of warmth and light. Housemen set about making the camp comfortable, unpacking a table from the *pukuru*, two high-backed chairs, several stools. They ranged bedfurs in a long row at the edge of the camp, and tethered the *hruss* on the other side. Sook stared into the brilliant light, trying to make out the faces of the people.

She could not find Zakri. There were two tall, slender men, but neither was he, and they both behaved like servants. They bowed often to two shorter men, one plump and dark, one even plumper, the fattest man Sook had ever seen, and pale as the snow on the hills around them. Those two were quickly seated in the tall chairs, and two others near them on stools. One of the Housemen started a cookfire and soon the seated men were holding cups of tea, looking at the House, but making no move toward it. Two burly Housemen took up positions at the edge of the *quiru*. They wore long knives strapped about them, and they stood facing out toward Soren.

Sook's hopes thinned, faded away like curls of smoke. She lowered herself into the window seat, suddenly weary. She gazed out at the newly made camp, and the men in it, and she understood all too well who and what they were. She had never been to the capital House of Nevya, in fact had never been away from her own House in her life, but she knew that such an exhibition of riches could come from only one place. It wasn't Zakri who had come, but Lamdon. Lamdon! Cantors and Magisters and Committee members. What did such people know of real trouble?

In the outer room of the apartment, she heard the itinerants talking and Cho's light voice in response. "It's just what we've been waiting for," he said. "Call the Singers into the Cantoris. You, Klas, give the carvers one last chance to be a part of this. Our goal has come to us!"

Someone asked a question Sook couldn't hear. Cho's answer was as clear and sharp as the icicles under Soren's eaves. "It's Magister Gowan. That dark man with him is Cantor Abram himself. Just where we want them."

Sook leaned forward, putting her forehead against the cold limeglass. The men from Lamdon were being served a meal, not a simple bowl of *keftet* but several different dishes spread out around them. She imagined what there might be for them to eat—grain for sure, dried fruit, perhaps nutbread with oil to dip it in. Her mouth watered, and a spasm of craving knotted her stomach. She wrapped her arms around her middle and set her jaw. They must not give in, neither she nor Mura nor the carvers nor the House members! They must stand on their own, and together. And they must warn those soft men from Lamdon! Didn't they realize Cho could strike at them even as they sat over their meal?

Two short raps sounded at her door, and the bolt slid back. Bree looked in. "Sook, I'm sorry, but no bath today. You probably saw?"

Sook jumped to her feet. "What's going to happen?"

Bree's plain features twisted. "We're having a meeting in the Cantoris. I don't feel good about this. That's Magister Gowan out there!"

"So I heard," Sook answered. She turned back to the window. "Which one is he?"

"The white one," Bree grunted.

"Spirit!" Sook exclaimed. "Did you ever know a man could grow so fat?"

"A few weeks at Soren, and he'd be skinny as a *wezel*," Bree retorted. "Like the rest of us. Anyway, I have to go. Sorry about the *ubanyix*."

"Bree, wait!" Sook cried. "Could you just—just forget—about locking the door? I promise I won't say a word. And with all this excitement . . ."

Bree looked back over her shoulder. The apartment was empty, but she hesitated. "I'm still in trouble for trying to help you the last time," she muttered.

"I know," Sook said softly. "But if he fails, and you've been kind to me—I know Singer Zakri will stand up for you!"

"Zakri?" Bree squinted at her. "You know, Sook, I have to agree with Mura. You put a lot of faith in a man you don't really know. And he's not even out there!"

Sook stiffened her back. "He will be! And I know what I need to know."

"They all say the same thing," Bree said sourly.

"Bree—just for me, then? If he finds out I'll tell him I unlocked it myself!"

Bree shook her head, muttering, "Six Stars! I'll probably be sorry for this. Just remember, if he puts someone else on this duty, you may not get any favors at all!"

Sook gave Bree a brilliant smile. "Thank you, thank you! Hurry to your meeting, now, Singer," she said. "I'll be back before you are. They'll never even know I'm gone!"

Sook found Mura and Eun and most of the carvers gathered around the long scarred table in the kitchens. They gave hushed cries of joy at seeing her, then drew her quickly into their whispered conversation. She glanced around to see that Nori was conspicuous by her absence, and that one or two carvers had also not come. She could hardly blame them for being afraid, but she was elated at the chance for action. Surely something would happen now!

Yul's death had aged Mura. The set of her mouth was bitter, her eyes under their wrinkled lids dark with grief. "We're going to send someone out," she said, "someone to tell them what's happening. That's the Magister of Lamdon out there, come at last!"

"Have you seen him?" Sook asked. "Any of you?"

No one had. "He's short and fat. And old. I don't think he's a match for Cho."

"But he's the Magister of Lamdon! Of the whole Continent!" one of the carvers protested. "How can the Singers oppose him?"

"This is just what Cho wanted," Sook told them. "I heard him say so."

"Surely he won't attack Magister Gowan!" Eun said faintly.

Sook thought for a moment, her fingers on her lips. "I don't think it's Magister Gowan he'll attack," she said. "The Magister of Lamdon isn't Gifted, only the Magister of Conservatory. Right?" She looked around the group for confirmation. "So the one he'll attack is the man with the Magister. The Gifted one."

"But who's with him? Who came as his Singer?"

"Not just his Singer. Cantor Abram, senior Cantor of Lamdon." Sook put her hands on her hips. "He's a fool, sitting out there on a great chair like he was up on the dais, nice and safe in his own Cantoris! Cho will make *keftet* out of him!"

Mura snorted. "That would serve him right," she said. "But maybe if we hurry we can prevent it. We were just deciding who should go."

"I'll go!" Sook cried immediately.

"No, you won't," said the carver. "They watch you too closely. You'll go back where they expect you to be. One of us will go."

"But," Mura said, "it shouldn't be one of the Gifted. He knows just how to hurt you."

"Then who?"

Mura stared at them. "I'm going to do it."

"Mura, no!" Sook protested. "Not you. Someone else, someone younger."

"She's right," the carver put in. "It should be someone who can run, who can get there quickly in the dark. In the cold."

"Me, then," Sook said again.

The heavy door to the kitchen swung open, and Bree's weathered face showed in the doorway. "Sook!" she hissed. "They're done! You need to hurry!"

Sook hugged Mura quickly, and nodded to the carvers. "I have to go. But, Mura . . ."

"Please!" Bree said urgently.

Sook cast an imploring glance back at Mura, but she ran. Taking the back staircase, she hurried up to the upper level and into Cho's apartment, closing her bedroom door behind her with some moments to spare before the itinerants came back. Sook listened to the sounds of them returning, the thudding of resettled furniture, the brush of their boots against the floor, murmured conversation. She knelt in the windowseat again. All afternoon she stayed there, staring into the *quiru* across the courtyard.

*

Raised voices roused Sook. She had fallen asleep, curled in the windowseat. Her neck was stiff. She groaned, and massaged it with both hands.

"Impossible!" came an imperious cry beyond her door. "The Magister will never agree, nor the Committee!"

Sook stumbled to her feet, bending to rub one tingling ankle. A glance outside showed her the Lamdon party's *quiru* now shone in a dusky sky. Long fingers of shadow, cast by the unusual light beyond the courtyard, stretched across the cobblestones.

"That's what we want, and that's what we'll have," she heard Cho announce, his high-pitched voice carrying easily to her ears. "Freedom to fix our own prices, whether itinerants or carvers; Soren as a base, without interference from the Committee; and the same rights Cantors have, private apartments, full privileges, and our own leader."

The Lamdon courier sputtered angrily. His voice did not carry so well, and Sook hobbled to the door on her stinging foot to press her ear to it.

"Are you prepared to make the sacrifices Cantors and Cantrixes make, then? To serve as they do?"

Cho's voice was cool and even. "But, courier, we do serve. We've served you, in fact. Did you drink from a carved teacup out there, in your great *quiru*? Did you eat from an ironwood plate? Use a spoon? A cookpot?"

"It's hardly the same," the courier shouted. "You're insane!"

"I?" Cho laughed and Sook heard his chair scrape the floor. She could picture him in his usual pose by the window, leaning against the frame, drawing his long black plait through his fingers. "I think it's you and your Magister—and perhaps your Cantors, out there—who aren't sane. You have no power over me."

"But what you're doing to these people, to this House—" The courier grew shrill in his frustration.

"Do you see them trying to escape, to run across that courtyard to join you?"

"They know we could hardly carry the whole House back to Lamdon."

"But they see you out there, you and your pale Magister and your weak Cantors. They see you eating and drinking like you were at some great feast, they see you fat and comfortable as they never are, and they understand even more why we need to do this."

"But—"

A bang, as of a fist on a table, startled Sook away from the door. "No more talk!" Cho said, loudly this time. "Go back and tell them. If they don't leave, and carry our message to the Committee, they'll regret it. If they need a demonstration, I'll give them one!"

"You're going to be sorry about this, Carver," the courier said.

There was a moment of silence. When he spoke again, Cho's voice was light once more. "You have it wrong. The regrets will be yours, and your masters', if they don't listen to me."

"Never!"

Footsteps sounded across the floor, and a door banged against the wall, and again in the doorjamb. Sook ran back to her window to see the courier march across the dappled courtyard, past the two guards and into the light of the *quiru*. The two younger Cantors rose to meet him, but the Magister and the senior Cantor remained in their chairs.

A knock at her door heralded the arrival of Bree, supper tray in hand.

"Bree! Did you hear all that? What's going to happen?"

"You'd better just keep out of it," Bree said dourly. "And that's what I plan to do, too."

"But how can you? You're a part of it!"

The Singer's lips pressed into a thin line. She set the tray down and pointed to the bowl and the cup on it. "Look at that!" she said in a low tone. "*Caeru* stew, tea. No fruit, no grain, no bread. We can't work, we can't travel, we can't eat. This isn't the way it was supposed to be."

Sook came closer to Bree, leaning forward to look up into her eyes. "Bree–you can fight back. We all can. You can help, talk to the others . . ."

Bree turned her face away. "Ship knows I'm in it now, and of my own will, too. I was all right with it—until Yul."

"But now?" Sook prompted her.

"Never mind. Eat your meal. I'll get the tray later."

Sook sat down on the bed and picked up her spoon. The stew was Mura's usual rich brown, and it smelled as spicy as ever, but she could see without touching it that it was only meat and broth. It didn't appeal to her. "I'm not hungry," she said.

"Best eat it anyway," Bree said from the door. "It's all there is."

Sook said, "Bree . . . are you sure you don't want to—"

Bree threw up her hand. "Don't even say it," she said. "A taste of his—discipline, he calls it—was enough for me, that day in the carvery. You don't know what it's like."

Sook sat with her hand in her lap, holding the spoon. "Tell me, then. What does he do?"

Bree leaned the back of her head against the door and closed her eyes. She said grimly, "It's like having your brains cut apart. It's like dying, only you're afraid you won't die and it'll go on forever. It's more than losing your Gift, which is bad enough; it's like losing yourself."

Sook shivered. "I'm sorry, Bree. I guess I'll never really understand."

"Spirit willing, you won't. Now you eat your stew, and I'll come back later."

But when she had left, Sook ignored the tray and went back to the window. The Housemen in the *quiru* were serving another meal to their Magister and the three Cantors. Sook was sure the Magister was drinking wine. It had been a long time since she tasted wine. Even worse, she knew it had been a long time since any of the itinerants had had any, and there was the Magister of Lamdon drinking it right in front of them.

She stood with her hands on either side of the window, and pointed her small chin at the fat man. "Magister or no," she muttered, "you're a great fool!"

Sook was wakeful when the rest of the House was bedding down. Her forced inactivity made it hard to sleep at night. She went back to the window seat when her meal tray had been removed to watch darkness fall over the Timberlands, and the stars come to life above the Continent. She watched as the Housemen beyond the courtyard fed their *hruss*, laid out the bedfurs, banked the cookfire. Thus it was that she saw Mura try to reach Lamdon's *quiru*.

It seemed she had slipped out through the stable doors and walked around the House to the courtyard. She crept along the edge of Soren's ragged *quiru*, and started toward Lamdon's bright one.

The guards who had stood watch all day were already in their bedfurs, and two new ones had replaced them. The other Housemen had gone to bed as well, leaving the Magister and the three Cantors sitting around the table. Mura was a slow-moving figure heavily muffled in borrowed furs. As she drew near the light, one of the younger Cantors stood to meet her. He came to the edge of the *quiru* and reached out of the warmth, stretching his hand into the cold and dark.

Before their fingers could touch, he reeled and fell back on his heels. He tripped over a stool and went down on the packed snow, where he lay without moving. The other Cantor ran to kneel beside him, then turned an ashen face, mouth working, up to the House.

Sook looked down to see that the double doors beneath her stood open to the night. Cho was on the steps, just at the edge of Soren's fragmented light. He raised his long arm, pointing and calling something out into the courtyard. Mura whirled, trapped in the darkness between the two *quiru*.

Magister Gowan came to his feet, with Cantor Abram beside him. He made a gesture, and one of the Housemen snatched up his heavy furs and ran, pulling them on as he went, toward Mura. Sook found that her knuckle was between her teeth, and she was biting on it, hard. She watched helplessly as Cantor Abram pressed his hands to his temples and bent double, and the other Cantor, the one kneeling by his colleague, cried out and slumped forward. Cho shouted again.

The Magister called out sharply and the Houseman on his way to Mura stopped in confusion. He looked from his Magister to Cho, taking in the condition of the Singers, waiting in the darkness for interminable moments for some decision. Sook knew there was no decision to be made. There was no choice. Without their Singers, they were all dead. Even the great Magister of Lamdon could not keep himself warm in the deep cold. Cho loomed in the open doorway, both arms out, head tipped back so Sook could see the curve of his long nose.

The Houseman backed away from Mura, taking slow and reluctant steps until he was within the circle of the *quiru's* warmth. Cho lowered his arms, and Cantor Abram straightened, shaking his head and rubbing his eyes. Magister Gowan shouted something, but there was no answer. The double doors below Sook were closing.

Cho meant to leave Mura in the courtyard, in the cold. He had attacked the Singers of Lamdon, and he would do it again if they tried to help her. Mura had become his demonstration, his sacrifice. With a cry of fury, Sook ran to her door.

No one had forgotten this time. The door to her bedroom was secure, the wooden bolt driven home in its socket, turned and braced in the locking slot. She couldn't get out.

Back she flew to the window, pounding on the limeglass with her fist. "Mura!" she shrieked. "Mura! Run to the stables, go to the stables!"

It was impossible for Mura to hear her, but she looked up at the window, and Sook saw the faint flutter of her eyes. She was already feeling the cold. Sook gestured wildly, pointing, to indicate that Mura should go back the way she had come, try the stable door.

The cook lifted and spread her hands. She mouthed, "Too late." She touched her heart, once, and then raised her fingers to Sook. She was saying goodbye.

"Mura, no! Try!" Sook screamed. She went on screaming until her throat ached, and the itinerants coming into the main room of the apartment banged on her door and demanded quiet. She ignored them, calling to Mura until her voice grew hoarse. Then she sobbed, kneeling on the window seat with her chin on her hand, staring at the macabre scene.

Mura walked slowly to the broad steps of the House. She seated herself on them, and drew the furs about her. Her back was straight, her head up. Sook could imagine the glare she turned on the Lamdon contingent. They stared in horror at the savagery of Cho's reprisal.

Even Sook's tears spent themselves eventually, but still she knelt at the window.

The end was not long in coming. Mura's rigid back curved slightly. She slumped, almost imperceptibly, within the inadequate shelter of the *caeru* furs. Irrelevantly, Sook wondered whose they were. They belonged to the stableman, perhaps, or to one of the Housemen who serviced the waste drop. They would come back into the House, those furs, and their owner would always know that Mura had died in them, frozen to death in the deep cold only a few steps from warmth and safety. Sook felt as if the cold had reached right inside the House, into her own breast. It made her heart ache unbearably.

Hours later, when all hope that Mura might have survived was past, Sook heard the outer door of the apartment open and close, and steps pass by as Cho and someone with him went into his bedroom. Not long after came Sook heard the sound of a girl's voice. She wasn't sure if it was Nori or some other Housewoman.

She rubbed the last vestiges of tears from her cheeks and whispered promises to herself. "I won't cry again," she vowed. "Not one more tear. He'll pay for this, Mura, for you and for Yul. I swear by the Ship!"

Sook kept vigil at her window through the night, her eyes and throat as dry as stone. She gazed down at the figure of Mura, slumped on the steps, and at the impotent figures of Magister Gowan and his Cantors. Over and over, through the long hours, she prayed for Zakri to come.

Chapter Twenty-one

Mreen leaned against Sira's back as they rode, lulled to drowsiness by the *hruss's* swinging gait. None of the travelers had spoken for hours. Only the rustle of an intermittent breeze stirring the irontree branches sounded in the silence. It was late in the afternoon when a faint grating broke the monotony. Sira lift her head and thrust back her hood.

She turned her head right, and then left, straining to hear it again. There— it was a scuffing, a scraping sound, the sound of bone runners sliding over stone left bare by the worn snow of late winter. Mreen wriggled, awakened by Sira's sudden tension.

Do you hear it, Mreen?

The little girl pushed her own furs away from her ears, but she shook her head.

Riders, Sira sent. *Many hruss, and pukuru.* She called to the others, "A traveling party is ahead of us, a big one—coming this way, I think."

Zakri put his hood back to listen. He shook his head. "I will take your word for it."

Theo reined in, dropping back until all of them were within three arms' length of one another. "Until we know who they are, better to ride close." He spoke calmly, but Sira heard the undertone in his voice, the slight huskiness. "Sira and Mreen, stay in the center," he directed. "Berk, there, to Sira's right. Zakri on the left."

I hear them now, Mreen sent. She tightened her arms around Sira's waist. Sira would have liked to reassure her, but it was clear the child was aware that, soon or late, they were riding into danger. She found Mreen's small hand, almost lost in the thick furs, and stroked it.

I am not afraid, Mreen sent stoutly.

No, I know you are not, Sira answered. *You are as brave as your stepsister.*

Do you mean Trisa? Is Trisa brave?

Sira patted her hand. *Indeed she is. Do you not know the story?*

Tell me!

And so as they rode forward, unsure of who was coming toward them, Sira distracted Mreen with the tale of Trisa's misery at Conservatory, her determination to run away, and her final success in accomplishing it. Mreen listened, sighing at Zakri's and Berk's part in the adventure.

When Sira finished the tale, Mreen sent, *Trisa was brave, but she was so silly! Who would want to leave Conservatory? It is the best place to be on the whole Continent!*

For you and for me, it is. But what is true for one Singer is not always true for another.

Theo spoke aloud, keeping his voice low. "Here they are." They all lifted their eyes to the approaching riders.

"Ship and stars!" Berk muttered. "Somebody's emptied their stables right out."

"Not quite," Zakri murmured. "Look who rides with them! Only one man I know of could fill furs that size. And the senior Cantor himself, out of Lamdon at last. The capital House has *hruss* and Singers to spare."

"So," Theo said. "Do they have him?"

Zakri scanned the riders. "I do not see him," he said. "But there is a man in a litter, there on the *pukuru*." He gestured to the left with his chin, keeping his hands on his reins. "I cannot see his face." He added in an urgent undertone, "Shield yourselves, and carefully. I will extend my shields around Mreen."

Mreen protested energetically. *I am shielded already!*

Good, Zakri sent back. *Then you will be twice protected.*

The man at the head of Lamdon's entourage kicked his *hruss* into a lumbering trot, hurrying toward them. He lifted his hand, and called out when he was within range. "Greetings from Magister Gowan v'Lamdon! What travelers are you?"

Theo raised his own hand, and answered, "Theo v'Observatory."

Zakri nodded approval of his caution. Theo hardly looked like a Cantor. His hair curled at his nape, cropped like an itinerant's, and his shoulders bulked inside his *caeru* furs. He looked like an itinerant.

The Lamdon man drew closer now, and his *hruss* slowed its heavy gait, jolting to a halt a few steps from Theo. The rest stopped too, facing him. Sira's and Zakri's shields were linked with Mreen's, twined together like the interlocking roots of the forest. Theo's own defenses stretched around them all, not precise, delicate Conservatory shielding but his own stubborn, stony wall of protection, toughened by experience. Sira felt Zakri's probe reach out past that barricade to touch the Lamdon rider's mind.

No Gift in this one, he sent, and they all relaxed a bit.

"Theo v'Observatory?" repeated the rider. He looked them over. "I've never met anyone from Observatory. I've heard some stories."

Theo grinned. "I probably told most of them," he said. He shifted in his saddle, sitting sideways with one foot dangling free of the stirrup, ready to chat. "You say you have Magister Gowan coming up there behind you?"

"So I do, and Cantor Abram to boot. We've had a nasty time of it at Soren."

Berk urged his *hruss* forward a step. "I'm Berk, courier for Amric," he said, letting his gruff voice carry over the snow to reach to the rest of the Lamdon party. "Why don't you take my respects to your Magister, and we can all make our camp together. I've had some experience with Soren myself, and I'd like to hear what's happening there."

"But first," Theo put in, "tell us who else is riding with you. Other Singers? Anyone from Soren?"

The man shook his head. "No one from Soren, that's for sure, though we tried. Two other Singers besides Cantor Abram, but one's hurt, pretty badly, they say. He looks all right to me, but he can't speak, can't ride."

It was told matter-of-factly, and the cold horror of it turned Sira's stomach. She looked ahead to the riders coming on, the litter scraping over rocks and snow behind them.

The rider said, "Strange business, that. All our Cantors look like they've seen an *urbear* in their bedfurs. Scared half to death."

"Do they?" Theo answered. "We will hear the whole story at the cookfire, no doubt."

The rider nodded assent, and turned his mount, thumping its flanks with his heels until it resumed its heavy-footed trot back toward Magister Gowan. Theo pointed to a broadening of the road that lay between the two parties. "We can make camp there," he said. "There should be room enough."

Berk still stared up the road, watching as the rider bowed to Gowan, pointed back at their own troupe, bowed again. "We'll hear no good news this day," he said. "But I'd guess we've nothing to fear with this lot. It might be best if they know who and what we are. We could use some authority behind us when we settle this little matter."

The Singers agreed. They followed Theo to the spot he had chosen, and by the time the Lamdon party reached it Zakri had raised a substantial *quiru* and Berk's cookfire was crackling nicely. They stood in formal ranks to meet Magister Gowan and Cantor Abram. Mreen hid behind Sira and Theo, peeking from behind their legs. Sira sent to Zakri, *I hope this will not be unpleasant. My last encounter with Abram was not even civil.*

He laughed under his breath. *Mine was downright offensive. I undid his hair for him.*

Theo cast them both a wry glance. *Wonderful. He will be so pleased to see you both.*

Two Housemen helped Gowan from his *hruss*. It was no easy task to provide him with a dignified descent from the high saddle. His great weight made them grunt and stumble, but soon enough he was standing on his own feet, his furs draping generously around his massive figure. Abram dismounted with slightly less fuss, and both dignitaries came forward on saddle-stiff legs to meet the newcomers.

It was evident immediately that Abram was a changed man. He bowed, and when he straightened, his eyes were shadowed and dull, with deep lines graven around them. Sira doubted the lines came only from the weathering of this journey.

"Cantrix Sira," he said heavily. "And Cantor Zakri v'Amric. Is this coincidence?"

Their answer was forestalled as a Houseman lugged a chair forward for Magister Gowan and helped him into it, arranging his furs, setting a carved footstool beneath his boots. Gowan eyed their group with eyes reddened by snow glare. His white hair looked oily, and he seemed shrunken, as if his abundant flesh had diminished, leaving his pale skin to lie in limp folds about his neck and chin. He did not speak.

"Cantor Abram," Sira said, "you will have guessed our purpose in being here. We will explain everything, but first I would like to present to you . . ."

She turned to Theo, ready to introduce him as Cantor for the first time outside Observatory. She saw his eyes crinkle and his lips twitch, ready to grin at Lamdon's reaction. Her own mood suddenly lightened, and the weight of her worries lifted. So much of her work she had done alone, but now they were together, she and Theo, and that meant they were stronger, more resourceful, more able than either of them could be on their own. Beside her stood her other student, Zakri, young and fine and capable. She was proud of them both, and proud of her work with them. Nothing Abram or Gowan might say could change any of that. What-ever challenge was to come, they would meet it together. She turned back to Abram.

"Cantor Abram, Magister Gowan. This is Cantor Theo v'Observatory. He has served in the Cantoris there these six years."

Theo bowed. Abram stared at him, then at Sira, saying nothing for a long, painful moment. When he spoke, his plump features barely moved. He said only, "Greetings, Cantor."

Sira's scarred eyebrow lifted. She had been prepared for criticism, denial, objections, not this drab acceptance, this colorless acquiescence. The senior Cantor's confidence, his self-assurance, were gone. She experienced an unwilling surge of sympathy for him, which she pressed down quickly. Surely nothing could be more humiliating to him than pity.

Mreen edged between Sira and Theo then, taking their hands in hers and gazing up at the dark man and the pale fat one. Abram caught sight of her and exclaimed, "In the name of the Spirit! What is this?"

I am Mreen, the child sent immediately.

Abram frowned deeply at her. Before he could remonstrate, Sira said, "Mreen is a Conservatory student. She sends because she cannot speak."

"Not at all?" They were Gowan's first words. "Is she always silent?"

"Always," Theo said with a chuckle. "A mixed blessing."

"And that—that light around her?" Gowan demanded. His voice was thin and querulous, and his jowls wavered as he looked from one face to another.

Sira said only, "Mreen's Gift is intense," and left them to make of it what they could.

Abram still frowned, but he bent his head to look more closely at Mreen. "How did she come to be this way?"

"She was born so," Sira answered. "As best we can tell. She has never uttered a sound."

The senior Cantor straightened and lifted his head. With a hint of his old arrogance, he asked, "Why is the child not with her class then, where she belongs?"

Berk stepped up beside Sira and bowed briefly. "We'd best tell you everything from the beginning," he said. His shrewd eyes assessed the Lamdon party. "I'd guess you have a story for us as well."

Once again the animation left Abram's face. "Indeed," he sighed. His shoulders bent as he turned away to signal to his Housemen. Zakri sent privately to Sira, *He wants to forget it all.*

She flashed him a look. *Suppose you wait for him to tell us about it before you eavesdrop on his private thoughts?* He smirked at her, and she shook her head in exasperation.

There were eight of the Lamdon Housemen, and they worked with speed and efficiency. In moments they transformed the campsite into a creditable simulation of a Magistral apartment, with chairs and stools ranged around a table, cups laid out, and meal preparations begun. Berk, Gowan, and all the Gifted but one had seats facing one another. Mreen climbed into Theo's lap and sat with one finger between her lips, watching the strangers. The light around her sparkled faintly. Abram moved uncomfortably in his chair as she turned her green gaze on him.

Zakri nodded toward the litter. "Someone is injured," he observed. The Housemen had laid the litter on a pad of furs near the cookfire. Its occupant was still, his head turned away, eyes staring blankly out into the dusk gathering over the Southern Timberlands.

Sira felt Zakri reach to touch the man's mind, and then withdraw. He gave a slight, almost imperceptible shrug.

"He was attacked." Abram's voice cracked as he spoke. "At Soren."

Magister Gowan leaned to one side, resting on the arm of his chair as if he had not the strength to support his own weight. His pale eyes flickered from one face to another. "They have no respect for me," he quavered. "Nor for the Committee. They wouldn't talk to my courier, and then . . . "

Lamdon's courier stepped up to the table. He alone looked energized, angered by what they had seen. "Have you been to Soren?" he demanded. "Do you know what they're doing?"

Zakri's answer was mild. "We did try to tell you," he reminded Gowan and Abram.

Gowan's folds of flesh trembled. "They locked her out," he whined. "In the cold."

They looked at him, mystified. "Who?" Theo asked. Gowan ran on without hearing him.

"I sent my Houseman to help her, but then my Singers . . . he was hurting my Singers! What could I do? I told him, I ordered him to stop, to let her come in, but he wouldn't listen!"

"Who was it?" Zakri asked sharply. "Who did they lock out?"

Abram lifted one shoulder. "I do not know her name . . . a cook, I think."

Zakri's face blanched white, then flamed. "Old? Young?" he snapped.

Abram shrugged again. "I have no idea. Have you felt what that man can do?"

"Yes," Zakri said shortly. His clenched fists were motionless on the table. Flashes of light glinted on his cheeks and hair.

Sira asked, "Will your Cantor recover, do you think?"

Abram shook his head wearily. "I do not know. How did you know he was a Cantor?"

Zakri struck the table a sharp blow with one fist, and the glimmers around him intensified. "We told you! There are no itinerants left outside of Soren!" He took a shuddering breath, and Sira felt his struggle to control his emotions. He was angry, but even more, he was afraid, not for himself, but for someone else. Abram and Gowan stared at him. When he had quelled his outbreak of light, he spoke more quietly. "Cho did the same thing to Cantor Izak. Izak is recovering, at Conservatory."

Abram's eyes brightened. "Recovering? Completely recovering?"

"He can talk, and he can walk. But his Gift, no. At least I do not think so. Cantrix Jana and I did all we could."

"Poor Jana—is she all right? Is she with him?"

"She is fine," Sira told him. She felt Theo's wry glance at her. She hesitated, then plunged in. "Cantrix Jana is at Observatory," she said bluntly.

"What? What?" Abram sputtered. He glared at her, at all of them.

Gowan's courier broke in, his voice loud, almost frantic. "How is this possible, any of it? You are Conservatory, all of you! How can a mere

Carver—a weak Gift, half-trained Gift—how can he have such power over you?"

"What is Cantrix Jana doing at Observatory?" Abram burst out. "She should be—"

Gowan moaned, "Everything is coming apart, I have no control. No one will listen, no one has any respect . . ."

Sira laid a hand on the table, palm down. Everyone fell silent, looking at it, then at her face. She spoke first to the courier, keeping her voice even. "You should never refer to the Gift in that way," she said. "Mistakes have been made, perhaps in testing Cho's Gift. But his training has been thorough, and it is exactly that which he is using against us."

"I do not understand you!" Abram cried. "He has no training!"

Sira glanced at him. "But he does," she said. "He is trained to guide an *obis* knife with his Gift. It is as precise a skill as raising a *quiru.*"

Zakri said levelly, "It is the perfect weapon against the Gifted. He assaults minds the way he wields an *obis* knife, and you may thank the Spirit for our own training, that makes it possible for us to protect ourselves."

"But Jana?" Abram asked.

"Cantrix Jana is serving in Observatory's Cantoris," Theo said. "It was her choice to—"

"Her choice! Hers? It is my duty to assign Cantrixes!" Cantor Abram's face grew red, and his eyes shone as if he would weep.

"There was no other way we could be free to come here," Theo said calmly.

Sira spoke again. "We intend to put an end to this, now. In our own way. We could not wait for Lamdon to make these decisions. People are suffering. We mean no disrespect."

Gowan whispered, "They locked her out. She sat on the steps and died. Froze to death in the cold, and we had to sit and watch . . ."

Next to Sira, Zakri took a deep, shuddering breath.

"We will do all we can," Sira said.

The Housemen began setting bowls of fragrant *caeru* stew before them. They laid platters of nutbread and dried fruit in the center of the table, and served wine to Gowan and Berk. There was a spicy brown tea for the Gifted. Sira sat with her chin in her hand, watching the elaborate service.

Might as well enjoy it, Theo sent to her privately. *Gowan certainly is.*

It was true. Only the Magister's appetite, it seemed, was unaffected by his experience.

More to the point, she answered Theo, *we will need all our strength.* But still she did not pick up her spoon. She glanced across the fire at the fallen Singer on his litter, and she felt the terrible emptiness where his Gift should have been. She looked at tiny, shining Mreen, perched on Theo's knee. Both Theo and Mreen met her eyes.

Sira, eat, Theo commanded.

It is good, Cantrix Sira, Mreen urged. *Try it.*

Sira smiled a little at them, and looked to her left, to Zakri. He joined in, forcing a smile to his own lips. *Eat, Maestra!*

She did as she was bid.

Mreen was right. The food was delicious. It was the ugliness of what had happened, and what was yet to come, that spoiled her taste for Lamdon's riches.

Chapter Twenty-two

Sook was kneeling in the window seat when they rode over the rise above Soren. She saw a tall, lean woman who sat her *hruss* easily, leaning back in her saddle and scanning the House from the crest of the hill. Her *hruss* turned its broad head back and forth, ears working, while the woman stared at Soren as if she could see right through its thick walls and into its troubled heart. Sook cupped her hands against the glass to shut out the glare, and squinted against the light, but she couldn't make out the woman's features inside the muffling circle of her *caeru* hood.

It was mid-day, and a tray rested untouched on the table behind Sook. She had heard the bolt secured after Bree left. Cho and his itinerants—and the carvers who had changed allegiance and now were at Cho's side every moment—had gone to the great room for their meal.

The stranger on the hill swept her furs away from her face as Sook watched, revealing short-cropped dark hair and an angular face, sharp planes of cheekbone showing clearly in the harsh light. A hint of white marked one of her eyebrows.

Sook was breathless with excitement. There were stories she had heard from travelers eating at the long table in the kitchens. They told of a Singer, a Conservatory-trained Cantrix who had abandoned the Cantoris and done heroic things. That Singer had a scarred eyebrow, marked with white by a *caeru's* claw.

The bolt in her door rattled sharply, making her jump. She hadn't heard the carvers return. The door crashed against the inner wall, and Cho staggered into the room. His mouth was strangely twisted, and he peered at her as through a thick fog. He grabbed for her, missing her arm and taking instead a painful, clumsy grip on her neck beneath her coil of hair.

"What is it?" she cried. "Let me go!" She struggled in his grasp, managing only to pull the hair at her nape more sharply. The sting of it brought tears to her eyes.

Cho only grunted. His dark skin was slippery with sweat, and he almost lost his hold on her as he dragged her by force through the apartment and down the corridor. The tears burned her cheeks and she screamed her outrage. "Stop it! You're hurting me!"

At the top of the stairs two rebel carvers met them. Cho let her go, but the carvers took her arms and half-dragged, half-carried her down the stairs. She kicked at them, catching one a glancing blow on his shin. He swore, and she turned her head to spit in his face, winning a brief moment of satisfaction from seeing her spittle drip down his cheek. He dared not release her to wipe it away. "Shame!" she hissed at him. His skin burned red, and he avoided her eyes.

Behind them Cho stumbled and made a gagging noise. Sook thought he might actually retch as they rushed down the staircase. She could only guess what it all meant, but surely, surely it had to do with the tall woman on the *hruss*.

Two itinerants, eyes wide and faces pale, threw open the double doors as they approached. The carvers hauled Sook outside, and for a moment she thought she was to suffer the same fate as Mura. The cold hit her like a fist; she had only her tunic and trousers on. Cho and the carvers hadn't taken time to put on furs either.

Cho came from behind to seize her by the hair, tearing the binding loose, thrusting her forward and holding her as he might dangle a cleaned fish over a cooking pot. Her neck was twisted to one side, and she lost her footing. When she found her balance again, she looked out past the court-yard to the top of the rise.

The tall woman was still there. Three other *hruss* stood beside hers.

Sook's heart leapt, and her pain and tears receded. Even the bite of the cold seemed to lessen as she saw that one of the riders push back to show his light hair and fine features. It was Zakri, Singer Zakri come at last! Sook smiled fiercely through the cloud of her tangled hair.

Cho panted as if from a physical struggle. It was not the effort of holding Sook. Something else was pushing him right to the edge of his endurance. He groaned, and swallowed noisily. Sweat dripped from his arm onto Sook's neck. He took a deep breath and shouted, so close to her ear that it hurt, "Stop!"

Sook knew as surely as anything that he was frightened, and she exulted. "Stop it now, or else this one—" He yanked Sook's hair so hard she thought her spine would crack. "This one will suffer the—"

He gasped, and swallowed again, then jerked Sook right off her feet.

The tall woman raised her hand, and Cho let out his breath in a rush. He released Sook without warning. She fell, bruising both her knees on the icy step. She scrambled to her feet again, and looked up the hill, full of hope.

Sira remembered well what it felt like to break another's mind. She remembered it too well, in truth: the power of it, the rush of energy, the sickening sensation that was like pushing someone off a cliff. It had been an irrevocable act, with irreversible consequences. It came back to her in her nightmares, the exhilaration, the violence, the guilt that overrode everything and lasted forever. It made her hold back when she exerted her power over Cho.

Cho's Gift was less sophisticated, less refined, and far less vulnerable than that other's. She did not know for certain she could break him, and she did not try. With Zakri and Theo lending her their strength, and Mreen under strict orders to keep her mind closed and apart, Sira applied her psi like a hook, a tether, taking hold of Cho and pulling him out of his lair as surely as he had pulled that poor girl by her long hair.

He was a canny opponent. He resisted her with a stubborn strength. He held her off just enough to drag his hostage out with him, though the effort had cost him. She felt Zakri's shielding waver, and the rush of his relief and then his renewed fear. She had no doubt Cho was capable of breaking the girl's neck before them all. She raised her hand to make certain Cho understood her action was deliberate before she released her grip on his mind.

Cho's victim collapsed on the steps, but was instantly on her feet again.

"Sook!" Zakri breathed. "Thank the Spirit!"

Berk rumbled, "Clever bastard."

Cho's high-pitched voice carried across the couryard and up the slope of dirty, much-trodden snow. "It won't work!" Sira heard the forced bravado that made his voice almost a shriek, and she glanced at Theo with her eyebrows lifted.

Theo grinned. "Scared him," he murmured.

The group on the hill sat motionless, looking down at the thin dark man with the long braid, the girl before him, the carvers and itinerants behind them. Through the open doors they saw House members putting their heads around just far enough to see what was happening.

"He's right enough," Berk muttered. "It's a stand-off. We'll have to try something else."

"They must feel the cold by now," Zakri said. "If they do not get Sook indoors, she will freeze."

Cho shouted again. "Get away from my House! You have no business here!" He grabbed Sook again to hold her in front of him with one arm. Her head reached only to his chest. Her hair fell over her shoulders and her dark eyes fixed on the riders on the hill.

"Who is she?" Sira asked.

"She is one of the cooks," Zakri said through clenched teeth. "He would not stop at killing her."

"We will not let that happen," Sira assured him. "But he is surprisingly strong. And someone is helping him, the same way you and Theo were supporting me."

"They're learning," Berk said.

"We will have to teach them a different lesson," Theo said calmly. "But perhaps not right at this moment."

They reined their *hruss* around, retreating from the hilltop, backtracking to a shallow clearing they had passed earlier. There they dismounted, Theo lifting Mreen down with a passing kiss on her curly head. They set about making their camp in silence.

Sira untied the bedfurs and pack from her saddle. As she set them down, she found Mreen standing beside her, her face tense. *Cantrix Sira,* she sent. *There is a child in that House.* Her little nimbus shifted around her, flecks of darkness disturbing its light. *There is a boy—a Gifted boy—and all this fighting is making him ill.*

Sira looked around for Theo. *Did you hear that?*

So I did. He came to kneel by Mreen. *Mreen, you must not open your mind to everything that comes your way. There is great danger here. This is a time to practice your shielding.*

I was careful, she sent. The green of her eyes had darkened almost to black. Strange lines were graven around her mouth and eyes. *You were all linked with that man, and I heard the boy. He is scared, and he hides in his room with a pillow on his head, but he cannot shut it out.*

Zakri finished the *quiru*, a modest one just large enough to encircle the people and the *hruss*. He came to join them, replacing his *filla* inside his tunic. *I am sure he could not hear the boy and Mreen. He was too busy with our Maestra.*

Nevertheless, Theo repeated. *It is not safe for her.*

But the boy needs us! Mreen insisted. *He is so scared and sick.*

Aloud, Sira said, "Yes, Mreen, and no wonder. We will do our best, but we must protect you, too." To Berk she explained, "Mreen hears the Gifted child in the House. He is suffering from the psi being used—Cho's psi."

Berk growled in his beard. Theo, too, set his jaw, the muscles flexing into knots. "I am going in there," he said. "To get the child out. I do not see another way."

Sira found a flat rock at the edge of the *quiru* and sat down on it, stretching out her long legs. "We cannot protect you at such a distance. It was all I could do to force him outside. There is a wildness to his psi, an abandon, that I have never felt before. He has no compunction."

"Zakri handled him," Theo pointed out.

"It was not easy," Zakri warned. "And he did not have help then. I am not so certain I could handle him now."

"Please, Theo, let us think of something else," Sira said. He did not answer and she sighed with a deep fatigue.

Berk and Mreen worked over the cookfire, side by side. Mreen's little halo glowed peacefully now as she fed softwood twigs to the flames, always her favorite chore. Berk said, "That's enough, little one. We don't want smoke to show them where we are." She dropped the last bits of wood into her pocket.

None of them felt hungry, but Berk made tea, "To help us think." Mreen served it, dimpling as she delivered the brimming cups, spilling only a few drops into the snow.

They sipped their tea and listened to the rustling of the irontree branches around them. In the Timberlands that sound never died down. The trees grew so closely that it was hard to tell, looking up, which branches belonged to which trunk. Above their clearing clouds gathered, and the lazy snowflakes of late winter drifted through the *quiru*, making tiny sputtering sounds as they dropped into the fire. Mreen sat crosslegged on her furs, rolling tiny balls of snow and tossing them into the fire to hear them hiss.

Berk said, "You're going to put out our nice little fire, Mreen."

She looked up hopefully, and he chuckled. "Yes, you can put in a few more sticks."

She stood and plunged her hand into her pocket. When she drew it out she was holding Cho's bit of carving in her hand, the little panel Izak had given her. She stared at it, her nimbus burning bright around her. When she looked up, her face was pinched and white.

Very clearly, she sent, *We must all go in. All at once.*

All the Gifted gazed at her, openmouthed. Berk looked around in consternation, and Zakri whispered, "She says we must all go in together." Berk, too, opened his mouth, and then closed it, shaking his head.

Theo went to Mreen and squatted beside her. *It is a brave idea, but I do not think we will be allowed inside. Cho is powerful, and he is a bad man. The House members do what he tells them because they are afraid. There is no one inside the House to help us get in.*

There is a Singer there. He is afraid of her, Mreen responded. Her eyes were as clear as new limeglass, and there was neither doubt nor hesitation in her sending.

Mreen, Soren is full of Singers! sent Zakri. *And they are all terrified, every one of them.*

This one is locked up, she answered. Her sending was so precise, so lucid, that Sira imagined even Berk could hear her. But the big man only watched, forced to wait until someone explained.

Zakri suddenly snapped his fingers, making them jump. Their eyes turned to him and he grinned. "Of course!" he cried. "Cantrix Elnor!"

Sira blinked. "Mreen," she said. "Could you hear her too? Is she still alive?"

For answer she held out the carving. *She was alive when he gave this to Izak.*

"I will try to reach her," Sira said.

"It might be the answer," Theo put in. His arm was around Mreen, the sleeve of his coat alight in her glow. "But now, Mreen, put the carving away." To Sira he sent, *I am worried for the child. This is too intense for her.*

Sira nodded, but she felt a fresh energy and a renewal of hope. Mreen obediently dropped the little panel into her pocket. Berk began preparations for a meal, and Mreen crouched beside him, dropping her bits of softwood into the fire, laughing her silent laugh as they burst into little stars of flame.

When they had eaten, Theo and Mreen scrubbed out the bowls and the cooking pot. Zakri measured out handfuls of softwood leaves for the *hruss*. Sira went to sit alone on the flat rock. She took out her *filla*, turning it for a moment in her long fingers, thinking and gathering her forces. Then she lifted the instrument and began an *Iridu* melody, slowly at first, then increasing the tempo until it was as bright and merry as the child playing by the cookfire. She cast her mind out with the careful precision learned over years of Conservatory training and practice. With perfect discipline, letting nothing distract her, she sought the mind of the older Cantrix.

Chapter Twenty-three

Who is there?

The sending was clear, but faint, from weakness or caution Sira could not yet tell. She answered, *I am Sira. Cantrix Sira v'Observatory, formerly v'Bariken.*

She waited for an answer. There were slight rustlings as the others prepared for bed, but Sira's focus was so narrow she heard nothing but the feeble voice in her mind. Her *Iridu* melody ended and began again. The old Cantrix's voice, despite its frailty, was as precise as the touch of a fingertip. It tingled delicately in her forehead, a familiar and distinct sensation, the unmistakable signature of Conservatory training.

I know your name. I am glad you are here, but this is dangerous. He hears everything.

Sira opened her eyes and signalled to Zakri. "Do you think you could occupy Cho, distract him so Elnor and I can talk?"

"Is she alive, then?" He came to sit beside her on the flat stone, and Theo followed to stand behind him. At the fire, Berk offered Mreen a handful of dried fruit from his saddlepack.

Sira said, "She is alive, but her sending is weak."

"She is rather old, after all," Zakri said.

"And she must be frightened," Theo added.

Sira nodded. "She has reason. No doubt Cho controls her by threatening her people."

"It is imperative he not know, then." Zakri took out his *filla* and looked at it, then smiled and put it back. "I think I can deal with our friend Cho. I am in the perfect mood for a game of knuckle and bone. Any wagers on the winner?"

Sira looked to Theo. "Will you follow, at a little distance? I do not know what will happen. His abilities are so odd, and now he has help. Zakri . . ." her voice trailed off.

Theo smiled down at her. "I will follow," he said.

"And no heroics," she warned. Theo chuckled, and winked at Zakri, but they promised.

She put her *filla* to her lips again. She played through the *Iridu* tune once, giving Zakri a chance to begin, before she sought out the captive Singer. *Cantrix Elnor? I think it will be all right now, at least for a time. Are you well?*

Again the thread of Elnor's thought was thin, but perfectly intelligible. *No one in this House is completely well,* she answered. *It is cold, and we are hungry. Our nursery gardens no longer grow.*

Your filhata?

They took it from me, and my senior's too. He is dead.

I heard. I am sorry.

Elnor was silent for a few seconds. When she sent again, it was like listening to someone whisper. Sira's brows drew together as she poured all her strength into listening. *Are you here to help us?* Elnor asked. *What can I do?*

Sira explained. The Cantrix was quick to grasp their plan, and eager to do her part. Sira wanted to ask her more, but Theo touched her arm in warning. She broke the contact.

"What is it?" she asked.

Zakri and Theo exchanged a look. "He knows we are here," Theo said. "He was at his evening meal, and at first he was not sure anything was taking place, but at the end—"

"He knew me," Zakri said. "He has grown much stronger. He cannot actually send clear thoughts, but he hears a great deal. I tell you, I hate feeling his mind anywhere near mine! It is like putting your hand into something rotten. And he is expecting a fight. As soon as he knew I was there, those others were there, too. Carvers, I am sure. Their psi is similar to

Cho's—that sort of wide focus . . . strong, but dull. The way they use it—it is like trying to cut bread with the side of your hand, sort of plowing through instead of slicing it neatly."

Theo gave a short laugh. "A colorful turn of phrase, my friend, but it describes the sensation well enough."

"Theo—now you have felt their power—do you think we can do this?" Sira asked.

"We can do it," he said. "We must. But there are none too many of us."

I want to fight, too.

All their eyes turned to Mreen, kneeling by the fire with Berk. She looked back at them with her little chin lifted.

"Mreen," Sira began. Berk looked around, startled.

"It is not safe for you, little one," Theo said firmly. "If you were listening, then you heard what Cantor Zakri said. This is an evil man, and he would not hesitate to hurt a child."

He is already hurting one, she sent.

"Let us not put another at risk, then," Theo told her. "Cantrix Sira and I will help Cantor Zakri, and Cantrix Elnor will do what she can. Your job is to help Berk with that *keftet* before we all starve!"

Mreen turned obediently to the fire again, but her face was grave. Sira rubbed her forehead with a weary hand.

"We will make it work, Sira," Theo assured her. "Between us, and Elnor. We will free Soren, and the little Gifted one. By this time tomorrow, it will be done."

"By the will of the Spirit," she sighed.

Theo patted her shoulder. "Exactly."

The task of getting into the House by way of the waste drop fell to Zakri. He crept around the frozen mound of offal and refuse, moving on silent feet past the inner wall of the eastern wing. It was early, and the narrow door was in near-darkness. The sun had risen above the mountains, but the space behind the House, between the two wings, was still in shade. Zakri shivered in his furs. Soren's inadequate warmth did not reach past its walls. There was no spill from the *quiru* to warm him.

Theo came to the stable door at the same time, leading two *hruss*. They reasoned that even if the stableman recognized him, it would be from his early years, when he was an itinerant. The stableman might be surprised, but hardly alarmed. Theo would stay with the *hruss* while Zakri slipped inside.

When they were in position, Sira walked boldly up the front steps and pounded on one of the tall doors with her fist. In the stables, Theo bent over one of the *hruss's* feet, ostensibly looking for a stone. He pressed his forehead against the shaggy flank, and listened. Zakri, inside the House now, flattened himself against the corridor wall, also following Sira with his mind. Cantrix Elnor was joined with them, the thread of her psi as fine and slender as a single hair of a *hruss's* tail. Together the four of them spun a web of power, wove a snare for their prey. Zakri tried to believe it was enough.

As they had hoped, Cho himself came to meet Sira in the hall. He was flanked by three others. Sira judged them to be carvers, since they, like Cho, wore long *obis* knives slung about their waists in slim leather scabbards. Two itinerants hovered on the stairs. All five were men, their faces rigid with tension. Since the day before, Sira was sure, they had known something was coming. Their fear was a presence, a cloud like the patches of darkness that marked the corridors. Nevyans were born and bred with deep reverence for a fully trained Gift, and they understood what Sira was.

Only Cho had no misgivings. He sneered at Sira. "Well, Conservatory. You've got nerve, coming into my House alone."

Sira lifted her head high to meet his eyes, confident that hers were as cold and hard as his own. She flicked a glance over the carvers, then the itinerants. "Are these your converts, Cho? Your faithful?" She spit out the words as if they tasted evil in her mouth. One of the carvers dropped his gaze to his feet, and the itinerants glanced at each other.

Cho's laugh was too high, a kind of adolescent snicker. His voice had almost no lower register, and it offended her ear. "So they are, Cantrix." He smiled. "Is that what I call you? Or is it Maestra?"

"It matters nothing to me what title you use." Sira's tone rang through the hall, and the itinerants shifted their feet, recognizing the power of it.

Cho shrugged, and stroked the thin plait that hung over his shoulder. "Fine—I'll just call you Conservatory, then. We'll go up to my apartment, and you'll be treated just as any courier might be, coming from one House to another. But remember—this is my House. I rule here."

Sira took a long and measuring look around her at the fractured *quiru*. She looked back at Cho with as challenging a glance as she could muster before she started up the stairs on her own, her long legs spanning two at a time. The itinerants jumped back hastily, to get out of her way, and she stopped, straddling three steps. "Do you really think," she asked them, "that I would indulge in the kind of abuse that your leader does?" She spoke over her shoulder then, to Cho. "But I suppose fear is a potent persuader if you have no other."

He laughed again, a titter as thin as his braid. He followed her up the stairs. At the top, he strode past her, leading the way. The carvers and itinerants followed at a cautious distance.

Inside the apartment, a plain woman with graying hair lay stretched on a couch. She leapt to her feet when they all trooped in, and Sira eyed her.

"This is Bree," Cho said. "Gifted, like yourself."

Bree flushed, and bobbed her head in a semblance of a bow. Sira turned away without responding and looked about her. "The *quiru* is little improved, even in your own rooms," she commented. "It looks to me, Carver, as if you have serious need of Conservatory."

Cho's smile faded, and he flipped his braid over his shoulder with an angry gesture. "You have nothing we want."

Sira pulled out a chair and sat down, stretching her legs out. "I wonder if your House members would agree," she murmured, and raised her scarred eyebrow at the others in the room.

Cho went to the window to lean against the casing. He tipped his head back to sight down his long nose at Sira. "I should warn you," he said with a smile. "My aides are ready this time, so none of your tricks . . . your Conservatory tricks."

"Tricks?" Sira said. "We call it training. Discipline."

He shrugged. "Call it what you like. Much good it does you now."

Sira folded her arms. "I have come for the child," she told him. "And for Cantrix Elnor."

"You can't have them."

"Since when on Nevya have innocent people been imprisoned?"

"Cantrix Elnor is sworn to serve Soren."

"But you are not allowing her to perform her duties."

Cho pulled a chair out with his foot. He sat in it and leaned far forward over the table until his face was level with Sira's. "She is there to serve if we need her. When I say. If I say."

Sira met his eyes. "Ah—so you do not have faith in this patchy mess of a *quiru*."

"Certainly I do," he said. "Just now, we are learning how to do things— many things—our own way, not Conservatory's way, not Lamdon's." He glanced around at his uneasy troupe. "It's a question of cooperation, isn't it, my friends? Teamwork."

"Indeed," Sira said dryly. "And the child? The little Gifted one?"

"He doesn't know what is best for him."

"And you think you do?"

"So I do."

Sira pushed back her chair and stood, her hands on her hips. The itinerants and carvers who leaned against the walls or waited in the doorway watched her warily. "Do you all want to live this way?" she demanded of them. "Your House cold, your freedom gone—"

"Gone?" Cho shrilled. "Their freedom isn't gone! They're just winning it now!"

"Truly?" Sira strolled around the table, and stopped in front of Bree. "Tell me, Singer. What freedom do you have now that you did not have before?"

Bree's plain face creased with misery. "Cantrix . . . " she murmured. "I'm sorry . . . "

"Oh, no need, believe me. This will all be ended soon." Sira stepped past Bree to address the man next to her. "You are a carver, are you not? Much call for your skills just now?"

"Don't say a word!" Cho snarled from behind them. "Nobody says anything!" The carver dropped his eyes to stare at the floor.

Sira went to the next, a heavy man with dark hair. "What is your name?"

His eyes pleaded with her, and she felt the tremble in his mind. "Ah. You are a Singer." she said. He nodded. "Your name?"

He began, "I'm Klas, Cantrix . . . " and then broke off. He sagged against the wall behind him, and his knees began to bend. His face went utterly pale, sweat beading quickly on his fleshy cheeks. Sira whirled to look at Cho.

Cho was on his feet. His eyes were narrowed, fixed on Klas. "Stop it!" Sira ordered. When Cho did not respond, she widened her own shielding to stop his attack on the itinerant. Cho turned the full force of his assault on her.

The brute force of his psi shocked her. Meeting it with her own was like being shoved head first into a stone wall. She stiffened her shields with an effort that made her head ache and her vision blur. It was no wonder these itinerants were cowed into submission.

Theo, who had followed everything, joined his energy to hers, and seconds later Zakri and Elnor did too. Together they broke off Cho's onslaught. With a gasp and a flaring of his thin nostrils, he gave it up. He stared triumphantly at Sira.

"So!" he exclaimed. "Conservatory didn't come alone, after all!"

Zakri! Theo! Sira sent swiftly.

On my way, Theo sent immediately.

And I, from Zakri.

Cho heard both. Before Sira understood his intent, he lunged for a door at one side of the room, thrusting back the bolt and going inside. Sira thought he was fleeing, and she was about to reach out for him with her psi, to attempt to force him out as she had the day before, when he appeared in the doorway, holding the girl Sook by the arm. He caught her close to him, at the same time pulling his long knife out of his belt with his free hand.

"Cho, no!" the Singer Bree exclaimed. Sira heard the terror in her voice, and her own anger flared again.

"If you do anything to harm this girl," she snapped, "I will break your mind like snapping an icicle over my knee, and the pieces will never mend!"

"I don't think you can do it, Conservatory," Cho answered. "But you're welcome to try!"

Cries and pounding feet from the corridor heralded Theo's arrival. He burst through the door, a crooked grin on his face, a cringing itinerant Singer dragged behind him. "Sorry to be late," he said breathlessly. "I had to pick this one's brain to find out where you were."

The itinerant pulled away, rubbing his arm, and casting fearful glances at Cho. "I couldn't help it," he whined. "I don't know how to shield myself!"

"Get out!" Cho commanded. With his eyes on Theo, he brought the long knife up to rest on Sook's breast, a hand's breadth from her slender throat. Despite the nearness of the black blade, a the girl's dark eyes shone with a sudden flash of joy. Zakri had just appeared in the doorway.

"Singer Zakri!" she cried, and Sira's heart turned over at the poignancy of her welcome. The girl did not know, did not understand.

"Let her go," Zakri growled. His voice was lower, older than Sira had ever heard it. Both Theo and Zakri took two steps closer to Cho.

The knife moved up, just under Sook's chin. The haft of it pressed into her skin, and her eyes widened. She made no further sound.

"There's nothing you can do," Cho said, very softly. "Before you can get to me, this blade will do its work."

Sira held up her hand. She commanded, "Enough! Enough have died in this House. We will not attack you. Lower the blade."

With agonizing slowness, Cho dropped the knife to Sook's breast once again. Sira felt Zakri's power building beside her, felt his overwhelming urge to slap the knife from Cho's hand with a burst of psi. The carvers came to stand on either side of Cho, and she felt the wall they built, the frightening power of combined kinetic psi they possessed. In truth, Lamdon and Conservatory vastly underestimated the Gift in these artisans.

Zakri, wait, she ordered.

Theo joined in. *Sira is right. This is too dangerous.* Cho smirked, hearing them.

Zakri released his pent-up breath. The three Singers faced the four carvers in a tense tableau, the dark-haired girl, the focus of their conflict, holding them apart. The scene froze for the space of several heartbeats, until Sook herself broke it.

"I don't care!" she cried, her voice breaking. "Let him kill me, Singer Zakri! Then you can get him!"

Cho laughed. "Feisty little piece, isn't she?" He brought his hand up from Sook's waist and gripped one of her small breasts, making her wince.

He began broadcasting a picture, very clearly, of Sook in his bed with his hands on her, doing degrading things to her body. His lip curled as he projected the image. None of the three carvers with him could receive it, but it flamed in Zakri's mind, and Theo's and Sira's, all too clearly. It was a fabrication, but it was detailed and obscene, the foul fantasy of a twisted and violent sexuality. Zakri tensed like a *tkir* about to spring, and Sira put her hand on his arm.

"Liar!" Zakri hissed.

"Maybe not," Cho said softly. "I'm perfectly capable of it, and she knows it." He laughed. "She's heard things, haven't you, little Sook?"

Sook's cheeks flamed, but her eyes on Zakri never wavered.

"If you don't leave, and now," Cho said, "I'll show your little friend here—" He jerked her hard, so that her head fell back against his chest. "—such a time as she'll never forget. You won't want her after that, will you?" At that, Sook closed her eyes.

Zakri's control broke. The air around him burned, brilliant sparks firing about his face. His psi gathered, that old involuntary surge that had so tormented him in his youth. It lashed out, striking at the *obis* knife in Cho's fist, to fling it across the room.

The support of the carvers had made Cho fearfully strong. The knife quivered, and moved in his hand, but it did not fall. He laughed and thrust it up under Sook's chin again. Zakri shuddered under Sira's hand, and his breath came fast. She felt his effort, and slid her hand down to grip his.

Let it go, Theo sent swiftly. *He will do it.*

I know. Zakri made a supreme effort that Sira could feel. The sparks disappeared, and his mind closed. Cho relaxed his grip slightly on Sook, and lowered the knife again. One tear slipped from her eye to make a lonely track down her cheek.

"And now," Cho said with a casual air. "You will leave, all three of you, or someone here will—lose his mind, shall we say?"

There was an audible intake of breath around the room. Theo touched Sira's back lightly with his hand, and she gave a slight nod. She turned to look at the frightened itinerants. "This is the future you have chosen, then!" she said to them. "Spirit have mercy on you."

With icy dignity, her back arrow-straight, she left the apartment, Theo and Zakri behind her. They made their way down the staircase, listening as they went. There was no sound from the Magisterial apartment except the sudden rush of feet when the itinerants were released from Cho's presence at last. Too angry even to speak, the three Singers strode down the corridor to the stables to retrieve their *hruss*. The stableman looked at them with eyes that were fearful and without hope. There was nothing they could tell him.

Chapter Twenty-four

"The only way is to get him alone," Zakri said. The Singers squatted or sat crosslegged around the cookfire, facing each other. "I thought if we went in together, he would be no match for us. But he uses the psi of those others as fuel for his own fire."

Berk, standing by the pile of tack, stretched out his massive arm and flexed his fist. "Perhaps physical force is what we need, and not psi force. I'm ready!"

Sira shook her head. "He holds them all hostage. If he is threatened, the Gifted around him will suffer. The itinerants especially are frightened of what he might do to them. He does not care how many minds he ruins—but he knows we do, and he uses it against us."

"If they could get themselves organized . . ." Theo said thoughtfully.

"They did try, once," Zakri told them. "A carver died. And now, he holds Sook because of me. Ah, Spirit, I wish I had his neck between my two hands right now!"

Sira ran her hands through her hair, and then looked down at her fingers, long and dark and supple, made for the strings of a *filhata*. "This is another lesson in the Gift. I have been lecturing Lamdon, and Conservatory, trying to get them to consider new possibilities—but I too have much to learn. Such a painful way to learn it! I have been arrogant, overconfident. Maestra Lu would have pointed out that my strength is also my weakness."

They were silent for some moments. Mreen was leaning on Theo, her curly head on his shoulder, staring into the fire. She gave a small sigh, and her little halo blurred and darkened, its light dimming to a pale shadow in the afternoon sunlight. Theo watched it change in response to the sombre mood around her. Suddenly he leaned forward, startling her. "I am sorry, little one," he said swiftly. "But listen, my friends. What is Cho's weakness?"

"Does he have a weakness?" Berk asked.

"Indeed he does," Theo answered. "He has one great weakness." A slow grin began on his face. He gave Mreen a squeeze. "It is in his Gift. His Gift, like all our Gifts, has its flaw."

They stared at Theo. Mreen's halo sparkled and brightened as she absorbed his excitement, and she wriggled in his arms. "Our friend Cho," he pronounced above her head, "is a most capable carver. But he cannot make *quiru*."

The white slash of Sira's eyebrow rose. Zakri said, "But, Theo, I do not see—"

Theo tousled Mreen's curls. She laughed silently, her small white teeth gleaming and her dimples twinkling. "You show them, Mreen," he urged her. "Show us what your Gift can do!"

Mreen smiled around the circle, making sure she had every eye before she scrunched her eyes closed, and pinched her lips tight with effort. Her nimbus began to darken, to fade. The sparks that danced through it slowed, dimmed, then went out. She repressed her energy until her halo was completely quenched, and she stood in ordinary daylight, without the least gleam of *quiru* light about her. They watched, holding their breath. Her eyes flew open to see their expressions, and she dimpled. The light around her began to shine again, and they laughed to see its aureole flare, as welcome and expected as the morning sun blooming above the eastern peaks.

"The *quiru*!" Zakri exclaimed.

"Indeed," Theo chortled.

Berk slapped his knee and roared. Even Sira, for whom a full smile was a rare thing, grinned until her cheeks hurt. It was the perfect weapon, aimed against the one vulnerable spot in Cho's defenses. It would not be an easy thing to accomplish, but it would be devastatingly effective. For some minutes, they laughed together, enjoying the moment. When they sobered, they began to lay their plans. Mreen followed everything with grave attention.

At the very end, Sira brought out her *filla* to try to reach Cantrix Elnor. They would need her. They would need every bit of strength they could draw upon. Before they left the campsite, Zakri made the *quiru* as strong and bright as he knew how, to last through the night.

A second time they approached the House in unison, just as the afternoon began to shade into twilight. Sira took a position to the north of the House, just at the edge of the courtyard. Theo approached from the west, through the door of the stables. He nodded to the stableman, one finger on his lips, as he passed the *hruss* and the tack room. The stableman watched him in hopeful silence as he moved into the corridor that led to the House. He found a private corner in which to work. On the south side, Zakri once again made his way around the waste drop. This time he sat down on the cold stone step of the back door.

Cantrix Elnor was ready, too. Her sending had been more frail than ever, but she assured Sira she was all right, and looking forward to meeting them all face to face.

They knew Cho heard them come, but spread out as they were, he hardly knew which of them to assault first. They intended that by the time he had called the carvers around him and organized a sortie, their work would have begun and his support would be eroded . . . all his support. Sook was the one at risk; but the swiftness of their attack was meant to occupy Cho, prevent his reaching her before they could. He would be on the defensive, trying to stop them, busy repairing the damage they were about to do.

Zakri began first. In his early years, this very phenomenon had been part of the curse of his untamed Gift, the wild and unpredictable talent that had earned him banishment from House and master more than once. He remembered with painful clarity what it had felt like, seeing the *quiru* die around him. He knew how to do this.

He bent his head, and closed down his hearing, his sight, his sense of warmth or cold. He drew in his thoughts, folding them in upon themselves like rolling up his bedfurs. He concentrated and reduced his Gift until it became a void at the back of the House, a black engulfing shadow that drew away every bit of light and heat from the nearby apartments, the corridors, the carvery.

In the west wing, Theo drained the *quiru* that sustained the kitchens. He had to thrust aside his repugnance, the fear every Nevyan was born with. Grimly, he repressed every nearby patch of light and warmth. They darkened and cooled with fearsome speed.

Cantrix Elnor, with strength born of desperation, drew the light and heat away from the upper corridors. Vestiges remained here and there, like puddles of melting snow, but the dark and cold that lurked outside every House, that haunted every Nevyan's dreams, began to spread.

Sira advanced across the courtyard to stand on the broad steps with her arms outstretched. Her Gift was the strongest of all. She was a full Cantrix, a Singer in her prime, and she threw herself into battle with all her resources. She slowed the tiny particles of the air around her in an utter reversal of the techniques she had learned so painstakingly years before. She felt the light fade from the great room, the Cantoris grow chill and dank, as if the limeglass windows were thrown wide. She focused her mind so fiercely that the cries of alarm from within the House hardly reached her. Her body grew cold, but she did not feel it. Not until her work was done did she feel the stiffness of effort in her neck and shoulders.

The cries from the House became wails, then shrieks. Children screamed in terror as shadows they had never known crept around them. Sira shut out their fear. She knew these people would never forget this night, when the dreaded darkness fell over their House.

She could not regret that now. She shielded herself, closed her mind to their suffering in the old manner. Zakri, too, had to brace himself against the emotions that poured from the House members. Theo, always vulnerable, found his face wet with tears, but still he held. Cantrix Elnor suffered the most, because she was weakened by hunger and age and grief, and because this was her House, her people. But even she did not relent, not for a moment.

The House grew cold between them. Cho stormed out of his apartment and raged about the corridors, ordering the itinerants to play, to work, to bring back the heat and the light.

Some tried. Fragments of melody sounded here and there, but the power of two Cantors and two Cantrixes was too great. The Gift turned inside out, darkness drinking in light, a terrifying revocation of the work of all Singers. It was a nightmare made real, and against the overwhelming fear of the cold, even Cho's weapon paled. Any light beginning to swell around the itinerants dimmed and died. Their fear made them tremble. The cold itself defeated them.

Vaguely, Sira became aware that Cantrix Elnor was no longer with them, no longer mirroring their work from her attic prison. She searched for her with her mind. She found Cho and two others, the Singers Klas and

Shiro, bursting into Elnor's room, carrying her bodily down the stairs from the attic, then down the main staircase. Through the ruckus of psi and fear and the din of frightened people, threaded Elnor's cry for help.

Sira, she sent, *they have me . . . they . . . .*

Sira threw open the double doors and strode into the hall.

Cho and the itinerants hauled Elnor into the Cantoris. The Cantrix was weak, her limbs trailing, her head falling back. A third man was halfway down the stairs, one hand sliding across the elegant banister, the other clutching a wrapped *filhata*.

Sira ordered, "Stop right there!"

The man threw her a wide-eyed glance. His feet were still, but he was poised to flee, up or down. "Please, Cantrix," he whined. "The *quiru*—"

Cho appeared in the doorway of the Cantoris, his features twisted with rage. "Bring me that, man! Hurry!" he commanded.

The itinerant put one foot on a lower tread. Sira snapped at him, "Do not move, Singer!"

He froze again, trapped like a *wezel* between two predators. Cho's eyes narrowed, and he hissed, "If you don't get down here, I'll wipe your idiot mind as clean as any *obis* blade!"

The man gasped, and sagged against the banister. Sira sent swiftly, *Zakri! I need you here!* Then she set her jaw and stretched out her shields to encircle the itinerant.

Cho's blow struck her an instant later. He must have known, have sensed what she was doing, and how it would weaken her. Protecting the itinerant taxed her strength to the utmost. She struggled for breath through a surge of nausea, fighting to focus her mind under the pressure of his attack. She saw nothing, heard nothing, but grappled desperately with the reckless force that was Cho the carver. She threw her inhibitions aside and struck at him, trying to break his hold on her and on the itinerant.

She failed. Her knees bent, and she grew dizzy, the floor tilting beneath her feet. She flung out her arms to orient herself.

Cho was too strong, and she was stretched too thin. Her shielding wavered, and she sent frantically, *Oh, Theo! I cannot hold . . . I am sorry . . .*

But before she broke, her groping hand found Zakri's shoulder, and her mind melded with his. Their shields joined, firmed and thickened, twining like the irontree suckers to make a whole greater than their individual strengths. It was Zakri who fired a burst of energy at Cho, as strong a volley as he could muster. Cho's attack collapsed under it. Sira's head abruptly cleared.

The itinerants Klas and Shiro flanked Cho in the doorway to the Cantoris. Cho's lean face was wet with sweat, but he was unhurt, and his eyes dazzled black with fury.

"You can't do this to me!" he hissed through the murky darkness.

"We are doing it!" Zakri exclaimed. "Look around you! It is as dark as night in this House. Give it up, Carver!"

For answer, Cho paced to the staircase and reached up past the banister to seize the *filhata* from the itinerant. The man cowered, shrinking from Cho.

"Elnor will sing," Cho snarled, "or she will die!"

Sira took two steps toward the Cantoris, keeping her wary eye on Cho. *Cantrix Elnor? Are you all right?* There was no answer. Cho moved behind her, and Sira hurried to reach the doorway before he did.

Elnor slumped on the dais where the itinerants had left her. She had fallen from the stool, and her hair spread in gray wisps on the floor about her head. She was not moving, and she sent nothing. Sira caught her breath.

The sound of *filla* came again in the upper corridor and in the hallway, threatening to undo their work. Theo still struggled from the west wing, but it was too much for any one Cantor to hold his own against the itinerants.

We must stop them! Sira ran into the Cantoris and leaped onto the dais, leaving Zakri stationed in the hall. Sira knelt beside Elnor, and began again, drawing in the light, fighting back the efforts of the Singers to repair the *quiru*. Zakri did the same. They drew in their shields as well, keeping them close and strong. Cho flailed at Zakri, then at Sira, but it did him no good.

The House members had fled to their own apartments to wrap themselves and their children in layers of fur, to hide under rugs to stave off the deep cold. The various sounds of the itinerants' *filla* faltered and died, and they, too, ran for the slender shelter of furs in their rooms.

Cho swore foully, and raced up the staircase.

Sook felt the cold seep into her little room from the top down, as if someone had lifted the roof off the House. She had no furs, but she threw her bedfur around her shoulders and ran to the windowseat to look down into the courtyard.

Below on the steps she saw Sira spread her arms, and saw the faint glow of *quiru* light around the walls of the House dim and vanish. Sook's lips stretched in a furious smile. "At last!"

She flew to her door and pounded on it. "Bree!" she cried. "Bree! Let me out! I want to see this, oh, please—Bree!"

The bolt rattled on the other side, and she pulled the door open to see Bree, her lips and nostrils white with fear, on the other side. "We're all going to freeze to death!" she moaned, and ran out of the apartment before Sook could answer.

Sook was close at her heels, seeing the darkness closing in on the House, the corridors dim and treacherous, the stones of the floor already frigid with the loss of warmth. Sook laughed aloud, triumphantly. She ran to the staircase and looked down.

Bree passed Cho on his way up. She glanced back once, hesitating a moment, but her fear was too great, and she fled toward her own room. Cho's lip curled when he saw Sook. The glitter in his eyes was the only light in the corridor.

"Well, little Sook," Cho cried. "Now it's just you and me!"

Her heart fluttered in her throat, but she stood as straight as she could. "It doesn't matter, anyway," she cried. "Singer Zakri will see you get what's coming to you!"

"Singer Zakri? Singer?" Cho laughed and seized her arm. "You fool! That's no Singer at all! Your Singer Zakri is a full-fledged Cantor!"

Sook felt suspended in the darkness, with nothing to hold on to. She staggered under his hand. "What?" she whispered. "You lie! You're a liar!"

Cho tittered, peering down at her face through the gloom. "I have no problem with lying," he said softly, squeezing her thin wrist, wrenching it upward. "But there's no need. You think he's for you, don't you, my girl? For you, a cook?"

"Zakri—Zakri's not—" she faltered.

"Oh, yes!" he crowed. "Zakri is! Zakri is Cantor Zakri, and no mate for you or for anybody!" His braid swung across his chest, and he threw it back, out of his way. He dragged her back down the corridor to the apartment, opening the door with his free hand. "So we'll just see how he likes this!" he exclaimed. He forced her across the room, flinging her into his own bedroom, slamming the door and shooting the bolt from the inside.

Sook stumbled over a stool and fell her length on the stone floor. Her head snapped back, striking the edge of the bedframe. A rushing filled her ears and she sank into a gray fog.

When she came to, Cho's body pressed hers into the soft furs of his bed, and he breathed sour gusts into her nostrils. His head lifted slightly, and his eyes narrowed. They were directed at her, but not seeing her. She knew that look—the itinerant Singers had suffered when he had that look. But she had no Gift to feel it! What was he doing? Who was he trying to hurt?

His hand gripped the collar of her tunic and he ripped it from neck to hem.

"O Spirit!" Zakri cried. He was still in the hallway, leaning against the wall, his eyes closed, his shields strong. Cho was sending him an image, a powerful scene that no shielding could shut out. Sook was on his bed, Sook with her head lolling, her face pale. Zakri tried to evade it, to disbelieve it, but Cho was in his mind, fastened to it with a tenacious strength worthy of a *tkir*. He was the *tkir*, Cho was, just as in Zakri's dreams. And he had Sook in his claws, tearing her tunic away from her body. This was no imagined deed, no empty threat. The sharp edge of reality made it vivid. Zakri gritted his teeth and his breath came fast.

He sent *Theo! I need your help! It is Sook—in Cho's apartment! We must hurry!*

Zakri ran, ignoring the cries and shouts from all over the House. He leapt up the stairs as fast as he could go, skidding at the top on the cooling stone. He raced down the hall toward Cho's apartment, bursting into it with a crash of the outer door.

The inner door was closed and barred. Zakri pounded on it with his fist, then pulled back his booted foot to kick it in. He heard Sook cry out in fear and pain, and he struck out with a blow of psi, hoping Cho was too occupied to block it. It was a broad swipe, fully intended to do as much injury as possible.

His strike met a parry of shocking strength. Cho had learned fast. Instinctively, Zakri shielded his own mind. He would be no good to Sook if his mind were ruined before he could get to her. He kicked at the door instead, using all his strength. It cracked under his heel, but it did not give.

Cho shouted, "Cantor Zakri! I'm going to do it right now while you beat on my door, and I'm going to let you see and remember every moment—to entertain you in your lonely Cantoris!"

Zakri tried to close his mind to the image, but he could not escape it. Cho tore at Sook's tunic until only the drape of her hair fell over her bare skin. He made Zakri watch, and feel the sinister pleasure he took in it. Zakri battered at the door again as Cho reached for Sook. He took a fistful of the fabric of her trousers and ripped it.

Zakri could bear it no more. With a convulsive thrust of energy, he broke the psi contact. He was kneeling by the door with his head in his hands when Theo dashed in, out of breath.

"What is it? What has happened?"

Zakri found that there were tears on his face as he looked up at the older Singer. "It is Sook—my friend—" He pointed to the cracked and splintered door. "She is there! You must help me, please!"

The bedroom lay in deep shadow. Sook blinked, thinking the blow on her head was still affecting her sight, and then, feeling the chill air strike her bare skin, she knew it was the failing *quiru* that made it hard to see. Cho leaned above her, and ripped her trousers from waist to knee with one hard jerk. She bared her teeth at him and he grabbed her hair, forcing her head up.

"Make plenty of noise, now, you little bitch," he panted. "We want your Zakri to hear everything!" He pushed her down with his weight.

He was too heavy, and too big, for her to resist. She felt as small and weak as a *caeru* pup, pinned by his body, with no purchase for her hands, nothing to push against or pull on. His long body covered hers, one hand in her hair, the other reaching for the tatters of her trousers.

Her left hand battered uselessly on his shoulder. Her right grasped at the bedfurs, searching for something to hold on to, something to fight with. She moved it desperately, seeking, searching . . . at last, finding.

The hilt was in her hand, the haft smooth and worn under her fingers. The scabbard, slim and black and hard, was pressing into the flesh of her hip, and would leave its mark in a long bruise when this was over. It was almost over. She was all but naked, and Cho was fumbling with his own clothes now.

Sook pulled the blade free of the scabbard and gripped the hilt in her right hand. With her left she found the long braid that lay on Cho's shoulder, and she pulled on it with all her might. His head twisted to her left, and he cursed with the pain of his pulled hair. When he lifted his arm, stretching to reach his plait and jerk it from her fingers, Sook did not hesitate. Just so had she spread the ribs of a *caeru* carcass, to carve the meat from the bones. When she thrust hard with the knife, it glanced upward, to his heart.

Cho gasped, and his body went rigid. His face above hers paled to the texture of glacial ice. When he released the breath, red, hot heart's blood gushed out over her hand. She screamed, not in fear but in rage and triumph.

At that moment, with Theo helping to guard his mind, Zakri used his special talent, his kinetic psi, to shove back the bolt that held the door, and he and Theo burst into the room.

Chapter Twenty-five

"Mreen? Mreen? Child, where are you?"

She heard the call, and her soft little heart gave a twinge, but she could not stop now. She had waited for just this moment, when Berk was occupied with tack and *hruss*, to make her dash for the House. The boy's misery was an ache in her mind, an insistent pull she could not ignore. Terrible things were happening in that House. She feared the boy might not survive them.

The thoughts and emotions of all the Gifted poured from the House, washed over the snow in a roiling deluge. She had to shield herself as strongly as she knew how, or find her own mind submerged in the flood. Much of what penetrated her shields was incomprehensible to her five-year-old mind. There was violence, that much she knew, and fear. And then there was the boy, whose own Gift was so undeveloped she could not even discover his name. He huddled in his room, weeping, shouting, anything to block out the chaos around him.

Boy! Boy! she sent, trying to attract his attention. *Hold on. I am coming. Boy, listen!* But he could not sort her small voice from the cacophony, the sea of uncontrolled psi.

There was no path where she cut through the irontree groves, and in places the snowdrifts were too deep for her short legs. She had to wade through them, sometimes having to get on all fours and crawl over the top of the snow. She grew hot and damp under her furs.

Slowly she made her way up the hill, reaching the crest just as Soren's *quiru* began to collapse. Twilight blanketed the surrounding hills in a violet haze, and Mreen shivered in her furs, watching it, though she was not really cold. She cast a glance behind her, hearing Berk call her name again and again.

I am sorry, she sent to him, though she knew he could not hear her. *I will be back soon.*

She hurried on. By the time she forded the crusted snow to reach the beaten snowpack of the courtyard she was breathless. She ran as fast as her aching short legs could carry her.

Soren lay in a muddy darkness. Mreen shuddered to see one of Nevya's great Houses without any gleam of *quiru* light shining from its windows, no comforting glow crowning its peaked roofs. It was an apocalyptic vision, the realization of the deepest fear of any child of Nevya. Mreen lowered her eyes, avoiding it. She clenched her small fists and raced over the unswept cobblestones and up the broad steps to the front doors.

One of the doors was ajar, left open by someone in a hurry. Mreen hesitated on the step, hating to put her foot into the dark hall. The swirl of psi around her, around the entire House, had not abated, but intensified. Somewhere, on the upper level, she sensed that the final confrontation was taking place. Her mind shied away from that conflict as her hand might pull back from a hot flame. She sought the boy instead, closing her eyes and concentrating, calling out for him, although she supposed he still would not understand.

Boy! Boy! Where are you? I am trying to find you!

"What in the name of the Spirit—"

Mreen opened her eyes and looked up to see a large man with black hair looming above her. She took an involuntary step backward.

"Who are you?" he demanded.

Mreen's nimbus, the only *quiru* light in the hall, shone brilliantly in the gloom. There was no other light. She was luminous, a lamp for the darkness. She gasped as she realized it, and took another step backward.

I am Mreen, she sent, but the man did not seem to hear her, though she could feel his anger and fear. Surely he had the Gift. But he bent forward and reached a meaty hand to take hold of her arm. She knew well that no Gifted person touches another without permission.

"Looks like you've got the only light in the House," the man growled. He hauled on her arm, and she winced with pain. No one, in her entire life, had ever laid a hand on her in that way. If she could have screamed, she would have, in sheer fury. "You're coming to see Cho," he said, and pulled her toward the stairs.

Mreen fought him. She kicked, and scratched at his hand with her nails. Black hairs covered his arm, and she tore at them. He cursed, some word she did not recognize, and bent down to take her around the waist. His forearm was just close enough. She sank her small teeth into it, shuddering at the taste of his skin and the texture of the coarse hairs that covered it.

For good measure, she focused on the spot of the bite, and made the broken skin as hot as her abundant psi energy could make it. He yowled with pain. He dropped her as he might have dropped a *caeru* cub that got its claws into him. She turned and ran, in the only direction she could, back out through the open door and into the night.

He swore, "Six Stars, girl, when I catch you . . ." He lumbered after her, out into the cold and dark.

Her halo was brilliant in the darkness, a clear beacon for her pursuer. She ran to the edge of the courtyard, then stopped, crouching, huddling on the cobblestones. She forced herself to focus, to draw in her light until it faded to nothing, leaving her invisible in the darkness.

It was almost more than she could bear. This was nothing like the demonstration she had made at the campsite. Everyone feared the dark, of course, but Mreen, in all her five years, had never seen true darkness. Light had always emanated from her like the twinkling of a star. Now there was no light to reassure her, not her own, nor that which should come from the Cantoris, nor even the cheery small flames of one of Berk's cookfires. She was shocked to find herself growing cold, a sensation she could not remember ever experiencing. A silent sob escaped her, and her teeth chattered. How, oh how, she wondered wildly, did other people bear it? She felt bereft. Her feet were numb already against the frigid stones, and the icy air burned in her chest. She struggled to stand upright. She knew, if this awful man did not give up the chase, that she could freeze to death, right here in front of the House, and no one would know until morning.

The man was struggling against his own fear. He called out twice, then hastened back into the dark House, where at least a semblance of warmth remained. But he remained in the doorway, peering out into the night, looking for her. She watched his sinister bulk, a shadow of menace in the doorway, and she despaired. She was too cold to cry, but her breath caught in painful spasms of shivering. She knew instinctively she must not get caught; if the bad man in this House had her in his control, nothing Cantrix Sira could do would be enough.

It was when she thought she could no longer control herself, when she thought she would have to surrender, give in to her need for warmth, that his footsteps at last retreated, and she thought she saw his dim form moving up the staircase. She waited, shivering, hugging herself inside her furs.

The moments passed. When she began to feel warm, she knew she had waited as long as she dared. She let out her breath all at once, and her nimbus flared, its consoling light and soothing warmth feeling like strong arms about her.

Mreen raced back to the open door and peeked cautiously inside. No one was in the hall, though she heard voices and running feet above the stairs. She trotted away down the nearest corridor, calling *Boy! Boy!* Above her, a ruckus of shouting mixed with a tide of psi. She tried to shield herself, but it was vivid and violent, with horrible images, the more terrible because she did not understand them. She was afraid she might be sick, right in the hallway. Then she heard him screaming.

"Stop it! Make them stop! Mama, Mama!"

She was in the wrong corridor. She heard his voice dimly through the cries and wails of other House members, and then only because his Gift lent it carrying power. She tried to fasten on it, to follow it.

Mreen looked behind her. No one had seen her light, and the man had not returned.

She could hear the boy clearly now, feel him. He was crying, sick and frightened. She retraced her steps, and ran frantically down the opposite corridor, all the way to the last apartment. Other people passed Mreen, running, calling each other's names. Some stopped to stare at her, but no one offered to touch her again. Their fear was as powerful as the darkness.

Mreen reached the closed door and heard the boy sobbing inside while a woman's voice pleaded with him. Mreen lifted the latch and pushed the door open.

The boy was perhaps five or six. He knelt on a couch in a muddle of bedfurs and pillows, his hands over his ears, his eyes squeezed shut. Tears and mucus ran down his face. A thin woman knelt beside him, trying to hold him as he rocked back and forth, wailing. "Oh, please, Joji, please," the woman cried. "Joji, stop! Joji, listen to me!"

Mreen shut the door sharply behind her and the woman looked up in alarm. "What is—who are you?"

Mreen went to the bed, touching her silent lips with her hand and shaking her head, trying to explain that she could not speak. She gazed intently at the boy, but his mother pulled him back, further away from her, shielding him with her arm. "What is it? What do you want?"

Mreen ignored her. *Boy!* she sent. *Joji! Can you hear me now?*

"Who are you?" the mother repeated.

Joji! Mreen sent, as loudly as she could. Her own shields were still young and untried, but she extended them as much as she knew how, trying to shut out some of the noise from the boy's mind, wary of leaving herself too vulnerable. She felt the mother's suspicious gaze on her as she concentrated. Her halo sparkled vividly, intensified by her efforts.

The boy's sobs subsided little by little as the noise in his head diminished. He wiped at his eyes, and his mother produced a bit of cloth from her pocket to clean his face. He sniffled, then sat up.

"Is it over? Is it—" His eyes stretched wide, sniffles forgotten, as he caught sight of Mreen. "Mama! Who's that?"

"I don't know," his mother said. She looked down at Mreen, who stood still beside the bed, powerless to explain herself.

Mreen stamped her foot in frustration. *Boy!* she sent. *Joji! I am trying to help you.*

"Oh!" he cried. "I can hear her, Mama—in my head!" He put out his hand to Mreen.

Mreen drew close to the bed, and reached up with her small hands to pull his head down. His mother gasped and pulled him away again, but Joji wriggled free of her. "It's all right, Mama, she only wants to talk to me!" He crawled forward on his knees through the tangle of the bedfurs. "What is it?" he asked Mreen.

She put her hands on his shoulders, bringing his head down to touch her forehead to his. Carefully, as clearly as she knew how, she sent, *I am Mreen. I came to take you away.*

Joji stared at her. He was dark, with soft brown eyes, and painfully thin, thinner even than his mother. He shook his head. "I can't do that," he told Mreen. "I can't leave Mama."

"Joji!" his mother exclaimed. "What are you talking about?"

He turned his head to look at her. "This is Mreen, Mama. She's Gifted."

The woman stared at Mreen in consternation. "Where did you come from? Why don't you speak?"

Mreen felt her shielding begin to waver, and she grasped Joji once again. *We have to hurry*, she sent urgently. *I am shielding you from all the psi, but I cannot keep it up. We have to leave before they catch us!*

"Then I have to take Mama," he said.

Mreen shook her head. *No, no. Tell her we will be back for her . . .* She drew a deep breath. *Tell her I promise.*

Joji stared at her for a long moment. Mreen was growing tired from the effort of keeping her shields up around them both, and she wavered. He gasped as the noise rose again on the periphery of his mind. He turned to his mother. "Mama, I'll be back for you. Stay here! Stay right here!"

His mother's tears shone in the reflected light of Mreen's nimbus. She clasped her arms about herself. "Oh, Joji, I don't even know who this is! And where are you going?"

"She's Mreen, I told you. She's shielding me, but she can't keep it up too long." He jumped down from the bed, turning back to pat his mother's arm. "We'll be back, Mama, we'll come back for you." He glanced at Mreen, and repeated, "I promise."

His mother put out her arm as if to stop them. Mreen turned her green eyes on her, fixing her with the intensity of her gaze, and the woman shrank back, a hand to her lips. *Tell her*, Mreen sent to Joji, *that it will be all right.*

Joji frowned, not understanding completely. Again Mreen touched her forehead to his. *Tell your Mama it will be all right. Cantrix Sira is here.*

Joji smiled at her, and turned to smile at his mother. "It's wonderful, Mama! I can hear her, clear as anything! And she says don't worry, Cantrix Sira is here."

The woman stared at him. "Joji—I don't know who that is, either."

He shrugged. "Me, neither, but I know Mreen!"

Mreen tugged at his hand. She was getting very tired, and thought if they did not get away soon, her shields would fail. Joji followed, looking back only once at his mother.

In the corridor, they ran, hand in hand, to the front doors and out into the dark. Joji pulled back suddenly, tearing his hand from Mreen's, when he saw that night had fallen over the snowy hills. He whirled, turning back to the House as if even the misery inside it was better than the terrors of the cold and dark outside. Mreen gripped his hand and pulled him close to her.

They slowed to a walk when they were down the steps. Mreen relaxed her shields and poured her energy instead into her own tiny *quiru*. It had lighted and warmed her since her earliest memory. It was much easier for her to intensify it now than it had been to quench it earlier. It bloomed full and bright about her and Joji, and in relative comfort, hands tightly joined, they made their way across the courtyard.

Mreen was exhausted. Her legs felt as heavy as *hruss* legs, plodding and thick. A sudden hoarse yell from the House made her heart thump hard in her breast. She glanced over her shoulder and saw that the hairy man had spotted them, and was coming out of the House and across the cobblestones.

Joji, hurry! Run! she sent. If he could not understand her precisely, he sensed her alarm. He yelped in fear, and together they raced for the shelter of the ironwood grove on the hill.

The big man's legs were much longer than theirs, and he could not be half so tired as Mreen was. She heard his feet slapping against the cobblestones. She and Joji ran as hard as they could, striving for the trees, not daring to separate for fear that Joji would be left in the cold. Mreen's breath came shallowly, and her short legs burned with effort. At the edge of the cobbled courtyard, she fell headlong from the stones to the snow.

The man exclaimed in triumph. She struggled to her knees.

Joji pulled her to her feet. "Come on, Mreen, you can do it! Come on, a few more steps!"

He tugged at her, and she was up, the two of them running together, Mreen staggering, Joji insisting. The man behind them cursed, and stumbled in the darkness. The children reached the shelter of the grove, and the man swore again as their little halo of light disappeared among the trees.

Mreen and Joji struggled on through the obstinate snowdrifts, until the House itself was obscured by the thick trunks of the trees. Only then did Mreen collapse on a huge sucker, sobbing soundlessly with what little breath she had left. Joji clung to her, amazed at his own daring in coming out with her, casting wide eyes back the way they had come to make certain the man could not see them.

For long minutes they rested, Mreen with her cheek against the rough bark of the sucker, Joji gripping her hand as if it were his only chance. When they could breathe again, and Mreen's legs felt stronger, they began the climb up the slope toward the campsite.

Mreen tried to find her own path, to retrace her footsteps, but her nimbus did not give enough light to make it easy. The snowpack was frozen stiff by the deep cold, slick on the surface, deep and spongy when they broke through the crust. Twice they fell, together. Once Joji rolled away, out of Mreen's halo, and his terror when he found himself in the darkness was a painful thing. Mreen had learned that fear herself not long before. He began to sob immediately with the shock of it. She clambered over the snow on all fours, to embrace him once again in her light, and they snuggled together, shivering, like two *caeru* pups lost in the drifts.

They wound slowly up through the trees, relieved when they saw at last the flicker of the *quiru* and the small steady fire within it. Mreen's heart ached to see Berk slumped beside the fire, his head in his hands. She must have been gone for hours. She pulled at Joji, rushing him, forgetting her exhaustion, hurrying into the light and warmth Zakri had refreshed before going down to Soren. Once they were safe in its circle, she dropped Joji's hand and flew to Berk.

She reached out to pat his grizzled cheek. His head flew up with a cry, and he swept her up in his massive arms. She hugged him back, hard. He buried his face in her shoulder and squeezed her until she thought she might never breathe again. When she could look into his face, she saw tears of relief standing in his eyes.

"You rascal!" he said hoarsely. "I thought you were gone! I—" He caught sight of Joji and broke off. "By the Ship! Who's this, then?"

Joji dropped his head, and stared down at his boots.

"Mreen!" Berk exclaimed. "You could have frozen, the two of you. It's dark—and cold!"

Mreen dimpled up at him, and he drew a ragged breath and hugged her close once again. "You kept him warm, didn't you, you little darling? You got him out of there, and you kept him warm! O Spirit, yours is a strange Gift!"

Berk held out his hand to the little boy. "Better come on over here by the fire, young man," he said. "Better tell me your name, since this one can't. You can speak, can't you?"

Joji took a hesitant step closer, then another. Tentatively, he put his hand in Berk's. "I can talk," he said shyly. "My name's Joji."

"Joji, is it," Berk said. "Well, Joji, you've had quite a time of it. But it's nice to have your company. Hungry?"

Joji nodded, and a smile brightened his thin face. "I'm really hungry," he said.

"Well, then. You just sit here and watch while Mreen and I make the *keftet*. We're good at it, aren't we, Mreen?"

Mreen nodded briskly, and ran to the saddlepacks for softwood. Berk watched her go, shaking his head, muttering to himself. He gave a shaky sigh, and looked down at the little boy she had rescued. "Ship and stars," he muttered. He patted Joji's shoulder and ruffled his hair before he went to fetch the cooking pot.

Chapter Twenty-six

Cho and Sook lay in a huddle in the half-light. Only the dull shine of Sook's bare shoulders and the river of darkening blood flowing between them were distinguishable to Zakri and Theo when they thrust the door open. Zakri froze in the doorway, afraid to know whose blood it was that stained the bedfurs. Theo pushed past him to reach for Cho and pull him away from the girl.

The carver was limp and heavy, a dead weight in his hands. Theo grunted as he lifted him, and turned him face up. The knife was still buried in his ribs and it caught on the tangled furs. Sook looked down at it, then at Cho's sightless eyes, and turned her head away.

Theo pulled one of the furs free to wrap around her nakedness. She searched his face as she accepted his ministrations, her eyes gleaming in the dusk. "Is he dead?" she asked in a breathless voice. "Did I kill him?"

Theo put his fingers under Cho's jaw, then slipped his hand beneath the loosened tunic, feeling with his palm just below the juncture of the ribs and the breastbone. There was no movement of heart or breath. Sook clutched the fur around her shoulders and wriggled as far away from Cho as she could get, stopping only when she bumped against the wall. Theo thought she looked very young, surely not older than four summers.

"You must not blame yourself," he told her gently. "He gave you no choice."

Her protest was no more than a whisper, barely audible. "No, no!" Tension constricted her throat. Her hands, holding the fur, were stiff. "Tell me! Have I killed him?"

Theo had to tell her. He tugged on the sticky bedfurs, pulling them up and over Cho's inert body. "Yes," he said. "He is dead."

She pounded the wall next to her with her fist, making Theo jump. "Thank the Spirit!"

He stared at her, understanding now the fire in her eyes. He had seen the same look on faces of hunters standing over their fresh kill, the hot flush of victory, the blaze of triumph. There was no regret in it.

Zakri found his feet at last and moved close to the bed. He glanced briefly at the mound of Cho's body, then away. "Sook, are you all right?" His voice cracked.

"Zakri!" She exclaimed. "He's dead. Cho's dead. Look at him—"

Zakri pulled back the furs to show Cho's waxen face. His narrow lips and thin nostrils had gone white. The black eyes that had struck terror into so many were now unmoving and dull, fixed forever on the view beyond the stars. His long braid lay twisted around his neck as if to choke off his last breath. But the knife still protruded from his side, blood drying on the hilt. There was no doubt about what had happened.

Sook had done it. Alone. Zakri could hardly take it in.

She came to her knees, the sheet bunched under her chin. Her stiff muscles now trembled violently. "I'm not sorry," she said, speaking too fast through dry lips. "I had to do it. He was an awful man, and he was going to hurt me! I'm not sorry, I'm not!"

Zakri stared at her, speechless. It was Theo who reassured her. "Of course you are not," he said. "You did what you had to do. But it was a hard thing, and frightening. You need some water, and fresh clothes. We can call a Housewoman to help you."

Sook crawled on her knees to the edge of the bed. "See—" she began. She found the floor with her feet and stood up, clutching the stained furs about her. She took one step toward Zakri.

Her legs collapsed. He caught her just in time to stop her falling to the floor, and swept her up in his arms as he might pick up Mreen. Sook's head lolled back and her loosened hair cascaded over his arm to brush the floor. Theo came to put his hand under her neck, to support her head as they lay her on the couch in the outer room.

"Stay with her," Theo told Zakri. "I will finish with—with what has to be done."

Zakri nodded, and knelt beside Sook, pulling an extra fur from the back of the couch to tuck around her. Theo returned to the bedroom, where Zakri could see him arranging Cho's long legs, straightening the bloody bedfurs. Theo hesitated briefly with his hand above Cho's face before he closed the staring eyes with his palm. At last he pulled the bedfurs all the way up over the body, leaving a long, narrow, lifeless mound.

Theo closed the bedroom door firmly and came back to the couch. The room began to brighten around them. Sook stirred and sighed. "What . . ." she whispered. "Where is . . .?" She struggled to sit up, and her eyes went wide as she remembered. She gasped, and cast a horrified glance back at the door to Cho's bedroom.

"It is all right now," Zakri said. "It is all over. See, the *quirunha* is going on even now."

The room was warmer, the chill being pushed back as if swept away by the warm, bright air that replaced it. Sook looked from Zakri to Theo and back again. Her chin began to tremble.

"Oh, Zakri," she cried. "I—I killed Cho, didn't I? I took his knife, and I—"

Zakri repeated, "It is all right, Sook! It is over now."

She stared at him, shaking her head. She tried to speak again, but her words dissolved in a torrent of tears. He knelt helplessly before her as she sobbed.

I do think, Cantor Zakri, Theo sent to him, *that it will not compromise your Gift to comfort the girl. She has had a terrible experience, and there is no one else here for her.*

Zakri cast Theo a grateful glance, then gingerly put his arms around Sook. She threw both arms around his neck, and wept out her loneliness and fear and horror. He held her, patting her shoulder, stroking her tumbled hair. The House warmed around them and the sounds of shouting and running feet in the corridors died away. By the time Sook's tears were spent, Soren was as bright as morning, and warmer than it had been for many months.

Theo left the apartment, returning just as Sook was wiping her face and trying to reorder the mass of her hair. "The House members have seen to the rest of them," he said obliquely.

Zakri stood up. He bent to rub his knees, which had grown stiff on the chill stone of the floor. "Are we needed, then?"

"Not for that. Sira would like us to come to the Cantoris—Cantrix Elnor is there."

"Good news," Zakri said. "Sook, shall we fetch a Housewoman for you?"

She shook her head, still shuddering slightly with the aftermath of weeping. "I have clothes, in there," she told him, pointing to the little bedroom which had been her prison. "I just need a moment. But I don't want to be alone!" She gave an involuntary glance at the closed bedroom door. "Will you wait for me?"

"Of course we will," Theo assured her.

When Sook had gone into the bedroom, Theo and Zakri went to the window and looked out into the night. The unkempt state of the courtyard was made clear by the generous spill from Sira's *quiru*.

What have they done with the others? Zakri asked.

They have rounded them up like wild hruss *and stabled them in the carvery,* Theo said. *No one else was hurt.*

Do they know about Sook? About Cho?

I told them only that he was dead.

Sook's door opened. She emerged dressed in a brilliant scarlet tunic and dark trousers. She had brushed her hair into a fresh binding, and scrubbed her face. Her eyes and lips were swollen and red, but she tossed her head as she looked back at the little bedroom. "I never want to see those walls again." Her voice was shaky, but growing stronger. "I've had enough of being a prisoner!"

Theo bowed to her, smiling. "So be it," he said. "May you live the rest of your life as free as the *urbear* on the Glacier!"

Sook managed a tremulous smile at him.

Together the three of them left the apartment and walked down the corridor to the broad staircase. The weeks of poor heat and light had left their mark in pockets of creeping mold and mildew that festered in corners and crevices. Dust and dirt lay everywhere, but the House members, pale and thin though they were, smiled and chattered, lively in their relief. They waved to Sook, and bowed to Theo and Zakri as they passed.

Zakri looked to his left when he reached the foot of the stairs. The carvery door was closed, bolted on the outside. Several House members stood guard before it. There were decisions to be made, reparations and punishments to be decided upon, but Zakri hoped those functions could be left to some other authority. Now that Sook was safe, and Soren free of its despot, he wanted only to return to his own House as soon as possible. He missed his own Cantoris, Cantor Gavn, even the sour Cantor Ovan.

In the Cantoris, Sira was still on the dais, a borrowed *filhata* in her lap. Cantrix Elnor, slight and gray-haired and weak, sat on one of the benches, facing her. A number of carvers were seated around Elnor at a respectful distance. They now sat, smiling, but keeping a watchful eye.

The *quiru* was complete. Sook, Theo and Zakri walked together up the aisle to the dais. Sira's brows rose at the sight of blood on Theo's clothes. He sent swiftly, *I will explain it all later.*

She stepped down from the dais to bow formally before the elder Cantrix. "Cantrix Elnor, I present to you Cantor Theo v'Observatory." Theo bowed also.

Elnor inclined her head. Her neck trembled slightly, and there was no color in her wrinkled cheeks, but she smiled. "I am glad to meet you, Cantor," she said. "And I thank you from the bottom of my heart for coming to the aid of my House."

"Glad to be of help," Theo responded. "And pleased to see you well."

She shrugged delicately. "Well enough. I will be better soon."

"And this," Sira began, holding out her hand to Zakri. "This is Cantor Zakri v'Amric—"

She was interrupted by an outburst from Sook. "No! It's not true!"

Zakri turned to her, stricken. "Sook! I could not tell you before—it was not safe, but—"

Sook's eyes blazed and her cheeks turned pink. "How could you let me think—let me feel—oh, be damned to you!" She whirled and ran from the Cantoris, leaving the Cantors and the carvers to look after her, dumbfounded.

Sira and Theo stared at Zakri. His cheeks flamed, and then paled.

"What have I done?" he begged them. "And what am I to do now?"

Sira had no answer. Theo said, "My friend, I think you had better go after her. She is hurt, and angry, but she needs to hear your explanation just the same."

Zakri looked at Cantrix Elnor, who watched the scene in confusion. The carvers around her exchanged glances and shifted uneasily in their seats. One of them rose as if to follow Sook, then sat down again.

Cantrix Sira, Zakri sent desperately. *I had no intention of deceiving the girl. I meant only to protect her.*

Sira answer was sympathetic. *I never doubted you, Zakri! But you must tell her that.*

Zakri bowed to Elnor and to Sira, and hurried up the aisle. Theo watched him go with a wry grin. *There is always one more surprise,* he sent to Sira.

Even for you, she answered.

Oh, yes? He folded his arms and cocked his head to one side. *I can hardly wait.*

Chapter Twenty-seven

Zakri found Sook in the kitchens, where they had first met, when she served him tea at the long, knife-scarred table under Mura's critical eye. Now Mura was gone, and Sook kept her back to him, fixing her gaze on the darkness beyond the window. He knew she was hiding her wet face and reddened eyes.

"Sook," he said softly. "I did not mean to deceive you. It never occurred to me—I mean, I never thought—"

Her arms were wrapped tightly around herself, and her shoulders slumped forward.

"Sook, please. Will you not speak with me, let me explain?"

She shook her head, and choked on a tiny sob. His heart ached with hers, and the air around him glinted with random flecks of darkness as he struggled for control. "Oh, Sook, listen to me," he pleaded. He was horrified to hear his own voice shake. He gulped. "Listen! We are friends, are we not?"

She spoke harshly, her voice rough with tears. "We were friends. You lied to me!"

"I never did."

"You let me think—you let me believe you were an itinerant, a working man, one of us!"

"I protected you. It was not safe for you to know what I was."

"I can take care of myself!" she snapped.

"Yes, I know." Suddenly weary beyond bearing, Zakri flung himself into a chair and buried his head in his hands. Sook glanced over her shoulder at him, and fresh tears welled.

"I thought—I hoped that you and I would be—" she stammered. She turned back to the window, unable to finish.

"I see that now," he said. "But I did not understand it before. You must understand that I do not—I never think of myself in that way. The Cantoris—the *filhata*—these are my life. To give them up, after working so hard to earn them, would be the greatest sacrifice of all."

"I see," she said. He looked up to see her straighten her shoulders and brush back errant strands of her hair with her two hands. "Well, then," she sniffed. "I'll just say goodbye to you, Cantor Zakri. We are very grateful to you and your friends."

"Sook!" he protested. He stood, and took a step closer to her, but she kept her face turned away. The curve of her cheek and the line of her slender neck tormented him. He whispered, "Please hear me. If I were not what I am, things would surely be different. But if Cantrix Sira had not trained me as she did, no one could have lived with me, not you nor any other person. My Gift was wild, out of control. I was a danger to everyone around me."

"I see," she said again. Zakri was dismally certain that she did not understand at all, and perhaps never would. It seemed he had failed her after all.

"I am sorry," he said. For answer, she sniffed again.

Zakri waited for a long moment, but she did not relent. He looked back once as he left the kitchen. Sook still stared out the window, her back straight and her head unbowed. Zakri felt her hurt, her loneliness, and her stiff pride. His own face was wet as he left her.

The Housekeeper of Soren, a woman who seemed still to be stunned by the events of the day, opened an empty apartment for Sira and Theo and their party. She produced clean bedding, but fresh clothes were not available. Apologetically, she explained there had been no soap, and thus no spare linens. They were glad to see the apartment had bedrooms enough for Zakri and Berk to have one, Sira and Mreen another. A long couch awaited Theo in the main room. It was late, and there was more work for them in the morning. The moment the door closed behind the Housekeeper, Theo threw himself on the couch and put his feet up on the carved arm. Sira stood by the long window, looking out.

Well? he demanded.

Her narrow lips curved upward ever so slightly and she cast him a sidelong glance. *Mreen was here,* she sent.

He sat up straight. *Mreen! When?*

Sira came to sit beside him. *When the* quiru *was down,* she answered. *She came and found the little boy . . . Joji, his name is. And she took him away, back to the camp.*

Theo stared in disbelief at Sira's face. *How—by the Six Stars, how is that possible?*

She pointed her long forefinger at him in mock admonition. *You gave her the idea with your* quiru *games. She got him outside, and she extended her light around him. They had quite a climb, from what she sends me, and she frightened Berk half to death, but they are safe now with Berk. I must find Joji's family and reassure them.*

Theo fell back on the couch, one hand pressed to his heart in mock suffering. *This is too much for an old Singer! That child will be the end of us all.*

More likely, Sira sent, *that child is the future of us all. Her Gift is beyond my understanding. She must have some great purpose in store for her. I only hope it gives her joy.*

Just like you, Maestra. You too have a great purpose. Has it given you joy?

She stretched out her narrow hand to touch his cheek, very briefly. *My dear,* she sent. She did not smile now, but her eyes were very bright. *No greater joy is possible, while we are together.*

Mreen and Joji and Berk arrived at Soren's doorstep before the next morning's meal was served. More introductions were made. The little boy was alight with happiness and excitement at the prospect of Conservatory. His mother was too relieved at seeing him safe to be upset at their imminent separation.

The great room hummed with talk and movement as House members hailed each other in celebratory fashion. Sira and Theo sat side by side, with Cantrix Elnor across from them. The Magister's seat they left empty. Many House members glanced at the carved chair at the head of the table, the same Cho had sat in for months, and their faces were grim. Sira wondered if there were no one at all to grieve the carver Cho's passage beyond the stars.

Sook herself served the central table. Her small body was straight, her face composed. "Good morning, Cantor, Cantrix," she said calmly as she placed bowls of *caeru* stew before them. "There are no vegetables or fruit at all yet. We've had to make the best of it, but we hope you'll come back when our nursery gardens have fully recovered."

Sira nodded to her. "Thank you, Housewoman," Theo said. "We will try to do just that."

Another Housewoman came after Sook with a pot of tea. This one kept her eyes averted from the empty chair, pouring tea with a nervous motion that spilled drops around every cup. Sira arched her brow.

Zakri, is this one afraid of us?

Zakri watched the girl's hasty retreat from their table. *That is Nori,* he sent. *She may be the only person in the House to be sorry Cho is gone.*

Do you not think those in the carvery are sorry? Theo asked.

No. I think by the time we arrived, everyone was so frightened of him that they are mostly relieved. Except now they have to face the Committee!

But they are Gifted. The Committee will be lenient with them—they will have to be! The shortage is still their main concern.

Sook looks fully recovered today, Sira put in.

Zakri sighed, and Theo reassured him. *She is a strong young woman, Cantor Zakri,* he sent. *She will be all right, in time. She has made up her mind to it.*

"Excuse me, Cantrix Elnor?"

An itinerant bowed to Elnor and to the rest of them. He smiled rather nervously, and bowed again. "I'm wondering . . . that is, a lot of us are wondering . . . can we go now, go back to our Houses, get back to work?" He gestured behind him to a table full of Singers. "We'd all like to know, actually."

Elnor lifted a tremulous hand. "I do not know," she said. "I will leave these decisions to you, Sira."

Sira and Theo exchanged a glance, and Theo nodded. "Yes," Sira told the itinerant. "It is time. You may all go as you see fit, and we wish you safe journey."

"Thank you, Cantrix." The Singer bowed again, and then he smiled broadly. "Tell me—does anyone want to send a message north? I'll be on my way to Manrus first thing tomorrow!"

Zakri said quickly, "Yes, indeed, if you will be riding by way of Amric!"

"So I will, Cantor," the Singer said.

"You have a long ride ahead of you," Theo commented.

"And I can't wait!"

There was laughter, and the itinerant bowed once more before going back to his own table. A burst of excited chatter and more laughter greeted him there, and the Cantors looked at one another.

"Things will be back to normal very soon, Cantrix Elnor," Sira said. "I am sure you will have a Magister, and a new junior, before the summer."

"I do hope so," Elnor said softly.

"Of course we will stay until you do," Sira added.

"Thank you, my dear. I am not sure I am strong enough to manage just yet."

Theo looked around at the House members. None of them looked strong, in truth, but he was certain that when their gardens were revived, their health would improve rapidly. Perhaps by summer, they could put all of this behind them. But for himself, and Sira, he could only guess what the summer might bring.

He had not shielded his thought, and Sira heard it. *Do you not think we will be back at Observatory by summer?* she sent.

Something is still to come, he answered. *But I do not know what it is, or where it will take us.* He pressed down his suspicion that it was not his own future that was in doubt, but Sira's. He had known for years that some great service still awaited her, and his instinct, or his Gift, told him it was near. She watched him, knowing he was hiding some thought. He smiled at her, and gave a slight shake of his head. *Nothing to worry about now,* he sent.

"Well, then," Sira said aloud. "I believe it is time for the *quirunha*." The great room hummed with talk and movement as House members hailed each other in celebratory fashion. Sira and Theo, with Cantrix Elnor, sat side by side at the center table. There was no Magister to take the traditional seat of authority, one of many problems still to be resolved by Lamdon. Itinerants were approaching to ask permission to leave the House. They wanted to resume their work, and several offered to carry messages. Sira and Theo, acting together, released any who wanted to go, and Zakri found one Singer planning to travel north who would carry a brief message for him to Amric, promising his early return. The House members had seen fit to lock up nine of the rebels in the carvery. They were to be Lamdon's problem. Most of them were itinerant Singers. The senior Cantor would have to deal with them.

When the meal was over, and it appeared that everyone who wanted to speak to them had done so, Sira and Theo rose from the center table to go to the Cantoris. They planned a special *quirunha*, and they had let the Housekeeper know they hoped all House members who were able would be in attendance. The second missing *filhata* had been found and tuned. With its mate it awaited them on the dais.

Berk, Zakri, Mreen and Joji followed them to the door of the great room. Sira's eye was caught by an odd movement to her right and she stopped in the doorway. She looked more closely at the people nearest the large window.

A man fell forward over the table, and the woman next to him pulled him upright again. She propped him against her own shoulder, and tried to get him to take a mouthful of *keftet*. As Sira watched, the meat and broth fell from his slack lips to splash back into his bowl. Patiently, the woman wiped his chin with her hand, and tried again.

Zakri stepped up next to Sira. *That man was one of Cho's demonstrations. He has been like that since I first came here.*

Did you try to help him?

No. There was no opportunity—and I fear his mind is past retrieval.

Sira and Theo looked at each other, and he nodded to her without speaking. "Mreen, Joji," he said, holding out his hands to the children. "Let us go on to the Cantoris and make sure everything is ready for the *quirunha*. Joji, are you strong enough to lift chairs and move stools about?"

"So I am, Cantor Theo," Joji said. "I'm very strong, Mama always says so."

Theo led them across the hall while Sira turned aside, with Zakri and Berk, to go to the man and woman by the window. As they approached, the woman looked up. She was of middle age, weathered and brown, and her eyes and face were worn with exhaustion.

"Forgive me for not standing, Cantrix," she said. "If I do not support Karl, he falls."

"I see that, Singer," Sira answered. She pulled out a chair and sat down. Zakri and Berk stood close behind her. "Can you tell me what happened to Karl?"

The woman eyed the three of them, then shrugged. "I guess it hardly matters now," she said. "I couldn't say before, or I'd get the same as Karl, and then I don't know who would have taken care of him—or me, for that matter."

"What is your name?" Sira asked.

"I'm Ana," she answered. "Ana v'Perl, it used to be. I don't know if they'll have me now." A flash of spirit showed in her eyes. "Karl wanted to come here, to follow Cho. He—" her eyes grew dull again. "He's my mate, Karl. I had to go where he went, didn't I?"

Sira nodded gravely. "I expect you did. I believe all the Houses will be delighted to have their Singers return."

Ana managed a tired smile. "Thanks, Cantrix. I hope you're right."

"Can you tell us what happened, then, Singer?" Berk asked.

She looked up at the big man. "I wanted to tell you before, when you were here. You're the courier from Amric, aren't you?"

He nodded.

"I didn't dare talk to you," she said. "It was that Singer, the one from Trevi."

Zakri caught his breath. "Iban!" he whispered.

She glanced at him. "Yes, that was it," she said. "Singer Iban. The thing was, Karl here had charge of making sure he didn't leave Soren, but then he got away, along with his relative. Cho didn't care about the other one, Clive I think his name was, because he wasn't a Singer. But he couldn't get home without Iban, of course. One day they just disappeared—they weren't anywhere to be found. Cho was furious. He kept saying if there was even one exception, the plan would be ruined. Every Singer had to be here, by will or by force. He sent Karl after Iban."

She paused, resetting her mate on her shoulder. Sira prompted her. "What happened then? What happened to Iban?"

"I only went because Karl and I always traveled together." She looked down at her mate's vacant features. "Always," she repeated sadly. "It's a long ride to Amric from Soren, and they were riding hard, but so were we. On the third day we caught up with them. I told Karl we should just let it go, let Iban go where he wanted, but Karl wouldn't hear of it. He said Cho was depending on him!" The last words were said bitterly, despairingly. "Then Cho used him, he used Karl, and this is what's left to me!"

"What do you mean?" Sira asked her. "How did he use him, at such a distance?"

Ana looked at her mate's hands lying useless on the table. Tears formed in her eyes, and she wiped them away with her sleeve. "He was a good Singer," she whispered. "A strong one, the best. That's why Cho wanted him." The others waited while she collected herself. "Cho used Karl's Gift to kill Iban. He struck with his own psi through Karl's, like . . . like calling out in a canyon, and hearing your voice echo off the far wall. Like skipping a stone across the Glacier. I suppose Iban's mind broke, though I had no way of knowing until you came looking for him. Karl—" she turned her hopeless eyes to Sira. "Karl has been like this ever since."

Berk rumbled something deep in his throat, but Zakri had no anger left. Wearily, he said, "Iban—our master—was brave to the end. It cost him his life."

"But had he not come to you," Sira reminded him, "Soren might have been lost forever. Cho grew stronger every day."

"Nevya must know about him," Zakri said. "He must be remembered as a hero."

"A hero indeed," Sira said. A shared memory of Iban, his expressive face and bright gray eyes, sprang up between them. But there was no time now for grieving. The matters of Soren's recovery were too pressing. *But we will always remember,* Sira sent to Zakri.

They took leave of Ana and her mate, leaving them to struggle on through their meal. They went across the hall to join Theo and Elnor in the Cantoris, to perform the one task that every Cantor or Cantrix must fulfill every day, without fail. Their personal feelings must always take second place to their duties.

Chapter Twenty-eight

The House members gathered in solemn rows to watch as the prisoners were taken from the carvery. Housemen and women lined the corridor in stony silence, holding their children by the hand or in their arms as the three carvers and six itinerants marched past with their eyes averted. The whisper of their boots against the stone floor was the only sound. Saddled *hruss* waited for them in the courtyard, where two itinerant Singers and six of Soren's strongest riders were already mounted, ready to begin the long ride to Lamdon. There the rebels would face the judgment of the Magistral Committee. Sira and Theo had debated this move. The number of riders was large, and available supplies were limited. They had decided to outfit the group one way only, and trust Lamdon to supply them for the journey home.

Theo stepped forward as the prisoners reached the double doors. He held out his hand to each of the itinerants as they passed. One by one, Klas, Shiro, and the three other men dropped their *filla* into his palm.

Bree came last. Her neck burned with shame, and she stared steadfastly at the floor. She pulled her *filla* from her tunic and held it out between two fingers without looking at it. Theo took it carefully, not touching her hand, and dropped it with the others into a leather pouch. It would be up to the Committee to decide if and when the *filla* would be returned. Bree swallowed and turned to the open doors with the three carvers trudging behind her.

"Wait!" Sook came running down the corridor from the kitchens, a towel still in her hands. "Wait, please!" she called.

She was breathless when she reached Bree, and put her small hand up to grip the Singer's shoulder. Bree looked away, shaking her head. "It's no use, Sook," she muttered.

Sook turned to Theo, then searched past him for Zakri. Zakri, with Berk and Sira, stood by the doors of the Cantoris with Mreen and Joji.

"Cantor Zakri," Sook said.

Zakri glanced once at Sira before he moved forward. "What is it, Sook? What can I do?"

"We have to help Bree," Sook said. "She helped me. She took me to see Mura, she unlocked my door, she brought me food. She even tried to stand up to Cho! I don't know what might have become of me if she hadn't been there."

Theo gave Bree a hard look. "Singer, do you have something to say for yourself?"

Bree lifted her head to meet Theo's eyes. "I'm getting what I deserve, if that's what you mean, Cantor," she said. "I helped Sook when I could, yes. But I was part of this from the start. It's just that—when I saw what was happening—I couldn't take it anymore. I should have done more . . . but it had gone too far." Her plain features were bleak.

"She doesn't need more punishment," Sook insisted. "She helped me, and she needs my help now." Her great eyes flashed at Zakri. She put out her hand as if to touch his sleeve, then jerked it back, remembering. "Please, Zakri. Make them let her go. For me."

Zakri lifted his hands in an appeal for understanding. "What can I do, Sook? These are not my decisions!"

"You have to do something. Please!"

Zakri flushed under the intensity of her gaze, aware of every eye upon them. "Cantor Theo," he murmured. "Is there anything we can do? Can you help me here?"

"Lamdon has to deal with them," Theo answered. "They are Gifted, and therefore subject to the highest authority. Sook could send along a letter, perhaps, some message asking for leniency in Bree's case."

Zakri looked hopefully at Sook. She considered for a moment, biting her lip. She glanced at Bree, and her chin lifted. "I'm going to go with them!" she declared. "I want to be there for the judgment."

Behind her the Housekeeper exclaimed, "But, Sook! Who will run the kitchens if you leave now?"

Sook put her hands on her hips and glared at the assembled House members. "Surely someone can manage during my absence!" The House members looked at each other. "You all ate when I was locked up for those weeks, didn't you?" Several put up their hands, about to speak, but Nori forestalled them. She came from behind the crowd. She cast a shy glance at Zakri as she passed him, and came to stand before Sook and Bree.

"I can do it, Sook," she said. "I want to."

Sook tossed her head. "Good. Then it's settled."

Zakri opened his mouth to protest Sook's plan, to remind her this would be no pleasant journey, but then he closed it without speaking. He had no say in this matter, either.

Theo smiled down at Sook. "Well, Housewoman, you have your way, it seems. Now you had better hurry, or the travelers will leave without you!" he said.

Sook gave him a brilliant smile, spun about, and flew down the corridor toward her own apartment. Zakri stood at Theo's shoulder as the rest of the offenders were ushered out into the courtyard to mount their *hruss*.

"Do you think they will listen to her?" he asked. "I fear the Magistral Committee will tear her to pieces."

Theo chuckled. "I think, Cantor Zakri, that your young friend will not rest until the Committee hears her out! She will be like a *wezel* in a *caeru* den . . . she is small, but she is persistent. When she gets those sharp little teeth into something, she will not let go until she is good and ready."

"I suppose you are right," Zakri said shakily, and laughed a little under his breath. "But I worry about her."

Theo clapped him hard on the shoulder. "My friend," he said. "You had best worry about the Committee—they have no warning!"

Within ten days of the restoration of the *quiru*, the gardens of Soren began producing vegetables once again. Limp, yellowing leaves turned green and firm, and sagging stalks straightened under the warmth and light that poured daily from Sira's and Theo's *quirunha*. Cantrix Elnor grew stronger, too. Like the plants in the nursery, she stood straighter and her color improved. When she joined them on the dais, her voice was unsteady at first, her intonation uncertain. But before many days passed she was singing securely in a high, clear voice. In due time she took a turn with one of the *filhata*, and on that day, she pronounced herself ready to welcome a new junior and take responsibility for her own Cantoris.

Messages flew between Soren and Lamdon, Lamdon and Conservatory, Conservatory and Soren. Sook returned to Soren in the company of a courier from Lamdon, bearing the news that the offenders had been censured and fined one hundred bits of metal, which should keep them busy for many summers. They had been released to go and earn their freedom, with the proviso that none of them ever visit Soren again. Only two, the Singers who had abandoned the Magister's party, received the ultimate sentence. Those two would be exposed in the Mariks, left to the deep cold as they had left the Magister and his mate and children.

Bree's fine was reduced to twenty bits of metal because of Sook's testimony on her behalf. When Sook told the story of the Committee meeting, her eyes flashed and tendrils of black hair flew about her face. Her cheeks had grown brown from the long days of riding, and her gaze was direct and confident. Zakri watched with pride, as if she were a treasured little sister. Theo watched them both, hiding a smile.

The carvers had been banished from Soren, from their home, in perpetuity. Their family members would have to decide for themselves whether to join them, whether to become members at whatever House might agree to take them in, or to forgo seeing them ever again.

I wonder if they know about Observatory? Theo sent to Sira, grinning at her.

I should imagine you will tell them.

Certainly. Observatory could do with some carvers of their own. And I doubt Pol would have any difficulty disciplining that lot!

The courier's greatest news for the House members was of their new Magister. The younger brother of the Magister of Arren was to be appointed in due course, and would arrive in the summer with his mate and their children and a retinue of servants. A search party had gone looking for the vanished Magister of Soren and his family as soon as there was a Singer available, but no trace had been found. The courier's features were stoic when he described the Committee's feeling that when the summer came the melting snow would reveal their remains. Those around the meeting table glanced at each other, shaking their heads.

Finally, the courier said, "Had Carver Cho not died in the battle for Soren, the Committee would certainly have had him exposed. As it is, they ruled that his body should be left in the hills, not to be buried when the thaw comes."

Sook, seated at the table with the dignitaries of her House for this one special meeting, kept her head high and her lips pressed together. Theo caught her eye and tapped his temple, reminding her that she had done what she must. She gave him a small nod of gratitude.

"And a Cantor?" Elnor asked. "Or Cantrix? Is Conservatory going to send me a junior?"

The courier bowed to her. "Your new colleague should arrive any day. Conservatory is providing his escort. And Conservatory requests that Cantrix Sira return with their riders."

Sira stared at him. "I? Go to Conservatory? Why is that?"

He bowed again. "I don't know, Cantrix," he answered. "They don't tell me everything."

Theo said, "It is a lot to ask, it seems to me. With no explanation!"

The courier spoke carefully. "I'm sorry, Cantor," he said. "It's what they told me to say."

Zakri grinned across the table at Sira. *What have you done now, Maestra?*

Sira arched her white-slashed brow at him. *Do not call me that! And I have no idea what this is about. I may not even go.*

Theo chuckled. *Oh, I do think you will go, Sira. And so will I! Who can resist a chance to visit Conservatory? Besides, we need to take Mreen back—and Joji.*

Sira regarded him thoughtfully. *You are right, as always. It has been a very long time since I have walked the halls of Conservatory.* She ran her fingers through her dark hair, and turned her head to look out the window. The first melt was beginning to pare away the snowpack. The dark green of the irontrees was already brightening, promising summer. *Would it not be lovely,* she mused, *to be in the open when the Visitor first rises in the east?*

Theo sent, *Indeed it would, my dear.* Zakri, listening as usual, quickly withdrew from their conversation. He smiled to himself, watching Sira and Theo. Sira's eyes were bright, and the sharp planes of her face were softer, the lines of weather and worry smoothed away. She looked very young just then, Zakri thought. For a brief span, she looked no older than Sook.

The moment passed. Theo turned to Zakri. "Cantor Zakri? Will you be coming with us?"

Zakri reluctantly shook his head. "I think it is time I went home—my home, which is Amric. Gavn has been alone with Ovan a long time."

Sira sent privately, *It will be hard to say goodbye to you.*

Zakri had to press down the fear that he might not see her again for years, perhaps ever. He forced a smile to his lips. *And to you, Maestra!* He could not push away the thought that Observatory was a long, long way from Amric, no matter how he reminded himself of his duty.

Theo sent to him, *Zakri. Conservatory is not more than a day's ride out of your way. Do come with us at least that far!*

He is right again, Sira sent. *Let us all ride together, one more time.*

Zakri laughed and gave in. *So I will! I see there is no resisting you two!* The air glimmered before him as if full of ice crystals catching the sun. He allowed the sparks to dance around him for a full minute before he quenched them.

The evening meal began in a festive mood. There was wine for the first time in months, a gift from the Magistral Committee, sent as a sign of encouragement and unity. Sook, for the first and only time in her life, sat at the central table to be served like the upper-level House members, her bright tunic a flame among the coal-dark colors. Theo made certain everyone spoke aloud throughout the meal, for her sake.

The Gifted were served tea, and the wine was measured out for the House members, poured into small ironwood goblets carved into charming shapes, no two alike. Sira admired the one at Sook's place. "Such a wealth of beautiful things here," she said.

Sook nodded. "It's a wonderful House," she said. "At least it was."

"It will be again," Theo assured her. "Just look around you."

Indeed, the great room was bright and warm, bustling with the talk and activity of a lively community. The mold that had taken root in the ceiling corners had been eradicated by much scrubbing, and the last bits of grime that had lain hidden in the darkness had been scoured away. The limeglass of the windows gleamed, and the stone of the floors shone smooth with polishing. Only the scarcity of fruit on the tables gave testimony to the time of hardship.

Will it be summer soon, Cantor Theo? Mreen asked.

Indeed it will. And we will all be at Conservatory soon.

Mreen leaned close to Joji, to touch her forehead to his. *Joji, summer is coming, and we are going to Conservatory!* He wriggled in his seat, bouncing as if it were all he could do to stay in the chair. Mreen frowned at him, and lifted one chubby forefinger. Joji froze in his place, and Theo, watching them, roared with laughter.

"What is it?" Sira asked. He tried to answer, but as soon as he drew breath, he laughed again, helplessly. Sira tapped the table with her fingers and looked around at the others. "Does anyone know what is wrong with Theo?"

"I think," Zakri said, also chuckling, "that you have an imitator!" He gestured with his thumb to Mreen.

"What do you mean?" Sira demanded.

"Never mind," Theo finally sputtered. "At least she chose a good model." He wiped his eyes, and lifted his teacup to Sira. "To our Maestra!" he cried. "May summer find you disciplining Conservatory as you have disciplined all of us!"

Zakri and Mreen laughed with Theo, and lifted their cups. Sira shook her head at them all, but she was smiling, and her eyes glistened in the rich yellow light of the *quiru*.

"We will see about that," she said softly. "It very well may be the other way around." She lifted her cup, and every House member did the same, whether tea or wine. "To Soren!" Sira said, and the cry was echoed around the room. "To Soren!"

Chapter Twenty-nine

They saw no reason to hurry as their party made its way northeast to Conservatory. The weather was warming, the air fragrant. Joji and Mreen crowed with excitement at every new scene they passed. Mreen gave up her treasured post behind Theo to Joji, and rode behind Sira or Zakri through the long days. In the evenings, they lingered long by the embers of the cookfire, looking up into the clearing sky. They found the Six Stars, and Conservatory's star, and then they slept gloriously late in the mornings, lulled into laziness by the sweet air that foretold summer.

Sira woke one morning to an insistent little hand on her cheek. *Cantrix Sira!* Mreen sent, bending close and patting her face softly. *Cantrix Sira! There it is!*

Sira sat up, blinking. Mreen's smile was enormous, her dimples flashing. She pointed, and Sira followed the direction of her short finger.

The sun had risen above the eastern horizon, and below it, trailing it like a distracted child, the Visitor traced the outlines of the Marik Mountains. Together, the two stars dissolved the early morning clouds into tatters of pink and gray. Sira caught her breath, and drew Mreen into the circle of her arm. The little girl knelt beside her, tucking her curls beneath Sira's chin.

That is the Visitor, is it not? she asked. *Summer is here, is it not?*

Indeed it is, dear one, Sira sent, hugging the warm small body close. *Indeed it is.*

Then I have two whole summers now!

Sira chuckled. *So you do.*

Shall I wake Cantor Theo and the others?

Sira smiled down at her and traced her round cheek with her finger. *In just a moment, Mreen. Just one more moment.* She looked back at the two suns shining above the distant peaks. Just there, she thought, just below the Visitor, is Observatory. They will be out in the courtyard today, looking up at the sky, celebrating, expecting our return. And in one more day, I will ride up to Conservatory. My true home. Every Singer's true home, as Mkel always says. And it may be the last time ever, for me.

It was a sobering thought, and she tried to thrust it aside. *Wake the others now, Mreen. They will want to see the Visitor.* Mreen dashed away to each of the others still dreaming in their bedfurs, and Sira reached for her boots. Summer at last! It was a time to rejoice. It was no time for dark thoughts.

A large company awaited them on the steps of Conservatory. Sira's heart lifted at the sight. House members, students, and teachers waited in formal ranks to receive her and her two students, the two Cantors who had never attended Conservatory. The two suns, shining together, gave luster to the colorful scene, the red and yellow and blue tunics of the House members, the deep colors worn by the upper-levels and the Gifted, the bared heads of all the people. Mreen and Joji were welcomed in a flutter of the youngest students. They looked like a flock of *ferrel* fledglings, circling their elders, swooping down on their new classmate and flying away with him. The *hruss* and all the gear swiftly disappeared as Sira, Zakri, Theo, and Berk bowed to Maestro Nikei, Maestra Magret, Cathrin and the others. It was a joyous reunion, but Sira knew in a heartbeat who was missing from the ceremonial gathering. Magister Mkel was not present.

Maestro Nikei? she began. He nodded, intuiting her query before she could form it.

That is why we sent for you, Sira, he sent. *Mkel is very ill, worse since we sent our message.* He glanced at Cathrin, who was bustling about shooing everyone indoors, making much of Zakri and Berk and Theo in her usual cheerful fashion. *Cathrin is being brave, but even she knows it will not be long now.*

Is there nothing we can do? Sira strode up the steps, formalities forgotten, to stand close to her old teacher. Maestra Magret joined them. They stepped aside, out of the flow of people.

Nikei has done all he can, Sira, Magret assured her. She patted Sira's arm in maternal fashion. *But Mkel wants to see you, and you can judge for yourself.* Sira nodded and turned to hurry indoors. *Sira!* Magret sent. Sira stopped in the open doorway to look down at her senior's lined, gentle face. *Be prepared,* Magret warned. *He is very ill indeed.*

Sira's throat tightened. She took a deep breath. *Thank you, Maestra.* More slowly now, she walked into Conservatory. As she passed, she laid her hand flat against the carved wood of the door, as if greeting an old friend. She cast her eyes up to the ancient plaque above her head to read once again the familiar words:

SING THE LIGHT,
SING THE WARMTH,
RECEIVE AND BECOME THE GIFT, O SINGERS,
THE WARMTH AND THE LIGHT ARE IN YOU.

Those lines were carved as deeply into her heart as into the ironwood of the plaque. Despite the sadness that awaited her, she savored this moment in which she entered Conservatory as an honored guest and alumna, no longer an outcast, no longer in disgrace. Her eyes filled with unaccustomed tears as she thought that she was, however briefly, truly home. She blinked the tears away and found Theo at her side.

What is it, Sira? he asked, standing close but not touching her. His blue eyes were dark as an evening sky. *What is wrong?*

She gave him a rueful shrug. *It is everything,* she answered. *Mkel is ill, and I am worried about him—but I am home, and all I can think of is how much I would like to stay!* More tears burned behind her eyes. She frowned and compressed her lips to compose herself.

Theo sent, *My dear, you look as fierce as that* tkir *that haunts Zakri's dreams!*

I know. But it is better than weeping like a first-level student in front of all these people.

They were following Magret and Nikei up the wide stairs then, their feet slipping easily into the worn spots of the treads. Sira looked around her, tasting the rich air of Conservatory, breathing in its essence. The arches of the doorways, the simply carved furniture, were of the simplest and most graceful designs, and the stone floor was devoid of rugs. In fact, rugs were never necessary at Conservatory. It was perfectly warm, perfectly and evenly lighted. Indeed, even now fragments of melody floated from the practice rooms, and with them came warm draughts that seemed infused, almost scented, by the music.

Yes, Theo agreed. *It is a magnificent place. I have always envied you your years here.*

At Mkel's apartment, Maestra Magret looked once, intently, into Sira's face. Sira nodded to her, indicating that she was ready. Nikei opened the door, and stood back for her to enter.

Sira was grateful for Magret's warning. Had this not been Mkel's own apartment, in which he had lived since her student days, and had she not expected to find him changed, she would have doubted her own eyes. He had always been well-fleshed, with thick hair, gray since she could remember, and lively eyes that saw and understood everything. But his illness had wasted him to a husk. He was so thin she wondered that he still lived. Only wisps remained of his hair, and his eyes fluttered, the lids falling as if he had not the strength to hold them up.

Is it Sira? Sira, are you here? he sent. She sensed that he had no breath to speak aloud. She moved to his bedside and knelt beside it.

Yes, Magister Mkel, it is I. I am here. I am terribly sorry to find you so ill.

He moved his hand from side to side, a negating motion. *That no longer matters. I only thank the Spirit you are here at last. I have been holding on to this life only . . . only . . .* It seemed he might be too weak even to finish his sentence. She waited, and finally heard, faintly, . . . *until you could come.*

Sira broke with custom by taking the spotted and wrinkled hand in her long smooth ones. *Why should that be, Mkel?* she asked, forgetting his title in the intensity of the moment. *Everyone here loves you, you have Cathrin, and Nikei—why should you need me to speed you on your journey?*

His fingers slipped against hers, trying to grip them. She did it for him, holding his hand tightly, wishing she could hold his spirit as well.

Sira, my dear . . . you will find out soon enough. But thank you for being here. Watch out—watch out for Cathrin, will you? Remember she has always cared for you . . . looked out for all of you . . .

Sira turned her head to find Nikei, near the door. She whispered, "Someone should fetch Cathrin, and quickly!"

Theo said, "I will do it, Maestro Nikei," and was gone in an instant.

Sira looked at Mkel once again, but his body was so wasted, his features collapsed and vacant, that she closed her eyes. She held his hand and saw, in her mind, the old Mkel, the vigorous man who had led and taught and set an example for all the Singers who had passed through Conservatory during his tenure.

Take care of them . . . he sent feebly. Sira heard the door open and close, and she felt Cathrin's warmth beside her, reaching for Mkel's other hand. Sira was distantly aware that Cathrin was weeping softly. But for Sira, the moment was one of pure psi contact, and the physical world receded into shadows.

What can I do for you, Mkel?

His breath rattled in his chest, and she thought for a moment it was over. Then she heard in her mind, very faintly, like a melody barely remembered, *Receive . . . receive the Gift . . .*

Sira did not know what it meant, but she accepted it as Mkel's farewell to her. She sent to him, *Safe and swift passage, Mkel,* but she believed his mind had already slipped away. A moment later his hand in hers went limp. Cathrin was sobbing brokenly, and Nikei came near to murmur comfort to her. Sira opened her eyes to see that Cathrin had pressed her face against Mkel's chest. It no longer rose and fell with his breath.

"Cathrin," she said gently. "Mkel's last thoughts were for you."

Cathrin lifted her tear-stained face to look into Sira's eyes. "Oh, no, Sira," she said, shaking her head. "Oh, no, they were not. I know better."

Sira began to protest, but Cathrin shook her head again. "Never mind, my dear," she said, wiping away tears that were quickly replaced with fresh ones. "I know what Mkel's thoughts were, and they were for Conservatory, just as they should have been. I'm so very grateful you came! He's been waiting."

Sira stared at Cathrin, and then at Nikei, mystified. Theo came to help her to her feet, and they stepped back to give Cathrin and Nikei time to say their own farewells.

What did he say to you, Sira? Theo asked.

He said he had been waiting for me, she sent. *And then—it was so odd—he said, Receive the Gift.* She felt stunned by sorrow and confusion, and she put her hand in Theo's, needing the warmth and the strength of his touch. *I do not know what he meant. I do not understand it at all.*

Theo pressed her hand. *He was close to death. Perhaps he did not know what he was saying.*

But why should he be waiting for me? He is surrounded by friends!

Theo had no answer for her.

The summer warmth caused the ground to thaw quickly. Within a week of summer's arrival, Nevyans hurried to inter their dead while it was possible. The bodies, which had lain frozen in the deep cold, were retrieved from their winter resting places and buried among the flourishing softwood shoots that sprang so quickly out of the softened tundra. It was good luck to be buried in a softwood grove, to return to the ground during the reign of the two suns.

Mkel's burial ceremony was a grand one. The senior Cantor of Lamdon came himself. All of Conservatory, House members, Singers, teachers, riders, and a number of itinerants gathered to bid the Magister farewell, trooping on foot from the courtyard in a long column, trudging after the *pukuru* which bore Mkel's body to its burial site. Cathrin had chosen the place carefully, on a slope overlooking the House, where, she said, Mkel could look down and see that Conservatory's work was properly carried on. Cathrin and Nikei and Magret were dignified and composed. Only the very youngest students wept. Joji and Mreen were wide-eyed and mystified by the whirl of events of the last weeks.

Sira kept an iron control of her feelings. Theo stayed close beside her, and though they sent little, she knew he understood her grief and confusion, mixed with her joy at these precious days in her old home, these last days with Mreen and with Zakri.

When the solemn rite was over, a quiet meal was served in the great room. Cantor Abram called all of the Gifted into the Cantoris the moment they were finished, leaving the House members to drink a commemorative glass of wine. Only Cathrin joined the Cantors and Cantrixes, the teachers and students, and the visiting itinerants who came to stand in rows facing the dais.

It was not a *quirunha*, and no *filhata* were in evidence. Abram stepped up alone to the dais and bowed to the assembly. They all bowed in return, and he gestured for them to be seated.

"We will speak aloud out of respect for our guests," he said, nodding to the itinerants who sat in a cluster far at the back. "And for Cathrin, of course, who has our deepest sympathy at this sad time." He bowed to Cathrin, who sat on the first bench with Maestro Nikei and Maestra Magret on either side. Sira and Theo were on Nikei's left, and Mreen crept close to sit in the circle of Theo's arm.

"My friends and colleagues," Abram went on. "The last years have seen great changes on the Continent. We at Lamdon have spent many hours discussing the challenges Nevyans face—"

Theo's elbow dug into Sira's side and she flashed him a look.

Abram said, "The shortage of the Gift has been of special concern, and it is Lamdon's feeling that in the next years we must examine the causes and possible remedies as closely as possible. We are particularly pleased by the renewal of trade and exchange of information with Observatory, and we . . ." He rattled on for several minutes, never saying anything in two words if five would accomplish the same.

Sira tried to keep her attention on the speech, but a strange sensation distracted her. She heard in her mind, but clearly, as if with her physical ears, the old song:

> SING THE LIGHT,
> SING THE WARMTH,

She almost looked behind her to see who was singing in the Cantoris, singing even while Abram droned on. Of course, she knew there was no one, but the song was so vivid!

> RECEIVE AND BECOME THE GIFT, O SINGERS,

Surely even Theo could hear it! She glanced at him, then at Magret, and Nikei, but their eyes were fixed on the dais. She looked down. Mreen's green eyes were wide, staring at her.

Do you hear it, Cantrix Sira? the child sent.

Sira caught her breath and nodded. Mreen heard it, too. Where did it come from?

> THE WARMTH AND THE LIGHT ARE IN YOU.

The melody faded away. It was achingly familiar, that song. Sira had learned it as a first-level student, and had sung it before an erudite audience at Lamdon when she had just four summers. She had taught it to Theo, and to Zakri, and last, to Mreen. It echoed in her mind now as if it was sent from the Spirit, from beyond the stars. It was Mkel's farewell.

Abram talked on. "We feel that the choice of Conservatory's next leader is a crucial one. It is always an important decision, of course, but in these difficult times even more so. After much weighing of possibilities, Magister Gowan, the Committee, and I, your senior Cantor, have decided to accept Magister Mkel's own nomination for his successor."

Nikei and Magret and Cathrin looked at Sira, and she arched her scarred eyebrow. They seemed very calm, she thought, considering the importance of this announcement. Probably Nikei or one of the other teachers—doubtless they already knew Mkel's choice—

Abram's chest swelled and he stepped to the edge of the dais. He raised his voice and announced in ringing tones, "My friends and colleagues! I present to you Conservatory's new Magistrix . . . Magistrix Sira v'Conservatory!"

He turned to her and bowed very low.

Chapter Thirty

At Abram's announcement, Sira rose to her feet very slowly, as if trying to stand in deep water. She felt every vertebra in her spine, every joint of hip and knee and ankle flex and expand to lift her upright. Her feet carried her to the dais without her being aware of making a conscious decision to go there. She saw herself bow to Abram, and then to the assembly, but she seemed to have left her real self standing at Theo's side. Nikei's and Magret's smiles were serene, Cathrin's tearful. The entire body of the Gifted rose to bow to the phantasm of Sira on the dais, while the real Sira, the essence of her, watched in shock.

The assembled people erupted in applause liberally mixed with exclamations of surprise. Not a few expressed dismay. The true Sira saw only Theo, registering the amazement that made his eyes wide, then the freezing of his features as he reined in his emotions. His usually open face became a closed mask. He bowed with the others, and when he straightened, though his eyes were open, she could neither see into them nor hear his thoughts.

Several moments passed before the dream Sira and the real Sira, reluctantly pulled from Theo's side, fused into one. Her face felt stiff, her body awkward as she bowed once again, and then looked over the faces in the Cantoris, trying to take in the import of what had happened, what had been said. Abram was saying something to her, and she nodded, but his words had no meaning. Nikei and Magret stepped up on the dais, to stand beside her as bulwarks against the tide of thoughts flowing around the room. She nodded to them as well, and it seemed she spoke, but none of it was real. Every detail was unutterably trivial . . . except for Theo's still face, his eyes blue-black, fixed on a point beyond her head.

Abruptly, Sira had to be away, away from the Cantoris, from the noise, both mental and audible, from the crush of people. With a muttered apology, she left Magret and Nikei standing with Abram on the dais. She glanced once at Theo, and then she fled, striding up the aisle on her long legs. She was not aware until she was already in the corridor, on her way to her old haven of the nursery gardens, that Mreen was with her, trotting frantically to keep up.

Mreen flashed a pleading glance, and Sira slowed her steps. The little girl, panting, took Sira's hand. *It is going to be all right, Cantrix Sira,* Mreen sent firmly. The words were sent as one adult might send to another. There was no doubt in them. Mreen's childish features shone with confidence. *You are the one. The Gift decided it.*

They reached the gardens, and Sira pushed open the door. Inside the air was rich and heavy, the farthest walls invisible in the nourishing haze of moisture and glowing *quiru* light. Sira and Mreen were alone. All the House members were still in the great room, all the Gifted left behind in the Cantoris. Hand in hand, Sira and Mreen walked between the flats of seedlings, the raised beds of root vegetables, the rows of tiny fruit trees kept close by the inner wall for warmth. Sira's legs grew suddenly weak, and she sat down abruptly on the nearest ledge. Mreen stood close by, stroking her arm.

Sira looked at her closely, seeing her, and everything, clearly for the first time since Abram's startling announcement. *Mreen! What is that in your hand?*

Mreen was holding a little *filla*, an old-fashioned one with tiny fragments of smooth metal worked around the stops. She held it up to Sira.

You remember this, do you not? Mreen asked, still in that strangely adult way. *This was Mkel's, and it was given to him by his own Magister, who had it from his Magister.* Her eyes glazed and grew distant, but there was no fear, only a pleasant dreaminess, in her expression. *So many hands,* she sent, shaking her curls. *So many Singers.* She dimpled at Sira. *And now you, Magistrix. You must have this.*

Mreen handed the little instrument to Sira, who took it with weak fingers. *Mreen—why?*

Because that is why Mkel gave it to me. Mreen suddenly laughed with her familiar soundless mirth. She was free of her burden, all at once, and the adult look faded from her face. *You will have to give me yours! Now I have no* filla *at all!*

Sira stared at her, and then at Theo who had come up behind her. *Theo—I am so glad you are here. Look what Mreen has given me!*

Theo looked at the little *filla*, and he bent to sweep Mreen up into his arms. *I see that. So this is why he gave it to you, little one.* He hugged Mreen. The look he turned on Sira was warm with love, but the old crooked grin was absent.

Yes! Mreen answered. She bounced in his arms. *Now let me go, Cantor Theo, please. I have to go to my lessons!*

He set her on her feet and she bowed to both of them, her nimbus as bright as the Visitor itself. She turned and ran up the path toward the distant door of the nursery gardens, then whirled and trotted back. She stopped in front of Sira, and sent with a little shrug, *Magistrix, it is true—I have no* filla *now.*

Sira brought out her own *filla*, hardly less worn than the one Mreen had just given her. She handed it to Mreen, and the child bowed, dimpled, and ran off once again, leaving Theo and Sira alone.

Sira met Theo's eyes, then dropped her gaze to the *filla* in her hand. She turned it over and over in her long fingers. Theo's shielding was a wall between them, a barrier to their usual closeness, and it hurt her to feel it. "You are unhappy," she said aloud.

"I am proud," he answered. He sat beside her on the ledge, and picked up a crumb of the rich soil of the bed behind them, rubbing it between his fingers into black dust. "You will be a wonderful Magistrix."

"Do you think so?" she whispered. "I am frightened half to death."

"I think that is natural," he said, with an attempt at a chuckle. "There is no more important job on the Continent."

"When we rode up to Conservatory," Sira mused, "I wanted nothing more than to come in and stay. And now—now that I will be staying— maybe for always—I do not know how to feel. I am torn in pieces!"

His face was close to hers, and he met her eyes, but he did not touch her. "You are thinking of Observatory," he said, "and our school."

"And of you, Theo." Her throat closed.

"I know," he said. He watched her tears spill over and roll down her face, but he did not reach out to wipe them away. She supposed it was because she was now Magistrix, and that made the difference.

He shook his head. He had heard her thought. *No, Sira, it is not that. What then?*

Theo stood up, stretching his arms over his head, rubbing his hands through his thick hair. She knew he was giving himself time to discipline his own emotions. He turned to face her, and the pain in his eyes was almost more than she could bear.

Sira, this is the destiny that has driven you all along. You are the reformer. You will restore the Gift to the Continent, and make our Houses safe. I— He managed a wry grin. *I am only an old itinerant. It is my destiny to love the Magistrix of Conservatory. We have been apart as much as we have been together. Now it looks as if we might be apart forever.*

Sira stood, too, and faced him. They were not any great distance from each other, but she felt that a chasm yawned between them, a gulf with no bridge. She hoped he would not ask, and he did not. Then suddenly she wished he would, and she chided herself. Of course he would not ask, because he knew perfectly well she would refuse. He knew her heart and mind as well as she herself did.

You know that I love you, too, Theo.

I know that very well.

But the Gift—

He held up his hand. *Shall I say it for you, Sira? Do I need to tell you that you would not be yourself if you made any other choice? Or even that I would be disappointed in you if you made another choice?*

She shook her head. Now he did smile at her, fully and generously. He dropped his shields, and she stepped forward, of her own volition. They came together, their arms tight around each other, for a precious and fleeting moment. She pressed her lips to his cheek, once. When they parted, his eyes burned fiercely, and Sira found fresh tears on her own face.

Chapter Thirty-one

Sira's investiture as Magistrix of Conservatory was to take place in three days. In the meantime, a thousand details were brought to her attention, needing her judgment, her decision. She had no time to contemplate what had happened, how a single stroke of fate had changed her life. Questions about the House, about the students, about her plans, rolled about her until she thought she would have no peace at all. Cathrin had already removed all of her personal things from the Magisterial apartment, though Sira protested her hurry.

Cathrin smiled at her. "This is what it is to be a Magister's mate, Sira."

Maestra Magret was there, and Maestro Nikei, sitting with Sira at the long table, helping to ease her into the demands of her new position. Magret and Nikei looked up sharply at Cathrin's words, and Nikei looked away quickly. "I think perhaps I will excuse myself now," he said hastily. He picked up the books he had brought with him and bowed quickly to the women before leaving the apartment.

Sira stared after him in confusion. "Why did Nikei leave like that? You would think an *urbear* was after him!"

Cathrin laughed a little. Magret said delicately, "We have been waiting, Magistrix, for a moment to speak with you. Nikei feels this is a discussion to be held among us women."

Cathrin put down the stack of linens in her hands, and came to sit close to Sira. "When it was Mkel's turn, Magistrix, all the women left the room."

"Oh," Sira said faintly. "I see."

Magret said, "Of course you are aware that the Magister of Conservatory, traditionally, takes a mate."

"Yes," Sira said.

"There has never been a Magistrix of Conservatory before, at least not in our memory," Magret went on. "Nikei and I, and the others, would like to know your wishes in this matter."

The two older women waited in a polite and respectful silence. Sira looked down at her hands, and out the window, then at Cathrin. "Cathrin, I would never want to say anything to offend Mkel's memory, please know that."

Cathrin nodded, searching Sira's face with her eyes.

"It is just that I want to use my Gift. It is not enough for me to simply oversee the school, and the training of the students." Sira smiled at little, ruefully.

"Maestra Magret knows that when I first left Conservatory, I burned with ambition. I wanted to sing for great audiences, to hear the acclaim of my colleagues, to prove that I was the best. The Spirit taught me, through all of the strange turnings my life has taken, that what is truly important is to sing, no matter for whom. The work, the music, is everything. I need to teach, to sing—to perform *quirunha*. Otherwise, the tasks of this office would be eternal punishment."

Magret nodded quickly. "I felt certain you would say exactly that, Magistrix." She rose, adding, "I will let the others know for you, shall I?"

Cathrin stopped her. "Wait, please, Maestra!" Magret turned back in surprise.

"Sira," Cathrin said, very softly. She paused, searching for the words she needed. "You know, being mated made Mkel's job all the easier. It's an enormous duty you have taken on, and it can be exhausting. Wouldn't you like to think about it?"

"So I have," Sira said quickly. "There was no decision to make."

"But," Cathrin insisted gently, "your special friend, Cantor Theo. Wouldn't you like to have him by your side, to help you to bear the load as I helped Mkel over the years?"

There was a silence. Sira could not sit still any longer. She pushed away from the table and went to look out over the summer-green hills, where the softwood shoots were already half as tall as she. For one fleeting moment, she wished she and Theo could simply ride away, out under the sky that was the same blue as his eyes, away from all problems and decisions and responsibilities. But she could not turn her back on this call, and she knew it. All her life she had answered the call of the Gift. She would not change that now.

She turned back to Cathrin and Magret. "I would," she said. "I would so like to have Theo's support, his help and his companionship, here at Conservatory. But I will never mate. It is not in me to make that compromise with my Gift. And how can I ask Theo to stay here, to abandon his work at Observatory? In truth, I am not sure he would want to do so either way, mated or unmated. He is Cantor Theo v'Observatory, not Magistrix Sira's mate!"

"I should tell you, Magistrix," said Magret, "that Lamdon believes you will move your school at Observatory, bring those Gifted children to Conservatory to be trained."

Sira's chin went up. "I will not. That would be throwing aside all that the Gift has taught us. If that is why they chose me, they were mistaken, and they will have to choose another."

Magret laughed. "Oh, they cannot choose another! Despite Cantor Abram's fine speech, Magister Mkel chose you, and they were bound to respect his wishes. But they did hope that your appointment as Magistrix would simplify things. You are such a puzzle to them all!"

Sira came back to sit again in the tall chair that had been Mkel's. "I believe I am to meet with Cantor Abram this morning, after the *quirunha*. I will explain to him, and to all of you, my plans for Observatory. But, Maestra, I hope I will have advice from you too, you and Maestro Nikei and all the others. It is important to me, and to Cantor Theo, to hear everyone's voice."

Magret bowed to her. "Magistrix, we will give you every support we can."

Magret was right. Abram's smug expression crumpled into an angry one when he learned that Sira and Theo had no intention of moving their students from Observatory. Sira was Magistrix already, though, despite the fact that the ceremony had not taken place, and he could not give vent to his feelings as he had when she was simply a rebel Cantrix without a Cantoris.

"Surely, Magistrix," he pleaded, his plump features pinched by his attempt to control his temper. "Surely it is better if all the Gifted are trained in one place."

Sira knew very well the power of her new position. It frightened her in the long night hours, but at this moment, she understood it was her job to use it. She trusted to her instincts. "Cantor Abram," she said levelly. "Why do you think Observatory, small House that it is, has seen such a flourishing of the Gift?"

Abram stared at her. "Does anyone know the reasons for such things? Those are the mysteries of life on the Continent!"

Sira met Theo's eyes and he winked at her. "I believe I do know," Sira said. She rose to pace to the window and back, to stand behind her tall chair, the Magister's—no, the Magistrix's—chair. She gripped it with her hands. The teachers and Cantor Abram, Theo, Berk, and Zakri were ranged around the meeting table. She swept them all with her glance.

"I am sure Cantor Theo would say that the *ferrel* builds more than one nest," she began. Theo grinned. "The way we have trained the Gift, the way in which we have used it on Nevya, has grown more and more narrow over the years. It is natural to try to control that on which we are dependent; but we have tried too hard. We have set too high a price on the Gift. We have misused our Singers, isolated them. For some, discovering their Gift is tantamount to a punishment, and therefore, the Gift does not appear."

"Punishment?" sputtered Abram. "I do not understand! The Gift has to be disciplined!"

"Yes. But discipline does not require ancient rules that have outlived their time."

"What rules, then? What rules do you wish to break?"

"Only the artificial ones," Sira said. "The ones that say the Gift can only be trained in one way, in one place. The rules that ignore realities, such as those that touched Trisa's life, or Zakri's, or Isbel's, or—" She nodded toward Theo. "Or Cantor Theo's."

Abram shook his head. Maestro Nikei said, "Mkel came to believe, in his last years, that change was necessary, and that Magistrix Sira was sent by the Gift to effect the change. When Mreen arrived, this child that is purely of the Gift, nurtured at Observatory and brought here by as revolutionary a figure as Cantor Theo—"

Theo chuckled aloud at that. Nikei smiled at him. "Indeed you may laugh, Cantor," he said. "When the Gift has you in its current, you must simply float on the tide. I doubt any of the great revolutionaries set out to be so. I doubt that Magistrix Sira set out to be a reformer."

Sira smiled at him. "You know I did not, Maestro Nikei," she said. "If I am, as you say, a reformer, then it is the work of the Spirit. I am no visionary." She paused for a moment, surveying the people around her. Very softly, she finished, "I am only a Singer, like each of you, willing to work hard and to listen to the Gift when it calls."

Theo smiled at Sira, his eyes the clear blue of the sky above the hills.

Abram said wearily, "What do you want, then, Magistrix? What are we supposed to do?"

Sira opened her hands, a gesture to include them all. "We will work," she said. "We will study and teach and practice as we have always done. Observatory's school will go on, with Theo and Cantrix Jana if she is willing. We will be open to surprises like Theo, and like Cantor Zakri. We will be more open in general, in fact, since I have learned from Theo that our healing can be much improved by being more open."

Abram scowled. Sira saw Zakri staring at him, and she suppressed a smile. No doubt later Zakri would tell her all that Abram had been thinking! She would scold him, but it would do no good. And she would not, in truth, mind knowing.

"I do not know what will happen," Abram muttered.

"No, Cantor Abram," Sira agreed. "Nor do I. We will simply have to try, and trust. It is all we can ever do."

*

The day of Sira's investiture as Magistrix of Conservatory dawned bright and warm, with the two suns brilliant in the sky. The Housemen and women, the young Singers, all the teachers, and the many visitors spent most of the morning bathing, planning what to wear and what to say, preparing to celebrate the ceremony and enjoy the feast afterward. Only Sira, with Theo and Nikei, was working, seated once again at the long table in her apartment.

"If you leave yourself open," Nikei was saying, "how can you bear the illness, and still do your work?"

"If you are closed," Theo answered him, "how can you know where the illness is?"

"You will have to show me, I think, Cantor . . ."

They were interrupted by a knock on the door, and Theo opened it to find a young Housewoman standing with her hands on her hips. "Yes?" he said.

"If the Magistrix doesn't come and bathe soon, there won't be any time!" she snapped.

Sira stood quickly. "Cantor Theo, please meet Ita. She is my new Housewoman."

Theo bowed to the girl, and she bowed in return, properly, but quickly. "Truly, Magistrix," she insisted. "It's late. You must come now! I won't have you looking like some kitchen worker—"

"All right, Ita." Sira arched her brow at Theo as she passed him. "I am coming."

Theo and Nikei listened to Ita scold Sira as they went down the corridor together. "It's really too bad about your hair, Magistrix," she was saying. "But there's nothing we can do about it now. I suppose it will grow, in time."

Theo laughed aloud. "I wish her luck with the hair," he chortled. "But it seems Sira will be obliged to obey someone, after all!"

It was a grand and colorful event, the invstituture of Magistrix Sira v'Conservatory. The dark tunics of the upper levels and the Gifted gave way, through the ranks of the assembly, to the brilliant hues of the Housemen and women. Magister Gowan's white hair and fleshy face contrasted sharply with Sira's tanned, lean figure on the dais. Magister Pol attended, on his first trip outside of Observatory. Sira's parents too, Niel v'Arren and his mate, were there. She had to struggle to find something to say to them. They were strangers to her, but they did not seem troubled by that. Their pride made them almost speechless in any case.

Mreen made Theo hold her up in his arms so she could see. Between them, Magister Gowan and Cantor Abram made the succession of the Magistrix of Conservatory official. The rite itself was short, but the congratulations and the cheering of the House members were long, cut off in the end only by the announcement of the meal.

Conservatory's kitchens had spared no effort, and the feast laid out in the great room was the richest Mreen had ever seen. She sat with her class, of course, but she watched Magistrix Sira at the central table with all the teachers, the dignitaries from Lamdon, her awestruck parents. Mreen thought Sira looked wonderful, tall and noble, born to be a Magistrix.

She watched Cantor Theo, too. He had a special place at Sira's right hand, and Mreen saw them glance at each other often, and she sensed the pain between them. It was wrong, somehow, that pain. Her own halo darkened when she felt it. Little shadows flitted around her despite her pleasure in the day. There was only laughter and vivacity around her, but Mreen was distracted from the rich *caeru* stew, the nutbread, the sweets she loved. At last she could bear it no more. She ducked under the table to scamper across the great room.

She tugged on Theo's sleeve, and he grinned down at her. *Well, hello, little one. Is the food at your own table not so good?*

She dimpled. *The food is wonderful!*

Then what are you doing here, with the old folk?

I know you are worried, you and Ca—I mean, Magistrix Sira.

Theo patted her cheek. *You know, even when we are happy, we each have our special sorrows, dear heart. Mine is that I must say goodbye to Magistrix Sira tomorrow . . . and to you as well!*

But, Cantor Theo, she sent urgently. *You are coming back!*

He looked at her quizzically. *Well, I suppose one day, Mreen. I am certain to come for a visit some day. Perhaps when you sing your first quirunha!*

She shook her head, her curls bouncing, her nimbus sparkling with energy. *Oh, no, Cantor Theo . . . very soon!*

How can you know that, Mreen?

She grinned at him, laughing her soundless laugh. *You are everywhere in Conservatory. I feel you in the classrooms, even in the practice rooms.*

Mreen, he sent carefully. *I have never been in any of those places.*

The little old woman peered out from behind the child's face again, in a way that had become almost familiar. *You will be, Cantor Theo. You will be.* Her nimbus shifted, dark and light together.

Mreen looked up to see that Sira, Magistrix Sira v'Conservatory, was listening to what she sent. Theo and Sira looked into each other's eyes, and they smiled. The pain between them evaporated like morning fog under the light of the two suns, and Mreen's halo frothed, glimmers and sparks of light doing a wild dance about her head, her floating red curls. The ancient expression vanished from her plump features, and her dimples flashed.

Suddenly, she was ravenous. She hurried back to her own table, eager for the lovely treats that awaited her there.

Author's Note

The Nevyan clef is a C clef, indicating the one pitch all Singers must be able to remember and reproduce accurately. Both the *filla* and *filhata* are tuned to C. The *filhata*'s central, deepest string is the bass C; from top to bottom, the *filhata* is tuned: E-B-F-C-G-D-A. The *filla* is tuned with no stops on C.

The modes are natural scales of whole and half steps; alterations, or accidentals, are considered variations and are used as embellishments, and can be half or quarter tones. Even those Singers without absolute pitch are required to memorize the C early in their training.

The modes are customarily employed in these ways:

> First mode, *Iridu: quiru*, sleep
> Second mode, *Aiodu: quiru*, healing
> Third mode, *Doryu*: warming water, treating infections
> Fourth mode, *Lidya*: entertainment, relaxation
> Fifth mode, *Mu-Lidya*: entertainment, relaxation

Glossary

caeru	Fur-bearing animal; source of meat and hides
carwal	Sea animal living mostly in the water
ferrel	Large predatory bird
filhata	Stringed instrument similar to a lute, used exclusively by Cantors and Cantrixes
filla	Small, flutelike instrument used by Singers
hruss	Large, shaggy animal used for riding and carrying, or pulling the *pukuru*
keftet	Tradition dish of meat and grain
obis knife	A knife made of slender long metal pieces, used in conjunction with psi to carve stone and ironwood
pukuru	Sled with bone runners
quiru	Area of heat and light created by the psi of Gifted Singers
quirunha	Ceremony that creates a *quiru* large enough to heat and light an entire House
tkir	Great mountain cat with long, serrated tusks
urbear	Silvery gray, very large coastal animal
wezel	Thin rodent-like animal

About the Author

Louise Marley's first career was as a singer of opera and concert music. Now an award-winning fantasy and science fiction writer, her novels often feature musical themes. She lives and writes in the Pacific Northwest.

CPSIA information can be obtained at www.ICGtesting.com
Printed in the USA
BVOW080306200912

300910BV00001B/44/P